RUBBED OUT

Books by Barbara Block

CHUTES AND ADDERS

TWISTER

IN PLAIN SIGHT

THE SCENT OF MURDER

VANISHING ACT

ENDANGERED SPECIES

BLOWING SMOKE

RUBBED OUT

Published by Kensington Publishing Corporation

RUBBED OUT

Barbara Block

KENSINGTON BOOKS
http://www.kensingtonbooks.com

Although the city of Syracuse is real, as are some of the other place names I've mentioned, this is a work of fiction. Its geography is imaginary. Indeed, all the characters portrayed in this book are fictional, and any resemblance to real people or incidents is purely coincidental.

KENSINGTON BOOKS are published by

Kensington Publishing Corp.
850 Third Avenue
New York, NY 10022

All Kensington titles, imprints and distributed lines are available at special quantity discounts for bulk purchases for sales promotion, premiums, fund-raising, educational or institutional use.

Special book excerpts or customized printings can also be created to fit specific needs. For details, write or phone the office of the Kensington Special Sales Manager: Kensington Publishing Corp., 850 Third Avenue, New York, NY 10022, Attn. Special Sales Department. Phone: 1-800-221-2647.

Kensington and the K logo Reg. U.S. Pat. & TM Off.

Library of Congress Card Catalogue Number: 2002101748
ISBN 1-57566-709-6

First Printing: November 2002
10 9 8 7 6 5 4 3 2 1

Printed in the United States of America

*To Hank and Paul Nielsen for their
friendship and support*

ACKNOWLEDGMENTS

I'd like to thank the following people for their help and assistance:

Dino Quarantiello for his coffee, without which I could not function, and his advice on gambling, which I'm sure will make it into my next book.

Charles Samuels for reading the book and pointing out my obvious errors.

Robert Strickland for his knowledge of materials and engineering and for propping me up when I really needed it.

My son, Lawrence Block, who is always my first and best reader.

I'd also like to especially thank my editor, John Scognamiglio, for his unwavering support and his suggestions, as well as for the freedom he's allowed me.

Chapter One

Everything bad in my life that's ever happened to me has started with a phone call. This was no exception.

It had been a slow week at Noah's Ark. So slow that I'd closed up shop early on Tuesday evening and taken my dog Zsa Zsa downtown to listen to some jazz at the Shamrock. But the band hadn't shown up and I'd downed a couple of Scotches, eaten a handful of pretzels in lieu of dinner, shared a beer with Zsa Zsa, and come home instead.

It was a little after eleven when I walked into the kitchen. The message light on my answering machine was blinking. I unwrapped my scarf and kicked off my boots as I hit the play button. Calli's voice, frantic sounding, floated out into the room.

"Robin," she said. "Where the hell are you? Lily's gone. Someone stole her out of the backyard. Call me as soon as you get in."

That had been two days ago and we'd been searching for her with increasing desperation ever since.

Tiger Lily was my friend's three-year-old pregnant golden retriever bitch, her baby. I loved her too. Apologies to Zsa Zsa, my cocker spaniel, but goldens are my favorite breed.

They are the true innocents of the world. With their goofy grins, they remind me of slightly dim-witted eighteen-month-old children dressed up in furry blond suits. Tiger Lily didn't have a mean bone in her body. She was sweet and trusting, the kind of dog who firmly believes that everyone in the universe adores her, and the thought of her alone, hurt, and afraid broke my heart.

I was hoping that someone had kidnapped her and was holding her for ransom, but when Calli didn't get a note it was clear that whoever had stolen her had something else in mind. Like keeping her and selling her puppies. Without papers the puppies would be worth a fraction of what they would be with them, one hundred dollars instead of eight, but maybe the someone who took them didn't know that. Or maybe they didn't care. Maybe they just needed a quick way to make a few bucks.

I could make a pretty good guess who that someone was, but Calli didn't want to hear about it. She didn't take bad news well in the best of times, and these weren't the best of times for her. She'd never been what you'd call tightly wrapped, but in the last couple of months the strings holding her together were fraying. On the other hand, not smoking wasn't bringing out the best in me either.

Friday turned out to be as slow as Tuesday had been at the store. If things kept up this way, I'd just make the month's expenses. I was cleaning out the gerbil cages when Calli called. Even before she told me her news, I could tell from the tone of her voice that she'd located Lily.

I reached into my jeans pocket for a cigarette and then remembered I wasn't doing that anymore and got out a piece of gum instead. I unwrapped the stick, folded it into thirds, and popped it in my mouth as Calli talked.

"She's chained up in back of this house on Fayette," she said.

"How'd you find her?"

"Luck." Calli took a deep breath and let it out.

"Luck?"

There was a brief pause; then Calli said, "What do you care how I found her? The important thing is that I did."

"Have you called the cops?"

"And give the low-life scum who did it a chance to sneak out the back with Lily while the police are banging on the front? I don't think so. We might never find her again."

"True."

"Damned right it is."

I snugged the phone under my chin while I filled the gerbils' food dish. They stood up on their hind legs waiting for me to finish.

"So what are you saying? Exactly."

"You know what I'm saying."

"No. I don't."

"I'm saying we need to get my baby back. Now. It's not as if you haven't done this kind of thing before," Calli said when I didn't answer.

"After all, what are friends for if you can't ask them to help you with a spot of robbery now and then?" I said as I put the cover back on the gerbil cage.

"I can ask Dirk when he comes back if you don't want to."

"No. I'll help." Anything Dirk touched turned bad.

"It'll be easy. All we have to do is pop in, grab Tiger Lily, and go."

"It's never that simple." This I did know.

"This will be. So when can you get here?"

I checked my watch. It was ten minutes after twelve. Manuel was due in the store in twenty minutes. It would take me about twenty-five minutes to get to Calli's, with a stop at my house to get what I needed. That should put us at the house a little before one.

Which would give us over an hour before the junior high students got out of school and started clogging the streets.

Since most of the adults would probably be at work, not too many people would be around. I bit a nail while I thought. Eleven at night would be better, but this was doable. I told Calli I'd be by her house as soon as Manuel came, and then I called him on his cell and told him to hurry it up. He blew into Noah's Ark ten minutes later.

"God, this weather sucks," Calli said as she scanned the street for a parking space. "I wish I was back in California."

"What do you expect? It's February in Syracuse."

"It's depressing." And she waved her hand in the air to indicate that she was talking about the block as well as the weather.

She was right. Most of the houses on the street needed painting. Torn plastic sheets flapped over windows. Trash bags spilled their guts onto the snow.

"I feel as if we're living in a black-and-white movie," Calli complained as she pulled the collar of her sheepskin jacket up and tucked her chin into it. Blue veins stood out on her forehead. "At least get the heater fixed in your car. If it's twenty degrees in here, it's a lot." And she blew a couple of smoke rings to emphasize her point.

Which reminded me of what I wasn't doing. God, this not smoking thing was making me crazy. Even with the patch I felt as if I had ants crawling up and down my skin. I took a deep breath and tried to focus on the scrawl of graffiti on the lamppost. It didn't help. Maybe lollipops would work. Either that or a gun to the head.

"Maybe we should use yours," I said.

"Yes, a Beamer would fit in so well."

"Dare I suggest you could get something less conspicuous?"

"One of the only benefits about living in a place like this is that I can afford a BMW."

"I suppose," I said and turned my attention back to the road.

We'd had twenty-three consecutive days of snow and the stuff was piled everywhere. With cars parked on both sides, the street reminded me of one of those narrow, windy mountain roads in Spain where only one vehicle at a time can get through and the other one has to back up.

"I hope Lily's all right," Calli said.

Out of the corner of my eye I could see Calli's lower lip quivering.

"She'll be fine."

"She better be." A moment later she indicated a space right before the bus stop. "Pull in over there."

"You're sure she's here?" I asked as I maneuvered the car around an overturned trash can. I could see it all now. *I'm sorry, your honor. My friend got the wrong house. We meant to rob the one next door.*

Calli nodded.

"Positive?"

"Absolutely."

"You gonna tell me how you found out?"

"No. And don't blame Dirk."

"I wasn't going to."

"Yes, you were."

"Okay. I was."

Chapter Two

Calli had always had bad taste in men, but Dirk was the worst of the bunch. Dirk? What kind of name is that anyway? It sounds like something out of a bad sword-and-armor movie. A drummer who'd last worked with a band called Tonto and the White Boys, Dirk lazed around Calli's house, ate her food, and made long-distance phone calls to Rome—the Rome in Italy, not New York State—on her phone when she was down at the paper. Oh, did I forget to mention the minor fact of him forging her signature on a couple of checks? But Calli had an excuse for that too.

I had not a doubt in the world that he or one of his white trash, redneck buddies was behind Tiger Lily's disappearance, but Calli refused to listen. I just couldn't figure out what she saw in him. He wasn't that hot. He certainly wasn't that smart. Or nice. Or helpful. Maybe he was great in bed, but I couldn't buy that either. He was too concerned with himself to be interested in someone else's pleasure. Anyway, if he were I would have heard.

"This isn't your business," she reiterated as we got out of the car.

I flinched as the wind hit. I definitely needed a warmer

jacket. The lining on this one was falling apart. "It is when you involve me."

She reached for the bolt cutters. "Then give them to me. Wait here. I'll get Lily back myself."

"Don't be ridiculous. It's a two-person job. Anyway, you don't know one end of these from the other."

"I think I can figure it out."

Calli wore high-heeled boots, believed shopping was an art form, and had trouble changing the lightbulbs in her kitchen fixture. She was most at home parked in her cubicle at the local paper, where she worked as a reporter.

The wind was making the lobes of my ears burn. I flipped the hood on my parka up and held on to my temper. "This is stupid. We both want the same thing: Tiger Lily home. Let's just concentrate on that. Okay?"

Calli's hand dropped to her side. "Okay."

I slipped the bolt cutter under my jacket. It made for awkward walking. I probably should have taken a smaller one, but I'd wanted to make sure it could do the job. I wanted to snip the metal and go in, not stand there struggling with the damned links. We were conspicuous enough as it was. I glanced at Calli as we walked down the street. The cold had leached the color from her skin. She looked like an advertisement for a vampire movie with her white skin and blood-red lipstick.

"Lily will be fine," I repeated. I didn't know what else to say.

"She's due in two weeks. I hope the stress doesn't make her deliver early."

"Me too."

"Dirk says he'll help."

"That's comforting."

"Can't you ever drop anything?"

"No."

"Even when I ask you to?"

"Don't you want to hear the truth?"

"Your truth?"

I shut up. Sometimes there's no talking to Calli.

"Fine then," Calli said.

I watched her hunch her shoulders up against the wind and keep walking. A moment later we arrived at the fence. It was as Calli had described it. Standard chain link. Except for one thing. There were five other dogs staked out in the small junk-cluttered backyard. I counted two nondescript, medium-sized black-and-tan mutts, a young black lab, a German shepherd with torn-up ears, and a beagle.

Tiger Lily started woofing the moment she saw us. Great big woofs. The other dogs joined in a few seconds later. The din was enough to alert everyone in a three-block area. All the dogs were tied up to metal stakes on short leads. No water or food bowls were in evidence. Even though it was minus seventeen with the wind chill factor, there wasn't as much as a blanket, let alone a shelter of any kind in sight. The snow around the dogs was stained brown with feces.

"You should have called Animal Control the moment you saw this," I said.

Calli put her hand on my arm. "I know. I'm sorry. I just wanted to get Lily. We'll call Animal Control once we get Lily in the car. An hour more or less won't make any difference."

"It would if you were the one freezing out there."

"Robin, be reasonable. I was afraid if I told you, you wouldn't do it."

"You should have allowed me the courtesy of making up my own mind."

As I turned toward the fence, I reflected that the problem with old friends is that you take things from them you wouldn't take from anyone else.

"Aside from everything else, given the noise the dogs are making, it's only a matter of time before someone comes over to find out what we're doing."

"I know." Calli buried her hands underneath her armpits and hopped up and down while I took the bolt cutter out of my jacket and got to work.

In a minute I'd made a hole big enough for Calli and me to crawl through. By now Tiger Lily was wagging her tail so hard, her hindquarters were wiggling from side to side. The other dogs were barking hysterically.

"Oh, Lily," Calli said and ran toward her. She wrapped her arms around Lily's neck and buried her nose in her coat. The golden licked Calli's cheeks. "You poor thing." And she started to cry.

I snipped the rope that was holding Lily with the bolt cutter and tapped Calli on her shoulder. "Let's go."

Calli stood up. Released, Tiger Lily jumped up and put her paws on Calli's shoulders and gave her another long lick. Her coat was matted and dirty, but a good bath and brushing would take care of that. The other dogs looked about the same.

"Don't you worry, guys," I told them. "You'll be out of here soon."

We had taken a couple of steps when we heard a woman yell, "Hey, what the hell do you think you're doing?"

Calli and I turned. A heavyset woman wearing a bathrobe and unlaced work boots was standing by the side door shaking a broom at us.

Calli grabbed onto Tiger Lily's collar. I noticed it was a frayed blue nylon. The people who'd taken her must have gotten rid of the expensive leather one Calli had purchased for her in Florence. I wondered what they'd done with it as Calli screamed, "I'm taking my dog."

The woman took a few steps toward us. Her hair was black. She had prominent cheekbones. I saw her mouth moving, but I couldn't hear most of what she was saying because her voice was being drowned out by the noise the dogs were making. But then she changed her mind because she whirled around and headed back inside her house instead. I didn't know what she was going to do, but I did know I didn't want to be around to see.

"Come on," I said to Calli. "Let's go."

We ran for the hole in the fence. Lily bounded along beside us. Delirious with joy, she was wagging her tail so hard, it was difficult for her to move and Calli had to keep urging her forward.

When we got to my car, I threw the bolt cutters in the back seat and Tiger Lily hopped in after them, while Calli and I got in the front. A moment later, Lily jumped up front and started lapping Calli's chin. Calli was laughing and trying to push her away, but it's hard to overcome a determined golden retriever.

After a couple of tries I managed to extract my cell phone from under Lily's ample rump and call Animal Control. Then I drove Calli and Lily home.

"Don't lie to me next time," I said to Calli as she got out of the car.

"I'm sorry," she said. Miss Meekness. But I could tell from the expression on her face that she was glad she'd done what she had.

I turned around and drove back to the house we'd just left. I wanted to make sure that Animal Control showed up, because sometimes they didn't.

This time the truck showed up twenty minutes later. I got out of my car and explained the situation to the officer. He was a tall, stoop-shouldered man who looked as if he'd been doing this job for too long. He shook his head when he saw the backyard.

"People," he said in disgust. "I don't know why they say we're the higher species. Last week, I found twenty dogs in a basement. No food. No water. We had to put most of them down."

He clamped his lips together, marched toward the house, and knocked. The door opened. The woman who'd shaken a broom at us, as well as a skinny, light-complexioned kid who I put at about twenty-one, came out.

"Madam," he said, "I'm Officer Driscoll from Animal Control, and I'd like to talk to you about the dogs you've got in your backyard."

"What about them?" the woman said. By now she'd changed into gray sweats.

"They look in pretty bad shape."

The kid gave Driscoll a sullen stare. "They're fine."

"Perhaps we can discuss this inside," Driscoll said.

"Fuck you," the kid said. Then he looked up and spotted me. "She's the one you should be hassling." He pointed a finger in my direction. "She stole a dog from us."

"She's the one who lodged the complaint," Driscoll said.

"You believe her 'cause she's white."

"Yeah," Driscoll replied. "That's it."

"She did," the woman said. "I saw her and her friend take one of my dogs."

"Did you steal a dog from them?" Driscoll turned and asked me.

"Absolutely not," I replied, giving him my most winning smile.

"There you go," Driscoll said to the boy and the woman. "Now, are you going to let me in there or am I going to have to call the cops?"

"You got no call to take our animals," the boy said. "We love them."

Driscoll grimaced. "If this is love, give me hate. So what's it gonna be?" he asked when the kid didn't answer. "You gonna let me in or not?"

"Not." And the kid ran back in the house.

"Damn," Driscoll said as the woman followed, slamming the door behind her. "My wife said my horoscope was predicting this was going to be a bad day."

The dogs in the backyard were still barking as the woman yelled through the door, "You better get out of here 'cause I got a gun and I sure do know how to use it."

"Great. Friggin' great. I got Annie Oakley here. What I want to know," Driscoll said to me as we walked toward his truck, "is how come I get all the morons."

I didn't have an answer, though it was a question I'd often asked myself.

Chapter Three

"You sure took long enough," Manuel told me as I walked into Noah's Ark. He was playing with one of the red-tailed boas we'd gotten in on trade a couple of weeks ago.

In all, it had taken a little over two hours for the police to talk the woman and the boy into coming out and to load the dogs in the truck.

"The situation was a little more complicated than I expected."

Manuel snorted as the snake slithered up his arm.

"It always is with you."

"There were five other dogs out there with Tiger Lily. I had to wait for Animal Control to come take them."

"That sucks. Were they in bad shape?"

"How happy would you be chained outside without any shelter, food, or water?"

"Someone should take a baseball bat to people who do things like that," Manuel commented as the boa wound itself around his upper arm.

"I think this woman is crazy." I peeled off my gloves and stuffed them in my pocket.

"And that makes what she did okay?"

"I didn't say that."

"But you got Lily?" Manuel asked as Zsa Zsa came out of the back room.

"When have I ever not accomplished what I set out to do?"

"Excuse me," Manuel said. "I forgot I was talking to Wonder Woman."

"Well, don't," I told him as I laid the bolt cutter on the counter and bent down to pet Zsa Zsa. She jumped up and lapped my chin. I rubbed the fur behind her ears for a little while before straightening up.

"And she's okay?"

"She's fine."

"How about the other dogs?"

"They looked worse than they are."

Manuel unwound the boa. It started moving toward his neck.

"Now me," he said. "I would have lifted Lily over the fence instead of using those."

He nodded in the direction of the bolt cutters. When you're seventeen, you think you know everything.

"She weighs over a hundred pounds."

"I could do that easy."

"Really? You weigh what? One-forty?"

He bristled and indicated my left hand. "At least then you wouldn't have gotten that."

I glanced down. I had a nasty gash on my thumb. I must have done it on the edge of the metal when I was trying to bend the links back. Suddenly my thumb began to throb. I rubbed it. Funny how things like that work. Something not bothering you until you know about it.

"That guy with the tattoo of a cross on his cheek was in," Manuel continued as the snake curled around his neck and began slithering down his shirt. "He wants to sell you some more angelfish."

"If he comes back, tell him the last fish he sold me had ick. Anything else?"

"Yeah." Manuel scratched his goatee. "*El Pendejo* called. He says he has a job for you." *Pendejo* is Spanish for putz, Manuel's favorite name for Paul Santini.

"Did he say what kind of job?"

"No. But he wants you to get in touch with him ASAP." Manuel pulled the snake out of his shirt by his tail and put him back on his arm. "I didn't think you were talking to him anymore."

"Santini?"

"No. The snake."

"That was last month."

"You should keep it that way."

"Why don't you like him?"

Manuel grimaced. "What's to like? The guy's a schmuck. He thinks he's friggin' Christ Almighty."

"I wouldn't go that far."

"I would." Manuel did an imitation of Santini's New Jersey accent. " 'Make sure you tell her I called or I'm gonna come down and tan your ass.' I mean, what's that about?"

"You could try giving me his messages."

Manuel grinned. "Then he should be nicer."

"So should you." I was picking up my backpack when Manuel said, "How much you think Lily's pups are going to go for?"

"Why? You want one?"

"No. Bethany does."

I groaned. Bethany was Manuel's girlfriend. Underaged girlfriend. Right now she was living with Manuel's mother because she'd gotten kicked out of her nice middle-class suburban house.

"Her birthday's coming up."

"We'll talk later." Manuel opened his mouth. "Later," I repeated.

Otherwise I'd say something I'd regret.

"Fine," Manuel said and ostentatiously turned away from me and started talking to the snake.

I didn't care. I went into the back room, poured myself a cup of coffee, and unwrapped the Snickers bar I'd bought earlier in the day. It was a little late for lunch, but what the hell. A girl's got to keep her strength up.

Paul Santini is an ex-cop who'd opened up his own shop a couple of years ago. He was an old friend of George's—they met on the force—but the friendship had ended when I slept with him.

I was pissed with George for walking out on me, and Paul was convenient, the closest guy around who was expressing an interest in me. So I was getting even. So what. Lots of people have done lots worse. The sex we had wasn't bad, but it wasn't good either. I'm not sorry it happened, but the fact that I do work for him means there are more levels to deal with than I'd like.

Paul specializes in security work, with a sprinkling of missing children and matrimonial stuff thrown in. He's licensed and bonded and advertises in the yellow pages and does all the rest of that professional stuff. Unlike me, who is unlicensed and get my jobs strictly through word-of-mouth referrals.

A while back my husband Murphy died and I inherited Noah's Ark. Not that I wanted to run a pet store, but I couldn't sell the place without taking a big loss. To make matters worse, one of my employees was killed and I was tapped for the murder. It's amazing what you can do when your ass is on the line. I discovered I had an aptitude for survival I didn't know I possessed. All those investigative skills I used as a reporter leaped into action.

I've been doing it part-time ever since in a low-key kind of way. I like finding things out and fitting those pieces together. Helping people now and then doesn't hurt either. I figure it helps with my karmic debt. Which is huge. I handle missing children and animals and the occasional missing spouse.

Once in a while I help Santini out. He pays me fairly well and, more importantly, he'll run checks for me on his computer. Of course I could get my own. I'm probably the only person in the known universe who isn't wired, but right now my cell phone is as far as I'm prepared to go technology-wise. It startles me to think that in my heart I'm a conservative instead of the liberal I always believed myself to be.

A couple of months ago, out of curiosity, I'd paid $39.95 to an on-line company to write a report about me. The next day they e-mailed me the result. It included my complete credit history as well as a list of every place I'd lived in the past eight years. And that list included the names, addresses, and phone numbers of all my neighbors. It was very impressive. And even though this kind of thing makes my job easier, it scares the hell out of me.

I was eating the last bit of my candy when Manuel popped his head in the back. "So what does he want?"

I threw the wrapper in the trash and licked my fingers. "I haven't called him yet. Why do you care anyway?"

"I figured maybe there'll be something in it for me."

"I thought you said he was an asshole."

Manuel shrugged. "He is, but if I only did business with the people I liked, I wouldn't be doing any at all."

A demonstration of trickle-down economics at its finest. I work for Santini and Manuel works for me.

They say pain bonds and maybe it does because Manuel and I had been shot by the same person and become friends when we were in the hospital recovering. Hobbling around the corridors together, we found we liked each other. I still can't figure out why. A high-school dropout, Manuel gets by doing a little of this and a little of that. Most of what he does is in the gray area between legal and illegal, although he's not averse to stepping over the line and has therefore acquired a fairly sophisticated knowledge of the judicial system.

He sure as hell knows more about what's going on in the street than I do, and he'll share that knowledge with me for a fee. Nothing Manuel does is for free. He's the quintessential entrepreneur. Right now he's working at the store for me while Tim is on vacation. I've offered to hire him on a permanent basis, but Manuel doesn't want to be tied down.

He prefers to drift in and out with the tides. Sleeping at different people's places, owning nothing, borrowing what he needs, ready to move at a moment's notice, waiting for his big opportunity, the one that's going to let him buy his SUV.

I can't do that anymore. I've gotten to the point where I need a certain degree of permanence. Maybe that's what middle age is all about—sleeping in your own bed at night and being happy about it.

I poured myself another cup of coffee, cleaned out the cut on my hand, picked up the phone, and called Santini. We arranged a meeting at his office down at the State Tower Building for six.

I was fifteen minutes late.

Chapter Four

The State Tower Building was constructed in the thirties. It would make a great movie set. It still has the marble paneling, the carved wooden ceiling, and the art deco lamps that define the architecture of that period. Unfortunately, Paul's office doesn't follow suit. It has a jerry-rigged feel to it. Definitely not the kind of place that would inspire me to spill my guts out, but I guess I'm in the minority because he does a pretty good business.

I walked through the waiting room with its lone picture and pushed open the door to the main office without bothering to knock. Today the place smelled of pepperoni pizza. Other days it smells of fried chicken or meatball subs. That's one of the things I like about Paul—he's not a health food nazi.

Paul was sitting at his desk fiddling with his computer. The wheels on his chair squeaked as he turned to look at me.

"What if I'd been with a client?"

"But you're not."

Santini looked like what he was: an ex-cop. He was heavyset. Big hands. Beefy features. Going to seed around the middle. What was it that had attracted me to him? Not his looks, that was for sure. Maybe his air of confidence. Maybe that's what I'd liked about George. God, just the thought of George made me want to reach for a cigarette. I wondered how many patches you could wear without getting sick. I took a deep breath and thought of other things.

The desk, the file cabinets, the couple of pieces of bad art on the wall, the run-down sofa, and the chairs hadn't changed since the last time I'd been there. Add in Paul's license, computer and printer, and the coffeemaker, and you had the sum and substance of his furnishings. The only thing new was the spider plant, and that was dying. I pointed to it.

"Maybe you should try plastic."

"I'll take it under advisement. You gonna take off your jacket or what?"

I realized I still had my ski parka on. I unzipped it, threw it on the sofa, and sat down in the chair next to his desk.

Paul leaned back in his chair and rested his right calf on his left knee. "So how are things going?"

"They're goin' the same way they always do."

Someone was yelling at someone on the sidewalk outside.

"They put a food pantry near here and then they wonder why no one comes downtown," Paul said. "By the way," he added. "You look like shit."

"Thanks. I like a man who gives me compliments."

"We should get together."

"We are."

"That's not what I mean."

"I know."

Paul tilted his chair back even further, folded his hands, and rested them on his belly while he regarded me. "You see George recently?"

"Why? What do you care?"

Paul picked at a nail. "Just making conversation."

"How about we stick to business?"

"Fine. If that's the way you want it."

"That's the way I want it."

He straightened up, turned around, and reached for a folder that was lying on his desk. "I'm surprised you got the message."

"I am too. You're not on Manuel's favorite-person list."

"I spend nights worrying about it."

"You should be nicer to him."

"I've known lots of Manuels. Sooner or later they all end up in the shit pile."

"Maybe they wouldn't if you gave them a chance."

"People make their own chances." Paul opened the folder and took the top page out. "Feel like earning a little extra cash?"

"What do you have in mind?"

"Something simple. Walter Wilcox. His wife's gone missing. I thought maybe you'd be interested in finding her for him."

"Why don't you want it?"

"Always suspicious. Because I'm up to my neck with an insurance fraud scam and I don't have the time. Being a nice guy, I thought of you."

I didn't say anything.

"Go over and talk to Wilcox, see what he has to say."

"Fifty-fifty split?"

Paul grinned. "I can find someone to do it cheaper."

"But then you wouldn't get to see me."

"True." He handed me the paper. "Everything you need is on it. After you talk to Wilcox, we can discuss the case over a drink at my place."

"Don't you ever stop?"

"No. Not until I get what I want. That's why I'm a success."

"Because you wear women down?"

"You shouldn't be so negative. You should give things a chance."

"I have."

"Not really. You don't know what you're missing. I was just hitting my stride."

"I'll call you after I speak to Wilcox."

Paul shrugged. "Suit yourself. But remember I'm always here for you. I'm not asking you to change, like some people I could mention."

"You mean George?"

"I didn't say that. You did."

"Good-bye, Paul."

The wheels on Paul's chair gave out with another squeak as he shifted position. "Hey, you can bullshit me if you want, but don't do it to yourself."

I grabbed my jacket and went out the door. The elevator was slow coming. While I waited for it I took out my cell phone and called Wilcox's number.

I was in the middle of leaving a message on his answering machine when he picked up. He sounded distraught, but then most people would in his situation. We set up a meeting for the following afternoon.

It was snowing as I left the building. Big fat flakes fluttered down, blotting out the sky and whitening the streets and the cars. I closed my eyes, lifted my head up, and stuck out my tongue. Spots of cold hit it and dissolved.

As I drove home, I thought about Tiger Lily. Then I thought about Zsa Zsa. We hadn't been out for a long walk in a while. Maybe I'd take her out to the field behind Nottingham High School. She liked that. And I got a kick out of watching her root around in the snow and scare the deer mice out of their winter nests. When it happened, it was always hard to tell who was more surprised, Zsa Zsa or the mice.

Chapter Five

It was snowing as I drove over to Walter Wilcox's office. We'd gotten six inches since last night and, according to the weather forecaster, were due for six more by this evening. The roads were gray with churned-up slush, but the houses, streets, and lawns were a pristine white.

Wilcox's office was located over on the north side of Syracuse, four blocks before the farmer's market. I'd passed by the building hundreds of times but had never really looked at it closely until now. It was an undistinguished, narrow, two-story rectangular affair constructed out of brick that someone had painted blue. But they must not have primed the walls correctly because the paint was flaking. It made the walls look as if they had a bad skin disease.

A dusting of snow covered a white stretch limo parked outside the front door. It was one of those big ones, the kind with the double wheels in back that was large enough to transport a football team. Mostly, they come out on the roads in the spring when the kids have their proms. For some reason they've always reminded me of millipedes. I wondered what it was doing here now as I studied the placard on the building wall.

Wilcox's office was located on the bottom floor of the building, while the upstairs was taken up by a real estate firm. I wiped the slush on the bottom of my boots off on the mat in front of the door and went inside. The receptionist glanced up from the pile of papers in front of her. She was an older lady with a haircut her stylist should have been shot for committing and a sour expression on her face.

"Yes?" she said, obviously annoyed at having me interrupt her work.

"Robin Light. I have an appointment with your boss."

"He's on the phone. He'll be out soon," she said and went back to her sorting. Miss Graciousness.

"Do you know his wife?" I figured that as long as I was here, I might as well get started on the job.

"Of course I know Mrs. Wilcox." The receptionist removed a staple from a set of papers and began separating them.

"Was she in a lot?"

"No."

"You two chat when she was here?"

The receptionist peered up at me over her reading glasses. "I'm busy. I don't have time to chat."

I tried a different tack. "I like the limo outside."

She didn't even bother looking up, just continued with her sorting.

"Is that how your boss goes to court?"

No response.

"Are you always this loquacious?"

"Not when I have work to do."

I stood there for a few more minutes waiting for her to say something, but she didn't—obviously she could withstand my penetrating stare—and finally I gave up and took a seat. The chair was impossible to get comfortable in. I tried distracting myself with the magazines on the table, but they were all *Field and Stream,* and old ones at that, and after leafing through them in a desultory fashion and wondering why anyone would want to do the kind of stuff they were writing about, I leaned back and studied my surroundings.

The cheap fake-wood paneling on the walls made the waiting room look like a sixties den. The brown shag carpet cemented the impression. And I thought they didn't sell it anymore. Or if they did, they shouldn't. The pictures on the walls, the kind you buy at one of those art stores in the mall, were on the same aesthetic level as the carpeting. The plants were plastic. This place was even worse than Paul's.

Given the décor, I figured Wilcox wasn't charging his clients a lot. Or if he was, it certainly wasn't going into the furnishings. On the other hand, he had enough cash lying around to hire Paul, and Paul didn't come cheap. Maybe Wilcox just had a bad sense of design.

Five minutes later Wilcox came out. He had the look of a drinker. He clasped both of my hands in his. They were unpleasantly moist. So were his eyes. He was a small man with a squarish face, a jawline that was beginning to soften, and a pronounced stoop to his posture that pooched his stomach out, making it look bigger than it already was.

His suit was cheap and ill-fitting, and his hair looked as if someone had gone over the top of his head with a thresher, but he had an expensive watch on his wrist, an item that must have set him back at least six figures, and expensive shoes on his feet. When he opened his mouth, his teeth looked stained and uneven.

My grandmother had always said you could judge a person by their shoes, but that was because Rolexes were before her time.

"So," he said as he led me into his office and closed the door. "Paul tells me you're going to find my wife."

"I'm going to try," I replied. "Hopefully, people will be more helpful than your secretary."

"Martha is protective."

"I would have chosen the word rude myself."

Wilcox shrugged. "Maybe, but I couldn't get along without her."

I changed the subject. "I take it you've been to the police?"

He nodded.

"And?"

"And they said there's nothing they can do. My wife isn't a minor. She hasn't committed a crime. No one's abducted her. All of which is true. But I'm concerned."

He drew his breath in as he indicated I should sit down on the plain wooden chair next to his desk. After I had, he sat in his chair and crossed his legs at the ankles.

I took a pen and notebook out of my backpack. "Why is that?"

"Why, indeed." Walter Wilcox clapped his hands together softly while he tried to decide what to say. I waited. A minute later he began to talk.

"Recently my wife began seeing a therapist. A psychologist. She hasn't been the same since."

"In what way?"

"She's become agitated." Wilcox bit his lip. "This man . . ." He gave the word a twist.

"The pyschologist . . ."

Wilcox nodded. ". . . Claims that my wife Janet was sexually abused as a child. Says that's the root of all of her problems."

"What kind of problems?"

"That's the thing." Wilcox flung out his hands. "I didn't think she had any. I mean, any more than the ones everyone has. Like last year, she went to a family reunion back home. She got some sort of twenty-four-hour stomach bug. But this psychologist told her it was her body's way of telling her she'd been abused."

"She told you this?"

"Yes."

"And that upset her?"

"Terribly. It's like she's become a different person. Maybe it's the pills she's taking."

I interrupted. "Which are?"

"Prozac and . . . I'm not sure about the other."

He looked at me for a comment, but I didn't say anything.

"All I know," Wilcox continued, "is she flies into these rages. She cries. She gets anxious. And the worst of it is, I don't think this abuse thing is true."

"Did you tell her that?"

"Yes. And I wish I hadn't." He rubbed the furrow between his eyebrows with his thumb. "She began screaming and yelling. Telling me I was part of the problem. Telling me I was just like her uncle. I left and came to the office. I had to. I just wanted to give her time to calm down, you know?"

I nodded encouragingly. It's something I'm good at.

"When I returned, she was gone."

"How did you know that she'd left?"

He frowned. "What do you mean, how did I know? It was obvious. Her car was gone. And she'd packed her suitcase."

"What did she take?"

"Some of her clothes. I'm not sure what exactly. I don't pay much attention to that sort of thing."

I could have told that from the way he dressed. "What else?"

"Her makeup. Hairbrush. Toothbrush."

"Did she take a lot of money with her?"

"Not that much. Two thousand dollars."

Two thousand dollars was enough to allow her to go somewhere, but it wasn't enough to live on. "Does she have another source of income?"

Wilcox shook his head. "Frankly," he continued. "I'm afraid she's suicidal. She's been talking a lot lately about life not being worth living. I don't want to have to . . ." He shuddered.

"I see. Can I ask why she went to this psychologist in the first place?"

"My daughter suggested him. Janet wanted to lose weight, and she hadn't been able to. She got on the Internet and that's when she decided that she was an emotional eater, so that's why she went to see this man. God, I wish she hadn't. I told her I liked her the way she was. I told her it didn't matter, but we were going to go to a wedding in six months and there was this dress she wanted to wear . . ." Wilcox's voice trailed off. "There were going to be some people there she hadn't seen in a couple of years. I guess she wanted to impress them."

"This must be hard on your daughter."

Wilcox nodded. "She feels terribly guilty."

"Can I speak to her?"

Wilcox made a vague gesture with his hand. "I'm not sure what her plans are. Exactly. Outside of the fact that she's going back to New York City soon."

"Perhaps I can speak to her before she does."

"Be my guest." Wilcox wrote down a number on a piece of yellow paper, tore it off the pad, and gave it to me. "She's staying at a friend's. But I just got off the phone with her. Stephanie hasn't heard from her mother either."

"Perhaps she can tell me something that would help."

Wilcox looked doubtful.

I pressed on. "Does your wife have any siblings?"

"No. She's an only child."

"Parents?"

"Both died a few years ago."

"Cousins?"

"I'll give you their names, but all they do is exchange Christmas cards." Wilcox leaned forward slightly. "Aren't you going to take notes?"

"When I need to, I will," I assured him. So far I hadn't

learned anything worth writing down. "Do you have any idea where your wife would have gone?"

"None. She's a homebody."

"Would her friends know?"

"She really doesn't have any."

I let that one go.

"Did she have a favorite place?"

"She likes the rose garden in Thornden Park in the summer. Did you know it's one of the ten best in the country?"

"No. I didn't. Was there someplace special you two went when you vacationed?"

"We haven't taken a vacation in years."

"Someplace she fantasized about going?"

Wilcox looked blank. I guess fantasy didn't count for much in their lives.

"Like Paris? Rome? San Francisco?"

"I don't think so. She didn't like to travel."

I didn't point out that she was traveling now.

"Did she take your name when she married you?"

"Yes."

"What was her maiden name?"

"Lyons."

I wrote that down.

"Why is that important?"

"Your wife might decide to start using it again."

The phone rang.

"She'll get it," Wilcox said, indicating his secretary.

It rang twice more before Martha picked it up.

"I'm sorry I can't tell you more," he said.

"Do you have a picture of her I can have?"

"At home. But it's two years old."

"That shouldn't be a problem. I'd like you to do something else for me as well. I'd like you to sit down and give me a list of people she knows, the name of her doctor and the psychologist she's going to, as well as the name of her college and high school. I need the license plate number of the car she took. Her Social Security number. Her credit card bills, old phone bills, her favorite restaurants, places she likes to go to, places she's always wanted to visit. In short, the more stuff you can tell me about her, the better my chances are of finding her."

"I'll have everything by tomorrow morning," Wilcox promised, looking up from the list he'd written down.

I stood.

"So you'll find her?" he said.

"I'll certainly try."

The limo was gone when I walked out the door. I decided someone in the real estate firm upstairs must have been closing a big deal.

Chapter Six

As I got into my car, I wondered if Janet Wilcox really was crazy or if her husband just thought she was. Women, you ask them why they left their husbands and they'll give you five hours' worth of reasons, easy. Most can go on for days detailing the causes. You ask guys why their wife left them, and they'll look at you and shrug their shoulders and say, "I don't know. She just went nuts." Like Wilcox.

Crazy or not, though, there was no question in my mind that Wilcox wanted his wife back even if he didn't understand what the hell was wrong with her. If he didn't want her back, he wouldn't be laying out the money he was. Since I've been doing this kind of work, I've found that money is as good a barometer of sincerity as anything, and a job like this could run Wilcox a substantial chunk of change.

I thought about the meds Wilcox said his wife was on as I turned the car over. It groaned in the cold. I rubbed my hands to warm them while I waited for the heater to kick in. One of these days I had to remember to buy a new pair of gloves. That could be the cause of her problem right there. Recently, I'd read somewhere that serotonin reuppers can spark manic episodes in people who are susceptible to bipolar disorder.

Maybe that was what happened to Janet. And now she was crashing.

On the way back to the store, I checked in with Paul, then dialed the number Walter Wilcox had given me for his daughter. She picked up on the second ring.

"Yes?" she said.

I introduced myself and explained why I was calling. "I'd like to see you if possible."

"I'm leaving to go back to New York City in an hour." She sounded nasal. As if she had a cold.

"I can come over now." There was a long pause on her end. I got the feeling she was searching around for an excuse to say no. "This won't take very long."

"Why can't we do this on the phone?"

"Because I'd like to meet you."

"Oh."

"It might help me to find your mother."

"I don't know anything. Didn't my father tell you that?"

"As a matter of fact, he did. I'd still like to talk to you, though."

"Oh, all right." Stephanie sighed and gave me her address. "But I'm telling you it's going to be a waste of time."

"I'm willing to take that risk." And I hung up before she could change her mind.

As I paused at a light, it occurred to me that Stephanie seemed amazingly unconcerned about her mother's disappearance. Which meant one of two things: either she didn't care or she'd heard from her. I guess I'd find out which soon enough.

On the way over to Stephanie's, I called Leonard's Animal Hospital to see how the dogs that had been taken out of the backyard on Fayette Street were doing. Leonard's Animal Hospital was where Animal Control took all the animals they picked up.

"Oh, you're the one that called it in," the vet tech who answered the phone said when I explained who I was. "We had to rehydrate the beagle, but everyone else looked worse off than they were. It's amazing what some food and water and warmth will accomplish."

"You forgot kindness."

"Ain't that the truth. Now all we have to do is find homes for them."

"What happened to the two people they arrested?"

"Well, I heard the woman is in the psych ward at Upstate—she totally bugged out. And the kid is downtown at the Public Safety Building." A dog started baying in the background. "Gotta go," the tech said. "If you hear of anyone who wants a dog, send him our way."

"Yeah, rescuing is the easy part."

"You can say that again."

I clicked off and called Manuel.

"Listen," I said to him. "You think Bethany would want one of the mutts that I rescued from the backyard?"

"She really wants one of Lily's puppies, but I have a couple of friends who've been talking about getting a dog."

"Call them up. I'll drive them over to the shelter if necessary."

"No need. They've got their own cars."

"Could you make a sign and put it in the store window?"

"I'm on it."

Maybe saving five dogs wasn't saving the world, but these days I'd take what I could get. The snow had let up, and the gray clouds were thinning. Occasionally I could see wisps of blue sky as I drove over to the university area. The streets were clogged with school buses discharging children, and it took me longer to get there than I anticipated.

The place Stephanie was staying in was located on Lancaster Avenue, a street made up of modest colonials occupied by professors, students, and docs from Upstate. It was situated on top of a small rise and nestled between two similar-looking houses. The house was a gray blue, but someone had painted the trim work a pale pink and surrounded the frame of the front window with a border of red flowers. Sometimes creativity should be discouraged.

Christmas lights still hung from the windows. There was a Neon in the driveway. The path to the house hadn't been shoveled, and my feet sank in the snow up to my ankles as I walked to the porch. I rang the bell. Stephanie answered at once. I don't know what I was expecting, but it wasn't someone who looked like her.

She was so thin, I could have circled her upper arm with my right hand. Her face was angular, her jaw prominent, and her nose, which was slightly red, looked as if it had seen the services of a plastic surgeon. She was wearing black jeans, a black turtleneck sweater, and black leather boots. New York City all the way. The lack of color in her clothes highlighted her cropped platinum hair and hazel eyes.

"I take it you're Robin Light," she said, motioning for me to come in.

I nodded. "Do you take after your mother's side of the family?" Because she certainly didn't take after her father's.

"No. Thank God," she replied as she took my coat and hung it on a hook in the hallway. "I'm adopted."

I followed her into the living room. The walls were covered with quilts. The rest of the furnishings—sofa, chairs, coffee table, and lamps—were Early American. Stephanie remained standing with her arms crossed over her chest. She looked as out of place as a piece of stainless in a packet of bows.

"So what do you do when you're not up here?" I asked her.

"I plan parties for people."

"It must be interesting work."

"It pays the bills." She ran a thumbnail down the side of

the arm of her black turtleneck sweater. "Like I said on the phone, I don't think there's anything I can tell you that will be of any help."

"And you don't have any idea where your mother would go?"

Stephanie shook her head. "We didn't talk much when I was younger, and once I moved out of the house we hardly talked at all."

"But you had to have talked about something."

"Well, yeah. When I was younger our conversations were about cleaning my room and coming home on time, and when I got older we talked about my hair and short skirts."

She cleared her throat. I waited.

"Really," Stephanie continued. "I mean, she's a nice woman. Don't get me wrong. But all I remember her doing is cooking and cleaning and watching television. A trip to the grocery store was a big outing for her."

"That's what your father said. So how come she took off all of a sudden? This doesn't seem like her."

Stephanie reached in her sleeve for a Kleenex and blew her nose. "I don't have a clue. Maybe she finally realized there's a big world out there."

"You don't sound as if you care very much."

"Of course I care." Stephanie's voice rose. "She's my mother. But I've learned not to spend my energy on things I can't do anything about."

Something told me that wasn't the whole story. Not even close to it.

"May I ask why you're up here?"

She shrugged. "It's no big secret. I brought a rug up from the City for a friend and I'm getting ready to drive back down." She looked at her watch. "And now, if you don't mind, I have to finish packing. I have a meeting in the City in five hours."

"Don't let me keep you."

Stephanie's eyes narrowed slightly. "I won't. I told you this was going to be a waste of time."

"Where did you get the name of the psychologist you recommended to your mother?" I asked as Stephanie ushered me out of the living room.

She stopped by the doorway and turned. "From a friend. Why?"

"No reason really. It's just that, according to your father, if it weren't for him your mother would still be here."

"How typical." She frowned and unconsciously straightened the edge of the quilt that was hanging on the wall. I thought it was the log cabin pattern, but I wasn't sure. I've never been a big quilt fan. "The man's never taken any responsibility for his actions and never will," she said with a certainty that spoke of old discussions.

"Meaning . . ."

"I really have to get going."

There didn't seem to be much more to say.

"Well, if you have any ideas . . ."

"I'll call you."

I gave her my card. She looked at it and slipped it into her pants pocket. Then she escorted me to the hallway.

"How's my father doing?" she asked as she handed me my parka.

"He's upset. Of course."

"Karma," she said as she held the door open for me.

I wanted to ask her what she meant but she shut the door before I could.

Chapter Seven

Zsa Zsa was stretched out in the store window gnawing on the edge of the two-foot rawhide bone I was using as a display object when I pulled up to the curb. By the time I'd walked inside, she was waiting for me. She wagged her rump and danced around my ankles while I knelt down and petted her. Manuel didn't bother looking up. He was too busy talking on the phone. The way he was hunched over it and the crooning sound of his voice told me he was speaking to Bethany.

When I got closer, he covered the mouthpiece of the receiver and said, "Have you found out about the puppies yet?"

"No. I haven't. Anyway, Bethany has to ask her parents. And they're definitely not going to say yes."

At this point I didn't think they'd buy Bethany a pencil set let alone a golden retriever puppy.

"She doesn't have to ask them anything. She's going to divorce them."

"What are you talking about?"

"I'll explain later."

"Where is she going to live? How is she going to support herself?"

Manuel help up his hand. "Relax. I've got everything covered." This did not fill me with a feeling of confidence. "And by the way," Manuel added, "George is waiting for you in the back."

And the day had been going so well up till now. "Great. Why'd you let him back there?"

"And I was supposed to do what to stop him?" Manuel demanded. "Like he's going to listen to me."

"You're right." George Samson probably outweighed Manuel by one hundred pounds or more.

"You know it."

"I wouldn't go that far."

My stomach was spasming as I walked into the back room. George and I had had a big fight four weeks ago. Our fight had been about a woman he claimed was a friend and I claimed was a lot more. That had been four weeks ago and we hadn't spoken since. Now he was sitting in my chair eating an apple, wearing the Irish Fisherman sweater I'd gotten him.

"What are you doing here?" I asked him. "Shouldn't you be in class or something?"

"I'm not teaching today." He took a last bite of the apple and tossed it into the garbage can. It hit the rim and bounced in.

"Then doing your research. Or correcting papers. Or working on a grant. Or whatever the hell it is you do." I could hear the nasty edge that creeps into my voice whenever I get upset.

"Would you like your chair back?" he asked quietly. He was almost always quiet. And in control. And I was almost always the opposite.

"If you don't mind."

He got up. "Why didn't you call?"

"Why didn't you?"

"I asked first."

"Fine." I took a deep breath and let it out. "We keep fighting and we never resolve anything, and frankly, I'm not sure I can keep doing this."

"Neither am I," George said softly.

"So why are you here?"

"I got worried. I just wanted to make sure you're all right."

"I'm fine."

George lifted the catalogues piled on the chair next to my desk, put them on the floor, and sat down.

"Calli told me you stopped smoking."

Whenever I'm not around George for a while, I forget what a big man he is. How much room he takes up. My office, which is not a large space, suddenly seemed smaller.

"I'm trying to."

"Good for you."

George is an African-American with black skin and features that are all angles and planes. Not the cuddly type. His mouth seems to rest in a scowl, although in the past year or two his expression has softened.

I still remember we'd been drinking at the local neighborhood dive one evening a couple of years ago when, apropos of nothing, he'd turned to me and said, "I can't help it if everyone is afraid of me." He'd grinned when he said it, obviously pleased with the prospect.

And he was right. He does scare people. If I didn't know him, he would frighten me. But he's a closet sweetie, someone who finds homes for stray kittens when no one is looking and lets Zsa Zsa sleep in bed with him because she's unhappy on the floor even though he doesn't like the smell of dogs. Sometimes, when things get too bad with his sister down in the Bronx, he allows his pain-in-the-ass nephew to stay with him as well, never mind that he can't stand Jamal's music, the way he dresses, or how he talks.

George played semi-pro football and then went on to become a cop and then got off the force because he couldn't stand it anymore. He's currently enrolled in a Ph.D. program in medieval history. Definitely an interesting man. Lots of incongruities that butt up against each other. He was also my husband's best friend. We got together after Murphy's death and have been parting and reconciling ever since. Calli tells me I've never been able to let go of Murphy and that's why I can't let go of George. Despite his roving eye. That he's a stand-in for Murphy. But then, Calli believes in ghosts too.

"When did you see Calli?"

"This morning at the gas station. She was filling up before heading up North."

"Better her than me." The North Country is a harsh place. "Is the paper doing another story on the casino?"

"I didn't ask her." George stretched his legs out. There was a mark on his cheek. I wondered if he'd cut himself shaving. Or it could be a scratch. I wanted to ask but didn't. "Your guess is as good as mine."

"God only knows there's enough material."

"This is true."

Even the *New York Times,* which runs more pieces on Botswana than it does on Central New York, had run a couple of items on The Sacred Feather Casino, not to mention the Teewakee Indian land claims. The Teewakees, claiming that treaties negotiated in Colonial times were illegal, were asking for their land back, land which happened to include the town of Wayne. Naturally, the people living there were a tad upset.

Some of them had put up signs on their houses and businesses. The signs said things like *No More Land for the Casino* and *Gambling Is a Sin.* Others had put up signs saying nastier things. It didn't help that there were white-power groups based up that way. Organizations had been formed. Lawyers hired. Threats made. The FBI had been called in to investigate.

I could see the locals' point, though. After all, they hadn't negotiated the treaty. But the Teewakee had a point too. They'd been cheated out of their land. This was definitely a lose-lose situation. No one was going to be happy whatever the result. I was thinking about that and about the concept of the sins of the fathers being visited on the children when George started speaking again.

"I hope she's not doing a series," he said. "She's going to hate being stuck out there without a Starbucks to get coffee in."

"The hell with Starbucks. How about a decent restaurant?"

The only things out that way were bars, bait shops, and gas stations. If you wanted a supermarket, you had to drive thirty miles. And then there was the weather. This time of year whiteouts were common. When Syracuse got five inches of snow, the North Country got fifteen. Add a wind that whipped the flakes into blizzard conditions and you had a recipe for disaster.

"I have a friend lives out around there," George said. "He tells me everyone is walking around with their shotguns loaded these days."

"Everyone always walks around with their guns loaded out there."

"Maybe so." George ran a finger under the edge of his turtleneck and pulled at it. "I wouldn't know. That's redneck country. As far as I'm concerned you could take that area and nuke it and no one would know the difference. In fact, it would be an improvement. They should get rid of all the people and give the place back to the deer."

"What have they ever done to you?"

"Personally? Nothing. I just don't like them."

"Why?"

"Because they don't like me."

"Good reason."

"Listen. I'm not the saintly old black family retainer in the movies that forgives everyone."

"I know that."

"Good." He dropped his hand and gave Zsa Zsa an absentminded pat. She licked his fingers. "Calli told me what happened with Tiger Lily."

"Did she tell you about the other dogs?"

"No."

Typical. I filled him in. "You don't know anyone who wants a dog, do you?"

"I don't, but I'll ask around."

"No students." Students took in animals and then went home at the end of the semester and threw them out on the streets. "What about you?"

"I don't have time for one."

"Of course you do."

"Okay. I have time, but I don't want to be bothered. Happy?"

"It's not about happy. I'd rather hear the truth than hear you make excuses."

George idly ran his finger down the spine of one of the catalogues. "That's what most people say, but they don't mean it."

"You believe that?"

"I know it."

I got up to get another cup of coffee. As I was going by him, George reached over, grabbed my wrist, and pulled me toward him. "I miss you."

"I miss you too."

I could smell his cologne. "Let's not do this."

He reached up and brushed a strand of hair off my fore-head. My insides felt like molten lead.

"I'm tired of this roller coaster that we're on. I want more."

"What if there isn't any more? What if this is it?" George pulled me down to his lap. "Would that be so terrible?"

"Yes." I knew I should get up, but I couldn't. It was like coming home.

Chapter Eight

George and I had dinner at a small Mexican restaurant on Westcott Street. For once the place wasn't crowded. I had salmon with fried sweet potatoes, George had swordfish, and we both had a couple of glasses of Belgium-style wheat beer. It was the first decent meal—no, scratch that; it was the first real meal I'd had in weeks. I'd been living on candy bars, coffee, and vitamin pills, with an occasional yogurt thrown in.

Whenever I get tense I have trouble eating, and I'd been tense a lot lately. Maybe it was the place with its copper bar and peach walls and tiny bouquets on tables, maybe it was the beer I was nursing, maybe it was being with George, but I finally began to relax a little.

George flagged the waitress and ordered two coffees and asked for the dessert menu.

"I ran into Paul the other day," he said to me after she'd gone. "He said you were working for him again."

I told him about Janet Wilcox.

"She's probably on the beach in Cancun shacked up with a Mexican beachboy."

"Sounds good to me. Sun. Sand. Sex. Margaritas. Maybe I

should try it too." Though I couldn't picture Janet Wilcox doing something like that from what her husband had told me.

George leaned across the table and punched me lightly on the arm. "After me, everyone is a letdown."

"My, what a big ego you have."

"Deservedly." George grunted. "I hope that prick is paying you well."

"I wouldn't be doing it otherwise. We're doing a fifty-fifty split. Finding her should be simple enough. Then I call the aggrieved husband and tell him where she is. Whatever happens after that is up to them."

George paused while the waitress placed the coffees in front of us and handed us the menu. We conferred and decided to split a pear apple crisp with whipped cream.

"Nothing is ever simple with you," he said when the waitress went off to get our dessert.

"You either."

"True." George picked up his cup and sipped his coffee. The cup disappeared in his hand. "Robin," he said.

"Yes?"

He shook his head. "I forgot what I was going to say."

"Getting old?"

"Guess so. I'm sure it'll come to me later." And he smiled and drained his coffee cup.

We chatted some more about Janet Wilcox. Finally the waitress brought our dessert. We ate every last bit of it and went back to my house.

"Manuel here?" George asked as we went inside.

"He's staying over at a friend's tonight."

"Good," George said.

And we went upstairs and made love.

Hours later I woke up to find George was already dressed.

"Robin," he said. He looked grave.

"Yes." My heart started fluttering.

He studied the window blinds for a few seconds.

"I wanted to tell you at the store yesterday. And then at dinner. But I couldn't."

His eyes moved to the wall. He was looking at everything but me.

"Tell me what?" I wrapped the sheet more tightly around me.

"I'm sorry," he said. "I really am."

"About what?"

"Natalie."

"Natalie?"

"The blonde."

"The one you said you weren't having a relationship with?"

"Yes."

"How long have you been seeing her?"

"Six months."

"Six months?"

"I never meant for this to get out of hand."

"Meaning?"

George rubbed the stubble on his chin with his hand, then took a deep breath and let it out. The sound filled the room. "I guess the best thing to do is just say it. Natalie's pregnant. It's my baby. We're going to get married. I don't know what else to do." He reached over and patted my shoulder. "I can't tell you how badly I feel. You have to believe that."

I didn't say anything. I couldn't find the words. I felt as if all the air had been squeezed out of me. I watched a squirrel run along the telephone line.

"I'm sorry," George repeated.

Then he was gone. I heard him close the downstairs door. I heard him drive off. So it was over. All those years. Just like that.

Zsa Zsa whimpered and nosed at my hand. I patted her head mechanically. "It'll be fine," I told her. But the way she was looking at me, I could tell that she knew it wasn't.

I threw the covers off me, got up, and took a shower. The bottle of shampoo I was using slipped out of my hands and fell on the floor. Rivulets of yellow ran toward the drain. I left the bottle, got out of the stall, dried myself, and got dressed. I knew I should cry or scream or do something. But I couldn't. I felt as if my guts had been ripped out, and there was a pain in my chest that wouldn't go away.

The phone was ringing when I walked into the store. I picked it up. It was George.

"I'm calling to see if you're okay."

"Don't call."

"Robin, I feel terrible."

I hung up. The phone started ringing again. After five rings the answering machine came on. I listened to George while I took a cigarette out of the pack I'd just purchased and lit up. When he was done, I erased his message and gave Zsa Zsa a treat. Then I got to work. Sweeping the floor comforted me.

Half an hour later, Walter Wilcox came by. As I watched him slowly walk across the floor, it occurred to me that we had something in common. We'd both had people we loved walk out on us. That should have made me more sympathetic. But it didn't. It made me not want to look at his face.

"So," he said, shoving the shoebox with the items I'd requested from him yesterday across the counter.

A faint odor of unwashed clothes and alcohol came off him. I wondered how much he'd been drinking last night. Certainly he didn't look as if he'd gotten a good night's sleep. His eyes were sunk back in his head, and the circles under them looked as if they'd been painted on skin that was pasty white from lack of sun.

"How long do you think it's going to take?"

"To find your wife?"

He scrunched his eyes against the light. "Who else are we talking about?"

"It was a rhetorical question."

"Sorry. I don't feel very well. I think I might be coming down with something."

Like a hangover.

"Did you speak to my daughter?"

I nodded.

"She wasn't much help, was she?"

"No, she wasn't. You were right about that."

"Janet and she never got along. It was tough. I felt bad for Stephanie." Wilcox stared into the shoebox as if it contained the past. "One day Janet would say it was okay for Stephanie to walk to her friend's house, the next day she'd throw a fit and insist she hadn't said anything like that." He gave a deprecatory shrug. "I tried to smooth things over, but I had to work."

"Stephanie told me she was adopted."

Wilcox nodded and unbuttoned his coat. It was standard lawyer's issue. Gray. Mohair. Conservative. Only there was a stain on the lapel, as well as a stain on his blue-and-white striped tie.

"She was. Janet really wanted a child. And sometimes she was a good mother . . ." His voice drifted off. "I don't know. I never figured out what the problem was."

"Why don't you just let me go through this stuff, and then we'll talk." I told him.

"Fine." His eyes never left my hands as I took the top off the box and laid it aside. "The photo's a couple of years old," he said as I lifted the picture of his wife out of the box. "She's gained weight since then. Maybe thirty pounds or so. That's why she went to that charlatan. But I told you that."

"Yes, you did."

Janet Wilcox was her husband's opposite. Neat to a fault.

In the picture her hair had been teased and shellacked into something that resembled a blond helmet. I didn't know women wore their hair that way anymore. It reminded me of photos I'd seen from the fifties.

Her face was perfectly made up, but that couldn't hide the nondescriptness of her features. She wasn't pretty. She wasn't ugly. She was plain. The frilly white blouse with ruffles around the neck that she was wearing belonged on someone younger and cuter.

I reflected that her daughter couldn't have been more different from her.

As I studied the photo, I thought about the comment George had made last night about Janet Wilcox running off to Cancun. He was one hundred percent wrong, I decided. Janet Wilcox did not look like the type of person who would ever shack up with a beachboy. Or anyone else for that matter. She looked like someone who wouldn't even buy a brand of toilet paper she wasn't familiar with, let alone go in for a romantic fling.

"I couldn't find another photograph. Janet didn't like having her picture taken."

"This will be fine." I laid the picture aside and looked at Wilcox. "Does your wife have an e-mail account?"

"She doesn't even know how to turn on a computer. We don't have one in the house."

"I notice you didn't include a list of her friends in here."

"I already told you. She doesn't have any."

I raised an eyebrow. "None?"

Wilcox relented. "Well, there are the women in her book group, but I don't know their names. She was a stay-at-home kind of person," Wilcox added. "I know that's unusual today, but it's true." He sounded defensive.

"What did she do at home?"

"Cleaned house, cooked. She watched a lot of TV. Especially those women's shows in the afternoon, the ones where everyone always has something wrong with themselves." That jibed with what the daughter said. "I was trying to encourage her to get her real estate license. At least it would get her out of the house."

I picked up Janet Wilcox's appointment calendar and leafed through it. Apparently Wilcox spoke the truth. It was mostly bare.

"Do you know where the book group met?"

"At Barnes & Noble on Thursday nights. But she stopped going a month ago. She said she didn't like the books they were choosing now. Too violent."

It wasn't much, but it was something. I made a note, then went back to rummaging through the box.

"How long is locating her going to take?" Wilcox asked.

"I don't know."

"You have to have some idea." Wilcox's tone was querulous.

"Not really." Zsa Zsa leaned against my leg. I bent down and scratched her rump. "Depending on what I come up with, it could take me two days, a couple of weeks, or six months."

"Six months?" he yelped "That's ridiculous. Paul said you'd do this fast."

Or maybe I'll never find her, I wanted to say as I picked a piece of packing tape off the fur on Zsa Zsa's leg. Sometimes people don't want to be found. Sometimes they just disappear into the ether. Sometimes they start a new life. Sometimes they die on the road and are buried in pauper's graves. Sometimes they're killed and buried in forests and bogs.

But mostly they come back. They go away and decide it was a mistake. The new lover turns out to be like the old husband or wife, or the freedom to do what they want turns into boredom and loneliness. Only their pride won't let them call home, so they start doing things like using their old credit cards, signaling to the people they left behind to come and get them. Sometimes the people they've left behind do. Other times they don't because they've discovered they're better off without them. But I wasn't being paid to say those things to Wilcox. I was just being paid to find his wife.

"I'll do the best I can," I told him.

Wilcox looked around the store. "You're going to be working on this full-time, aren't you?"

"Yes. My associate will be taking over my retail duties." Associate indeed. Good thing he couldn't see Manuel.

"Why six months?" he continued. "This is a simple job."

"Then you do it."

"You're right. You're right. I'm sorry. I apologize." He took off his hat and unbuttoned his jacket. "Since Janet's gone, I haven't been sleeping well. I'm just worried that she's done something stupid."

"I know you are. I'll try and wrap this up fast—mostly cases like this are fairly simple—but I can't promise anything until I see what I have."

That seemed to satisfy him because he said, "I'll call you first thing tomorrow morning for an update," as he wiped his brow with the back of his forearm.

"By all means." I gave him a big, insincere smile. "I look forward to it."

I began to understand why Paul had given me this job.

After Wilcox left, I made myself a large pot of French roast and drank it down while I went through the papers Wilcox had given me. On a first, casual pass, none of it yielded much in the way of information, but I pulled the phone bills out to take a more detailed look at them. Then I called Paul and asked him to run a check on Janet Wilcox's license and credit cards and see what turned up.

"Sure, I can do that for you," he told me. "So what did you do last night?"

"Nothing," I lied. I wasn't talking about George with him. "I went to bed early. What can you tell me about Wilcox?" "Good old Walter?" I heard a creak as Paul turned his chair around. "Not too much to tell."

"He's a friend of yours? You didn't tell me that."

"More of an acquaintance really."

We chatted for a few more minutes, and then I hung up and phoned the psychologist Janet had been seeing. He must not have been very busy because he picked up on the second ring.

He had one of those professionally soothing voices. I wondered if there's a required class psychologists have to take to get that tone—Calming Voice 101.

I told him I was having anxiety attacks because I didn't think he'd talk to me if I told him the real reason I was coming to see him. As luck would have it, he happened to have a cancellation at five that afternoon. I told him I'd see him then and hung up.

I spent the next hour cleaning out the fish tanks and fending off my creditors, smoking cigarettes, and trying not to think about George.

Chapter Nine

I was lighting my fourth cigarette of the hour when the kid from the house on Fayette Street walked through the door and started toward me.

"I thought you were in jail," I said as I reached for the phone.

"I got bailed out."

"Stay where you are," I warned, "or I'm phoning the police."

"You got no call to do that." And he threw a crumpled-up piece of newspaper on the counter.

I smoothed it out with my right hand while I kept hold of the phone with my left. Down at the bottom of the page was a three-line item mentioning the incident. Although it didn't give his name because he was underage, it mentioned Robin Light, proprietor of Noah's Ark, as the complainant. Wonderful.

"You her?" the kid said.

"No. I'm the Queen of Sheba. I'm just filling in here. What do you want?"

I shoved the paper back toward him. Now that he was closer, I could see he was wearing a threadbare jacket and sneakers. Little hairs were starting to come in on his skull. I wondered if they itched.

"Why'd you have to fuck everything up?" he demanded.

"Why'd you have to steal my friend's dog?"

"I didn't. Myra found her. Maybe you should have asked her before calling Animal Control."

"I would have called them anyway."

"He jabbed his finger at me. "You had no right to do that. They were Myra's babies. They was the only thing she had."

"Then she should have taken better care of them. They could have died out there."

"She was doin' the best she could."

"She was doing a bad job."

The kid hit the counter with the flat of his hand. The gecko that was on the ceiling skittered away in alarm.

"People like you are always big with advice, but you never help out," he cried. "Now she's crazy, and it's your fault."

"Look. What do you want?"

"I want to tell you what you did."

"Well, you have. So how about leaving."

His face scrunched up, and he whirled around and ran for the door.

I threw the article in the trash and started mopping the floors, but the kid's words, the ones about always being big with advice, lingered in my mind. Calli had said that to me too. So had Murphy for that matter. Oh, well. I went back to thinking about where Janet Wilcox could have gone. It was more productive.

When Manuel arrived, I cut out and headed for Woodchuck Hill Road. It was time to talk to the neighbors and see what they had to say about Janet Wilcox.

Woodchuck Hill Road has two ends. The cheap end and the expensive end. The Wilcoxes lived on the cheap end, which is still more expensive than my neighborhood. The houses there are closer together, as opposed to the doctors' end, where the houses are separated from each other by an acre or more of woods and the only things you see out your window are trees.

It had started snowing again, a slow, steady drift. I had a vision of the snow piling up and up, shrouding everything, until silence was all that was left. As I turned onto Woodchuck Hill Road, I went by two cars that had slid into a ditch.

Janet Wilcox's house, as well as the ones around it, all looked as if they'd been built by the same builder. Three- and four-bedroom wooden colonials with attached garages. Only the trims on the houses were different. And the outside plantings. Other than that they were all the same.

I started with the house on the left of the Wilcoxes. The young woman who opened the door looked to be about nineteen. She was blond and blue-eyed, and except for the ring through her right nostril, a ring that would have done Ferdinand the Bull proud, she could have been in a contest for All-American Girl.

"Put a plug in it, Sam," she yelled before turning her head back to me and asking what I wanted.

I told her.

Her eyes widened. "Boy, and I thought nothing ever happened around here."

"So you know Janet Wilcox?"

"I've seen her pulling in and out of her driveway."

"You've never spoken?"

"Except to say hello. I'm the au pair." She said it as if that explained everything.

"Pretty fancy."

"I thought so too until I started working." Her grin flickered off. She wrinkled her nose. "Too many romance novels. That's my problem. You probably want to speak to Mrs. Goldstein, but she isn't in right now. You'll have to come back later."

Before I had a chance to ask her when Mrs. Goldstein would be returning, the sound of wailing hit the air. The girl turned and ran toward it. I followed. Two five-year-old twins were locked in combat over a ball.

The au pair put her hands on her hips and glared at them. "You're both going to your rooms if you don't stop that right now."

They didn't.

"I mean it."

The twins kept fighting. The au pair grabbed one of them and held him under her arm sideways like a football. The volume of screams increased. I gave the au pair my card, told her I'd be back to speak with Mrs. Goldstein, and left before I suffered permanent ear damage.

It was wonderfully quiet outside. The snow had stopped falling. The branches of the trees were etched in white against the steel-gray sky. One by one, I watched the street-lights come on. Darkness comes early this time of year. I slogged from one house to another, my feet leaving a trail of prints, but got about as far as I had with the first place I'd visited. Either no one was home, or if they were, they didn't know the Wilcoxes well. None of the women I spoke to even knew that Janet Wilcox was gone.

"Oh, my," two of them said when they heard.

By the time I'd covered the area, it was almost five o'clock. I got back in my car and drove over to Janet Wilcox's psychologist on East Genesee.

Peter Simmone's office was a step up from Wilcox's. Better furniture in the waiting room. Beige carpet on the floor. Neutral darker beige sofa. White walls with a hint of tan. Innocuous pictures of generic landscapes on the walls. Soft track lighting. Warm temperature. A box of Kleenex on one of the end tables. For those sudden fits of emotions?

I hung my parka on the coatrack, sat down, and picked up the only reading matter. The book was entitled, *You Can*

Be Your Own Best Friend. I put it down and tried to think about my strategy, but my eyes kept closing. The warmth was making me sleepy. I was on the way to dozing off when Peter Simmone opened the door to his office and beckoned me in.

His appearance went with the soothing voice I'd heard on the phone. He was about five-eleven, in his late forties, early fifties, with a slight paunch above the belt of his brown corduroy pants. His wedge-shaped nose dominated his face. His beard was salt-and-pepper. Ditto for his hair. He looked like an easygoing kind of guy, but his eyes weighed and measured me. I had the feeling they didn't miss much.

"So," he said, indicating that I should take a seat on the leather sofa while he sat down in the chair across from me. "Tell me about these attacks you've been having." I guess he didn't believe in wasting time.

I handed him my card. "Actually, I didn't come to see you about anxiety attacks."

He read it slowly, his frown increasing, then reread it before handing it back to me. "Then what did you come to see me about?"

"Janet Wilcox."

He waved his hand in the air. "I already told her husband that I can't—"

"Her husband is ready to sue," I interrupted.

Simmone looked at me incredulously. "Sue?"

When in doubt, lie. That's my motto.

"For loss of marital services."

"Excuse me?"

Now I had his full attention. "Loss of his wife's services. He claims his wife was fine before she started seeing you. He claims that you implanted the idea that she was abused as a child and that that idea has so unsettled her that she stopped being able to function. She no longer cooks, cleans, or fulfills her marital obligations. And now that she's run away . . ."

"Run away?"

"I guess you don't keep track of your clients very well." I tapped my card on my front teeth. "He's hired me to find her."

The frown turned into a scowl. "I still don't get what that has to do with me."

"Well, if you could help me locate her, Wilcox might be willing to drop his lawsuit."

Simmone glared at me. "Are you threatening me?"

"Hardly. I'm doing you a favor."

"Even if I did know, which I don't, legally I'm not allowed to reveal anything."

I leaned forward. The sofa was too deep to sit in comfortably. "You are if she's a danger to herself or others."

"She's not."

"Her husband says different. He says she's suicidal."

"Her husband has his own set of issues to deal with."

I wondered if therapists had to take another course in how to talk and not say anything. "So, you're telling me he's lying."

"I'm telling you he's not a professional."

Simmone half turned in his chair, picked up a pencil off his desk, and began fiddling with it. The air coming through the heat vents in the room made a whooshing noise. I tried a different tack.

"And the fact that she's run away doesn't concern you?"

Simmone put the pencil down. "I'd have to know more about why she left before I rendered an opinion."

"I take it you're not going to help me?"

"No. I've already made that abundantly clear to her husband. It would be a breach of ethics."

"Suit yourself. I hope you have good malpractice insurance because you're going to need it."

"This is ridiculous."

I stood up. Being in the room was like being in a womb. It was making me claustrophobic.

"Not to Walter Wilcox." I placed my card on Simmone's desk.

From the expression on his face, I'd laid a dead mouse on his desk. He pushed it away with the tip of his finger. "People like you . . ." he began. But I didn't give him time to finish.

"Do yourself a favor," I told him, "and call me if you remember anything. Or find anything out."

"I can tell you right now, you're not going to be hearing from me."

"Okay. But I wouldn't want to be you if this woman dies."

"Out," ordered Simmone pointing to the door. Very dramatic.

When I left, he was reaching for the phone.

Probably to call his lawyer.

Chapter Ten

I was on my way back to Noah's Ark when I got a call on my cell. It was the au pair from the Goldstein house.

"Remember how you were asking me about Janet Wilcox?" she said.

"Yes."

"Well, I lied when I told you I didn't know anything."

"Okay." The SUV in back of me honked as I maneuvered my way around an Explorer that was turning left. "You've got my attention."

"Give me a hundred dollars, and I'll tell you something interesting."

"That's a little steep, isn't it?"

"Not for this. If you don't like it, you don't have to pay me."

"That seems fair."

We arranged to meet at the entrance to Wegmans Supermarket in ten minutes. I got to the grocery store early. It was a little before dinnertime and the place was jammed with shoppers. I had to circle the lot three times before I found a parking place on the far end. I waited inside the doors, next to the grocery carts, and watched people streaming in and out.

The adults looked tired and drawn after their day at work, and the children looked cranky and fidgety. Everyone was in a hurry, anxious to get home. The carts going by me were full of frozen dinners and prepared foods, and then I saw a man walking out with a loaf of bread under one arm and a string bag containing artichokes, carrots, and circles of brie and I thought of George.

George and his food. He liked shopping for it. He liked cooking it. He liked feeding me, the only man I'd ever gone with who had. He made himself dinner every night. Sometimes on Sunday afternoons in the winter he baked bread. It had been nice coming into his house, smelling the flour and the yeast. I wondered if his wife and child would like it. God. Better not to think about him. At all. Better to pretend he'd died. I was reaching for a cigarette when I spotted the au pair coming through the door.

She was dressed in jeans, sweater, matching gloves and scarf, and a black microfiber jacket.

"I'm buying milk for Mrs. Goldstein," she said, indicating that I should follow her inside.

I skirted a woman in a camel-hair coat and business suit balancing a screaming six-month-old on one hip and a bag of groceries on the other. Lines of exhaustion creased her face. Maybe my grandmother was right. Maybe you can't have it all.

"So what do you want to tell me?" I asked the au pair.

She looked away. "I wouldn't ordinarily do this, but there's this concert I want to go to, and Mrs. Goldstein doesn't . . . well, she doesn't give me any money. I mean, she gives me a little, but taking care of the twins all day . . . It's not that I don't like them. I do. They're adorable. But I feel as if I'm going crazy. I have to get out. And Don't Go There are playing in Buffalo and my friend has a car. . . ."

I put up my hand to stop the flow of rationalizations. "First off, tell me your name."

"It's Kira. Kira Brown."

"Okay, Kira Brown. What you're doing is a good thing."

Kira fingered her nose ring. "I guess you're right." She brightened. "I mean, Mrs. Wilcox could be in trouble."

"Yes, she could."

"This is just . . . it feels dirty somehow. Like Judas and the twelve pieces of gold."

"I think it was thirty pieces of silver."

"Whatever."

She dropped her hand and began fiddling with the zipper on her jacket.

We were standing in front of the produce stand while people eddied around us. Berries from Chile. Peaches from Argentina. Apples from Upstate. Twenty years ago you'd be lucky to get oranges in the winter.

"This isn't really about her," Kira continued. "I mean, it is but it isn't."

"Then what?"

"I think I know why she left."

Kira paused again. I waited.

"Her husband. He has a girlfriend."

"How do you know?" I will not think about George. I will not think about George, I repeated to myself.

"Because she's a friend of mine. She works down at Le Bijou."

Le Bijou is an all-nude bar that opened up fairly recently.

"What's your friend's name?"

"Do I have to tell you?"

"If you want your money, you do."

Kira bit her lip. "She's going to kill me."

"She doesn't have to know how I found out."

"You won't tell her?"

I put my hand up. "Swear. You'll be doing a good deed."

Kira took a deep breath. "Alima. Her name is Alima."

"Does she have a last name?"

"Matterson. Wilcox, he's really nuts about her. Last week he gave her a diamond ring. A big one."

"How old is she?"

"My age. Nineteen. He's come on to me too. But that was before he hooked up with Alima." She wrinkled her nose at the idea. "Don't tell her that, though."

"I won't," I assured her. Cute.

I thought of Wilcox's daughter. She was—what? Twenty-five? Twenty-eight? I wondered what she would say. Then I wondered if she knew. Given her attitude toward her father, something told me that she might.

"How do you know Alima?"

"We went to high school together. Actually, she was the one that got me my job with the Goldsteins. She used to baby-sit for them when the twins were younger."

"So what got her into her present line of work?"

"Her boyfriend suggested it. She's got a really good body, and she was short tuition for vet tech school."

"Whatever happened to student loans?"

"She doesn't like to be in debt." Kira leaned into the dairy case and reached for a gallon of milk. "It's not like it's a big deal," she added.

"If you thought that, you wouldn't care if she knew that you told me."

"It's not that. She's a private person." Kira clasped the gallon of milk to her breasts as if it were a baby. She searched my face worriedly. "So, is what I told you worth a hundred dollars or not?"

"Enjoy the concert." I counted out five twenties and put them in her hand. "Where can I get hold of Alima?"

Kira hesitated. I reached for the money.

"I can always take it back."

"She'll be at Le Bijou tonight around ten."

"Thanks."

"I don't know why I feel so bad," Kira fretted.

"I don't either."

And I left her with her guilty conscience and went out the door. Flakes of snow drifted down under the lights. Two little children dressed in snowsuits stood with their faces turned up trying to catch snowflakes with their tongues, while their mother loaded groceries into the car. Zsa Zsa did that too. When I got home I'd take her for a walk.

As I got in my car, I decided it would be interesting to hear what Wilcox had to say about his nineteen-year-old sweetie. And whether there was anything else he'd "forgotten" to tell me. His house wasn't that far away from Wegman's. I looked at my watch. It was conceivable he was home by now. I backed out of my parking place and drove over there.

The lights were on. I parked in the driveway behind his Nissan. He hadn't shoveled a path to his front door, and his footsteps were clearly visible in the snow. I added mine to his, climbed the two front steps to his porch, and rang the bell. He answered the door with a glass in his hand. He looked surprised to see me.

"That was fast," he said. He slurred the words together. I wondered how many drinks he'd already had.

"I have a few more questions. Can I come in?"

"Of course. *Mi casa es su casa.*" And he bowed.

The table in the hallway of his house was overflowing with unread mail and newspapers. The strains of opera filled the air. I didn't know which one because I've never liked the stuff myself. I sniffed and caught a faint scent of unemptied kitchen garbage cans.

"You found something?" he asked, taking another sip from his glass. His jacket was off. I could see he'd added another stain to his tie.

"In a matter of speaking." I nodded toward the glass. "After-work cocktail?"

"A Manhattan without the cherry. It's the cherry that makes the drink, but I seem to have run out. I'll make you one if you want."

I shook my head even though I wanted one. Once I started drinking, I had a tendency to keep going and I still had some things I had to do. It was at least seventy in the house. I took off my parka. Wilcox didn't offer to hang it up. I suspected his wife had taken care of the social amenities as I threw it on the banister and went into the living room. Wilcox trailed after me.

The place was a decorator's dream. Everything in the room had been color-coordinated. The needlepoint pillows on the sofa picked up the pattern in the drapes, which picked up the colors of the pictures on the walls. Even the colors of the picture frames on the fireplace mantel matched.

"Janet spent a long time putting this room together." Wilcox drained his glass and gestured to the coffee table, which was covered with empty beer and soda bottles, Styrofoam containers, and empty pizza boxes. "We're not supposed to eat in here. She'd kill me if she saw this. I'm going to clean it up before she gets home."

"I'm surprised she hasn't killed you already."

He went over to the bar and mixed himself another Manhattan. I noticed his hands were shaking slightly as he put another ice cube in his glass.

"Aren't you going to ask me why?"

"Is something wrong?"

"Does the name Alima mean something to you?"

Wilcox took a big swallow of his drink.

"Should I know who that is?"

"I hope so, considering she's your little cutie on the side. Tell me, was your wife mad when she found out? I bet she was. Is that why she ran off?"

"I told you why she left."

"I don't believe you."

"Why would I lie?"

I ticked off the reasons. "Because you're embarrassed. Because you're ashamed. Because you don't want to admit to yourself that you've been stepping out with someone younger than your daughter." Then I gave him my standard honesty spiel. "Believe me, I don't care what you've done. But if you want me to find your wife, you have to tell me the truth. If you don't, you're just wasting your money and my time."

Wilcox closed his eyes for a second. His shoulders slumped. It was as if someone had pulled the plug.

"Okay." He took another sip from his glass. "I didn't tell you because I was embarrassed. I made a mistake, a really bad one. But this was the first time . . . I ever . . . oh, hell." He swallowed. "I didn't think it would make a difference. I didn't think it would matter."

"What else haven't you told me?"

"Nothing." He put his hand up. "I swear. Really. You have to find her for me. You just have to." And he stared into his glass. "I need her back."

I felt a trickle of pity for Wilcox, and then I thought about George and the trickle dried up.

Chapter Eleven

I finished off the day by going to see Alima Matterson. There was a slim possibility that she might know something about Janet Wilcox's whereabouts, and even if she didn't, talking to her seemed better than going home and staring at the four walls. Which I'd be doing soon enough anyway.

I got to Le Bijou a little before ten. The place was located off Erie Boulevard, shoved back from the main street and bordered on one side by a welding business and on the other by a printing company.

The parking lot was only half shoveled. Judging from the number of cars in it, business was not booming. The place looked like a warehouse for dry goods. The sign out front— LE BIJOU. LIVE ALL NUDE REVIEWS ALL THE TIME—and the picture of the girl on the wall were the only things that said different. As I entered, I noticed that a couple of corner slats on the lower wall were working their way loose.

The place was as erotic as a hardware store. The walls were covered with fake wood paneling. A sheet outlining rules of conduct was prominently posted in the entranceway. The space was large and sparsely furnished. No attempt at decoration had been made. There was the stage, a bare platform where a bored-looking girl was doing a desultory dance with a fire pole; the bar, which featured coffee and juice (liquor being off limits in joints like this); and the VIP rooms, where the girls did their lap dances.

The description Kira had given me of Alima turned out to be fairly accurate, and it didn't take me long before I spotted her cozying up to a guy at the bar. The guy was in his forties and looked like a mid-level insurance salesman.

Alima had her face turned up toward him and was gazing at him as if he were a god. Calli does that too. I've always wanted to go up to the guy she's talking to and say, "Don't you realize she's putting you on?" But maybe I'm just jealous because I've never mastered "the look." Alima had, though. For sure.

"Yes?" she snapped when I got near her.

She wasn't what I would have picked for Wilcox. Usually men go for women like their wives, only fifteen years younger, so I'd figured him for something conservative. But she wasn't. I couldn't imagine Janet Wilcox wearing the equivalent of safety pins through her cheek, a ring through her nose, or stretchers in her ears even when she was younger.

This girl was prettier as well, with small, regular features and large eyes that offset her blotchy skin and the scar above her upper lip where her cleft palate had been fixed. Her body was good. Certainly a lot lusher than Wilcox's wife's, voluptuous without being flabby. But it was the kind of body that would turn to fat by the time she was twenty-five if she didn't hit the gym three or four times a week.

"I'd like to talk to you about Walter Wilcox," I told her.

"You don't look like the police."

"That's because I'm not." I took out my card and gave it to her. "He hired me to find his wife."

"So?" She handed the card back. "What does she have to do with me?"

"I was hoping you might know something."

"About her? Why would I?"

Before I could answer, the bartender ambled over. He was as big and as tall as he was wide. Tanned. Relaxed. Balding. Fortyish. The gold chain he was wearing around his neck served to emphasize its girth.

"You okay?" he asked Alima. "She bothering you?"

Alima nodded. He looked at me and jerked his thumb toward the door.

"Leave."

I opened my mouth.

"Now," he added before I could say anything. "You want to talk to Alima, talk to her on her own time. This is a place of business, and you're interfering with it."

I glanced around. "It doesn't look that busy to me."

He took another step forward. "I've never thrown a woman out, but that doesn't mean I won't."

"Fine." I put both hands up. "I'm going. You mind if I leave my business card?"

"Put it on the bar."

I did. I certainly wasn't going to argue with him, especially since he looked as if he could shot-put a small building.

"Call me if you think of anything," I told Alima.

She sniffed and turned back to the man she'd been talking to. When I left, she had taken his hand and was leading him to the VIP room for a lap dance. A sign on the wall said, TWENTY BUCKS PER SONG. When you considered the fact that a song usually lasted no more than three minutes, I decided I was definitely in the wrong field. I wondered if this was how Alima and Wilcox had met, and if he was the only guy she was playing. Somehow I didn't think so.

I drove back to the store, picked up Zsa Zsa, went home, and watched old Cary Grant and Rosalind Russell movies till three in the morning while I drank Scotch and ate a bag of chocolate chip cookies. It was a surprisingly good combination. I passed out on the sofa with Zsa Zsa snuggled up behind my knees.

I woke up to the phone ringing. I opened one eye and stared out through the picture window. It was dark. The streetlights were still on. It felt like four in the morning, and I felt like shit.

"What?" I croaked into the receiver.

"Did you find anything yet?" It was Wilcox.

"What time is it?" I was still logy. My head was throbbing and my throat was dry.

"I don't know. Seven o'clock." I wondered how long he'd been up.

I groaned. "You gotta be kidding me."

"You said to call."

"Not this early." I hung up and burrowed my head in the pillow. I was just falling back asleep when the phone rang again. Why I answered it, I don't know. It was Paul.

"How's the Janet Wilcox thing coming along?" he said, speaking way too loudly.

I moved the phone away from my ear. "Why are you up this early?"

"I never went to bed."

I turned onto my back and rubbed my eyes. It didn't help. Everything still looked blurry. Maybe I was getting nearsighted in my old age.

"Robin, are you there?"

"I'm going back to sleep. Call me later." And I hung up. The phone rang again. Probably Paul. But it could have been the Pope for all I cared. I disconnected it, stumbled upstairs, and crawled into bed. Zsa Zsa jumped up and curled up on the pillow next to me. When my alarm went off at nine o'clock, I felt marginally more human. Four cups of coffee later, I was ready to function. I spent the rest of the day making phone calls from the store, trying to track down Janet Wilcox and failing.

I started with her daughter, Stephanie, who was down in New York City. She sounded even more annoyed with me this time around.

"I don't suppose you've heard from your mother yet?"

"No. I haven't. Now, if you'll excuse me, I'm on the other line." And she clicked off. Bet she didn't send Janet a Mother's Day card.

I spoke to two of her cousins. Wilcox had been right. They just corresponded over Christmas. They'd stopped trying to get Janet to come out and visit them a long time ago.

"What's the point?" one of them said. "All she does is complain."

"About what?" I asked.

"Everything," she replied. "Absolutely everything. And then she denies she said anything. She's a very difficult person."

I managed to locate three members of her book group. They didn't know anything about Janet Wilcox either. They didn't discuss their personal lives when they met. But they could say this about her: She was always well prepared for their discussions, unlike some people they could mention, who actually lied about reading the book. If I could imagine that. I said I could and tried Janet Wilcox's physician and got as far with him as I had with her psychologist.

At this point it was four o'clock in the afternoon, and I decided to go over the credit card receipts Wilcox had collected for me again. I'd done it before and nothing had popped up at me, but I was running out of options.

It was a fairly simple task because Janet Wilcox didn't charge that much. Most of her purchases seemed to center around her house and involved things like dishes and sheets and picture frames. She bought her clothes at Talbot's and her shoes at Easy Spirit. Both stores that catered to conservative, suburban women of a certain age—as the French like to say.

Occasionally Janet Wilcox splurged and bought herself a couple of boxes of chocolates and a book, but I could tell from the receipts that the books were paperbacks. Her only real luxury appeared to be getting her hair done every week at the Final Cut Beauty Salon.

I was musing about the name being one I would never have chosen for a beauty parlor when it hit me. Sometimes women tell their hairdressers things they don't tell anyone else. A cliché, but that didn't make it any less true. I got out the phone book and looked up the address for the salon. It was over in Eastwood. Close enough. I told Manuel I'd be back in an hour and drove over.

The place had that familiar permanent-wave smell. It took me back to when I used to go to the beauty parlor with my mom. I'd hated every minute of it, from the shampoo to the dryers, which burned the back of my neck. My mother always wanted me to get my hair curled. I always wanted it straight. The last time I'd gone, I'd come out looking like a poodle. That was when I was thirteen. The next time I'd gone back, I'd been twenty-six.

The salon was tiny. A strictly two-person operation. Two sinks. Two cutting stations. A line of chairs along the far wall. A large wicker basket filled with kids' toys. Another one filled with magazines. It was the kind of place that catered to the locals. The walls were painted lilac and hung with framed photos of Tuscany landscapes. A vase at the reception counter was filled with a bouquet of ferns and spider chrysanthemums.

A collection of vintage Bakelite and rhinestone jewelry was neatly displayed in a glass case below the cash register. ASK ABOUT OUR PRICES, said the hand-lettered sign standing by them. A badly bleached blonde somewhere in her seventies was getting her hair cut when I walked in.

"I'll be with you in a minute," the hairdresser said to me as he lifted a lock of her thinning hair and snipped at its ends.

I sat down on one of the chairs and waited. The man trimmed and studied his cut. Hair rained down on the black plastic cape covering the woman's shoulders. Occasionally she'd brush a piece off her nose.

"Chris, I think you're going to like this," he said to her, his face a picture of concentration.

"You're sure?" the woman said. "I want to look nice for my niece's wedding."

The hairdresser patted her shoulder. "You'll look gorgeous, darling. I promise. You'll be the belle of the ball."

Somehow I doubted it. The woman had a receding chin and the eyes of a basset hound. But that was what she needed to hear because she beamed. The hairdresser put down his scissors and reached for a bottle of conditioner. He squirted a dab of it into the center of his hand, then proceeded to massage it into the woman's scalp.

"So," he said to me as he worked. "What can I do for you?"

I told him.

"Janet," he said as he turned on his hair dryer and began fluffing out the woman's hair. "Of course I know Janet. She's a regular."

"So you think you'll be able to help me?"

"Possibly." He assessed my hair with a practiced eye. "You need to have your split ends trimmed."

I reached for my ponytail and studied the ends. "They're fine."

"They're damaged."

"No more than a quarter of an inch," I conceded.

Over the years I've noticed that people tend to be chattier

when they're comfortable, and they're comfortable when they're doing the things they're used to doing. Usually I cut my hair myself, but if I needed to get my hair trimmed to get the information I wanted, so be it. I've done a lot worse in my time.

"No problem," he said before turning back to his customer.

I watched while he finished her up. He back-combed her hair, then brought it forward and sprayed each curl into place. It was like watching someone construct a building.

"You work it, girl," he said as the woman reached in her purse to pay.

She was still giggling as she walked out the door. He had made her feel good. Maybe that was why Janet Wilcox had come here each week. To get what she couldn't get at home.

"Remember," I reminded him as I sat down in the chair. "Not more than a quarter of an inch."

He picked up my hair, weighed it in his hand, then undid the rubber band, fanned it out, and studied it some more. "Half. You should use a better conditioner. Your hair is really dry. I have one you might like."

"Fine." I'd take it out of my expense money along with the haircut. "Janet Wilcox."

"My. Aren't you the persistent one." He sprayed water on my hair with a mister. I felt like a fern.

I must have made a face because he said, "Just wetting it down, dear. By the way, my name is John, and yours is—?"

"Robin."

"You have a card?"

When I gave it to him, he glanced at it and slipped it into his pocket. "A real private detective. The boys at the club are going to love this."

And him too, I'd wager. He had closely cropped hair that had been bleached white, a diamond stud in his left ear, and a tight ass his black pants showed off. His black T-shirt hugged his ribs. Very Manhattan. Just like Janet's daughter Stephanie.

"Okay John. How long have you've been doing Janet Wilcox's hair?"

He twisted the silver AIDS bracelet on his left wrist around. "You mean that Palm Beach crash helmet do she insists on having?" He rolled his eyes. "God. I've been spraying those curls for ten—no, eleven years. Or is it twelve? I don't want to do the math. It's too frightening. Scary how fast time goes, isn't it?"

I agreed that it was.

He gestured with his free hand. "The principessa has a standing appointment every Thursday at nine-forty-five in the morning. Not that her majesty is ever here on time."

He fastened a black nylon cape over my shoulders and told me to look down. Then he began to cut. I could hear the snick-snack of the scissors.

"Frankly," he continued. "I'm surprised she left. I didn't think anything could pry her out of that house of hers. The way she talks, you'd think it was the Taj Mahal."

I looked up.

"Don't do that," John said. "I don't want to cut you."

I went back to looking at my knees.

"Well, at least her husband is having a rest," John added.

"I take it you don't like her."

"Let's just say that she wants me to do back flips through burning hoops and then doesn't tip me." He clicked his tongue against his teeth. "I just couldn't imagine living with her. She's one of those people that polish their grievances up like precious stones and take them out every time they have a chance."

"It sounds as if she and her husband were a match."

He grunted, put his scissors down, and ran both hands through my hair, pulling it out to either side as he studied my reflection.

"Do you think she's suicidal?" I asked thinking of what Wilcox had told me.

"Oh, please. She's a bitch." He pronounced it be-atch. "People like that don't kill themselves, they drive other people to it."

Okay.

"Do you have any idea where she could have gone?"

He laughed. "Oh, yes. I think I can make a pretty good guess."

And he told me what I wanted to know.

Chapter Twelve

Except for a woman wading through a snowbank to get to her car, the sidewalk was empty when I stepped outside the salon. The weatherman had promised it wouldn't get below twenty. The weatherman had lied. It felt as if we were into the single digits, but maybe that was because of the wind, which had kicked up again.

I jammed my hands in my pockets and headed for my vehicle. By the time I got there—a minute at most—my earlobes were stinging. After I pulled out onto James Street, I called Walter Wilcox at his office, but his secretary informed me he'd already gone home. I tried him there.

He picked up on the third ring. "Mike," he said, sounding out of breath, as if he'd just run up the stairs.

"No. This is Robin Light."

"Sorry."

An SUV cut me off. "Idiot!" I yelled at the guy.

"What?" The phone crackled.

"Nothing." I tried the heat. It still wasn't working. By the time it got going, I'd be where I had to go. "I might have a lead on your wife."

Wilcox exhaled. "Thank God. I've been so worried. Where is she?"

"Down in the City."

"You mean New York City?" Alarm undercut the relief in his voice.

"Yes."

"That's impossible."

"Not according to my sources."

"But she hates that place. I could never get her to go down there."

"Well, she's down there now."

"Are you sure?"

"Moderately."

"All those people."

"Eight million." Or was it more? Or less? I forget.

"How will you find her?"

"I think I can narrow down the odds considerably."

Opera was playing in the background. I wondered if Wilcox ever listened to anything else. I wondered if he had a glass in his hand. I was willing to wager he did.

"Then you know who she's staying with?"

"I've got a name."

"How did you get it?"

"From her hairdresser."

"Janet's hairdresser?" I could hear the question in Wilcox's voice, and then he spelled it out. "You're sure she's reliable?"

"He," I corrected as I sped through a yellow light because I was afraid I'd skid out if I stomped on the brakes.

All those years and Wilcox still didn't know anything about someone his wife had seen once a week every week for at least ten years. If that didn't encapsulate the problem with his marriage, nothing did. "Yeah," I said, remembering the hairdresser's tone when he'd spoken about Janet. "I think he's reliable. And anyway, it's the only lead I've come up with so far."

"That's good. That's very good." I could hear the slur of alcohol in Wilcox's voice. "I want you to go down there and find her."

I thought about leaving the store. I thought about the fact that I'd been spending too much time away from Zsa Zsa. I thought about the fact that the weather forecast was predicting a nor'easter coming up from the Carolinas. I thought about the fact that I'd been running on four hours of sleep a night for the past week.

"Sorry, but you're going to have to count me out. I'm sure Paul can find you someone to take over."

"I don't care if he gets me Sherlock Holmes. You're the person I hired, you're the person I want."

"Listen . . ."

"It's just going down to the City, for God's sake."

I heard ice cubes clinking in a glass. Wilcox must be refreshing his drink.

"I know what it is."

I pulled into the Dunkin' Donuts parking lot. I needed a large coffee and two chocolate-peanut doughnuts, and I needed them badly. I also needed to sit someplace warm and defrost my toes and my fingers. Especially my toes. Which felt like pieces of wood.

"It's not a big deal."

"Then you go."

"I can't. I have things to do up here."

"So do I."

"This is important."

"I realize that, Walter," I began when Wilcox interrupted.

"God love you. I won't forget this," he cried. His vowels had become softer. He was starting to run his words together. "Call me the moment you've located her. And whatever you do, don't talk to her. I don't want to scare her." And he hung up before I could reply.

I stared at the phone for a minute. Paul could deal with this. Wilcox was his client, after all. I went inside and got three doughnuts instead of two. I sat by the window and ate them and watched the lights of the cars going by and thought about New York City at dusk. When I lived down there, it had always seemed like the loneliest time of the day to me. It still did. I crushed my napkin, stuffed it into my empty coffee cup, tossed the cup in the trash, and drove over to Paul's office.

The State Tower Building was emptying out as people went home for dinner. Paul was on the phone when I walked through his office door.

"Wilcox," he mouthed. I moved some newspapers off a chair and sat down while he told Wilcox not to worry. That he'd take care of everything.

"Get someone else. I'm not going," I announced to Paul when he got off the line. "I already told him that. He just refuses to listen. Or he's too drunk to listen. I don't know which."

"Not even for a two hundred and fifty dollar bonus?"

"Get real, Santini."

"Okay. Five hundred."

"I may be cheap, but I'm not that cheap."

"A thousand extra for two days' work? Robin, come on. It's not that big a deal," Paul said. "Manuel can fill in for you."

And he reached in his back pocket, took out his wallet, counted out ten one-hundred-dollar bills, and laid them on the desk one at a time. Watching him, I realized he looked tired. Maybe it was the light, but the lines around his mouth looked deeper, the circles under his eyes darker.

The money was too good to turn down, which I'm sure Paul knew. And besides, it had occurred to me that maybe I needed to get out of Syracuse for a while. Sometimes any change of scenery is a good one. Especially when everywhere I went reminded me of George.

"Why do you care about Wilcox?"

Paul drummed his fingers on the desk. "I don't. I just like to keep my clients happy. Besides, he has some important friends."

I snorted. "Like who?"

Paul rattled off the names of some local politicians as I folded up the bills and put them in my pocket.

"That's supposed to impress me?"

"No. But it's good for business." Paul reached into his bottom desk drawer and brought out a bottle of twenty-five-year-old Scotch. "A gift from a grateful client of mine." He grinned. "Let's drink to success. We can both use it."

I certainly could. I looked at the bottle. It was warm in here. The radiator was making a comforting hissing noise. I could taste the peaty aftertaste of the Scotch. I could feel the warmth in my mouth and throat. So I said, sure. Why not? It had been a crappy week.

I took off my parka and threw it on the sofa. Paul pulled two glasses out of another drawer. They were smudged. I decided I didn't care. The alcohol would kill whatever pathogens were on them.

"Straight?" he asked.

"Is there another way?"

"Not for me." He poured two fingers into my glass and handed it to me. "How's old Georgie doing?"

"I wouldn't know. I haven't seen him lately. Why are you asking?"

"Just making conversation."

"Oh." I wondered if Paul knew about Natalie. It wouldn't have surprised me if he did. Paul knew everything. I don't know how he did, but he did. He was like Manuel that way.

Paul raised his glass and I raised mine.

"To truth," he said.

"I like success better."

"To success then."

We drank. Paul refilled our glasses. We lifted them again.

"To finding Janet Wilcox," I proposed.

"To big fees," Paul said.

We drank to that.

"Do you ever worry that you're drinking too much?" Paul asked.

"Sometimes. You?"

"Sometimes."

I raised my glass and he poured me another shot, then did the same for himself.

Half an hour later I was stepping out of the elevator of the State Tower Building with my bonus, plus fifteen hundred dollars' worth of expense money, and the information I needed about the man Janet Wilcox was allegedly staying with in my backpack.

I went home, walked Zsa Zsa, had another couple of nightcaps, and fell asleep on the sofa watching television.

Chapter Thirteen

That night I dreamt about Murphy. I was sitting in the middle of an island so small that there was only room for me. Murphy was standing over me telling me something about a wall and the color purple and that I shouldn't worry about the thing underneath when Zsa Zsa woke me up barking at a snowplow going down the street. My heart was still racing as I looked outside. The sky was white; the air was filled with flakes.

It looked beautiful and would drive lousy. I reached over and clicked to the Weather Channel. The announcer was predicting possible blizzard-like conditions as far down as the metropolitan area. Read New York City. Better and better. Especially since two inches of snow tended to paralyze the City.

I got on my boots, put on my parka, and walked outside with Zsa Zsa. She jumped in and out of the drifts. Little clumps of snow clung to her ears and nose.

"What do you think?" I asked her. "Should I go or stay?"

She woofed.

"Go. I agree. Nothing like a change of scenery to change your viewpoint."

And I motioned for her to come back in. I dried her off with a big towel and went into the kitchen. I was just about to make myself some coffee, then go upstairs and tell Manuel what I was going to do, when Bethany waltzed into the kitchen.

"You were asleep when I came in," she explained.

I stopped grinding the beans. "What are you doing here?"

"We have a snow day. It was on the television last night."

"That's not the issue. You shouldn't be here."

"Manuel's mom said it was okay."

"Did she?"

I didn't think it was, but I bit my tongue. It was too early in the morning to talk about this.

"You think I'm lying?" Bethany demanded, putting her hands on her hips.

"I didn't say that."

"Sorry."

"I like your hair."

She smiled. "Thanks."

One thing was for sure. She looked better now than she had when her parents had hired me to find her last year when she'd run away. She'd lost weight since then as well as the platinum hair, the big gold earrings and chains, and the baggy clothes she'd been sporting. Despite what her father said, maybe she and Manuel were good for each other.

Of course, Manuel wasn't why she'd gotten booted out of her nice, middle-class Cazenovia household. That had to do with her generally lousy attitude. And it was pretty bad. But I don't know. If I had a kid, I don't think I'd give up on her so easily.

Bethany ran her finger down the handle of one of the mugs out on the counter. "I'm sixteen."

"I know how old you are."

"I'm not a kid."

"In the eyes of the law you are. And what is this stuff Manuel was telling me about you divorcing your parents?"

Bethany slouched against the counter. "I can go to court and have myself declared an emancipated minor. My father told me he doesn't care. And my mother always follows everything he says."

"Are you going to?"

"Maybe."

"And who's going to support you?"

"Me. I'll get a job at the mall."

"What about school?"

"I'll finish up at OCC." Bethany studied her nails. "Manuel's mom says I can stay with her a little bit longer."

"And then?"

"I'll figure something out." Bethany reached over and took my hand. "Manuel said he's going to get me a golden retriever puppy." She beamed. "I've always wanted one, but my father would never have one in the house. Too much hair."

"Bethany, having a puppy is like having a baby."

"I know." Her smile got wider.

I didn't know what else to say. She reminded me of myself at that age, and it was too painful to watch.

She leaned against the kitchen counter. "So what are you up to?"

"I'm getting ready to go down to the City."

"On a case?"

I nodded.

Her eyes widened. "Cool. I'll make your coffee for you and bring it up to you."

"Sure. Thanks." I turned to go upstairs and pack.

"And don't worry," Bethany called after me. "I'll take good care of Zsa Zsa. And I'll make sure Manuel does the dishes and shovels the sidewalk."

It was too bad she couldn't be like this with her own parents, I thought as I got a suitcase out of my closet, but I guess that wasn't going to happen. At least not any time soon. Zsa Zsa jumped on the bed and whined while I threw clothes into the suitcase. She knew I was going. By the time I got back down, Manuel was in the kitchen eating cereal.

"Maybe you should wait for the weather to clear," he said.

"I'll be fine. I'll call you when I get into the City."

Bethany came over and gave me a hug. "You be careful."

"I will." I hugged her back and knelt on the kitchen floor and hugged Zsa Zsa. She smelled like popcorn. "You be a good girl and take care of the house," I crooned in her ear. She licked my chin. "Mommy will be back soon."

She walked me to the door. When I pulled out of the driveway, she was on the chair looking out the window. Even though she was in good hands, I felt bad about leaving her.

Usually to get to New York City from Syracuse takes anywhere from four and a half to five and a half hours depending on the route you take, the time of day, and the weather. This time it took me seven. I probably should have taken the New York State Thruway. The State does a good job of keeping it clear in bad weather. Instead I went down through the Catskills on Route 17. In the spring, summer, and fall, it's a beautiful ride—a winding mountain road that goes through what is, for my money, some of the best scenery in New York State.

But not today. Today the road was littered with cars that had slid off into ditches. Given them and the periodic whiteouts, I drove at a prudent forty-five miles an hour. But by the time I reached the town of Liberty, New York, the snow had turned to flurries. The flurries, in turn, changed to a hard rain that thrummed on the hood of my car as I hit the Palisades Parkway.

My car headlights reflected off the wet asphalt. I had to hunch forward to see. When I reached the top level of the

George Washington Bridge, my eyes were aching from the effort of focusing. The river was shrouded in fog, the Manhattan skyline hidden in the gray mists. Traffic moved slowly on the Henry Hudson Parkway—at least that hadn't changed—and I watched the lights from the apartments on the Palisades wink on and off as if they were sending Morse code.

I got off at the 96th Street entrance and went across town. Even though this side of the City had become fashionable, it still looked bleak in the rain, a picture of gray on gray, with people scurrying to where they had to go. I was glad I was in my car instead of out walking.

The apartment Janet Wilcox was supposedly camping out in belonged to a man named Salvatore Quintillo. According to Janet's hairdresser, Quintillo was a friend of Janet's from college. According to Paul, Quintillo was a one-time painter who now sold decorator art to doctors and dentists. He worked out of his apartment on 81st Street between Third Avenue and Lexington, as well as renting office space in the back of a small gallery on 95th Street.

I'd had an apartment three blocks away from Quintillo's before I moved upstate. I had good times there. Sad ones. Painful ones. Ones I had no desire to revisit.

But there were also the calls from the credit card companies, not to mention the sales tax I owed New York State and the five hundred dollars I owed the power company. So here I was. Back in my old neighborhood. The Upper East Side.

I'd read somewhere that this ZIP Code had the largest concentration of rich people in America. I believed it. When I was growing up, it hadn't been like that. It had been middle-middle class, with lots of mom-and-pop stores and restaurants—mostly Hungarian—where you could get an entire meal for eight dollars. Now there were food boutiques that displayed apples as if they were precious jewels and neighborhood restaurants that charged $10.50 for a BLT.

My mother was one of those rich people. She lived on Park Avenue. Eight blocks away from Quintillo's. A five-minute drive. A seven-minute walk. She lived in a white-glove building. Doorman. Elevator man. The whole schmeer. You walked into the lobby and you felt as if you should be talking in whispers. My mother's living room was as big as my dining room and living room combined. That place held a lot of memories for me. Most of them bad. That was one of the reasons I'd come to Syracuse. To put as much distance between her and me as possible.

I took a deep breath and turned my mind to what Paul had told me. From what he'd been able to ascertain, Quintillo did a good business helping Park Avenue docs maintain the upscale tone to their offices that enabled them to charge as much as they did. My question, given what I'd heard about Janet, was why were those two friends? What bound them together? According to everyone I'd talked to, Janet Wilcox had no friends. None at all. From everything I'd been told about her, I would have expected her to be staying in a hotel.

Too bad she wasn't. Then I could have sat in the lobby, read a book, and waited for her to come down.

Chapter Fourteen

Before cell phones, running a stakeout by yourself was difficult, not to mention terminally boring. All that sitting with no one to talk to. No one to trade jokes with. That's not true anymore. You can talk to your heart's content. As long as you have the money to pay the bill.

But you still can't read. At least nothing you have to concentrate on. Crossword puzzles are okay. But there are only so many of those you can do. I suppose I could always whittle. Or knit. I can see it now. Sam Spade's book of knitting patterns for revolvers and other assorted weapons. They have tea cozies. Why not gun cozies?

Actually, I used to knit. For a brief period when I was trying to be domestic. I even knit a sweater for Murphy. It ended up with very long sleeves and a short body. It would have fit a gorilla perfectly. I gave it up after that—the knitting, that is. If I'd been smart, I would have worked on the knitting and given up Murphy instead.

Another bad thing about being alone on a stakeout is there's no one to run out and get food. You have to stock up beforehand. Although these days, with a cell phone, you can probably get a delivery to your car, though that's not a good way to remain inconspicuous.

And then there's the pee factor. That's huge. If you're a guy you can pee into a Coke bottle. I've heard some women do that too. Not me. I'm not that hardcore. I figure, screw it. You gotta go, find a restaurant, buy a coffee and a Danish, and use the rest room.

The block Janet Wilcox's building was on was strictly residential. Which meant there were no coffee shops or restaurants I could sit in, no stores to linger in. I'd either have to stand outside—which I wasn't inclined to do because I'd be fairly obvious and because it was still pouring and I didn't fancy getting pneumonia—or find a place to park the car, not an easy thing in a place where legal spots are a rare commodity.

On the good side, 201 East 81st Street was a five-story brownstone instead of one of those large, fancy-schmancy apartment buildings with both a main and a service entrance. On the bad side, it looked exactly like the one I'd lived in. More memories. But the good side of that was that I was familiar with the layout.

There were usually three or four apartments to a floor, with the superintendent living in the basement apartment. Number 201 seemed to be following the same pattern—a fact attested to by the garbage cans lined up along the iron railing that cut off access to the outside, downstairs steps.

Which meant there was only one way to get in and out of 201. I decided to make sure. I double-parked my car in front of the building and ran up the steps. The door, wood and glass, stuck when I pushed it open. I brushed the raindrops off my jacket, stepped inside, and got a serious case of déjà vu.

The entrance hall was the exact duplicate of the place I'd lived in all those years ago. It had the same nondescript green textured paper on the walls. I remember hearing a decorator friend of mine call it Urban Blight. The wallpaper books called it Wheat Grass. Takeout menus were stacked on the radiator, just the way they are in everyone else's building. The place had the same mailboxes with the illegible names written in the little white spaces, the same intercom system. The intercom system was there to give the residents a feeling of security. But like most feelings of security it was false because people were always forgetting their keys and buzzing to be let in. Like I was going to do now.

I ran my finger down the names. There were eighteen. Quintillo's was listed as 3B. I pressed the buzzer and waited. No one answered. I chose another button at random.

"Yes," a voice came back a few seconds later.

"This is the sister of . . ." I consulted the intercom. "Tom Bernstein in 5B. I forgot my key. Can you let me in?"

"Oh, for God's sake . . ."

"I'm sorry," I said in the most contrite voice I could muster up.

I heard some grumbling and the door buzzed open. I went inside. Four bikes and a stroller were stored by the steps. The walls of the inner hallway were painted ballpark-mustard yellow, a slightly darker, but no less ugly shade of yellow than the walls in my place had been. I peeked behind the stairs. No entrance. No steps leading down to the basement. The people living here had to take their wash to a laundromat. What a pain that had been.

I decided it would be prudent to go upstairs and scope out the locale of Quintillo's apartment. I had a pretty good idea where 3B most likely was, but I wanted to make sure. Sometimes landlords cut up these apartments in funny ways so that they can get even more money.

It turned out I could have saved myself the climb. I'd been right. Quintillo had the middle apartment. Its windows faced toward the back instead of toward the street, just as mine had done. The six months I'd been out of a job, I'd spent hours every day watching five stray, mangy-looking cats tearing at the garbage bags people threw out the window, stalking rats almost as large as they were, and snoozing under the shade of a couple of spindly sumac trees that had erupted out of the asphalt.

Ergo: I couldn't see Janet Wilcox from the street and she couldn't see me. I stood in the hallway listening to the indistinct sounds of the radio drifting under the door of Quintillo's apartment. The radio didn't mean anyone was in. Lots of people keep their radios on when they aren't home. Or they used to. I imagine they still do.

Some do it so their pets will have company; other people do it to convince burglars that someone is home. The ones that had ransacked my apartment hadn't been fooled. I was thinking I should have tried the TV when I heard steps coming down the stairs and left. Better, I reasoned, not to have to explain what I was doing there.

On the way out, I passed a man coming in. He was dressed in a gray overcoat and had one of those men's hats with ear flaps on his head.

"Nasty weather," he said, smiling at me and revealing a mouth filled with too many teeth.

I nodded noncommittally.

"Just moved in? I don't remember seeing you before."

"Visiting."

But when I turned again, the smile was gone and he was appraising me as he fumbled with his keys. Or maybe I'd just imagined it in the dim light. When he saw me watching him, he gave a curt little nod and swiveled around so his back was toward me. I decided I was becoming paranoid in my old age as I hurried down the steps and into my car, investing more in a simple transaction than I should.

I called Wilcox from my cell to tell him I'd arrived.

"Remember," he said. "Phone me when you see Janet. Don't do anything else."

"I remember."

"I'll ring you up in a couple of hours to see how things are going."

I don't think he heard me mutter, "Terrific" as I clicked off. I couldn't wait to spot Janet and get the hell out of there. I drove around the block, parked in front of a Greek coffee shop, and got two large coffees, three cheese Danishes, a couple of chocolate bars, and a large hamburger and fries to go. I paid with a fifty.

"Don't you have anything smaller?" the guy behind the counter growled.

"No." I'd forgotten that no one in New York City likes anything larger than a twenty.

He rolled his eyes and slapped my change down. I counted it. It came to $31.13. I checked the receipt. If I lived down here again, I couldn't afford to eat.

The counterman was scowling at another customer when I walked out the door. I drove back to 81st Street, double-parked diagonally down from the building, and settled in to wait. By now it was three o'clock in the afternoon, and the schoolkids were coming home. I ate my hamburger, which was lousy, and munched on my French fries while I watched them, some walking in groups, others walking hand in hand with their mothers, others with their maids.

Everyone was walking hurriedly, heads bent down, sheltered under umbrellas, anxious to get out of the rain. Then I watched people walking their dogs. My mother wouldn't let me have a dog. I'd begged and I'd pleaded, and finally I wore her down and she'd relented.

I'd come home one day from school to a tired-looking, splay-backed Springer spaniel that had been kenneled way too long. Her name was Cindy, and I loved her anyway. I loved her even though she wasn't a puppy. I loved her even though she was too tired to play. Six months later I walked in the door after school and Cindy was gone. Just like that. Banished back to the kennel. Too much trouble, my mother had said.

I took a sip of coffee and wondered what had happened to

her, as I watched a woman drag an unwilling poodle down the street. And then I wondered what my mother was doing. How she was doing. I should call her. Drop by. I was thinking about that when my cell rang. It was Calli telling me Tiger Lily had gone into labor and she'd called the vet. I told her to keep me updated and she signed off before I could ask how much she was asking for the puppies.

Two minutes later the phone rang again. This time it was Wilcox.

"Have you seen her?" he demanded. "Have you seen my wife?"

I told him I hadn't.

"Are you sure? Are you sure she's staying there?" I pictured him rubbing his hands through his hair. "Maybe I should have gone with someone else after all."

"Maybe you should have. It still isn't too late." I powered off. If it came to that, I'd deduct my expenses and give Paul back the rest of the money.

The phone rang again. Wilcox.

"I'm sorry," he blubbered. "I'm just upset. You understand."

I understood that he was falling into the abyss.

"You should get yourself some help."

There was a moment of silence then Wilcox said, "Pardon?"

I didn't say anything.

"How come you can do twenty good deeds and one bad one and it's the bad one that counts?" Wilcox asked.

"I don't know."

"My minister doesn't know either."

"I'll call you when I have something to tell you."

"Please. I'll be waiting."

I turned the phone off and slipped it into my backpack.

Twenty minutes later, someone pulled out and I got a parking space a little way down from the building. I spent the next three hours finishing off the cheese Danishes, the chocolate bars, and the coffee, and trying to stay awake. Which was difficult. My eyelids kept closing and my head would start to drop. If it hadn't been as cold as it was in the car, I would have dozed off.

I was rubbing my hands together, trying to warm them up, when I noticed a man and a woman going into 201. I leaned forward and squinted, trying to get a better look at them. The woman looked vaguely similar to Janet Wilcox except her hair and makeup were different. But the man was an exact fit for Quintillo.

Looked as if it was time to move. I got out of my car and headed for the door. The woman I made for Janet Wilcox and the man I was now certain was Quintillo were still in the outside hallway. Quintillo was struggling to get a large manila envelope out of his mailbox while the woman was fumbling around in her bag. Probably for the keys.

"Jesus," he was complaining to no one in particular. "Fucking mailman. He does this every fucking time."

He had just opened his mouth to say something else when the woman saw me. Her head snapped up. Quintillo's gaze swiveled in my direction. I moved toward him.

"Maybe you can help me."

Quintillo's eyes flicked back and forth, as if he was expecting something bad to happen and he wanted to be ready for it. "Maybe. What do you want?"

Now that I was closer, I could see that the woman was indeed Janet Wilcox. The eyes, the mouth, and the chin were all the same. Only she'd reinvented herself. She looked twenty years younger. Her hair was blond and blunt cut. She was wearing bright red lipstick and black eyeliner. She had on a black microfiber raincoat that her daughter would have found acceptable and boots with high heels.

"Sorry to bother you." I gave them both my brightest smile. "I'm looking for a Patricia Hagerd in 5F."

"There is no 5F here," Quintillo told me.

"Are you sure?"

"Positive."

"Is this 222 East 81st?"

"No. It's 201."

I laughed, apologized, and left. The moment I got back to my car, I called Wilcox.

I expected he'd answer on the first ring. He didn't. His answering machine picked up instead. I left a message.

"Walter, this is Robin Light. I've found your wife. Ring my cell phone and let me know what you want me to do."

I called Paul next. He didn't answer either. I left the same message on his machine that I had on Wilcox's. Great. Now what? Stay? Go?

A moment later, Quintillo came out the door and decided the question for me. He looked up and down the street as if he wanted to make sure no one was keeping tabs on him. I ducked my head, but not fast enough. I could tell from the slight stiffening of his body that he'd spotted me.

I waved and pulled out. "Just looking for the address," I yelled to him.

By the time I'd reached the corner, he'd headed back inside. I drove around and called Wilcox again. No answer. I left another message.

"Are you coming down? Do you want me to go up?"

I tried Paul again. Nothing. Now I was getting annoyed. Wilcox was probably passed out somewhere leaving me holding the bag.

I drove around aimlessly while I tried to decide what to do. Undulating lines of yellow taxis, call lights flickering in the rain, snaked in and out, picking up and letting off people. Buses, lit from the inside like a Hopper painting, stopped at corners. Women in high heels and tight cloth coats scurried along holding tiny black umbrellas.

I went through the park and saw the blaze of trees around Tavern on the Green dressed up in their hundreds of white lights. Murphy and I had eaten there our last night in New York City. I went down Fifth Avenue past the Metropolitan Museum of Art, with its grand façade and kept on going. Around 59th Street I turned onto Madison Avenue and cruised up it, looking at the fancy shop windows. It was hard to believe, but there'd been a time when I'd worn stuff like that. And looked good in it too.

My instructions had been to find Janet Wilcox. I'd done that. I had no idea what Wilcox wanted me to do next. Stay in the City overnight? Talk to his wife? Start back upstate? Which was when I realized that somehow or other in my meanderings I'd contrived to drive by my mother's building on 74th Street off Park Avenue.

I stopped on impulse and got out of the car and walked under the canopy. The doorman came out of the building to greet me. He was younger, instead of one of the usual gray-haired brigade. Someone I didn't know. I don't know why I was expecting someone I did.

"Can I help you?" he asked.

There was a slight brogue in his voice. My mother's co-op always had Irish help. They were considered classier. I had to admit this one looked good enough to eat in his uniform with the gold braid on his shoulders and his hat, not to mention the white gloves.

"Yes. I was wondering if the Browns are in."

"I'm sorry. They've stepped out. Would you like to leave a message?"

"No, thanks."

"Are you positive?"

"Absolutely."

He watched me get back in my car and drive away.

I felt relieved and sad all at the same time. I turned onto Park Avenue and drove uptown. The traffic had thinned. Park was one of those streets where the traffic always moves.

Maybe because it's mostly apartment buildings. I remembered how much I'd enjoyed looking at the flowers in the dividers in the summer and the Christmas trees in the winter when I was a little girl. I thought I owned the City then, that I'd always be here.

I was going to live in a brownstone by Central Park and have dinner parties for interesting people and be a great writer. Of course the brownstone would have a working fireplace. The place would smell of lilacs in the summer and spruce in the winter.

Then, when I met Murphy, the fantasy changed. We were going to buy a farm and raise goats—never mind that neither of us had ever lived in the country, much less farmed.

I was thinking about that when I realized that I'd been driving up the FDR Drive and was turning onto the Third Avenue Bridge and going out of the City.

I reached for the phone and called Walter.

"Last chance," I told his machine. "Talk to me or I'm out of here."

There was no answer.

I told myself fine. For all I knew, he could be on his way down here. Or he could be out cold.

I could have turned around and checked into a hotel. It would have been the smart thing to do. I was really too exhausted to drive. But I didn't want to.

I wanted to get out of the City and away from the people and the noise and the memories. I wanted to go someplace quiet. I wanted to go home.

I called the house and got Bethany and told her I'd be back up in Syracuse in about five hours.

I'd fulfilled my part of the deal. The rest was up to Wilcox.

Chapter Fifteen

I took the Thruway back. There weren't many cars on the road and I spent the time rocketing through the night, trying not to think about my mother and what had gone wrong between us.

It seemed to me as if she'd wanted someone else as her daughter, someone I could never become. Somewhere along the way, I'd quit trying. Sad for her and sad for me. Then I thought of Murphy and George, which wasn't much better, so I reached over and turned the radio all the way up and put my foot on the gas and didn't think of anything at all.

It had been drizzling when I left the City, but now it had stopped raining. The sky was black with patches of gray. A sliver of moon looked as if it was suspended by a string. Once in a while, I spotted the twinkling lights of a plane flying overhead. After Albany, the mounds of snow on the sides of the road grew bigger as I headed farther upstate.

The roadway was cleared and salted. I did a solid eighty-five to ninety all the way back to Syracuse. Around Utica I got a call on my cell from George.

"I don't know what to do," he said.

I took a deep breath. I could feel the heaviness in my chest expanding.

"I can't help you."

"Please, Robin." He sounded as if he was crying.

I started to cry too. I couldn't talk because words wouldn't come. I clicked off the cell and threw it on the seat. By the time I reached home, I'd gotten myself back under control. Bethany, Manuel, and Zsa Zsa were waiting for me when I pulled in. I almost felt as if I had a family.

Bethany took my jacket when I walked in the door and handed me a bowl of soup.

"Minestrone. You look as if you could use this," she said.

I sat in the living room and devoured it.

"It's good, isn't it?" Manuel asked me.

"Very."

Manuel put his arm around Bethany. They were sitting on the sofa next to me.

"She made it. From scratch." He sounded so proud.

Bethany beamed.

"You find the person you were looking for?" she asked.

"Right where she was supposed to be. Did Wilcox call?"

Bethany shook her head. "No one did." She took the bowl from my hand. "You should go to bed. You look exhausted."

"I am." And I went upstairs.

I kicked off my shoes and stretched out on my bed. It felt wonderful. I closed my eyes. I knew I should get up and take my clothes off, but I was too tired to do it. The next thing I knew I was asleep.

Zsa Zsa woke me up at eight in the morning by cleaning my ear. I told her to cut it out and buried my face under the pillow, but she sat there growling and tugging on my sleeve with her teeth until I finally sat up.

"There. Are you satisfied?"

She wagged her tail, stretched out on the bed, put her head

between her paws, and watched me crawl out of bed. I stripped off my clothes and stood under the shower until the hot water gave out. I dried my hair and braided it; then I found some clean clothes, jeans and my old black cashmere turtleneck sweater buried in the back of the drawer. I'd forgotten how much I loved wearing it, it was so soft, until I slipped it on.

As I went downstairs I could hear Manuel's alarm clock going off. I let Zsa Zsa out, made myself a pot of coffee, and toasted two slightly stale bagels and ate them with some honey and cream cheese. By this time it was a little after nine and I was feeling marginally better.

"You want me to open Noah's Ark?" Manuel asked as he came into the kitchen. His eyes were full of sleep.

"If you wouldn't mind. I want to wrap up the Wilcox thing." I looked around. "Where's Bethany?"

"She went back to my mom's house. It's easier for her to go to school from there."

"I'll be in the store around twelve."

"Good." Manuel took a cereal bowl out of the cabinet, opened the refrigerator door, grabbed the milk, and put both of them on the kitchen table. "Because Bethany and I have an appointment with the lawyer at two."

"Manuel . . ."

He raised his hand. "Her parents don't give a shit about her, but they won't let her go either. At least this way she can do what she needs to."

"This is an awfully big step."

"I know. But she's got me to help her."

I looked at Manuel. All of a sudden he seemed like an adult. I don't know. They needed each other. Maybe it would work.

"It'll be all right, Robin. I know it will."

I gave Manuel a brief hug. "I hope so."

"I do too," he said softly.

I dropped my arms and he grabbed the box of Frosted Flakes off the kitchen table and began pouring it into his cereal bowl.

"See you soon." I put on my boots and my parka and went out to start up my car. First I turned on the heater and the rear-window defroster and then I got the scraper out and cleaned off the windows. Ah, winter in Syracuse. You gotta love it.

I was pulling out of the driveway when Calli called. "I just wanted to let you know. Lily had six puppies."

"So how does it feel to be Grandma?"

"Great. It was so exciting watching them being born. They're so ugly, like little rats, but I love them anyway. I've already used up two rolls of film. Will you be their godmother?"

"Godmother?" I laughed. "Are you having them baptized too?"

"I'm having their christening robes made now."

"Good. I'll get a new outfit."

"What? Another pair of jeans?"

"For you I'll wear black leather."

"So you will?"

"I'd be honored. When can I see them?"

"How about this evening? And Robin, Lily's being so good. I'm so proud of her. When I think that if it wasn't for you . . . I just get the chills."

"Don't, Calli."

"You're right. You're right. Stay in the present moment. The past doesn't matter. We create our own truth."

If I could, I would take all of Calli's self-help books and consign them to the garbage can.

"I wouldn't go that far." It has been my experience that if you don't pay attention to the past, it'll come around and bite you in the ass.

"You know what I mean. And Robin." Calli lowered her voice, "You were wrong about Dirk. He's being wonderful.

He didn't even care that I spent the night sleeping with Lily. He said he understood."

"I'm glad." I tried to sound sincere. I wanted to be wrong. God, did I ever. I just knew I wasn't.

Calli and I talked for another couple of minutes about the pups. After she hung up, I tried Wilcox's house again. Still no answer. I phoned his office. According to the message on the answering machine, no one came into the office until nine-thirty. Of course, I could leave a message if I wanted, and Mr. Wilcox would get back to me as soon as possible. Great.

By now I was beginning to feel a little uneasy. How drunk could Wilcox have gotten? First, I couldn't get him off the phone and now I couldn't reach him? I lit a cigarette and headed over to his house. It was closer than his office. I figured I'd check there—who knew? Maybe he'd gone on a bender and was passed out on the bathroom floor—and then I'd run by Paul's office and slip my report under his door.

The streets I traveled through were all shoveled. Fresh snow piled on top of the old, hiding the trash and the slush. Everything looked clean and white. Little drifts of snow blew off the fir trees and the wires. Flakes danced in the clear blue sky. Very charming. A regular Currier and Ives print. As long as you were on the inside looking out.

It took me ten minutes to reach Wilcox's house. I parked on the road and waded through a foot of snow to get to his door. If he'd gone out, he'd done it in someone else's car, because his was still in the driveway. No one had plowed it out.

I could have felt the hood of the car to make sure it was cold—Paul probably would have—but it seemed unnecessary. I could hear the television playing from where I was standing. I rang the bell. No one answered. I rang it again, even though I didn't expect anyone to come to the door. I was right. No one did.

I touched the door handle. It moved slightly, which was when I realized that the door wasn't completely closed. Later,

the cops asked me why I hadn't waited and called them before going in, like any normal person would have done. I did-
n't have a really good answer. I felt as if I was caught in a
drama and I had to play out the scene. I pushed the door
open and went inside.

Even from my position in the hallway, I could see something bad had happened. One of the chairs in the living room
was on its side. So was the coffee table. Magazines and papers had been scattered all over the floor. There was a splatter mark on the wall where someone had thrown something.
Shards from one of the mirrors on the wall lay on the floor.

Two of the dining room chairs were lodged on top of the
sideboard, looking as if they'd been thrown there, while a
third, with one of its legs missing, was lying on its side. Pieces
of shattered china and crystal were spread over the floor and
the table. A landscape was impaled on one of the chair
finials. So much for Janet Wilcox's decorating scheme.

The kitchen hadn't fared much better. The cupboard doors
were hanging open. The floor and the counter were littered
with cans and boxes. Smashed plates and glasses covered the
floor and the kitchen table. Given their spread, it looked as if
someone had heaved them at someone else. I spotted what
looked like a smear of blood on the edge of the counter. Then
I noticed another one on the floor. I was squatting down to
look at it when the refrigerator turned on. The noise made
me jump. I straightened up.

"Wilcox!" I yelled.

I didn't get an answer. But I hadn't expected one. When I
wiped my hands on the side of my jeans, I was surprised to
see that I was sweating. I straightened up and tried to recreate what had happened. Wilcox coming to the door, opening
it, letting people in. And then the fight. Somehow I didn't
think that Wilcox had won.

It turned out I was right.

He hadn't.

Chapter Sixteen

Sometimes I still see Wilcox's body in my dreams. I think I always will.

I found him upstairs.

The acrid odor of burning flesh engulfed me when I stepped inside his bedroom. And there was the heat. Then I saw Wilcox.

Someone had stripped him naked, slapped duct tape over his mouth, and staked him out on his bed over a portable electric heater, the kind people use to heat their garages and bedrooms. The heater was turned up full blast. I couldn't imagine the agony he must have felt as he was slowly roasted alive.

I noticed cigarette burn marks on his legs and feet, and someone had cut large strips of skin off his chest and arms and stomach.

From the look on Wilcox's face, it had taken him a long time to die.

I began to gag. I averted my eyes from the body on the bed, yanked the plug from the heater out of the wall socket, then stumbled out of the room and threw up in the middle of the hall.

The kind of violence where you get mad and shoot some-one I can understand, but not something like this. As I walked down the stairs, I noticed tiny splatters of blood on the wall. Wilcox's, no doubt. I thought I was okay, but I had trouble extracting my phone from my pocket. When I finally got it out, my fingers felt thick and clumsy as I punched in the numbers to Paul's cell phone.

This time he answered.

"Wilcox is dead," I told him. "I'm going to call the police. I just wanted to let you know first."

"What do you mean?"

"What I said."

"Wait. Let me call them."

"Go ahead."

"Where are you?"

"At his house."

"Stay there. I'll be right over."

"Make it fast."

I clicked the phone off and tried to concentrate on other things. Like Tiger Lily and her puppies and how nice it would be to go to Maui, but my mind kept going back to what I'd seen upstairs. I couldn't help myself.

Ten minutes later, I heard Paul's car pulling up outside.

"He's upstairs," I said as he came through the door. "Second room on the right. And be careful where you step."

Paul took the steps two at a time.

He came back down a couple of minutes later.

"Jesus," he said.

I noticed there were beads of sweat on his upper lip, and the veins in his nose were redder.

"That poor sonofabitch." He reached for his phone and called the police.

"I thought you said you were calling it in when I spoke to you," I said as I lit two cigarettes and handed him one.

"I wanted to take a look first. Now I'm sorry I did." He

took a puff. "We shouldn't smoke in here," he said. "We'll contaminate the crime scene."

I got up and we headed outside.

"Jesus," Paul repeated. "All my years on the force, I don't think I've ever seen anything like that."

"I wish I hadn't seen it."

"What made you come over?"

"I couldn't get you. I couldn't get Wilcox. I guess I just wanted to tell him I found his wife."

Paul took another puff of his cigarette, snubbed it out with his fingers, and put the butt in his pocket. "No sense in confusing forensics," he explained. He squared his shoulders. "Listen, about not being able to get me . . . I'm sorry. I've been in the hospital till this morning. Kidney stones." He shook his head. "God, they hurt like a sonofabitch. They say it's the worst pain you can ever have."

"Not the worst," I said thinking of Wilcox.

"No. Not the worst," Paul said softly. "You're right about that."

Both of us stood there for a minute not saying anything.

"It's cold out here." Paul rubbed his hands together. "Let's wait in my car."

I nodded and we walked toward his Explorer, taking care to retrace our footsteps.

When we got inside, Paul reached under the seat and came out with a flask. He unscrewed the top, took a swig, and handed it to me.

"For the cold," he said.

I took a gulp and handed it back.

"Feel better?" Paul asked.

"Marginally."

He took another swig and passed it back to me. I took another drink. It was the same stuff that we'd had in his office. I could feel my insides begin to loosen up.

Paul hadn't shaved and the shirt and pants he was wearing looked as if he'd picked them off the top of the laundry pile.

"It's amazing what a person can live through before he dies," he said.

"We should all be equipped with circuit breakers. Too much and we switch off."

"We are, but if you're good, you know how to circumvent them. That's the art."

I shivered and reached for the flask. It was something I didn't want to think about. "Who would do something like that?"

"I don't know. Wilcox must have really pissed someone off."

"Still . . ."

"Maybe the cops will get lucky," Paul said. "Maybe one of the neighbors noticed a strange car parked in the driveway. Or on the road. From the looks of it, whoever did this was here for a while."

"I hope I don't run into them."

Paul reached over, took the flask out of my hand, and took a big swallow. "Me either," he said as he wiped his mouth with the back of his hand. "Me either."

A snowplow lumbered by down the street. I lowered the window and tossed what was left of my cigarette out in the snow.

"Some guys, they just have no luck. No luck at all."

"I've always thought you make your own," Paul said.

"Maybe." I lit another cigarette and thought about how much I wanted to call George all of a sudden.

Chapter Seventeen

The Dewitt police arrived before I had time to finish my cigarette. Paul and I got out of the Explorer to greet them. Paul did all the talking. We stayed outside while they went in. They didn't look too steady when they came out.

They secured the scene and called the Criminal Investigative Division, who rolled in within ten minutes of the call. An Officer Profit took down my initial statement while waiting for the CID unit to show up. I told him about the front door to Wilcox's house being opened and about why I had walked in. I told him about why Wilcox had hired me, I told him about the trip down to New York, about finding Janet Wilcox, and about my concern at not being able to contact Walter Wilcox.

Profit looked up from his writing. "Because you thought he was passed out?"

"It crossed my mind."

"He'd been drinking a lot?"

"Enough the last couple of times I saw him."

"He seemed nervous to you? Scared?"

"Nervous. Mostly nervous."

"Did you have a feeling why that was?"

"I put it down to being anxious about finding his wife. In retrospect, I was wrong."

"So he never said anything about people threatening him?"

I shook my head. "Not to me."

"And you found his wife?"

"She's staying with a guy called Quintillo down in New York City." And I gave Profit Quintillo's phone number and address.

"Any other family?"

"A daughter." I was giving him Stephanie's number when one of the officers went into the kitchen. He must have hit the play button on the answering machine because I could hear myself saying, "Wilcox, are you there? Pick up the phone." My voice sounded tinny.

I wondered if Wilcox's killers had heard me. Thinking about it gave me an uncomfortable feeling in the pit of my stomach.

"You think there's a relationship between Wilcox's wife's disappearance and what happened upstairs?" Profit asked me.

"I don't think I know enough to know," I replied.

"Terrific." Profit snapped his notebook shut. "A philosopher. Anything else?"

"I pulled the heater plug out of the upstairs wall."

He nodded, pointed to the wall in the hallway, and instructed me to stand over there. I did as I was told. A few minutes later, Paul came over and stood next to me.

"No one is answering at Quintillo's apartment," he said.

"Maybe Quintillo and Janet went out to a movie or something."

"Maybe." Paul was chewing gum. I asked for a piece. He dug in his pocket and brought out a package of Bazooka bubble gum. "This is all I have."

As I unwrapped it, a detective, a young guy wearing a navy blue blazer, a crisp white shirt, a blue-and-red paisley tie, and a pair of gray slacks came over and asked me to recreate my route through the house.

"How long are you going to keep Paul and me here?" I asked as I mounted the steps.

"Probably another half hour. How do you know Santini?"

"Through George Samson." It was a measure of how I was feeling that saying George's name didn't bother me.

"How's George doing?"

"Well enough. How do you know him?"

"Mutual friends. What's your connection?"

"He was friends with my husband."

"Small world." And the detective gestured for me to go ahead of him.

Wilcox's bedroom had become a busy place since I was in there last.

As I walked through the door, one of the techs was saying to his partner, "My wife is threatening to make me take swing dancing lessons."

"Get some balls. Tell her no."

"Hey, I'm not the one that can't go out because I have to do the laundry."

"At least I have clean clothes."

His partner laughed and got out his camera. "So how's your kid's skiing doing?"

The tech grinned. "I think he's going to make it to the state finals."

Both men looked up briefly when I came in then returned to going about their business. I showed the detective where I'd stood and what I'd touched, which wasn't much.

Maybe it was the effects of shock, but this time I didn't feel anything as I gazed down at Wilcox. I indicated the rope that had been used to bind Wilcox's hands and feet. It was heavy duty, industrial-strength twine.

"You think the person that did this brought that with them?"

"Probably," the detective said. He looked around. "It doesn't strike me as the kind of thing you'd find in a place like this."

As I was going down the stairs, the EMTs were bringing the stretcher up the steps. I flattened myself against the wall to let them pass. Walter Wilcox was headed for the Medical Examiner's office and his autopsy—not that there was much question about what had killed him. Why was another matter.

I wanted to talk to Paul some more, but he and his cop friends were schmoozing it up, and he showed no disposition to leave. I lingered for a while hoping I could snag him, then gave it up as a bad job.

I was on my way out the door when he called out to me, "Hey, don't go hog wild with the rest of the expense money. I need it back."

"Gee. There goes my trip to the Keys. Don't worry, I'll have your invoice for you tomorrow."

Outside, the driveway had been roped off with crime-scene tape. There were two more squad cars, plus the ambulance outside. A policeman was directing traffic. The neighbors who were at home had come out of their houses and were standing around, clustered in tight little knots, watching the proceedings. I recognized a few of the faces from before. I could tell they recognized me too, but before anyone could come over a camera crew arrived and I slipped away. This would definitely be the lead story on the six o'-clock news.

"Jeez," Manuel said when I walked into Noah's Ark. "What the hell happened to you?"

"I look that bad?"

"You look awful."

I went into the bathroom and glanced in the mirror. He was right. I did. I was sheet white, which emphasized the

dark circles under my eyes. I spent the rest of the day working at the store. There was something soothing about the
routine and about being with the animals.

Zsa Zsa seemed to know something was wrong, and she
spent the day alternately following me around, rubbing up
against my leg, and bringing me her toys to play with. The
beating in my chest had almost slowed to normal levels by
the time I put the CLOSED sign on the door.

I was looking forward to going over to Calli's to see the
pups. I'd made up a little gift basket to take to Tiger Lily consisting of a variety of dog treats. I was busy arranging them
when the phone rang. Expecting it to be Calli, I picked it up.

Silence reigned on the other end of the line. I could hear
someone breathing and the sound of traffic. Whoever was
calling was probably using a cell phone.

"George, is that you?"

A car started honking.

"Last chance."

Nothing.

I hung up.

I didn't know whether I wanted to cry or scream.

Chapter Eighteen

I was sitting cross-legged on the floor in Calli's spare bedroom petting Tiger Lily's head while six naked blobs of protoplasm rooted around her belly, sucking on her teats. She wasn't doing badly for a first-time mother. I know humans who have done a lot, lot worse.

She'd made a cozy nest for herself between the bed and the wall, a space of about twenty-four inches. Like the Three Bears nursery rhyme said, the space wasn't too big and it wasn't too small. It was just right. In addition, it was out of the line of sight of the door and protected on three sides by two walls and the bed.

"You are such a good girl," I crooned in her ear.

I could feel the tension I'd been carrying in my neck dissipating as I inhaled the odors of dog and puppy, milk and newsprint. Lily furrowed her forehead, put her head down between her paws, and looked at me imploringly with those eyes the color of dark chocolate.

"It could have been worse. You could have had ten." She just looked at me. "I know, I know," I told her as I untangled a matt behind her ear. "Motherhood is a pain in the ass. But the pups will be gone soon. Six, seven weeks. Eight at the most. I promise."

She sighed the same sigh I'd heard from my grandmother. Then, resigned to her fate, she sighed for the second time, turned around, and nudged at the nearest pup with her nose. It let out a squeak and kept on sucking.

I took one of the treats I'd bought for Lily out of its package and gave it to her. She took it from my hand delicately and ate it slowly, without great enthusiasm. Clearly it was okay, but not great. She probably would have liked something from Purina better, but at the moment corporate was out and homespun was in. The dog world followed the same fashion laws as everything else.

I'd been thinking the other day that in a way we'd gone back to the time when my grandmother had fed our dog the leftover scraps that she got from the butcher combined with whatever we were having for dinner that night. Only things are more artful now. And expensive. Sincerity and simplicity are today's new marketing ploys. You get that perfect five-hundred-dollar meditation mat, and enlightenment will automatically follow.

In line with that concept, the packaging on Laura's Doggie Delights had the requisite length of sisal cord around the top and a label made of coarse brown paper. Of course the label was handwritten. What else?

According to it, Laura's Doggies Delights were an all-organic peanut-butter biscuit that contained only healthy, natural ingredients. They'd been mixed by hand, rolled out in Laura's own kitchen, and baked in her oven. I was thinking I wouldn't be surprised to hear that they had been baked on a brick hearth, powered by hardwood oak logs cut with a hand saw and split with an axe, when Calli opened the door a crack and slipped in.

"Aren't they wonderful?" she asked, gesturing toward the

puppies. "I wish I could stay home with them all day. And by the way, Zsa Zsa is not pleased. At all."

"I figured she wouldn't be."

She'd shot me a poisoned glance when I told her she had to stay downstairs and flounced off, but there was nothing I could do. Bringing her into Lily's nursery was not an option. Not unless I wanted a quick trip to the doggie emergency ward to have Zsa Zsa sewn back up. Lily was nice, but she wasn't that nice. New mothers, whatever the species, in general do not take kindly to intrusions. In fact, I was flattered that she let me in the room. I wouldn't have been surprised if she hadn't.

"What's she doing?"

"Sitting on my sofa and sulking."

"I'll make it up to her."

Calli plopped down on the floor next to me. "Sounds like the guys I know. Something more interesting comes along and away they go. Then they think they can make it up to you with flowers."

"Are we talking about Dirk?"

"Don't be ridiculous." She gestured to the puppies. Two had finished nursing and were busy fighting with each other. "So what do you think?"

"I think they're wonderful."

"Me too." She massaged her lower back with her left hand, then leaned against the bed. "God, I'm exhausted."

"You still driving up North?"

"Unfortunately. Yesterday I thought I was going into a ditch for sure. I don't know why anyone lives up there."

"The Native Americans do it because they have to, and the others do it because they're antisocial and like the idea of being able to do what they want."

"I think they would use the word self-reliant."

"Yes, white power groups would. So, how's the story going?"

Calli shrugged. "Slowly. Everyone has something bad to say about everyone else. Checking out the facts is hard. Not that it matters anyway. Mike told me he heard a rumor they're thinking of killing the series. But what do I know? Why should they tell me? I'm just writing the damned piece after all."

She yawned. "Between work and the puppies, I think I've gotten a total of four hours sleep for the past three nights. But it's been worth it." She closed her eyes for a few moments and rubbed them gently with her knuckles before opening them. "Did I tell you, I prepared a whelping bed down in the rec room in the basement, just like the vet told me to do, but she liked up here better. On the carpet."

"That's okay. My first dog, Elsie, had her litter in Murphy's closet. She wouldn't let anyone in there for three weeks. Anytime anyone tried, she'd run out and nip them. Murphy had to go out and buy new clothes."

Calli giggled.

"I thought it was pretty funny too, but Murphy didn't."

Calli lightly ran her fingers along the top of the carpet. "I think I might have to have this ripped up, not that I liked this color anyway," she reflected. "What would you call it?"

"Puke yellow?"

"I don't know what I was on when I picked it out."

"For sure something that wasn't very good."

As I watched Calli, I realized that I hadn't seen her looking so happy in a long time. Maybe there is something to motherhood after all. Especially if you can mother vicariously.

Calli reached over and stroked under Lily's chin. Then she lifted up one of the puppies. Lily's body tensed. Her eyes never left the pup Calli was holding. "I'm thinking of keeping one," she told me before returning it to Lily. "Actually I'd like to keep them all."

I recalled the chaos surrounding Elsie's puppies. "Believe

me, you won't when they get bigger and start running around."

"Maybe." Calli brushed a strand of blond hair off her forehead. "We'll see."

"Manuel wants one. For Bethany."

"What do you think?" Calli asked.

"I think I'll end up with the dog."

"Zsa Zsa would not be pleased."

"No one likes being replaced." I took a deep breath as George's face flashed through my mind. The pain in my chest returned.

"Are you all right?" Calli asked.

"Fine. I just got something in my eye."

"You need a tissue?"

I shook my head.

"This is about what happened yesterday at Wilcox's, isn't it?"

I nodded, grateful not to have been the one who lied. Discussing yesterday was easier than discussing George. If I told Calli about George getting married, it would be real. I couldn't deal with that yet. Maybe I don't do well with relationships, but I do real well with denial.

Calli had been out of the office all day, so the first she'd heard about what had happened at Wilcox's house was on the six o'clock news. Though my name hadn't been mentioned—I'd been called a concerned neighbor—she'd recognized Wilcox's name from one of our previous conversations and, being the nosy person she was, she'd called me immediately to find out what was going on. I'd been too tired to talk then. Now I wasn't.

Even though she'd found out some of the details in the interim I told her everything anyway. When I got to the part about how Wilcox had died, Calli clapped her hands over her mouth.

"Oh, my God," she cried.

"I know."

"I can tell you one thing. I'll never eat barbecue again."

"That's a terrible thing to say."

Calli shuddered. "You'd have to be a real sicky to do something like that."

"Yeah. We're definitely talking psychopath."

Calli crossed her arms over her chest and rubbed them. "But I'll tell you one thing. Seeing that would give me nightmares for months."

"I don't get nightmares," I lied.

"What a crock of shit."

Calli was right. I'd been plagued with them ever since my father died. Something like Wilcox just brought everything back. I watched Calli pick one of Lily's golden hairs off her black cashmere sweater and set it carefully on the rug.

"I should have gotten a black lab. That way the dog hair wouldn't show," she reflected as she picked another hair off her sleeve. "I swear I could knit a sweater from Lily's fur." She brightened. "And speaking of sweaters, they're on sale at Good Stuff." Good Stuff is a high-end boutique out in Fayetteville where Calli does most of her shopping. "Let's go out there Saturday afternoon. You could use some retail therapy."

"I don't have the money." I was going to need everything I'd earned from this job to pay my bills.

"You have Santini's expense money."

"I have to return most of it."

"Robin, I'm deeply disappointed in you. All those years on the newspaper. Does the phrase creative padding mean nothing to you?"

"What happened to your morals?"

"I don't have any when it comes to clothes."

"Or men."

"That too. And proud of it."

I couldn't help laughing.

Calli is a great believer in shopping as a cure for every-thing—that or a pedicure. I used to think that was terminally shallow, but now I'm not so sure she isn't on to something. You can't control the big things in your life, but you can control the color of your nails and the cut of your skirt.

Sometimes distraction is a good thing. And anyway, I could use a new sweater. I had exactly four in my dresser drawer. When I lived in New York City, I'd had so many, I'd ended up storing some of them in my oven. I think I lost interest when I married Murphy. He hated me spending money on stuff like that and I hated buying cheap stuff, so I ended up not buying anything at all.

"Maybe you're right," I conceded.

"Of course." Calli tapped her fingers on her thigh. "I always am. Wilcox," she mused. "Is there something about him I should know?"

"I can't imagine what."

The manner of his death seemed the most notable thing about him.

"You'd tell me if there was, right?"

"Don't you ever stop working?"

"Once in a while."

Calli might look like a Barbie Doll, but she has the mind of a Mac computer. Except, of course, when it comes to herself. I was thinking about how it always works that way when I heard the downstairs front door open and close.

"Is that Dirk?"

Calli shook her head. "No. His kid."

"I didn't know he had kids."

Calli held up three fingers. "By two different women." I must have given her a look because Calli added, "Don't worry. He's not staying here, not that you should talk, with Manuel."

"That's different."

"No, it isn't. Anyway, he just came by to get something Dirk left for him."

"And speaking of Dirk, where is the crown prince of music?"

"Playing a gig somewhere out in Tully. Things seem to be picking up for him."

"Glad to hear it," I said with as much sincerity as I could manage.

"He's even thinking of cutting a CD and distributing it himself. That stuff is so much easier to do with the web. I just loaned him some money to register his CD with ASCAP."

"Wonderful."

Calli put her hand on my arm. "Please, Robin. Give him a chance. He really is trying. And you should see him with Lily."

"It's just that you're my friend and I don't want to see you getting hurt again."

"I know." She patted my arm, then smoothed down the front of the sweater she was wearing. "You have to believe I know what I'm doing."

"I do."

"No, you don't, but thank you for lying."

There was the sound of something falling downstairs.

"I swear that kid can't cross the room without falling over his own feet," Calli told me. She leaned over. "What's going on down there?" she yelled.

"Nothing. I tripped over the rug and knocked over a chair," Dirk's son yelled back.

A moment later, I heard footsteps clomping up the stairs.

"Calli, I can't find the folder," he said. "Are you sure my dad left it?"

The voice sounded familiar.

Then he stuck his head in the door.

It was the kid from Fayette Street.

Chapter Nineteen

The kid and I stared at each other. His nose was red from the cold. So were his hands. He was still wearing the same cheap jacket he'd had on when he came to see me in the store. It was probably the only one he had.

"What are you doing here?" he demanded when he saw me. He looked confused.

"I could ask the same of you." I turned to Calli. "This is the kid that was in the house where we found Tiger Lily."

I looked at her biting her lip and knew that she knew.

"But I'm not telling you anything you don't already know, am I?"

The kid indicated me with his chin. "Calli, she a friend of yours?"

Calli didn't answer him. She looked away. As if she hadn't heard. As if he didn't exist.

"Yes, I am," I told him. "I guess she didn't tell you that."

He scuffed his feet on the carpet. "I don't know what you're talking about."

"Sure you don't."

Calli coughed. "Dirk says the whole thing was a mistake," she said to me.

Lily whimpered softly. The tension in the room disturbed her. I put out my hand and petted her.

"What do you mean, mistake?" I asked Calli.

"A misunderstanding."

"I see."

Calli got busy taking more of Lily's hairs off her sweater.

"Who paid the kid's bail?" I asked her.

"Hey, I got a name," the kid protested.

We both went on with our conversation as if he wasn't there.

"I did," Calli admitted.

"You weren't going to tell me, were you?" I asked her.

Two spots of color grew on her cheeks. "Only because I know how you get."

"How I get?"

"Yes. You're always so self-righteous about everything."

"You don't think being lied to should upset me?"

"What I told you wasn't a lie. Tiger Lily got out of my yard."

"I thought you said she was stolen."

Calli held up her hands and let them drop back into her lap. "I thought she was. But stolen or lost, what difference does it make? She was gone. I had to get her back."

"It makes a big difference."

"The result was the same. She was missing."

"Don't play those semantic games with me."

Calli glared at me.

I glared back.

I pointed to the kid. "Did he tell you where Lily was? Is that how you knew?"

Lily gave a tentative thump of her tail at the mention of her name and licked my hand. I gave her a quick hug.

"Well, is it?" I asked Calli.

Calli studied the wall, while the kid looked at both of us—

not quite sure what to do. I almost felt sorry for him. He was in way over his head.

I went on. "So what was this whole business with stealing her back? Why not just go up to the front door and knock?"

Calli nodded her head in the kid's direction. "Because he didn't want Myra to know."

"The woman who came to the door?"

"Yes," Calli whispered.

"Who cares what he wanted?"

"Hey," the kid said. "That isn't nice."

"I'm not in a nice mood."

I pushed myself up and headed for the door.

"Where are you going?" Calli asked.

"Out of here." And I walked into the hallway.

"Robin, please," Calli called as she came after me. She put her hand on my shoulder. I spun around. "Robin, he was trying to help."

I gestured to the kid, who was standing close to Calli with his hands jammed in his pockets. "I bet."

Calli put her hand on my arm. "Robin," she said. "He found Lily at Myra's house. He told me where she was."

I turned toward the kid. "And I'm supposed to believe that?"

"It's true," he insisted. "Myra found her wandering the streets. She was gonna sell her," he mumbled.

"Why'd you come to the store?"

He shrugged. "I told you. I thought I could do something to help Myra out."

"You're just an all-around great guy, aren't you?"

The kid didn't say anything. I looked at Calli.

"You should have told me."

She picked up her hands and let them fall.

I started for the stairs. "Myra is Dick's second wife. I was embarrassed," Calli called after me.

"Friends trust each other."

Maybe I should have been more understanding. Maybe I should have gone back up. But I didn't. I was so hurt and angry that I couldn't think of anything else to say. Instead I whistled for Zsa Zsa, walked out the door, got in my car, and drove home.

It was extremely cold out, and the weatherman said it would get even colder tomorrow. Nothing was moving outside. Everyone was inside keeping warm. Bethany and Manuel were cuddling on the sofa watching television when I walked in the door. The air smelled of popcorn.

"You want some?" Bethany asked. "I just made it."

"Thanks, but no thanks." I hung my jacket up and went straight to the liquor.

"Are you sure?" Bethany said.

"Positive."

"The lawyer said Bethany could become an emancipated minor if she wanted to."

"Great."

"He said to think it over."

"Good idea."

"Well," Manuel said as I unscrewed the top of the bottle. "Is Calli going to let us have a puppy?"

"I wouldn't count on it if I were you." I poured myself a triple.

"Why not?"

I took a sip. Then I took another. I could feel the knot in my chest loosening. It occurred to me as I took my fourth sip that my drinking was moving from the "like to" to the "need to" category.

"Why?" Manuel repeated.

"I'll tell you later." And I took my drink and went upstairs. I could hear Zsa Zsa's nails on the risers as she followed me.

I wasn't in the mood to talk to anyone at the moment.

Chapter Twenty

Maybe I wouldn't have dreamt about George if he hadn't called me just as I was falling asleep.

"Don't hang up," he said when I picked up.

"Did you call me before at the store?"

"No. Why?"

"Because I could hear someone breathing on the line. Then they hung up. I thought it might be you."

"I wouldn't do something like that."

I didn't say anything.

"Robin, are you still there?"

I pushed Zsa Zsa off my pillow and rested my head on it. "I'm here."

"What are you thinking?"

"That talking to you is incredibly painful."

"I'm sorry. I just called to find out how you are."

"Why?"

"Because I care about you. I always will. Don't you know that?"

"You have a funny way of showing it. Why shouldn't I be fine?"

"They mentioned your name on the eleven o'clock news."

"Great. What did the story say?"

"Not too much. Just that you had discovered Wilcox's body."

"Nothing else?"

"It was, and I'm quoting, a brutal murder."

"That's a fairly accurate assessment."

"What happened?"

I couldn't help myself. I told him.

"Jeez," George said when I was through. "What the hell did Paul get you mixed up in?"

"I'm not mixed up in anything. It's over."

"I hope so."

"And anyway, I don't think Paul knows any more about what happened than I do."

George's laugh was humorless. "He always knows. Is there anything that I can do for you? Anything that you need?"

I wanted to say, yes, there is. I need you to make things the way they were before.

"Not that I can think of," I told him instead. "Paul's taking care of the legal side of things."

"He should." George hesitated. Then he said, "All right. I suppose it's good night."

"So how's Natalie?" I asked.

"Natalie's fine."

"Good."

I couldn't bring myself to ask about the baby.

"Can we have dinner one night?" George asked.

"No, we can't."

"Robin, I'm so sorry."

"I wish you'd stop saying that. It doesn't help."

"I don't know what else to do."

"You've already done it."

I pressed the off button on my phone. I punched my pillow up and turned onto my side. Zsa Zsa turned over on her back and made the low-pitched growling noises she does when she wants me to rub her belly.

"How would you like a puppy?" I asked as I complied.

She growled some more.

"Okay. Okay."

Still. A little golden puppy would be nice. I could bring it to the store. I wondered how badly Zsa Zsa would take it. Eventually she'd get used to the idea. She might even like it. It would give her someone to play with. And it would make me feel less guilty about leaving her. There are perks to not being an "only." Eventually, I fell asleep to the accompaniment of the wind moaning through the trees.

In the dream I had, George and I were wandering through a long, narrow room that seemed to go on forever.

"I have to go now," he told me.

"Wait. I have to give you your clippers."

He didn't say anything. Suddenly I noticed that the walls of the room were full of doors. Some had mirrors. Some were painted red; others were painted gold and purple. Somehow I hadn't seen that before. When I looked back, George was gone. My heart started beating faster. I knew something terrible was going to happen if I didn't find him. I went over and opened the door on my left. A black wind whooshed out and threatened to suck me in. I just barely managed to close it and turned to the door on my right.

"No, no, no," a voice from somewhere said.

But I knew I had to. I had no choice. I grasped the clear glass handle and turned. The door slowly swung open. I looked down. Blood was running out of it. It trickled around my bare feet and began to grow. There was more and more.

First the blood was around my ankles; then it came up to my calves and my knees. I tried to close the door, but now I couldn't reach the knob. It was an inch too far away. I tried to move, but I couldn't take a step. I woke up when the blood was reaching my mouth.

I bolted upright and turned on the lamp. My heart was beating so hard, I was having trouble catching my breath. It was as quiet as death in my bedroom. Zsa Zsa licked my hand. I gave her an automatic pat, put on a T-shirt and a pair of flannel pajama bottoms, and went downstairs.

The television was still playing. Manuel must have forgotten to turn it off when he and Bethany went upstairs. I poured myself a small Scotch, lay down on the sofa, got the remote, and clicked on to the Weather Channel and watched pictures of the clouds floating overhead in the sky with the sound off and read the little white letters that came across the screen. In Cairo it was in the 80s. In Syracuse it was fourteen degrees with a wind chill factor of five below zero. Snow storms and squalls were predicted for Onondaga County through tomorrow night. Why I lived here I didn't know.

At some point I must have fallen asleep again because I woke up to Manuel standing over me.

"Have a bad night?" he asked.

"Nightmare."

"Bummer. Are you opening this morning? Because I got some errands I have to do."

"No problem." I sat up and put my head in my hands. My back hurt from sleeping on the sofa, and my eyes itched from lack of sleep.

"You shouldn't do this kind of stuff anymore," Manuel observed.

"Look for people?"

He nodded.

"It usually doesn't turn out this way."

"Seeing something like that. Once would be too much for me."

"I think it might be too much for me too."

"People who do things like that . . ." Manuel hesitated a second while he searched for the right phrase. "You don't want to get in their line of sight."

"You don't want to get within a hundred miles of them."

I thought about what George had said about Paul as I got up and peered through the living room blinds. It was snowing again. It was the kind of day that made you want to stay in bed curled up with a good book.

Did Paul have a handle on what was going on? I really wanted to believe George was wrong.

"You think the cops are going to get whoever did Wilcox?" asked Manuel, interrupting my thoughts.

I watched my neighbor come out and start up his car. He was bundled up so that only his nose showed.

"I certainly hope so."

And I dropped the slat down and got ready to go to work.

Chapter Twenty-One

Aside from a couple of calls from a reporter on the local paper, to whom I refused to speak, and a visit from the detective, the rest of the day went by uneventfully. I'd made three sales, one of them a big one, repaired a water filter, cleaned out the gerbil and hamster cages, swept out the bird room, fed the reptiles, and had almost figured out why the crickets kept escaping when Manuel walked through the door at one-thirty in the afternoon.

I pointed to the fifty-gallon aquarium sitting on the floor next to the counter.

"A woman named Mrs. Brown is going to come by and pick this up in about an hour."

Manuel nodded. "Where are you going to be?"

"I thought I'd go down to Paul's office and finish things up."

"Good idea."

I had to give him my bill, plus refund the expense money I was carrying around. I was afraid that if I kept it any longer, I'd spend it.

"The roads are bad," Manuel cautioned as he went into the back. "Be careful driving."

"What are you, my mother?"

"You need one. How about the puppies?"

"Calli and I had an argument."

"So?"

"So we're not talking to each other."

"That's means I can't get a puppy?"

"You can get one from someplace else. I'm not asking her."

"Maybe I will."

"Go ahead."

Manuel muttered something under his breath and went to check on the boas.

The snow on the streets was greasy, and I slid all the way down to the State Tower Building. This time I put my car in the garage attached to the building. I figured it was easier to pay the four bucks than to have to clean my car off when I came back outside.

Paul glanced up from his computer screen when I came through the door of his office. Today the place smelled of cheap Chinese food. I noticed the plant was gone.

"First step in redecorating," I said, pointing to where it had been.

"Call me Miss Stewart. I was just trying to phone you," he said, clicking the computer off.

"And here I am."

"You're not answering your cell."

"That's because I left it at home."

"What's the point of having it if you don't carry it with you?"

I shrugged. "Sometimes, I'm just not in the mood to be reached. Like you weren't when I was down in the City," I added pointedly.

"I already explained I had a medical emergency." And he gave me his tough-guy frown.

"I didn't think tough guys got kidney stones."

"Well, I'll tell you one thing. You're not tough when you get 'em."

I crossed over to his desk and handed him an envelope. "Here's my bill and the expense money I didn't use." Despite Calli's suggestion, I was giving it all back.

Paul waved his hand. "Keep it. There's something else I want you to do."

I carefully placed the envelope on top of a pile of manila folders. Paul pretended not to see it.

"Thanks for the offer, but I think I'm done playing Nancy Drew, girl detective, for a while."

Paul indicated the chair by the side of the desk. "Sit down."

"Another time. I told Manuel I'd be right back."

"Fuck Manuel."

"You can try, but I don't think he'd agree. You're not his type."

"I'll try not to be hurt."

"I always thought you went for the tall blondes anyway."

Paul drummed his fingers on the arm of his chair. "We need to talk."

"You may need to, but I don't."

He spun his chair around to face me. "Robin, for God's sake. For once, can you not play games?"

"I could, but why wouldn't I want to? Or have you considered the possibility that I don't want to hear what you have to say?"

"You don't know what I have to say," Paul said.

"And I'd like to keep it that way," I replied.

"Why?"

"Because I've had enough. I'm on overload."

"Aren't we all."

Paul sat up straight, opened the bottom drawer of his desk, got out the bottle of Scotch and two glasses, and poured each of us a shot.

"It's a little early," he said. "But what the hell."

"What the hell indeed."

I pulled up a chair and sat down in it. Something on Paul's face told me this wasn't going to be good.

"Aren't you going to take off your jacket?"

"No. I won't be staying that long."

"Suit yourself."

Paul handed me my glass. I noticed that his hand shook slightly when he did. I took a sip of Scotch and watched the snowflakes swirling past the window. In the outside corridor, a woman wearing heels tapped her way by. I wondered if I could still walk in them without breaking my ankle as I waited for Paul to speak.

Finally I said, "I'm listening."

Paul took a swallow from his glass, grimaced slightly, and rolled it between the palms of his hands.

"What I want you to do will be a piece of cake," he said. "You've done most of the work already."

"The only thing I've been working on is Wilcox, and Wilcox is, as you very well know, dead."

Paul finished his drink, put the glass down, and poured himself another shot.

"But his wife isn't. I want you to find her."

"Haven't you heard what I've been saying to you?"

Evidently he hadn't, because Paul went on as if I hadn't spoken. "She's changed residences. The police haven't been able to locate her."

"Well, that's their problem, not mine."

"Robin, listen . . ."

I held up my hand. "Forget it."

"Robin . . ."

"You want to find her, you go. Or get someone else."

"Listen . . ."

"No way. No how." I drained my glass. "Thanks for the drink, but I'm out of here."

I was starting to stand up when Paul slammed his hand down on his desk. The thud resonated in the silence of the office.

"Will you please do me the favor of shutting up . . ."

The edge of fear in his voice made me sit back down. I don't think I ever heard him scared before. The radiator clanked as I leaned forward in my chair and studied Paul's face.

"This isn't about Janet Wilcox, is it? It's about you."

He turned away and got busy studying the view out the window, not that there was much to study. We weren't talking tropical island here.

"How bad is it? How bad?" I repeated when he didn't answer.

Chapter Twenty-Two

I watched Paul's shoulders rise and fall as he took a deep breath and let it out.

"Bad enough," he admitted. He still wasn't looking at me. "And there's something else you need to know."

I remembered the call I'd gotten at the store. The one I'd thought had been from George and wasn't.

"I'm involved too, aren't I?"

"In a peripheral way."

"How peripheral?"

Paul swiveled his chair around, reached out, and took my hands in his. "I really didn't mean for this to happen. You have to believe that."

It occurred to me that he sounded like George. One excuse after another.

Manuel's comment about not wanting to be in the line of sight of certain people floated through my head. Well, it looked as if that was exactly where I was.

"I think you'd better tell me what's going on."

"That's what I've been trying to do."

He let go of my hands, filled my glass again, screwed the top of the bottle back on, and put it back in the drawer.

"You know the expression, there's no fool like an old fool? Well, it's true."

I waited.

"Wilcox was a fool."

"Alima," I guessed.

Paul nodded.

"And his wife found out."

Paul nodded again.

"And that other story, the one Wilcox told about his wife being suicidal? That wasn't true?"

"Not to my knowledge." Paul cracked a knuckle. "Janet was just very, very pissed."

"That doesn't seem unreasonable given the circumstances. Most women would be."

I know I had been. I'd tried to brain Murphy with a heavy pot when I found out he'd been sleeping with one of my friends. Unfortunately, my aim had been bad.

"Actually," Paul continued, "I don't think she really gave a shit about Walter. I think she didn't like the fact that he was spending money on his girlfriend. Plus it was a pride thing. Her husband taking up with a lap dancer."

"Would she have felt better if he had taken up with a Supreme Court judge?"

"Maybe. With Janet, status always counts." Paul fiddled with his sleeve. "The problem is that when she took off, she took some of Walter's property with her."

"Okay."

"But this property really wasn't Walter's."

"Whose is it?"

"That's not important."

"I think it is."

Paul ran his finger over the edge of the desk and brushed a speck of dust away.

"These are not nice people, I take it?" I said.

"Well, they're not winning the citizenship award of the year."

"And now they want their property back."

Paul nodded.

I always stun myself with my brilliance.

"Which is why Wilcox was so anxious for me to find his wife."

Paul nodded again.

"Were they the ones that did Wilcox?"

Paul slumped down in his chair and swiveled from side to side. He looked profoundly tired.

"I doubt if they did it. But I'm sure they hired the people who did."

"So why aren't you telling this to the police?"

"I don't have any proof." He sat up and spread his hands out in front of him. "Just lots of suppositions."

"Oh, I think you have a little bit more than that."

Paul went back to studying the window. The view looked bleak. Mostly gray skies, gray sidewalk, empty streets. Everyone was staying in. They'd probably caught a case of the winter blahs. There was a lot of that going around Syracuse these days.

He kept his eyes glued to the outside. "They think I helped Wilcox steal the money."

"Did you?"

"No."

"Then why do they think that?"

"They said that Wilcox told them."

Paul and I were both silent for a moment. I knew we were both thinking the same thing. In Wilcox's circumstances, we both would have rolled in our mothers to make the pain stop. Contrary to what some people say, pain does not ennoble, pain degrades.

"I got a call," Paul said. "They told me I'd better get their stuff back. Or else."

"Why don't you go to the police?"

Paul gave me a contemptuous look. "Get real. People like that want you, they get you."

"You could leave town for a while."

"And do what?"

"Sit on the beach. Sightsee. Climb Mount Everest. Learn the accordion. Take swing dancing. Whatever."

"With what money? I have five dollars in my checking account."

"I thought you were doing well. What about the big security contract you've been working on?"

Paul got the bottle back out and poured himself another drink. He didn't pour one for me and I didn't ask. He was busy wiping a drop off the rim of his glass—Mr. Neat—when he spoke.

"I made some bad investments."

"What kind?"

"The double-down kind."

"Jeez." Paul was one of those guys with a system. "I thought you always told me you don't gamble when you can't afford to lose."

"Everything was going well. I was raking it in . . ."

"And then you weren't."

"Exactly." Paul gulped his Scotch down. At this rate, he'd be through the bottle before dinner. "I should have left the table."

"And the guys you owe want you to recover the money for them."

"We'd be even."

"And if you don't?"

"Let's just say, you and I wouldn't be having any more fun."

I rested my hands on my knees and watched a seagull land on the roof of the building across the way. They seemed to be everywhere these days. Them and the crows and the pigeons. They were taking over the friggin' city.

"Maybe you'd better start at the beginning."

Paul put his glass down. "It's simple. Walter Wilcox was the lawyer for two numbnuts Russian mobsters."

"We have Russians in Syracuse?"

"Direct from Moscow via Brighton Beach."

"I thought we had the Mafia."

"No, dear. They were in Utica and Buffalo, maybe thirty years ago. Now we have the Russians and the gang-bangers." Paul took a paper clip off his desk and absentmindedly began straightening the bends out. "I think they came up here because they couldn't make it in the City. Anyway, Walter had a small lapse in judgment and decided to skim about two hundred fifty thousand dollars in cash from them."

I wondered what a large lapse in judgment would be.

"Because of the girl."

"Because of the girl. He wanted to go away with her."

"So what did Walter do with the money?"

"Ah." Paul rubbed his finger around the rim of his glass. "Here we come to the crux of the problem. He had it down in his basement. Hidden among his tools."

"Get out of town!"

"It's true."

I rolled my eyes. "Why not a mattress? Don't tell me. He had a phobia against safety deposit boxes?"

"He thought this would be a better option."

"You'd think a lawyer would be a little smarter."

Then I thought about the ones I knew. Most of them were so arrogant that they believed they could get away with anything. Which ended up making them stupid.

"I take it you didn't advise him otherwise?"

Paul got huffy. "I wasn't involved at that point."

I finished the story for him. "Let me guess. When his wife left, she took the cash along."

"Yes."

"I can see that. Saves on court costs. No messy adjudication."

"No. Just a lesson for Walter."

"Quite a lesson."

Paul brushed his hair back with the flat of his hand. "It certainly was."

"So now they want their money back."

"Yup."

"And you want me to get it."

"No. I want you to find Janet Wilcox. That's a different thing altogether."

"Why can't you?"

"Because Janet Wilcox knows me. We've met a couple of times. The moment she sees me, she'll take off."

"It seems to me as if she already has."

"True," Paul conceded, "but you have a better chance of getting close to her than I do."

"Why?"

"Because you're a woman. She'll see you as less threatening."

"That's probably true."

Paul cracked his knuckles again.

"And if I find her, then what?"

"Call me. I'll fly down and get her to give up the money."

"The inimitable Santini touch?"

Like George, he was more than capable of violence. Unlike George, he didn't mind exercising that capacity.

Paul shrugged and ran his thumb along his lower lip. "In this case, I'm prepared to do whatever works."

I thought of Janet Wilcox. She seemed like someone who would fold at the first sign of pressure.

"I have a feeling it won't be a problem."

"I hope so." And Paul threw the paper clip down on his desk. "I sure as hell hope so."

"Me too," I said, thinking of Wilcox.

Chapter Twenty-Three

Paul reached in his desk, took the bottle out again, and poured himself another shot. Maybe opening and closing the drawer was his exercise for the day.

"Want one?" he asked me.

I shook my head. I was pleased to note I hadn't gotten that bad yet. "You should slow down."

"Look who's talking."

"At least I don't get drunk in the middle of the day."

"Don't quibble."

"Quibble? You doing 'Improving Your Vocabulary in 100 Days' again?"

"I keep seeing Walter." Paul downed another shot and wiped his mouth off with the back of his hand.

"I get it. You're playing on my need to rescue things and put them right."

"It's nice to know that you got something out of that therapist you were seeing."

"Not enough to stop me from getting involved with you."

Paul saluted me with the empty glass. "Think of me as the next step in your spiritual growth."

"How much time do we have?"

"Three days," Paul said.

"Piece of cake."

"That's what I've been thinking."

"So then there's no problem."

"Exactly. And just to make sure." Paul opened his middle desk drawer, reached in, and came out with a Glock. "Here," he said, putting it in my hand. "Take this."

"Why am I going to need it?"

"Just in case. I was a Boy Scout, remember?"

"They must have been hard up for members."

Paul tried for a smile and failed.

I slipped the gun into my backpack. Never mind that I wasn't licensed to carry a handgun. The truth is, I don't like guns. I think they make you overconfident and get you into situations you shouldn't be in in the first place. Plus it's too easy to have an accident with them.

On the other hand, given what had happened to Wilcox, I was prepared to make an exception. Flexibility, I read somewhere, is the hallmark of the high-functioning professional.

"And Robin," Paul said. "Remember. Aim for the chest. At twenty feet you can't miss."

"Don't worry. I'm not planning to."

And I wasn't. I was prepared to shoot first and worry about the explanations later. I got up to leave.

"I'm sorry," Paul repeated as I reached the door. "I really am. I thought this would be simple. If I had known, I never would have . . ."

I cut him off with a gesture. Everyone was apologizing. Maybe that was better than not. I don't know. But it didn't help remedy the situation.

"Fine," he said. "I understand."

While I was waiting for the elevator, one of my grandmother's phrases flitted through my mind. She'd always said, "Lie down with dogs, get up with fleas." Once again she'd been right, I reflected as the elevator doors slid open.

I nodded to the three people inside and got on.

"Cold enough for you?" a woman said to me.

"Not really."

Syracuse humor.

We rode down the rest of the way without saying another word to each other.

Manuel was not happy when I told him I had to leave again.

"When is Tim coming back?"

"In another two weeks."

Tim was my other employee. He'd been out of town for a while taking care of personal problems. I hadn't asked what they were, and he hadn't volunteered. I finally squared it with Manuel by promising to get some extra help in for the next couple of days.

"Are you taking Zsa Zsa?"

"I can't."

He yanked up his pants. Why he insisted on wearing them with the crotch down to his knees is something he has yet to explain to me.

"Boy, she's going to be pissed at you."

"I know."

Nothing like throwing a little guilt into the equation, I always say. I wondered if Manuel had been a Jewish mother in his last life.

"She likes me but . . ."

I thought of the weapon in my backpack. "Listen, Manuel, if anything happens . . ."

"Yes?"

I stopped. "Forget it."

But it was too late. Manuel was on full alert. "Hey, what's going on?" he demanded.

"Nothing. Absolutely nothing. I'm just having a bad day."

I didn't want to tell Manuel what Paul had told me because I knew if I did he'd want to come down with me, and I didn't want him to get caught up in this. Things were bad enough as they were. Anyway, if something happened to him, who would take care of Zsa Zsa?

"You havin' a lot of those recently."

"No kidding."

He looked me in the eyes. "You in trouble?"

I looked back at him and lied. Like Calli. But there are lies and then there are lies.

"No," I said.

"Because me and my homies . . ."

"I'm fine. Honest."

"All you got to do is say the word."

"I know."

Finally I managed to convince him I was okay, and he moved off to take care of the shipment of iguanas that we'd just gotten in. I went into the back, wrote out some checks for orders that were coming in over the next two days, and arranged for someone I knew to work at the store. Then I went home, made a reservation at the Gramercy Park Hotel down in the City, and forced myself to take a nap.

Even though I wanted to get going right away, I was afraid that if I did, I'd go off the road because I'd fallen asleep at the wheel. I woke up two hours later, took a quick shower, changed into my good black pants and my oatmeal-colored cashmere sweater, and put on the two hundred fifty dollar boots that Calli had forced me to buy, which I'd heretofore worn exactly once.

God. Calli. I missed her. Maybe she was right. Maybe I was a self-righteous bitch.

I dialed her number. No one answered. I left a message on her machine saying, "Let's talk."

Somehow that made me feel better. Then I called Manhattan information and asked if there was a new listing for Janet Wilcox. Not that I expected there to be. But sometimes people do strange things, especially when they're nervous. There wasn't. I did the same for the rest of the boroughs and got the same result. Nothing. Oh, well. Worth a try. I lit a cigarette, packed my suitcase—I seemed to be doing a lot of that all of a sudden—slipped on my black leather jacket, and wound the red mohair scarf that George had given me as a birthday present around my neck. But I couldn't keep that on. It was too painful. I put it back in my drawer and picked out an old knit wool scarf that I'd bought at Marshall's, my favorite discount store.

It was a little after seven o'clock at night when I pulled out of my driveway. Before I got on the Thruway, I stopped at Dunkin' Donuts and got two large coffees with cream and sugar and four chocolate-peanut doughnuts to go. Dinner. I asked for a glass of water and swallowed a couple of vitamins that I'd taken to carrying with me and, confident that I'd taken care of my nutritional needs, continued on my way.

Unlike the last time I drove down, I made good time. The roads were clear, the weather was fine, and the traffic was minimal. It was a little after eleven by the time I pulled into the City. I'd spent most of the drive trying to figure out how I was going to locate Janet Wilcox.

According to the information Paul had acquired, she hadn't been using her credit card, so if she'd bought an airline or bus or train ticket, or rented a car, she'd done it with cash, meaning there was no record of her transaction—or at least none that he could access. Ditto with hotels. Which was too bad.

For all I knew, she could be on the Costa del Sol by now, although I didn't think she was. She didn't impress me as a woman who'd go someplace new. I saw her as staying with the familiar. Of course, she hadn't impressed me as the kind of woman who'd take off with her husband's money either.

I had two leads. Quintillo and her daughter, Stephanie. Which was better than nothing. Hopefully, one or the other would know where she'd gone. I was pretty sure that was the case, because most people have a need to keep in touch with their nearest and dearest, even when it isn't in their best interests to do so. I also wasn't too worried about persuading Quintillo and/or the daughter to speak to me. I'm fairly good at convincing people to tell me what I need to know.

My question was: What had made Janet Wilcox leave Quintillo's apartment in the first place? Had something spooked her, or was leaving part of her master plan? If she had been spooked, I hoped the thing that had done the spooking wasn't me.

As I ate the second half of my third doughnut, it occurred to me that Janet Wilcox had to have known where the money came from. Or at least she had to have known that her husband was involved in something illegal. After all, no one leaves that kind of change lying around if they're legitimate.

I could see her going down one day to clean the basement and discovering the money sitting there. A late Christmas present. She probably hadn't said anything to Walter about her find. She'd retired upstairs to think. Because she probably already knew about Alima.

So she'd come up with her plan, her "fuck-you-Walter" plan. I could see the vindictive smile playing on her lips. I wondered if she knew, or cared, that something bad might happen to her husband and the father of her child.

Paul was right. Janet Wilcox was one very pissed-off lady.

Chapter Twenty-Four

The first thing I did when I got into the City was head over to Quintillo's place. I rang the buzzer to his apartment, but no one answered, which meant he was either still out for the evening or asleep. I was about to ring someone else's buzzer when a young couple came along and opened the inner door. I slipped in after them. They didn't seem to mind. I don't think they even noticed. They were too busy locking lips. I admired their skill as I followed them up the stairs. I'd always found it hard to do both those things at the same time.

No light was showing under the crack between the floor and the door of Quintillo's apartment. I rang the bell. No one answered. I stood very still and listened. I didn't hear any sounds. Either Quintillo was a deep sleeper or he was out. I turned and went down the steps and headed into the street.

The bare branches of the gingko tree in front of the building glowed under the street light. People were walking by, mostly couples out on dates. Dog-walkers urged their charges to do their business so they could go upstairs. I thought about Zsa Zsa. I wondered how long it would take her to forgive me for deserting her. Then I wondered what she'd think of New York City if I brought her down. I listened to the snippets of conversations floating in the air. In Syracuse, everyone would be inside and asleep by now.

I could have double-parked my vehicle and waited for Quintillo to return, but I decided I'd catch up with him in the morning. The nap I'd taken earlier hadn't been enough. I needed to sleep in the worst way. Otherwise, I'd begin making mistakes, and I didn't have time to do that right now.

The Gramercy Park Hotel is a shabby, aging queen of a building, and I love her. I love her partly because of the mix of people she gets, partly because she's still funky and hasn't been rehabbed to the point where every ounce of her character has been drained away, and partly because Murphy used to work there as a night clerk while he was taking courses at Hunter College during the day. I'd spent a fair amount of time with him hanging out behind the front desk, and coming here reminded me of him.

After I checked in, I unpacked, got out my flask, called down to the desk and got some ice, filled my glass half full with Scotch, turned on the TV, and lay down on the bed.

The room was shabby in a comforting kind of way. The dresser had nicks in the wood. The prints on the wall were generic landscape scenes. The white chenille cover on the bed reminded me of the ones on my bed when I'd been little. The curtains were a brown-and-white check. The mattress itself was old and had a few lumps in it, but it was serviceable for the time I was staying. I was halfway through *East of Eden* and was feeling pleasantly sloshed when my cell rang. I looked at the number. George. I could feel my mood evaporating as I heard his voice.

"Manuel asked me to call," he told me. "He's worried about you."

"He must be very worried to turn to you."

"He is."

"Funny. Last I heard, he was calling you an asshole."

"I'm hurt."

"You shouldn't be. He's right. If he's that worried, why isn't he calling himself? You're slipping," I said when George didn't reply. "You're usually a better liar."

"Okay," George said. "You got me. I'm the one that's concerned. All he said was that you were down there again. Given everything that's happened, I got to wondering."

"I have a ticket to the opera."

"Seriously."

"Seriously, why do you care?"

"That's not fair."

I leaned over and took another sip of Scotch. Someone in the room next door must have turned on the shower. I could hear the water running.

"Yes, it is, George, but if you want to know, I'm helping Paul."

"That certainly sets my mind at rest."

"Too bad."

I could hear the sound of George's television through the wire.

"Let him solve his own problems."

"Maybe I don't want to."

"What the hell has he gotten you involved in?"

"That is none of your business."

On screen, James Dean was discovering that his mother was a prostitute. Seeing the expression on his face made me want to cry.

"I told you Paul was no good," George continued.

"Funny. He says the same thing about you."

It occurred to me they were fundamentally the same. Both players, both men who got off on the adrenaline rush.

"Robin, come home."

"I will in a couple of days."

"Do it now."

"If you're so worried about me, why don't you get on a plane and come down here then?"

"I'd like to." Here George hesitated.

I finished the sentence for him.

"But there's Natalie. Tell me, does she know you're speaking to me?"

"Robin . . ."

"Does she?"

"No."

"You have to decide what you want: to be in my life or out of it. You can't have it both ways."

"I told you. I care about you. I always will. I want to be your friend."

"That's not going to happen."

I hung up, drained my glass, and poured myself another drink.

I went back to watching *East of Eden*. But it wasn't the same. Finally, I clicked the television off and closed my eyes. A fire engine went by. Someone's car alarm went off. Two men started fighting underneath my window. I heard glass shatter. Someone shrieked. Then there was silence. I didn't bother getting up to look. I really didn't care if they bled to death on the sidewalk as long as they did it quietly. What was even worse was that I didn't care that I didn't care.

Instead, I turned on my side and pulled the covers over my head. I was in my early forties. I didn't have a husband. I didn't have children. I didn't even have health insurance, for God's sake. I had a business that was on the verge of going under. I was in debt. I hadn't spoken to my mother in—how many years? Maybe my mother had been right.

Maybe I shouldn't have married Murphy. Maybe I should have married the Park Avenue lawyer and joined the country club and hosted dinner parties and done charity work. Volunteered at the temple. Become chairman of a committee or two. Had a child. Maybe even two. Eventually get a job as an editor somewhere. Or work as a receptionist in an art gallery. Even if I got divorced, I'd still be in better shape than I was now.

But I hadn't loved the Park Avenue lawyer. I'd loved Murphy. I pulled the covers back down and clicked the television back on. That was the problem. That had always been the problem. I always went with my emotions.

Maybe love was an overrated commodity. In the Middle Ages, people had considered it a form of insanity. Maybe it was. Look at what it had done for Wilcox. He'd been going along—not great, but okay—and he'd met Alima and his life had spun out of control. He'd done things he'd probably never considered doing. And for who? A girl who made her living rubbing herself on men's crotches, a girl whose main goal in life was to separate men from their money.

And on that edifying note, I drifted off to sleep.

Chapter Twenty-Five

I got up in a better mood than I'd gone to bed in. There's something about the anonymity of hotel rooms, with their promise of possibilities, that always cheers me up. I don't know what that says about me, but it's probably not good.

I took a long, hot shower, got dressed in my snazzy clothes, took the elevator downstairs, and had a big breakfast consisting of fresh-squeezed orange juice, two fried eggs, a toasted English muffin, home fries, bacon, and three cups of coffee with cream while I read the *New York Times* in a coffee shop not too far away from the hotel. I was finishing my last cup when Paul called me on my cell.

"How's it going?"

"It's not." I took a last sip and pushed the cup away. "I'm just about to get started."

"Do you know what time . . . ," he began before I cut him off.

"Hey, feel free to jump in whenever you want."

There was silence on the other end of the line.

"I'll call you when I have some news." I pressed the off button and motioned for my check.

The sun was out and the temperature was in the high thirties. I whistled as I drove uptown. Third Avenue looked good. Traffic was moving. Sun glinted off the tops of the skyscrapers. The mica embedded in the pavement sparkled. Waiters were out in front of their restaurants hosing down their part of the sidewalk. Clusters of people stood outside office buildings taking early cigarette breaks. I automatically reached for my pack and lit up. Solidarity in all things.

I noticed a street vendor on the corner. They were all over the place. This one was doing a brisk business selling coffee and doughnuts to people coming out of the subway. I wasn't certain, but I didn't think we'd had so many of those when I lived here. Shop windows sported expensive merchandise. People on the streets were walking with their heads held higher than they were yesterday.

I double-parked in front of Quintillo's building, trotted up the steps, and buzzed Quintillo's apartment. No one answered. I hoped he hadn't taken off with Janet. I checked my watch. It was a little after nine. Maybe he'd gone off to work. I called the work number Paul had given me and asked.

"Mr. Quintillo," a woman with a snotty British accent told me, "never arrives before ten-thirty in the morning."

"Really? How lovely for him."

The woman's accent became a little more North Country and a little less Sloane Ranger.

"I believe he works out at the health club every morning. May I tell him who's calling when he comes in?"

"Dr. Ozma's office manager."

"Dr. Who?"

"Ozma." I spelled it out. "O-Z-M-A. The famous Park Avenue plastic surgeon."

"Of course."

Sometimes you just have to amuse yourself.

"I'll be in touch."

And I clicked the off button on my cell phone at the same

time I looked at my watch. It was nine-thirty. I had a little over an hour to kill. I decided to spend it at the Metropolitan Museum of Art. When I was a kid, I'd loved the Egyptian Wing. No one ever went there. It was quiet and dim—my private world.

The guards hadn't cared when I'd perched on the foot of the statues made of marble. I would go there on Saturday mornings and dream I was Nefertiti, Queen of Egypt, or scare myself by making myself believe a mummy was going to chase me.

But the exhibition had changed over the years. It had upscaled just like the rest of Manhattan had. Now, the wing was bright and busy, full of tourists and swarms of chattering schoolchildren. Now, it cost way more than it should to get in, given that the Metropolitan Museum of Art is supposed to be a public institution. The suggested entrance fee was $10.25. I slid a dollar toward the volunteer. She gave me a scathing look. I smiled back. Scathing looks don't do much to me anymore.

"I'm one of the poor huddled masses," I explained.

She wasn't appeased. Reluctantly, she handed me my button. I put it on the lapel of my jacket and walked by the guards.

Everything in the Egyptian Wing was clearly labeled and arranged in chronological order. It's true you could learn more. But it lacked the mystery it had before. Or maybe it was just that I was older. But it was still a pleasant place to be, and I whiled away a little under an hour drifting through the rooms looking at the jewelry and the drawings on the papyrus.

When I was done, I made my way out to my car and drove over to the gallery Quintillo housed his business in. Even though it was located in the low nineties instead of down on Gallery Row, the place still looked posh. A still life from a relatively minor French seventeenth-century painter was displayed in the window with the lavishness that a Delacroix would have deserved.

The gallery itself was carpeted in light green. A slightly grayer shade of green was on the walls. Pictures of more second-rate seventeenth- and eighteenth-century painters in extremely expensive, ornate frames hung on the walls. Toward the middle of the room sat the woman who I assumed was the one I'd previously spoken to. The desk she was sitting behind was Georgian, and there was an enormous bouquet of fancy tropical flowers in the middle of it.

The woman herself was slim and blond and dressed in the usual New York City black pants and a black sweater. What a surprise. She measured me as I approached, and from the expression on her face I could tell that she found my shoes, pants, and jacket acceptable. I wondered if she would have frozen me with her disdain if she hadn't. She folded her hands in front of her and smiled.

"May I help you?"

"I certainly hope so. I called earlier."

"Oh, yes."

She looked at her watch. It was thin, just as she was, and gold and probably cost more than my car. Somehow I didn't think she'd earned the money for it working here.

"Mr. Quintillo is running a little late," she informed me. "I'm expecting him in at any moment."

"That's all right. I'll wait." And I moved off to study the paintings on the walls.

Fifteen minutes later, Quintillo barged in. He was carrying a take-out container of coffee in one hand and a briefcase in the other. He looked shorter than I remembered, and as I watched him I realized that his arms were longer than average. He was going bald on top. He'd had what hair he had left cut close to his head under the misconception that it made him look hip, instead of like a man trying to hide the fact that he was going bald. His eyes were close set and looked puffy, as if he hadn't been getting a lot of sleep. His face was clean shaven.

He was wearing fancy clothes—a cashmere coat and, from what I could see, an expensive blue suit, striped shirt, and paisley tie—but his walk didn't match his clothes and I got the distinct impression he would have been happier in jeans, a sweatshirt, work boots, and a baseball cap.

The receptionist nodded at me and explained who I was. I watched Quintillo's forehead furrow as he tried to place me. I wouldn't have been surprised if he recognized me from the night I spoke to him—people in his line of work usually have a good memory for faces. But he didn't. Maybe it was because I was dressed differently now and my hair was up and pulled away from my face.

I smiled and moved toward him. We shook hands.

Here we go, I thought.

Chapter Twenty-Six

Quintillo frowned, crossed his right arm over his waist, leaned his left elbow on it, and tapped his chin with the fingers of his left hand. "This is going to bother me. I know I've seen you before."

"I live around here," I said.

"That must be it," Quintillo replied. There was a tinge of doubt in his voice. But he didn't pursue it. I was a possible customer, after all.

After exchanging a few niceties, I explained what Dr. Ozma wanted for his waiting room. Preferably something French. Something tasteful. Something soothing.

"Ozma." Quintillo cocked an eyebrow. "I don't remember hearing that name."

"Well, you should." I acted surprised. "He was mentioned in *Vogue* and *Elle* recently. Why don't we go in your office and discuss things."

Quintillo demurred. "I usually prefer to talk to my clients directly. That way I can get a feel for their personalities. I find it works better."

I gave him my most winning smile.

"I'm sure in most cases it does, but Dr. Ozma was very

specific in his delegation of this responsibility to me. Unfortunately, his time is taken up with the press of his commitments."

Quintillo smiled back, but it was a teeth-only smile. His heart wasn't in it. I could see he didn't like having his way of doing business interrupted.

"Fine," he said. "Perhaps I could have a phone consultation with him at some time."

"I'm sure that can be arranged."

At this point the receptionist, who had been following the conversation, suggested using one of the rooms off the main gallery. If we'd been in a car dealership, they would have called it the closing room. I don't know what they called it in the art world, but the principle was the same. Get in there and make that sale.

Quintillo gave her a grateful look. I followed him into one of the rooms along the periphery of the gallery. Quintillo closed the door behind us. The colors were the same as the colors outside, but the walls were bare and the lighting was subdued.

I gave him my jacket and he hung it on a hook by the far wall and did the same for his.

"We don't have a closet," he said apologetically as we both sat down.

A moment later, the receptionist knocked and opened the door. She was carrying a tray with two white bone-china cups, a silver coffeepot, sugar bowl and creamer, and a plate of cookies. Quintillo gave her another smile. We were all doing a lot of smiling around here.

He poured me a cup of coffee and put it in front of me. I added cream and two teaspoons of sugar and took a sip. It was good. It was better than good.

I was reflecting that the rich live better than you and me as he poured himself a cup. "I'm afraid I didn't get your name," he said.

"I'm sorry. It's Robin. Robin Light."

"Now," he said, beaming at me. "Robin, can you go into a little more detail about what it is that Dr. Ozma wants."

"Love to."

He waited.

I took another sip of coffee and said, "You, my friend, are in some serious shit."

A flash of recognition shot through his face.

"Jeez," he said. "You're the woman . . ."

"Who had the wrong building," I finished for him.

Better late than never.

"I knew you looked familiar."

"I was wearing different clothes."

His eyes flicked across my face and back. Suddenly he wasn't Mr. Smooth-Talking Art Dealer anymore. He was working-class New Jersey.

"Fuck. There is no Dr. Ozma, is there?"

"Nope."

"Ozma from Oz," Quintillo said. "Not a bad name for a plastic surgeon."

"I like to think of myself as a genius in my own quiet way."

"And you're—"

"Oh, I'm still Robin Light." I took out my card, the one that said I was a private detective, and shoved it across the table. "Right now, I'm working for a guy called Paul Santini."

"You don't look like a private detective," Quintillo said.

"Then I guess we're even because you don't look like an art dealer."

"Fair enough. Now that we've established that we don't look like we should, I want you to get out." And he jerked his thumb toward the door.

"I don't think so." I took another drink of coffee. "What blend are you using? This is really very good."

He started to rise. "I'm getting Amanda to call the police."

"You can if you want, but that would be a profound mistake on your part."

I snagged a cookie and bit into it. I tasted butter and oatmeal and walnuts and raisins and something I couldn't define. Then I got it. Orange peel. I reached for another cookie and ate that too as Quintillo considered what I'd said.

"All right," he said as I tried out what looked like a brown-sugar shortbread. "You got five minutes to tell me what you want."

I dusted the crumbs off my mouth and wiped my hands on the linen napkin the receptionist had so thoughtfully provided.

"I think you already know. I need to locate Janet Wilcox."

"Unfortunately, I don't know where she is."

"I don't believe you. By the way, where did you get these cookies? They're delicious."

"A bakery on Third Avenue between 79th and 78th Streets. I've already spoken to the police. I'll tell you what I told them. I came home from work, and Janet Wilcox wasn't there. I have no idea where she went."

"It's very important that I find her."

"Maybe it is, maybe it isn't, but that has nothing to do with me. I sell art, I don't run a missing-persons bureau."

"Perhaps you should."

And I leaned forward and told him about what had happened to Wilcox. I could see him getting paler as I spoke.

He opened his jacket and loosened his tie.

"How do I know you're telling the truth?"

"Call Paul Santini and ask him." I gave him the number.

He looked even worse when he got off the phone.

"I can't believe it," he said to me. "People like that. They should take them out to the Pine Barrens and cap 'em." He shook his head. His voice trailed off.

I popped another shortbread cookie in my mouth. It literally melted on my tongue. I wondered how much a pound of them cost. Probably a lot. On the other hand, what else was expense money for?

"Here's something else to consider. The people who did that to Wilcox are really anxious to have their property returned. Right now, they don't know about you, but believe me, I can remedy that in an instant."

"So what? I have nothing to do with this."

"I don't think they're exactly discriminating in the fixing-blame department, if you get my meaning."

"But they don't know who I am," Quintillo protested. Then enlightenment struck. "You wouldn't," he said, looking at my face.

I smiled again. Given the atmosphere, it seemed like the right thing to do. "I will if I have to."

"I don't believe you."

"Why?" I pointed to my breasts. "You're making a mistake if you think that having these automatically makes me a compassionate person."

"Shit," Quintillo said.

He bit his thumbnail.

I took another sip of coffee while I was waiting and watched Quintillo dab at a nonexistent spot on his tie.

"I knew I should never have said yes when she called me up," he told me. "See, this is why it's hard to be nice. The only thing it gets you is in trouble."

"I don't think the Pope would agree. Why did she leave your place?"

Quintillo put his cup and saucer back on the tray. "My apartment is really small. A tiny one-bedroom. After a while she got tired of sleeping on the sofa."

"So you and she aren't . . ."

"God, no." Quintillo shook his head. "She's not my type. I'm not sure that she's anyone's type. We're just friends."

"I heard she doesn't have many of those either."

"I don't think she does."

"So how come you and she were?"

"We were never *friend* friends. She has an interest in art. I think I'm the only person she knows she can discuss it with. But we hadn't talked in—I don't know." Quintillo stopped to calculate. "At least five years."

"And then she just pops up. Weren't you surprised when she called you?"

"Sure I was."

"And you just let her come down."

"Hey, I'm a nice guy."

"So you said." I got up and leaned against the wall and folded my arms across my chest. "Here's what I think. I think she offered to pay you to let her hide out in your place, and you said okay."

"Why would I do something like that?"

"Because you need the money."

Quintillo gestured around the room. "Does this setup look like I'm a guy who needs money?"

"No. But this isn't your setup. I'd wager you're just renting the use of the space and the receptionist. Given what you do, you couldn't afford something like this. If you could, you'd be living on Park Avenue instead of 81st Street. So how much did she offer you? Five hundred? A thousand?"

Quintillo pursed his lips.

I walked over to the table and sat back down. "Hey, this is New York City. Everyone hustles. That's one of the things that makes this place so great."

I could see Quintillo thinking over what I'd said. "Fifteen hundred," he told me after a moment had gone by. "She offered me fifteen hundred."

"Hard to resist."

"Exactly."

"And did she tell you why she was doing this?"

"Janet said she was leaving her husband, and she was

afraid he'd find her. In my place she'd be harder to trace. She said she only needed to stay there for a couple of nights."

"Did she say anything else?"

"While she was there? Mostly she talked about her husband. About what a creep he was and how'd she'd given him the best years of her life and now he'd taken up with this slut. Frankly," Quintillo told me, "I stopped listening. It reminded me too much of what my ex-wife said to me before she took me for every friggin' thing I ever owned."

I tried to keep the conversation on course. "Where did Janet go?"

"She didn't tell me. Honestly."

I smiled at him. "You know, whenever anyone says 'honestly,' it makes me think the opposite."

"Are you saying I'm lying?" Quintillo demanded.

"Lying is a harsh term. Maybe obfuscating."

If you can't scare people with a gun, wow them with big words, I always say. I poured myself a half cup of coffee and drank it before continuing.

"Here's what I think you're thinking. You're thinking instead of telling me where she is, you're going to race up to where Janet Wilcox is and get more money from her. Don't do it. Don't be stupid. You don't want to wind up like Wilcox. You don't want to get involved with these people. It's not worth it."

Quintillo sighed. I watched him weighing his options.

Finally, he said, "She never told me where she was going, but I saw the address. She wrote it down on a slip of paper. I think I can remember what it was."

I grabbed three more cookies on the way out.

Chapter Twenty-Seven

I went back to my car and checked in with Manuel.
"So how are things going back in Syracuse?"
"Nothing new. Except Calli came by the house."
"What did she want?"
"To talk to you."
I really had to call her. I reached for the pack of cigarettes on the seat, took one out, and lit it as Manuel continued chatting.
"Bethany asked her if she could have one of Lily's puppies, and she said probably yes. We're going over there this afternoon to look at them."
"Do you know how much time and money it takes to raise a puppy, especially the first year . . ."
"Don't worry about it," Manuel said.
"Because I'm not getting stuck . . ."
"You won't. It'll be fine. Bethany wants to name the puppy Tara. What do you think?"
"I think I don't want to talk about this right now."
"Well, when can we talk about it?"
"When I get back."
"You promise?"

"I swear."

"We'd better," Manuel said. "And Robin," he added, "don't worry. Bethany and I already cleaned up the wax on the stove."

"What wax?"

But Manuel didn't answer because he'd already hung up. I could have called Manuel back and asked him what he was talking about. But I didn't. Because the truth was, I've learned there are some things it's better not to know. As I stubbed out my cigarette and chucked the butt out the window, I decided that if Sam Spade had to deal with teenagers, he wouldn't have been so cool.

I checked in with Paul next. He didn't pick up his phone or his cell. I wondered if he was in the hospital again with another kidney stone. As I was leaving a message on his voice mail filling him in on what was going on, it occurred to me that maybe he was at the casino.

I'd had a black-sheep uncle who couldn't keep away from the poker table. Eventually, a fisherman found his body floating in the East River a year after he'd disappeared. Hopefully, Paul would wise up before something like that happened to him. Probably wouldn't, though. Most people have to be looking at the abyss before they decide it's time to change.

I was sitting in my car thinking about my next step when a guy in a Range Rover pulled alongside of me and rolled down his window. I don't know. Maybe he thought he was going on safari. I hear there are lots of lions in Central Park.

"Hey, lady," he yelled. "You pullin' out or what?"

"Pulling out."

I let him have the parking space and went to find Janet Wilcox. Maybe I'd do better with her.

According to the address Quintillo had seen, she was hiding out on Belmont Avenue in the Bronx. When I'd lived in New York City, Belmont Avenue was in the borough's Italian section. The section probably still was Italian, since Italians tend to hold on to their territory. Turned out I was correct.

Ethnicity aside, it was an odd choice for Janet to have made, and I was surprised that she had ended up there. Even though the area is mentioned in guidebooks, it's definitely off the beaten path. Being an out-of-towner, I would have thought Janet Wilcox would have stuck to Manhattan, maybe venturing as far afield as Park Slope in Brooklyn at the most. The only thing that people who don't live in the City know in the Bronx is Yankee Stadium. Maybe Quintillo had suggested it.

As I turned onto the Madison Avenue Bridge, I thought about how my mother and I used to drive up this way to see my aunt, years ago when she and her husband had lived in the Bronx. And then I thought about the fact that George's mother and sister lived not that far away from where I was heading.

I'd met them once in passing three years ago. I suppose the fact that I hadn't met them again should have told me something. Of course, I'd never had much to do with Murphy's family either. Hadn't wanted to. Or my own, for that matter. I'm not big on families. In my experience they tend to bring out the worst in people. Or at least the worst in me, if we're being precise.

Sometime or other while I'd been inside the gallery talking to Quintillo, the morning sun had disappeared. It had clouded up again. The water in the Hudson River looked choppy and cold. An empty barge, muscled along by a tugboat, was making its way downstream to the ocean. The buildings across the way on the Palisades seemed mirage-like in the thin winter light.

These days the City has turned its back on its rivers. When I was growing up, New York City was still a major world port. I remember going down to the piers to see the ships off-loading when I was twelve. Seeing the names. Cairo. Karachi. Bangkok. Vowing I would travel to those places one day. Who'd have thought I would end up in Syracuse.

By now it was a little after eleven-thirty and traffic was still fairly light. I was on East Tremont Avenue when Paul called me on my cell.

"So where is she?" he asked.

I told him.

"Belmont Avenue? Where the hell is that?"

There was static on his line, and his voice pulsed off and on.

"In the Bronx."

"The Bronx? Isn't that crack land? I didn't think people lived there anymore."

I glanced at a small boy holding his grandmother's hand as they crossed the street.

"Some do."

"Well, just remember. I'm not paying you to do anything cute. Verify the address and call me."

I told him I would and clicked off. For the next twenty minutes or so, I drove around trying to find Janet Wilcox's address. The houses, neat and tidy, looked the way I remembered them. Despite the weather, the stores on Arthur Avenue were bustling with people bundled up against the wind, pushing those mesh shopping carts on wheels that I've only seen in New York City. The live poultry market was still there. So was the pizzeria where Murphy and I used to go. The pharmacy that had had the bottle of leeches in the window with the sign leaning against it saying, FOR MEDICINAL USE ONLY, was still there as well.

I finally located the house Janet was supposed to be staying in. It was a compact, two-family brick affair with a tiny front yard enclosed by a chain-link fence. An attached garage stood off to the left. The driveway was empty. In the downstairs window, someone had posted a sign that read, APARTMENT FOR RENT. INQUIRE WITHIN.

I found a parking spot about a block away, maneuvered my car into it, and walked back. You could have eaten off the streets. All the houses I went by had curtains on their windows and doormats with cute little sayings on their front steps. Some of the people hadn't taken down their Christmas decorations yet.

The house I was looking for had a picture of Santa Claus on his sleigh pasted across its front window. A small spotlighted statue of the Virgin Mary sat in the yard off to the right. The gate groaned when I opened it. I went up the path to the front steps. There were two mailboxes attached to the front wall. One had the name Lazzarro neatly printed on the name slot. There was no writing on the other one.

I was about to ring Lazzarro's bell when, out of the corner of my eye, I saw Janet Wilcox rounding the corner. She was wearing a brown cloth coat with a bright turquoise woolen scarf wound around her neck and matching suede ankle-length boots on her feet. The scarf and the boots looked expensive and were designed to catch the eye. Part of her new look, no doubt, though in her circumstances I would probably have gone with inconspicuous.

Her shoulders were stooped against the wind and her arms were full of grocery bags. When she saw me, her eyes widened and she slowed down fractionally. So much for calling Paul, I thought as I watched Janet Wilcox bend her head and begin studying the pavement as if the cracks in it could provide the answer to her problems.

Obviously, she remembered me from the other night. She kept on walking, slowly increasing her pace. By the time I'd gotten through the gate, she'd left the pavement, wormed her way between two parked cars and was halfway to crossing the street. I caught up with her just as she reached the other side.

"Janet Wilcox," I said.

She looked up at me. Her features seemed softer somehow. Her skin was blotchy from the wind, but her hair wasn't moving. I guess her hairspray habit was hard to break.

"I'm sorry," she told me in a pleasant voice as she shifted her parcels around slightly. "You're mistaken. You have the wrong person. My name is Cecelia."

"Well, Cecelia you must have an identical twin." I dug the picture of her that Wilcox had given me out of my backpack and showed it to her. "See. Same mouth. Same eyes. Same chin. Same overreliance on hairspray."

She took the picture and gave the appearance of studying it before handing it back. "She does look like me, doesn't she?" Janet allowed.

"She is you."

"I can see where you'd make a mistake."

"Your friend Quintillo told me I could find you here."

"Quintillo?" She cocked her head and smiled brightly. "I'm sorry. I don't know anyone by that name."

"You stayed at his apartment. Remember. I saw you and him in the hallway. He was trying to get his mail out of the mailbox."

She shook her head. "I don't know what you're talking about. I've been here for a while."

"Great. But I still need to speak to Janet Wilcox."

The softness left her eyes. She compressed her lips into a thin line. I could see her weighing the possibilities. Finally she said, "My mother always said: Lie down with dogs, get up with fleas. She was right."

"What a coincidence! So did my grandmother. Maybe we're related three generations back."

Janet Wilcox sniffed at the suggestion.

"Fine. But be that as it may, I still need to speak to you."

Looking at Janet's pinched mouth, narrow lips, and suspicious eyes, I could see why Wilcox had gone off with Alima, though I had an idea the only difference between the two women was the packaging. That probably made all the difference, though.

"I'll give you one hundred dollars if you'll go away," Janet Wilcox told me.

"You think I come that cheap?"

"A hundred dollars is a good amount."

"Only if you live in Nairobi. Not that it matters because I can't do it." And I put my card in her hand.

She didn't even glance at it, just let it flutter to the curb.

I bent over and picked it up. "You know you can get fined for littering."

"Why can't you?"

I turned the collar of my jacket up and stuck my hands in my pockets. "Take your money? For a variety of reasons."

"All the worse for you." And she hunched her shoulders against the wind that had started kicking up.

"I think I like talking to Cecelia better."

"She's not available now."

"Okay." I nodded toward Lazzarro's house. "So how did you find this place anyway?"

"That's none of your business."

Guess my charm wasn't working. "It's cold out here. Let's go inside."

"Why should we? I just told you we have nothing to talk about." Janet Wilcox's voice was harsh, but now that I was listening more carefully I heard a tinge of shrillness. Push a little and she'd break. She took a step back. "Now get away from me or I'll call the police."

"Go right ahead," I told her. "They've been looking for you. As I'm sure you know."

"I know nothing of the kind."

A woman hurried along the street, gave us a casual look, and moved on. We could have been two friends having a minor disagreement.

I waited to see if Janet asked me why the police were looking for her, but she didn't. I took that to mean she knew they'd called Quintillo's apartment, which also meant she knew about her husband being dead. Nice lady. They must have had a great marriage. No wonder her daughter was the way she was.

"How about we go in your apartment before my fingers drop off?" I suggested again.

I reached over and took hold of her elbow. Her body stiffened. I realized she looked like my fifth-grade elementary-school teacher, the one who had made me sit in the corner every chance she got. To teach me to not talk back, she'd said. Obviously her plan hadn't worked very well. Neither was Janet Wilcox's for that matter.

"Don't you dare touch me," she huffed.

I wasn't impressed. I'd been told a lot worse by a lot nastier people. My backpack was hanging off my left shoulder. I gestured to it with a nod of my head.

"I have a Glock in here. A gun," I clarified for her benefit.

"I know what a Glock is."

"Good. Now, I don't want to use it, but I'm cold and irritable and I will if I have to, so I suggest you do what I say."

Janet Wilcox drew herself up. "You wouldn't dare."

"Don't bet on it." She was right, but she didn't know that. I tried to look sufficiently menacing. "Why wouldn't I? Because you're such a pleasant person?"

She was quiet.

"Look around," I told her, indicating the street. "No one's out. No one would see anything. Think about it."

Evidently I made the correct impression, because after a few seconds, she turned on her heels and marched back across the street. I followed. We were both silent as she fitted her key into the lock to her apartment.

"They should take down the For Rent sign," I said.

She didn't reply. Some people just don't know how to do chitchat.

We walked up the steps with her in front. Just in case she decided to run. She fitted another key in the door and we were inside her apartment. Janet headed toward the kitchen and I followed. We went through the living room. The décor was Italian rococo. The walls were covered with flocked wallpaper. A matching sofa and love seat were upholstered in damask. A glass-topped coffee table sat in front of the sofa. A bookcase toward the far wall held a fifteen-inch television. I didn't see a sign of clothes or books or papers.

"Not planning on staying long," I commented.

Janet Wilcox kept going as if I hadn't said anything.

"I hear the Caribbean is nice this time of year, though I think your money would go further in Mexico. Or Costa Rica. Excuse me, I forgot—your husband told me you didn't like to travel, but then I bet he thought you didn't like to steal either."

She ignored me, put her packages on the kitchen table, unbuttoned her coat and scarf, and carefully hung them on the back of the chair.

I placed my backpack on the floor next to the doorway. It was beginning to hurt my back.

"Aren't you going to ask me what I want?" I said to her.

"I've already told you I have no desire to speak to you, so why would I ask you anything?"

"Don't you want to know about your husband?" I asked. "No."

She began unpacking her food. A box of macaroni. A jar of tomato sauce. A tin of canned beef stew.

I picked it up and read the label. Three-fourths of the ingredients were words I couldn't pronounce. "I didn't know anyone actually ate this stuff."

Janet Wilcox took the can out of my hands and banged it down on the table.

"He's dead, you know."

She kept on unpacking. Not even a moment of hesitation.

"But of course you do. Don't you care?"

"It has nothing to do with me."

"I think it does."

She turned and faced me. "You forced your way in here. You threatened me."

"And your point is?"

"My point is, I don't have to say anything to you and you can't make me."

"I think we've established that I can, but let's not go into that right now. Do you know how he died?"

"How many times do I have to tell you I'm not interested?"

"He was tortured to death."

Janet Wilcox picked up the can of tomatoes and put it on the top shelf of the cabinet across from the sink.

"He was tortured to death because of the money you took from him. He spent a long time dying."

Not even a flinch. I could have been talking about squashing a gnat.

She returned to get the box of macaroni. "I wanted Mueller's, but all I could find was this foreign stuff."

"I need to get back the money that you took. The people your husband took it from are very unhappy."

"That's not my problem."

"Now, that's where you're mistaken."

And that was when things started to go really wrong.

Chapter Twenty-Eight

I heard a "Hello, ladies," and spun around.

Paul was standing in the middle of the kitchen doorway with his arms folded across his chest and a shit-eating smile on his face.

To this day I still don't know how come I didn't hear the front door opening and closing or him coming up the stairs.

"Glad to see me, Janet?" he asked.

"Not particularly," I replied. "What are you doing here?"

"Hey, Light, in case you didn't notice, I'm not addressing you," he snapped, the smile suddenly gone. "I'm talking to Janet." And he put the smile back on as if it was a pair of false teeth he was taking out of the jar.

"Light?" I said. "So formal. What happened to Robin?"

He ignored me and watched Janet. The vein below her right eye was twitching. She swallowed and edged closer to me. I may have made her nervous, but not as nervous as Paul was making her.

"Don't want to answer?" Paul continued.

She swallowed but didn't say anything.

"That's too bad 'cause I'm real glad to see you." He made a show of looking around. "You know, this place isn't half bad, though the wop décor would get to me after a while. Especially the guinea wallpaper. How'd you find it? Still don't want to answer me?" Paul went on when Janet didn't reply. "That's okay. Even though some people would consider that rude. You still have a little time."

He unzipped his jacket and hooked his thumbs on his belt. The jacket was one of those heavy black leather ones. The kind cops wear. He had a one-day growth of beard, his eyes were bloodshot, and he looked as if he'd slept in his clothes. Glancing past him through the kitchen window, I noticed a cat stalking a pigeon pecking on something on the ground. The cat got within half a foot before the pigeon flew away. Something told me it wasn't going to be that easy for Janet and me.

"Janet," Paul said. "Remember how you used to make me take my shoes off when I came in your house, even when I wiped my feet, even if I was just going to stay for five minutes?"

She pressed her lips together till they were nothing more than a thin line.

"It used to drive me crazy. All that lacing and unlacing." Paul indicated his feet. "See. My boots are still on."

Despite herself, Janet looked toward the door. Wet footprints and ridge-sized clumps of gray slush that had fallen from Paul's Dr. Martens marked his trail across the floor.

"Didn't even bother to wipe them off on the doormat," he told her. "What you gotta say about that?"

"Nothing," Janet whispered.

I had to strain to hear her.

"Goddamned right," Paul said.

"I thought you were in Syracuse," I said.

Dumb comment.

"And I thought you weren't going to talk to Janet," Paul said.

"Evidently we were both wrong."

He grinned. I couldn't help thinking he needed to have his teeth cleaned.

"I love technology, don't you?" he said. "It gives one so many more options. Now you can do anything from anywhere."

"I'm enraptured by it."

"Nice word choice. You should have stuck with being a writer."

"I'm beginning to think so too."

My eyes strayed to my backpack for not more than a fraction of a second, but it was enough for Paul to pick up on.

"You wouldn't be thinking of using my own weapon on me, would you?" he asked as he reached down and scooped it up.

"The thought never crossed my mind."

"Sure it didn't. Not keeping it with you was careless, Light. Very careless."

"I know. I should have foreseen you were going to turn out to be a shiftless, lying sonofabitch."

He opened the backpack and peered in. "I'll take that as a compliment. How much crap do you carry in here anyway?" he said as he pawed through it. "Here we go." And he took out the Glock he'd given me in his office and stuffed it into his jacket pocket. "You should get a shoulder harness like the detectives in the movies do."

"I can't. It would spoil the line of my clothes."

"I wouldn't have thought that was a concern of yours."

"It is," I protested.

" 'Course it is." Paul sucked in air between his teeth. "That's what I always said to myself every time you walked into the office. Paul, there's a woman that has an overdeveloped fashion sense." He looked me up and down. "Although I have to admit you look better than you usually do. Here."

He dug in his pocket and came out with a set of handcuffs. "Put these on," he said, tossing them to me.

"That's not necessary."

"Oh, yes, it is."

"And if I won't?"

"Now is not the time to be doing one of your numbers," he warned. "I will hurt you if I have to."

"You're such a putz."

Paul's smile vanished again. "I don't think you're in a position to call anyone names. Now put them on."

He was right. I wasn't. I did as I was told.

"Satisfied?" I said showing him my wrists.

He came over and tightened them. "Now I am."

He tossed my backpack to me. I caught it with both hands.

"It's safer this way. For both of us," Paul said. "No accidents."

"How reassuring that you have my welfare at heart," I said.

"Isn't it?"

Janet's eyes darted from me to Paul to me again.

"What game are you running?" I asked him.

"Game isn't the word I would use." Paul picked something out of his front tooth with his fingernail.

"Then what is?"

"Actually, I got to thinking after you left my office that maybe you were right after all. I should leave town. Take a vacation. See the world. Learn new things. I really don't have anything holding me in Syracuse. You want to come along?"

I indicated the handcuffs with my chin. "You certainly know how to persuade a girl."

Paul shrugged. "Some women like it that way."

"I'm not one of them."

He smirked. "Yes, you are. You just don't know it yet."

"Now I can understand why you're so lousy in bed."

I wondered why I still hadn't learned to watch my mouth as Paul's smirk changed to a scowl. He clenched his fists, took a step toward me, then stopped.

"You're not worth the energy."

Worked for me.

He laughed. "I don't know what I saw in you in the first place. I can do better."

"I know I can."

"You haven't so far."

"That's a matter of debate. Aren't you worried that they're going to kill you?"

Paul turned up the corners of his mouth into an imitation of a smile.

"No, dear. If Mikhail kills anyone, he'll kill you and her."

Wilcox had used the name Mike on the phone. Mike was Mikhail in Russian. Coincidence? Not likely.

"They won't be able to find me," Paul said.

"But I will. I'll make it my mission in life."

Paul's eyebrows shot up. He smiled for real this time. "I'm trembling in fear and trepidation."

I could feel myself flushing.

"And even if you do, so what? What are you going to do? Call the police?"

"No. Turn you over to the Russians."

"You won't."

"Don't bet on it." More than anything, I hate being made a fool.

"Your conscience won't allow it."

"You'd be surprised what my conscience will allow."

"I would be. In any case, I think you're overestimating your ability in the detection department."

"Not really. I've found everyone I've ever looked for. I don't see why you should be an exception." I'd have given anything for a cigarette at that moment. "George said you were bad news."

"And George was right. You should have listened to him, but then, that's another of your problems. Besides being careless, that is. You don't listen to people."

"Let's not turn this into a see-how-fucked-up-Robin-is discussion, if you don't mind. Though one thing is clear. I shouldn't have listened to you."

"This is true. Isn't that right, Janet?"

Up to this moment, she'd been standing perfectly still, the way a rabbit freezes when a fox sees it. As if not moving makes the rabbit invisible. I noticed that Janet's hands were shaking. She crossed her arms over her chest and buried her hands in her armpits.

"I'll take the money now, if you don't mind," Paul said to her.

"I don't know what you're talking about," she replied.

If she'd asked me, I would have told her she'd given Paul the wrong answer, but she didn't.

"Really?" he said.

"Really."

"How inconvenient for you." He swept his free hand around the room. "So if I looked around this apartment, I won't find it here?"

"Go ahead," Janet replied. "Look all you want." Her voice had a slight tremble in it.

Paul moved his mouth up in an imitation of a smile. "Don't waste my time. It puts me in a bad mood. I have things to do and places to see."

"I told you, I don't have the money."

"I know you do."

"I don't."

"Last chance."

When Janet didn't say anything, Paul crossed the floor and

casually backhanded her across the face. She staggered back from the force of the blow.

"Some men don't hit women," he informed her. "Believe me, I'm not one of them."

I moved toward Paul, but he'd taken the Glock out of his jacket and was pointing it in my direction. "You. Stay where you are."

"Fine." I lifted my hands. "I was just getting a glass of water anyway."

"Of course you were," Paul said. "It's what I would do in the circumstances."

I wondered what I'd do with the handcuffs off. Half of me felt really bad for Janet, while the other half of me remembered what had happened to her husband and thought that Janet Wilcox was getting a small taste of what she had coming.

"The next one will be worse," Paul promised Janet.

"I told you, I don't have the money."

"That's too bad."

Paul kept an eye on me as he moved toward Janet Wilcox. She tried to scuttle away from him, but she had nowhere to go. This time Paul put his weight into the blow. I heard the *whap* of his hand on her flesh and saw her head fly back. She slid down the cabinet door and landed on the floor.

"Please," she cried as she hid her face in her hands and tried to curl up in a ball.

But she wasn't fast enough.

Paul smiled, lifted his foot, and casually kicked her in the stomach with the tip of his boot. The kick was hard, but not hard enough to rupture anything.

"Consider that foreplay," he said.

Janet's legs jerked.

"The frogs I killed when I was a kid used to do that," he observed as he stepped back.

"Now, we're about to get into the real deal," he informed her as a thin stream of bile came out of her mouth. Paul turned toward me. "Tell her this is just a taste of what's going to happen to her. Tell her," he ordered. His face was expressionless. "Unless, of course, you like seeing this."

I didn't, despite what Janet had done.

I took a deep breath.

"He's right," I told Janet. "Tell him where the money is. He's not going to stop until he gets what he wants."

Paul nodded.

"You should listen to her," he said to Janet. "For once she's making sense."

He raised his foot to kick her again.

"At least let her get her breath back so she can talk," I pleaded.

He consulted his watch, then smoothed his hair back with the hand that wasn't holding the gun. "I'll give her five minutes. No more."

It was dead quiet in the kitchen. Paul looked around. "We could use a little music, don't you think, ladies? Something to liven things up a little. Where's the radio?"

"There isn't one," I said.

"She telling the truth?" he asked Janet.

She nodded weakly.

Paul shook his head. "How can you live without music? It's nectar to a man's soul."

Janet looked as if she was going to throw up again. The refrigerator turned itself on. Janet's ragged breathing filled the room.

Now it was my turn to look at my watch. We'd been in Janet's apartment for less than half an hour. Somehow it seemed a lot longer.

"I'm waiting," Paul said to Janet. "Hurry it up."

Janet groaned. After thirty seconds or so, she lifted herself up on her hands and knees. She stayed like that for a moment or two, head hanging down, slightly swaying back and forth. A line of drool made its way out of the corner of her mouth and hit the floor. I went to help her.

"She does it on her own," Paul said. His eyes were flat.

Looking at him, I realized the Paul I thought I knew was gone. I've seen snakes that have had friendlier expressions.

"How did you get to be like this?" I asked him.

He kept one eye on me and one eye on Janet while he answered.

"I always have been. I've just come out of the closet."

"You should go back in."

"I like myself this way better."

"Well, I don't."

"I didn't expect you would."

"How come I never noticed?"

Paul shrugged. "People see what they want to."

"You'll gamble this money away too."

"Always the optimist," Paul said.

Finally, after a minute or so, Janet Wilcox managed to pull herself up using the cabinets. Her stockings were ripped from where she had fallen and her skirt was twisted around, but every hair on her head was still in place.

"What the hell are you using on your hair, shellac?" Paul asked her. "You should sell that stuff to the Air Force."

Janet wiped her chin off with the back of her hand. "I told Walter he shouldn't have gotten involved with you."

"He shouldn't have gotten involved with Alima," Paul replied.

He moved toward her, his weight casually balanced on both feet.

"You should be reported to the authorities," she said.

Now that she had her breath back, she was doing a passable turn as an indignant middle-class suburban matron. I couldn't decide if she was stupid or brave. I don't think Paul knew either.

He shook his head slowly from side to side. Incredulous. "You really don't get it, do you? No one gives a shit about you. Especially me. Especially now." He rubbed the bridge of his nose with the thumb of his left hand. "In fact, I'm betting that if old Walter was here, he'd be paying me to do this."

Janet studied the sink and didn't say anything.

"You killed him."

"That's not true," she said.

"Oh, it most certainly is. If you hadn't taken that money, your darling husband would be alive today."

"I didn't know that would happen."

Paul snorted. "In your heart you did. And even if you didn't, which I don't for one second believe, so what? According to the law, ignorance is not a defense. You're at least guilty of manslaughter. What do you say, Robin?"

"I say you should quit playing at being judge and jury and leave her alone."

"And I say she deserves some payback." Paul turned and faced Janet again. "I bet you liked that they roasted him. I bet you thought he deserved it."

"No. No," Janet cried, shaking her head back and forth. "I didn't. I just wanted him to be sorry for the way he treated me."

"Well, he certainly was that. Actually," Paul said, his face a study in boredom, "the truth is, I don't really give a shit why you did what you did." He balled his left hand into a fist and lifted it up so it was almost level with Janet's chin. "Now, are you going to tell me what I want to know or do I have to break your friggin' jaw for you?"

She turned to me.

"Will he?" she asked.

"Absolutely," I said.

Her mouth quivered. Her shoulders sagged. She'd reached the threshold of her endurance.

"All right," she told him. "I'll tell you where the money is."

Paul smiled and flexed his fingers.

"Believe me, I never thought you wouldn't."

After she told him, he hit her anyway just for the hell of it.

Chapter Twenty-Nine

Paul had his gun hidden under his jacket and pointed toward us as he marched Janet and me down the stairs.

"At least let me put on my jacket," I complained. "It's twenty degrees out there."

"You're a tough girl. You'll survive," he said, pushing me toward the door.

"You're an asshole, you know that."

"So you've said," Paul told me as he opened the door to the street. It was empty. "Don't even think about yelling," he warned as he hustled Janet and me to his car, which was parked right in front of the house. "Because I *will* shoot you."

I didn't say anything.

Paul nodded in the direction of the sidewalk. "Try and run if you don't believe me," he said to me. "See what happens."

"That's all right. I'll take your word."

Paul smirked. "That's what I thought," he said. "No guts."

"Is that an expression for being stupid?"

Paul's face clouded over. "Don't push it," he said as he

loaded us into his car. "You first," he said, indicating me, "and her second."

Then he slammed the passenger door shut, walked around to the other side, and got in. If we were going to run, now would have been the time to do it, but it was clear to me from the dazed expression on Janet's face that she wasn't capable of putting one foot in front of the other, let alone running, and I think Paul knew that too.

"Why don't you let us go?" I said to Paul. "You don't need us now."

"I'll tell you when I don't need you."

I held up my hands. "At least loosen the cuffs a little. They're cutting off my circulation."

Paul cocked his head to one side and widened his eyes. "And the magic word is?"

"You should only eat shit and die?"

Paul slapped me across the face. It wasn't that hard, but it was hard enough. My eyes began to water.

"And don't even think about kicking me," he warned. "Because I'll beat the living crap out of you."

"Would that make you feel good?"

"You have some mouth on you, you know that?" Paul said as he turned on the car.

"Comes from being a native New Yorker."

"Another reason they should take this place and sink it in the ocean."

Janet coughed. We were sitting so close, her shoulder was rubbing up against mine. I could smell the mix of vomit, old perfume, and fear coming off her. Her turquoise boots, the emblem of her new life, were stained with yellowish drips.

"Are you going to kill us?" she whispered.

Paul laughed. "Why the hell should I do that? You two aren't worth the trouble."

"Nice to know we're important," I said to him. I lifted both hands and pulled on the neckband of my turtleneck.

"Could you at least open the windows a crack?" The lack of air circulation was getting to me.

Paul glared at me, but he did as I'd asked. I guess the smell was getting to him too.

I took a deep breath as the cold air poured in. Then I stretched my legs out to get the kink out of my calf. I watched but didn't say anything as Paul took a left instead of a right at the corner. Unlike Manhattan, the Bronx is an easy place to get lost in, and I could tell that the deeper we got into the borough, the more nervous Paul was becoming, a fact that gave me a certain amount of pleasure. If I got really lucky, someone would come along and shoot him.

Soon we were in the middle of Fordham Road. The street had been a shopping center when my aunt and uncle had lived up here. It still was. Only now the complexions of the people doing the shopping were different. The Jews and Italians had given way to Dominicans and African-Americans.

"Did you know that the Bronx is the only borough of New York City that's attached to the mainland?" I said. I forget where I'd read that.

Always inform when possible, that's my motto.

"So now you're a friggin' tour guide," Paul said as he tried to read a street sign. A good quarter of them were gone.

"At least I'm not a kidnapper."

"I'll pull over and make those bracelets tighter if you don't shut up," he warned, his eyes still on the road. "Fuckin' city," he muttered. "I wouldn't live here on a bet. What the hell is University Heights Bridge? I don't remember that being there when I came up."

"You could always ask someone," I said. "Or maybe you'd like me to drive."

"I told you to shut the fuck up," Paul snarled. "The next time I hit you, it'll be a lot harder."

Obviously city driving wasn't bringing out the best in him.

"Charming as always," I said as I clenched and unclenched my hands trying to keep the circulation in them going.

Janet didn't say anything at all. She sat with her hands folded in her lap and her eyes facing front. She could have been in church. Every once in a while she'd lightly touch the places Paul had hit her, as if reminding herself of what had happened. Her lower lip was bleeding, and the bruises on her face had turned red and puffy. By tomorrow they'd be purple, green, and yellow. Not Janet's colors. Not anyone's for that matter. Unless you were an M&M.

As I watched Paul blunder around the streets, I wondered how in God's name I could have gone to bed with this man. What had I seen in him? How had I been so wrong about him? There must have been signs. Manuel had seen them. So had Calli. They'd tried to warn me. And of course I hadn't listened. People had tried to warn me about Murphy too. I hadn't listened to them either. Out of Murphy, George, and Paul, I was down two to one. Not a good score.

The traffic had gotten heavier and the skies had grown darker. Except for an occasional muttered, "Fuck," Paul was quiet as he tried to find his way down to Manhattan. We drove around for twenty minutes or so before he finally managed to get us on the Henry Hudson Parkway.

"Congratulations," I told him. "I always love taking the scenic route."

"Shut up," Paul growled.

And here was another thing. How had I managed to go with someone with such a limited vocabulary? In all ways.

"You never could take a compliment," I told him while I watched the stream of cars, haloed in their own headlights, crossing the George Washington Bridge.

When I was younger I'd loved crossing the bridge on the top level and seeing the lights of the Palisades spread out before me as we drove to New Jersey to visit my cousins.

Farther on, even though it was dark and cold, scattered

handfuls of kids were throwing footballs to each other around Riverside Drive. Around 90th Street I felt a pang as I spied a man walking a blond cocker spaniel. I hoped Zsa Zsa was doing all right with Bethany and Manuel.

"If we get off here, we can stop at the Museum of Natural History," I said to Paul as we came up on the 79th Street Boat Basin. "Don't you want to see the dinosaurs? I bet Janet would."

"The only thing I want to see is the back of this place," Paul commented as he changed lanes again.

I moved my hands up and down. The tips of my fingers were starting to go numb. "Me, I'm kinda glad to be back."

"You would be." Then he kept his left hand on the wheel and pointed at Janet with his right one. "Why'd you do it?"

She gave no indication of having heard him.

"Answer me when I talk to you," he barked.

"I thought you weren't interested."

"Well, I am now."

"You want to know why I took the money?" Janet's words came out slowly, each one enunciated.

"No. I want to know why you bought a boat."

She kept staring straight ahead.

"I'm waiting," Paul said.

Janet took a deep breath and let it out.

"Don't get me angry," he warned.

She dabbed the blood off her lip. Finally she spoke. "I took the money because it wasn't fair."

"What wasn't fair?"

"I made Walter a nice home. I gave him a daughter. I cooked his meals and washed his dirty underwear. I listened to his complaining. I deserve something for that."

Paul snorted. "You sound like my friggin' ex-wives. Always whining. Did you ever think that maybe Walter wanted something else?" Paul asked, swerving to avoid a car that was cutting us off.

"He never said he was unhappy." Janet's lower lip was trembling. She clasped and unclasped her hands. "He should have told me."

Paul threw a quick glance in her direction. "Maybe he did. Maybe you weren't listening."

"He didn't." Janet's voice rose. "He threw me away for that . . . that . . . thing. Like an old sweater."

"Old sweater? Give me a fuckin' break. You can do better than that."

But now that Janet was started, she wanted to keep going. "He told me I bored him. I bored *him?* What about him boring me? Do you know how old that . . . that person is? She isn't even eighteen. She's younger than his daughter. It's disgusting."

"So it would have been okay if he'd picked someone older?"

Janet's nostrils flared. "I deserve a little happiness too."

"My sentiments exactly," Paul said. "Which is why I'm doing what I am. Glad to see we agree on something."

Janet bristled. "We have nothing in common."

"I think we do," Paul said. "After all, we're both willing to do anything to get what we want."

"That's a lie."

"Is it?"

I could feel Janet's body growing rigid as she went back to looking straight ahead of her.

We got off the West Side Highway and turned left onto 42nd Street. The street was jammed. Cars were double-parked on either side, narrowing the available lanes. Everyone was sitting on their horns. Just in case people didn't realize they weren't moving. I checked my watch. We'd been in the car for a little over forty-five minutes, and the way we were going it would probably take us another half an hour—at least—to reach our destination.

Paul was cursing again. "I hate this fuckin' shit," he said as he honked at the taxi in front of us.

"That's going to do a lot of good," I told him.

He hit the horn again. Just to show that he didn't have to listen to me.

"Why the hell did you have to pick the Port Authority?" Paul said to Janet.

I could feel her leg shaking through her coat, but her face was expressionless.

"It was convenient," she told him.

"How was it convenient? You didn't come here by bus. You drove."

"I took a taxi down here."

"You did?"

"Yes."

But there was a catch in Janet's voice. She should have nodded instead.

I could see awareness dawning in Paul's eyes.

"You're lying to me, aren't you?" he said.

"Why would I do that?" she said.

"You stupid fuckin' bitch," he said, his eyes still on the street.

"I didn't," she protested.

"Don't bother denying it." Paul's face was taut with rage. "All this time you've been jerking me around. Making me ride around like some sort of friggin' loser. God, you're going to regret this."

Janet watched a bicyclist in a bright orange down jacket weave in and out of the traffic.

"No, you are," she finally said.

"We'll see about that."

"Yes, we will." She touched her lip and laughed. The effect was disconcerting.

"Did you know?" Paul said to me.

I turned toward him.

"How would I know? You're the hotshot detective here."

"You think this is funny, don't you? Let me tell you, you're not going to think it's funny when I get through with you," Paul warned.

"Don't take out your stupidity on me," I protested.

And that was the point at which Janet opened the door and stepped out. I'm almost positive I heard her say, "Go to hell." But I can't be sure.

Chapter Thirty

It's odd what your mind holds on to in moments like this. I remember feeling a rush of cold air and turning and seeing the empty space where Janet had been sitting.

I remember seeing the door on her side swinging shut and thinking, *It's not latched,* at the same time I was thinking, *That's funny. Where the hell has she gone?*

I never saw her actually step out into the street.

I must have screamed Janet's name because Paul glanced over. He looked almost comical with his mouth hanging wide open. Then he swore and slammed on the brakes.

"I don't fuckin' believe her," he cried as I pitched into the dashboard.

We came to a dead stop.

Even though we hadn't been going very fast, probably under ten miles an hour, we'd still been moving. I don't know what Janet expected to happen. Maybe she'd been watching too many movies, but in real life when you step out of a moving vehicle you fall.

I watched her stumble and go down on her hands and knees.

"What the fuck is wrong with you, lady?" a bicyclist

screamed at her, missing her by probably not more than a quarter of an inch.

She picked herself up and studied her skinned knees. Then she turned her hands over and studied her palms. As if she had all the time in the world. I don't know how she could have missed the bus lumbering toward her. She had to have seen it. Or heard it. Not that it would have made much difference if she had. It was too late. She couldn't have gotten out of the way.

The words, "Watch out!" flew out of my mouth.

I think she heard me because she half turned in my direction. By now the bus was almost on top of her. The bus driver's eyes widened as he realized what was about to happen.

His brakes screeched as he tried to stop. But he couldn't. At least not in time.

There was a *thwack* as the bus hit Janet. She slid down and her body disappeared under the bus. Like in a cartoon. The bus kept going, dragging her along. It seemed to take forever before it stopped, although it probably wasn't more than thirty seconds. When it did, the doors opened and the bus driver ran out, followed by a swarm of passengers.

"Fuck. Fuck. Fuck." Paul's face was red. He slammed the wheel with the flat of his hand. "I can't believe she did that. What the hell was she thinking?"

"That she didn't want to get beaten up by you?"

He blinked. "If she had just done what I asked her to, none of this would have happened."

"Is that the way you see this?"

Instead of answering, Paul pointed to where Janet had been sitting. "Give me her pocketbook. Maybe there's something in there we can use."

I held it up to him and he snatched it out of my hands and pawed through it, looking for his salvation. But it wasn't there. Janet Wilcox had to have had the neatest pocketbook

of any woman I'd ever seen. The only things in it were a lipstick, a compact, and a comb. Paul threw it down in disgust.

"I should have cuffed you two together," he said. "I just
never thought . . ." His voice trailed off. He shook his head.
His skin had gone from red to sheet white. He rubbed the
side of his nose with the joint of his right thumb.

"I didn't think she'd be that friggin' dumb. Stupid bitch."
Paul stared straight ahead as if he was contemplating his future and it didn't look very good. "She's killed all of us."

"Let's not exaggerate."

"You're right," he replied although he didn't sound convinced.

"Maybe she's still alive."

Santini shook his head. "No way. Not with what happened to her."

I raised my hands. "How about uncuffing me so I can go
see."

He sighed. "What the hell. Why not? Everything's gone to
shit anyway." And he reached over and unlocked the
bracelets.

I rubbed my wrists. "Are you coming?"

"Yeah. Sure. This will be the perfect end to the perfect
day."

I got out of the car and threaded my way through the
crowd that was gathering. Paul followed. It was chaos.
People were honking their horns. Pedestrians were screaming
at each other. People still in their cars were leaning their
heads out of their windows demanding to know what had
happened.

The bus driver was on his knees with his shoulders and
head under the bus; so was another man. They both
reemerged a moment later. The bus driver shook his head.

"I don't believe this," the driver was saying to the people
around him. The back of his shirt had worked itself free and

was hanging below his jacket. "I just don't believe this. Seventeen years without so much as a dented fender. I have three years to go until retirement and now this. She just stepped out. One second I was thinking about getting coffee, and the next second she was there. She came out of nowhere. Nowhere." He turned to one of the passengers. "You saw. You saw what happened, didn't you?"

The passenger, a Sikh, nodded while he nervously plucked at his eyebrows.

An Asian woman standing behind him had whipped out her cell and was talking to someone in Chinese.

A little farther away, a white twenty-something female in a fur jacket, gold chains, and black leather pants had her cell out as well. "I'm going to be late," she was saying. "Don't freak, Mom. The bus driver ran over someone. No. I'm not lying."

"I'm going to see her face forever," the driver wailed to the assembled crowd. "Why would she do something like that?" His hand went to his chest. His face got pale. "I feel sick."

"You may be having a heart attack," a middle-aged man said. "Come sit over here." And he led the driver back to the bus.

"Jeez, now something's wrong with the driver," the twenty-year-old was saying. She started tapping her nails against her thigh. "No, *Mother*, I am not making this up. Of course I want to come to the family dinner."

I knelt down where the bus driver had been and looked under the bus. Santini had been right. Janet Wilcox was no longer among the living. There was no doubt about that at all. Well, I suppose if you have to go, better to go this way than the way her husband had. In the background I could hear the sound of sirens. Someone must have called the police. They'd be here soon.

I got off my knees and melted back into the crowd. Paul materialized beside me.

"You were right," I told him. "She's dead."

"No way she couldn't be." He bit his lip. "What the hell was she thinking?" Paul asked me again. "All she had to do was give me the money."

He seemed sincerely bewildered. He thought he had everything factored in, and it turned out he hadn't. Even though it was freezing out, Paul's forehead was beaded with sweat. He wiped it away with the back of his hand.

"She always hated to part with a buck. You know she gave Walter an allowance? He'd give her his paycheck, and she'd give him fifty bucks a week for expense money. Fifty bucks."

"My grandmother would have said she was frugal."

Paul snorted. "I'll tell you one thing. I'm sorry I ever met Walter. I'm sorry I let him talk me into getting involved in this mess." And he started walking toward his car.

I caught up with him. "Where are you going?" I asked. "We have to wait for the police."

He gestured at the crowd. "You see anyone paying attention to us?"

No one was. They were all either staring at the bus or talking among themselves.

"You wait for the cops if you want to and explain what happened to them. I'm getting out of here."

"But . . ."

"But what? I'm out of here."

"Where are you going?"

"I don't know. But don't worry. When I figure it out, I'll be sure and let you not know."

"You do that."

I watched Paul get back in his car. Somehow or other he managed to maneuver it through the traffic. A minute or so later he was gone from view. Maybe I should have stayed, but the more I thought about the situation, the more I decided Paul was right. This was not a time for explanations; it was a time for leaving. Nothing I said was going to help Janet

Wilcox. She was beyond that now. What I needed to do was get my jacket, get my car, and get out of the city.

I headed across town, caught the Number Six train uptown, got off, and walked over to Belmont Avenue. A bitter wind swept down through the streets. By the time I got to Janet Wilcox's apartment I was numb with cold. The first thing I did when I got inside was go straight to the heat register in the kitchen and stand over it until I could feel my toes and fingers again.

As I waited for my blood to start flowing, I stared at Janet Wilcox's groceries. What was the line about undone tasks? I had to resist the urge to finish putting them away. Instead I did a quick search of the place on the off chance that the money was here, which it wasn't. Then I grabbed my jacket and took off. I didn't want to stay any longer, because I was nervous that the people living in the apartment downstairs would come back and I'd have to explain my presence.

As I drove out of the Bronx, I turned on the radio and tried not to think about what had just happened. About my gullibility. About my responsibility for what had just occurred. If I hadn't gone looking for Janet Wilcox, she'd be alive today. Or maybe not. She'd pretty much signed her death warrant, not to mention her husband's, when she'd stolen that money. I'd just executed it.

I started fiddling with the radio, but I couldn't find anything I wanted to listen to. I kept trying, but finally conceded defeat and turned the radio off right after I got on the New York State Thruway.

My grandmother would have said there was no use crying over spilt milk. But I hadn't believed that when I was eight years old and I'd left the top of the chameleon cage off and Tito had gotten out and died, and I sure as hell didn't believe it now.

I was thinking about how I'd looked all over the apart-

ment for him when I glanced down and realized two things:
One, I was going over eighty-five miles an hour, and two, my
gas tank was almost empty. Ten minutes later I was lucky
enough to come up to a rest stop. I pulled in and parked.
There probably weren't more than twenty cars in a lot that
could have taken two hundred. They looked lonely, huddled
together against the night.

I went in, bought two large cups of coffee and a pack of
cigarettes and went back to the car. I peeled off the cello-
phane on the cigarettes in the car and broke open the seal
and the foil wrap. The sharp smell of tobacco drifted through
the car. After I smoked my cigarette, I filled up the tank and
called Manuel and told him I was on my way home.

He said that was good, because one of the aquariums in
the store had sprung a leak and he'd had to transfer all the
fish to the other tanks. And oh, yes, by the way, Zsa Zsa had
actually caught and eaten a mouse and as a result had had di-
arrhea all over the place. I don't know what she was thinking
of. Like me, she did better with highly processed food.

She greeted me when I walked in the house. I petted her
for a little while, chatted with Manuel, then went straight upstairs and lay down on my bed.

Manuel came up and stood in the doorway. "Bethany and
I are thinking of moving in together."

"So she's submitting her petition to Family Court?"

Manuel shook his head. "She decided not to."

"Why?"

"Her mother asked her not to."

"That must have made Bethany feel good."

"It did."

"You know if you move in together her father can have
you arrested for statutory rape."

"No. She has to press charges. Anyway her mother said it
was okay with her."

"It's still a bad idea."

"Why?"

"I just told you."

"No, you didn't."

I closed my eyes. I could feel a headache coming on. I hoped it wasn't a migraine. I hadn't had one of those in a while. "Can we talk about this tomorrow?"

"Sure," Manuel said. "But we're serious."

"I know."

I didn't say anything else. I could feel Manuel hovering in the doorway, waiting for me to open my eyes again. When I didn't, he left. A few seconds later I heard Zsa Zsa coming up the stairs. She jumped on the bed and put her head right next to mine on the pillow. I curled myself around her.

"I'm sorry for leaving you," I said.

She licked my chin. One thing about dogs. They forgive you.

I fell asleep to her belching in my ear. Considering what I'd just been through, the sound was oddly soothing.

I kept expecting dire repercussions, but there weren't any. At least not right away. No one—not the police, not Paul's "friends"—came around to talk to me. Which made me more nervous than if they had.

The local paper ran a story in the metro section about the deaths of Walter and Janet Wilcox. And while there were speculations about the relationship between the two fatalities, the story didn't follow up on that angle, confining itself to talking about the tricks that fate plays. I wondered if the police felt the same way or not, but I wasn't in a position to ask them. Except for George, Paul was my only other lead in, and obviously I wasn't going to be asking him for anything.

That afternoon I went looking for Santini.

I was pretty sure the sonofabitch wasn't going to show up back here, but I wanted to make certain. There were a couple of things I wanted to clear up. I tried his office and his house. His office door was locked, and his car wasn't in his garage.

Two of the neighbor's kids making snowballs in the yard next door volunteered the information that Mr. Santini had asked them to shovel out his driveway. He'd told them he'd be gone for at least two weeks, maybe more, and given them twenty dollars in advance.

"What about his mail?" I asked. "Are you supposed to collect it?"

"He didn't say anything about that," one of the kids answered.

"He just said to shovel his driveway," the other one added.

Which meant the post office was probably holding it. Which meant he'd been planning on clearing out when he'd sent me down to New York City.

I'd been his stalking horse. For sure. The knowledge did not put me in a good mood.

I checked at his favorite bars, but no one had seen him there either. One of the bartenders I spoke to said that Paul had told him he was going to be doing a job and would be away for a while.

On a hunch I checked at Le Bijou, the strip club Alima worked at. It seemed like the type of place Paul would go. Now that I thought about it, I wondered if Paul had introduced Wilcox to this place, because it didn't seem like the kind of activity a man like Walter would engage in without a push.

The same guy who had thrown me out the first time came around the bar to meet me. He looked as big now as he had then.

"What is it with you?" he said when I asked him if he'd seen Paul Santini. "Does this place look like Information Central?"

I made a show of looking around. "You mean it's not?"

The place reeked of loneliness. I'd seen more connections happening at shoe sales than I did between the woman dancing on the stage and the two men watching her. At least lust is something. There was nothing there at all.

The guy pointed to the door. "I told you once, and I'm telling you again, get out of here. And this time stay out."

I didn't argue. What was the point? There was nothing I could do to make him talk if he didn't want to.

I like to think that intelligence, guile, and cunning triumph over strength, but some days I wish I was six-five and three hundred and fifty pounds. It would make my life a hell of a lot easier.

The third day, the deadline Paul had told me we had, came and went without anything happening. I began to relax a little. Who knows, maybe he'd made the whole thing up.

It was possible, I started thinking, that maybe the whole Russian mob thing was just a scam to make me find Janet Wilcox for him. It wouldn't surprise me at all.

I spent the next couple of days making it up to Zsa Zsa and Manuel. I took Zsa Zsa for a couple of long walks, shared a beer with her at a bar down in Armory Square, got her a couple of new dog toys and a new collar. This one was covered with seed pearls. I could tell she thought it was pretty nifty by the way she pranced around. The mouse incident was pretty much put behind us.

As for Manuel, I gave him a two-hundred-dollar bonus, took him and Bethany out to dinner at Ruby Tuesday's, and bought him a DVD player. After all, I was spending Paul's expense money. I really didn't care.

Actually, I wanted to get rid of it. It felt like blood money to me. In the end, I donated what was left over to one of the no-kill animal shelters. At least that way it would do some good.

Zsa Zsa, Manuel, and I settled back into our routine.

I'd begun thinking everything was going to be all right when the call came.

Of course.

Isn't that the way things always go?

Chapter Thirty-One

It was one of those bleak mid-winter, midweek days, the kind where the sky is an expanse of gray and it seems as if it will snow forever and you wonder what the hell you're doing living in a place like this.

I was killing time watching another sputter of flakes falling outside the store window. It wasn't a lot. Just enough so I'd have to clean off the car again when I went outside. Not that I was complaining. Up north, they'd gotten a foot or so dumped on them. Zsa Zsa and I had eaten lunch half an hour ago. One Big Mac for me, one for her, and we'd split a large order of fries.

The day was going slowly. I'd done the *New York Times* crossword puzzle and gotten my taxes ready for my accountant, not to mention cleaned, watered and fed the animals and washed the floor. I kept looking at the clock expecting it to be five. But it wasn't. I had six more hours before I could go home. I'd just taken ten dollars from a customer, given him fifty cents' worth of change and bagged the new ferret toys he was buying when the phone rang. I picked up as the customer walked out the door.

"Noah's Ark," I said.

"Is this Robin Light?" someone with a heavy Russian accent asked.

I took a deep breath. It looked as if I'd been wrong. It looked as if Paul hadn't made up the story about the Russian mobsters after all. Too bad for me. I was hoping he had. I snugged the phone between my ear and my shoulder and reached for my cigarettes.

"Who wants to know?"

"Joe."

I lit up and inhaled. A kitten we were keeping for someone jumped up on the counter, knocked my matches over the edge, and watched them fall.

"I hear Joe is a well-known name in Russian. So is Mike."

The voice chuckled. "I was told you had a good sense of humor."

"Who told you?"

"I will let you guess."

"What if I don't like guessing games?"

The kitty jumped off and began batting the matches around.

"Then you shouldn't play them."

"Fair enough. So what can I do for you?" As if I didn't know.

"A friend of yours has something of ours. We would like it back."

I could have taken a leaf out of Janet Wilcox's book and pretended I had no idea what he was talking about, but what was the point in doing that? Look at where it had gotten her.

"I'm sure you would, but he's not my friend," I said. "And I don't have anything."

"That's too bad."

"Go talk to him."

"That will not be possible, I think."

A chill went up my spine. I took another puff from my cigarette, then ground it out on the top of the soda can next to

the register. I don't know why, but it was making my throat
feel raw.

"And why is that?"

"Because . . . because . . ." the man who called himself Joe
paused, searching for the correct phrase. "He . . . he has gone
on a long trip."

"You saw him?"

"To say good-bye."

Somehow I didn't think we were talking Aruba here. Poor
Paul. I wondered where they had gotten him. And how.
Knowing Paul, he'd probably gotten drunk and called them
up to tell them how I had the money. And they'd said, we understand. Come. Tell us all about it over a drink. And that
had been that. Paul had always thought he was smarter and
tougher than he was.

"I see," I said.

"I'm glad you do."

"We should talk," I said.

"*Da*. We should. That is why I am calling."

I remembered my grandmother had always hated the
Russians. She'd lived in a little town that sat on the border
between Poland and Russia. Sometimes the border had been
on one side, sometimes the other. But she'd never thought of
herself as Russian or Polish. She thought of herself as Jewish.
Now that I thought about it, I'd only heard her speak
Yiddish in the house. Never Russian. I wondered if she'd
known any.

There was a Russian Orthodox church five blocks away
from our apartment. She always crossed to the other side of
the street when we went by it. Once I'd asked her why.

"*Cossacks*," she'd said and spat three times on the sidewalk.

I'd cringed in embarrassment and pretended I wasn't with
her. I wanted to have a grandmother who didn't sip her tea
through a sugar cube, who was American.

I couldn't stop thinking about how hurt she must have felt when I arranged the meeting.

When I hung up, I called George. I may be many things, but suicidal isn't one of them. Contrary to what some people think.

I met Joe's friends down in Armory Square at a cigar bar called The Impresario. On the weekends the place is always packed, but this was nine-thirty on a snowy Wednesday night in Syracuse, and not too many people were there. The bartender was killing time polishing glasses, talking to a couple of kids who looked as if they should have been home studying, and keeping an eye on the television over the bar, all at the same time. He nodded to me as I went by. George didn't. He took another sip of his beer and continued watching the television.

The men I was looking for were sprawled on a sofa in the back. They were smoking cigars and sipping what I assumed to be brandy out of snifters. There were three of them. All three were dressed in black turtleneck sweaters and dark pants. Two looked to be in their early thirties while the third man I put at mid- to late-fifties. Except for a scar that went down the length of his left cheek, the older man had finely drawn features while the other two had noses and mouths that looked as if they had connected with one fist too many. All three had slicked-back, dark hair.

The older one waved me over.

"You want to try some brandy?" he asked as I sat down in an armchair facing him.

"That would be nice." I took out a cigarette. The man closest to me leaned over and lit it with a gold lighter. I noticed he was wearing a Rolex on his wrist. If it was a counterfeit, it was a good one.

The older man signaled to the waitress. "In Russia people

eat and drink." He indicated the coffee table in front of us. "There, the whole table would be covered with food."

She came over and the man ordered a brandy for me.

"It is more civilized, I think." He looked at me. His eyes were shrewd. He smelled of money. "Do you know Russian peoples?"

"My grandmother came from Russia."

"You are Jewish, no?"

"Yes."

"I can tell. It is not the same thing as being Russian."

"So she said."

He picked a piece of lint off his sweater. "I do not mean this in a disrespectful way."

"Then how do you mean it?"

"As a matter of fact. Jews are different. Like the Ukrainians are different. Or the Turkish people." He took another puff of his cigar. "I myself am part Jewish. On my father's side. One generation back. Just as she is Italian," he said, pointing to the waitress who was putting my brandy on the coffee table in front of me. "Are you?" he asked.

"Part Italian," she said and scurried away.

"See," he said. "I am always right. I have an eye for these things." He pointed to his eye, then indicated my drink. "Try it."

I took a sip. "It's good." And it was. I'd forgotten how complex a good brandy can taste.

He looked pleased. "Fifty year. Americans think Russians only drink vodka and eat caviar and borscht. They see *Doctor Zhivago,* and they think they know about Russia. They think they know about the Russian people. They are wrong. They know nothing. How can they know when Hollywood has an Arab playing a Russian?

"Russians are a serious people. Tough." He hit his chest with the flat edge of his fist. "Not soft like you Americans.

We go through hard times. Always hard times. When the French come to Moscow, the people burn everything—their food, their houses, everything—because they would not let the French have their city. The Russians would see their children starve first.

"We have lived through the Tsars. We have lived through the Fascists. We have lived through the Communists. Do you know the secret to the Russian peoples?"

I shook my head.

"We are not afraid of death. This makes us strong." He took another sip of his brandy and put the glass down on the coffee table. "You have heard of the Russian Mafia, yes?" he asked.

"I have read about them," I replied carefully.

He made a dismissive gesture with his hand. "Your reporters make them out to be idiots. That is a mistake. People who know them are respectful." He took a puff of his cigar and knocked the ash off into an ashtray. "Do you know why?" he asked and then answered his own question. "They are smart and they are not sentimental. Now the Italians are a sentimental people. The Russians are not. Someone he owes an Italian money and he does not pay. The Italian warn and warn and warn. The Italian gives lots of chances. Then if the customer does not pay, they kill him. Big deal. Now it is over for this man. He does not have to worry anymore. But the Russian, he is not like this." And he waved a finger in the air. "He is very different.

"The Russian, he only give one warning and the man, if he does not pay, he does not kill him. He kills first his children and then his wife. And if still the man is not paying, he kills the mother and the father. The man that owes, he has more . . ." He searched around for the word. "How you say . . . he has more incentive to pay back the money that way. And the Russians, they are not caught because they always make it seem someone else is doing it. Either that or these people, they just disappear. No one ever find them. They become . . . like in your McDonald's hamburgers."

Suddenly veggie burgers began to have a greater appeal.

"Russian mob people know how to do things like this. They are good. This is because many Russian Mafia, they are ex-KGB. They are efficient. They know how to run things. I think this is interesting, don't you?"

"Very." I stubbed my cigarette out in the ashtray. I almost would have liked it better if he had threatened me. "But I don't see what this has to do with me. May I speak frankly?"

The man nodded.

"My friend was stupid. He handled things badly, so badly that the person he was interested in stepped in front of a bus."

"*Da,*" the older man said. "We know this."

"Then you must also know that I don't have anything to do with this situation." I picked my next words carefully. "I can understand your being upset at your loss, but sometimes, as a businessman, these things occur, and when they do one has to take a write-off."

The older man took a sip of his brandy, savored it for a few seconds, then swallowed and blotted his lips with a napkin. "This is true. But one does not take this write-off until one has explored every avenue for getting one's money back. We think you are smarter than your friend."

"My friend was a professional. I was just helping him out."

"Then perhaps you will do us the favor of helping us out as well."

"Of course I would like to, but unfortunately I have a business to run."

"People buy these snakes and things that you sell?"

"How do you know what I sell?"

"Good businessmen do their research." He toyed with his glass for a second before taking another sip. "I have a problem finding good help. Do you?"

"Everyone does," I replied cautiously, wondering where the conversation was going. "It's the nature of the times."

"It is especially frustrating when you find someone good and they disappear."

"Disappear?"

The older man nodded. "It happens."

I was about to reply when a phone rang. The younger man on his left reached over and picked up the cell phone lying on the table next to his drink. He spoke for a minute in Russian, then handed the phone to the man I'd been talking to.

"Please excuse me," he said to me and then switched to Russian. A minute or so later, he handed me the phone. "For you," he said. "Go on," he prompted.

I took a deep breath and lifted it to my ear.

"Robin," Manuel said. Then there was a click and nothing.

Chapter Thirty-Two

The older man took the phone out of my hand and slipped it into his pocket.

"As I was saying," he said to me. "Good help is hard to find. It would be a pity if you lost yours."

"If anything happens to Manuel . . ."

The man put his hand on my shoulder and patted it reassuringly. I flinched and the man smiled.

"Nothing will happen as long as you do what you are supposed to," he told me.

"And if I can't?"

The man removed his hand and studied his fingernails. They were square and clean and looked as if they'd seen the attentions of a manicurist recently. "I hope you will." And he got up and began putting his coat on. The other men rose as well.

"Come," the older man said to me. "I will walk you out of the bar."

"I don't believe you," I said.

The older man shrugged. "Go and check. But don't spend too much time doing it."

George was chatting with the bartender as we walked by.

The older Russian paused at the door and nodded back toward him.

"I met a black American once in Moscow. He was big too. The Africans that came to study at our university in Moscow were a smaller people. Why do you think that is?"

"I don't know."

"I read somewhere that it is because you Americans bred them that way when they were slaves." The man began buttoning his black leather trench coat. "So I'm hoping the next time I talk to you, you will have good news for us."

"And when will that be?"

"Today is Wednesday. You will hear from us on Sunday."

"What if I come up with something before then?"

This time when the man smiled, I realized he was wearing an upper plate. "You Americans are an impatient people." And he slipped on his gloves and turned up the collar of his coat.

"Do you have a name?"

"Everyone has a name." He paused while he thought. "You may call me Ivan. To Americans all Russians are called this, no? So you may call me this too." He reached over and shook my hand. "It has been very nice talking to such an attractive lady. I am sincerely hoping that our business will come to a pleasant end. It would be a pity if it did not." Then he nodded to the man on the left, who moved forward and opened the door for him.

As soon as the door closed, George got up and hurried after them. He came back a moment later.

"I got the first two letters of their license plate," he said. "I couldn't see the rest. A car pulled in front of them."

I felt like throwing up.

"I don't believe this."

George looked at me carefully and put his hands on my shoulders. "What's happened? What's wrong?" he asked. "You have a funny expression on your face."

"They have Manuel," I said. "I heard his voice on the phone."

We went through the motions of checking Manuel's whereabouts even though in my gut I knew it would be a waste of time. We went to Noah's Ark first because that was where Manuel was supposed to be. The place was locked up. The lights were off. There was a white rectangle on the door. When we got closer I could see it was a note.

"Don't touch it," George said.

"I wasn't going to." I read it aloud with George looking over my shoulder. *"Dear Robin,"* it said. *"I'm sorry I have to go off and leave you like this, but I have personal business I have to take care of. Love, Manuel."*

"Manuel's handwriting?" George asked.

I nodded. He'd never signed anything else he'd sent me, "Love."

"These Russians are good," George said. "I'm impressed."

I could see George's breath dissipate in the night air. The branches of the tree in front of the store glistened under the street lamp.

I read the note again, somehow hoping there was some secret information imbedded in it I could decode. I was reading it for a third time when I heard scratching on the other side of the door. I looked through. It was Zsa Zsa. She must have been sleeping in the back and heard our voices. I don't know how I could have forgotten about her. She rushed out when I opened the door and ran around my legs in an ecstasy of welcome.

"Poor thing," I said as I knelt down and embraced her. Thank God they'd left her alone. Finally she quieted down and I went inside.

The first thing I noticed was that the cash drawer was open and the money gone. Whoever had kidnapped Manuel had tried to make it look as if he'd taken off with the day's earnings. Other than that, everything else was in place. Manuel had gone without a fight. I pictured it.

A man coming in. Manuel asking what he wanted. "This," the man says, drawing a gun from his jacket and aiming it at Manuel. Manuel saying, "Take what you want." The man shaking his head, telling Manuel to get a pencil and paper. Making Manuel write the note. Manuel watching him emptying the drawer. Then marching Manuel outside to the waiting car.

"Come on." George tapped me gently on the shoulder. I noticed he had Manuel's note in one of the plastic bags I used for crickets. "Not that there's going to be anything on here we can use," he said, indicating the bag with his chin. "But you never know."

I didn't say anything.

George squeezed my shoulder. "We'll find him."

"Yes, we will." I took a deep breath to stave off the fear that was growing in my stomach. Fear was the enemy, I told myself. Get too afraid and you can't think.

On the way home, I called Manuel's mother's house. No one was home. Then I remembered. The family had gone to a funeral in Puerto Rico. I just hoped George and I found Manuel before they got home. I couldn't imagine telling Manuel's mother that he'd been kidnapped and was being held hostage.

I called his friends next. No one had heard from Manuel today. I called people he did business with. They all said he hadn't been around since yesterday.

"What do you think?" George asked as we pulled into my driveway.

"What I thought before. That they have him."

As I opened the car door for Zsa Zsa, the front door of my house flew open and Bethany stepped out. She had her hands on her hips and an aggrieved expression on her face. Dressed in jeans and one of Manuel's old shirts, her face devoid of makeup, she looked about twelve.

"Do you know where Manuel is?" she demanded as George and I walked inside. "I've been waiting here for two hours. We were supposed to go to the movies."

George and I looked at each other. He took off his jacket and carefully hung it in the closet. I did the same. Neither of us wanted to be the one to tell her. Bethany scanned our faces. Her expression changed as she realized something was wrong.

"What happened?" she asked. She put her hands up to her mouth. "Tell me," she demanded. "Was Manuel in an accident? Is he dead?"

"No," I replied.

"Then what? Did he go off with another girl? Has he got himself arrested?"

I shook my head and told her what had happened. Her face crumpled. She began to sob.

"It's not fair," she kept repeating. "It's just not fair. He's the only person that was ever nice to me."

I took her in my arms and held her and stroked her hair as she burrowed her face in my shoulder. Soon my sweater was damp with her tears.

"We'll find him and bring him back," I murmured. "You'll see. We will. I promise." And for a few seconds I almost believed myself.

Finally, when Bethany's sobs had subsided, I went into the kitchen and got her a glass of water and a damp paper towel for her eyes. Then I led her to the sofa.

"Here," I said, giving her the towel. "It'll help with the swelling."

"I don't care about my eyes," Bethany said, pushing it away. "I don't care about anything." But she took small sips of water from the glass I handed her.

George sat down on the coffee table across from her and leaned forward, his arms dangling between his knees, his face soft with sympathy. For a couple of moments he just sat. Finally he spoke.

"Bethany, I know this is hard, but I want you to take a minute and collect yourself and see if you can think of anything that can help us find Manuel. Any little fact. Anything at all," he said.

Bethany took another sip of water, then sat clasping the glass in her hands. "I'm sorry. I can't think of anything," Bethany whispered.

"That's okay. That's fine. Maybe you will later. When was the last time you spoke to Manuel?"

Bethany thought. "About seven. We were going to a ten o'clock movie."

Tears started flowing down her cheeks. I watched them drip down her chin and onto her hands.

"Anything else?" George asked as I sat down beside her.

"No."

I took the water out of her hands and put it on the side table. "Maybe you should think about going home. It might be easier for you."

Bethany's head shot up. Her eyes flashed.

"No. I have to stay here. It's okay, isn't it?" she pleaded.

I remembered sleeping in Murphy's shirt for weeks after he died. Taking comfort in his smell. Trying to pretend nothing had happened. This was the same thing.

"I'll see what I can work out. But I'm going to have to call your parents and let them know where you are."

"Why bother? They don't care."

"Be that as it may, I still have to phone them."

"And anyway," Bethany said. "You need me to take care of Zsa Zsa." And she reached over and clasped my hands in hers.

George got up and put in a call to one of his friends who

was still working with the Sheriff's Department. He paced
the living room as he talked, his expression getting grimmer
and grimmer. Twenty minutes later, he hung up and put the
cordless on the coffee table.

"Phil will help unofficially," he said. "But given the circumstances, there's only so much he can do. I'll go down tomorrow and file a missing-person report, just to have some
paper."

Bethany started crying again. This time Zsa Zsa, who'd
been sleeping on the rug behind the armchair, came over and
started licking Bethany's cheeks. Bethany tried pushing her
away, but Zsa Zsa persisted and eventually, out of self-de-
fense, Bethany stopped crying, at which point Zsa Zsa curled
up next to her. Half an hour later, I looked over to see
Bethany asleep with her head tipped back against the sofa
and her mouth open.

"We should get someone in to stay with her," George said
looking down at her. "So she won't be alone."

I nodded.

"I have a student I could ask."

"She'll stay here?"

"She will if I ask her to." George bent over and picked up
Bethany and carried her up the stairs. I went up behind him,
and Zsa Zsa went behind me.

I opened the door to Manuel's bedroom. "Put her in here."

George gently laid her down on the bed. I took off her
shoes and socks and covered her with the comforter. Zsa Zsa
jumped up and gave Bethany a good-night lick.

"Poor kid," George said as we went down the stairs.

"Poor Manuel."

He'd warned me to stay out of their line of sight, and he
was the one that was in it. God, what a mess. I went in the
kitchen and called Bethany's parents to let them know where
she was. It was my bad luck that her father answered.

"Robin, of course you're free to do what you want, but I

think it's a mistake to let her stay with you," her father told me. "She has to learn the consequences of her actions sometime."

I didn't bother pointing out that Manuel's kidnapping had nothing to do with anything his daughter had done.

"She thinks you won't take her back."

"That's not true. Not true at all. As I've repeatedly told her, she's welcome to come home when she learns some responsibility."

"Which means?"

"Going back to the school in Florida."

"But she doesn't like it there."

"She should have thought of that before she ran away from home. I can't have her here disrupting our lives anymore. It's too hard on her mother."

"So you're suggesting I kick her out onto the street?"

"I'm suggesting you do whatever falls within your comfort zone." And he hung up.

Sanctimonious ass. I placed the cordless back on its cradle. I'd choose Tiger Lily over Bethany's father as a parent any day of the week. The scary thing was that this guy made his living giving other people advice on how to raise their children.

I poured a double shot of Scotch for George and me, then brought the drinks and the bottle into the living room.

George took a sip from his glass. "No matter how much I try, I'm never going to like this stuff. Although I'll grant you, the color is pretty." He began tapping his fingers on the glass. "I'd love to get my hands on Paul."

"I don't think anyone is going to be doing that. I don't think anyone is ever going to find him. He's probably scattered all over the Northeast by now."

"But you don't know for certain."

"No. I don't," I admitted. And I probably never would.

George took another sip of his drink. As he put the glass

on the coffee table, Zsa Zsa jumped up on the sofa, turned around three times, and snuggled up against George's thigh. George gave her an absentminded pat. She wagged her tail, put her head between her paws, and closed her eyes.

"These people don't leave many loose ends around, do they?" George said as he scratched Zsa Zsa's back.

"Apparently not." I thought about Paul calling them dumb. He had seriously underestimated them. So had Wilcox for that matter.

"I'll see what I can find out about the Russians. That can't be too hard."

I got up and dropped the shades on the living room windows down. Suddenly I felt exposed, having people being able to look in.

"Here's my question," I said, turning to face George. "Why Manuel? Why not someone else?"

"Simple. Because you care about him. Because these guys know if they have him, you'll do what they want to the absolute best of your ability."

"I know that. But how do they know that? Whoever took Manuel knows me."

George picked the glass up and rolled it between the palms of his hand. "Paul knew that you and Manuel were tight," he said. "He could have told the Russians."

"Yeah. He could have. Maybe he did. But that doesn't lead anywhere."

"Meaning?"

"I have another idea." And I went upstairs and woke Bethany up.

Chapter Thirty-Three

"Are you sure about this?" George asked as he turned onto East Genesee Street. We were in his car, heading toward the house I'd found Tiger Lily in.

"No, I'm not sure at all. But the kid's a possible link, and that makes him worth talking to."

I've always thought that if you keep moving and talking to people, eventually you bump up against something that shows you where to go next.

"You don't even know if he lives there."

"I guess we'll find out soon enough."

"Do you know how many skinny white kids with shaved heads there are in this city?" George asked. "How do you know that the one Bethany saw Manuel talking to is the one we want?"

"I don't."

George turned the corner onto Fayette Street. No one was out. We were the only car on the road. At one o'clock in the morning, everyone was home asleep. I lit a cigarette and exhaled. George waved the smoke away with his free hand.

I opened the window a crack.

"Better," George said.

"I figure if I'm wrong, we're in the same place we were before, but if I'm right, we're a step ahead."

"Are you sure this doesn't have to do with Calli and Dirk and showing Calli what a putz she hooked up with?"

"I'm positive." I took two more puffs, lowered the window a little more, and flicked the cigarette out onto the road. Somehow or other smoking wasn't doing it for me anymore. Maybe I needed to change brands. "Does Natalie know you're doing this?"

George took his eyes off the road for a second to look at me. "Where did that come from?"

I shrugged. "I'm curious."

"I suppose you have a right to ask. And *this* meaning what we're doing now?"

I nodded.

"Yeah. I told her." He pulled into a parking space right in front of the door of the building the cops had taken Myra out of.

"What did she say?"

He turned off the ignition. "That you're using this as an excuse to get me back."

"Is that what you think too?"

"No." George pushed open the car door. "If I thought that, I wouldn't be here."

"So how does it feel being a father?"

George ducked his head. "I don't want to talk about it."

"You're going to have to at some point."

"Maybe, but not now."

"When are you getting married?"

George took a deep breath and let it out.

"Can we just concentrate on the business at hand?"

"Sure. If that's what you want."

"It is."

We both got out. A limb from the oak we were standing

beneath cracked from the cold. It sounded like a rifle shot. George and I both jumped.

"Nervous," George said.

"Yeah. Aren't you?"

"Tough guys don't get nervous."

"Excuse me, I forget," I said as we walked by a discarded Christmas tree lying on the side of a six-foot mound of snow. Pieces of tinsel drooped from its branches. The angel on top had lost her wings and halo.

I skirted the garbage bags scattered nearby and followed the shoveled path toward the house. Torn plastic flapped from the upstairs windows. Cut-up black plastic garbage bags covered the downstairs front windows. There was a spotlight on the porch that lit up half the walkway. An old beat-up Pontiac was parked in the driveway. I waded through the snow and touched the hood. It was still warm.

"Someone's home," I said.

"It would appear so." George leaned on the doorbell. It played the first couple of bars of the *William Tell* overture.

"Nice to know someone has a sense of culture." George looked around. "You sure this place isn't a dope house?"

"Pretty sure."

It did look like one, though.

"Well I hope it isn't 'cause I left my shotgun at home." George leaned on the bell again.

No one came to the door.

"The inhabitants of this domicile are, I am sure, all in bed preparing for another productive day," George said as he stamped his feet to keep them warm.

"No doubt."

"So whadda ya think?" George said, doing his New York City imitation. "Do we stay or go?"

I pointed to the stairwell. The light was on and through the plastic sheeting I could see the faint shadow of a person coming down the stairs.

"Stay," George said.

"Maybe he's coming to answer the door."

"I've always thought you were a closet optimist."

George leaned back, brought his weight forward, and rammed the door with his shoulder before I could reply. A hairline crack appeared down the door's center.

"Hollow core," George said. "They don't stand up." And he brought up his foot and kicked it in. "Bad quality hollow core at that," he said as he took a step inside. I was right behind him.

I heard the sound of pounding feet and got a glimpse of the sole of someone's sneaker disappearing around the corner into the hall.

"Guess you were right. Guess he wasn't going to answer," I said.

Of course, if someone were breaking my door down, I wouldn't be answering either.

"Guess not," George agreed. Then he yelled, "Stop!"

The person kept going. What a surprise. If he had stopped, I would have fainted from amazement. Does anyone, ever, except on TV shows? George and I went after him. He went through the hallway and into the kitchen. When we got there, he was fumbling with the lock to the back door. I finally got a look at him in profile. It was Dirk's kid. I would have slapped myself on the back if there'd been time.

"We need to talk to you," I told him.

"Fuck you," the kid threw over his shoulder.

"I'd prefer not."

The kid didn't turn around. George and I had gotten halfway across the kitchen when he threw the back door open and darted down the steps.

"He's not very polite, is he," George said as we ran across the yard where Tiger Lily had been chained up.

"No, he's not."

"And he is the person with whom we wish to speak?"

"Definitely."

"Good," George said as we hopped the fence and took off down the street after him. "Because I'd hate to think I was doin' this for nothing."

"I thought you liked exercise."

"I like jogging. I like tennis. I don't like this."

The kid went up a side street, took a left onto Genesee, ran a block, then headed back in the direction of Fayette.

"I wonder if he runs track?" I gasped. I had a stitch in my side. I had to give up smoking.

"He should if he doesn't." George wasn't even breathing hard. The perks of leading a healthy life. He pointed. "He's going in there," he said as the kid turned into a driveway between two houses.

We followed him in. The driveway was dark and littered with debris. Suddenly I heard a "Damn," and turned around. George was on the ground, rubbing his ankle. An overturned baby carriage was next to him.

"I'm fine," he said, waving me on.

I ran about ten more feet and halted. The driveway branched out into two small backyards and dead-ended in a hurricane fence. Behind it a dog that was doing a good imitation of the Hound of the Baskervilles was hurling himself against the slats with enough force to make them shake. I was willing to bet the kid hadn't gone over the fence. He wasn't that crazy.

I made out a garden shed to my right and four poles supporting a tarp to my left. An old army Jeep was sitting underneath it. The kid had to be here somewhere, hiding in the shadows. I just couldn't see where. I took a couple of steps out of the light and flattened myself against the wall of the house and motioned for George to stay where he was. I preferred to have the kid come to me if possible instead of blundering around in the dark and possibly missing him.

Five minutes dragged by, then ten. I wasn't wearing gloves

or heavy socks, and my fingers and toes were aching. I'd just about decided the hell with it, I was going to go in and get that little sonofabitch, when I heard faint rustling sounds coming from the direction of the shed.

Then I heard the crunch of footsteps. They were coming in my direction. I would have said a prayer of thanks if I could have moved my lips. Now I could see the kid's face. He was looking this way and that. His body was ready to move at the slightest sound. I held my breath as he came closer. When he was right beside me, I stepped out and grabbed his wrist.

"Didn't anyone ever tell you patience is a virtue?"

He grunted and brought his arm back to punch me, but George grabbed him by the back of his jacket and yanked him away before he could.

"I could have taken care of that," I told George.

"I can let him go if you want."

"No. That's okay."

"You sure?"

"Positive."

"Hey," the kid cried. "What about me?"

"Good question." And George jacked the kid up against the wall.

The kid quieted down. I've noticed George has that effect on people.

He looked from George to me and back again and said, "Why the hell can't you leave me alone?"

"Because I'm drawn to your magnetic personality," I told him.

The lights came on in the house we were standing next to.

"Maybe we should move before someone calls the cops," George suggested.

"Good idea."

"Let's go back to his house." And he indicated the kid with a nod.

"It isn't my house," the kid said.

"Shut up." George grabbed the back of the kid's neck and started marching him down Fayette Street. "What's your name anyway?" George asked him.

"Why you askin?'"

George shook him.

" 'Cause I am."

"All right. Quit that. You're making me sick to my stomach."

"Too bad." George shook him harder. "Tell me what I want to know, and I'll stop. Otherwise I'll keep going."

"Okay. Okay. It's D," the kid said.

"Like in D-E-E? I thought that was a girl's name."

"Like in the letter D."

"Is that what it says on your birth certificate?"

The kid didn't say anything.

George gave him another shake. The kid flopped around like a scarecrow.

"Well, is it?" he asked.

"No," the kid said sullenly.

"Then what is?" George gave him another shake.

"I tole you to quit that," the kid said.

"Then answer the question."

"Okay. It's Dirk Junior. Satisfied?"

George grinned. "If that was my name, I'd be calling myself D too."

The kid didn't say anything. We got to the house and went inside. There were holes cut in the inside walls at random, allowing for a view of the next room without having to walk into it. Someone had ripped up a section of the floor in the living room. In the dining room I looked up and saw the tub in the bathroom through the hole in the ceiling.

"Interesting décor," George said to me as he pushed Dirk Junior into one of the few chairs that had its stuffing intact. "Is this what they mean by post-modern apocalyptic?"

Dirk Junior scowled. "What you talking about?"

George favored him with a genial smile. "Apocalyptic. Referring to the Apocalypse. The last book of the New Testament. The Book of Revelations. If you read, you'd know things like this."

"You're really crazy," Dirk Junior told George. "Hey," he said brightening. "I know. This is some kind of new TV show, right?"

"Wrong," George said.

"Then what the fuck you want with me?" Dirk cried

"Careful," George said. "Your bravado is showing. Me, I don't want anything with you. She's the one that does."

I stepped forward. "I understand you and Manuel know each other."

"Manuel? Who the fuck is that?"

George rapped him on the top of his head with his knuckle. "Mind your mouth."

Dirk Junior scrunched down and rubbed his head. "That hurt."

"It was supposed to."

"You a cop?"

"I was."

"I can always tell."

"I don't care what you can tell. I want you to answer her question."

"I don't know no Manuel."

George rapped him harder. "To improve your memory."

The kid moved farther down in the chair. "I could have you arrested for doin' this."

George came around to the front of the chair and leaned over Dirk Junior. "I've had a long day," he said in a soft voice. "And I rather be home, so believe me when I tell you I'll do whatever it takes to shorten things up here. Now are you going to answer the question or not?"

The kid licked his lips. He looked so pitiful cowering in the chair I almost felt sorry for him.

"Well?" George asked.

"Oh, yeah." The kid sat back up and snapped his fingers. Now he was Mr. Cool. "Now I remember," he said to me. "The kid that worked in your store. You shoulda said that in the first place."

"My error."

"Damned right."

"How'd you meet him?"

"We bumped into each other at The Night Watch and got talking." The Night Watch was a dance club. "He was gonna sell me a palm viper."

Great. What a good idea. Selling a venomous snake to someone like that. I just hoped that when I found Manuel, he'd be alive so I could kill him myself.

"Not now he's not. He's missing."

"So what's that got to do with me?"

"That's what I'm trying to find out." I clenched and unclenched my fingers to warm them up. "Do you know any Russians?"

"Like people from Russia?"

"That's what I just said."

The kid looked at me as if I were crazy. "Why would I know that?"

"You might have run into them."

"Where? Fayette Street?"

I gave up and tried another tack. "You talk to anybody about Manuel?"

The kid shook his head.

"Did you know he was living with me?"

"We didn't talk about that kind of stuff."

"What kind of stuff?"

"Personal stuff."

"What did you talk about then?"

Dirk Junior studied the ceiling while he thought. "Reptiles. Bands. Things like that."

"Anyone ask you about him?"

"Like who?"

I sighed. George was right. This was turning into a dead end.

"Okay," I told him. "At least tell me how Tiger Lily wound up in your backyard."

"Myra's backyard."

"Fine," I agreed. "Myra's backyard."

The way he told the story was long and confusing, but given what I knew it was plausible.

Not that it helped me at all.

Chapter Thirty-Four

"Well, that was a waste of time," George said as he put the key in the ignition of his car.

"You're telling me something I don't know?" I turned up the collar on my jacket.

"Obviously not." George nodded and changed the subject. "Have you spoken to Calli?"

"No. But I should. She was over at the house when I was down in New York."

"So why haven't you?"

I slumped down in the seat and rubbed my arms. "I don't know. I guess I'm still mad at her for lying to me."

George fiddled with the heat.

"Not to mention getting involved with another loser." I glanced at George. He didn't say anything. "Calli said I'm too judgmental. Do you think so?"

"Let's say I think you're attached to your view of reality."

"That's a diplomatic way of saying yes. Why? I'm being pretty good with you, considering."

George touched the tips of his fingers together as he watched a car coming up the street. It slowed down as it went by us, then sped up again.

"I think we're on dangerous ground here. We should change the subject."

"You're right. We should." Two teenagers coming out of a house across the street gave our car the once-over. They probably thought we were narcs. I took a deep breath and let it out. White wisps hung in the air for a few seconds before dispersing. "Okay. You believe what Dirk Junior told us about Tiger Lily?"

"No. You?"

"Not really. Although it's possible."

"Personally, I think his story is bullshit. I think he stole the dog and then pretended to tip Calli off, and she made up this whole other story to tell you so you wouldn't lecture her about Dirk."

"I'm thinking I'd like to give the kid the benefit of the doubt."

"Sucker."

"Maybe."

Actually, the more I thought about Dirk Junior's story, the more I decided George was right. According to Dirk Junior, he and Myra had gone to Calli's house to collect money that Dirk owed Myra, but Dirk didn't have it and Myra decided to take Tiger Lily instead, because she knew she'd be able to sell Lily's puppies.

At first Dirk said no, but Myra kept going and he capitulated, spineless jerk that he is. So Myra took Tiger Lily and chained her up outside. Luckily for Lily, according to Dirk Junior, he had a soft spot for goldens. After listening to her cry for two days, he couldn't stand it anymore. But he knew that talking to Myra was like talking to a tree, so he made an anonymous call to Calli, which was where I came in to the picture.

"This thing is such a mess." I rubbed the back of my neck. I could feel a headache coming on.

"Here, let me do that," George said. He drove with one

hand and massaged my neck with the other. "That good?" he asked.

"Much better."

"Naturally. I'm the best."

"Not to mention humble."

A short time later we pulled into my driveway. George took his hand off my neck and pinched the bridge of his nose. He looked like a man who needed to sleep for twelve hours straight, get up, have something to eat, and go back to bed for another twelve.

"I'll see what I can find out about the Russians," he said.

"Maybe something you turn up will lead us to where they stashed Manuel."

"Maybe," George said, but he didn't sound convinced. He leaned his head back on the seat.

I lit another cigarette. The smoke swirled in front of my face and vanished—just like Manuel had, while I ran down my to-do list for George.

"I'll talk to the daughter and the art dealer again. Maybe I can shake loose something from one of them on what Janet Wilcox did with the money."

"You think the two hundred and fifty thousand could be down in the City?"

"I have to assume that's the case."

"She could have mailed it somewhere."

"The idea has occurred to me."

For all I knew, Janet Wilcox could have buried the money in the middle of the rose garden in Thornden Park, but that wasn't a productive line of thought and I wasn't going to follow it. I stubbed my cigarette out, cracked the window, and tossed the butt into the snow.

"I don't know why I keep smoking these things."

"Because you're an idiot."

"Thanks."

"Any time."

I watched one of my neighbors pull into her driveway and carry her miniature poodle into the house.

"The Russians probably found out about Manuel from Paul," I said.

George shifted his weight around in his seat. "It seems like the most logical possibility," he allowed.

We sat in silence for the next five minutes, neither of us wanting to get out of the car.

Finally I blurted out what I couldn't get the little voice inside my head to stop whispering in my ear. "Truth. You think Manuel's still alive?"

"Truth? Absolutely," George said. "Nothing is happening to him until you get them their money."

"And then when they have it . . ."

"*Adios, muchacho.*"

"And *muchacha,* I'm thinking."

George smiled. It wasn't a reassuring sight. "That's not going to happen."

"I hope not."

"I won't let it."

"Good to know." I opened the door. The cold air rushed in. "Give my regards to Natalie," I said as I got out.

George grunted. "Lay off, will you."

"I was just being polite."

"No, you weren't. You were being bitchy."

"Okay, Dad. I was bitchy."

I watched George pull out of the driveway and go down the street. When the tail lights of his car vanished, I went inside my house. I hadn't put the bottle of Scotch George and I had been drinking away. It was still on the dining room table. I grabbed it and one of the glasses and went upstairs. I peeked into Manuel's bedroom on the way to my own. Bethany and Zsa Zsa were cuddled together in his bed. I tiptoed in and straightened out the comforter. Zsa Zsa opened her eyes, woofed a soft hello, closed her eyes, and went back to sleep.

I clicked on the light in my bedroom and poured myself a drink. I sipped the Scotch while I got ready for bed, but it didn't help. That click in my head that turns everything off didn't come.

I kept tossing and turning as I thought about Paul and the drinks we'd had together in his office and how I'd believed what he'd told me. Some women had no luck with men. I wondered if I was one of them, and then I wondered how the Russians had gotten hold of him and how long it had taken him to die. Then I started thinking about Manuel and where he was and how scared he must be feeling and how when it came down to it this whole thing was my fault and how the clock was ticking away.

Finally I couldn't stay in bed anymore. I threw off the covers, got up, retrieved a yellow legal pad and a pencil from the drawer of my nightstand, and wrote down everybody and everything that I knew about the case. I wrote down Quintillo, Paul and Walter and Janet Wilcox and their daughter Stephanie, as well as Alima, Calli, Dirk, Dirk Junior, and the Russians.

Next I drew arrows connecting people together and wrote down every piece of information, no matter how insignificant, I had about those connections. There was something there. Something that would point me in Manuel's direction. There had to be.

Unfortunately, I couldn't see what it was. It was like having a name on the tip of your tongue but not being able to remember it. Finally, I put the pad on the bed beside me, turned off the light, and closed my eyes. Maybe if I relaxed, it would come to me. It didn't, but eventually I fell asleep anyway.

* * *

I woke up the next day feeling worse than I had when I went to bed. Around nine, after I'd walked Zsa Zsa and talked to Bethany, I started making phone calls. I couldn't get hold of Quintillo, but I did connect with Stephanie's roommate, who told me Stephanie had come back to Syracuse to sort through her parents' belongings.

"Wow," the roommate said to me. "Are things weird these days or what?"

"Very weird." And I hung up.

I could have called Stephanie, but face to face is always better, so I drove over to her parents' house instead. A quarter-sized patch of blue sky was visible in the east. The tree branches were wearing little caps of snow. The asphalt on the main streets was grayed out with salt. As I made a turn onto East Genesee, I spotted a black-and-gray tabby cat gingerly treading its way between two garbage cans, halting every ten steps or so to shake the snow off its paws.

I stopped at the nearest Mini Mart to get some coffee and a doughnut. When I got back in the car, I turned on the radio. The announcer was yammering on about how if it continued snowing the way it had been, we were going to hold the record for the most snow for this month of all the Upstate cities. What a thrill.

From the expression on Stephanie's face when she answered the door, she felt the same way about me that I'd felt about what the radio announcer was saying.

"I don't want to speak to you," she informed me. "You bring bad luck."

"That's a new one."

"It's true."

"You don't believe that, do you?"

Stephanie pursed her lips and looked away.

"I thought not."

The black turtleneck sweater she was wearing made her

look haggard. I'd be willing to guess she'd lost at least five
more pounds since the last time I'd seen her.

"I think you might be interested in what I have to say."

She sniffed. "Doubtful. I'm busy. Now go away." And she
tried to slam the door in my face.

But I had my foot jammed in the door already, so she
couldn't. Doc Martens definitely have their uses.

"I'm sorry. I can't do that," I told her as I pushed it open
and stepped inside. "There are things we have to talk about."

"What things?" Stephanie asked. She seemed a little more
uncertain now that I was in her house.

"Your mother, for one."

"I have nothing to say about her."

"I think you do."

"I'll call the police," Stephanie threatened, but I could tell
from the quaver in her voice that she really didn't mean it.

She was holding herself rigidly, as if she was afraid she'd
shatter if she took a wrong step.

"Go ahead."

I walked into the living room. Stephanie followed behind
me. A black leather suitcase sat in the middle of the room.
Other than that, the place looked pretty much the way it had
the day I'd found her father.

"Did you just get in?"

"About half an hour ago."

"You must have left the City early."

Stephanie looked at me, then looked away. "I haven't been
sleeping well lately." I could tell that even that simple statement cost her.

"Join the club. You staying here?" Given what had happened, I knew that I wouldn't want to.

"It's just for a night or two."

I indicated the room with my chin. "It must be hard to
come back to this. Why aren't you staying with your friend?"

"She's away. What's it to you anyway?"

I favored her with one of my dazzling smiles. "Tell me, how come you wouldn't stay with your Dad when your mom left, but you're willing to stay here now?"

Stephanie flicked a piece of lint off her sweater. "You're the detective. You tell me."

"Did you dislike your father that much?"

Stephanie leaned against the wall and folded her arms over her chest. "Why do you care?"

I looked around some more. "I'm just trying to understand."

"Understand? There's nothing more to understand. They're both dead."

"I know."

"So what do you want with me?"

"I was wondering why you came up."

"The same reason anyone would. To straighten things out."

"I think maybe you had another reason."

"You're right." Stephanie tapped her nails on her upper arms. "I enjoy the snow. Can't get enough of that stuff."

"Yeah. You look like a skier." I ran a finger along the back of one of the chairs. "You been upstairs yet?"

Stephanie swallowed and shifted her weight from her right to her left foot. "I'm planning on sleeping on the sofa."

"So you know what happened."

"The police told me . . . They told me some. I didn't want to hear all of it."

"That was smart." I unzipped my parka.

Over the years, I've come to realize that truth can be an overrated commodity. There are some pictures it's better not to have rattling around inside your head.

Stephanie hugged herself. "I had to go down and identify my mother. I've never done anything like that before."

"Most people haven't," I said gently.

"She called me the morning before she died, you know."
I stayed silent, waiting for her to continue.

"But I wasn't home. The message on my machine said she needed to talk to me." Stephanie bit her lip. "I should have called her back, but I just didn't want to deal. She was nuts, you know. Really crazy. It was like my mother was different people, and you never knew who you were going to get. I should have called, though. Getting a caterer for the Nelsons' anniversary party could have waited."

Stephanie walked over to the sofa, picked up one of the cushions off the floor, and put it back where it belonged. "Not that it matters now. She didn't give a shit about me. I don't know why I should care about her." She was about to replace the second cushion when I heard a noise.

"Are you expecting someone?" I asked.

Stephanie shook her head rapidly from side to side.

A moment later Alima waltzed into the living room. I noticed she was holding a key in her hand.

Chapter Thirty-Five

———

"Who the hell are you?" Stephanie demanded, as she took in Alima's piercings, her skin-tight black leather pants, fire-engine-red sweater, red boots, and fake leopard jacket. "How did you get in here?"

"The normal way. Through the door."

"It was locked."

"No shit. Your daddy gave me a key."

"Why would he do that?" Stephanie asked, her voice a study in confusion. "Are you the cleaning lady?"

Alima put her hands on her hips and curled her lips up in a sneer. "Cleaning lady? Do I look like a cleaning lady to you?"

Stephanie took a step back. "I'm sorry. I just can't think of any other reason you'd have a key."

Alima looked at her, then looked at me and grinned. She had sharp canines, something I'd never noticed before. I wondered if she'd had them filed.

"You want to tell her or should I?" she asked me.

"Why don't you?"

I was interested to hear what she was going to say. Besides, I didn't have the heart.

"Fine. I will." Alima swept her hair off her face with the back of her right hand and paused to fix a barrette, building the tension. "I was your father's friend," she said to Stephanie.

"My father's friend?"

"You know. The reason your mother left." For all the expression in Alima's voice, she might as well have been talking about the weather.

For a second I was sorry I'd let Alima do the talking. It was like watching a lynx getting ready to eviscerate a rabbit. I could see the muscles in Stephanie's throat working as she swallowed, trying to take everything in.

Alima tipped her head to the side and fingered her nose ring in an absentminded way. "Your father said your mother told you about me. I guess she didn't, huh? You two couldn't have been very close."

"How old are you?" Stephanie asked, looking at Alima carefully for the first time.

Alima tossed her hair off her face again. "Old enough to get what I want."

Watching her, I remembered what it had been like to be that sure of myself, of my sexual power.

"I can't believe my father would go out with someone like you."

"Someone like me?" Alima raised an eyebrow. The ring through it moved as well. "What's that supposed to mean?"

"What do you think?"

"I think I'll just pretend you didn't say that." Alima held out her hand. Stephanie ignored it. "Perhaps another time," Alima said putting it down by her side. "In any case, since I was driving by I decided to stop and meet you. I thought it was about time. Especially since we're going to be doing business together."

"Business? We're not doing anything together. Get out."

Stephanie pointed to the door. "Get out right now and leave the key to the house on the table."

"I don't think your daddy would want that."

"I don't give a damn what he wanted."

"You should."

"All I know is what I want, and what I want is for you to get the hell out of here. Now."

Alima looked about as concerned as a cat did upon hearing the word no. "You don't mind if I take a quick look around the house, do you?"

"Didn't you hear what I said?"

"Yes, but I have a cleaning crew coming next week, and I want to make sure the to-do list I'm giving them is complete. Of course, if necessary, I suppose I could postpone them for another week or so, but then I'd have to get a different painter in. I'm sure you understand." Alima turned to me. "I think this place should bring a good price after it's put back together, don't you?"

"What are you talking about?" Stephanie demanded.

Alima's eyes widened. She put her hand to her mouth. "Oh, my God, you mean your father didn't tell you?" she asked in a fake concerned voice. "He left the place to me."

I felt like slapping her.

"That's impossible," Stephanie said. She held out her hand and steadied herself against the arm of the chair.

"No, it's not. Call the lawyer."

"My mother wouldn't have let him do something like that."

"Janet had nothing to say about it. The house was in his name."

Stephanie shook her head. "No. You're lying."

"Am I?" And Alima took her cell out of her bag, hit the power button, and dialed. "Here," she said, holding her StarTAC out to Stephanie. "Talk to the lawyer in charge of probating your father's estate. Ask him. Go on," she said when Stephanie hesitated. "You want to know, don't you?"

Stephanie's hand was shaking as she took the phone and walked into the kitchen. I could hear her saying, "No, he wouldn't. He didn't," over and over again. She looked sick when she came out.

"Told you," Alima said, retrieving her phone from Stephanie's hand.

I don't think Stephanie even noticed.

"How could he have done something like this?" she asked as she sank into the sofa and buried her face in her hands. I noticed she'd bitten her nails down to the quick.

Alima took it upon herself to answer.

"Simple," she said. "He was in love with me. I made him feel important. Not like you or your mother." She put out her hand and studied her nails. "You can fight this in court. But it's going to cost you money. If I were you, I'd settle for the money your mother stole from your father and let it go at that. If you can find it."

Stephanie lifted her head up. Her eyes were dull with shock. "I don't know what you mean," she said.

As I watched Alima weigh Stephanie's answer, I wondered, if you act like fifty when you're eighteen, do you act like eighteen when you're fifty?

Finally Alima said, "I can't believe you don't know what I'm talking about."

"I don't. You're just saying all this stuff to confuse me."

"Am I?"

"Yes, you are."

Alima leaned forward slightly. "Tell me," she said, "what do you think your father did?"

"He was a lawyer."

"He was a lawyer for two Russian mobsters."

Stephanie's eyes widened. Two small red dots appeared on her cheeks. She jumped off the sofa and strode over to where

Alima was standing and shook a finger in front of Alima's chest.

"You're lying," she cried. "I don't know why you are, but you are. I know what he did. I used to spend time in his office. He wrote wills for little old ladies and did house closings and handled divorces and did stuff like that."

Alima shrugged. "Maybe that's the way he started off, I'm not saying it isn't, but people who handle wills for little old ladies don't die the way he did."

Stephanie bit her lip and turned her head away. "I don't believe you. I won't believe you," she said.

Alima gave her a pitying look. "So much the worse for you," she told her before turning to me. "It's your turn," she said to me. "You try and explain the realities of life to her," she said. "I've got other things to do with my time. And by the way," she said to Stephanie, "you should do something about the way you dress. You look like a crow."

"Fuck you."

I grabbed Stephanie's arm just as she was bringing her hand up to punch Alima in the face and dragged her back to the sofa. It took me a half an hour to settle Stephanie down and another half an hour to convince her that Alima was telling her the truth. From the expression on Stephanie's face, I had the feeling it would have been kinder if I'd taken out a gun and shot her.

"My mother never said anything to me about money. She really didn't." I watched Stephanie's eyes well up and the tears begin to fall. They dripped down her cheeks and fell on her sweater. "She told me she had a little money saved up. I thought she was using that.

"I tried to be a good daughter," Stephanie continued, her fingers plucking spasmodically at her pants legs. "I really did. But everything I did was wrong. I never knew what she wanted, and after a while I gave up trying."

Alima paused at the entrance to the living room on her

way up the stairs. She took one look at Stephanie and rolled her eyes.

"Grow up," she said to her. "So your family life stunk. So what? Suck it up and move on."

Stephanie didn't give any sign of hearing her.

"My father was worse, though," she continued. "One day, when I broke a dish, he told me adopting me was my mother's idea and he'd only done it to shut her up. I've never forgotten that."

"He was probably angry," I said.

Stephanie shook her head. "It was more than that. He meant it. I never remember him hugging me. Not even once." She closed her eyes for a few seconds, then opened them. Her cheeks were speckled with little dots of mascara that had fallen off her eyelashes. "I should have stayed in the City," she whispered. "I should never have come back here."

"Why did you?"

Stephanie wiped her cheeks with the back of her right hand, smearing the dots into larger splotches. Her skin glistened with the moisture from her tears.

"I just . . . I didn't . . . I couldn't believe." She took a deep, shuddering breath. "I don't know. I guess I thought coming here would make it real. It would have been better the other way." Her face collapsed and she started to sob.

I couldn't get her to stop, and I couldn't leave her the way she was. After about an hour of trying to get someone to sit with her, I was desperate. I finally dialed Peter Simmone, the psychologist her mother had gone to, and explained the situation. Despite our past meeting, he told me to bring Stephanie over. A point for him.

I managed to coax her into my car. He was waiting for us when I got there. The last I saw of Stephanie, he'd put his arm around her and was guiding her into his office. She was leaning into him, as if she'd fall down without his support.

I turned around and went back to the Wilcox house. I had

a question for Alima, but she'd already gone. Luckily for me, there were no locks on the bottom windows. I pushed one open and went inside. I spent the next hour and a half going over the house from top to bottom, just to make sure the money wasn't there.

It wasn't.

Or if it was, I couldn't find it.

Chapter Thirty-Six

George and I met at the pizza shop near Nottingham Plaza. He was ten minutes late, and I was starting on my second slice when he walked through the door. I waved to him and he nodded to me before giving his order to the girl behind the counter. A moment later he put his plate containing three slices topped with pineapple and ham down on the table and slid into the booth opposite me.

"How can you eat that?" I asked.

"This from a woman who lives on chocolate doughnuts and coffee?" he said as he took off his jacket and carefully laid it next to him on the seat.

"Chocolate is good for you, or haven't you heard?"

"Really?" I watched George peel off the top of a small container of blue cheese dressing and dip his pizza in it. "So what's going on?" he asked.

"I just talked to Stephanie. I don't think she knows anything."

"She could be lying," he said as he took a bite. A line of red-colored oil slid down his chin. He wiped it away with his napkin.

I thought about the expression on her face when Alima mentioned the money. "I don't think so."

"Why?"

I recounted the conversation between Stephanie and Alima.

"Plus I went through the house. The money's not there."

"No reason it should be. If it were me, I'd have it in a bank in the Bahamas by now."

"If it were me, I'd be in the Bahamas by now."

"This is true," George said. He took another bite. "This Stephanie, she could be a really good liar. I've known people that could convince their own mothers they were somebody else's child."

"If what you say is true, why would she be up here?"

George shrugged. "People do illogical things all the time."

"That's helpful."

"But true."

"Maybe. My gut feeling is she doesn't know."

"Your gut feeling? That's what you're going on here?"

"What else do I have?"

George considered that for a moment. "Nothing else, I suppose, when you get right down to it. So what now?"

"I'm going to fly down to New York City and talk to Quintillo."

He took another bite, then reached over for my soda. "You mind?" he asked.

I shook my head and he took a sip.

"And if you come up dry, what then?"

"I'll worry about that when it happens. So what about you? Did you find anything out?"

"Some dibs and dabs. But not a whole hell of a lot, unfortunately. I think I can put names to two of the guys at the bar, but that's it. No addresses, no vehicles, no nothing. They've both got warrants out on felony assault, fraud, and extortion. One of them is a possible ex-KGB."

"Wonderful."

"Phil says he thinks they got in beef with some of their brethren in Brooklyn and decided to set up shop here until things cooled down."

"They probably couldn't resist the climate."

"Pining away for all that snow and ice."

"Reminds them of home."

George finished off his first slice and started in on the second. He was a neat, methodical eater. Which is hard to do with pizza.

"And that's it?"

"I'm hoping to have the names of the other guys for you by tonight."

"It would be nice if you could turn up an address."

"I'm working on it."

"I mean they have to live somewhere."

"How about under a trash can?"

"My money would be in a Dumpster."

George drizzled some more blue cheese dressing on top of his second slice, folded it, and took a bite.

"Don't worry," he told me. "Phil and I are going out later. We'll shake something loose."

"Why's he doing this?"

"He owes me."

"And?"

"He's hoping to pick up some information he can use."

"Anything else?"

"He was a friend of Paul's."

"Makes sense." I glanced at my watch.

"What time's your plane?"

"I still have an hour before I have to be out at Hancock."

"Good. I'll drive you," George said

It almost felt like old times, I thought as I watched George polish off the remains of his last slice.

*   *   *

It was cold in New York City, the kind of raw cold that bites through your bones and makes you want to stay inside, turn on the TV, and order in Chinese. I was waiting for a cab outside the terminal at LaGuardia and wishing I'd brought along another sweater when my cell rang. It was Bethany. She sounded hysterical, but then, that wasn't unusual these days.

"You just got a dozen gladioli delivered to the house," she said. "The note said, *Thinking about you, Manuel*. Gladioli are what people send to funerals."

"Not necessarily," I told her even though that was my association with them as well.

"He's going to die."

"Bethany, he's going to come out of this. These people are just playing with our minds."

"Well, they're doing a good job. I threw them in the trash."

"Okay. Leave them there, but don't throw them out."

"I shouldn't have done that, should I?" And she started to sob. So much for being tactful.

"No harm done." I took a deep breath.

Bethany cried louder. I moved the cell away from my ear.

"Bethany, where's the girl that's staying with you?"

She stopped crying long enough to answer me. "She went off to class. I was just going to go to school when these came. I don't know what to do."

"Don't do anything. I'm calling George. He'll be over."

Bethany sniffed. "He doesn't have to. Really."

"I can see that. He'll be glad to." And I hung up and phoned George.

"I'm not a baby-sitter," he said.

"She shouldn't be by herself now, and there's something else as well." And I told him about the note and the flowers.

"It probably won't lead to anything, but I'll see if I can

trace them. Maybe someone got stupid and used a credit card."

"Maybe," I said although I didn't think so.

"It would be a nice change."

He hung up and I called Bethany back. "George will be over in about twenty minutes."

"Okay." Her voice was very small.

"How's Zsa Zsa?"

"She's fine."

"Good. I'll call you later."

"Promise?"

"Promise."

I wanted to say something else, but I couldn't think of anything except, "Don't worry."

Sometimes words really are inadequate. Or maybe it's that I can't think of the right ones when I need them. As I slipped my cell into my coat pocket, the two people standing in front of me got into a cab. A few seconds later, another cab pulled up in front of me and I slipped inside. In the best-case scenario, the trip into the City from LaGuardia takes twenty minutes, but we were in rush-hour traffic, and that wasn't going to happen this time around unless we sprouted wings.

Traffic had congealed around us and we advanced in fits and starts. I spent the next hour watching the numbers on the meter grow and wondering how Manuel was and thinking about what the flowers and the message meant. Like Bethany, I didn't think the choice of flowers was accidental.

Listening to the wailing of the music coming from the radio of my Pakistani driver mixed in with cars honking their horns didn't improve my mood. I'd just asked the driver to turn his music down when we hit a two-car pile-up before the tolls, and that slowed us down even more.

Finally, we inched our way through and got onto the FDR. But that wasn't much better. It must have been pouring in the

City earlier in the day because there were large puddles on the road that the cars were slogging through, and I finally told the cabbie to get off at the 96th Street exit and take Third Avenue down to Quintillo's apartment.

I didn't know if he'd be there or not, but aside from the gallery it was the only address I had for him. As it turned out, he wasn't. At first I was upset, but his absence turned out to be a good thing. By dint of a good story and three hundred dollars, I managed to convince the super that I was Quintillo's long-lost sister, and he unlocked the door of Quintillo's apartment and let me in to wait. It would be a pity, we both agreed, for me to have to wait outside in weather like this. Especially since it had taken me so long to find him.

The place was hot and stuffy, the way apartments get in New York City when the heat comes on in the winter. Looking around, I'd forgotten how small apartments in the City could be. Even though it was a one-bedroom, the entire place could fit in my living room with space left over to spare. I took off my jacket, stashed it on the sofa, and got to work looking for Janet Wilcox's money. Unfortunately, something that small could be anywhere.

I decided to start in Quintillo's bedroom and then go through his living room, kitchen, and bathroom—in that order. I worked as quickly as I could, but I could see it was going to take a while because Quintillo's place was jam-packed with drawings, canvases, and pieces of sculpture. Evidently he was using it as a storeroom for the artworks he was selling out of the gallery.

I wondered how the hell Quintillo managed to get dressed in the morning, as I edged my way around five bronzes, one of which looked like a Rodin. I looked through his drawers, which were filled with drawings, and tried his closet, which contained sporting equipment, an ironing board, five cases of books, two suits, and three pairs of jeans. Welcome to City living. I checked under the mattress as well, found nothing except some old socks, and moved on to the living room.

I glanced at my watch as I came out. It had taken me half an hour to go through Quintillo's bedroom, and the only thing I knew now that I didn't know before was that he had an awful lot of unsold stock on his hands. As I walked into the living room, I heard footsteps out in the hall. A second later I heard a key turning in the latch. The master of the house had returned.

"Hi," I said when he came through the door. "You wanna do Chinese or Mexican tonight for dinner?"

Chapter Thirty-Seven

Quintillo's mouth dropped open. His eyes widened. He clutched his chest. For a moment, I thought I was going to have to call the EMTs because he was having a heart attack.

"How the fuck did you get in here?" he demanded when he'd recovered enough to talk.

"Oh. I'm your long-lost sister, didn't you know?"

He threw the mail he'd been clutching down on the table and reached in his pocket and pulled out his cell.

"I'm calling the management company right now."

"Don't be mad at the super. He really thought I was your sister."

"You're full of shit. How much did you give that little spic to let you in?"

"That's so un-PC."

"Shut up."

"You know your forehead gets red when you get angry? It's kind of cute." And I gave him my most winning smile. For some reason Quintillo didn't fall down at my feet.

"I'll tell you one thing," he said. "I'm getting my locks changed tomorrow. Let that little spic just try and get a spare key from me. And he can say good-bye to his Christmas bonus."

"I take this to mean we're not dining together?"

Quintillo took a step toward me and shook a finger in my direction.

"I could have you arrested. In fact, I'm going to."

"For what? Breaking and entering? Stealing?"

"How about unlawful entry?"

"Okay," I conceded. "There is that. You could call the police—that's true. Only then you wouldn't know how much trouble you're in."

Quintillo rubbed his chin with the knuckles of his right hand. "Trouble? I'm not in any trouble. You're the one that's in trouble."

"Yes, you are. You're in the Janet Wilcox kind of trouble."

He snorted. "We've been over this already. I told you everything I know about Janet. You have any more questions, go ask her."

"I'd love to, only I can't."

"And why is that?"

"Because it's hard to talk to dead people. Mediums are so unreliable these days."

"She's not dead," Quintillo sneered. "You're trying to con me."

"Am I?" I pointed to his phone. "Call her daughter and find out." And I gave him Stephanie's number in Syracuse.

Quintillo punched in the numbers and waited. "No one's home," he announced.

"So leave a message and she'll call back."

"I don't believe you."

"Why would I lie?"

His eyes moved around the room inventorying the contents as he mulled the question over.

"I didn't take anything," I said.

"I didn't say you did." He pulled the beige cashmere scarf he was wearing around his neck off and folded it in two. "All right," he conceded when he was done. "What happened to her?"

"She walked into the path of an oncoming bus on 42nd Street."

Quintillo gave all his attention to laying the scarf on the back of a green leather armchair. Then took off his coat, carefully folded it in two, and placed it over the scarf. When he was through, he looked at me.

"You know, now that you mention it, I remember hearing something about something like that on the radio, but I wasn't really paying attention."

"Neither was she. That was the problem."

"Poor Janet," Quintillo mused. "She was one of those people that nothing ever worked out for."

He walked into his kitchen, got a glass off the sideboard, and opened the freezer. I heard the click of ice cubes going into the glass. Then he came back out, took a bottle of Stolichnaya off the desk in the living room, poured himself a couple of fingers, and drank half of it down.

"Want one?" he asked.

"I'll pass. Too much to do."

"Suit yourself," Quintillo said and took another sip. "It's unbelievable when I think about it," he said to me. "This woman whom I haven't seen in—I don't want to tell you in how many years—calls me up out of the blue and asks me if she can stay with me and out of the kindness of my heart . . ."

"And fifteen hundred dollars," I interjected.

Quintillo continued as if I hadn't said anything, ". . . I say yes, and since then all I've gotten is trouble. She was like Typhoid Mary, trailing misfortune in her wake."

"That analogy isn't really correct. Typhoid Mary has gotten a really bum rap. It turns out that . . ."

Quintillo held up his hand. "It's been a long day, so do me a favor and spare me the history lesson. I'm not interested."

I didn't say anything.

Quintillo finished the rest of his Stoli and poured himself another finger. "Just tell me what you want. I have an opening down in Soho I have to get ready to go to."

"Basically, I have a problem I'm hoping you can solve for me."

"And why would I want to do that?"

"Because otherwise you'll be a very unhappy person."

"And your reason for saying that?"

I looked around his apartment. "So how's your business doing anyway? I wonder if all these works of art have their provenances in order."

"They're fine," Quintillo said, but I could tell from the way he said it that it wasn't true.

"All of them?" Most art dealers are part charm, part high-powered salesman, and part con man.

"Yes. All of them. Get to the point."

"The point is this. Janet Wilcox took two hundred and fifty thousand dollars that didn't belong to her, and now the people she took it from want it back."

"So you told me."

"If they don't get it, they're prepared to kill a very dear friend of mine."

"That's too bad, but what makes you think I have it?"

"Because she stayed with you."

"That's pretty shaky."

"Maybe, but it's the only thing I've got."

"I told you. I haven't seen this woman in years. Why should she give me two hundred and fifty thousand dollars?"

"She could have asked you to hold it for her."

"I wouldn't trust me with that. Why would she?"

"Maybe she told you it was something else."

"She didn't. The only thing she left behind was a package of dried fruit. You're welcome to look through it if you want."

"Maybe she hid it somewhere and didn't tell you."

"I guess that's possible," Quintillo conceded. "Although I don't see why she would do something like that."

"Me either," I conceded. "But it's a possibility I'd like to eliminate."

Quintillo shrugged. "You want to look around, be my guest. Just don't take too long."

"Thanks."

I didn't tell him I'd already started.

"What I want to know is why the hell Janet Wilcox chose me?"

"I think she thought you were her friend."

"That's sad." Quintillo fished an ice cube out of his glass with the tip of his finger and put it in his mouth. "My dentist tells me this is a bad habit," he said as he began to crunch down on it. "He says I'm going to chip the enamel on my teeth."

Then he turned on the television and stood in front of it and watched the news as I went through the rest of his place. I had a feeling it was going to be a waste of time, and it was. I went through the motions anyway, because I couldn't afford to leave any possibility unexamined.

"No luck, huh?" Quintillo asked when I was done.

"Nope."

"I didn't think you'd find anything."

The radiator next to the window in the living room clanked. I skirted the chair and stood next to Quintillo.

"What did Janet Wilcox do when she left here?"

Quintillo's eyes left the screen for a moment.

"How do you mean?"

"Did she say anything? Do anything?"

Quintillo thought for a moment. "She told me she'd rented a place for herself and thanked me for allowing her to stay here. That's about it."

"What else?"

"She had this big suitcase, so I offered to take it down for her while she went and got her car. It seemed the least I could do." Quintillo screwed up his mouth while he tried to recall the sequence of events. "I think it took her about fifteen minutes to get it. She'd had to park up around 85th and First. Actually, I think driving in city traffic freaked her out.

"She buzzed me from downstairs and I came down with the suitcase and put it in her trunk. Then we hugged and she thanked me again and drove away, and that was the last I saw or heard of her."

"What kind of car was she driving?"

"Nothing very sexy. One of those Volvo station wagons that soccer moms drive."

"Anything else?"

Quintillo shook his head. "Not that I can remember."

I gave him my card. "If you remember anything, anything at all, please call me."

"Is there a finder's fee or anything like that?"

"Two thousand dollars."

I didn't have it, but I'd get it.

"Fine." Quintillo slipped my card in his wallet. "If I hear of anything, I'll be in touch."

That had been a waste of time, I decided as I went down the stairs. I was walking out the front door of the apartment building and wondering if it was too late to catch the next flight back to Syracuse when it hit me.

Janet Wilcox's car. I'd forgotten all about it. It was the only place I could think of that I hadn't looked. Hopefully, the police hadn't impounded it yet. On the way up to the Bronx, I called George and asked him to check my notes for the license plate number of Janet Wilcox's vehicle.

Chapter Thirty-Eight

George hadn't called back by the time I left Quintillo's apartment. I thought about phoning him to see what the holdup was, but managed to control my impulse. Not easily, but I did. I was also not happy to see that it was raining again. Cabs were scarce, and by the time I got one, my jacket was damp and my hair was wet.

I watched the beads of water clinging to the windows of the cab I was in as we charged up Third Avenue. Deliverymen on bikes darted between the moving cars. People at intersections jumped over large puddles caused by the storm sewers overflowing. Pedestrians huddled under umbrellas trying to keep the rain off. Red and yellow lights from the cars reflected off the wet asphalt. Neon store signs glowed in the dark.

As we moved through Spanish Harlem, the stores got smaller, the traffic lighter, and the sidewalks had fewer people on them. Turning onto a side street I watched three men, their hair slick with water, struggling to unload a sofa from a moving van while an elderly woman stood in the doorway of a run-down building holding the door open for them.

A little farther up, two squad cars were parked kittycorner

to a vacant lot, partially blocking traffic. A group of people were arguing with the two policemen. A woman wearing a down jacket over what looked like a nightgown was being held back by a teenage boy. He reminded me of Manuel. The icy feeling in the pit of my stomach started to grow again. I took a deep breath and made myself focus on Janet Wilcox's car.

God, I hoped that the police hadn't impounded it. Down in Manhattan, they came and towed you away in a heartbeat. I was counting on traffic rules and enforcement being a little laxer in the Bronx.

As the taxi headed onto the Third Avenue Bridge, a large neon sign winked on and off through the fog. I was just thinking it reminded me of a Cyclops when George called.

"I was getting worried," I told him.

"Well, it might be helpful if you organized things a little better," he said to me. "It would make things easier to find. Just a suggestion."

"I'll bear that in mind for the next time."

"Which I hope there isn't going to be. Got something to write with?"

"I will in a second." I fished a pencil and piece of paper out of my backpack. "So how's life in the snowbelt?" I asked George as I scribbled down the numbers he'd just given me.

"Snowing. We've got another five inches so far today."

"Glad I'm down here."

I could hear the squeak of George's chair as he turned. He must be sitting in front of his computer.

"The flowers turned out to be a bust. No big surprise there. The order was phoned in, and the credit card turned out to be stolen."

"Why am I not surprised?"

"To make matters even better, Phil tells me that in Russia they have this thing where you send even-numbered flowers for funerals and odd-numbered floral arrangements for happy occasions."

I asked the question even though I knew what the answer would be.

"How many gladioli were there?"

"Ten."

"Wonderful."

The knot that seemed to have taken up permanent residence in my stomach got a little bit tighter. George coughed. I could hear the murmur of the television going in the background.

"These guys are really cute," George said. "They send us a reminder, and we can't prove anything. I should have had Phil waiting outside. He could have followed them."

"We didn't know they'd taken Manuel."

"Yeah, but we knew they didn't want to talk to you about coming to their house for tea."

"I take this to mean you haven't made any more progress."

"We turned up another name, but we can't attach an address to him."

I realized I was tapping my fingers against the car window. I couldn't seem to stay still.

"Syracuse isn't that large."

"It's large enough. It's not New York City, but it's not Oren either. It's harder to get lost, but not impossible. Anyway, they could be living in Clay or Minoa or B'Ville. We're going to start going through every strip joint in the county tonight. Maybe they're hanging out in one of them."

"Tough assignment."

"That's what I said." There was a click on the line. "Hold on," George said, "it might be Phil." But it wasn't.

"You think Phil's outfit would spot us the two hundred and fifty thousand if we can't find the money in time?" I asked George.

"I don't know. There isn't much in it for them."

"Mafia guys."

"Low-level Mafia guys."

"Well, you know what they say. If you want to find out what the CEO of a company is doing, ask the cleaning staff."

"You just made that up."

"It doesn't mean it isn't true." The taxi lurched to one side, and I grabbed the door handle to keep from sliding across the seat. "I don't understand why they don't have information on these guys. They must have wives and girlfriends. I'm sure they're calling them."

"I'm sure they are, but there's only so far Phil can go unofficially. As it is, he's stretching the line pretty thin. For another thing, these guys are using their cells, not land lines. And thirdly, when we get down to it—we can't tie these clowns to anything. We can't tie them to Wilcox's death. We can't tie them to Santini's disappearance. We can't tie them to Manuel's disappearance. We can't even tie them to the friggin' flowers, for Christ's sake."

"I know. I know." I changed the topic to one a little less depressing. "How's Bethany doing?"

"The same way she was when I came over this morning. Badly. The only thing that's keeping her together is taking care of Zsa Zsa."

"More guilt. Just what I need. Thank you so much," I said to George as the taxi headed into the Bronx.

I was looking out the window. Piles of garbage bags were stacked in front of five-story brick buildings. Spindly trees glittered under the streetlights. Most of the cars parked along the curbs were cheaper than the models in Manhattan, and the people out on the street were dressed for warmth instead of style.

"Anytime," he said. He paused for a moment, then said, "Maybe I should talk to some of Manuel's friends. See if they know anything."

"I already have. They don't."

"It never hurts to reinterview."

"I don't think they'll talk to you."

"Oh, yes, they will." George's voice was grim.

"Fine." I gave him the list. Even though George would never admit it, I knew his lack of success finding anything was gnawing away at his guts. "I'll call you when I find Janet Wilcox's car."

"You do that," George said and clicked off.

Ten minutes later the driver dropped me in front of the house Janet Wilcox had stayed at. The lights in the lower apartment were on. It looked as if someone was home. I climbed the steps and knocked. An elderly, heavyset woman in jogging pants and a bright fuchsia sweatshirt with the slogan *Grandmother of the Year* emblazoned across her chest, answered the door. She had a towel slung over one shoulder and was holding a wooden spoon in the other. The smell of roasting chicken floated out of the door.

"Yes?" she said peering up at me.

I glanced at the name on the mailbox. "Are you Mrs. Marino?"

"If you're selling anything, you'll have to come back when my husband's home."

"It's nothing like that." I introduced myself as Janet Wilcox's sister.

"Her sister?" Mrs. Marino studied my face. "You don't look like her sister."

"Half-sister. Same mother, different fathers."

Mrs. Marino shook her head. "All these—what do they call them—blended families. Things were a lot less complicated in my day, I can tell you that. You got married and you stayed married. Period. Whether you liked each other or not. Not that anyone asks my opinion." She narrowed her eyes and inspected me carefully. "So why are you here again?"

I gave her the story I'd come up with in the taxi. "My sister was supposed to meet us down in the City for a family gathering. She never showed up, and when I couldn't get her on the phone I decided to come up and see what's going on."

"Why not call the police?" Mrs. Marino wiped her hands on the dish towel on her shoulder.

I gave an apologetic shrug. "I don't want to say anything bad about her, but she was going out with this man . . . and frankly, I'm afraid she might have taken off with him again."

Mrs. Marino grimaced. "Just like my sister, may she rest in peace. Ran off with a gambler who left her with three children." She shook her head. "I swear some women don't have the sense that God gave them."

"My sister doesn't."

Mrs. Marino clicked her tongue against her teeth. "I haven't seen her in days. Not that I usually keep track, you understand," she said quickly. "I always tell my tenants a person rents a place from me and it's like she isn't here."

Why didn't I believe that?

Mrs. Marino made an adjustment to her towel. "The only reason I've been looking for her is that I need to talk to her about the rent. She's only paid up for one month, so I need to know what her plans are. If she's not going to stay, I have to get the place cleaned out."

"I'll get her daughter to call you."

Mrs. Marino nodded.

"I was thinking, do you know if my sister took her car?"

"How should I know that?"

"I assume she was storing it in your garage."

"Oh, no." Mrs. Marino put a wisp of gray hair back under her hairnet with her free hand. "There's no room down there for something like that."

"Do you know where she put it?"

Mrs. Marino shrugged. "I suppose on the street along with everyone else's." She turned to go. "If you don't mind, I have a chicken in the oven . . ."

I took a step forward. "I was wondering if I could just go upstairs for a moment and look around."

Mrs. Marino gave me another hard look, then gestured for me to come in. The house was immaculate. The hall table and the tables in the living room were all overflowing with family pictures. I followed her into the kitchen. A pan full of hand-rolled pasta was drying on the kitchen table. An old cast-iron pan on top of the stove was bubbling with sauce. If my stomach wasn't turning and twisting, it would have made me want to eat.

"You know," she said as she opened a drawer and took out a small, square tin can. "I'm seventy-six years old." I watched her pry the lid off and go through the contents. "Ah, here we are," she said. She handed me a key on a piece of red wool.

"You don't get to be my age without learning to mind your own business. I've done that with my children and their spouses and my grandchildren and I've found it works out just fine. Things have a way of arranging themselves the way they want to anyway regardless of what we do."

She pointed to the key. "Don't forget to return this when you're done."

"I won't."

"They cost money to make, you know. And I either want the next month's rent, or I want your sister's belongings out of here, you understand?"

"Perfectly."

"Good. My mother always said that a woman alone was trouble." She turned and opened the oven door. "If you wouldn't mind letting yourself out, I have to baste the chicken."

I did as requested.

Things looked exactly the way they had the last time I'd been in Janet Wilcox's flat. As far as I could see, nothing had been moved. But this time I really went through the place. I opened up every cabinet and went through every drawer. I took them out and examined the sides and the bottoms to make sure Janet hadn't taped the money to the bottom of them.

I looked behind the two sinks and in the toilet bowl tank. I took all the pillows off the sofa and easy chairs and ran my hands in the cracks formed by the junctures between the bottom and the sides. Then I tipped them over and looked underneath.

I lifted up the rug in the living room and the bedrooms. I stripped the bed and tipped the mattress off the box spring. I went through the hall and the bedroom closets inch by inch, but all I found were dust bunnies and a couple of old gum wrappers. I tapped on the baseboards and the walls, but they were solid. Last but not least, I went through Janet Wilcox's suitcase. I folded and unfolded every piece of clothing in it. I went through her toiletry bag and looked in her shoes.

I wanted to believe her suitcase had some sort of secret compartment, but I knew it didn't. It was just an ordinary piece of luggage that she'd probably bought at some place like Marshall's. The only thing that was unusual was that I couldn't find an address book or anything of that ilk. I knew she hadn't been carrying it in her bag. Maybe she'd kept it in the car.

By the time I was done putting everything back in order, my arms were aching, my nose was itching from the dust, and I was no nearer to finding the two hundred and fifty thousand dollars than I had been when I'd come up here.

"You find anything that would help you?" Mrs. Marino asked as I handed her the key.

"Unfortunately not."

"Don't worry. Your sister will call you when this guy dumps her. Believe me. I know." And she closed the door and went back to her cooking.

* * *

The rain had stopped , but it was still cold and damp. I zipped up my jacket and turned up the collar and put my gloves on and began my search for Janet Wilcox's car. I started on the block I was on and then began walking in ever widening circles. Of course, there was a chance that the car wasn't even on the street. Wilcox could have stored it in a garage or the police could have towed it. But right now, in light of any evidence to the contrary, I had to assume that Janet Wilcox had off-loaded her suitcase, then parked her car nearby—relatively speaking.

Occasionally I'd pass a dog-walker or someone coming home with a bag of groceries, but mostly the streets were quiet. People were in their houses eating dinner or watching television. I wondered what Manuel was eating as I walked through the streets. Not much, I was willing to wager. The only thing I was grateful about was that Manuel's mother was still away. I couldn't imagine what I would say to her when she came home.

I touched base with George and Bethany. Nothing new in Syracuse. Finally, an hour and a half later, I lucked out and located Janet Wilcox's car. It was parked five blocks away, at the end of a residential street, right behind an alternate-side-of-the-street-parking sign. The windshield was covered with tickets. Another week or so of that, and the city would prob-ably get around to towing it.

I peeked inside. The seat and the floor, unlike Janet Wilcox's house or the flat she'd been staying in, was littered with bottles and newspapers and pieces of paper. I had the odd feeling that this was the place Janet Wilcox had really lived in. That this was her home. I wondered if I'd find her address book as I tried the door. It was locked.

I glanced around. No one was out on the street and even if they were, it was dark out, which would make it difficult to see what I was doing. I hoped the car wasn't alarmed as I took the little handy-dandy tool that Manuel had given me out of my backpack and stepped off the curb and walked over to the driver's side.

If it were alarmed, I'd just walk away. If anyone came after me, I'd deny it. One of the advantages of being white, female, middle-aged, and marginally middle class, is that people don't link you with criminal activity. They leave that for the young, teenage blacks and Hispanics.

I looked around one more time. The street was empty. I popped the lock and waited. Nothing went off. I opened the door, slid inside, and quietly closed the door behind me. The odor was the first thing that hit me. It had a musty smell to it, which was overlaid with the odors of mildewing fabric and old pizza, but since the windows were electronic and I couldn't open them, I was just going to have to live with it. Anyway, I've been in places that have smelled a lot worse.

I left the interior cars lights off—it seemed better to attract as little attention as possible—and started going through the stuff on the seat and on the floor. It turned out to consist mostly of old newspapers, empty soda bottles, and candy wrappers, plus an old towel that smelled of mildew.

I leaned over and opened the glove compartment next. I found the usual stuff people keep in there. An insurance card made out to one Janet Wilcox. The car manual. Receipts for repairs. A Ziplock bag full of quarters for the parking meters. A couple of old candy wrappers. And then, stuffed in the back, I found something that looked as if it could be a possible lead.

Chapter Thirty-Nine

I called George as I walked toward the subway.

"Listen," I told him. "I found a copy of a UPS transaction form in the glove compartment of Janet Wilcox's car. She sent a package shortly after she arrived in New York to a woman out in Adams, a Mrs. Bonnie Gilbert."

"The name doesn't ring a bell."

"No. But the timing is right, so it might be what we're looking for."

"I don't get it. Whatever happened to wire transfers? Who would send a quarter million dollars in cash through the mail?"

"Maybe someone who's desperate. I think we should go talk to this lady."

"You want me to drive out there now?"

I looked at my watch.

"It's too late. Why don't you hold off until tomorrow morning? I'm figuring on taking the bus up from Port Authority."

"The bus? Boy, you travel in style."

"That's what everyone always says about me. It's the only thing that's running. I should get in to Syracuse somewhere around six-thirty in the morning. Why don't I call and you come and pick me up and we'll drive up to Adams together."

"See you in the a.m." And George clicked off.

I was a couple of blocks away from the subway when I called Stephanie and told her about the car and her mother's clothes.

"Let Alima handle it," she snapped, hanging up before I could reply.

I'd like to think I'd be more charitable, but the truth is I'd probably act the same way in similar circumstances. I stowed my phone, got my Metrocard out and went down the stairs to the subway station.

When I lived in the City, I used to ride the subway all the time, but it had been a while since I had. When I'd left, the subways were dangerous. They're a lot safer now, but the platforms still look grim with their white tile walls and cement floors and dim lighting. The Number 6 is one of the busiest lines in the City, but it was way past rush hour, and there were only a handful of people on the platform. We all stayed close to each other—but not too close. Just near enough to keep within easy eye range.

About twenty minutes later, a train rumbled in. The car I stepped into was new, but kids had already scratched their tags into the glass in the windows. It looked worse than the graffiti. And you couldn't wash it off.

I had nothing on me to read except the UPS paper I'd gotten from Janet Wilcox's car. After I got tired of doing that, I spent the rest of the time watching the people across from me. A group of teenagers were laughing and talking, but everyone else was slumped in their seats looking pale-faced and slack-jawed, their faces devoid of expression, anxious to get home.

I called George when we got to Utica, and he was waiting for me when my bus pulled in. He handed me a coffee and a bagel with cream cheese as I walked through the door into the terminal.

"Here," he said. "I figured you could use this."

"Thanks."

"How can you sleep on a bus?"

"Have enough Scotch and you can sleep on anything."

George grunted.

"Just kidding."

"No, you're not."

"Okay. So I'm not. What's going on up here?"

"Nothing. You were right about Manuel's friends. Nobody knows anything."

"Too bad. I was hoping I was wrong."

"Me too."

We stopped by my house so I could take a shower and change my clothes. By the time I'd finished talking to Bethany and petting Zsa Zsa, it was a little before nine. George and I left my house ten minutes later. We stopped at the Mini Mart and got some more coffee and hit the road. Right after we got on Route 81, George got a call on his cell.

He nodded and said, "Okay," into the receiver a couple of times. Then he said, "Thanks. We'll be in touch," powered down, and tossed his phone on the seat next to him. "That was Phil," he said to me.

"I thought maybe it was."

"I asked him to run Bonnie Gilbert through the computer for us."

"And?"

"And nothing. She's an old lady. A ninety-one-year-old lady, to be precise."

"You're kidding."

George took a sip of his coffee and changed lanes.

"Nope. Why would Janet Wilcox be sending the money to a ninety-one-year-old woman out in the middle of God-knows-where?" he said.

"Maybe we're wrong. Maybe she wasn't sending her the money. Maybe she was sending her a knitting pattern."

"Now there's an example of blatant ageism, if I ever heard one."

"You going to report me to the PC police?"

"Immediately." George handed me his coffee, and I put it back in one of the cup holders. "The Russians should be calling soon."

"I'm aware of that."

"Phil and I have been talking."

I waited. The mounds of snow piled up on the margins of the road were black with car emissions. George took his eyes off the road and looked at me.

"Even if it turns out that this Bonnie Gilbert has the money, we still have some serious decisions we have to make."

"I know," I said to George.

George went back to looking at the road. "I know you know."

"I just want Manuel back. I don't care about anything else."

"That's what we're going to try to ensure."

It was quiet in the car for a few seconds. I could hear the tires turning on the macadam. I opened the window a crack, then reached into my backpack, got out a cigarette from the pack, and lit it.

"Phil wants to bring everyone in on this," I said as I put the match in the ashtray.

George didn't say anything.

"He already has, hasn't he? Hasn't he?" I repeated.

George reached over and turned on the radio. "He didn't have a choice."

We spent the rest of the trip in silence.

* * *

The town of Adams is situated up north. It's located on Route 11, between Pulaski and Watertown, one of those places that, if I had to guess, had sprung up on the crossroads to service the travelers coming through. But then the Thruway got built, leaving Route 11 to its own devices. Now the town is a cluster of houses and a few stores hanging on as best they can.

We found Bonnie Gilbert's house without any trouble. As we pulled up on the side of the road, I realized we should have called to make sure she was there, but then it occurred to me: Where the hell would a ninety-year-plus woman be going? George turned off the ignition and looked at me.

"So what are we going to say?" he asked.

"I'm waiting for inspiration to strike."

"You don't have a plan?"

"No. Do you?"

"No." George opened the car door. "This is going to be interesting."

The cold air rushed in. It was so icy, it hurt to breathe. The sky was a wash of pale blue. The house, a brown-shingled affair, was surrounded by cedars that had been allowed to grow taller than they should have. The driveway contained a battered pickup truck and an old station wagon. Two snowmobiles sat off to one side.

As George and I walked up the steps to the porch, a dog started barking. The barking got louder as I rang the bell.

I heard a "Just a minute." A few seconds later, a tired-looking, middle-aged woman came to the door. An apricot-colored miniature poodle followed on her heels.

"Yes?" she said.

"We're looking for Bonnie Gilbert," I told her.

"I'm sorry," she said. "But she isn't seeing anyone right now. You'll have to come back another time."

"We came from Syracuse."

"You should have called first. She's sick." And she closed the door in our faces.

"That went well," George remarked as we walked back to the car.

"Didn't it though."

"So what do you think?" George asked when we were sitting in his car again.

"I think I'd like to know who that woman is."

"Me too." He put his key in the ignition switch and turned on the engine. "I think it's time we talked to the locals."

"I saw a grocery store two blocks back."

"My thought exactly."

The store was small to begin with and felt even smaller when I stepped inside because it was crammed from bottom to top with everything from canned soup to antifreeze. Turn too fast and you'd knock something over.

The man standing behind the counter looked as if he'd been standing in the same spot for the last thirty years and would be there for the next twenty. His face reminded me of one of those apple dolls that they sell at county fairs, all crumpled in on itself. His eyes widened when I came in. They got even wider when he saw George.

"What can I do for you folks?" he asked.

He propped his elbows on the counter and waited for our answer. We were probably the first new people he'd seen in the last couple of weeks. Maybe even longer.

"I'll take a pack of Camels," I said.

"You're not from around up here, are you?" he asked. Then he answered his own question. "Most people living in the area buy these at the reservation store," he said as he got the Camels down from a shelf and put a pack of matches on top. "It's getting so it hardly pays for me to carry them. Damned governor," he muttered. "But you don't want to hear about my problems. So what brings you up this way?"

"The newspaper in Syracuse sent us," I said as I pushed a twenty-dollar bill across the counter.

"Syracuse?" He made it sound as if he were talking about the South Pole. "What do they want with us?" he asked as he gave me my change.

"Well, I don't think it would be telling if I said that we're up here to interview Bonnie Gilbert."

"Bonnie Gilbert?" The man snorted. "What on earth for?"

"The paper wants to do an article on people in their nineties. Their views on how the world has changed. That kind of thing."

"Well, you people down in Syracuse aren't very sharp, are you? Bonnie's in her fifties."

I looked incredulous. "You're kidding me, right?"

The man cackled gleefully. "If she's in her nineties, I got to tell you she's done a darn good job of fooling me."

"Can I ask what she looks like?"

"Maybe five-five. Dull brown hair. Got these front teeth that are bucking out."

I pretended to think. "Doesn't sound like the description we've got. Sure you're right?"

The man squared his shoulders. " 'Course I'm right. She comes in here most every day."

"Well, you should know." I pocketed my cigarettes and my change. "Thanks. I guess I should call my editor and see what he wants me to do."

"Guess you should. In her nineties, eh?" He was still laughing when George and I left the store.

"We go back," George said as we drove away.

"Absolutely."

This time when Bonnie Gilbert came to the door, George shouldered his way in.

"I told you, Bonnie Gilbert isn't feeling well," she cried. "Now get out of here or I'm going to call the police."

George corrected her. "What you said, to be precise, was that she wasn't receiving visitors."

I chimed in. "We talked to the guy in the grocery store. He pretty much described you as Gilbert," I told her. "My problem is, according to the information I received, you're supposed to be ninety years old."

Bonnie Gilbert put her hands on her hips and tried to look tough, but the expression on her face betrayed her. She was looking at us as if we were the nightmare she knew would arrive on her doorstep someday. For a moment, I felt as if I'd wandered into somebody else's dream.

"I don't know what you're talking about," she insisted.

"I think you do." George raised an eyebrow and clicked his tongue against the roof of his mouth. "Ninety years old, and you don't look a day over fifty. How about that. I'm sure there are lots of people who'd love to hear your secret."

Bonnie Gilbert absentmindedly picked up the poodle that had been dancing around her feet and cradled it in her arms.

"Who are you?"

"People that have developed an interest in you," I replied.

As I watched her, I couldn't help thinking that whatever her age, she hadn't led an easy life. She wasn't wearing any makeup. A rectangular patch of sunlight from one of the windows was playing across her cheeks, exposing every line and pore and age spot in her face. Her brown hair was dull and brittle and looked as if someone had hacked at it with a dull scissors.

The clothes she was wearing—jeans, a man's flannel shirt, and a down vest—had been washed so many times, the colors were a memory of what they'd been. Bonnie Gilbert looked as bleached out as her clothes.

"Listen," George went on. "We don't care who you really are or what you've done."

"You have no cause to talk that way to me," Bonnie Gilbert protested in a cracking voice.

"Sure I do," George said.

I stepped forward. "We want the package Janet Wilcox sent you."

Bonnie Gilbert widened her eyes in a pantomime of innocence. "What package?"

"This package." And I held out the UPS receipt.

Bonnie Gilbert put the poodle down and took the slip from me. Her lips moved as she read it. While she did, a large, long-haired, black-and-gray cat skirted the edge of the room, jumped up on one of the windows, and fixed us with a baleful glance.

"They must have delivered it to someplace else," she said. "See." She pointed to the bottom. "I never signed for it."

"Really." George rocked back and forth on the balls of his feet as he stared at Bonnie Gilbert. After a few seconds she began to fidget. "You like history, Bonnie?"

"History?" She sounded confused. Unsure of where George was heading.

"I do. I make my living teaching it. Maybe I like it because it's like a gigantic puzzle. You get certain pieces together, and suddenly everything becomes clear. You're in your fifties, aren't you?"

Bonnie licked her lips. "Why?"

George ignored her question and kept on going. "That would put you in your late teens or early twenties in the seventies. A time of great upheaval in this country, what with the war and all."

"So?"

"There were all these people running around then, thinking they were going to save the world. Robbing banks to get money to help finance their causes. Setting off explosives. Sometimes people got killed."

Bonnie didn't say anything.

"The FBI never caught all the radicals. Some of them went to Canada, and others of them got birth certificates and

Social Security numbers of people who had died and constructed whole new lives for themselves."

"What does that have to do with me?" Bonnie Gilbert whispered.

"Nothing. I'm just talking about history." George scratched his cheek and gave her a speculative look. "I hear the FBI is still offering rewards for information leading to the capture of those fugitives. But I'm sure you know that."

"Why would I?"

"You tell me."

Bonnie Gilbert hugged herself, ignoring her poodle, who was standing on her hind legs, scratching at her jeans.

"What happened in the past isn't our concern," George continued. "But we'll make it our business if you don't hand over the package you got from Janet Wilcox."

Bonnie Gilbert looked close to tears as she scurried out of the room. A few seconds later she was back.

"Here." She put the package in George's hand.

He unwrapped it. The money was there.

"It was supposed to be for Janet's and my old age," she told me. I guess she thought I was the nicer one. "We were going to buy a house in Florida."

"Unfortunately, I don't think that Janet will be joining you," I said.

She gave me a blank look.

"She stepped out in front of a bus in New York City."

"I don't believe you."

"Believe it. It's true."

Bonnie Gilbert swallowed a couple of times. She looked dazed.

"Can I ask you why Janet sent you the money?"

She shook her head and stared out the window. The cat did the same. A blue jay perched on the branch of one of the cedars for a few seconds, then flew away. I repeated my ques-

tion. Bonnie Gilbert acted as if I hadn't spoken and continued looking out the window.

"I need to get that apple tree cut down come spring. It's
half dead," she mused. Her voice was flat. "Maybe I'll get
me one of those Japanese maples. I always liked those,
though they do tend to be kinda fussy. I'll ask Kent. He'll
know."

"The package," I said. "Why did you get it?"

She finally looked at me.

"I thought you'd know. You seem to know everything
else."

"I don't."

"I'm Janet's half-sister."

"I didn't think she had any siblings."

"Just me." Bonnie Gilbert began playing with the zipper
on her down vest. "Same father. Different mothers. Mine
moved out to Seattle. We lost touch. When I came back from
Canada, I took a chance and called her. We were the only one
each of us had. Even if we couldn't tell anyone."

When George and I left the house, Bonnie Gilbert was sitting in the living room staring at the wall, while her poodle
jumped off and on her lap.

"Tell me," I asked George as we headed for his car. "How
did you know?"

"I didn't. I took a guess."

"Based on what?"

"Her age. The fact that she assumed someone else's identity. It was the only explanation that made sense."

George and I got into his car.

"What do you think she did?" I asked as we pulled away
from the curb.

"I don't know. Maybe robbed a bank. Set off explosives.
Possibly killed someone in the commission of a crime."

"Are you going to tell anyone about her?"

George shook his head. "Living up here. You ask me, it's worse than being in prison."

"The FBI wouldn't agree."

"I'm aware of that."

I leaned over and kissed George on the check. "You're a nice man."

"That's what I keep trying to tell you."

"I know."

Suddenly I was overcome with the need to sleep. I leaned my head on George's arm and closed my eyes. The week had finally caught up with me.

Chapter Forty

When my cell went off, George and Phil stopped talking and focused their attention on me. I grabbed it off the coffee table.

"Hello," I said.

It was the call I'd been waiting for. I nodded to Phil and George. They sat down on the sofa next to me, one on each side.

"You have our possession?" the Russian asked.

"Yes."

"Good. We will arrange a transfer."

"I want proof of life first."

"Proof of life?" he scoffed. "What you think this is? A movie?"

"Hey, quid pro quo. I don't get what I want, you don't get what you want." I pressed the off button and let out the breath I didn't know I'd been holding.

"You did good," Phil said to me.

He was so sure of himself. At least he acted the part. Closely shaved. Impeccably dressed, with a knife pleat in his pants and shoes shined to a high gloss. I wondered what he was like when he was home alone.

"What if he doesn't call back?" I said.

I realized my hands were shaking. I wiped my palms on my jeans. They were slick with sweat.

"He will," Phil said. "He has to." And he picked up the remote and went back to clicking channels. "You gotta have some balls."

"Fuck you."

He laughed and settled in to watch something on the History Channel. Half an hour later, my cell rang again. It was Manuel.

"Robin," he said.

The connection was poor. He sounded as if he was underwater.

"Oh, my God. How are you? Where are you?"

But he didn't answer.

"Manuel?"

"This is what you wanted?" the Russian asked.

"Yes," I whispered as Zsa Zsa climbed up in my lap. She began to whine.

Outside, my neighbor began using his snowblower on the sidewalk in front of his house. The noise made it hard to hear. I ducked my head and covered my left ear with my hand.

"Good. We will call you tomorrow at two o'clock and tell you where to meet us."

"Wait a minute," I said. "That's not acceptable."

"Tomorrow. Two o'clock." And the Russian hung up.

"Shit." Phil got up from his chair and started pacing. "This makes it a little more complicated," he said as I placed my cell back on the coffee table. "But nothing we can't handle." He tapped his fingers on his thigh and paced some more. "These guys are strictly small time. They're gonna be a piece of cake."

I shook my head. "I don't know. They don't seem so small time to me."

"Trust me. They are." He reached into his pocket, pulled out his phone, pressed a number, and talked into it. "We're on," he said.

"You think the Russians know about Phil?" I asked George after he left.

"I don't see how they could. I think they want to run you around. Give you another night to stew about things. The crazier you get, the easier it is for them."

I reached for my cigarettes. "I think they're succeeding."

He patted my shoulder. "I've got to go. Natalie wants me to help her with some stuff. I'll come back when I'm done if you want."

"Don't bother. I'll be fine."

"Really?"

"Yes, really," I lied.

Fuck him, fuck the Russians, fuck everybody.

After George left, I went into the kitchen and got a glass and some ice cubes. Then I got the bottle of Scotch and sat back down on the sofa and filled the glass half full and took a gulp. But it didn't silence the small, persistent voice in my head that kept saying I'd just made the biggest mistake of my life. Or rather of Manuel's. That no matter what Phil said, no matter how smooth he talked, in the end his buddies would get what they wanted and I'd leave without Manuel.

The problem was, I couldn't go to the hand-off alone. No matter which way I figured it, it came down to the same thing. I needed someone watching my back, someone with firepower. Preferably a lot of someones.

Truth was, there was no reason for the Russians to keep me alive once they had the money. In fact, they had every reason not to. First they'd kill me and then they'd kill Manuel. Unless they saw I wasn't alone. Then they'd kill Manuel. Just to be pissy. Because that's the way they did things. God. I realized Zsa Zsa was butting my hand with her head.

"I know," I said. "I'm not paying you any attention."

I scratched underneath her chin while I sipped my Scotch. I was just thinking that it was going to be a very long night when Zsa Zsa started barking. I heard a key in the lock. A minute later Bethany walked into the living room. She'd been out visiting a friend. I told her what was happening as she dropped her backpack on the armchair.

Her face crumbled. She burst into tears. Not the reaction I would have expected.

"I can't stand this anymore," she sobbed. "All the waiting. I just can't."

I didn't want to hear it, especially because she was saying what I was feeling, but I bit my tongue, got up, and hugged her instead. This is what people must mean when they talk about being mature. Her jacket felt cold from being outside.

"It'll be fine," I said.

"What if it isn't?"

"Don't say that."

She raised her face to me. Her eyeliner was smudged. She had black circles around her eyes. "Why?"

"It'll bring bad luck."

"You don't mean that."

"Of course not." But part of me did.

I'd just gotten Bethany settled on the sofa when the door-bell rang. Bethany and I looked at each other.

"I'm not expecting anyone," she said.

"Me either." I took a peak out the window. George's car was in the driveway."

"It's okay."

Bethany nodded. I went to get the door.

"I was scared you were the Russians."

"Phil has a couple of guys stationed down the block."

"You could have told us."

"Sorry," George said stepping inside.

He had a pizza box in one hand and a liter of soda in the

other. "I figured you and Bethany might be hungry," he explained.

"But what about Natalie?" I asked as he put the boxes on the coffee table in front of us.

"Nothing. She wanted me to go shopping with her. I told her I had other things to do."

"She must have been pissed."

George shrugged. "She'll live." He handed me a soda. "Time to switch off the Scotch. You don't want a hangover tomorrow."

"You're right. I don't." While Bethany went into the kitchen to get some napkins, I twisted the top off the soda bottle and poured some into my glass.

"You realize," George said, "there are people out there that see you doing what you just did, they'd kill you on principle."

"You mean you're not supposed to drink Coke and twenty-year-old single-malt Scotch together?"

" 'Course you are. It says it in my guide to fine wines and spirits."

I took another sip and put my glass down. "God, I wish this was over."

George slipped off his shoes. "Me too."

The Russians called at two o'clock on the dot the next day.

"At least you have to give them credit for being punctual," George observed.

"Yeah. It makes murder and kidnapping seem almost okay."

They instructed me to drive up Route 11 to Oneida Shores, which is forty to fifty minutes from where I live. At first I was surprised by their choice of site. I thought the Russians would have picked someplace closer. But when I thought about it some more, I could see why they'd done what they had.

Oneida Shores is a county park set on Oneida Lake. I'd been up there maybe three or four times in all the time I'd lived in Syracuse. Once to run Zsa Zsa, and the other times to visit someone who had a camp on the shore.

The topography was flat. There weren't a whole lot of things to hide behind up there. Most of the flora consisted of scrub with some maples and an occasional willow tree thrown in.

Phil and his buddies would be pretending to be ice fishermen and snowmobilers, which are the two major groups using the park in the winter. Oneida is known for the fishing both in the summer and the winter. In the summer all the camps on the shoreline are in use. They're stacked so closely together that you can look into someone else's kitchen and see what that person is making for dinner, but in the winter things are quieter.

It suddenly occurred to me that it would be hard for Phil to pick out the Russians, but then the Russians would have the same problem with Phil because everyone out on the ice looks the same. They're all wearing parkas with their hoods up. They're all wearing pac boots. They're all sitting on upturned twenty-gallon buckets with their backs to the wind.

And if that wasn't bad enough, the weather forecaster was predicting a lake-effect storm moving into the area. Lake effect is something that's peculiar to the Upstate area. One of those storms can drop three feet in a day. It can snow so hard, you can't see in front of you. Literally. You could be driving along and not know where the road is. And then it's over. Just like that.

My instructions were to go down to the shore right by the left parking lot and wait. Someone would come, and we would make the exchange. The money for Manuel. They saw anyone, they'd leave and it would be adios, Manuel.

According to Phil, his people would move in once I had Manuel.

Easy. Not to worry. So why was I chain-smoking one cigarette after another?

The drive up to Oneida Shores took longer than I expected.

It was snowing when I left Syracuse and it got worse as I headed up north. The plan was that George would follow me up. I concentrated on the road in front of me and tried not to think about what was waiting for me ahead.

Even though there wasn't much traffic on Route 11, what there was was crawling along. Once I got out of the Village of North Syracuse, I picked up a little more speed because there were fewer cars on the road, but I was still going below the speed limit.

Now there were car dealerships and places that sold tractors and mobile homes. An abandoned drive-in stood off to the right. Motels with names like the Bel-Air and Fisherman's Paradise stood empty, waiting for the summer. As I got closer, there were a couple of places selling boats. At the last place, the owner had placed a nineteen-foot runabout in front of his yard. It looked marooned in the snow. By now the snow was coming down harder and my window wipers were working overtime.

I turned on my cell to call George. Which was when I got my first jolt. The light on it was flashing. The battery was running low and I'd forgotten to charge it. Even worse, I didn't have the thing you plug into the cigarette lighter. I wanted to kick myself.

"I'm almost there," I said to him.

"I know," he said. "I can see you. Phil called to tell me his guys should be pulling into the park in five minutes or so."

"Why the hell aren't they there already?"

They'd taken I-81—which was faster.

"There was a five-car pile-up."

"That sucks."

"Don't worry. They'll be there. And in the meantime you still got me."

"I thought Natalie did."

I could hear the intake of George's breath. Then he said, "Where'd you put the gun I gave you?"

"Not touching that one, are you?"

"The gun, Robin."

"In the trunk."

"Seriously."

"Seriously. Listen, my battery is running out. I gotta get off."

"Robin, you . . ."

"Don't say anything." And I clicked off.

Five minutes later, I made the turn into the park. The entrance kiosk was deserted and the gate was up. In the winter entrance is free. Snow half covered the slide and the jungle gym in the children's playground. It drifted up against the side of a gnarled willow tree. I could see deer tracks and the trails left by cross-country skiers. A little farther off were deep ruts left by snowmobiles.

I wondered where George was as I headed over to the boat ramp. He hadn't made the turn in. Maybe he was waiting outside the park for Phil. Maybe there was another way in I didn't know about. I lit a cigarette as I looked over the parking lot. Except for a handful of trucks and SUVs, it was deserted.

The vehicles probably belonged to the ice fishermen who had parked there and off-loaded their equipment onto the ice—except, of course, for the vehicles that belonged to the Russians. I figured there had to be at least two of those. But all the vehicles were empty. No one was sitting in any of them.

I wondered if the Russians had arrived as I scanned the

lake. It was one vast sheet of ice. The ice was different shades of white—lighter in some places, darker in others, almost blue in some. Little shacks cobbled together out of odds and ends were set down on it here and there. Occasionally, through the snowflakes, I caught a glimpse of a dark shape moving around. An ice fishermen, I assumed. In the background I could hear the roar of someone's snowmobile. A faint odor of gasoline hung in the air.

Then out of nowhere it started snowing very hard. Everything became white. The sky. The ground. The lake. They were all one color. My phone rang again. I picked it up.

"Where are you?" I said, expecting it to be George.

"Where should I be?"

It was the Russian.

"Listen carefully," he said when I didn't reply. "I want you to get out of your car and walk straight out on the lake and we'll meet you."

I opened the window and flicked my half-smoked cigarette out into the snow. "Where's Manuel?"

"He'll be there."

I scrutinized the area again. I couldn't see anyone. All the trucks were locked and empty. The Russians had to be out on the ice. Probably felt right at home too.

"Let me talk to him."

"Just do what I'm telling you to," the Russian said. He sounded hoarse, as if he had a cold.

"Not unless I can speak to him."

"You want to hear him die?"

"I'd rather hear him sing the Sharks and Jets song from *West Side Story.*"

"You don't believe I'd do it."

"No. Then you won't get what you want."

"You want to take that chance?"

We were playing a game of chicken, and I turned away first.

"No," I whispered. "How far do you want me to walk?"

"Until we meet you. Oh. And tell your friend to stay away."

"What friend?"

"Because we speak with an accent doesn't make us stupid." And the Russian clicked off.

I called George.

"Where the hell are you?" I asked him.

"Outside the park. Waiting for Phil. He'll be along any minute."

"Great. By the way, they know you're here."

"They're guessing."

"They said to tell my friend to stay away."

"They still could be guessing," George said.

"No. They know. They want me to walk out on the lake."

"Stall for time."

"I don't think I can."

"You have to."

The beeping in my phone got louder.

"What can I say?"

"I can barely hear you."

"This phone is going dead."

There was no response on the other end of the line. I'd lost the connection.

Not good. Not good at all.

Chapter Forty-One

I watched the flakes coming down. It had been snowing yesterday afternoon when Phil was sitting in my living room. He'd been sprawled out in the armchair when I asked him about the down side of the operation he was proposing.

"There is no down side. It's a piece of cake. No problems." To emphasize the point, he'd adjusted his tie. I could still see it. It was yellow with fine brown lines running through it. "It'll run smooth as silk."

I raised an eyebrow. "Smooth as silk?"

"Yeah." Obviously Phil didn't do irony. "I guarantee it."

"And if it doesn't?"

"It'll be fine."

And he'd smiled at me as if I was an idiot to believe anything less. Yeah. Right. Things were going really well.

If I walked out on the ice, I'd be a sitting target. If I didn't, Manuel would be dead. Of course he could be dead already. No. I refused to think about that possibility. I wished I'd brought the bottle of Scotch with me. Another possibility I refused to think about.

It started to snow harder. Now the snow was coming down so fast, it was impossible to see. I felt as if I were in the middle of one of those paperweights I'd loved when I was a little kid. Lake effect. I hoped it didn't last long. Storms like this could stop within ten minutes or go on for three hours.

I lit another cigarette and took the gun George had given me out of the glove compartment and laid it across my lap. That way I'd be able to get to it quickly if I needed to. Then I took the car out of park and put it in drive.

It had been an extremely cold winter, so the lake should be frozen solid. Driving out onto the ice should be all right. The Russians were out there. And ice fishermen did it all the time. Not to mention the snowmobilers.

I remember a man I met in a bar one night when Murphy and I were shooting pool telling me he lived to fish. Especially in the winter. He loved watching the auger bore through the ice. He loved seeing that dark circle of water below come into being. Like discovering a hidden world, he'd said. He loved lowering his rod down, never knowing what was waiting for him. He loved the solitude and also belonging to something at the same time.

He'd said that one day he'd looked out over the ice. Every twenty feet or so there'd been a man sitting on an upturned twenty-gallon drum. And they were all wearing their parkas with their hoods up. And they were all sitting in the same direction with their backs against the wind. All of them were bent over their holes in the ice, watching their rods bob up and down. And it occurred to him that they were like the crystalline structure in a snowflake. Separate, but bound together.

Then he'd gone on to say that the ice was a living thing. It constantly moved and shifted. Cracks came and went. Ledges formed. Rotten spots popped up. Sometimes there were hot springs underneath. You had to be able to read it. At which point he'd apologized for talking so much and wandered off.

I wished he was here now. I could certainly use some help.

But even so, I still stood a better chance in my car than out of it. Out of my car, I stood no chance at all.

I was wondering how much my car weighed as I drove onto the lake. Probably too much. I could feel the difference in the way the car drove as soon as the tires hit the ice. I felt as if I was sliding along. So far I didn't hear any cracking sounds. What had that guy said? Ice breaking sounded like a rifle shot? So that was good.

How long did you have in the water before you got hypothermia? Three minutes? Five minutes? I'd read somewhere that if you fall off a fishing boat in Alaska, they don't go back for you. There's no point. Not that it mattered. Most of the people who go through the ice in their cars don't come back up again. You read about one or two of them every year over breakfast. Well, if that happened, I wouldn't have to worry about lung cancer, would I?

I stubbed my cigarette out and drove some more. I thought I was driving straight, but I wasn't sure, because I was beginning to lose my bearings. Several years ago, I'd been rafting down a river in a cave in Belize. It had been pitch black. You couldn't see your hand in front of your face, and when I'd come out I'd been turned around in the wrong direction and hadn't even known it.

I felt like that now. Only everything was white. I didn't see how the Russians were going to find me, because I certainly couldn't find them. Or how Phil or George were going to get the Russians. Even if my cell were working, it wouldn't help in weather like this. God, I hoped this stopped soon. Then I made out a wavering outline of something looming up in front of me. As I got closer, it got clearer. Jesus. It was a shack. Where the hell had that come from? I didn't remember anything being in front of me.

As I slammed on the brakes someone rear-ended me. I heard a whoosh as the air bag exploded. My head snapped back as if someone had punched me in the jaw. I was pinned to the seat. I couldn't move. But, the car was.

A moment later it plowed into the building. A big board landed across the hood, right next to the windshield. Another one glanced off the top of the windshield. The insurance company would be so pleased, I thought, as I noticed the radiating crack appearing on the left-hand side of the window. Part of the shack's roof came down in front of me. Then, just as suddenly as my car had picked up speed, it stopped.

I was trying to untangle myself from the air bag when my door flew open. Someone grabbed my arm and yanked me out of the car. I stumbled and fell to my knees. As I did, I noticed the front tire on the driver's side was in a hole in the ice. Then I heard the click of a gun and thought about my gun, which was probably down on the floor, under the front seat by now. Way to go, Robin.

The older Russian, the one who had done most of the talking the night I'd met him at the bar, said, "Get the money," to someone I couldn't see.

He was dressed in a gray parka and had a hat pulled down over his head and a scarf wrapped around his mouth. If it weren't for the accent, I'd never have known who he was.

"I didn't bring it," I told him, even though I was sure he knew I was lying. But it was the only thing I could think of to say.

Which was when I realized my jaw was throbbing. Then I realized that at some point or other the storm had let up as quickly as it had come. Which meant George could find me. He had to be around here somewhere. Unless . . . no. I refused to think that.

The person the Russian had been talking to lifted me up by my collar. I was still woozy from the crash. I stumbled, and he jerked me up again.

"We don't believe you," he said.

"It's true."

"Look in the car," the older Russian ordered.

Who was he talking to? There must be a third person there as well. Off in the corner somewhere. Which was why I couldn't see them.

"Where's Manuel?" I asked.

The older Russian laughed.

"Is he dead?"

"You Americans. Always so afraid of dying. Of growing old."

"So you said. Spare me the philosophical discourse."

"It makes you weak."

"We're weak? At least we didn't lose most of our country."

The Russian went into a diatribe about the Ukraine and Chechnya, but I wasn't listening. I was paying attention to the ice under my feet. The boards from the shack that looked like a thrown deck of cards littering my car and the ice. Flakes of snow swirling around my face. The boiled wool smell of the coat of the man standing behind me. The feel of the barrel of his gun between my shoulder blades. He pressed it into my spine.

"Maybe we don't kill you," he whispered into my ear. "Maybe we just leave you paralyzed for life. Da? Then we come back and fuck you when we want."

"Is that the only way you can get a woman to sleep with you?"

"What you say?" the man asked.

"You heard me. And by the way, where'd you learn to handle a gun? Central Casting?"

Before he could do anything, I leaned back into the gun and kicked at his leg as hard as I could. After all, what did I have to lose? I'd be dead anyway soon. At least this way it would be over faster. I bent my leg at the knee and brought it straight back with as much force as I could manage. I felt a crunch as the sole of my shoe connected with bone.

The Russian gasped as I whirled around. I grabbed for his gun, but it wasn't there. He'd dropped it on the ice. As he was bending down to get it, the older Russian raised his and fired. Little pinpricks of hot metal from the car peppered my face as I dove under it and began wiggling to the other side. I figured my only chance was to try and get to the gun George had given me. The Russian wouldn't miss next time.

Someone grabbed at my foot and I kicked at him. As I moved along, it dawned on me that my legs were wet. I put my hand down. I felt water. Then my fingers felt a fissure. I moved forward a little and reached down into the crack. Oddly, the water felt warmer than the air. This was not good. Not good at all. I was wondering how bad a shape the ice was in as the Russians screamed at each other. Too bad I couldn't understand what they were saying.

I was coming up on the other side of the car when one of the Russians stepped on my shoulder, pinning me down.

"I think you should know that the ice is breaking," I told him as he dragged me up by my hair.

He was smiling. He threw me across the hood of the car and raised his gun. I tried again.

"If the car goes in the water, you won't get your money."

I could hear his breath. I could smell the alcohol on it. You know how they say your whole life passes in front of you in moments like that? It's not true. All I thought was, I hope Bethany keeps Zsa Zsa.

I heard a shot. But I didn't feel anything. Maybe when you're dead, you don't, I thought. Instead I felt a heavy weight pressing me to the car. Something was dripping on my neck. Which was what made me realize I was still alive. Nothing drips when you're dead. Or at least you can't feel it.

I managed to twist partway around. The man who had been going to shoot me was lying on top of me. He looked like a badly done horror movie character. There was a hole in his chest and part of his forehead was gone, but the eye that was still there was staring at me.

I was pushing him off me when I heard another shot. I turned toward it in time to see the older Russian, the one I'd talked to in the bar, fall. Then there was another crack and the third Russian, the one I thought was in the corner, fell.

I ran over to him first. He was dead. No doubt about that, considering the way his face looked. So were the other two guys. Suddenly George and Phil and a dozen guys in black were there.

"Are you all right?" George asked.

"Fine. But Manuel . . ."

I heard a roar. Everyone turned. A red pickup truck was heading toward us. Two men were sitting in the front seat.

Out of the corner of my eye, I watched a man dressed in black crouch down and take aim at the truck.

"Don't shoot!" I yelled as I ran toward him.

But I got there too late.

I reached him just after he got off a volley of shots. As I pushed his arm down, I saw a crimson splatter on the windshield of the truck coming toward us. The horn blared as the driver's head hit it as he slumped onto the steering wheel. Then one of Phil's guys appeared beside me and started dragging me away.

"Leave me alone," I shouted.

"You need to calm down," he said. Like I was hysterical.

"I need to find Manuel."

"Let us handle the situation."

I was in the middle of trying to pull my arm free when the door on the passenger side of the oncoming truck swung open. The man who'd been sitting in the passenger seat jumped, rolled a couple of times, and lay still.

The truck kept coming toward us. Everyone scattered. The next thing I knew, it had crashed into my car. When I looked again, the man who had jumped out was reaching toward his waistband as he started to get up.

"Don't!" one of Phil's guys yelled.

"Freeze!" another of them yelled.

But he didn't stop. He yelled something in Russian and kept reaching for his waistband.

"No!" I screamed as two people opened fire.

The Russian's body jerked and twitched as the bullets hit him. The smell of cordite hung in the air. I wrenched away from Phil's man and ran over to the Russian. He was lying on his side. Blood was streaming out of his nose and his ears, forming a pool on the ice. I knelt down beside him.

"Where's Manuel?" I asked.

He blinked. I reached down and shook him.

"Tell me!" I screamed.

Suddenly George was beside me. I hadn't heard him come up.

"He's dead," he said.

"He can't be."

"I'm sorry. He is."

As I got up, I looked down. My hands were covered with his blood.

"Maybe Manuel is in the first car."

"He's not," George said.

"I want to see."

"They checked. He isn't there."

"Maybe he's in the trunk."

"Robin . . ."

I brushed George's arm away. "I'm going to look."

And I started for the car. I hadn't taken more than three steps at the most when it started getting lower and lower and lower. And then it disappeared. Without a sound. Poof. Just like that. It was gone into the water.

The ice had been pristine when I'd driven out on it. Everything had been perfectly white. But now there were patches of red and black. Pieces of timber were scattered all over. A faint odor of gasoline hung in the air. I realized that men in parkas and heavy boots, ice fishermen, had started gathering near where Phil's people were.

Phil walked up to where George and I were standing.

"I'm sorry things got fucked up," he said to me.

As if that was supposed to help. I didn't answer him. I couldn't. Instead I turned to George and held out my hand.

"Give me the keys to your car," I told him.

"Why?"

"I'm going to find Manuel."

"Odds are he's dead, Robin," Phil said.

"Don't say a word to me."

"You have to accept it."

"I won't." I looked at George. "I need the keys." I could see the pity in George's eyes. "Don't," I said as he handed them to me.

"Are you sure you want to do this?"

"Yes."

"Okay."

He handed them to me and I slipped them in my pocket. "Thanks," I told him.

"You can't go," Phil told me. "We need you here."

"Like you have a right to tell me what to do." And I started walking away.

"I can make you stay," Phil called after me.

I turned around. "You just try."

And I turned back around and kept on going.

I heard George say, "Let her go."

It wasn't until I got to George's Taurus that I realized I was crying.

Chapter Forty-Two

I dreaded the idea of going home and having to tell Bethany that I'd failed, that Manuel wasn't coming home. I couldn't face saying the words that would make Manuel's death real, so I went to the store instead. I didn't know where else to go. It was a mistake. I saw Manuel leaning on the counter by the cash register talking to his friend on the phone. I saw him shelving stock.

"How come I have to do this?" he was saying to me. "Why can't you?"

I heard him asking me for a twenty-buck advance.

"Just this once, Robin. You know I'm good for it."

I saw him sitting in my chair with his feet on the desk eating a sandwich when I went in the back room.

I heard him say to me, "You want to stay out of some people's line of sight," as I looked at myself in the bathroom mirror.

My face and my jacket were flecked with blood. One side of my face was purple from where the air bag had hit it. Clumps of my hair were sticking out of my head in odd directions. I took my jacket off and threw it in the corner. Then I washed my face and combed my hair and changed into the spare clothes I keep in one of the cabinets for emergencies. It didn't make me feel better.

Next, I fed the fish and made sure that all the animals were okay. Bethany had been doing Manuel's job of taking care of the animals, and while I trusted her, it didn't hurt to make sure. I watched myself doing everything as if I was a third party.

When I was done, I made myself some coffee and took the cup and went back into my office. I didn't turn on the light. Instead I sat in the dark and thought. I thought about what had gone wrong and why and what I could have done to prevent it. Right before I'd driven off in George's car, Phil had come over. It had taken an enormous amount of self-control on my part to keep from punching him.

He'd leaned his elbow against the window frame, bent down, and told me he'd do what he could to find Manuel. But I didn't see how. Everyone who knew where Manuel was was dead. There was no one to talk to. And the Russians who were still alive were probably on their way out of here by now. I know I would be if I were them.

I took the butterfly knife Manuel had given me a couple of years ago for my birthday out of the desk drawer and weighed it in my hand.

"I got it for you," he'd said. "Just in case you need a little extra something."

I'd asked him what was wrong with flowers and candy, and he'd laughed.

When I told Calli and George, they both thought I was crazy to take it. But I'd been touched by the present.

"Butterfly knives are like switchblades. You can get arrested for carrying one of those," George had said.

"I can get arrested for crossing in the middle of the street too," I'd told him.

"This isn't the same thing."

"You're right. An AK-47 would have been better. More efficient."

George frowned. "You're missing the point."

"Which is?"

"It's illegal. You shouldn't let Manuel give you things like that. It encourages bad behavior."

While I could understand what George was saying, I'd thought then and I think now that you accept what people can give you. From Manuel, this knife was a gesture of affection. He would have been hurt if I'd given it back.

"I'm not returning it," I told George.

"Have it your own way," he'd snapped. "You always do." And we'd watched television in silence for the rest of the night.

I ran my finger around the holes that decorated the length of the metal hasp. Then I took off the clasp at the bottom of the knife and began flicking it back and forth, watching the blade come out and go back in as it opened and closed. The knife had what looked like an eight-inch blade, though I'd never measured it. But it was enough to do some serious damage if you stuck it in the right place. I closed the knife, pushed the clasp up, and slipped it in my sock, around my ankle, where my boot ended. It felt comforting to be carrying something of Manuel's on me.

I started thinking about him and about how long we'd known each other. About how he'd been a street punk when we'd met. About how he'd saved my life and I hadn't saved his. Then I thought about Manuel's mother and Bethany. What was I going to say to them? This was my fault. If it hadn't been for me, Manuel would never have gotten kidnapped.

I should never have believed Phil. I should have done more to find Manuel. But most of all, I should never have taken the job from Paul Santini. I should never have gone to Wilcox's office. And after I found his body, I should have pulled out. I shouldn't have allowed Paul to talk me into going down to the City. Although by that time it was too late. The moment I walked into Wilcox's office, I was involved. I wished the Russians had gotten me instead. But of course they wouldn't do that. They know it's always worse for the one left behind.

I closed my eyes. My eyes. My hands. My feet. Even my hair felt heavy. As if I weighed five hundred pounds. All I could do was sit there in the dark and listen to the noises. I heard the swish of the pumps running in the fish tanks. There were rustles and squeaks as the hamsters and the mice went about their business.

The parakeets were chirping. I could picture them pecking at the birdseed in their food dishes. Their colors reminded me of the Yucatan. I could catch a plane and fly down there. Lie on the beach for a couple of days. Get skin cancer. Janet Wilcox would have been better off if she'd done that. At least she'd be alive.

I inhaled the smell of cedar shavings and the aroma of the water in the tanks. I was thinking of the time Manuel had let a barrelful of crickets escape when my cell phone started ringing. I reached into my backpack and turned it off. Let whoever was calling me leave a message. A moment later the phone out front started ringing. Five rings later, the answering machine clicked on. Bethany's voice floated out into the dark.

"Robin," she said. "Robin, are you there? Pick up."

And she started to cry. I knew I should speak to her, but I couldn't make my hand reach for the phone. Then the answering machine shut off and it was blessedly quiet. But not for long. The phone started ringing again. The answering machine clicked on again. Whoever invented it should be shot.

"God damn it!" Bethany cried. "Talk to me. Where the

hell are you? Turn your goddamned cell phone on. Fuck you, Light. Just fuck you."

Then the answering machine clicked off again, but I knew she'd keep calling. I fumbled in my backpack and found a cigarette and lit it. As I took a puff and watched the smoke curling up in the dark, it occurred to me that the more people you lose in your life, the harder it gets, not the other way around. This was something you never got used to.

The phone rang again. This time it was George wanting to know how I was. I didn't answer him either. Why couldn't everyone just leave me alone?

I would have sat in the dark forever, but the phone kept ringing and ringing. Finally, I managed to get myself up and out of the store. I drove around for a while, not knowing what else to do. The city plows had done their work. The streets were relatively clear and traffic flowed easily.

People were shoveling out their driveways and clearing off their cars, while little kids bundled up in snowsuits, boots, hats, and gloves were building snow forts. According to the announcer on the radio, the storm had deposited seven inches of snow in Syracuse, more up north. No kidding.

I tried to keep from yawning and failed. My eyelids started drooping. I reached over and rolled down the window to keep myself awake. All I wanted to do was go to bed. I was surprised when I looked at my watch to see that it was just a little before six. Somehow it seemed as if it should be eleven. This day had gone on forever.

The lights in the window of a bar on the north side of town attracted my attention. The place was snugged between a grocery store and a rundown colonial. Someone had replaced the rotten wood with boards painted different colors, giving the place a patchwork look.

I parked the car in front of a hydrant and went in. The six people sitting at the bar glanced at me when I came through the door and then went back to watching television. They looked as if they were used to minding their own business.

I sat down at the far corner and ordered a beer. If I had to guess, I'd say that the place had been fitted out twenty years ago and hadn't been touched since. There were tears in the bar stools that had been mended with duct tape and big gouges on the bar itself. The pictures hanging on the wall were covered with grime. A fine layer of dust and smoke hovered in the air.

As the bartender put my beer in front of me, I remembered that one of Manuel's friends lived two blocks away from here. A short kid with a permanent limp from the motorcycle accident he'd been in, he and Manuel had been talking about getting a car and driving cross-country next summer.

Suddenly I felt as if I couldn't breathe. I threw a five-dollar bill on the bar and went out to George's car without touching the beer I'd ordered. The fresh air made me feel better. So did driving. I cruised in and out of streets. The North Side was a good place for that, since everything turned and looped. They say only the dead know Brooklyn. Well, the North Side isn't that bad—but if you don't live in it, you need a map. Then, I'm not quite sure how, I was passing Wilcox's office. I stopped and backed up and stared at the place. It looked the same as it had when I first went in there.

Wilcox had worked for the Russians. Which meant that he had their names on file. Somewhere. Maybe all their names. Maybe even some that hadn't been on the lake. I was sure the cops had gone over everything.

Still.

It wouldn't hurt to have another look.

It wasn't as if I had anything better to do at the moment.

Chapter Forty-Three

Walter Wilcox's office turned out to be surprisingly easy to break into. For openers, the place wasn't alarmed and even though the door had a dead bolt, the windows had nothing on them in the way of locks. Even better, they were all about three feet off the ground. In addition, no one was around, nor were they likely to be since this area was largely commercial. All I had to do was boost myself up and I was in.

Which is what I did. Then I lowered the blinds in the office that weren't already down and got to work. Wilcox's phone book and computer were gone, taken by the police no doubt, but his files were still there. I pulled up a chair, made myself as comfortable as possible under the circumstances, and spent the next couple of hours going through them.

By the end of that time, I had a crick in my neck, my eyes hurt from reading fine print in bad light, and I was extremely glad I'd never become a lawyer. But that was all I knew. Judging by the content of the files, it appeared as if Walter Wilcox was the model of what he presented himself as—a hard-working attorney in private practice.

He must have kept the records of his transactions for the

Russians hidden somewhere in his house, because according to these files, all Wilcox did was close on houses and draw up wills and adoption papers. He shepherded people through separations and divorces—if they weren't too complicated. He also took care of traffic tickets and the occasional misdemeanor. His business seemed strictly limited to dealing with individuals and their problems.

There was only one thing that broke that pattern: His business dealings with the real estate company upstairs. He did all their house closings and record keeping. Not that that meant anything. Probably a matter of convenience for the people upstairs. Why get in a car and drive when you could walk downstairs to get what you needed done? Still it was something.

I leaned back in Wilcox's chair and let my mind drift to the first time I'd walked in here. I'd made a crack to the secretary about the stretch limo waiting outside. I'd asked her if that was how Wilcox got to court. She hadn't found it funny. Coming out of Wilcox's office, I'd wondered if the real estate company owned it. Not that they weren't entitled to. It was just another anomaly.

Anomalies are usually just random incidents without significance. On the other hand, it wouldn't hurt to go upstairs and poke around the real estate office. I was definitely on a roll here. I'd already broken into one office. What was one more? If I couldn't get inside, I'd turn around and head for another bar.

But I was saved from that fate by the graciousness of the gods. The lock on the office door was a cheapo special, and I managed to open it without too much trouble. The moment I walked into the inside office, I knew I was on to something. The place didn't have the feel of any real estate office I'd ever been in. It had the feel of something provisional, something that could be abandoned without a backward glance.

The office consisted of three interconnecting rooms. The

front room contained a couple of cheap particle-board desks, two vinyl chairs, plus a small scatter rug and a card table covered with empty Styrofoam cups, envelopes, and magazines. Add a tatty-looking sofa shoved over into the far corner, and you had the sum and substance of the furnishings.

The second room had two cots in it. The beds had sleeping bags on them instead of bedding. There was an overturned plastic box between them that functioned as a table. It had a half-empty bottle of vodka on it. A clue? Whaddaya think? The third room was empty. I did a quick check of the bathroom before going back to the main room. There was toothpaste, shaving cream, mouthwash, soap, shampoo, and towels. Someone had been living here.

I went back into the first room and went over to the bridge table. One of the magazines was *Time*. But the title of the other one was in Cyrillic. Ah-ha! Another clue. Finally. You look long enough, and sooner or later one pops out. So this is where some of the Russians had stayed.

And then something else hit me. There was no phone in the place. Novel way for real estate agents to do business, I decided. Your clients reach you through mental telepathy.

And there was another thing. Something I couldn't identify. I stood there for a few seconds and then it came to me. The place smelled like the Russian who had been holding me. It was a combination of cigar smoke and alcohol and something vague and indefinable.

So what had the Russians used this place for? A crash pad, obviously. But then why set this place up as an office? Why not just rent a flat? Maybe because they had business holdings of some kind. Like the limo, maybe? I wondered what else they owned. I hadn't been paying attention when I'd flipped through their file downstairs.

And then it occurred to me that this was how Walter Wilcox had become acquainted with the Russians. I could see it happening. They'd moved in over him, invited him out for drinks, and suddenly before he knew it his life was taking a different direction.

They must have seemed exciting to him. Exotic. Like something out of the movies. A temptation he couldn't resist. Suddenly he had a secret life. And a girlfriend. Things he'd never had. Things he'd fantasized about having. And by the time he'd woken up and realized with whom he was playing, it was too late. He couldn't dig himself out.

I ran down the stairs and went back to Wilcox's office to take a look at the files for the real estate company again. They could have stashed Manuel in one of their properties. It was a long shot, but it was the only shot I had.

I grabbed the file and opened it up. I couldn't find a mention of a car-for-hire company. But according to what I read, Wilcox had closed on six properties for them in the last year and a half. Maybe there were more, but checking that out would have to wait until tomorrow morning.

I took a pen off Wilcox's desk and jotted down the addresses and phone numbers on a scrap piece of paper and put it in my pocket. Then I put the file away, returned the chair to where it had been, and turned off the lights. As I walked out of Wilcox's office, I thought about calling George, but that would have meant explaining what I'd been doing for the past hours, and I wasn't in the mood to do that. I decided I could always call George if anything came up.

It was snowing again when I stepped out onto the pavement. I watched the flakes drifting down under the streetlights for a few seconds before I drove off. The first three addresses were on the North Side, close to where I was, so I checked them out first. One was a strip club, the other featured an "all-nude review," and the third had a sign on the window that said, ALL NAKED GIRLS, ALL THE TIME. Maybe the Russians were building their own little nudie-bar empire.

In addition, all three had signs in their windows advertising wide-screen TV. Judging from the cars in the parking lot, all three places were busy. Naked women. Big screen TVs. I mean what else could a guy want?

They seemed like unlikely places to put Manuel. But then, I never would have guessed that the Russians owned the real estate company upstairs from Walter Wilcox either. I started with the strip club. It had an entrance on the side where the girls came and went. It was locked, but when I knocked, one of the strippers let me in. She looked about fifteen going on forty.

"I'm looking for my son, Manuel," I said.

She shrugged. "Try out front."

"He said he was going to meet a girl that worked here. Maybe you know her? She's . . ."

"Save it." The girl tugged at the belt of her terrycloth bathrobe. "I'll get Mario. He's the one you should talk to."

"That's all right. I'll find him."

She tossed her hair back from her face. "If that's what you want," she told me in a seen-it-all voice. "I have to get ready to go on. I'm next."

I followed behind her as she walked into the dressing room. There were three other women in a room as big as a galley-sized kitchen. None of them paid me any attention as I wandered down the corridor. The entrance to the stage was off to the right. I peeked out. A bored-looking girl in a cowboy outfit was getting ready to remove her top to a souped-up rendition of "Home On the Range." The men in the audience seemed equally unenthusiastic. I moved on.

There were two doors on the left-hand side. I opened them both. One was the bathroom. The other one was the supply closet. I walked a couple more feet. There was another door at the end of the hallway. When I opened it, a guy who could have been a linebacker for the Pittsburgh Steelers looked up from his laptop.

"Who the hell are you?" he asked.

I could think of a lot of possible answers to that question, none of which would get me the information I wanted, so I favored him with a sweet smile and lied.

"I'm looking for my son." I described Manuel. "He's infatuated with this stripper. I don't know her name or where she works, but I thought if I walked around . . ."

The man cleared his throat. I could tell from the expression on his face that this was the first time he'd heard a story like this and he figured he'd heard them all.

"I'm sorry, lady. I ain't seen anyone like that back here."

I did a good hand-wringing demonstration. "He hasn't been home in two days."

The man's eyes darted back to the screen and away. "I see him, I'll tell him to call his ma."

"I'd appreciate it."

"Now, if you don't mind . . ." He turned back to the computer screen.

"You promise?" I said.

"I promise," he said without looking up.

"He needs to graduate."

That may have been laying it on a bit thick.

If he'd been a woman, he would have rolled his eyes. Instead he said, "Close the door behind you on the way out."

I talked to a few more people before I left. No one had seen Manuel. Or if they had, they weren't saying.

The next two clubs pretty much followed the same pattern. I came in through the rear entrance and told people I was looking for my son. Reactions ranged from mild sympathy to amusement to annoyance, but no one threw me out and I talked to a lot of people. No one had seen anything. The problem was, I didn't know whether to believe them or not.

The fourth and fifth addresses turned out to be one-story rental properties over in Eastwood. I knocked on both doors. One was occupied by a family of five. A young couple lived in the other. Both families appeared to be recent Russian immigrants, but they spoke enough English to understand what I was saying to them.

Even though it was on the late side, both families let me into their houses when I told them I was looking for an undocumented worker and I'd been given this address by his friends. Maybe it was my winning smile that made them open the door, or maybe it was the fact that I told them that if they didn't cooperate I'd call the authorities. I could tell they didn't know whether to believe me or not, but they didn't want to take the chance. I went over the houses from top to bottom. Manuel wasn't there.

"Was he here?" I asked at both places.

"*Nyet.*" Everyone shook their heads.

"Would you tell me if he had been?"

The people at both places smiled politely and nodded. Of course they would.

I didn't believe them. I tried a different tack.

"Your landlord got killed today."

They kept smiling.

I wondered if they understood me.

I explained again, this time using sound effects.

Their smiles stayed the same.

I smiled back.

We all smiled. It was great. A regular love fest. All that good feeling.

I left both houses not knowing much more than I had when I'd come in. The only thing I was fairly confident of was that if Manuel had stayed in either place, the families didn't know where his captors had dragged him off to. The kidnappers wouldn't have told them, and these guys had learned to mind their own business in Russia. Being smart people, they were sticking to the same rules now.

Which left me with one more place to go. The address I had was over in the general vicinity of Syracuse China, which was near Eastwood. I took my time driving there. It wasn't because the roads were bad—which they were—it was that this was my last hope. If Manuel wasn't there, I was going to have to admit he probably wasn't going to be turning up anytime soon. Just like Paul Santini. But when I looked at the building, I began to feel a small ray of hope.

Chapter Forty-Four

To get to the building, I had to take a left onto a small, badly plowed road called Cumberland Avenue. I'd driven about twenty feet when I saw the place I was searching for. A flat-roofed, one-story affair made out of corrugated sheets of metal, it looked like a warehouse. There was nothing in any way remarkable about it. You could drive by it every day for ten years and never notice it.

A small sign on the left-hand side read, PLASTICS, INC. Somehow that kind of enterprise didn't seem to fit in with the Russians I'd come to know and love. But what the hell, maybe they were diversifying. From what I could see, there were two entrances into the place. A door in the front and a loading dock in the back.

A large parking lot set off the building from the main road. The tarmac of the parking lot in back of the place gave way to scrub. There was one other building all the way down on the opposite side of the street, but aside from a WILL BUILD TO SUIT sign the road was empty. I wouldn't be surprised if there were deer, quail, rabbit, and pheasant here in the summer.

I studied the parking lot. The snow was deep. It hadn't

been plowed for a while. Which, for my purposes, was a bad sign. I drove in a little way, stopped the car, and got out to take a better look.

Now that I was studying the snow more closely, I saw tire marks that led from the road to the warehouse and back again. Although the tracks were partially filled in with the day's accumulations, they were still visible. By tomorrow they'd be gone. But someone had been here recently.

I got out my phone and called Phil. I got his machine. Which didn't surprise me. Now that I thought about it, he was either still processing paperwork—corpses make lots of paperwork—or he was at the bar drinking with his cronies. And he probably wouldn't come even if I could reach him. Especially after this afternoon out on the ice. As far as Phil and his merry band of men were concerned, the show was over, the bad guys were dead, and Manuel was a regrettable casualty. Sad, but that's the way it went. So sorry.

And if I wanted to go around with a bug up my ass because I couldn't accept reality—well, that was my problem. Maybe Phil would come out now to humor me, just as a favor to George. But that was doubtful. The day had been too long. Maybe he'd come out tomorrow. Or maybe he wouldn't come at all. Whaddayathink? I mean, why should he, really? On my say-so? Not bloody likely.

I left Phil a message anyway and tried George's cell. The phone rang until his voice mail came on. I left a message filling him in on what was happening.

"Call me," I said.

Then I tried his house. His bride-to-be answered. Was I having a good day or what?

"Who is this?" she asked.

I told her. She wasn't pleased.

"You know," she told me, her voice getting snippy, "he has better things to do than run around looking for you."

It's nice to know she was one of those women who kept her opinions to herself.

"Is that what he's doing?"

She let out a noise that was something between a snort and a whinny.

"Just stay out of our lives."

"A little possessive, aren't we?"

"I'm going to be his wife."

"So he said."

"Good. Because he has a family now. Which means he won't have time for you or your problems." And she hung up.

Charming. I almost, the operative word here is almost, felt sorry for George. Too bad for him. Date someone because she has boobs the size of Kansas, and you get what you deserve.

I sat in the car pondering whether or not I should call Natalie back and decided against it. I had a feeling Natalie wasn't going to be into delivering a message from me no matter what it was. Hopefully, George would check his voice mail at some point and get back to me.

I got out, took the pry bar that I'd spotted on the backseat of the car, and tramped through the snow up to the front door. The lock was cheap and it didn't take much for me to jimmy it open. I pulled the door open and stepped inside

It was as cold on the inside as it was outside. Not to mention dark. I couldn't see anything. Not even my own hands. The phrase "pitch black" flashed through my mind. I felt around the wall for the light switches, found and flicked all of them on. The place lit up. It was as big as a football field. And just as empty. I wanted to cry. I don't know what I'd been expecting. Maybe Manuel sitting trussed up in a chair in the middle of the room. But he wasn't there.

I walked in a little farther. It was clear the place was a

warehouse. There was a forklift parked over by the far wall, and the walls on either side of me were lined with rows of industrial shelving that were stacked with white bins and cartons. Wooden pallets were stacked underneath some of the shelving as well as piled near the center of the room.

A card table was set up by the loading bay. I headed toward it. Maybe there was something there. A stack of invoices was lying in the center of the table. I gave them a quick look through. They all had to do with the shipping and receiving of various kinds of polymers. Whatever else the Russians were doing, they were running a legitimate business.

Next to the invoices was an empty bag of Oreo cookies and an almost empty carton of milk and a couple of pens, a pad of yellow lined paper, and a new deck of cards, none of which told me anything I didn't already know, except that someone had had some time on their hands.

I walked over to the shelving, took down one of the white containers and pried the top open. Inside was a sealed plastic bag full of red powder. I put the top back on the container, replaced it, and went on to the next. It had a different color powder. The one next to that had the same color powder as the first one.

Boy, I was really getting someplace. I tried the boxes next. Some of them contained molds. Others had dyes. Others had things I couldn't identify. I walked back to the middle of the room and looked around again. There was nothing here that wasn't supposed to be. Or at least if there was, I couldn't see it.

I took my gloves off and stuffed them in my jacket pocket. Then I fished around in my backpack for my cigarettes. A belt of Scotch wouldn't have hurt either. Maybe I should start carrying a flask. No. That would be the beginning of the end.

As I lit a cigarette, I wondered how I was going to tell

Manuel's mother that not only was her son dead, but that she didn't even have a body to bury. And Bethany. God, Bethany. I could see the look in her eyes when I walked through the door. It made me want to get back in George's car and keep going.

Maybe that was why I couldn't make myself leave the warehouse yet.

"Just because you want it to be one way, doesn't mean it is," I heard my mother whispering in my ear.

"Yes, it does," I'd always reply.

Maybe that was why she'd called me stubborn. Actually she'd used the word "incorrigible," if we're being accurate. I prefer to think of myself as tenacious.

I smoked my cigarette halfway down, and flicked it away. It landed on the cement floor, smoldered for a few moments, and went out. I started walking around again aimlessly, not sure what I was looking for, but unable to abandon the search.

In the next hour or so I reread the invoices on the card table. I checked out the forklift. I opened more boxes and pried the covers off of more white plastic containers. I read the labels on them. None of it told me where Manuel was. In disgust, I kicked at a paper cup lying on the floor.

It rolled toward the shelving and stopped next to something that looked like a small, crumpled-up piece of paper. I walked over, squatted down, and picked it up. Only it wasn't paper. It was a small, white, dice-like cube. Except instead of having dots on it, it had a capital "B" on its six sides.

About a month ago Bethany had showed me a bracelet she'd bought for Manuel. It had consisted of seven white cubes, each with a letter that spelled out her name. They'd been strung together on a leather thong.

"You think he'll wear it?" I asked.

Bethany had looked at me as if I was crazy.

"Of course he will," she'd said. "I'm giving it to him." And he had. Even though he'd told me it made him feel silly.

I got down on my hands and knees and looked around. The cold from the concrete floor seeped through my jeans as I spotted another cube under the shadow of a wooden pallet. I reached over and grabbed it. This one was a lower-case "y." I scanned the floor. All I saw was gray concrete with hairline fractures. The rest of the letters had probably rolled under the wooden pallets.

I tightened my fingers around the dice until they bit into the palm of my hand. I felt dizzy. Manuel had been here and I'd missed him. Now it was too late. If only I'd thought of going to Wilcox's office sooner, I could have gotten here in time. Suddenly it seemed terribly important to retrieve the rest of the letters. It was the least I could do for Bethany.

I carefully put the dice in my jacket pocket, got up, and started pulling at the top pallet, but it was wedged in tightly under the bottom of the shelf. After a few minutes of tugging it became apparent to me that I couldn't move it. I'd have to take the shelf off first. Not a big job because the shelves were attached to the main poles by a slot-and-groove mechanism. They would be easy to dismantle once I had the boxes off.

It took me five minutes to off-load the shelf and another five minutes to work the shelf loose. It had gotten jammed in, and I had to wiggle it back and forth before I could ease it out. Then I started moving the pallets. They were heavy and awkward. My back was hurting as I dragged the last one out onto the floor.

Then I walked back over and saw what was under it.

Chapter Forty-Five

For a second I just stared, the way you do when you see something you don't expect to. Then I realized what I was looking at: a hole next to the wall that was maybe three feet by four feet wide and three feet deep that had been dug out of the concrete and earth.

My heart started beating faster as I made out the outline of Manuel. He was lying on his side. He'd been hog-tied with his hands and feet lashed together. I jumped down into the hole and touched his neck. His skin was cold, but I could detect a faint pulse. I lifted his head. His mouth was covered with duct tape. I removed it. He didn't even flinch.

"Manuel," I said.

Nothing.

I took my knife out of my boot and cut Manuel's bonds and straightened out his arms and legs and rubbed them to get the circulation going. The rope had dug into his wrists almost to the bone.

"Jesus." I wanted to cry.

I put the knife down beside Manuel, took off my jacket, and covered him with it. I stroked his hair. It was matted with dirt.

"Okay, kid," I told him. "Come on. We're going home."

I'd just put my hands under his arms to pull him out when a voice coming from somewhere above me said, "No. You're not."

I looked up to see Dirk Junior grinning down at me. He was wearing a big goose-down parka and pac boots and a watch cap pulled over his ears. More importantly, he was pointing a Glock at my head. Why is it that everyone seems to have a 9mm these days?

"You should get your hearing checked," he told me.

"I can do that right now if you'd like."

He snorted.

"I'll take that as a no."

"Very good."

I tried smiling at him while I stretched my fingers out and worked the knife I'd laid by Manuel's side toward me. It seemed to be taking forever. It was dark down in the hole and I hoped Dirk Junior couldn't see what I was trying to do, but it wasn't dark enough because the next thing he said was, "What the hell are you doing?"

"Nothing." My hand closed around my knife.

"Right. Bring your hands up slowly. Both of them," he said when I showed him my left one.

I brought up the hand with the knife.

"Very good." He nodded toward a spot on the cement floor. "Put it there. Now," he yelled when I didn't move fast enough.

I did what he asked. He stuck out his foot and worked the knife toward him with the toe of his boot. Then, without taking his eyes off me, he bent over, picked it up, and put it in his jacket pocket.

"Thanks," he said. "I can always use one of these and you won't have any use for it soon."

"How sweet. Can I at least have a cigarette?" I asked.

"I don't think so. How'd you figure out Manuel was

here?" and he gestured around the warehouse with his free hand.

"Wilcox's records. I don't understand. Why the Russians? Why this?" I asked.

Dirk Junior shrugged. The hat gave his face a thuggish quality.

"What's to understand? I needed some money. The Ruskies needed a little help. I gave it to them."

"How much of the $250,000 were you going to get?"

"They were giving me a thousand dollars finder's fee for telling them about Manuel."

"That's not a lot considering the charges you're going to be facing."

"Plus I got to do one of their 'E' and 'Special K' routes," Dirk Junior said, as if I hadn't spoken.

Special K is one of the names the kids give an animal tranquilizer that's all the rage these days.

"Nice to have a career."

"Hey, I need the money. Somebody like me—you gotta get it any way you can."

"Because you just have to have that new car."

"Because I got my old lady to support. No one else is, that's for sure. Hey. Stay where you are," Dirk Junior ordered as I started to straighten up.

I did what he told me to. I didn't have much of a choice.

"Tell me," I asked. "Did the Russians ever plan to let Manuel go or were they just going to put him in this hole and leave him to die?"

Dirk Junior didn't answer.

"Were they?" I repeated.

"What difference does it make?"

"I want to know for my own sake. That's all."

"Yeah," Dirk Junior answered. "They were."

"Did you know that they were going to kill him when you gave them Manuel's name?"

"Naw." Dirk Junior wiped his nose with the back of his free hand. "I wouldn't have given it to them if I had."

"So why didn't you do something when you found out?"

"You mean like go to the police?"

"Yeah. You could have made an anonymous call."

He laughed. "What world are you living in? I was in it already. It was too late. Shit happens. You got to roll with it. That's how all the big-shot CEOs get ahead."

Wonderful. The final flowering of capitalism.

I nodded in Manuel's direction. "You know, if he dies you're implicated in a homicide."

"They have to find the body to charge me."

"Not necessarily."

"Hey. Don't try and fuck me over. I read the law. I know what's what."

"Is that why you're here? To get rid of Manuel?"

"I got responsibilities."

"Not to the Russians. They're dead."

"I know. That's what my old man's bitch said."

"Are you referring to Calli?"

"Does he have another one?"

"Not that I know of."

"You don't know much, do you?"

"Evidently not."

Dirk Junior rubbed his cheek with his free hand. "Well, I figure someone else will be buying this property or renting it out. Having a corpse here . . ."

"Manuel's not dead."

He shrugged again. "Whatever. Anyway. It's messy. You never know where things like that will lead."

"You're a prudent guy."

Dirk Junior didn't answer. I don't think he knew what prudent meant. His eyes strayed to Manuel. "He don't look so good."

"Being buried alive usually isn't good for the constitution."

"That's a fact." Dirk Junior scratched under his hat. "By the way. Just in case you're interested, I was the one that took Tiger Lily."

"I kinda thought you had."

He smirked. "No, you didn't. You believed what I told you."

"No. I wanted to believe what you were telling me. That's different. Maybe that's because I wanted to believe something good about you."

"Good?" He sniggered. "You sound like your friend. 'Dear, it's not too late to make something of yourself.' He mimicked Calli's voice. "'We just want the best for you.' Fuck her! She wants the best for me, what the hell she doin' hangin' around with my old man? He should be takin' care of my old lady. If he did what he was supposed to, I wouldn't be doin' this."

"Is that what this is about? You're pissed at your old man?"

"No. It's about money."

"That's what Marx said."

"Who cares about Marx? Fuck him. Fuck you. Fuck everyone." And he began pulling back on the Glock's trigger.

"Hey," I cried, "don't you want to know how I knew that Manuel was here?"

"You already told me."

"Did I?"

"Yeah, you did."

I shrugged.

"Didn't you? Didn't you?"

"If you say so."

Dirk Junior licked his lips. "You said you found out through Wilcox's records. Where are they?"

"His records? In his office."

"Where is it?"

"You expect me to tell you?"

"Damned right I do." From where I was standing I could see his Adam's apple bob up and down. "I'll shoot your fuckin' arm off first if you don't."

"Well, as long as you put it that way." And I gave him the address.

"How'd you get in."

"I had a key," I lied.

Dirk Junior held out his hand. "Give it to me."

I turned toward Manuel.

"Don't move," Dirk Junior ordered.

"It's in my jacket pocket."

"I'll get it. Get back," he ordered.

I moved off a little bit.

"Further."

I took another step back. "This is as far as I can go."

Dirk Junior had his gun on me as he jumped down into the hole. He pointed the Glock at me as he rummaged through my jacket pockets with his free hand.

"You're jerking me around. There's nothing here," he said after a couple of moments had gone by.

"Sure there is. You're just not looking hard enough."

He nodded toward Manuel. "You come look."

"Whatever you want."

"And keep your hands up."

I raised them slightly. As I moved toward Dirk Junior, I thought about Manuel and Bethany and Zsa Zsa. What would happen to her if I died? And Bethany. Where would she go? Not to mention the animals in the store. God, I didn't even have a will.

"Hurry up," Dirk Junior said. "I want to get going."

I hoped he was a good shot. I hope he didn't leave me to bleed to death. I wondered where he'd bury Manuel and me.

Probably in a dump somewhere. And no one would ever know where we were. I was about six inches away from Dirk Junior now, close enough to see his eyes shifting this way and that and his gun hand shaking. Before I had time to think about what I was doing, I'd brought my hand up and chopped at his wrist. His hand went down. The gun discharged. He screamed, took a couple of steps backward, and toppled onto Manuel.

"You shot my foot off," he said as the gun fell out of his hand.

I reached over and took it.

"Just be happy I'm not shooting you in the head," I said while I dialed 911.

Chapter Forty-Six

The police got to the warehouse first, followed by George, Bethany, and Phil. Or maybe the order was reversed. I can't remember. I don't know how much time elapsed before everyone came.

I spent it trying to keep Manuel warm and thinking about the time we'd gone to Mexico together and how I'd thought he'd be interested in the country and that it would be good for him to see his Hispanic roots. Instead he'd hated everything about Mexico except the tequila and couldn't wait to get back to Syracuse and his friends.

I'd wanted to expand his horizons and he'd been perfectly happy with them the way they were. As I hugged Manuel tighter, I noticed that I had Dirk Junior's blood on my sleeve. I turned and looked at him. He'd managed to crawl out of the hole and get about ten feet away before he'd gone into shock and collapsed.

George and Bethany got there just as the EMT guys were loading Manuel onto a stretcher.

"Oh, my God," Bethany cried when she saw him. She would have thrown herself on the stretcher if George hadn't restrained her. "I want to go with him."

"We'll meet them at the hospital," George told her as Phil came toward us. "You won't be able to see him for a while anyway."

Phil still looked crisp and polished after the long day he'd put in. He was the only one among us who did. I wondered how he managed to look that way as he pointed to the hole Manuel had been in.

"I'm betting they used that to cache the drugs they were selling. And I'm betting they have other hiding spots like this around the place."

"Most likely," I said, and I told him what Dirk Junior had told me about getting a piece of the Russians' drug trade.

Phil turned toward Dirk Junior, who was being wheeled out into a waiting ambulance. "The EMT guys think he's going to lose his foot," he commented.

"He should lose more than that," George said.

Phil grunted and turned back to me. "You okay?"

"As okay as the circumstances warrant."

"You want to get checked out at the hospital first, or you want to talk?"

"Talk."

George opened his mouth to say something, but before he could, Phil said, "Why don't you and Bethany go to the hospital. Robin will meet you there."

George nodded. Then he gave me a hug and kissed the top of my head.

"He really likes you," Phil told me as George and Bethany walked away. "But you know that."

"I guess I do."

Phil rubbed his hands together. "Let's talk in my car. This place is colder than my refrigerator."

I walked into Crouse's ER room an hour later. George was sitting in one of the seats in the waiting room. He was leaning forward. His hands were clasped and hanging down between his knees. He got up when he saw me and came over to where I was standing.

"Bethany's in with Manuel now."

"How's he doing?"

"All right. Considering. He's tougher than I thought."

Relief flooded through me, followed by a wave of tiredness. Suddenly I felt exhausted. The only thing I wanted to do was go home and go to bed. George headed for the doors that separated the waiting room from the treatment rooms. I followed him in.

"Listen," he said when we were on the other side. "I know this is a really bad time for this, but there's something I have to ask you."

"What?"

A nurse came by and we moved toward the wall. George licked his lips. I waited. I was so tired my bones ached.

"It's a simple question. All you have to do is answer yes or no."

"Okay."

I backed up against the wall for support and tried to keep awake.

Finally George said, "Do you love me?"

"What?"

"You heard me."

"And that's your question?"

"Yes."

"What the hell difference does that make?" I cried. Then I lowered my voice. "You're having a baby with someone else."

"Just answer me. Please."

"Why now?"

"Because I have to know."

I was so angry I could hardly talk. I started to move away. I didn't want to be near George. For a second at the warehouse I'd forgotten about Natalie. Now it was all back.

"You just don't quit, do you? You really are a piece of work. You know what? You and Natalie deserve each other. I'm going to see Manuel, and then I'm going home."

George caught hold of my arm.

"Let go of me," I demanded.

His hand fell away.

"Robin. Please. I need to know."

I looked up at him.

"Why?"

His face was impassive.

"Because I do. Just answer me. You owe me that much."

"I don't owe you anything, and that's not an answer."

"You have to trust me."

"Yeah, right. That's a funny line coming from you."

"I know I haven't acted well."

"That's one way of putting it."

George didn't reply. He swallowed and looked away. His shoulders slumped. I closed my eyes. I didn't want to look at him anymore. It was too painful. It would be so much easier to lie and say, I hate you. Go to hell. And it wouldn't be a lie. I did hate him. But it wouldn't be the whole truth either.

I thought of all the games we'd been playing for what seemed like forever. I was tired of them. George and I were like hamsters on a wheel. We just went round and round in circles. It was time to get off. I opened my eyes.

"Okay," I said. "I love you. More or less. Satisfied?"

"Very." And he leaned over and kissed me lightly on the lips. "Manuel's in room twelve. I've got some business I have to take care of." And he started walking away.

"What business?"

"I need to talk to Natalie."

"About what?"

"Arrangements."

"What do you mean, arrangements? Why do you always have to be so fucking cryptic?"

"Don't worry. I'll take care of everything."

"Like what?"

But George hadn't heard me. He'd already gone through the doors.

What an asshole. But I realized I was smiling for the first time in a long time and I didn't know why.

I was walking toward Manuel's room when Calli came running toward me. Tears were streaming down her face. Dirk was behind her.

"They called me from the paper. Are they all right?"

"They?" I replied.

"Manuel and Dirk Junior."

"I think they're both going to be okay," I said slowly, looking from Dirk to Calli and back again. Somehow I had a feeling that the person who had called her hadn't told her the whole story.

Dirk patted Calli on the shoulder. "I'm going to see my son," he told her and moved off down the corridor.

"His son is in serious trouble," I told Calli.

Her hands went up to her mouth.

"What kind of trouble?"

"He tried to kill me, and he's involved in Manuel's kidnapping."

She bit her lip. "He'd never do anything like that."

"Well, he did."

Calli looked at me in disbelief.

"He was going to shoot me."

She groaned. "Poor Dirk. He really loves that kid."

"That kid was going to shoot Manuel and rebury him."

"No."

"Yes. And by the way, he blames you for everything that's happened."

"Me?" Calli yelped.

"You. According to him, if Dirk wasn't living with you and was taking care of Myra, none of this would have happened."

"That's ridiculous," she protested.

"I'm not saying it isn't. I'm just saying that's what he thinks."

Calli's fingers pulled at the sheepskin piling edging her jacket. "I've tried to be nice to him. I've tried to get him to go back to school." She shook her head.

"I've got to go see Manuel. He's in room twelve, in case you're interested. And by the way. Dirk Junior did steal Tiger Lily after all."

Calli just looked at me. I felt really bad for her.

"I don't know what to do," she whispered.

"Well, you know what my advice is."

She absentmindedly unbuttoned her jacket.

"You have to talk to Dirk."

"I do, don't I?"

"I think so." And I went to check on Manuel.

Chapter Forty-Seven

When spring arrives in Syracuse, people come out to greet it. After six months of snow and cold and clouds, we feel as if we've earned the green leaves and blue skies. It's like going from living in black and white to living in Technicolor.

It was the third week in April. I'd spotted my first robin yesterday. This morning, as I'd been drinking my coffee, I'd heard a flock of geese overhead. The last pile of snow on the shady side of the house was gone, and even though the lawns were still too soggy to rake, everyone on my block was out, picking up the trash left from the winter, washing windows and cars, or just puttering around.

I was standing on the front lawn of my house with Zsa Zsa, trying to admire the crocuses and the delicate yellow-green of the new leaves on the trees and not have an anxiety attack as I watched George and Manuel unload one of George's dressers off the U-Haul they'd parked in my drive-way.

"I'm putting this one in our bedroom and the other one in the guest room," George said as he and Manuel went by me.

"You're sure they'll fit?"

The dresser was one of those huge, dark mahogany Victorian pieces. I hate Victorian furniture. I always have. But since it came from George's grandmother, I couldn't say anything. I think this is what they mean by compromise.

"Remember. We measured them out," George reminded me.

"Right."

I took a deep breath and exhaled and silently repeated the mantra I'd been telling myself for the past months. "This living-together thing is going to work out fine. Once we get the furniture arranged. Once we get into a routine. Everyone has a period of adjustment."

Of course, as Calli had pointed out, it would have been easier if George and I had just bought a house together and started fresh. But we hadn't. Mostly because with George's child support payments to Natalie, he couldn't afford to. I had a feeling those payments weren't going to last too long.

From what I could see, she was as domestic as a scorpion. From the way she was talking, I wouldn't be surprised to wake up one morning and find a basket with the baby on the doorstep—something else I was trying not to think about. I mean, what the hell do you do with something like that anyway? Teenagers, I could deal with. Dogs, I was good with. But babies? Just the thought of one gave me the heebie-jeebies.

I moved back a couple of inches to avoid getting banged in the leg with the dresser as Manuel came by me. He looked the way he had before his ordeal. It had taken a few months, but he was back to his old self. At least on the outside. Inside was a different matter. But I was hopeful that over time, those scars would fade as well. I was thinking it would be good if I could convince him to go talk to someone when John, my neighbor across the way, waved at me.

I waved back. He put down the rag he'd been polishing his

car with and started across the street. I'd been wondering how long it would take him to come over and find out what was happening. But Bethany beat him. She suddenly appeared at my side dragging Tara, her golden retriever puppy, behind her on a leash.

"She just ate grass. What should I do?" she asked me.

She was wearing a plain white T-shirt and a pair of faded jeans. The pout she'd sported had disappeared, along with fifteen pounds. She'd cut her hair very short, and even though her mother and father had been horrified, I thought the style looked good on her.

"Not that it matters what we think," her father had said to me, "now that she's living with you."

I was trying to reconstruct how that had happened when she tugged at my sleeve and brought my mind back to the present.

"What should I do?" she repeated.

"Nothing. She'll puke it up. All puppies do that. Don't they?" I crooned at Tara.

I put my hand down and she gave it a lick, at which point Zsa Zsa growled. She wasn't fond of Tara, a fact that Tara couldn't comprehend. A true golden retriever, she believed that everyone loved her. Tara rolled over on her belly, then got back up and started attacking the bottom of Bethany's jeans. Bethany reached down and pried Tara off. The puppy was big for her age. Even though she was just four months old, she looked like six. She was definitely going to be a big girl.

"I was thinking we could take her to dog class," Bethany said. She looked at George coming out of the house. "Unless you won't have time."

"I'll make the time."

"Because if you don't . . ."

"I will," I said firmly.

"Just you and I."

"Deal. Bethany, just because George is moving in doesn't mean that—"

"I know." She looked at me as if I was an idiot. "And by the way, we should get a bigger hot-water heater. There's not going to be enough hot water for all of us."

"I'll think about it."

"And can we go see Tiger Lily later?"

"Maybe. We'll see how the moving goes."

Bethany nodded. "Because I'm sure Tara would like to see her mom." She paused for a minute. "I'm glad that guy Dirk left."

"Me too."

"Calli isn't."

"She'll get over it."

Bethany wrinkled her nose. "Why did she hook up with someone like that?"

"I think you have to be older to understand."

She rolled her eyes. "God," she said. "You sound just like my mother." And she ran off with Tara leading the way.

I was thinking how complicated my life had gotten when John materialized next to me. He leaned over and gave me a poke in the ribs with his elbow.

"You getting some new furniture?" he asked. "Or is someone moving in?"

"Can't stand not knowing something, can you?"

He grinned. "You're damned right I can't."

"Someone's moving in."

John rocked back on his heels and adjusted the brim of his baseball hat. "The black guy?"

"Yup."

John smiled. "He play golf?"

"Yes."

"Is he any good?"

"Very."

At that moment, Manuel and George came out of the house. John moved toward them.

"Can I give you guys a hand?"

They started chatting, but I wasn't listening.

Who knew? Maybe everything would work out. Maybe George and I would live happily ever after.

If we could just figure out how to fit all his stuff in my house.

THE PERIPHERAL
NERVOUS SYSTEM

THE PERIPHERAL NERVOUS SYSTEM

Edited by
John I. Hubbard
Department of Physiology
University of Otago
Dunedin, New Zealand

PLENUM PRESS • NEW YORK AND LONDON

Library of Congress Cataloging in Publication Data

Hubbard, John I   1930-
   The peripheral nervous system.

   Includes bibliographies.
   1. Nerves, Peripheral. I. Title. [DNLM: 1. Peripheral nerves. W1500
H875p 1974]
QP365.5.H8   612'.81   74-6258
ISBN 0-306-30764-2

© 1974 Plenum Press, New York
A Division of Plenum Publishing Corporation
227 West 17th Street, New York, N.Y. 10011

United Kingdom edition published by Plenum Press, London
A Division of Plenum Publishing Company, Ltd.
4a Lower John Street, London W1R 3PD, England

Printed in the United States of America

Contributors

Eric A. Barnard
*Departments of Biochemistry
and Biochemical Pharmacology
State University of New York
Buffalo, New York, USA*

Christopher Bell
*Department of Zoology
University of Melbourne
Victoria, Australia*

T. J. Biscoe
*Department of Physiology
University of Bristol
Bristol, England*

J. G. Blackman
*Department of Pharmacology
University of Otago Medical School
Dunedin, New Zealand*

Geoffrey Burnstock
*Department of Zoology
University of Melbourne
Victoria, Australia*

Mohyee E. Eldefrawi
*Section of Neurobiology and Behavior
Cornell University
Ithaca, New York, USA*

Lloyd Guth
*Laboratory of Neurochemistry
National Institute of Neurological
Diseases and Stroke
Public Health Service,
Department of Health, Education and Welfare
Bethesda, Maryland, USA*

Arthur Hess
*Department of Anatomy
Rutgers Medical School
New Brunswick, New Jersey, USA*

John I. Hubbard
*Department of Physiology, Medical School
University of Otago
Dunedin, New Zealand*

Carlton C. Hunt
*Department of Physiology and Biophysics
Washington University School of Medicine
St. Louis, Missouri, USA*

Ainsley Iggo
*Department of Veterinary Physiology
University of Edinburgh
Edinburgh, Scotland*

David M. Jacobowitz
*Laboratory of Clinical Science
National Institute of Mental Health
Bethesda, Maryland, USA*

Margaret R. Matthews
*Department of Human Anatomy
Oxford University
Oxford, England*

P. B. C. Matthews
*University Laboratory of Physiology
Oxford University
Oxford, England*

Syogoro Nishi
*Neurophysiology Laboratory,
Department of Pharmacology
Loyola University Medical Center
Maywood, Illinois, USA*

Denis Noble
*Fellow of Balliol College, Oxford University
University Lecturer in Physiology
Oxford, England*

Sidney Ochs
*Department of Physiology
Indiana University Medical Center
Indianapolis, Indiana, USA*

Henry deF. Webster
*Head, Section on Cellular Neuropathology
Laboratory of Neuropathology
and Neuroanatomical Sciences
National Institute of Neurological
Diseases and Stroke
Bethesda, Maryland, USA*

J. G. Widdicombe
*Department of Physiology
St. George's Hospital Medical School
London, England*

Preface

The peripheral nervous system is usually defined as the cranial nerves, spinal nerves, and peripheral ganglia which lie outside the brain and spinal cord. To describe the structure and function of this system in one book may have been possible last century. Today, only a judicious selection is possible. It may be fairly claimed that the title of this book is not misleading, for in keeping the text within bounds only accounts of olfaction, vision, audition, and vestibular function have been omitted, and as popularly understood these topics fall into the category of special senses.

This book contains a comprehensive treatment of the structure and function of peripheral nerves (including axoplasmic flow and trophic functions); junctional regions in the autonomic and somatic divisions of the peripheral nervous system; receptors in skin, tongue, and deeper tissues; and the integrative role of ganglia. It is thus a handbook of the peripheral nervous system as it is usually understood for teaching purposes.

The convenience of having this material inside one set of covers is already proven, for my colleagues were borrowing parts of the text even while the book was in manuscript. It is my belief that lecturers will find here the information they need, while graduate students will be able to get a sound yet easily read account of results of research in their area.

JOHN I. HUBBARD

Contents

SECTION IIA—JUNCTIONAL TRANSMISSION—STRUCTURE

Chapter 6
Ultrastructure of Ganglionic Junctions **111**
   Margaret R. Matthews

SECTION IIB—JUNCTIONAL TRANSMISSION—FUNCTION

Chapter 7(i)
Neuromuscular Transmission—Presynaptic Factors **151**
   John I. Hubbard

Section I

Peripheral Nerve

Chapter 1

Peripheral Nerve Structure

Henry deF. Webster

Head, Section on Cellular Neuropathology
Laboratory of Neuropathology and Neuroanatomical Sciences
National Institute of Neurological Diseases and Stroke
Bethesda, Maryland, USA

1. INTRODUCTION

Recent research dealing with the morphology of peripheral nerves has been concerned largely with their cellular constituents and has emphasized the morphological correlates of functional and metabolic activity. Application of new cytological techniques has expanded morphological horizons rapidly, and current concepts have benefited also from the study of reactions of peripheral nerves to experimental alteration and disease. A complete review of the structure of peripheral nervous tissue is beyond the scope of this chapter. Here, cellular morphology of mammalian nerve is the main concern, and recent research has been favored in selecting references to include herein. Current texts can be used to supplement the introduction to the histology of peripheral nerve that is provided below. Other books and reviews deal with certain aspects of nerve structure in much greater detail and also provide many additional references (Schmitt and Geschwind, 1957; Lehmann, 1959; Causey, 1960; Speidel, 1964; Murray, 1965; Bischoff, 1970; Gray, 1970; Jacobson, 1970; Peters *et al.*, 1970; Billings, 1971).

2. HISTOLOGY AND DEVELOPMENT

The light microscopic appearance of transversely and longitudinally sectioned peripheral nerves is shown in Fig. 1. Nerve fibers are arranged in

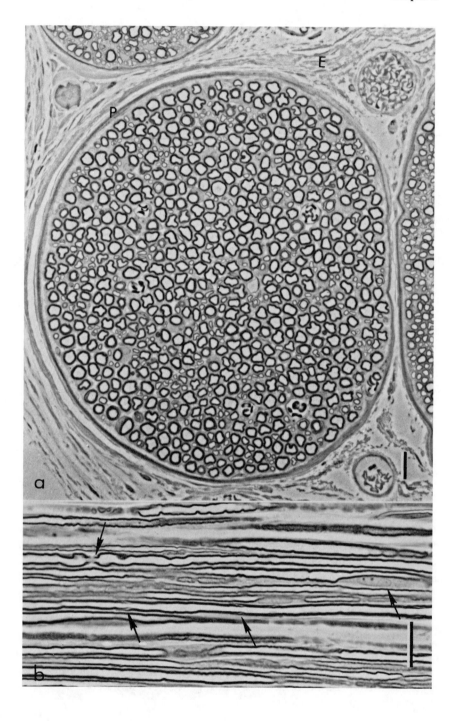

bundles that are embedded in loose connective tissue, the epineurium. The perineurium is the dense, lamellated, fibrous sheath that surrounds the nerve fibers and endoneurial connective tissue in each bundle or fascicle. Many fibers (axons) in the fascicles of most nerves are myelinated. Each segment of an axon's myelin sheath is formed by one Schwann (neurilemma, satellite, sheath) cell. The regularly spaced axonal regions between adjacent myelin segments are the nodes of Ranvier. The internodal distance corresponds to the length of the Schwann cell, and its nucleus is located midway between nodes. Other Schwann cells surround the numerous small axons that remain unmyelinated. The endoneurium includes the collagen, fibroblasts, vessels, and mast cells that fill the spaces between Schwann cells and their nerve fibers.

The relationships between Schwann cells and axons are established during development. As expected, there are wide variations among species, in different nerves of the same animal, and, in special cases, along the same axon (Bunge, 1968; Peters *et al.*, 1970; Schnepp and Schnepp, 1971; Waxman, 1973). Figure 2 illustrates the important morphological events leading to the appearance of mature myelinated and unmyelinated fibers in mammalian nerve (Geren, 1954; Robertson, 1957; Peters and Muir, 1959; Peters and Vaughn, 1970; Webster, 1971; Webster *et al.*, 1973). Initially, groups of proliferating Schwann cells form sheaths that surround and then subdivide bundles of axons. Axons destined to become myelinated are larger in diameter and frequently are located in individual furrows within the Schwann cell sheath. When a Schwann cell establishes a 1:1 relationship with one of these larger axons, it stops dividing, becomes separated from its neighbors, and forms myelin, a derivative of its surface membrane (Geren, 1954; reviewed by Robertson, 1962; Peters and Vaughn, 1970; Webster, 1971). The fiber bundles and their Schwann cell sheaths become smaller as more and more Schwann cells surround and myelinate single axons. When this sorting process is completed, the remaining Schwann cells provide furrows on their surfaces for smaller axons that remain unmyelinated. This sequence of events progresses distally along a nerve, and by the end of development both the myelinated and unmyelinated fibers have acquired mature sheaths consisting of chains of individual Schwann cells.

Generally, myelin formation begins when axons are 1–2 μm in diameter (Duncan, 1934; Matthews, 1968). The available evidence indicates that myelin

Fig. 1. Transverse (a) and longitudinal (b) sections of sciatic nerve shown at low magnification. Vertical scales at lower right represent 20 μm. In (a), the epineurium (E) contains vessels, fibroblasts, and collagen. The perineurium (P) surrounds fascicles of nerve fibers which are separated by endoneurial connective tissue. The longitudinal section (b) includes a node of Ranvier (upper arrow), a Schwann cell nucleus (right arrow), and Schmidt-Lantermann clefts (lower arrows).

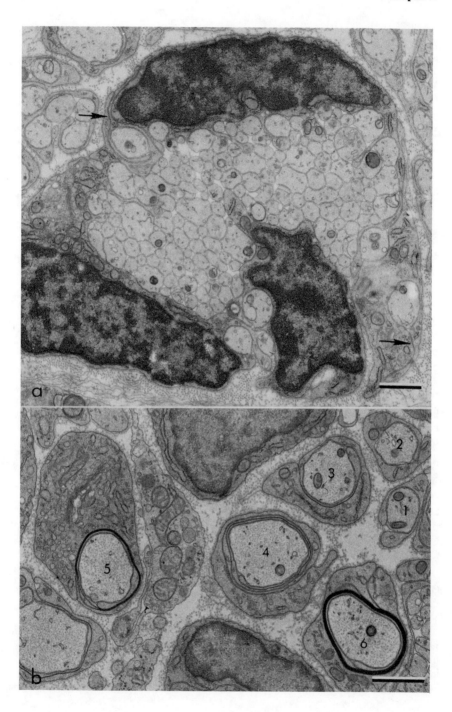

sheaths are first observed around axons destined to become the largest in a nerve (Thomas, 1956). As axons elongate toward their end organs, new myelin segments are added; during subsequent growth of an axon, its Schwann cells and their myelin segments increase in length but not in number (Thomas and Young, 1949; Thomas, 1955). After an axon becomes myelinated, its conduction velocity increases dramatically. Impulses jump from one node of Ranvier to the next, a process termed "saltatory conduction" (see Chapter 2.6). From a functional standpoint, three important dimensional parameters are the axon's diameter and the myelin sheath's thickness and length. Recently, Williams and Wendell-Smith (1971) used several techniques to measure these dimensions and compared the results with those obtained *in vivo*. They found that the ratio of axon diameter to sheath thickness was similar in rabbit dorsal and ventral roots but differed distally in skin and muscle nerves. Also, when axons of the same diameter were compared in sensory and motor nerves the latter had thicker sheaths. These and other differences were attributed to variations in local growth patterns of these axons, Schwann cells, and their myelin sheaths. Although thicker, longer myelin segments usually surround larger axons that conduct faster, their observations emphasize that a single dimensional parameter at one point along a nerve cannot be used to classify populations of myelinated fibers.

3. THE AXON

A neuron's axon originates at a funnel-shaped hillock that can be identified in light microscopic sections by its lack of basophilic material (Nissl substance) and by the absence of granular endoplasmic reticulum in electron micrographs. In multipolar neurons, there are two distinctive features of the initial segment (Palay *et al.*, 1968). Microtubules converge in the tapering hillock and occur in clusters along the length of the initial segment. In addition, there is a thin layer of dense material under the initial segment's plasma membrane. When studied at higher magnification, this undercoating is granular, about 200 Å thick, and is separated from the axolemma by approximately 80 Å; it also is stained by ethanolic phosphotungstic acid (Powell and Sloper, 1973). Palay *et al.* (1968) suggested that the undercoating represents a surface specialization concerned with the initiation and propagation of the action

Fig. 2. Transverse sections of developing nerve. In (a), processes of five Schwann cells surround an axon bundle. Between the two lower nuclei, three axons are segregated in separate furrows. Schwann cells surrounding single larger axons have formed long mesaxons (arrows). Six axons in (b) illustrate the stages in myelin formation. The mesaxon forms (1,2) and elongates to form a loose spiral (3,4) that becomes compact except for separation of the layers near the mesaxon (5). When the spiral includes six to eight layers (6), its entire circumference is compact. Scale bars, 1 μm.

potential; it was found only in initial segments of multipolar neurons and at all nodes of Ranvier. Sensory neurons, whose action potential originates elsewhere, do not have undercoated initial segments that contain fascicles of microtubules.

Beyond the initial segment, the axon contains filaments, tubules, mitochondria, agranular endoplasmic reticulum, occasional lysosomes, and multivesicular bodies that are similar to those found in other parts of the neuron (Figs. 3–5). There are clusters of ribosomes in the axon hillock that become less frequent and are only occasionally found beyond the axon's initial segment in mature animals (Zelena, 1972).

3.1. Filaments and Microtubules

Neurofilaments and microtubules (neurotubules) are the major constituents of axons and have been the subject of much recent research (Wuerker and Palay, 1969; Wuerker, 1970; see reviews by Schmitt and Sampson, 1968; Wuerker and Kirkpatrick, 1972; Shelanski and Feit, 1972). In electron micrographs, neurofilaments are long, thin threads. In cross-sections, they are circular, measure about 90 Å in diameter, and have clear centers. Their walls are about 30 Å thick and contain globular subunits that may have short radiating arms. Physicochemical studies of neurofilaments from axoplasm of the giant squid suggested that the globular subunits are coiled in a helix, and, recently, acidic proteins with molecular weights of about 25,000 and 73,000 have been isolated (Huneeus and Davison, 1970). In addition, 50-Å microfilaments have been found in growth cones of cultured neurons; growth can be inhibited reversibly by cytochalasin B (Yamada et al., 1970) and chemical evidence indicates that the microfilaments are actin (Fine and Bray, 1971).

Microtubules are 240-Å cylinders of indefinite length. They have a clear center that may contain a dot. The walls of microtubules are about 60 Å thick and are made up of 11–14 circular subunits. Cross-bridges between adjacent microtubules are present in the fascicles found in the initial segment (Palay et al., 1968) but are uncommon elsewhere. Changes in temperature (Rodriguez-Echandia and Piezzi, 1968), mitotic spindle inhibitors (Wisniewski et al., 1968), and an anesthetic, halothane (Hinckley and Samson, 1972), will dissociate microtubules and have been useful in studying their function and composition.

The chemistry of microtubules is included in two reviews (Barondes and

---

Fig. 3. Transverse sections, adult sciatic nerve. Next to a small myelinated fiber in (a), processes of another Schwann cell form individual furrows for a number of axons that are unmyelinated. Scale bar, 0.5 μm. In (b), neurofilaments, neurotubules, and the myelin sheath's lamellar structure are shown at higher magnification. Scale bar, 0.1 μm.

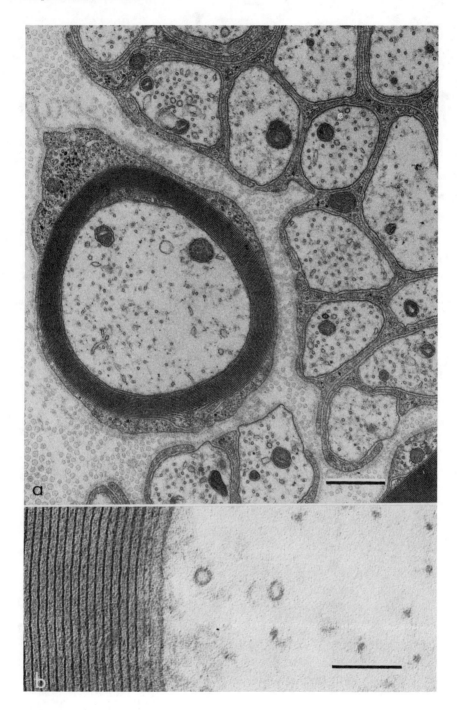

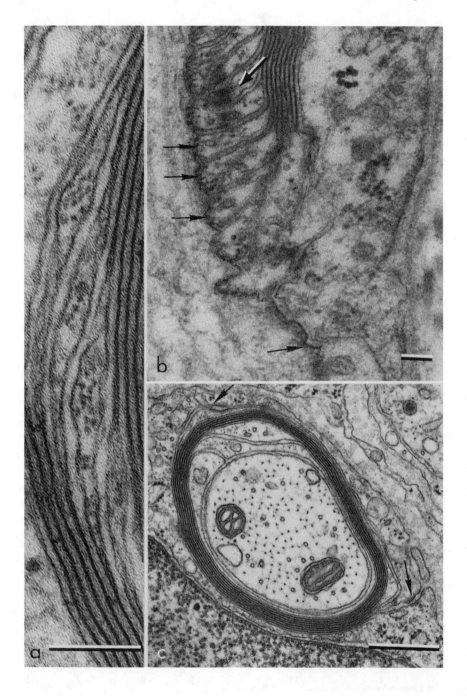

Feit, 1970; Shelanski and Feit, 1972). In brief, two different isolation procedures have been used to study microtubular subunits. In the first, microtubules are isolated directly from sperm tails, flagella, or brain after stabilization; the second depends on the capacity of microtubules to bind colchicine. Current evidence suggests that the tubulins obtained with both procedures are similar. Microtubular protein (tubulin) from brain is a dimer; the molecular weight of the two subunits is 55,000–60,000 and they differ slightly in amino acid composition. Finally, more recent experiments have shown that isolated brain tubulin can polymerize *in vitro* and form microtubules (Weisenberg, 1972).

Several observations have suggested that a structural relationship exists between neurofilaments and microtubules. The latter are more prominent in developing axons and decrease in relative density during subsequent growth (Peters and Vaughn, 1967). Also, masses of filaments are observed when microtubules are disrupted by mitotic spindle inhibitors (Wisniewski *et al.*, 1968); when studied *in vitro*, this effect is partially reversible (Daniels, 1973). However, these filaments and neurofilaments differ biochemically and interconversion has not been observed directly. The distribution of microtubules and neurofilaments in myelinated and unmyelinated axons of varying size has been studied quantitatively in transverse sections of sciatic nerves (Friede and Samorajski, 1970). In both fiber types, the sum of the number of neurofilaments and microtubules correlated best with an axon's area. The ratio of microtubules to neurofilaments was much higher in unmyelinated than in myelinated axons, and in the latter decreased slightly during maturation. Clusters of microtubules were observed frequently, and their association with axonal mitochondria (Raine *et al.*, 1971) was confirmed. It is also of interest that cross-bridges between microtubules and synaptic vesicles have been described in spinal cord axons of the lamprey (Smith and Hasinoff, 1971).

Growth of neuronal processes and maintenance of their extended form are two important functions postulated for microfilaments, microtubules, and neurofilaments. Axonal growth cones have small motile projections that contain microfilaments composed of actin-like proteins (Yamada *et al.*, 1970; Wessells *et al.*, 1971; Fine and Bray, 1971). Movement of these microspikes

---

Fig. 4. In (a), a Schmidt-Lantermann cleft is sectioned transversely. Tangentially arranged pockets of cytoplasm containing a few ribosomes are surrounded by continuous membranes that join to form major dense lines in compact myelin on both sides of the cleft. In the longitudinally sectioned node of Ranvier shown in (b), a few desmosomes are found in the terminal myelin loops (heavy arrow). A series of rings (upper thin arrows) is located between these loops and the axolemma, which has an undercoating (lower thin arrow) beyond the last loop. In (c), junctional complexes are located at the mesaxon's origin (lower arrow) and in the outer layer of myelin in this transverse section of developing nerve. Scale bars for (a), (b), and (c) are 0.1, 0.1, and 0.5 μm, respectively.

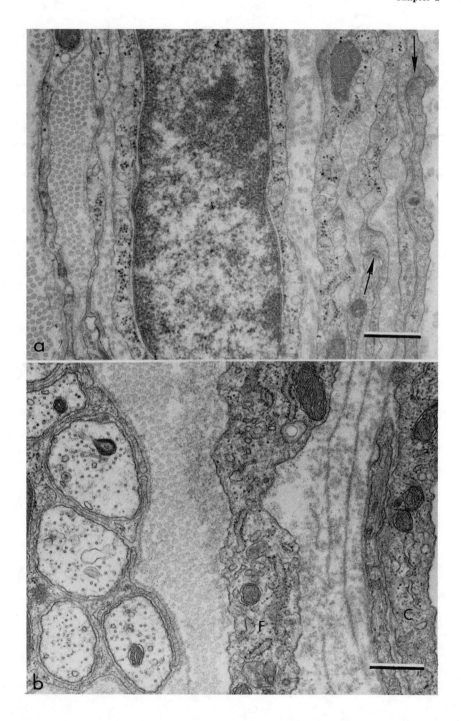

and extension of the growth cone are reversibly inhibited by cytochalasin B. Microtubule assembly is also required for elongation of the axon since colchicine prevents the process of growth and produces reversible retraction without an initial, direct effect on growth cone function. Neurofilaments appear to be less important during axon growth than in the subsequent maintenance of its shape. As mentioned above, they appear later in development than microtubules and are most numerous in the largest axons.

Transport is a third function suggested for microtubules and filaments and is of sufficient importance to justify more detailed analysis in Chapter 3. Much of the literature dealing with the morphology of axoplasmic flow is included in reviews by Lubinska (1964), Barondes (1967), Davison (1970a), Lasek (1970), Weiss (1970), Dahlström (1971), and Ochs (1972). Many investigators have suggested that microtubules play the leading role in axoplasmic transport, but morphological evidence to support this concept has been difficult to obtain. Recently, Fernandez studied the fine structure of axonal microtubules in crayfish nerve cords at intervals after flow was experimentally altered (Fernandez et al., 1970, 1971). In regions where the slow movement (1 mm/day) of ^{3}H-leucine was inhibited by cold or colchicine, the microtubules appeared normal. When both fast (10 mm/day) and slow components were blocked by vinblastine, loss of microtubules and crystal formation were observed only in axons near the injection site after 1 h. In more distant regions, where inhibition of transport persisted for more than 16 days, examination of axons at intervals revealed some that appeared relatively unaffected. In many axons, however, microtubules were present but had lost their slender, lateral filamentous projections and were surrounded by varying amounts of flocculent material. Thus one injection of vinblastine blocked axon transport for more than 16 days without dissociating microtubules. Their surface structure was altered, however, and the fine filamentous network located there under normal conditions seems to have an important role in this system's transport mechanism. Neurofilaments were not observed in these axons, and, to date, there is little, if any, direct evidence to support the suggestion that neurofilaments participate in axoplasmic transport.

The role of neuronal organelles in axonal flow has also been described in a series of recent reports by Weiss and Mayr (1971a,b,c) that supplement an earlier review (Weiss, 1970). Counts showed that the total number of microtubules in six axons almost exactly equaled the sum of the number present in their distal branches. They considered microtubules to be unbranched con-

Fig. 5. In (a), the perineurium is sectioned transversely and consists of layers of longitudinally oriented collagen alternating with fibroblasts joined by tight junctions (arrows). The epineurium is to the right. In (b), a basal lamina covers the capillary endothelium (C) and the Schwann cell surrounding the unmyelinated axons but is not present on the surface of the endoneurial fibroblast (F). Scale bars, p.5 μm.

tinuous cylinders extending from a neuron's soma to one of its endings. By contrast, the spacing of filaments remained constant in spite of wide variations in an axon's transverse area, suggesting that filaments were discontinuous and metastable.

3.2. Other Organelles and the Axolemma

Mitochondria in axons are thin, may be several microns long, and are usually unbranched. They contain longitudinally oriented cristae and relatively few dense granules. Counts have revealed that unmyelinated fibers contain more mitochondria per square micron of transversely sectioned axoplasm than myelinated axons (Samorajski and Friede, 1968; Zelena, 1968). In the latter, motochondria are more numerous at nodes of Ranvier, and in both types of fibers they help provide the energy required for conduction and for the fast component of axoplasmic transport (Ochs, 1971).

Axons also contain vesicles and cisternae of agranular endoplasmic reticulum arranged in longitudinal rows that are more prominent at nodes of Ranvier and near endings. A few multivesicular bodies and lysosomes are found there, also. The distribution of these organelles and the appearance of high acid hydrolase activity in them immediately after axonal injury suggest that they are involved in the transport and turnover of some of the axon's protein constituents (Holtzman and Novikoff, 1965; Holtzman, 1971). The agranular reticulum may also be concerned with the formation of dense-cored vesicles (Teichberg and Holtzman, 1973).

The axolemma is the axon's plasma membrane and is similar to that covering the rest of a neuron's surface except at nodes of Ranvier or endings. It measures 70–80 Å, is trilaminar, and is asymmetrical in electron micrographs of osmium-fixed nerves. A relatively clear region is found between two lines, and the one next to the cytoplasm is usually denser and slightly wider. Recently, coated invaginations of the axolemma have been observed along the internodal surfaces of myelinated axons in young mice; they may represent sites of pinocytotic exchange between a Schwann cell and its axon (Waxman, 1968).

At nodes of Ranvier (Figs. 1 and 4), the axon becomes smaller and its surface differs (see reviews by Peters and Vaughn, 1970; Waxman, 1973; as well as Hess and Young, 1952; Robertson, 1959; Williams and Kashef, 1968; Williams and Hall, 1970). In brief, observations on both living and fixed myelinated fibers have shown that the degree of nodal constriction is greater in large axons with thick myelin sheaths. Carbohydrate-containing basement membrane material is found between the terminal villous processes of adjacent Schwann cells (Langley and Landon, 1967), and beneath the axolemma there is an undercoating similar to that observed along the axon's initial segment. Where the myelin sheath ends on either side of the node, there are round densities between the axolemma and each terminal loop of myelin. These densities, called transverse bands, may be arranged in a spiral, and they are thought to limit the penetration of tracers into the internodal periaxonal space (Hirano and Dembitzer, 1969).

As mentioned above, axonal organelles are more numerous near endings and may play a role in the turnover of its constituents and remodeling (Sotelo and Palay, 1971). The histology and fine structure of neuromuscular junctions and other endings of axons in the peripheral nervous system are described separately in Chapters 4, 5, 6, 10 and Section III.

4. SHEATHS OF AXONS

4.1. Schwann Cells

Rows of Schwann cells, similar to those encapsulating neurons in ganglia, extend as a sheath along all of the neuronal processes in the peripheral nervous system. Variable numbers of small axons that remain unmyelinated occupy longitudinal indentations along Schwann cells that are cylindrical and contain a centrally located nucleus surrounded by organelles (Figs. 3 and 5). Other rows consist of tubular Schwann cells that have surrounded a larger axon and formed adjacent segments of its myelin sheath (Fig. 3). Nuclei of Schwann cells often contain more than one nucleolus, and in aldehyde-fixed preparations the distribution of chromatin is patchy and peripheral clumping is frequently observed. Ribosomes study the outer leaflet of the nuclear envelope, which is interrupted by pores. The perinuclear cytoplasm contains a prominent Golgi apparatus and cisternae of granular endoplasmic reticulum, as well as occasional cilia (Grillo and Palay, 1963). Most of the Schwann cell's mitochondria lie in the perikaryon or in the paranodal cytoplasm. They usually have transverse cristae, a dense matrix, and occasional granules. They are generally shorter and narrower than those in neurons. A few lysosomes and multivesicular bodies are also present along with microtubules, filaments, clusters of ribosomes, and glycogen particles. Elsewhere along the Schwann cells that surround myelinated axons, the layer of cytoplasm is relatively thin and contains microtubules, filaments, ribosomes, and an occasional mitochondrion or lysosome.

A basal lamina varying in width and density covers the Schwann cell's trilaminar surface membrane (Figs. 3–5). Similar material extends over some unmyelinated axons and is found at nodes of Ranvier, where it separates the axon surface and terminal processes of adjacent Schwann cells from the endoneurial collagen (Fig. 4). This material is rich in carbohydrates and can be stained with a number of reagents such as alcian blue, ruthenium red, and phosphotungstic acid at acidic pH (Pease, 1970; Landon and Langley, 1971; Luft, 1971).

4.2. Myelin

Many electron microscopic studies have established that peripheral myelin originates from the Schwann cell's surface membrane (Geren, 1954; reviewed by Robertson, 1962; Peters and Vaughn, 1970). Initially, the mesaxon elongates to form a spiral around the axon (Fig. 2); further growth leads to apposition of the layers and the compact structure shown in Fig. 3. In micrographs of osmium- and permanganate-fixed nerves, the Schwann cell's surface membrane is trilaminar and asymmetrical. Its outer layers are opposed in the mesaxon and produce the less dense, intraperiod lines in compact myelin. The cytoplasmic faces of the surface membrane unite at the end of the first spiral turn and form the interperiod or major dense line of myelin. Thus the repeating radial period of 125–150 Å includes two "unit" membrane leaflets. Early studies using polarized light and X-ray diffraction had shown that, in myelin, bilayers of radially oriented lipid molecules alternate with layers of tangentially arranged proteins (reviewed in Mokrasch et al., 1971); Robertson subsequently demonstrated that both osmium and permanganate stain the external polar regions of the lipid layers even though the dimensions and density of the layers differ (see Robertson, 1962). Recently, better methods have improved myelin preservation in electron micrographs; the 170–180 Å period corresponds to that observed in fresh nerves by X-ray diffraction and double intraperiod lines are separated by about 20 Å (Napolitano and Scallen, 1969; Revel and Hamilton, 1969; Peterson and Pease, 1972). The relative absence of protein within the lipid bilayers has also been shown by Branton (1967). In electron micrographs of freeze-fracture preparations of nerves, myelin membranes are smooth and free of particles found in other membranes, including the Schwann cell's plasmalemma.

The chemical composition and metabolism of myelin have been reviewed recently (Davison and Peters, 1970; LeBaron, 1970; Mokrasch et al., 1971). In peripheral nerves, lipids constitute about 75% of myelin's dry weight and virtually all the rest is protein. The major lipids are cholesterol, phospholipids, and galactolipids, and models of the myelin membrane usually show them in a molar ratio of about 2:2:1. Current evidence suggests that the cholesterol content is higher in the external leaflet of the lipid bilayer (Casper and Kirschner, 1971) and that the inner, cytoplasmic layer contains more cerebrosides.

About 70–80% of the protein in myelin is proteolipid, which has been difficult to isolate and characterize (Mokrasch et al., 1971). Basic (Folch-Lees) and acidic (Wolfgram) proteolipids have been described, and in peripheral myelin the concentration of the latter is slightly higher. Probably, the proteolipids exist in myelin in an extended B-like configuration. Their distribution in peripheral myelin may be asymmetrical; observations during swelling suggest that the external surface of each lamella contains more acidic than basic proteolipid.

Other basic proteins have been isolated that are antigenic, have molecular weights of about 6000 and 11,000, and constitute about 20% of peripheral myelin's total protein (Eyelar, 1970; Oshiro and Eyelar, 1970). Recent observations indicate that basic protein is found on the external surface of the myelin membrane (Dickinson *et al.*, 1970). Others have suggested that it is better protected from the circulation on the cytoplasmic side; this location also seems more reasonable because of the asymmetrical distribution of lipids and the intense staining of the interperiod line by osmium.

The metabolism of myelin formation and its subsequent maintenance in the adult have been more thoroughly investigated in the central than in the peripheral nervous system (Davison, 1970*b*; Mokrasch *et al.*, 1971). The available evidence suggests that myelin is not made *de novo*. Instead, the initial turns of the mesaxon spiral may resemble the Schwann cell's plasma membrane biochemically.

Compared to mature myelin, this early or "myelin-like" membrane probably has a higher protein-to-lipid ratio and contains more phosphatidylcholine, less cerebroside, and almost no sulfatide or basic protein. As the myelin spiral becomes compact and grows, the basic protein, cerebroside, and sulfatide content rises and the amount of phosphatidylcholine decreases.

The mature myelin sheath is much more inert metabolically than other membranes (Smith, 1968; LeBaron, 1970). Its stability has been attributed to its high content of lipids and their slow turnover. However, a small proportion of lipids, especially phosphoinositides, the sulfate in sulfatides, and some fatty acids, are exchanged more rapidly. This small, active pool may be located near cytoplasmic interfaces in the sheath's outer or inner layers or close to the Schmidt-Lantermann clefts, which are described below. In general, proteins in myelin have a faster turnover rate than lipids. The basic proteins are the fastest, and, in contrast to the lipids, incorporation of precursors can be inhibited by cycloheximide (Smith and Hasinoff, 1971).

Usually, the myelin sheath is circular or oval in transverse section. Most of its irregularities disappear during the final phase of development (Webster, 1971), and in the mature sheath redundant loops or folds are generally limited to the paranodal regions of large fibers (Webster and Spiro, 1960). Similar variations in sheath contour have been observed recently *in vivo* (Williams and Hall, 1971*a*).

In longitudinally sectioned fibers, the compact array of myelin layers is interrupted by tangential clefts, the incisures of Schmidt-Lantermann (Fig. 4; Robertson, 1958; Hall and Williams, 1970). In these clefts, myelin lamellae alternate with small cytoplasmic pockets that form thin, spiral connections between the layers of Schwann cell cytoplasm that lie inside and outside the myelin sheath. Junctional complexes, dense material, tubules, and occasional multivesicular bodies have been observed in these incisures, and they become more prominent in living fibers which are traumatized or immersed in hypotonic solutions (Hall and Williams, 1970).

Paranodally, the myelin lamellae terminate in spirally arranged loops beginning with the innermost layer and ending with the outer layer at the nodal gap (Fig. 4) (Geren-Uzman and Nogueira-Graf, 1957; Robertson, 1959; Williams and Kashef, 1968; Berthold, 1968). In small fibers, the loops formed by successive layers all touch the axon surface and participate in forming the terminal bars described above. Many loops fail to reach the paranodal surface of large axons; this may be due in part to distortion during tissue preparation. Junctional complexes are often found between adjacent loops which contain dense material, granules, a few tubules, and vesicular profiles.

4.3. Function of Schwann Cells and Their Myelin Sheaths

The most important function of Schwann cells in vertebrate nerves is to form and maintain myelin sheaths. Schwann cells must continue to interact with the axons they myelinate since myelin breakdown and Schwann cell changes accompany degeneration of axons produced by nerve transection (Wallerian degeneration). Fragmentation of myelin lamellae is associated with the earliest axonal changes at nodes of Ranvier (Webster, 1962). An increase in the number of Schmidt-Lantermann clefts precedes the breakdown of the myelin sheath into ovoids (Webster, 1965); both the incisures (Hall and Williams, 1970) and the margins of ovoids (Holtzman and Novikoff, 1965) show an increase in acid phosphatase activity. Further myelin fragmentation and breakdown are associated with Schwann cell hypertrophy and hyperplasia. The basal laminae of Schwann cells persist as a longitudinal framework (Thomas, 1964) that helps orient proliferating Schwann cells (Bradley and Asbury, 1970) and regenerating axons. The new myelin segments are thinner (Schröder, 1972) and shorter than their predecessors even though they are formed by the same process. Recent morphological studies of Wallerian degeneration emphasize the importance of Schwann cells (Singer and Steinberg, 1972) and include *in vivo* observations (Williams and Hall, 1971*a,b*). The temporal and spatial sequences of axonal changes have also been described (Donat and Wisniewski, 1973) and reviewed (Joseph, 1973).

Alterations in Schwann cell number, size, and shape are less striking if myelin breakdown occurs in the presence of an intact axon (segmental demyelination). Fragmentation of paranodal myelin lamellae is followed by breakdown of the affected segment within the Schwann cell. Myelin remnants are then sequestered and taken up by macrophages. During this type of demyelination, the axon which remains normal is displaced toward the Schwann cell surface prior to remyelination (Webster et al., 1961; Webster, 1964).

Thus myelin breakdown and regeneration can be produced by damaging axons or Schwann cells. Other observations suggest how they may interact under normal conditions to maintain myelin metabolically and assist in the turnover of its constituents. Singer and his collaborators (1966, 1968) found that after intraperitoneal administration of radioactive amino acids, Schwann cells, myelin sheaths, and axons were labeled in both normal nerves and in distal segments of transected nerves. Also, tracers when injected endoneurially are found in Schwann cells, between lamellae of the myelin spiral (Revel and Hamilton, 1969; Olsson and Reese, 1971; Hall and Williams, 1971; Singer et al., 1972); they may gain access to the periaxonal space along the paranodal transverse bands (documented initially in the CNS by Hirano and Dembitzer, 1969; Reese et al., 1971); and, finally, they can be found in axons and their neuronal perikarya after centripetal transport (Kristensson and Olsson, 1971). The presence of pinocytotic invaginations on the axolemma also suggests that exchange occurs along internodal surfaces of axons (Waxman, 1968). Thus routes exist for transport and exchange between extracellular space, Schwann cells, myelin, and axons.

The motion of Schwann cells, myelin sheaths, and their incisures in living fibers may enhance metabolic exchange in myelin lamellae and could also influence flow in the axons they surround. Rippling, undulating movements of the myelin sheath were observed years ago by Speidel (see 1964 review). Murray and her collaborators noted similar movements in mature fibers after myelination in vitro; Schmidt-Lantermann clefts were often located near myelin overgrowths in mature sheaths and were thought to fluctuate and play a role in remodeling the sheath (reviewed by Murray, 1965). Her later observations characterized these movements in greater detail (Murray and Herrmann, 1968). Every 10–15 min, rippling pulsations traveled along the Schwann cells and reversed direction frequently. As each ripple passed over a partially open cleft, it was squeezed shut temporarily. Singer and Bryant (1969) also studied sheath movements in vitro by gently exposing myelinated fibers in sciatic nerves of Xenopus frogs. Most sheath movements occurred near Schmidt-Lantermann clefts, and their activity was highly variable. Generally, the incisures were closed and slitlike. Opening occurred about once in 8 h, varied in duration, and was accompanied by inward swelling that compressed the axon. More recently, Williams and Hall (1970, 1971a; Hall and Williams, 1970) used oblique incident illumination to examine myelinated fibers within intact nerves in vivo. During 2–6 h of continuous observation, the contour of myelin sheaths remained stable; undulations, rippling movements, and peristaltic movements (Weiss, 1972) were not observed. Incisures did not change in location or number; the majority were "closed," a few were "moderately open," and there was little change in their state of dilation during the period of observation. Thus there appears to be little movement of mature Schwann cells and myelin sheaths when they are located in nerve fascicles, and it seems unlikely that the motion described affects transport significantly.

4.4. Connective Tissue Sheaths

The fine structure of connective tissue sheaths in the peripheral nervous system has been studied (Thomas, 1963; Burkel, 1967; Waggener, 1967), and their permeability has been of great interest (Klemm, 1970; Olsson and Reese, 1971). The extracellular compartment that surrounds Schwann cells and their axons is the endoneurium (Fig. 5). It is relatively large, and the collagen within it contributes to the elasticity of nerves that are stretched repeatedly during normal body movements. Endoneurial fibroblasts resemble those found elsewhere; they have ellipsoidal nuclei, thin processes, large mitochondria, long cisternae of granular endoplasmic reticulum, and no basal lamina. Occasional pericytes and mast cells are found near vessels. Collagen and lamellated fibroblasts form alternating layers in the perineurium (Fig. 5). Tight junctions between adjacent perineurial and endothelial cells prevent tracers from penetrating the perineurial and blood–nerve "barriers" (Waksman, 1961; Olsson and Reese, 1971). Proximally, in spinal roots, there are fewer fibroblasts and less endoneurial collagen. The outer sheath is also thinner than the perineurium and its cellular organization becomes modified as it merges with the pia (Maxwell et al., 1969; Haller and Low, 1971; Haller et al., 1972). Distally, the connective tissue sheaths become thinner and generally disappear before nerve fibers terminate at their endings (Kerjaschki and Stockinger, 1970).

5. REFERENCES

Barondes, S. H., 1967, Axoplasmic transport, *Neurosci. Res. Prog. Bull.* **5**:307.
Barondes, S. H., and Feit, H., 1970, Metabolism of microtubular protein in mouse brain, in *Ciba Foundation Symposium on Alzheimer's Disease and Related Conditions*, pp. 267–278, Churchill, London.
Berthold, C.-H., 1968, Ultrastructure of the node–paranode region of mature feline ventral lumbar spinal-root fibres, *Acta Soc. Med. Upsal.* **73**:37 (Suppl. 9.)
Billings, S. M., 1971, Concepts of nerve fiber development, 1839–1930, *J. Histol. Biol.* **4**:275.
Bischoff, A., 1970, Peripheral nervous system, in: *Ultrastructure of the Peripheral Nervous System and Sense Organs* (A. Bischoff, ed.), pp. 3–166, C. V. Mosby Co., St. Louis.

Bradley, W. G., and Asbury, A. K., 1970, Duration of synthesis phase in neurilemma cells in mouse sciatic nerve during degeneration, *Exptl. Neurol.* **26**:275.

Branton, D., 1967, Fracture faces of frozen myelin, *Exptl. Cell Res.* **45**:203.

Bunge, R. P., 1968, Glial cells and the central myelin sheath, *Physiol. Rev.* **48**:197.

Burkel, W. E., 1967, The histological fine structure of perineurium, *Anat. Rec.* **158**:177.

Casper, D. L. D., and Kirschner, D. A., 1971, Myelin membrane structure at 10 Å resolution, *Nature New Biol.* **231**:46.

Causey, G., 1960, *The Cell of Schwann*, E. and S. Livingstone, Edinburgh.

Dahlström, A., 1971, Axoplasmic transport (with particular respect to adrenergic neurons), *Phil. Trans. Roy. Soc. Lond. B* **261**:325.

Daniels, M. P., 1973, Fine structural changes correlated with colchicine inhibition of nerve fiber formation *in vitro*, *J. Cell Biol.* **58**:463.

Davison, P. F., 1970a, Microtubules and neurofilaments: Possible implications in axoplasmic transport, *Advan. Biochem. Psychoparmacol.* **2**:168.

Davison, A. N., 1970b, The biochemistry of the myelin sheath, in: *Myelination* (A. N. Davison and A. Peters, eds.), Charles C Thomas, Springfield, Ill.

Davison, A. N., and Peters, A., 1970, *Myelination*, Charles C Thomas, Springfield, Ill.

Dickinson, J. P., Jones, K. M., Aparicio, S. R., and Lumsden, C. E., 1970, Localization of encephalitogenic basic protein in the intraperiod line of lamellar myelin, *Nature* **227**:1133.

Donat, J. R., and Wisniewski, H. M., 1973, The spatio-temporal pattern of Wallerian degeneration in mammalian peripheral nerves, *Brain Res.* **53**:41.

Duncan, D., 1934, A relation between axone diameter and myelination determined by measurement of myelinated spinal root fibers, *J. Comp. Neurol.* **60**:437.

Eyelar, E. H., 1970, Amino acid sequence of the basic protein of the myelin membrane, *Proc. Nat. Acad. Sci. USA* **67**:1425.

Fernandez, H. L., Huneeus, F. C., and Davison, P. F., 1970, Studies on the mechanism of axoplasmic transport in the crayfish cord, *J. Neurobiol.* **1**:395.

Fernandez, H. L., Burton, P. R., and Samson, F. E., 1971, Axoplasmic transport in the crayfish nerve cord: The role of fibrillar constituents of neurons, *J. Cell Biol.* **51**:176.

Fine, R. E., and Bray, D., 1971, Actin in growing nerve cells, *Nature New Biol.* **234**:115.

Friede, R. L., and Samorajski, T., 1970, Axon caliber related to neurofilaments and microtubules in sciatic nerve fibers of rats and mice, *Anat. Rec.* **167**:379.

Geren, B. B., 1954, The formation from the Schwann cell surface of myelin in the peripheral nerves of chick embryos, *Exptl. Cell Res.* **7**:558.

Geren-Uzman, B., and Nogueira-Graf, G., 1957, Electron microscope studies of the formation of nodes of Ranvier in mouse sciatic nerves, *J. Biophys. Biochem. Cytol.* **3**:589.

Gray, E. G., 1970, The fine structure of nerve, *Comp. Biochem. Physiol.* **36**:419.

Grillo, M. A., and Palay, S. L., 1963, Ciliated Schwann cells in the autonomic nervous system of the adult rat, *J. Cell Biol.* **16**:430.

Hall, S. M., and Williams, P. L., 1970, Studies on the "incisures" of Schmidt and Lanterman, *J. Cell Sci.* **6**:767.

Hall, S. M., and Williams, P. L., 1971, The distribution of electron-dense tracers in peripheral nerve fibres, *J. Cell Sci.* **8**:541.

Haller, F. R., and Low, F. N., 1971, The fine structure of the peripheral nerve root sheath in the subarachnoid space in the rat and other laboratory animals, *Am. J. Anat.* **131**:1.

Haller, F. R., Haller, A. C., and Low, F. N., 1972, The fine structure of cellular layers and connective tissue space at spinal nerve root attachments in the rat, *Am. J. Anat.* **133**:109.

Hess, A., and Young, J. Z., 1952, The nodes of Ranvier, *Proc. Roy. Soc. Lond. B* **140**:301.

Hinckley, R. E., and Samson, F. E., 1972, Anesthetic-induced transformation of axon microtubules, *J. Cell Biol.* **53**:258.

Hirano, A., and Dembitzer, H. M., 1969, The transverse bands as a means of access to the periaxonal space of the central myelinated nerve fiber, *J. Ultrastruct. Res.* **28**:141.

Holtzman, E., 1971, Cytochemical studies of protein transport in the nervous system, *Phil. Trans. Roy. Soc. Lond. B* **261**:407.

Holtzman, E., and Novikoff, A. B., 1965, Lysosomes in the rat sciatic nerve following crush, *J. Cell Biol.* **27**:651.

Huneeus, F. C., and Davison, P. F., 1970, Fibrillar proteins from squid axons. I. Neurofilament protein, *J. Mol. Biol.* **52**:415.

Jacobson, M., 1970, *Developmental Neurobiology*, Holt, Rinehart and Winston, New York.

Joseph, B. S., 1973, Somatofugal events in Wallerian degeneration and axoplasmic transport: A conceptual overview, *Brain Res.* **59**:1.

Kerjaschki, D., and Stockinger, L., 1970, Zur Struktur und Funktion des Perineuriums, *Z. Zellforsch.* **110**:386.

Klemm, H., 1970, Das Perineurium als diffusions Barriere gegenuber Peroxydase bei epi- und endoneuraler Applikation, *Z. Zellforsch.* **108**:431.

Kristensson, K., and Olsson, Y., 1971, Uptake and retrograde axonal transport of peroxidase in hypoglossal neurones: Electron microscopical localization in the neuronal perikaryon, *Acta Neuropathol.* **19**:1.

Landon, D. N., and Langley, O. K., 1971, The local chemical environment of nodes of Ranvier; a study of cation binding, *J. Anat. Lond.* **108**:419.

Langley, O. K., and Landon, D. N., 1967, A light and electron histochemical approach to the node of Ranvier and myelin of peripheral nerve fibers, *J. Histochem. Cytochem.* **15**:722.

Lasek, R. J., 1970, Protein transport in neurons, *Internat. Rev. Neurobiol.* **13**:289.

LeBaron, F. N., 1970, Metabolism of myelin constituents, in: *Handbook of Neurochemistry* (A. Lajtha, ed.), Vol. 3, pp. 561–573, Plenum Press, New York.

Lehmann, H. J., 1959, Die nerven Faser, in: *Handbuch der mikroskopischer Anatomie des Menschen* (W. Mollendorff and W. Bargmann, eds.), Vol. 4, pp. 415–701, Springer-Verlag, Berlin.

Lubinska, L., 1964, Axoplasmic streaming in regenerating and in normal nerve fibers, in: *Mechanisms of Neural Regeneration* (M. Singer and J. P. Schade, eds.), Progress in Brain Research, Vol. 13, pp. 1–71, Elsevier Publishing Co., Amsterdam.

Luft, J. E., 1971, Ruthenium red and violet II: Fine structure localization in animal tissues, *Anat. Rec.* **171**:369.

Matthews, M. A., 1968, An electron microscopic study of the relationship between axon diameter and the initiation of myelin production in the peripheral nervous system, *Anat. Rec.* **161**:337.

Maxwell, D. S., Kruger, L., and Pineda, A., 1969, The trigeminal nerve root with special reference to the central–peripheral transition zone: An electron microscopic study in the macaque, *Anat. Rec.* **164**:113.

Mokrasch, L. C., Bear, R. S., and Schmitt, F. O., 1971, Myelin, *Neurosci. Res. Prog. Bull.* **9**:440.

Murray, M. E., 1965, Nervous tissues *in vitro*, in: *Cells and Tissues in Culture* (E. N. Willmer, ed.), Vol. 2, pp. 373–455, Academic Press, London.

Murray, M. R., and Herrmann, A., 1968, Passive movements of Schmidt-Lantermann clefts during continuous observation *in vitro*, *J. Cell Biol.* **39**:149a.

Napolitano, L. M., and Scallen, T. J., 1969, Observations on the fine structure of peripheral nerve myelin, *Anat. Rec.* **163**:1.

Ochs, S., 1971, Characteristics and a model for fast axoplasmic transport in nerve, *J. Neurobiol.* **2**:331.

Ochs, S., 1972, Fast transport of materials in mammalian nerve fibers, *Science* **176**:252.

Olsson, Y., and Reese, T. S., 1971, Permeability of vasa nervorum and perineurium in mouse sciatic nerve studied by fluorescence and electron microscopy, *J. Neuropathol. Exptl. Neurol.* **30**:105.

Oshiro, Y., and Eyelar, E. H., 1970, Allergic encephalomyelitis; a comparison of the encephalitogenic A1 protein from human and bovine brain, *Arch. Biochem. Biophys.* **138**:606.

Palay, S. L., Sotelo, C., Peters, A., and Orkand, P. M., 1968, The axon hillock and the initial segment, *J. Cell. Biol.* **38**:193.

Pease, D. C., 1970, Phosphotungstic acid as a specific electron stain for complex carbohydrates, *J. Histochem. Cytochem.* **18**:455.

Peters, A., and Muir, A. R., 1959, The relationship between axons and Schwann cells during development of peripheral nerves in the rat, *Quart, J. Exptl. Physiol.* **44**:117.

Peters, A., and Vaughn, J. E., 1967, Microtubules and filaments in the axons and astrocytes of early postnatal rat optic nerves, *J. Cell Biol.* **32**:113.

Peters, A., and Vaughn, J. E., 1970, Morphology and development of the myelin sheath, in: *Myelination* (A. N. Davison and A. Peters, eds.), pp. 3–79, Charles C Thomas, Springfield, Ill.

Peters, A., Palay, S. L., and Webster, H. deF., 1970, *The Fine Structure of the Nervous System; The Cells and Their Processes*, pp. 70–88, Harper and Row, New York.

Peterson, R. G., and Pease, D. C., 1972, Myelin embedded in polymerized glutaraldehyde-urea, *J. Ultrastruct. Res.* **41**:115.

Raine, C. S., Ghetti, B., and Shelanski, M. L., 1971, On the association between microtubules and mitochondria within axons, *Brain Res*, **34**:389.

Reese, T. S., Feder, N., and Brightman, M. W., 1971, Study of the blood–brain and blood–cerebrospinal fluid barriers with microperoxidase, *J. Neuropathol. Exptl. Neurol.* **30**:137.

Revel, J. P., and Hamilton, D. W., 1969, The double nature of the intermediate dense line in peripheral nerve myelin, *Anat. Rec.* **163**:7.

Robertson, J. D., 1957, New Observations on the ultrastructure of the membranes of frog peripheral nerve fibers, *J. Biophys. Biochem. Cytol.* **3**:1043.

Robertson, J. D., 1958, The ultrastructure of Schmidt-Lantermann clefts and related shearing defects of the myelin sheath, *J. Biophys. Biochem. Cytol.* **4**:39.

Robertson, J. D., 1959, Preliminary observations on the ultrastructure of nodes of Ranvier, *Z. Zellforsch.* **50**:553.

Robertson, J. D., 1962, The unit membrane of cells and mechanisms of myelin formation in: *Ultrastructure and Metabolism of the Nervous System* (S. R. Korey, A. Pope, and E. Robins, eds.), Vol. 40, pp. 94–158, Williams and Wilkins Co., Baltimore.

Rodriguez-Echandia, E. L., and Piezzi, R. S., 1968, Microtubules in the nerve fibers of the toad *Bufo arenarum* Hensel: Effect of low temperature on the sciatic nerve, *J. Cell. Biol.* **39**:491.

Samorajski, T., and Friede, R. L., 1968, Size-dependent distribution of axoplasm, Schwann cell cytoplasm, and mitochondria in the peripheral nerve fibers of mouse, *Anat. Rec.* **161**:281.

Schmitt, F. O., and Geschwind, N., 1957, The axon surface, *Progr. Biophys.* **8**:165.

Schmitt, F. O., and Samson, F. E., 1968, Neuronal fibrous proteins, *Neurosci. Res. Prog. Bull.* **6**:113.

Schnepp, P., and Schnepp, G., 1971, Faseranalytische Untersuchungen an peripheren Nerven bei tieren verschiedenger Grosse. II. Verhaltnis Axondurchmesser Gesamt-durchmesser und Internodallange, *Z. Zellforsch.* **119**:99.

Schröder, J. M., 1972, Altered ratio between axon diameter and myelin sheath thickness in regenerated nerve fibers, *Brain Res.* **45**:49.

Shelanski, M. L., and Feit, H., 1972, Filaments and tubules in the nervous system, in: *The Structure and Function of the Nervous System* (G. H. Bourne, ed.), Vol. 6, Academic Press, New York, pp. 47–80.

Singer, M., and Bryant, S. V., 1969, Movements in the myelin Schwann sheath of the vertebrate axon, *Nature* **221**:1148.

Singer, M., and Green, M. R., 1968, Autoradiographic studies of uridine incorporation in peripheral nerve of the newt, *Triturus, J. Morphol.* **124**:321.

Singer, M., and Salpeter, M. M., 1966, The transport of ^{3}H-1-histidine through the Schwann and myelin sheath into the axon, including a re-evaluation of myelin function, *J. Morphol.* **120**:281.

Singer, M., and Steinberg, M. C., 1972, Wallerian degeneration; a re-evaluation based on transected and colchicine-poisoned nerves in the amphibian, *Triturus, Am. J. Anat.* **133**:51.

Singer, M., Krishnan, N., and Fyfe, D. A., 1972, Penetration of ruthenium red into peripheral nerve fibres, *Anat. Rec.* **173**:375.

Sloper, J. J., and Powell, T. P. S., 1973, Observations on the axon initial segment and other structures in the neocortex using conventional staining and ethanolic phosphotungstic acid, *Brain Res.* **50**:163.

Smith, M. E., 1968, The turnover of myelin in the adult rat, *Biochim. Biophys. Acta* **164**:285.

Smith, M. E., and Hasinoff, C., 1971, Biosynthesis of myelin proteins *in vitro, J. Neurochem.* **18**:739.

Sotelo, C., and Palay, S. L., 1971, Altered axons and axon terminals in the lateral vestibular nucleus of the rat: Possible example of axonal remodeling, *Lab. Invest.* **25**:653.

Speidel, C. C., 1964, *In vivo* studies of myelinated nerve fibers, *Internat. Rev. Cytol.* **16**:173.

Teichberg, S., and Holtzman, E., 1973. Axonal agranular reticulum and synaptic vesicles in cultured embryonic chick sympathetic neurons, *J. Cell Biol.* **57**:88.

Thomas, P. K., 1955, Growth changes in the myelin sheath of peripheral nerve fibers, *Proc. Roy. Soc. London B* **143**:380.

Thomas, P. K., 1956, Growth changes in the diameter of peripheral nerve fibers in fishes, *J. Anat. Lond.* **90**:5.

Thomas, P. K., 1963, The connective tissue of peripheral nerve: An electron microscopic study, *J. Anat. Lond.* **97**:35.

Thomas, P. K., 1964, Changes in the endoneurial sheaths of peripheral myelinated nerve fibres during Wallerian degeneration, *J. Anat. Lond.* **98**:175.

Thomas, P. K., and Young, J. Z., 1949, Internode lengths in the nerves of fishes, *J. Anat. Lond.* **83**:336.

Waggener, J. D., and Beggs, J., 1967, The membranous coverings of neural tissues; an electron microscopy study, *J. Neuropathol. Exptl. Neurol.* **26**:412.

Waksman, B. H., 1961, Experimental study of diphtheritic polyneuritis in the rabbit and guinea pig. III. The blood–nerve barrier in the rabbit, *J. Neuropathol. Exptl. Neurol.* **20**:35.

Waxman, S. G., 1968, Micropinocytotic invaginations in the axolemma of peripheral nerves, *Z. Zellforsch.* **86**:571.

Waxman, S. G., 1973, Regional differentiation of the axon: A review with special reference to the concept of the multiplex neuron, *Brain Res.* **47**:269.

Webster, H. deF., 1962, Transient, focal accumulation of axonal mitochondria during early stages of Wallerian degeneration, *J. Cell Biol.* **12**:361.

Webster, H. deF., 1964, Some ultrastructural features of segmental demyelination and myelin regeneration in peripheral nerve, *Progr. Brain Res.* **13**:151.

Webster, H. deF., 1965, The relationship between Schmidt-Lantermann incisures and myelin segmentation during Wallerian degeneration, *Ann. N.Y. Acad. Sci.* **122**:29.

Webster, H. deF., 1971, The geometry of peripheral myelin sheaths during their formation and growth in rat sciatic nerves, *J. Cell Biol.* **48**:348.

Webster, H. deF., and Spiro, D., 1960, Phase and electron miscroscopic studies of experimental demyelination. I. Variations in myelin sheath contour in normal guinea pig sciatic nerve, *J. Neuropathol. Exptl. Neurol.* **19**:42.

Webster, H. deF., Spiro, D., Waksman, B., and Adams, R. D., 1961, Phase and electron microscopic studies of experimental demyelination. II. Schwann cell changes in guinea pig sciatic nerves during experimental diphtheritic neuritis, *J. Neuropathol. Exptl. Neurol.* **20**:5.

Webster, H. deF., Martin, J. R., and O'Connell, M. F., 1973, The relationships between interphase Schwann cells and axons before myelination: A quantitative electron microscopic study, *Develop. Biol.* **32**:401.

Weisenberg, R. C., 1972, Microtubule formation *in vitro* in solutions containing low calcium concentrations, *Science* **177**:1104.

Weiss, P. A., 1970, Neuronal dynamics and neuroplasmic flow, in: *The Neurosciences: Second Study Program* (F. O. Schmitt, ed.), Rockefeller University Press, New York, pp. 840–850.

Weiss, P. A., 1972, Neuronal dynamics and axonal flow: Axonal peristalsis, *Proc. Natl. Acad. Sci. USA* **69**:1309.

Weiss, P. A., and Mayr, R., 1971*a*, Neuronal organelles in neuroplasmic ("axonal") flow. I. Mitochondria, *Acta Neuropathol. Suppl.* **5**:187.

Weiss, P. A., and Mayr, R., 1971*b*, Neuronal organelles in neuroplasmic ("axonal") flow. II. Neurotubules, *Acta Neuropathol. Suppl.* **5**:198.

Weiss, P. A., and Mayr, R., 1971*c*, Organelles in neuroplasmic ("axonal") flow: Neurofilaments, *Proc. Natl. Acad. Sci. USA* **68**:846.

Wessells, N. K., Spooner. B. S., Ash, J. F., Bradley, M. O., Luduena, M. A., Taylor, E. L., Wrenn, J. T., and Yamada, K. M., 1971, Microfilaments in cellular and developmental processes, *Science* **171**:135.

Williams, P. L., and Hall, S. M., 1970, *In vivo* observations on mature myelinated nerve fibres of the mouse, *J. Anat. Lond.* **107**:31.

Williams, P. L., and Hall, S. M., 1971*a*, Prolonged *in vivo* observations of normal peripheral nerve fibres and their acute reactions to crush and deliberate trauma, *J. Anat. Lond.* **108**:397.

Williams, P. L., and Hall, S. M., 1971*b*, Chronic Wallerian degeneration—An *in vivo* and ultrastructural study, *J. Anat. Lond.* **109**:487.

Williams, P. L., and Kashef, R., 1968, Asymmetry of the node of Ranvier, *J. Cell Sci.* **3**:341.

Williams, P. L., and Wendell-Smith, C. P., 1971, Some additional parametric variations between peripheral nerve fibre populations, *J. Anat. Lond.* **109**:505.

Wisniewski, H., Shelanski, M. L., and Terry, R. D., 1968, Effects of mitotic spindle inhibitors on neurotubules and neurofilaments in anterior horn cells, *J. Cell Biol.* **38**:224.

Wuerker, R. B., 1970, Neurofilaments and glial filaments, *Tissue Cell* **2**:1.

Wuerker, R. B., and Kirkpatrick, J. B., 1972, Neuronal microtubules, neurofilaments, and microfilaments, *Internat. Rev. Cytol.* **33**:45.

Wuerker, R. B., and Palay, S. L., 1969, Neurofilaments and microtubules in the anterior horn cells of the rat, *Tissue Cell* **1**:387.

Yamada, K. M., Spooner, B. S., and Wessells, N. K., 1970, Axon growth: Roles of microfilaments and microtubules, *Proc. Natl. Acad. Sci. USA* **66**:1206.

Zelena, J., 1968, Bidirectional movements of mitochondria along axons of an isolated nerve segment, *Z. Zellforsch.* **92**:186.

Zelena, J., 1972, Ribosomes in myelinated axons of dorsal root ganglia, *Z. Zellforsch.* **124**:217.

Chapter 2

The Nerve Impulse

Denis Noble

Fellow of Balliol College, Oxford University
University Lecturer in Physiology
Oxford, England

1. INTRODUCTION

Since the famous eighteenth-century controversy between Galvani and Volta, it has been well known that electrical events are involved in nerve transmission and that the application of electric current will excite nerve and muscle cells. By about the end of the nineteenth century, it had also become apparent that the response of individual nerve or muscle cells to electric currents of different magnitudes is *all or nothing*. Currents below a certain strength fail to excite; currents above this *threshold* evoke a full response. The earliest workers also observed that the current threshold depends on the duration for which the current is applied. Weak currents must be applied for a longer period of time than strong currents. From this work emerged the familiar strength–duration curve in which the threshold strength is plotted against duration. Lapicque and others showed that this curve is explained by supposing that the excitation process involves the accumulation of charge and that this occurs with an exponential time course, characterized by a time constant (the strength–duration time constant, $\tau_{\text{S--D}}$). Rushton later pointed out that there must be a minimal length of nerve that lies at or above threshold before propagation can be initiated.

The theory that propagation occurs by axial flow of electric current was suggested by the nineteenth-century physiologist Hermann. Hodgkin (1937) later provided excellent experimental evidence for the electrical theory of propagation.

The purpose of this chapter is to describe how some of these important observations on nerve excitation may be related to, and explained by, the current theory of excitation. To do this, we shall use brief accounts of the cable theory of passive properties, the Hodgkin–Huxley theory of ionic current flow, and more recent developments that attempt to combine the two theories to give explanations of the initiation and spread of excitation. A considerably more advanced account will be found in Jack et al. (1974).

2. PASSIVE ELECTRICAL PROPERTIES

The generation and propagation of the nerve impulse involve the flow of electric current within the axoplasm and across the cell membrane. The physics of this process is now very well understood, but we still know relatively little of the chemistry of the membrane transport processes.

The axoplasm acts as a simple resistance whose value, r_a, is expressed per unit length (centimeters) of nerve. Applying Ohm's law to the flow of axial current, i_a, we obtain

$$\frac{\partial V}{\partial x} = -r_a i_a \tag{1}$$

where V is the transmembrane voltage (millivolts) and x is distance (centimeters). In this treatment, we shall equate the transmembrane voltage to the axoplasm voltage and neglect fields in the extracellular space. If positive current flows in the direction of increasing x, the voltage must decrease with x and the sign in equation (1) must be negative.

As the current flows along the axon, it will be increased or reduced by current flowing inward or outward across the cell membrane. At any point, therefore, the density of membrane current (i_m) is given by the change in i_a:

$$\frac{\partial i_a}{\partial x} = -i_m \tag{2}$$

The negative sign in this equation arises from the convention that an outward membrane current is a positive current and this requires that i_a should decrease with x.

Equations (1) and (2) give us two equations for i_a. To combine them, we must differentiate (1) to give us another expression for $\partial i_a/\partial x$:

$$\frac{\partial^2 V}{\partial x^2} = -r_a \frac{\partial i_a}{\partial x} \tag{3}$$

and we may then eliminate $\partial i_a/\partial x$ to obtain

$$\frac{1}{r_a} \frac{\partial^2 V}{\partial x^2} = i_m \tag{4}$$

The membrane current is the sum of the accumulation of charge on the capacitance of the membrane and the leakage of charge as ionic current i_i through the membrane channels, i.e.,

$$i_m = i_c + i_i = c\frac{\partial V}{\partial t} + i_i \tag{5}$$

where c is the membrane capacitance per unit length of nerve.

From (4) and (5), we obtain the general equation for current flow:

$$\frac{1}{r_a}\frac{\partial^2 V}{\partial x^2} = c\frac{\partial V}{\partial t} + i_i \tag{6}$$

The first term represents membrane current flow due to local circuit gradients in the nerve. We shall therefore refer to this component as the local circuit membrane current.

Most of the experimental and physiological situations of interest in nerve excitation may be represented as solutions to equation (6) or to various simplifications of this equation. This is illustrated in Tables I and II. Table I defines three simplifications of common interest:

1. In the steady state, e.g., when a constant current has been applied for a long period of time, there will be no variations in voltage with time and the capacity current is then zero.

Table I. General Equation for Current Flow in Nerve Fibers and the Simplifications Corresponding to Steady-State, Space-Clamp, and Voltage-Clamp Conditions

	Membrane current	=	Local circuit current (plus any electrode current)	=	Capacity current	+	Ionic current
	i_m	=	$\dfrac{1}{r_a}\dfrac{\partial^2 V}{\partial x^2}$	=	$c\dfrac{\partial V}{\partial t}$	+	i_i
Steady state $\left(\dfrac{\partial V}{\partial t}=0\right)$	i_m	=	$\dfrac{1}{r_a}\dfrac{d^2 V}{dx^2}$	=	0	+	i_i
Space clamp $\left(\dfrac{\partial^2 V}{\partial x^2}=0\right)$	i_m	=	i_e	=	$c\dfrac{\partial V}{\partial t}$	+	i_i
Voltage clamp $\left(\begin{array}{l}\dfrac{\partial V}{\partial t}=0\\[4pt]\dfrac{\partial V}{\partial x}=0\end{array}\right)$	i_m	=	i_e	=	0	+	i_i

Table II. Solutions, Applications, and Results for Various Cases of Physiological Importance

Conditions	Solution or application	Results
Linear cases		
Steady state; $i_i = V/r_m$	$V = V_0 e^{-x/\lambda}$	λ ($\therefore$ r_m/r_a)
Uniform; $i_i = V/r_m$	$V = V_0 e^{-t/\tau_m}$	τ_m ($\therefore$ $r_m c$)
Steady state and uniform	$V = r_m i_e$	r_m (hence c and r_a)
Full linear cable	Hodgkin–Rushton equation	Rate of spread of electrotonus
Nonlinear cases		
Voltage clamp; $i_i = F(V, t)$	$i_e = i_i$	i_i as function of V and t
"Steady state"; $i_i = F(V)$	$i_e = i_i$	Voltage threshold, liminal length, safety factor for conduction
Full nonlinear cable	Real nerve	Excitation and conduction

2. If we achieve spatially uniform applications of current to the fiber, there will be no voltage gradients and $\partial V/\partial x$ (and hence also $\partial^2 V/\partial x^2$) $= 0$. This condition requires either that an axial metal electrode be inserted so that the axoplasm is shortcircuited or that the length of nerve polarized be sufficiently small for spatial variations to be negligible. In both cases, the membrane current is now supplied by an electrode and the local circuit current becomes replaced by the electrode current, i_e.

3. When both these conditions hold, there are no voltage variations with distance or time. This is achieved by the voltage clamp technique in which the voltage in a uniformly polarized cell is held constant by the use of electronic feedback. The electrode current is then equal to the membrane ionic current and may be used to measure i_i.

For all these three situations (and for the general case when none of these simplifications applies), we may distinguish between two cases. When the membrane voltage is small compared to the threshold, the $i_i(V)$ relation is nearly linear. The solutions for this case are known as "linear cable theory." The general case, when i_i is a nonlinear function of V, gives rise to nonlinear cable theory.

The various combinations of cases that are of interest physiologically are summarized in Table II. For the linear cases, we may write

$$i_i = \frac{V}{r_m} \tag{7}$$

and equation (6) becomes

$$\lambda^2 \frac{\partial^2 V}{\partial x^2} = \tau_m \frac{\partial V}{\partial t} + V \tag{8}$$

where the *space constant*, λ, is given by $(r_m/r_a)^{1/2}$ and the *time constant*, τ_m, is given by $r_m c$.

In the steady state, $\partial V/\partial t = 0$ and we then have

$$\lambda^2 \frac{d^2 V}{dx^2} = V \tag{9}$$

for which the solution is

$$V = i_e (r_m r_a)^{1/2} \exp\left(-x/\lambda\right) \tag{10}$$

where i_e is the electrode current applied at the point $x = 0$. This solution may be verified by differentiating (10) twice to obtain (9). The expression $i_e(r_m r_a)^{1/2}$ is the value of V at $x = 0$. The ratio of $V_{x=0}$ to i_e is the input resistance, R_{in}, of the nerve. Hence

$$R_{\text{in}} = (r_m r_a)^{1/2} \tag{11}$$

This is an important result since it shows that the input resistance (and hence the voltage response to a current—synaptic, sensory, or electrode—applied at one point) varies as the square root of the membrane resistance.

The voltage decays exponentially, and by measuring the distance at which V falls to $1/e$ of its initial value we obtain λ and hence $(r_m/r_a)^{1/2}$. We may then obtain r_m and r_a as

$$r_m = R_{\text{in}} \lambda \tag{12}$$

and

$$r_a = \frac{R_{\text{in}}}{\lambda} \tag{13}$$

These are the relations used to obtain r_m and r_a experimentally when current may be applied to a nerve at one point (see Hodgkin and Rushton, 1946).

When current is applied uniformly, $\partial V/\partial x = 0$ and (8) simplifies to give

$$i_e = \tau_m \frac{dV}{dt} + V \tag{14}$$

which for a sudden change in i_e from zero (i.e., a step change) has the solution

$$V = i_e r_m [1 - \exp(-t/\tau_m)] \tag{15}$$

i.e., the voltage changes exponentially with time. i_e is now expressed as electrode current per unit length of nerve (to have the same units as i_m), and in the steady state

$$V_\infty = i_e r_m \tag{16}$$

from which we immediately obtain another way of estimating r_m. The time constant, τ_m, is measured as the time required to charge the membrane to $V_\infty(1 - 1/e)$, i.e., 0.63 V_∞, and the membrane capacitance may then be estimated as

$$c = \tau_m/r_m \qquad (17)$$

Finally, when neither of these simplifications can be made, we must solve the full equation (8). This was done by Hodgkin and Rushton (1946), and their result is plotted in Fig. 1. The important point to note is that the voltage does not change exponentially. Near the electrode, it changes very quickly, reaching 84% of its steady level in one time constant. As we move further from the electrode, the charging process becomes slower. This is expected since the membrane capacitance at a distance from the electrode must be charged through a progressively larger axial resistance. Its charging will be slower just as the filling of a water tank is slowed by the water first passing through a narrow, high-resistance pipe.

The relevance of the Hodgkin–Rushton solution to the initiation of excitation will be discussed later.

3. VOLTAGE-CLAMP ANALYSIS OF THE IONIC CURRENT

Under voltage-clamp conditions, $i_e = i_i$ and the electrode current then measures i_i as a function of voltage and time. This simplification is one of the justifications for using the voltage-clamp technique. It is not, however, the

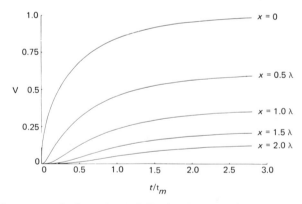

Fig. 1. The time course of voltage change following the onset of a constant current applied to an axon at one intracellular point. The curves were obtained by plotting the Hodgkin–Rushton equation (Hodgkin and Rushton, 1946, equation 4.1) for distances $x = 0$, 0.5λ, 1.0λ, 1.5λ, and 2.0λ. Note that the voltage rises rapidly toward its steady-state value at points close to the current source but rises more slowly and after a delay at a distance from the source.

only justification. The time dependence of the ionic currents was found to be expressible in terms of rate coefficients of conductance change that are unique functions of the membrane potential. This means that a specification of the rate coefficients using constant voltages may be used to predict the time course of current change during any sequence of voltage changes, including of course the action potential itself.

The total ionic current in nerve fibers is found to be composed of three components:

$$i_i = i_{Na} + i_K + i_l \tag{18}$$

where i_{Na} is the sodium current, i_K the potassium current, and i_l a small "residual" or "leak" current carried by chloride and other ions. The sodium and potassium currents are time dependent. Thus the potassium current is described by the equation

$$i_K = \bar{g}_K n^4 (E - E_K) \tag{19}$$

where $\bar{g}_K$ is the maximum conductance to potassium ions, E_K is the potassium equilibrium potential given by the Nernst equation

$$E_K = \frac{RT}{F} \ln \frac{[K]_i}{[K]_o} \tag{20}$$

and n^4 is the fraction of the potassium channels that are conducting. The interpretation of this equation is that four "gating" mechanisms determine the state of each channel. Each may be "open" or "closed," and all must be open for the channel to conduct. However this is not the only possible way in which the current may be successfully described (see Tille, 1965; Hoyt, 1968; Goldman, 1964).

The fraction of gates in the open state (n) obeys a first-order equation:

$$\frac{dn}{dt} = \alpha_n(1 - n) - \beta_n n \tag{21}$$

where α_n and β_n are opening and closing rate coefficients that are functions of the membrane potential only; α_n increases on depolarization of the membrane, while β_n decreases. This result would be expected if the gating groups are charged so that their probability of being in a particular position in the membrane is voltage-dependent. Hodgkin and Huxley (1952) did not derive equations for α_n and β_n. They simply fitted plausible equations to the empirical results. In this respect, the theory is a semiempirical theory and does not attempt to derive all the properties of the nerve membrane from first principles. The processes determining g_K are illustrated schematically in Fig. 2.

The behavior of the sodium current was found to be similar to that of the potassium current, except that one of the gates must be supposed to close on

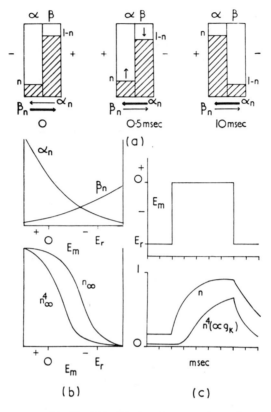

Fig. 2. Processes assumed in Hodgkin–Huxley theory to determine potassium conductance. (a) Response of n reaction to sudden depolarization. Initially, the fraction (n) of groups (or sites) in the α (active) state is small since α_n is small and β_n is large. Depolarization increases α_n and decreases β_n so that n rises exponentially to a larger value. Relative magnitudes of rate constants (α_n and β_n) are indicated by thickness of arrows. (b) Top: Variation of rate constants with E_m. Bottom: Variations of n_∞ [$=\alpha_n/(\alpha_n + \beta_n)$] and n_∞^4 with E_m. (c) Response of n and g_K to sudden depolarization. Note: Curves in this illustration are not accurate solutions to the Hodgkin–Huxley equations; they have been drawn freely to indicate major features of the theory more clearly. From Noble (1966).

membrane depolarization. If the opening "gates" (m) open faster than the closing gate (h) closes, we obtain a transient conductance increase. The equation used in this case is

$$g_{Na} = \bar{g}_{Na}m^3h \tag{22}$$

where m and h obey equations similar to (21).

Using their empirical estimates of the rate coefficients α_n, β_n, α_m, β_m, α_h, and β_h, Hodgkin and Huxley were able to calculate the ionic current for any sequence of voltage changes and to use this calculation to give i_i in the full cable equation (6). The membrane voltage may then be computed as a function of voltage and time. The results were highly successful in reproducing the nervous impulse and its propagation (see Fig. 3).

The Hodgkin–Huxley equations are, however, fairly complex. They may only be applied to the particular excitable tissue for which the voltage-clamp analysis has been obtained, and the solution of the equations requires a considerable amount of computing. There is, therefore, a need to consider simplifications that allow some of the important features of excitation and propagation to be obtained more readily and applied more generally. Simplified systems do not, of course, allow accurate estimates of excitation parameters to be obtained, but they do allow relatively simple explanations to be given.

4. MOMENTARY CURRENT–VOLTAGE RELATIONS

The particular simplification we shall use here depends on the fact that the sodium activation reaction (m) is considerably faster (τ_m is about 0.2 ms) than the sodium inactivation (h) or potassium activation (n) reactions (τ's for these reactions are several milliseconds). For the purpose of giving an explanatory account, we shall use current–voltage relations given by assuming

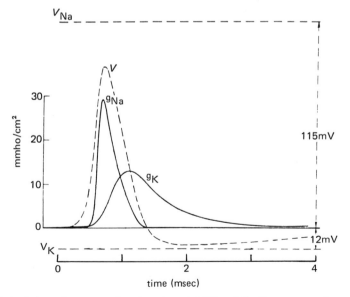

Fig. 3. Calculation of propagated action potential (V) and the time course of g_{Na} and g_K given by Hodgkin–Huxley equations (Hodgkin and Huxley, 1952). From Hodgkin (1958).

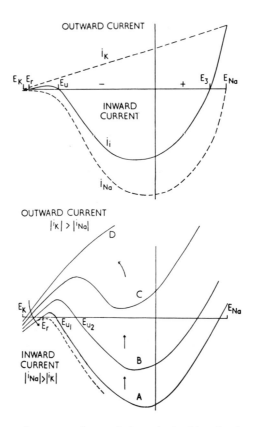

Fig. 4. General form of current–voltage relations obtained by allowing "fast" variable m to vary with E_m at its steady-state value m_∞, while "slow" variables n and h are constant. Top: Construction of momentary current–voltage relation (solid curve) by addition of individual ionic current–voltage relations (interrupted curves). Bottom: Changes (A–D) in momentary current–voltage relation as n increases and h falls. A is obtained when n and h have their resting values; C and D correspond to values of n and h at the end of the action potential. Interrupted curve shows form of A when $[Ca]_o$ is low. From Noble (1966).

that the m reaction is infinitely fast while the n and h reactions are held "frozen" at particular values. Such current–voltage relations will resemble those obeyed momentarily by the membrane a short interval of time (of the order of 0.2. ms) following a step change. They may therefore be called "momentary current voltage relations." The term "quasi-instantaneous" has also been used for this purpose.

The general form of the relations generated in this way is illustrated in Fig. 4. The top diagram shows the construction of a net ionic current–voltage diagram from the individual Na and K currents. E_K is negative, and at potentials positive to E_K, i_K is outward. Since n is held constant (at a relatively low value corresponding to the resting membrane) i_K is a linear function of E. E_{Na} is positive, and at all potentials negative to E_{Na}, i_{Na} is inward. Since m_∞ increases as the potential is varied from very negative toward positive values, the $i_{Na}(E)$ relation is very nonlinear. Near E_{Na}, i_{Na} is small because the driving force, $E - E_{Na}$, is small. At potentials near E_K, i_{Na} is small because g_{Na} is small. In between these two points, i_{Na} passes through a maximum. The net current–voltage relation cuts the voltage axis at three points, V_A, V_B, and V_D. V_A is the resting potential. V_B is the potential at which the net ionic current changes from inward to outward. This point must therefore be the voltage threshold for uniform excitation. V_D is the potential to which the system changes once V_B is exceeded.

It should be emphasized that a current–voltage diagram of this kind is obeyed only momentarily (and then only approximately). Once the membrane is depolarized, h falls and n rises. We may therefore construct a family of $i_i(E)$ relations for various pairs of values of h and n that will apply approximately at successive points of time following depolarization. This is shown in the bottom diagram of Fig. 4. As h decreases, i_{Na} falls; as n increases, i_K rises. Both changes lead to a shift in the outward current direction and toward a more linear set of relations.

We shall illustrate the use of these diagrams by considering the conditions for the initiation and propagation of action potentials. Since it is difficult to obtain analytical results using the Hodgkin–Huxley equations (even when simplified as described here), we shall use a simple cubic equation to represent the ionic current (see Noble, 1972):

$$i_i = \frac{1}{R}\left[V - V^2 + \left(\frac{V}{2}\right)^3\right] \qquad (23)$$

This relation is plotted in Fig. 5, and it can be seen that its shape is very similar to the momentary current–voltage relation at the beginning of excitation.

5. THE THRESHOLD CONDITIONS FOR EXCITATION

As already noted in the previous section, the potential V_B is the threshold voltage for excitation by currents applied uniformly to the membrane. However, this is an extremely unusual situation in physiological circumstances. Excitatory current from sensory or synaptic potentials is applied nonuniformly since it is generated locally. Moreover, in most neurophysiological experiments, nerves are excited at one point by metal or glass electrodes. The voltage is not therefore uniform and, for subthreshold currents, will decay

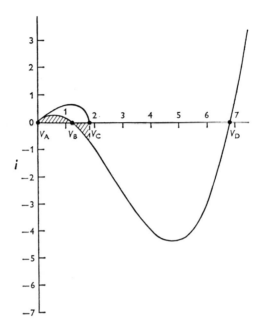

Fig. 5. Diagram showing relation of threshold potential for excitation in a cable (V_c) to the ionic current–voltage diagram. The curve intersecting the voltage axis at three points (V_A, V_B, and V_D) is given by equation (23) and closely resembles the momentary current–voltage relation of an excitable cell. The curve intersecting the voltage axis at V_A and V_C is the relation between current applied at one point of the axon and the voltage at that point. Note that the cable threshold (V_c) is given by the point at which the hatched areas are equal. From Noble (1972).

with distance from the excitatory current. This will insure that the inward excitatory current generated by strongly depolarized regions near the current source will be offset by outward current generated by less strongly depolarized regions. The threshold condition will then be that the net ionic current integrated over the whole fiber length becomes inward. This is illustrated in Fig. 6 (bottom), which shows the situation at threshold where the amounts of inward and outward current are equal. Clearly, to achieve this situation a certain minimal length of nerve must be depolarized beyond V_B to generate enough excitatory current to achieve excitation. This is the length (x_{LL}) defined by Rushton (1937) as the *liminal length* for excitation.

To show what determines the liminal length, we consider a further simplification of the current–voltage diagram shown in the upper diagram of Fig. 6. The relation is represented by two linear segments that fit the curve at the resting and threshold voltages V_A and V_B. The spatial variation below

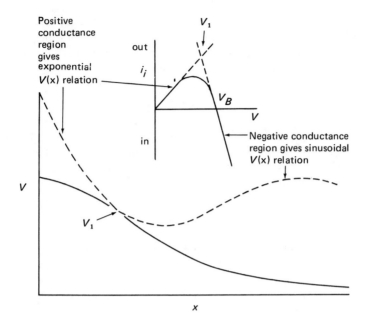

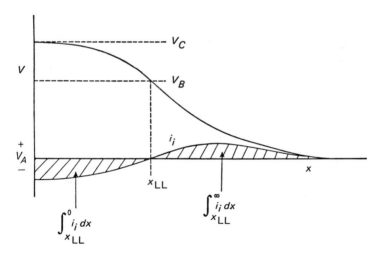

Fig. 6. Top: Diagram illustrating the way in which the spatial variation in potential in an axon near threshold is approximately given by a cosine solution generated by the negative conductance near threshold (V_B) and an exponential solution generated by the positive conductance near the resting potential (V_A). Bottom: Diagram illustrating the liminal length, x_{LL}, for excitation. V_C is the threshold voltage at $x = 0$ (see Fig. 5), V_B is the voltage at which i_i changes direction. x_{LL} is the length of axon that generates inward ionic current flow. At threshold, the hatched areas are equal. From Noble (1972).

the point V_1 will be given by the exponential solution already given as equation (10) above. Above V_1, the cable is also a linear one but differs from the resting cable in having a negative membrane conductance. This changes the sign of equation (9):

$$\lambda_B^2 \frac{d^2V}{dx^2} = V \tag{24}$$

where $\lambda_B = (-g_1 r_a)^{-1/2}$ and $-g_1$ is the slope of the current–voltage relation near threshold. λ_B^2 is therefore negative, and the solution we require is one which simply changes sign on being differentiated twice. This requirement is satisfied by the circular function $\cos(x/\lambda_B)$ since $d^2 \cos(y)/dy^2 = -\cos y$. In this case, the appropriate solution is

$$\Delta V = (V_C - V_B) \cos(x/\lambda_B) \tag{25}$$

where ΔV is the voltage $V - V_B$ and V_C is the threshold voltage at $x = 0$.

To obtain an approximate result for the variation of V with x at threshold, we simply match the two solutions (as shown in Fig. 6) to produce a continuous curve which starts as a cosine and ends up as an exponential.

Note that the length of the fiber that is depolarized sufficiently to generate inward current is simply the first quarter-cycle of the circular solution. Since the cycle period will be $2\pi\lambda_B$, the liminal length must be given by

$$x_{ll} = \frac{\pi\lambda_B}{2} \tag{26}$$

and, remembering the definition of λ_B given above, we obtain the result that the liminal length is inversely proportional to the square root of the conductance at threshold. Since this is determined by the magnitude of the sodium current, x_{ll} will be approximately inversely proportional to $(\overline{g_{Na}})^{1/2}$.

Now we have already shown that the time taken to depolarize the membrane to a particular potential depends on the distance from the current source (see Fig. 1). Hence the larger the liminal length, the longer will be the time taken to achieve the threshold state. This leads to the expectation that the time constant of the strength–duration curve for excitation should be strongly dependent on the liminal length and hence on the value of $\overline{g_{Na}}$ (see Fozzard and Schoenberg, 1972; Noble, 1972).

This is indeed the case. Figure 7 shows strength–duration curves for various assumed liminal lengths (top) and the variation of the strength–duration curve time constant with x_{ll} (bottom). The values shown by the points correspond to the values of liminal length obtained for various excitable cells. Squid nerve has a liminal length approaching 1.0λ and the strength–duration time constant τ_{S-D} in this case is similar to the resting membrane time constant, τ_m. In the case of skeletal muscle, g_1 is relatively large compared

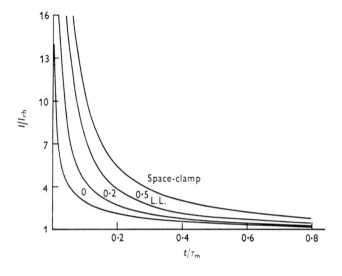

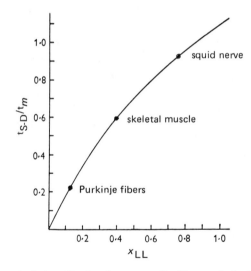

Fig. 7. Top: Theoretical strength–duration curves for fibers polarized at one point with liminal lengths x_{LL} = 0, 0.2, and 0.5λ. The "space-clamp" or uniformly polarized case is also shown. The curves were obtained by calculating the time taken for each current strength to depolarize the liminal length point beyond the ionic current threshold V_B, assuming the fiber to respond as in Fig. 1. Bottom: The strength–duration time constant (τ_{S-D}) as a function of liminal length. τ_{S-D} is expressed as a fraction of τ_m, x_{LL} is expressed as a fraction of λ. The points correspond to the values calculated for squid nerve, skeletal muscle, and cardiac Purkinje fibers. Modified from Fozzard and Schoenberg (1972.)

to g_m and the expected liminal length is only about 0.4λ. $\tau_{\text{S-D}}$ is therefore smaller than τ_m. This phenomenon has been known experimentally for a long time. Thus Davis (1923) and Grundfest (1932) found that the strength–duration time constant for muscle depends on the way in which the current is applied and is considerably shorter for focally applied current than for widely applied current. A much smaller effect was observed in nerve.

This effect is particularly dramatic in cardiac Purkinje fibers (Fozzard and Schoenberg, 1972) for which the liminal length is only about 0.1–0.2λ. The value of $\tau_{\text{S-D}}$ for focally applied current is then only about $0.2\tau_m$.

6. FACTORS DETERMINING CONDUCTION VELOCITY

From Fig. 5 and 6, it is clear that one condition for the initiation of a propagated action potential will be that the area of inward current in the current–voltage diagram should be larger than the area of outward current. The amount by which the inward current exceeds the outward current in turn determines the speed of propagation. Thus an excitable cell that generates only a little more inward current than is minimally required will conduct slowly. Since conduction is then easily subject to agents (such as nerve blockers) that reduce the excitatory current, the cell is said to have a low *safety factor* for conduction. Conversely, a cell generating a large inward current has a large safety factor. In squid nerve, the sodium conductance g_{Na} may be reduced by more than 75% before conduction fails. The safety factor in this case is therefore large.

However, cells with similar safety factors do not necessarily conduct at the same velocity. The cable properties of the fiber are also important. The influence of the cable properties may be shown by considering the equation for current flow during an action potential traveling at a constant conduction velocity θ. The distance, x, traveled in time t is then given by

$$x = \theta t \tag{27}$$

and we may replace $\partial^2 V/\partial x^2$ in equation (6) by $1/\theta^2 \, d^2V/dt^2$. Hence

$$\frac{d^2 V}{dt^2} = \theta^2 r_a c \left(\frac{dV}{dt} + \frac{i_i}{c} \right) \tag{28}$$

If we assume i_i/c to be the same in different fibers (in particular, we assume the safety factor to be the same), $\theta^2 r_a c$ must be a constant. Hence

$$\theta \propto \left(\frac{1}{r_a c} \right)^{1/2} \tag{29}$$

Now r_a varies inversely as the cross-sectional area, i.e., as $1/d^2$, where d is

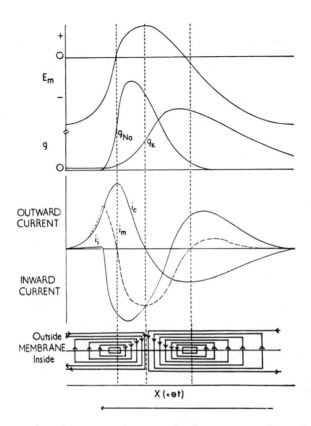

Fig. 8. Changes of conductances and currents flowing across membrane during propagated action potential. Interrupted vertical lines indicate corresponding points on the curve. The lowest diagram shows local circuit currents flowing between different regions of membrane. The first stage of depolarization, the "foot" of the action potential, occurs before any appreciable rise in g_{Na} or i_i occurs. During this time, the membrane current is generated by other areas of membrane where large conductance changes have already occurred. This local circuit depolarization then triggers changes in conductance that generate the rest of the action potential. The extent to which the propagated action potential differs from the "membrane" action potential (i.e., one that does not propagate) can be readily appreciated from the fact that during a "membrane" response i_m is zero and i_i and i_c are always equal and opposite. This is true at only two points during a propagated response. The abscissa is x, and since $x = \theta t$ it is also proportional to time. From Noble (1966).

fiber diameter. Also, c varies as the fiber circumference (since the capacitance is simply proportional to membrane area); i.e., c varies as d. Hence $r_a c$ varies as $1/d$, and we obtain

$$\theta \propto (d)^{1/2} \qquad (30)$$

i.e., the conduction velocity increases as the square root of the fiber diameter (but see discussion in Jack *et al.*, 1974).

The sequence of events occurring during a propagated action potential in a nonmyelinated fiber is illustrated in Fig. 8. The first potential change is an exponential rise known as the "foot" of the action potential. During this time, the ionic conductance remains small and the ionic current is small, while the capacity current rises nearly to its peak and accounts for almost all the membrane current. This phase represents the invasion of the membrane by local circuit current from the approaching action potential. As dV/dt reaches its peak, the main rise in g_{Na} occurs. The delay between the rise of potential and the rise in g_{Na} represents the delay between V changes and changes in m and is determined by the time constant of the m reaction, i.e., about 200 μs. The increase in g_{Na} results in a large inward movement of sodium ions so that i_i changes from a small outward value ($|i_K| > |i_{Na}|$) to a large inward value ($|i_{Na}| \gg |i_K|$). However, the capacity current is still outward so that i_i and i_c are now flowing in opposite directions. Thus during the last part of the rising phase of the action potential the depolarization is largely attributable to the inward movement of sodium ions rather than to charge spreading from other regions of the fiber. Therefore, the discharge of the membrane capacity occurs in two stages: first by local circuit current supplied by areas of membrane already active, then by the local inward flow of sodium current consequent upon depolarization. The speed at which these events occur, and hence the speed of propagation, clearly depends on the magnitude of the capacitance to be discharged and on the magnitude of the inward sodium current.

One way of increasing the speed of propagation, therefore, is to reduce the capacitance of the nerve. This is achieved in myelinated fibers, in which the nerve axon is enveloped in closely packed layers of Schwann cell membrane, leaving the axon membrane directly open to the extracellular fluid only at discrete intervals (the nodes). This arrangement greatly increases the thickness of the membrane dielectric at the internodes and so reduces the capacitance. The depolarization produced by local circuit current is then considerably faster and the propagation speed is increased.

This increase in propagation speed occurs provided the increase in r_a (due to the reduction in the fraction of the cross-sectional area filled by axoplasm) is not too great. In small nerves, a significant decrease in c will be achieved at the cost of a large increase in r_a and the conduction velocity will be reduced below that of an equivalent nonmyelinated axon of the same external diameter. In large nerves, the membrane thickness can be increased significantly with a proportionately smaller increase in r_a. Hence myelination is only effective in increasing conduction velocity in fibers larger than a certain size. Rushton (1951) has given a theoretical treatment of this problem which suggests that the critical diameter should be about 1 μm.

The actual relation between θ and d for myelinated nerve is not so easy to obtain. Rushton (1951) obtained the relation

$$\theta \propto d \tag{31}$$

Coppin and Jack (1972) have described experiments showing that the relation obeyed in practice is approximately

$$\theta \propto d^{1.5} \tag{32}$$

Thus the conduction velocity increases more steeply with fiber diameter than in the case of unmyelinated fibers.

7. REFERENCES

Coppin, C. M. L., and Jack, J. J. B., 1972, Internodal length and conduction velocity of cat muscle afferent nerve fibres, *J. Physiol.* **222**:91p.

Davis, H., 1923, The relationship of the "chronaxie" of muscle to the size of the stimulating electrode, *J. Physiol.* **57**:81p.

Fozzard, H. A., and Schoenberg, M., 1972, Strength–duration curves in cardiac Purkinje fibres: Effects of liminal length and charge redistribution, *J. Physiol.* **226**:593.

Goldman, D. E., 1964, A molecular structural basis for the excitation properties of axons. *Biophys. J.* **4**:167.

Grundfest, H., 1932, Excitability of the single fibre nerve–muscle complex, *J. Physiol.* **76**:95.

Hodgkin, A. L., 1937, Evidence for electrical transmission in nerve, *J. Physiol.* **90**:183.

Hodgkin, A. L., 1958, Ionic movements and electrical activity in giant nerve fibres, *Proc. Roy. Soc. B* **148**:1.

Hodgkin, A. L., and Huxley, A. F., 1952, A quantitative description of the membrane current and its application to conduction and excitation in nerve, *J. Physiol.* **117**:500.

Hodgkin, A. L., and Rushton, W. A. H., 1946, The electrical constants of a crustacean nerve fibre, *Proc. Roy. Soc. B* **133**:444.

Hoyt, R. C., 1968, Sodium inactivation in nerve fibres, *Biophys. J.* **8**:1074.

Jack, J. J. B., Noble, D., and Tsien, R. W., 1974, *Electric Current Flow in Excitable Cells*, Clarendon Press, Oxford.

Noble, D., 1966, Applications of Hodgkin–Huxley equations to excitable cells, *Physiol. Rev.* **46**:1.

Noble, D., 1972, The relation of Rushton's "liminal length" for excitation to the resting and active conductance of excitable cells, *J. Physiol.* **226**:573.

Rushton, W. A. H., 1937, Initiation of the propagated disturbance, *Proc. Roy. Soc. B* **124**:210.

Rushton, W. A. H., 1951, A theory of the effects of fibre size in medullated nerve, *J. Physiol.* **115**:101.

Tille, J., 1965, A new interpretation of the dynamic changes of potassium conductance in the squid giant axon, *Biophys. J.* **5**:163.

Chapter 3

Axoplasmic Transport—Energy Metabolism and Mechanism

Sidney Ochs

Department of Physiology
Indiana University Medical Center
Indianapolis, Indiana, USA

1. INTRODUCTION

Two systems of material transport are present within nerve fibers (Schmitt, 1968; Grafstein, 1969; Ochs, 1969; Barondes, 1970; Lasek, 1970; Dahlström, 1971a). In mammalian nerve fibers, isotope labeling shows the presence of a slow transport system with materials carried down the fibers at a rate of approximately 1–12 mm/day and a fast transport system with a well-defined rate close to 410 mm/day (Ochs, 1972a). The mammalian system which will be discussed for the most part in this chapter has an advantage in that the rate is readily measured as a crest or a wave of labeled materials in the nerve *in vitro* whereby the mechanism can be more readily analyzed.

Some general properties regarding axoplasmic transport are shown in Fig. 1. One important principle is that the mechanisms of synthesis in the cell body are separate from those of material transport within the nerve fiber. Additional processes are present in the terminal. The different regions and functions are shown in diagrammatic fashion in Fig. 1, where A represents the cell body, B the axon with its apposed Schwann cell and myelin sheath, and C the nerve terminal (the neuromuscular junction and muscle fiber in the example shown).

The nerve cell body has a high rate of protein synthesis at the ribosomes associated with endoplasmic reticulum, at site S in somal region A. The entry

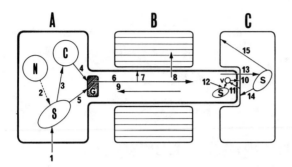

Fig. 1. Diagrammatic representation of the neuron. Cell regions show (A) cell body, (B) nerve fiber, and (C) terminal region with a synapse on a muscle fiber. In A, upon entry of precursor (1), the nucleus (N) controls (2) synthesis (S), with an arrow (3) showing a compartmentalization (C) of synthesized material. These materials move into the axon (4,5) with the Golgi apparatus (G) having a control over their egress to the axon. Both fast and slow transport systems of transport move materials down the nerve fiber (6). Arrows to the membrane (7) and to the Schwann cell (8), with the myelin sheath shown by horizontal lines, indicate control over their functions. A backward axoplasmic transport is indicated by an arrow directed to the cell body (9). In the terminal region C, vesicles (V) are shown effecting synaptic transmission (10), with a reconstitution of transmitter (11). Synthesis of some components in the terminal is indicated by S, with some contribution of materials shown (12). An arrow from the nerve entering the cell (13) indicates trophic materials with, in some cases, control over synthesis (S) in the muscle. Receptor materials are indicated by arrows 14 and 15 inserted into the membrane.

of precursor (amino acid) is indicated by an arrow (1), and N (the nucleus) containing DNA serves to indicate its control (2) over the kinds of materials made. Compartment C indicates where incorporated proteins and possibly other materials are stored (3) for later egress to the axon (4). A gate controlling the export of materials from the cell body into the axon of either just-synthesized materials (4) or those which have entered a compartment (5) for later egress to the axon is presumed to be the Golgi apparatus (G) (Droz, 1965; Ochs *et al.*, 1970*b*).

The arrow directed down the axon (6) represents both fast and slow transport systems, which carry down enzymes and other materials needed to maintain the functional viability of the fiber. This includes components entering the membrane (7) to maintain its function.

The membrane has recently been viewed as composed of phospholipids arranged tangentially as a bilayer with globular proteins embedded in it (*cf.* Fig. 2 in Singer, 1972). These proteins could, depending on their nature, confer selective permeability to Na^+K^+ and other ions involved in excitability, or perform special functions, e.g., the Na^+K^+-activated ATPase involved in sodium pumping. Proteins are all likely to have a turnover, and the proteins in the membrane would thus require replenishment. This is the view represented by Fig. 1, where some part of the proteins carried down by axoplasmic transport is indicated as being inserted into the membrane.

Other substances carried down the fibers which are required to maintain their viability are those concerned with the more general needs of energy maintenance, the enzymes and components required for glycolysis and oxidative phosphorylation. Mitochondria in which oxidative phosphorylation is carried out are moved down the fiber at a slow rate (Barondes, 1966; Jeffrey *et al.*, 1972). This also seems to be the case for the glycolytic enzymes as indicated by LDH (Khan *et al.*, 1971).

The Schwann cells in which myelin is layered around the myelinated nerve fibers also appear to be controlled by materials carried into them from the nerve fiber (8). This is shown by the characteristic Wallerian degenerative changes which start a few days after interruption of the nerve in the part of the fiber distal to the transection. The axon exerts a control over myelination and the thickness of the myelin sheath (Friede, 1972).

An arrow in the backward or retrograde direction (9) represents a mechanism for the movement of materials back into the soma, possibly as part of a feedback mechanism controlling the level of synthesis in the soma. Such a mechanism could explain the chromatolysis and increased levels of production of nucleic acids and protein seen in the cell body after transection of nerve fibers. The "signal" for such chromatolysis ascends to the cell body in the transected fibers rather than by an indirect route through the circulation (Ochs *et al.*, 1961; Cragg, 1970). In the terminal region C, vesicles (V) are shown emptying their content of transmitter substances across the synapse (10) to effect excitation (Chapter 7(i)). An arrow (11) shows the reconstitution of transmitter, which is acetylcholine (ACh) in the case of the neuromuscular junction. Synthesis (12) of transmitter components or of some part of the vesicles in the terminals (S) may be controlled by local influences as well as by the downward transport of materials. An arrow (13) indicates the entry of several trophic substances from the nerve into the postsynaptic cell to control its function and, in the case of sensory terminals, into the secondary cells controlled by the nerve terminal (Gutmann and Hnik, 1963; Guth, 1968, 1969; and Chapter 11).

References to these topics may be found in other chapters and in the papers and reviews noted above (*cf.* Ochs, 1972*b*, 1973). In this chapter, emphasis will be placed on the fast axoplasmic transport system in mammalian nerve fibers, its dependence on oxidative phosphorylation, and recent evidence for the "transport filament" hypothesis, the mechanism considered to be responsible for fast axoplasmic transport. The possible relevance to slow transport is also discussed.

2. FAST AXOPLASMIC TRANSPORT

2.1. Characterization

To study fast axoplasmic transport, labeled precursor (^{3}H-leucine) was injected near either the neuron cell bodies of the cat lumbar seventh (L7) dorsal

root ganglion or into the ventral horn of the spinal cord near the L7 motoneurons; then, after several hours, downflow was shown by a crest of labeled
activity in the sciatic nerve (Ochs, *et al.*, 1969; Ochs and Ranish, 1969). The
crest represents labeled proteins incorporating the precursor, and it advances
at a regular rate at close to 410 mm/day. This was shown by the displacement
of the crest with time when nerves were taken at increasing intervals after
injection of the precursor (Fig. 2). In a comparative study where fast axoplasmic transport was studied in the longer lengths of sciatic nerve present
in larger monkeys, the goat, and large dogs, a similar crest was found, moving
down with a rate close to 410 mm/day (Ochs, 1972c). This applies to both
sensory and motor fibers, the latter seen after injecting labeled precursor near
the L7 motoneuron cell bodies of the spinal cord. Using radioautography, the
rate of fast axoplasmic transport was found to be independent of nerve fiber

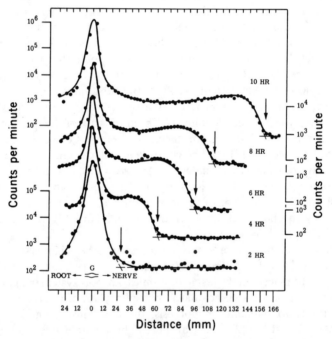

Fig. 2. Pattern and rate of transport. Distribution of radioactivity in the dorsal root
ganglia and sciatic nerves of five cats taken between 2 and 10 h after injecting ^{3}H-leucine
into the L7 ganglia (G). The activities present in 5-mm segments along roots, ganglia,
and nerves (abscissa) are given (ordinate) on logarithmic scales. The ordinate scale for
the nerve 2 h after injection is given at the left bottom with divisions in counts per minute.
At the left top, a scale is given for the nerve taken 10 h after injection. Partial scales are
shown at the right for the nerves taken 4, 6, and 8 h after injection. From Ochs (1972a).

diameter, i.e., to have the same rate in fibers ranging from 3 to 23 μm (Ochs, 1972c).

The ³H-leucine taken up by the cell body is incorporated into protein and polypeptides which are then transported out into the fibers. This was shown directly by subcellular centrifugation of roots or nerves taken at different times after injection of ³H-leucine. Activity was found in the "nuclear" (N), "mitochondrial" (M), "particulate" (P), and high speed supernatant or soluble (S) fractions (Ochs et al., 1967; Kidwai and Ochs, 1969). The soluble fraction had the highest relative level of labeled activity at later times, as expected from its movement by the slow transport mechanism. A smaller proportion was carried down in the S fraction by fast axoplasmic transport. The incorporation into the soluble proteins of the S fraction was shown by trichloroacetic acid precipitation followed by hydrolysis of the precipitate and identification of ³H-leucine in paper chromatograms. Protein incorporation was also reported by Bray and Austin (1968) and McEwen and Grafstein (1968). A fractionation of the soluble protein and polypeptides into different classes of protein was made using gel filtration and isoelectric focusing (Kidwai and Ochs, 1969; Ochs et al., 1969; James and Austin, 1970; James et al., 1970; Sabri and Ochs, 1972). A wide variety of proteins are labeled (Karlsson and Sjöstrand, 1971a), the different types of protein and polypeptides carried down by the fast and slow transport mechanism, these changing to some extent with time (Sabri and Ochs, 1972).

A relatively higher level of labeling was found in the P fraction at early times corresponding to downflow by the fast axoplasmic transport mechanism (Ochs et al., 1969). Some part of the P fraction contains vesicular components or precursors of the vesicles related to synaptic transmission. This is suggested by the accumulation of vesicles above a dammed region of the nerve, first described by Van Breeman et al. (1958) and more recently by Pellegrino de Iraldi and de Robertis (1968). However, not all of the P fraction constitutes transmitter vesicles, because a similarly high level of activity was found in the P fraction carried down by fast axoplasmic transport in the sensory fibers (Ochs et al., 1969; Sabri and Ochs, 1973).

In any case, the relatively high level of labeling of the P fraction requires further attention. Acetylcholinesterase (AChE) is present in the P fraction of motor nerve fibers, and in accord with its synthesis in the somas and a continuous downflow into the fibers, AChE was found accumulated proximal to nerve ligations (Lubińska, 1964). A fast rate of AChE was reported by Johnson (1970) working in this laboratory, and Lubińska and Niemierko (1971) recently gave a rate of 260 mm/day for its transport. A similar rate was reported for downflow of catecholamines (Dahlström and Häggendal, 1966) and for protein (Lasek, 1970). Using double ligations of cat sciatic nerves, a faster rate of transport of AChE was found (Khan et al., 1971; Ranish and

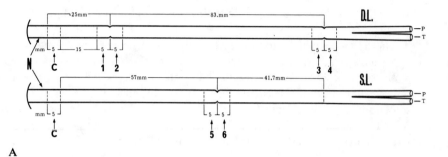

A

B

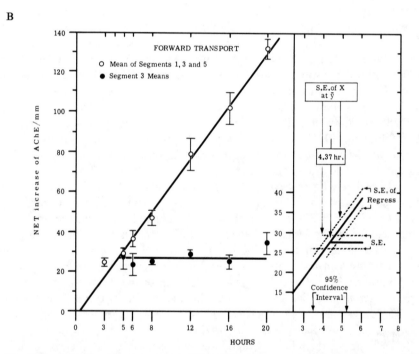

Fig. 3. Acetylcholinesterase transport. (A) Schematic representation of sciatic nerves (N) shows sites of ligations and sample designations. Segments 1, 3, and 5 are proximal samples. Segments taken were 5 mm long. P and T are peroneal and tibial branches, and D.L. and S.L. signify doubly and singly ligated nerves, respectively. (B) Net accumulations of AChE in segments proximal to ligations from 3 to 20 h. A regression line is shown for the combined values from segments 1, 3, and 5. The line drawn for the means of segment 3 is after 4–5 h, parallel to the time axis. The insert (right) shows the standard errors of both lines and the 95% confidence interval with respect to time. ○, Accumulation proximal to upper ligation in doubly ligated nerves or proximal to single ligation; ●, accumulation proximal to distal ligation within the doubly ligated nerves. From Ranish and Ochs (1972).

Ochs, 1972). The determination is shown in Fig. 3B, where an accumulation of AChE activity is seen to occur above the upper ligation (Fig. 3A) in linear fashion over a period of 20 h. Within the ligated segment, the accumulation of AChE just above the distal ligation leveled off after 4–5 h. This is a pattern expected if part of the AChE is free to move by a fast axoplasmic transport mechanism and becomes piled up at the distal ligation within the isolated nerve segment. By taking the distance between the ligations and the time when the accumulation leveled off, the rate computed was 431 mm/day, reasonably close to the 410 mm/day rate found using isotopes. Approximately 15% of the AChE activity present within the motor nerve fiber was calculated to be free to move by means of the fast axoplasmic system, 10% in the forward direction and 5% in the retrograde direction. The remainder of the AChE in the fibers is either being moved down by slow transport or fixed into membranous structures (Brzin et al., 1967; Kasa, 1968).

A variety of substances, some necessary for energy metabolism, some related to lysosomes, various other enzymes, glycoproteins, and other polysaccharides, have been studied from the point of view of transport by the fast or slow systems (Johnson, 1970; Dahlström, 1971a; Geffen and Livett, 1971; Samson, 1971; McEwen et al., 1971; Elam and Agranoff, 1971). It will be of interest to systematically assess the rate of downflow of a variety of identifiable substances with the same direct technique.

2.2 Mechanism and Energy Supply

A hypothesis has recently been advanced for fast axoplasmic transport based on an analogy with the sliding filament theory of muscle (Ochs, 1971a, 1972a). The microtubules and/or neurofilaments are considered to be the stationary element of a sliding filament pair, with a hypothetical "transport filament" synthesized in the cell bodies moving down along the microtubules and/or neurofilaments by means of cross-bridges. Particulates, proteins, and polypeptides synthesized in the cell bodies are bound to the transport filament and thus carried down the nerve fibers (Fig. 4). The finding that all this heterogeneous group of materials is being carried down the fibers by fast axoplasmic transport at the same fast rate indicates that a common carrier is involved.

Such a mechanism requires energy for cross-bridge activation, most likely as $\sim$P in ATP. Evidence for this view has been obtained in in vitro studies, where it was found that the usual crest pattern and rate of transport occur as long as oxidative metabolism is maintained (Ochs et al., 1969; Ochs and Hollingsworth, 1971). Anoxia produced by N_2, sodium azide, cyanide, or dinitrophenol causes a rapid block of fast axoplasmic transport within 15 min. In such experiments, the L7 ganglia are injected with ^{3}H-leucine, and

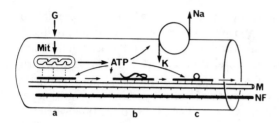

Fig. 4. Transport filament hypothesis. Glucose (G) enters the fiber and after glycolysis and oxidative phosphorylation in the mitochondrion (Mit), the ATP produced supplies energy to the sodium pump shown controlling the level of Na^+ and K^+ in the fiber and as well to the "transport filament." These are shown as black bars to which various components are bound and so carried down the fiber: The mitochondria (a) temporarily attaching as indicated by dashed lines to both forward and retrograde moving transport filaments and thus giving rise to a fast to-and-fro movement (though with a slow net forward movement), and soluble protein (b) shown as a folded or globular configuration as well as polypeptides, and small particulates (c) more firmly bound to transport filaments. Thus a wide range of components are carried along at the same fast rate. Cross-bridges between the transport filament and the microtubules and/or neurofilaments affect the movement in similar fashion to the sliding filament theory of muscle, the required energy supplied by ATP. The cross-bridges are shown arising from both microtubules as spurs or side arms seen in high-resolution electron micrographs.

an *in vivo* downflow for a period of 2 or 3 h is allowed. The nerves are then removed and placed in chambers containing 95% O_2 plus 5% CO_2 for a further period of *in vitro* transport, usually 3 or 4 h. As can be seen when the nerve is exposed to N_2 to block oxidation, the crest does not move down much more than it did during the 2 h of downflow *in vivo*, and no further movement takes place *in vitro* (Fig. 5). The rapid block of fast axoplasmic transport which occurs when oxidative phosphorylation is interrupted indicates that there is only a limited amount of $\sim P$ available when the supply of ATP is shut off by blocking oxidative phosphorylation.

A different time course is seen when iodoacetic acid (IAA) is used to block glycolysis (Ochs and Smith, 1971*a*). This agent produces a characteristic slope in the downflow pattern, with a complete block after 1.5–2 h (Fig. 6). The decrement in outflow is not due to a delayed entry of IAA into the nerve fibers, as shown by the block within 5–10 min of the enzyme glyceraldehyde-3-phosphate dehydrogenase (GAPD) and thus of glycolysis in nerves exposed to IAA (Sabri and Ochs, 1970). The delay in the failure of fast axoplasmic transport after blocking metabolism with IAA is considered due to the utilization of endogenous metabolites, acetyl CoA and α-ketoglutarate, which can enter the tricarboxylic acid cycle below the site of glycolysis block. When these intermediates are depleted, ATP production stops and fast axoplasmic transport fails. By supplying the IAA-treated nerve preparation *in vitro* with a sufficient amount of *l*-lactate or pyruvic acid, the blocking action of IAA can be reversed as these metabolites enter the tricarboxylic acid cycle below

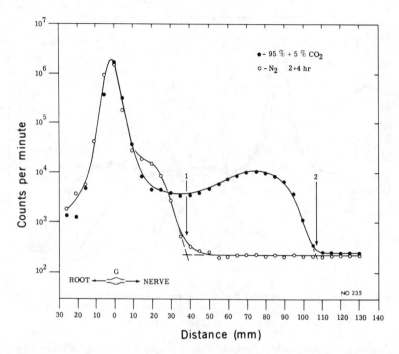

Fig. 5. *In vitro* transport and anoxia. Nerves removed from cats 2 h after injecting their L7 dorsal root ganglia with ^{3}H-leucine. One nerve (●) was placed in a chamber containing 95% O_2 plus 5% CO_2 for an additional 4 h, kept moist with Ringer–lactate solution at 38°C. The rate of transport *in vitro* was that expected of fast transport in the animal (arrow 2). The other nerve (○) was similarly treated except that it was exposed to N_2 while in the chamber for 4 h; the crest advanced no further beyond the 2 h of downflow which had taken place in the animal (arrow 1). From Ochs (1972a).

the point of glycolysis block. This can be seen in the generalized scheme of metabolism of Fig. 7, where the sites at which the metabolic inhibitors are known to act are indicated. Anoxia brought about by N_2, CN, or sodium azide is through their action at the terminal cytochrome oxidase step. The agent DNP acts to uncouple oxidative phosphorylation, and IAA blocks glycogen at the GAPD step. Several other agents at present under investigation are also shown. One is 2-deoxy-D-glucose (2-DG), an analog of glucose. It enters the cells to become phosphorylated to compete with endogenous glucose-6-phosphate at the phosphoglucose isomerase step (Wick *et al.*, 1957; Nirenberg and Hogg, 1958). Another possibility is that 2-DG can act on hexokinase and thus reduce the transport of glucose into cells (Gimeno *et al.*, 1966). However, cat sciatic nerve has sufficient endogenous glycogen and glucose plus, possibly, other metabolites to maintain a supply of ∼P for at

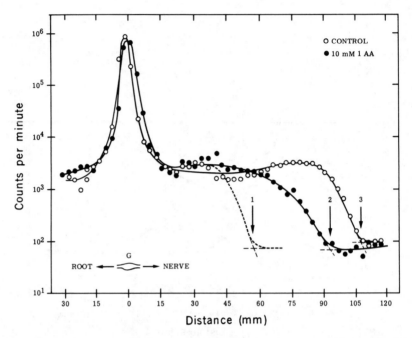

Fig. 6. Block of glycolysis with IAA. Transport *in vitro* is shown in nerves removed 3 h after injecting cat L7 dorsal root ganglia with ^{3}H-leucine. One nerve was placed in a chamber with 10 mM IAA for 3 h ($\bullet$), and arrow 2 shows a diminished downflow compared to the control nerve ($\bigcirc$) (arrow 3). The dashed line and arrow 1 indicate the extent of the downflow expected for the 3-h downflow which had occurred *in vivo*. From Ochs and Smith (1971*a*).

least 5 h and, in some cases, for more than 9 h. A block of fast axoplasmic transport with 2-DG would thus most likely indicate an interference with the endogenous utilization of glucose.

In *in vitro* experiments on fast transport with 2-DG, block occurred at 3–4 h instead of at 1.5–2 h when IAA was used (Ochs, 1972*d*). This later time of block and the high levels of 2-DG needed to effect such a block suggest either that the pentose shunt can prolong the supply of ATP or that the block due to 2-DG is produced by some other mechanism of action.

Another agent indicated in Fig. 7 is fluoracetate (FA), which was selected to block the tricarboxylic acid cycle. This most likely occurs at the aconitase step (Peters, 1955; Goldberg *et al.*, 1966). With FA present in the medium in *in vitro* experiments, fast axoplasmic transport was blocked in 0.75–1.25 h (Ochs, 1972*d*). This time of block is significantly longer than the time of 15 min within which transport fails when oxidative phosphorylation is blocked and

suggests that intermediates entering the tricarboxylic acid cycle can supply
the oxidative chain with reducing equivalents for 0.5–1.0 h or so before they
are exhausted and ATP production ceases. Alternatively, there may be a time
required for the conversion of FA to fluorocitrate to effect a block of aconitase. However, Wolfe and Elliot (1962) note that brain tissue does not con-
vert FA to fluorocitrate, and determination of whether FA does act to block
aconitase in peripheral nerve will require further study.

Support for the concept that a supply of ATP is critical for the maintenance of fast transport was obtained by measuring the levels of ATP and CP
($\sim$P) in nerve after blocking oxidative phosphorylation and glycolysis (Sabri
and Ochs, 1971, 1972). When nerves were made anoxic with N_2 or CN, the
combined level of ATP and CP was reduced to approximately half of control
levels within 15 min, i.e., when fast axoplasmic transport failed. On the other

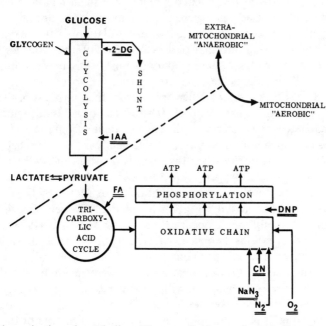

Fig. 7. Schematization of metabolism. The overall scheme of metabolism shows glucose,
either exogenous or from glycogen stores, entering the glycolytic pathways. There is also
a pentose shunt as shown. The result of glycolysis is pyruvate, which enters the tricarboxylic acid cycle in the mitochondrion. Reducing equivalents enter the oxidative chain
for conversion of ADP to ATP at three sites. Oxidative block at the terminal (cytochrome
oxidase) step by N_2 anoxia, CN, or azide is indicated. The agent DNP acts as an un-
coupler, preventing ATP formation. Glycolysis block is shown produced by 2-deoxy-D-
glucose (2-DG) and by iodoacetic acid (IAA). The agent fluoracetate (FA) blocks the
tricarboxylic acid cycle.

hand, when glycolysis was blocked with IAA, the combined level of ATP and CP fell to half of control values in 1.5–2 h—namely, at the time when fast axoplasmic transport was blocked.

The similarity of the times required for the combined level of ATP and CP to fall to half and for the block of fast transport suggests that a critical level of $\sim$P is required to maintain fast axoplasmic transport. Presumably, the remainder of the $\sim$P is compartmented in the axon or in Schwann cells and is a little more resistant to prolonged anoxia or to glycolysis block. With a further period of anoxia or glycolysis block, a further fall in the combined level ATP and CP occurs with no apparent break in the curve as had earlier been found by Stewart et al. (1965). This change is reversible if anoxia is relieved within an hour, as shown by a recovery of ATP and CP toward normal levels (Sabri and Ochs, 1972).

The local nature of the supply of $\sim$P to the mechanism underlying fast axoplasmic transport was investigated by making a small region of the nerve anoxic, just ahead of an advancing crest of activity. This was done by covering the nerve with strips of plastic coated with petrolatum so that oxygen was prevented from diffusing into that part of it (Ochs, 1971b). After an in vitro downflow of several hours, a sharp peak of dammed activity was found at the forward edge of the anoxic region with a steep fall to baseline levels just distally inside it (Fig. 8). An inference drawn from the sharpness of the fall of activity just inside the anoxic region is that oxygen or ATP does not diffuse for more than a few millimeters into the covered region from the well-oxygenated region just outside it. The transport filament carrying its labeled components thus remains in situ when the axon is deprived of ATP. When the region is uncovered and oxygen again becomes available to generate ATP, fast axoplasmic transport resumes without delay, as shown by the advanced position of the crest of activity (Fig. 8). Reversibility is seen after 4–5 hr of anoxia with sufficiently long recovery times (Leon and Ochs, 1973).

The dependence of fast axoplasmic transport on metabolism was further shown by the effect of temperature on the rate of fast axoplasmic transport in vitro (Ochs and Smith, 1971b). Sciatic nerves were taken from cats after injection of the dorsal root ganglion with ^{3}H-leucine and 2 or 3 h of downflow allowed in vivo. Then the nerves were taken from the animals and placed in chambers allowing in vitro downflow for a further 2–4 h. One of the nerves from each of the animals was kept at 38°C, the other at 28°C or at a temperature close to 0°C. A marked effect of temperature on the rate of transport was found. A Q_{10} of 2.0 was determined for the temperature range of 28–38°C and a Q_{10} of 2.3 for the temperature range of 18–28°C. Flow was stopped below a temperature of 11°C (Ochs, 1973). A similar Q_{10} had been reported by Grafstein et al. (1972) for fast transport in the optic system of the goldfish, also indicating that metabolism is involved.

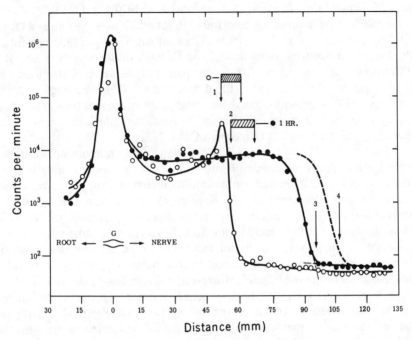

Fig. 8. Local anoxic block and damming of activity. Nerves made locally anoxic by covering with plastic strips coated with petrolatum at the positions indicated by the hatching and bars. One nerve (○) remained covered for all of the 3 h of *in vitro* downflow (arrow 1). The covering over the other nerve (●) was removed after 1 h (arrow 2). Arrow 3 shows the extent of movement of its crest. Arrow 4 and the dashed line indicate the expected downflow if the nerve had not been made temporarily anoxic. From Ochs (1971*b*).

In nerves kept at low temperatures, ATP and CP levels were essentially unchanged, indicating that the supply of ~P was not primarily affected by temperature (Ochs, unpublished results). According to the transport filament hypothesis, the slowing of the rate of transport at lower temperatures results, therefore, from a reduction in the rate of utilization of ATP, presumably at the cross-bridges between the transport filament and the microtubules and/or neurofilaments. It is of interest in this regard that the rate of tension increase in isometric contractions of frog sartorius muscle has a Q_{10} of 2.5 (Hartree and Hill, 1921). A similar Q_{10} close to 2 was found for the rate of shortening of the sarcomere (Close, 1965). Rat skeletal muscle appears to have a higher Q_{10} (Hill, 1972).

In further analogy to muscle, the utilization of ATP by the transport system in nerve requires the presence of an ATPase with actomyosin-like properties. Such an Mg^{2+}, Ca^{2+}-activated ATPase was found in brain neurons (Puszkin *et al.*, 1968; Berl and Puszkin, 1970), and a Mg^{2+}, Ca^{2+}-activated ATPase has recently been found in cat sciatic nerve (Khan and Ochs, 1972*a*). The Mg^{2+}, Ca^{2+}-activated ATPase of cat nerve which is present in the P fraction is ouabain insensitive, and the lack of effect of Na^+ and K^+ differentiates it from the Na^+, K^+-activated ATPase which is also found in lesser amount in sciatic nerve (Iqbal and Ochs, 1973). The Mg^{2+}, Ca^{2+}-activated ATPase present in nerve has most of the properties seen in contractile systems including its inactivation by sulfhydril-blocking agents, e.g., mersalyl, and other agents (Khan and Ochs, 1972*b*).

How Mg^{2+}, Ca^{2+}-activated ATPase relates to the microtubules is under investigation. An involvement of microtubules in transport is indicated by the action of colchicine and vinblastine to interrupt axoplasmic transport (Karlsson and Sjöstrand, 1971*b*; Kreutzberg, 1969; James *et al.*, 1970; Dahlström, 1971*b*). Colchicine and vinblastine are presumed to act by a disassembly of microtubules (Samson and Hinkley, 1972), although this does not occur in all nerves, e.g., in crayfish ventral cord axons where block of transport occurs without disruption of microtubular morphology (Fernandez *et al.*, 1970). On the other hand, Hinkely and Green (1971) showed in rabbit vagus nerves that when colchicine blocked transport the content of microtubules was reduced. An important finding was that electrical activity remained, indicating that the blocking action of colchicine is not effected indirectly through a block of energy metabolism. An apparent blocking effect of colchicine on Mg^{2+}, Ca^{2+}-activated ATPase in mammalian nerve (Khan and Ochs, 1972*a*) was later traced to an action on the enzymes used to assay the ATPase; colchicine is, in fact, relatively ineffective (Khan and Ochs, 1972*b*). A lack of effect of colchicine on the ATPase of actomyosin extracted from skeletal muscle had earlier been reported (Forsheit and Hayashi, 1967). Vinblastine is also relatively ineffective toward Mg^{2+}, Ca^{2+}-activated ATPase (Khan and Ochs, 1972*a*). Present evidence therefore shows that ATPase is located either on the cross-bridges, on the transport filament, or on sites on the microtubules and/or neurofilaments not occupied by colchicine or vinblastine.

A disassembly of microtubules may be brought about by low temperatures (Rodriguez-Echandia and Piezzi, 1968; Tilney and Porter, 1967). This was studied in nerves *in vitro*, in which fast axoplasmic transport was reduced or blocked by bringing the nerves in which transport had been initiated to a temperature just above 0°C for a period of 1–3 h followed by a return to a temperature of 38°C for a further period of time (Ochs, 1973). A prompt resumption of fast axoplasmic transport occurred at the usual temperature, with the crest falling short of the controls at 38°C by the time during which the nerve had been kept at 0°C. Therefore, if nerve microtubules do in fact disassemble at low temperature and the transport filaments come free in the axoplasm, they presumably can find their way back onto the microtubules when they reassemble at the higher temperature to resume transport. The absence of a lasting effect of low temperature on the resumption of fast axoplasmic transport is in accord with the results of Fernandez et al. (1971), who found in similar cold-treatment experiments that crayfish nerves had normal-appearing microtubules and there was no lasting block of slow transport.

If the transport filament requires a Mg^{2+}, Ca^{2+}-activated ATPase, a binding of divalent ions reducing their level below that adequate for enzyme activity should block fast axoplasmic transport. However, the use of EDTA or EGTA in the medium in *in vitro* experiments gave equivocal results. Further, while oxalate was effective in causing a reduction in rate and a block of transport in concentrations of 10–30 mM (Ochs, 1972a, and unpublished experiments), this agent also reduced the level of ATP and CP in the nerves. While this indicates an entry of oxalate, it suggests that oxalate could, perhaps, act in an indirect fashion by reducing the divalent ion required at some enzymatic step and lowering $\sim P$. A Ca^{2+} binding is still possible because the decrease of $\sim P$ produced by oxalate was only half as great as that seen when transport was blocked by an interruption of ATP production by anoxin.

2.3. Transport and Membrane Function

Intermediary metabolism leading to the production of ATP in nerve tissue appears to be qualitatively the same in brain tissue, ganglion, or nerve fiber, although the level of metabolism is lower in ganglion and nerve (Brink, 1957; Larrabee, 1958; Horowicz and Larrabee, 1958; Quastel and Quastel, 1961; Friede, 1966; McIlwain, 1966; Lowry, 1966; McDougal et al., 1968; Lajtha, 1970–1971). The rate is still lower in frog nerve, which was used in the bulk of earlier studies (*cf*. Gerard, 1932), when compared with mammalian nerve (Cranefield et al., 1957; Stewart et al., 1965; Okada and McDougal, 1971).

As indicated in the model shown in Fig. 4, part of the ATP which is produced by oxidative phosphorylation is required to supply the sodium pump with $\sim P$, and this has been estimated to take about half (Baker, 1965) or most (Ritchie, 1967) of the ongoing metabolism. These estimates rest on assumptions made as to the number of Na ions extruded per $\sim P$. In any case, some part of the ATP production is required to supply $\sim P$ to the mechanism underlying fast axoplasmic transport indicated by the cross-bridges between the transport filament and the microtubules (Fig. 4). The dependence of the nerve on ATP supply was studied in cat sciatic nerves made anoxic with N_2 (Ochs et al., 1970a). Fast axoplasmic transport and action potentials both failed in less than 15 min. In these studies, nerves were placed in chambers containing 95% O_2 plus 5% CO_2 in equilibrium with water vapor and kept at

38°C by temperature-controlled water circulated in hollow walls (Fig. 9). Action potentials could be elicited from nerves suspended on the electrodes of the chamber while fast axoplasmic transport was also going on—for up to 4 h. When the 95% O_2 plus 5% O_2 gas environment was replaced by N_2, α action potential responses were reduced and were completely blocked within 10 min (Fig. 10). This time was briefer than usual. Usually mammalian nerves survive anoxias of 15–30 min in N_2 (Gerard, 1932; Wright, 1946, 1947). A much more prolonged maintenance of resting and action potentials is seen in giant axons after interruption of oxidative metabolism and the sodium pump (Hodgkin and Keynes, 1955). This difference is most certainly due to the much greater volume of axoplasm in the giant nerve fiber so that a longer time is required for K^+ and Na^+ concentrations to change.

   In the experiments on transport in the chamber of Fig. 9, small increases

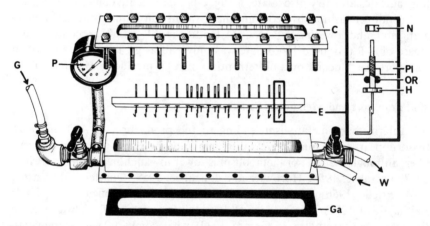

Fig. 9. Chamber for action potential recording and *in vitro* transport. The upper portion of the chamber is made of plastic and contains pins passing through it at 1.5-cm intervals. Curved silver electrodes are soldered to the bottom of the pins. The sciatic nerve removed from the animal is placed on the curved portions of the electrodes and thus is suspended in approximately the center of the chamber when the top is set over the bottom of the chamber with an intervening gasket. Screws set around the metal part over the plastic cover fasten to the bottom part of the chamber to seal it. Valves at either end control the entry and exit of gases which are used to flush and fill the chamber. Typically, the gas used to maintain transport is 95% O_2 plus 5% CO_2. After the chamber is flushed and filled to a small excess of pressure above atmospheric pressure as indicated by the gauge, the valves are closed. A small amount of Ringer's solution is placed on the bottom of the chamber and vapor comes into equilibrium with the gases present in the chamber, preventing the nerve from drying. The walls of the bottom are hollow, and through it a heated water supply regulated at 38°C is circulated by a pump. Connections made to the projecting pins from the top to a stimulator and preamplifier lead to an oscilloscope so that the nerve can be stimulated and recorded from at various places along its length. The insert E shows details of the electrode connections.

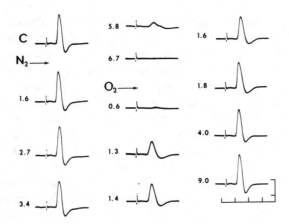

Fig. 10. Effect of N_2 anoxia on action potential responses. Control responses represent maximal α action potentials. The distal electrode was near the injured cut distal end of the nerve and responses were close to monophasic. At the arrow at the left, the 95% O_2 plus 5% CO_2 gas mixture was replaced with N_2. At the time in minutes shown at the left of the traces, the responses began to diminish in amplitude and at 6.7 min were completely blocked. The chamber was then reflushed with 95% O_2 plus 5% CO_2 and action potentials responses recovered back to control levels.

of pressure, i.e., to about 0.5 atm above atmospheric pressure, had little noticeable effect on either action potentials or fast axoplasmic transport. However, when high pressures of 95% O_2 plus 5% CO_2 (3–8 atm) were employed in these chambers, there was at first a small excitability drop over a period of several minutes which leveled off and then, after 1–3 h, depending on the pressure, a fall to zero response. At this time, there was also a block of fast axoplasmic transport (Ochs and Heckaman, 1972). The levels of ATP and CP found in the nerve decreased to about half of control values, indicating a failure of supply of $\sim$P. The effect of the higher pressures to decrease ATP production is brought about through oxygen poisoning of metabolism (Haugaard, 1963) and not through pressure *per se*.

The rate of fast axoplasmic transport does not change much as a result of increased nerve activity. Nerves in the chamber of Fig. 9 were stimulated to give maximal action potential responses at 100 pulses/s for a period of 3–4 h, and the rate of fast axoplasmic transport was reduced about 10% (Ochs and Smith, 1971b). This small decrease does not seem to be related directly to a reduction of the level of $\sim$P, because the content of ATP and CP was not much reduced (Ochs, unpublished experiments). In comparable experiments, no effect at all on the transport of AChE was reported to result from similar periods of prolonged repetitive stimulation (Jankowska et al., 1969).

If ATP is supplied to the sodium pump and to the transport mechanism in the fibers as shown in Fig. 5, it might be inferred that a block of the Na^+, K^+-activated ATPase of the pump with ouabain might increase the level of ATP, and if more $\sim P$ were available to the fast axoplasmic transport mechanism this might possibly increase its rate. However, ouabain in concentrations adequate to block the sodium pump causes a decrease in the rate of fast axoplasmic transport in cat (Ochs, 1972a) and frog nerves (Anderson and Edström, 1973) a finding which at present remains unexplained.

An excitable membrane is not a necessary condition for fast axoplasmic transport, nor do variations in excitability control the rate of transport. When active Na entry across the membrane was blocked by either tetrodotoxin (TTX) or procaine, the pattern and the rate of fast axoplasmic transport remained unchanged (Ochs and Hollingsworth, 1971). In experiments similar to ours, fast axoplasmic transport was not blocked in nerves exposed *in vitro* to lidocaine at concentrations adequate to block action potentials (Fink *et al.*, 1972). However, at concentrations above 0.1% there was a decrease and at 0.6% a block of fast axoplasmic transport which was associated with a disruption of microtubules. With halothane, no block of fast axoplasmic transport was found at a concentration of 3% when action potentials were blocked, while with higher concentrations of 7.8–10% block occurred with evidence of loss of microtubules (Kennedy *et al.*, 1972). Incidentally, in these experiments the rate given for fast axoplasmic transport in the controls was 408 mm/day, in close confirmation of the rates we found for fast axoplasmic transport *in vivo* and *in vitro* (see above).

Our recent studies of *in vitro* transport were carried out with nerves placed in 25-ml Erlenmeyer flasks containing Krebs–Ringer solution vigorously bubbled with 95% O_2 plus 5% CO_2. With the NaCl in the Krebs–Ringer medium replaced by KCl, the resulting depolarization had no effect on the pattern or rate of fast axoplasmic transport (Ochs, 1972e). In these experiments, when all external ions were replaced by an isotonic sucrose medium fast axoplasmic transport was still maintained at the usual rate. Membrane polarization is thus definitely shown not to be required for transport. A small deviation from isotonicity, of ± 25–50 mM, had little effect, but larger deviations of ± 100 mM and more caused a reduction in the rate and then a block. These osmotic effects are likely to have been brought about by change in the internal environment involving elements of the mechanism proposed to account for fast transport (Fig. 4).

3. SLOW AXOPLASMIC TRANSPORT

3.1. Characterization

Investigation of the slow transport system preceded the discovery of fast axoplasmic transport. As shown by tracer techniques with ^{32}P (orthophosphate) as precursor (Samuels *et al.*, 1951; Ochs and Burger, 1958; Ochs *et al.*, 1962), the incorporated phospholipids (Miani, 1963, 1964) and other phosphate compounds, phosphoproteins, inositol phosphate, etc., are moved down the axons by the slow transport system at a rate of several millimeters per day. The form of outflow is an exponentially declining function with a decreasing slope, as the time allowed between the injection of precursor near cell bodies and removal of nerves or ventral roots for determination of outflow pattern is increased over a period of days and weeks (Ochs *et al.*, 1962). Other earlier studies made using tritiated or ^{14}C-labeled amino acids had also shown a slow outflow (Koenig, 1958; Waelsch, 1958; Droz and Leblond, 1962). It was only later, when larger amounts of ^{3}H-leucine were used and earlier times studied, that the presence of fast and slow outflows was recognized by the break in the outflow slopes and the different changes of the two components with time (Ochs, 1967; Lasek, 1968; Ochs and Johnson, 1969).

The rate of slow transport is unfortunately not so readily characterized as the rate of fast axoplasmic transport. Miani (1963) considered the farthest extent of outflow seen in 1 day as the measure of rate, but this "faster" outflow represents a different interpretation of the same data. The half-activity point of the slopes of outflow was used as a measure of rate in our ^{32}P studies, with a value of 4.5 mm/day derived for (slow) transport (Ochs *et al.*, 1962). This estimate was close to the rate of 1–3 mm/day given by Weiss and Hiscoe (1948) on the basis of an apparent volume increase of nerve fibers in the dammed region above partial nerve constrictions.

3.2. Mechanism

Weiss and Hiscoe (1948) suggested that the whole of the axon "grows" out inside the fiber, a process also described as a perpetual growth or a proximodistal convection (Weiss, 1961). A peristalsis of the fibers was envisioned as the process underlying such bulk movement (Weiss, 1969). However, the inference of a perpetual growth or a convection of axoplasm in the sense of Weiss conflicts with the exponentially declining outflow found for slow transport. Another inconsistency was indicated by the results obtained using "beading" (Ochs, 1965). Upon stretching a nerve and then quickly freezing it at very low temperatures (toward $-160°C$) before preparing the tissue for histological examination by freeze-substitution, a series of constrictions or beads are seen to be excited by the stretch. This technique in essence causes a partition of the nerve contents, with a greater concentration of the linear elements, the microtubules, and/or neurofilaments remaining in the constrictions and more of the soluble components moved into the expanded part of the beads. In nerves in which slow transport has carried down labeled protein before stretching and beading, the microtubules and/or neurofilaments are found to be labeled to a lesser degree than the soluble or particulate components in the axoplasm of the expanded part of the beads (Ochs, 1966). This indicates a nonuniformity in the composition of transported substances with respect to the filamentous and soluble components. More recently, the studies of Martinez and Friede (1970) have clearly shown that there is accumulation of some of the formed elements and enzymes present in nerves above a ligation and not of others. The differences in the types of materials accumulated led them to conclude that a continuous outgrowth of all of the axoplasm as envisioned by Weiss was incompatible with their findings (cf. Spencer, 1972). In studies in the author's laboratory, ligated nerves were subjected to freeze-substitution in order to best preserve the shape of nerve fibers, and a different picture has emerged from that seen by Weiss and Hiscoe (1948). The freeze-substituted nerves show beading and form changes but not the exaggerated swellings and tortuosities indicative of an increase in fiber volume as might be due to a continuous movement of the axoplasm down inside the axion, which Weiss and Mayr (1971) consider "similar to a flow of lava or of glaciers." What is seen is evidence of re-generation of fibers (Ochs, unpublished observations).

If the concept of a continuous outgrowth of axoplasm is rejected, a hypothesis other than that of bulk flow is required to explain slow transport. Such a hypothesis must account for the exponentially declining outflow. The hypothesis now put forth is based on the complex movement of the mito-chondrion shown by optical studies. Using Nomarski techniques, particles of mitochondrial size are seen to have a rapid movement in either direction (Burdwood, 1965; Kirkpatrick et al., 1972). If mitochondria and other com-ponents are temporarily bound to the transport filaments, its backward and forward movements could give rise to the slow net movement in the proximo-distal direction (Barondes, 1966; Jeffrey et al., 1972; Khan et al., 1971), and the declining exponential outflow pattern typical of slow transport.

This "transport filament shuttle" mechanism can account for the different sensitivities to temperature shown by fast and slow transport. Using ^{32}P downflow as a measure of slow transport, a Q_{10} of 1.3 had earlier been esti-mated (Ochs et al., 1962), while the rate of fast axoplasmic transport was found to have a Q_{10} of 2–2.3 (Ochs and Smith, 1971b). A similar difference in the Q_{10} of fast and slow transport in the fish visual system was also reported by Graf-stein et al. (1972). The mitochondrion presumably in its rapid movements forward and backward requires ATP as does fast axoplasmic transport, and its rate would be expected to have a similar high Q_{10}. However, with the rates of both the forward and backward movement reduced at a lower temperature, the net slow movement may show a smaller Q_{10}.

Colchicine has been reported to block fast transport but not slow trans-port, as shown by the accumulation of marker components for the mitochondria at a ligature when a region of the nerve above that site was injected with the mitotic blocking agent (Kreutzberg, 1969). This could be interpreted as a lack of effect on slow transport if it were indeed a bulk movement. However, a block would not be expected if slow transport is in fact brought about by the movement of mitochondria back and forth below the site of colchicine injection.

While the proposed mechanism to account for slow transport seems to fit reasonably well with the known phenomena, much more investigation is required to critically test the model presented to account for the underlying molecular events.

4. REFERENCES

Anderson, K.-E., and Edström, A., 1973, Effects of nerve blocking agents on fast axonal transport of proteins in frog sciatic nerves in vitro, Brain Res. 50:125.

Baker, P. F., 1965, Phosphorus metabolism of intact crab nerve and its relation to the active transport of ions, J. Physiol. 180:383.

Barondes, S. H., 1966, On the site of synthesis of the mitochondrial protein of nerve endings, J. Neurochem. 13:721.

Barondes, S. H., 1970), Axoplasmic transport, in: Handbook of Neurochemistry, Vol. 2 (A. Lajtha, ed.), p. 435, Plenum Press, New York.

Berl, S., and Puszkin, S., 1970, Mg^{2+}-Ca^{2+}-activated adenosine triphosphatase system isolated from mammalian brain, Biochemistry 9:2058.

Bray, J. J., and Austin, L., 1968, Flow of protein and ribonucleic acid in peripheral nerve, J. Neurochem. 15:731.

Bray, J. J., and Austin, L., 1969, Axoplasmic transport of C^{14} proteins at two rates in chicken sciatic nerve, Brain Res. 12:230.

Brink, F., 1957, Nerve metabolism, in: Metabolism of the Nervous System (D. Richter, ed.), p. 187, Pergamon Press, New York.

Brzin, M., Tennyson, V. M., and Duffy, P. E., 1967, Ultrastructural, cyto chemical, and microgasometric studies of acetylcholinesterase in isolated neurons of the frog, Internat. J. Neuropharmacol. 6:265.

Burdwood, W. O., 1965, Rapid bidirectional particle movement in neurons, J. Cell Biol. 27:115A.

Close, R., 1965, The relation between intrinsic speed of shortening and duration of the active state of muscle, J. Physiol. 180:542.

Cragg, B. G., 1970, What is the signal for chromatolysis? Brain Res. 23:1.

Cranefield, P. F., Brink, F., and Bronk, D. W., 1957, The oxygen uptake of the peripheral nerve of the rat, J. Neurochem. 1:245.

Dahlström, A., 1968, Effect of colchicine on transport of amine storage granules in sympathetic nerves of rat, Europ. J. Pharmacol. 5:111.

Dahlström, A., 1971a, Axoplasmic transport (with particular respect to adrenergic neurons), Phil. Trans. Roy. Soc. B 162:325.

Dahlström, A., 1971b, Effects of vinblastine and colchicine on monamine containing neurons of the rat, with special regard to the axoplasmic transport of amine granules. Acta Neuropathol. Berl. Suppl. 5:226.

Dahlström, A., and Häggendal, J., 1966, Studies on the transport and lifespan of amine storage granules in a peripheral adrenergic neuron system, *Acta Physiol. Scand.* **67**:278.

Drachman, D. B. (ed.), 1973, Symposium on trophic function of the neuron, *Ann. N.Y. Acad. Sci.* (in press).

Droz, B., 1965, Accumulation de protéines nouvellement synthétisées dans l'appareil de Golgi du neurone: Étude radioautographique en microscopie electroniqué, *Compt. Rend. Acad. Sci. Paris* **260**:320.

Droz, B., and Leblond, C. P., 1962, Migration of proteins along the axons of the sciatic nerve, *Science* **137**:1047.

Elam, J. S., and Agranoff, B. W., 1971, Transport of proteins and sulfated mucopolysaccharides in the goldfish visual system, *J. Neurobiol.* **2**:379.

Fernandez, H. L., Huneeus, F. C., and Davison, P. F., 1970, Studies on the mechanism of axoplasmic transport in the crayfish cord, *J. Neurobiol.* **1**:395.

Fink B. R., Kennedy, R. D., Hendrickson, A. E., and Middaugh, M. E., 1972, Lidocaine inhibition of rapid axonal transport, *Anesthesiology* **36**:422.

Forsheit, A. B., and Hayashi, T., 1967, The effects of colchicine on contractile proteins, *Biochim. Biophys. Acta* **147**:546.

Friede, R. L., 1966, *Topographic Brain Chemistry*, Academic Press, New York.

Friede, R. L., 1972, Control of myelin formation by axon calibar (with a model of the control mechanism), *J. Comp. Neurol.* **144**:233.

Geffen, L. B., and Livett, B. G., 1971, Synaptic vesicles in sympathetic neurons, *Physiol. Rev.* **51**:98.

Gerard, R. W., 1932, Nerve metabolism, *Physiol. Rev.* **12**:469.

Gimeno, A. L., Lacuara, J. L., Gimeno, M. F., Ceretti, E., and Webb, J. L., 1966, Effects of 2-deoxy-D-glucose on isolated atria, *Mol. Pharmacol.* **2**:77.

Goldberg, N. D., Passoneau, J. V., and Lowry, O. H., 1966, Effects of changes in brain metabolism on the levels of citric acid cycle intermediates, *J. Biol. Chem.* **241**:3997.

Grafstein, B., 1969, Axonal transport: Communication between soma and synapse, in: *Advances in Biochemical Psychopharmacology*, Vol. 1 (E. Costa and P. Greengard, eds.), p. 11, Raven Press, New York.

Grafstein, B., Forman, D. S., and McEwen, B. S., 1972, Effects of temperature on axonal transport and turnover of protein in goldfish optic system, *Exptl. Neurol.* **34**:158.

Guth, L. (ed.), 1968, "Trophic" effects of vertebrate neurons, *Neurosci. Res. Prog. Bull.* **7**:1.

Guth, L., 1969, "Trophic" influences of nerve on muscle, *Physiol. Rev.* **48**:645.

Gutmann, E., and Hnik, P. (eds.), 1963, *The Effect of Use and Disuse on Neuromuscular Functions*, Elsevier, Amsterdam.

Hall, Z. W., 1973, Multiple forms of acetylcholinesterase and their distribution in endplate and non-endplate regions of rat diaphragm muscle, *J. Neurobiol.* **4**:343.

Hartree, W., and Hill, A. V., 1921, The nature of the isometric twitch, *J. Physiol.* **55**:389.

Haugaard, N., 1963, The toxic action of oxygen on metabolism and the role of trace metals, in: *Oxygen in the Animal Organism* (F. Dickens, and E. Neil, eds.), Pergamon Press, New York.

Hill, D. K., 1972, Resting tension and the form of the twitch of rat skeletal muscle at low temperature, *J. Physiol.* **221**:161.

Hinkley, R. E., and Green, L. S., 1971, Effects of halothane and colchicine on microtubules and electrical activity of rabbit vagus nerves, *J. Neurobiol.* **2**:97.

Hodgkin, A. L., and Keynes, R. D., 1955, Active transport of cations in giant axons from *Sepia* and *Loligo*, *J. Physiol.* **128**:28.

Horowicz, P., and Larrabee, M. G., 1958, Glucose consumption and lactate production in a mammalian sympathetic ganglion at rest and in activity, *J. Neurochem.* **2**:102.

Iqbal, Z., and Ochs, S., 1973, Axoplasmic transport of Na-K activated ATPase in mammalian nerve, *Fed. Proc.* **32**:366.

James, K. A. C., and Austin, L., 1970, The binding *in vitro* of colchicine to axoplasmic proteins from chicken sciatic nerve, *Biochem. J.* **117**:773.

James, K. A. C., Bray, J. J. Morgan, I. G., and Austin, L., 1970, The effect of colchicine on the transport of axonal protein in the chicken, *Biochem. J.* **117**:767.

Jankowska, E., Lubińska, L., and Niemierko, S., 1969, Translocation of AChE-containing particles in the axoplasm during nerve activity, *Comp. Biochem. Physiol.* **28**:907.

Jeffrey, P. L., James, K. A. C., Kidman, A. D., Richards, A. M., and Austin, L., 1972, The flow of mitochondria in chicken sciatic nerve, *J. Neurobiol.* **3**:199.

Johnson, J. L., 1970, Changes in acetylcholinesterase, acid phosphatase and beta glucuronidase proximal to a nerve crush, *Brain Res.* **18**:427.

Karlsson, J. O., and Sjöstrand, J., 1971*a*, Characterization of the fast and slow components of axonal transport in retinal ganglion cells, *J. Neurobiol.* **2**:135.

Karlsson, J. O., and Sjöstrand, J., 1971*b*, Axonal transport of proteins in the optic nerve and tract of the rabbit, *Acta Neuropathol. Berl. Suppl.* **5**:207.

Kasa, P., 1968, Acetylcholinesterase transport in the central and peripheral nervous tissue: The role of tubules in the enzyme transport, *Nature* **218**:1265.

Kennedy, R. D., Fink, B. R., and Byers, M. R., 1972, The effect of halothane on rapid axonal transport in the rabbit vagus, *Anesthesiology* **36(5)**:433.

Khan, M. A., and Ochs, S., 1972*a*, Mg^{2+}-Ca^{2+}-activated ATPase in mammalian nerves: Relation to fast axoplasmic transport and block with colchicine, *Abst. Am. Soc. Neurochem.* **3**:93.

Khan, M. A., and Ochs, S., 1972*b*, Mg^{2+}-Ca^{2+}-activated ATPase in mammalian nerve and its relation to fast axoplasmic transport, in preparation.

Khan, M. A., Ranish, N., and Ochs, S., 1971, Axoplasmic transport of AChE, LDH and MAO in mammalian nerve fibers, *Soc. Neurosci. Abst.* **1**:144.

Kidwai, A. M., and Ochs, S., 1969, Components of fast and slow phases of axoplasmic flow, *J. Neurochem.* **16**:1105.

Kirkpatrick, J. B., Bray, J. J., and Palmer, S. M., 1972, Visualization of axoplasmic flo*w* *in vitro* by Nomarski microscopy: Comparison to rapid flow of radioactive proteins, *Brain Res. (Eng.)* **43**:1.

Koenig, H., 1958, The synthesis and peripheral flow of axoplasm, *Trans. Am. Neurol. Ass.* **83**:162.

Kreutzberg, G., 1969, Neuronal dynamics and axonal flow. IV. Blockage of intra-axonal enzyme transport by colchicine, *Proc. Natl. Acad. Sci. USA* **62**:722.

Lajtha, A. (ed.), 1970–71, *Handbook of Neurochemistry*, Vols. 3–5, Plenum Press, New York.

Larrabee, M. G., 1958, Oxygen consumption of excised sympathetic ganglia at rest and activity, *J. Neurochem.* **2**:81.

Lasek, R., 1968, Axoplasmic transport in cat dorsal root ganglion cells: As studied with (^{3}H)-1-leucine, *Brain Res.* **7**:360.

Lasek, R. J., 1970, Protein transport in neurons, *Internat. Rev. Neurobiol.* **13**:289.

Leoni, J., and Ochs, S., 1973, Reversibility of fast axoplasmic transport following differing durations of anoxic block *in vitro* and *in vivo*, *Soc. Neurosci. Abst.* **3**:147.

Lowry, O. H., 1966, Energy metabolism of the nerve cell, in: *Nerve as a Tissue* (K. Rodahl and B. Issekutz, eds.), Harper and Row, New York.

Lubińska, L., 1964, Axoplasmic streaming in regenerating and in normal nerve fibres, in: *Mechanisms of Neural Regeneration* (M. Singer and J. P. Schadé, eds.), *Progr. Brain Res.* **13**:56.

Lubińska, L., and Niemierko, S., 1971, Velocity and intensity of bidirectional migration of acetylcholinesterase in transected nerves, *Brain Res.* **27**:329.

Martinez, A. J., and Friede, R. L., 1970, Accumulation of axoplasmic organelles in swollen nerve fibers, *Brain Res.* **19**:183.

McDougal, D. M., Holowach, J., Howe, M. C., Jones, E. M., and Thomas, C. A., 1968, The effects of anoxia upon energy sources and selected metabolic intermediates in the brains of fish, frog and turtle, *J. Neurochem.* **15**:577.

McEwen, B. S., and Grafstein, B., 1968, Fast and slow components in axonal transport of protein, *J. Cell Biol.* **38**:494.

McEwen, B. S., Forman, D. S., and Grafstein, B., 1971, Components of fast and slow axonal transport in the goldfish optic nerve, *J. Neurobiol.* **2**:361.

McIlwain, H., 1966, *Biochemistry and the Central Nervous System*, 3rd ed., Little, Brown and Co., Boston.

Miani, N., 1963, Analysis of the somato-axonal movement of phospholipids in the vagus and hypoglossal nerves, *J. Neurochem.* **10**:859.

Miani, N., 1964, Proximo-distal movement of phospholipid in the axoplasm of the intact and regenerating neurons, *Progr. Brain Res.* **13**:115.

Nirenberg, M. W., and Hogg, J. F., 1958, Inhibition of anaerobic glycolysis in Ehrlich ascites tumor cells by 2-deoxy-D-glucose, *Cancer Res.* **18**:518.

Ochs, S., 1965, Beading of myelinated nerve fibers, *Exptl. Neurol.* **12**:84.

Ochs, S., 1966, Axoplasmic flow in neurons, in: *Macromolecules and Behavior* (J. Gaito, ed.), p. 20, Appleton-Century-Crofts, New York.

Ochs, S., 1967, Axoplasmic transport of protein and the beading phenomenon, in: Axoplasmic Transport (S. Barondes, ed.), *Neurosci. Res. Bull.* **5**:340,377.

Ochs, S., 1970, Fast axoplasmic flow of proteins and polypeptides in mammalian nerve fibers, in: *Protein Metabolism of the Nervous System* (A. Lajtha, ed.), p. 291, Plenum Press, New York.

Ochs, S., 1971a, Characteristics and a model for fast axoplasmic transport in nerve, *J. Neurobiol.* **2**:331.

Ochs, S., 1971b, Local supply of energy to the fast axoplasmic transport, *Proc. Natl. Acad. Sci. USA* **68**:1279.

Ochs, S., 1972a, Fast transport of materials in mammalian nerve fibers, *Science* **176**:252.

Ochs, S., 1972b, Fast axoplasmic transport of materials in mammalian nerve and its integrative role, *Ann. N.Y. Acad. Sci.* **193**:43.

Ochs, S., 1972c, Rate of fast axoplasmic transport in mammalian nerve fibres, *J. Physiol.* **227**:627.

Ochs, S., 1972d, Block of fast axoplasmic transport by interruption of metabolism with 2-deoxyglucose, fluoroacetate and azide, *Am. Soc. Neurochem. Abst.* **3**:109.

Ochs, S., 1972e, Membrane properties (excitability and osmoticity) and fast axoplasmic transport *in vitro*, *Soc. Neurosci. Abst.* **2**:255.

Ochs, S., 1973, Cold block of fast axoplasmic transport: Reversibility and effects of colchicine and vinblastine, *Soc. Neurosci. Abst.* **3**:147.

Ochs, S., 1974, Systems of material transport in nerve fibers (axoplasmic transport) related to nerve function and trophic control, *Ann. N.Y. Acad. Sci.* (in press).

Ochs, S., and Burger, E., 1958, Movement of substance proximo-distally in nerve axons as studied with spinal cord injections of radioactive phosphorus, *Am. J. Physiol.* **194**:499.

Ochs, S., and Heckaman, P., 1972, Block of nerve excitability and fast axoplasmic transport by increased O_2 and CO_2, *Biophys. Soc. Abst.* **12**, 192a.

Ochs, S., and Hollingsworth, D., 1971, Dependence of fast axoplasmic transport in nerve on oxidative metabolism, *J. Neurochem.* **18**:107.

Ochs, S., and Johnson, J., 1969, Fast and slow phases of axoplasmic flow in ventral root fibers, *J. Neurochem.* **16**:845.

Ochs, S., and Ranish, N., 1969, Characteristics of the fast transport system in mammalian nerve fibers, *J. Neurobiol.* **1**:247.

Ochs, S., and Smith, C. B., 1971a, Fast axoplasmic transport in mammalian nerve *in vitro* after block of glycolysis with iodaocetic acid, *J. Neurochem.* **18**:833.

Ochs, S., and Smith, C. B., 1971b, Effect of temperature and rate of stimulation on fast axoplasmic transport in mammalian nerve fibers, *Fed. Proc.* **30**:665.

Ochs, S., Booker, H., and DeMyer, W. E., 1961, Note on the signal for chromatolysis after nerve interruption, *Exptl. Neurol.* **3**:206.

Ochs, S., Dalrymple, D., and Richards, G., 1962, Axoplasmic flow in ventral root nerve fibers of the cat, *Exptl. Neurol.* **5**:349.

Ochs, S., Johnson, J., and Ng, M.-H, 1967, Protein incorporation and axoplasmic flow in motoneuron fibers following intra-cord injection of leucine, *J. Neurochem.* **14**:317.

Ochs, S., Sabri, M. I., and Johnson, J., 1969, Fast transport system of materials in mammalian nerve fibers, *Science* **163**:686.

Ochs, S., Ranish, N., Hollingsworth, D., and Helmer, E., 1970a, Dependence of fast axoplasmic transport in mammalian nerve on metabolism and relation to excitability, *Fed. Proc.* **29**:264.

Ochs, S., Sabri, M. I., and Ranish, N., 1970b, Somal site of synthesis of fast transported materials in mammalian nerve fibers, *J. Neurobiol.* **1**:329.

Okada, Y., and McDougal, D. B., 1971, Physiological and biochemical changes in frog sciatic nerve during anoxia and recovery, *J. Neurochem.* **18**:2335.

Pellegrino de Iraldi, A., and de Robertis, E., 1968, The neurotubular system of the axon and the origin of granulated and non-granulated vesicles in regenerating nerves, *Z. Zellforsch. Mikroskop. Anat.* **87**:330.

Peters, R. A., 1955, Biochemistry of some toxic agents. II. Some recent work in the field of fluoroacetate compounds, *Bull. Johns Hopkins Hosp.* **97**:21.

Puszkin, S., Berl, S., Puszkin, E., and Clarke, D. D., 1968, Actomyosin-like protein isolated from mammalian brain, *Science* **161**:170.

Quastel. J. H., and Quastel, D. M., 1961, *The Chemistry of Brain Metabolism in Health and Disease*, Charles C Thomas, Springfield, Ill.

Ranish, N., and Ochs, S., 1972, Fast axoplasmic transport of acetylcholinesterase in mammalian nerve fibers, *J. Neurochem.* **19**:2641.

Ritchie, J. M., 1967, The oxygen consumption of mammalian non-myelinated nerve fibers at rest and during activity, *J. Physiol.* **188**:309.

Rodriguez-Echandia, E. L., and Piezzi, R. S., 1968, Microtubules in the nerve fibers of the toad *Bufo arenarum* Hensel, *J. Cell Biol.* **39**:491.

Sabri, M. I., and Ochs, S., 1970, The action of iodoacetic acid on glyceraldehyde 3-phosphate dehydrogenase (GAPD) in mammalian nerve, *Physiologist* **13**:299.

Sabri, M. I., and Ochs, S., 1971, High energy phosphates in anoxic and iodoacetate treated mammalian nerve, *Trans. Am. Soc. Neurochem.* **2**:104.

Sabri, M. I., and Ochs, S., 1972, Relation of ATP and creatine phosphate to fast axoplasmic transport in mammalian nerve, *J. Neurochem.* **19**:2821.

Sabri, M. I., and Ochs, S., 1973, Characterization of fast and slow transported protein in dorsal roots and sciatic nerve, *J. Neurobiol.* **4**:145.

Samson, F. E., 1971, Mechanism of axoplasmic transport, *J. Neurobiol.* **2**:347.

Samson, F. E., and Hinkley, R. E., 1972, Neuronal microtubular systems (Editorial views), *Anesthesiology* **36**:417.

Samuels, A. J., Boyarsky, L. L., Gerard, R. W., Libet, B., and Brust, M., 1951, Distribution exchange and migration of phosphate compounds in the nervous system, *Am. J. Physiol.* **164**:1.

Schmitt, F. O., 1968, Fibrous proteins—Neuronal organelles, *Proc. Natl. Acad. Sci. USA* **60**:1092.

Singer, S. J., 1972, A fluid lipid–globular protein mosaic model of membrane structure, in: Membrane Structure and Its Biological Applications (D. E. Green, ed.), *Ann. N. Y. Acad. Sci.* **195**:16.

Spencer, P. S., 1972, Reappraisal of the model for "bulk axoplasmic flow," *Nature New Biol.* **240**:283.

Stewart, M. A., Passonneau, J. V., and Lowry, O. H., 1965, Substrate changes in peripheral nerve during ischemia and Wallerian degeneration, *J. Neurochem.* **12**:719.

Tilney, L. G., and Porter, K. R., 1967, Studies on the microtubules in heliozoa. II. The effect of low temperature on these structures in the formation and maintenance of the axopodia, *J. Cell Biol.* **34**:327.

Van Breeman, V. L., Anderson, E., and Reger, J. F., 1958, An attempt to determine the origin of synaptic vesicles, *Exptl. Cell Res. Suppl.* **5**:153.

Waelsch, H., 1958, Some aspects of amino acid and protein metabolism of the nervous system, *J. Nerv. Ment. Dis.* **126**:33.

Weiss, P., 1961, The concept of perpetual neuronal growth and proximo-distal substance convention, in: *Proceedings of the Fourth International Neurochemical Symposium, 1960* (S. S. Kety and J. Elkes, eds.), p. 220, Pergamon Press, New York.

Weiss, P., 1969, Neuronal dynamics and neuroplasmic ("axonal") flow, in: *Cellular Dynamics of the Neuron* (S. H. Barondes, ed.), Vol. 8, p. 3, Academic Press, N. Y.

Weiss, P., and Hiscoe, H. B., 1948, Experiments on the mechanism of nerve growth, *J. Exptl. Zool.* **107**:315.

Weiss, P. A., and Mayr, R., 1971, Neuronal organelles in neuroplasmic ("axonal") flow. I. Mitochondria, *Acta Neuropathol. Berl. Suppl.* **5**:187.

Wick, A. N., Drury, D. R., Nakada, H. I., and Wolfe, J. B., 1957, Localization of the primary metabolic block produced by 2-deoxyglucose, *J. Biol. Chem.* **224**:963.

Wolfe, L. S., and Elliott, K. A. C., 1962, Chemical studies in relation to compulsive conditions, in: *The Chemistry of Brain and Nerve*, 2nd ed. (K. A. C. Elliott, I. H. Page, and J. H. Quastel, eds.), p. 694, Charles C Thomas, Springfield, Ill.

Wright, E. B., 1946, A comparative study of the effects of oxygen lack on peripheral nerve, *Am. J. Physiol.* **147**:78.

Wright, E. B., 1947, The effects of asphyxiation and narcosis on peripheral nerve polarization and conduction, *Am. J. Physiol.* **148**:174.

Section IIA

Junctional Transmission— Structure

Chapter 4

Neuromuscular Junctions and Electric Organs

Arthur Hess

Department of Anatomy
Rutgers Medical School
New Brunswick, New Jersey; USA

1. INTRODUCTION

The neuromuscular junction has been much studied anatomically and physiologically, not only because of its influence on muscle action, but also because of its ready accessibility as a peripheral synapse and the significant information that it contributes to synaptic morphology and function in general. Fine structural studies employing the electron microscope and histochemical studies, usually involving the localization of cholinesterase, have contributed most significantly in recent times to our knowledge of the anatomy of the neuromuscular junction. These studies have dealt not only with the structure of the myoneural junction itself, but also with the distribution and location of the nerve terminals on the muscle fibers. Variations have been found, both in the structure and in the disposition of the nerve terminals, and these varieties of endings have attracted attention because they are correlated in many instances with functional variations in the action of the muscle fibers.

2. THE TYPICAL NEUROMUSCULAR JUNCTION

The most common kind of myoneural junction typical of most endings of the vertebrate muscle fiber will be described first and then variations on this theme will be discussed.

2.1. Distribution and Location of Nerve Terminals

Most muscle fibers are individually innervated by a single end plate which usually occurs in the mid-length of the muscle fiber. Hence a band of innervation occurs, located in the middle of the muscle and differing in shape depending on the mode of origin and insertion of the muscle fibers (Coërs, 1967).

2.2 The Axon

2.2.1. Internal Structure and Organelles

The terminal axon arborizes over the surface of the muscle fiber in the synaptic gutter. The axoplasm contains numerous mitochondria of typical structure, a dearth of neurofilaments (although some can be found), and synaptic vesicles about 300 Å in diameter containing a lightly electron dense material enclosed by a membrane (Fig. 1). The vesicles are usually distributed randomly in the terminal axoplasm near the muscle fiber, but recently "active zones" of accumulated vesicles near the presynaptic cleft have been described (Couteaux and Pécot-Dechavassine, 1970). The synaptic vesicles have received much attention because they might represent the storage form of the neuromuscular transmitter and release acetylcholine (ACh) in quantal amounts. Exocytosis of the content of the vesicles into the synaptic space has been suggested (Couteaux and Pécot-Dechavassine, 1970). Increased ACh release at the neuromuscular junction produces a fall in vesicle numbers, while an increase in synaptic vesicle numbers adjacent to the presynaptic cleft occurs in preparations fixed at various times following a long period of nerve stimulation (Jones and Kwanbunbumpen, 1970). A process of endocytosis may also occur, and "coated" vesicles have been found in nerve terminals. These are best seen with peroxidase treatment (Zacks and Saito, 1969), where this reagent gains access to the synaptic space and attaches to the nerve terminal membrane, which apparently then pinches off to form a vesicle within the terminal coated by peroxidase. "Coated" vesicles can also be found normally in the terminal axon, and these are supposedly coated by amorphous material found in the synaptic space. There has been much speculation regarding the changes which must occur in the length of the terminal axonal membrane, since exocytosis implies that the membrane of the synaptic vesicle fuses with the terminal axonal membrane to extrude its contents into the synaptic space causing increase in membrane length, and endocytosis demands that the terminal axonal membrane pinch off to form a vesicle which passes into the axon causing decrease in membrane length [see Chapter 7(i)].

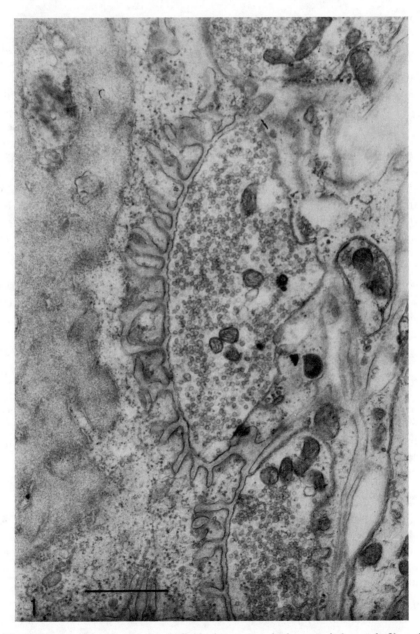

Fig. 1. Electron micrograph of an individual nerve terminal on a twitch muscle fiber of the garter snake showing the terminal axonal organelles, the synaptic vesicles, and the amorphous substance in the space between nerve terminal and muscle fiber. The line on the photograph indicates 1 μm.

2.2.2. Sheaths

The nerves entering a muscle form a plexus from which terminal medullated fibers emerge to innervate individual muscle fibers. Near the muscle fiber, the myelin sheath terminates before the arborization of the end plate. When the light microscope was the only means of investigation, it was usually said that the so-called neurilemmal sheath on the terminal axon outside of the myelin sheath became continuous with the sarcolemma of the muscle fiber. The electron microscope has revealed that there are no naked nerve terminals and that the telodendrion or terminal arborizing branches of the nerve fiber are covered by a sheath of terminal Schwann cells or teloglial sheath, which caps the surface of the terminal portion of the nerve fiber away from the muscle fiber (Robertson, 1960). This teloglial sheath is covered by the sheath of Henle or innermost layer of endoneurium surrounding the terminal axon and continuous with the endomysium covering the sarcolemma of the muscle fiber. Hence the myelin sheath and Schwann cells terminate to liberate the nerve fiber and allow its approach to the muscle fiber, while the connective tissue layer on the nerve and muscle is continuous. All motor nerve endings are, therefore, hyper- or epilemmal, rather than hypolemmal (under the sarcolemma), and no fusion of axoplasm and sarcoplasm exists.

2.3. The Synaptic Space

The space between nerve terminal and muscle fiber or primary synaptic cleft is about 500 Å wide (Fig. 1). In this space is a moderately electron dense material similar to that of basement membrane material or ground substance which can either fill the synaptic space or be separated from axonal membrane and sarcolemmal membrane by a distance of about 200 Å (Robertson, 1960; Zacks, 1964; Csillik, 1967).

2.4. Postjunctional Muscle Fiber

The motor nerve terminal complex is called the "motor end plate." The structural modifications of the postjunctional muscle fiber are called collectively the "sole plate" or the "subneural apparatus." Sole plate structural modifications consist of changes in the muscle fiber membrane or sarcolemma and of the sarcoplasm in the immediate vicinity of the nerve terminal.

2.4.1. Sarcolemmal Infoldings

The space or primary synaptic cleft of 500 Å between nerve terminal and muscle fiber is greatly increased in extent by invaginations from the primary synaptic cleft of the sarcolemma into the muscle fiber to form postjunctional sarcolemmal infoldings or secondary synaptic clefts (Robertson, 1960; Zacks, 1964) (Fig. 2). These vary greatly in frequency of occurrence and in length in different vertebrates and indeed in different muscles of the same animal. Generally, they can penetrate about 0.5–1 μm into the muscle fiber and can be separated from each other by distances of about 1000 Å or more. The infoldings are generally slightly dilated at their deepest portion of penetration into the muscle fiber. The sarcoplasm of the sole plate, then, is thrown into a series of short evaginations passing between its invaginated sarcolemmal folds. The sarcolemmal membrane on the tip or outer border of these evaginated fingers of sarcoplasm frequently appears thicker (with accumulated dense material attached to its inner surface) than the remainder of the muscle sarcolemmal membrane along the sides and depths of the postjunctional sarcolemmal infoldings or away from the area of the sole plate.

The amorphous, moderately electron dense ground substance extends continuously into the secondary synaptic clefts from the primary clefts and hence is always intervening between the pre- and postsynaptic membranes of nerve and muscle and between the invaginations of the sarcolemma.

2.4.2. Sole Plate Sarcoplasm

The sarcoplasm of the muscle fiber in the area immediately under the nerve terminal is characterized most strikingly by an absence of myofilaments. Mitochondria are scattered. Free ribosomes and cisternae of granular endoplasmic reticulum are conspicuously accumulated in this area of the muscle fiber. The Golgi apparatus of the muscle fiber is frequently located in this area. Lastly, many nuclei, called "sole plate nuclei," are located in this area. While there are other areas of the muscle fiber devoid of myofilaments or where ribosomes, Golgi apparatus, mitochondria, and nuclei occur, it is the sole plate under the nerve terminal which is usually the most extensive area in the muscle fiber exhibiting these features.

3. VARIATIONS OF MOTOR END PLATES

While virtually all motor endings on vertebrate striated muscle fibers have almost all or many of the above features, alterations in this scheme have been found. In many instances, these variations in structure of the neuromuscular junction have been related to the physiological characteristics of the muscle fiber which they innervate.

3.1. Variations from Class to Class

There are so many variations from vertebrate to vertebrate that it is difficult to find an underlying reason or to compose a scheme for this variety.

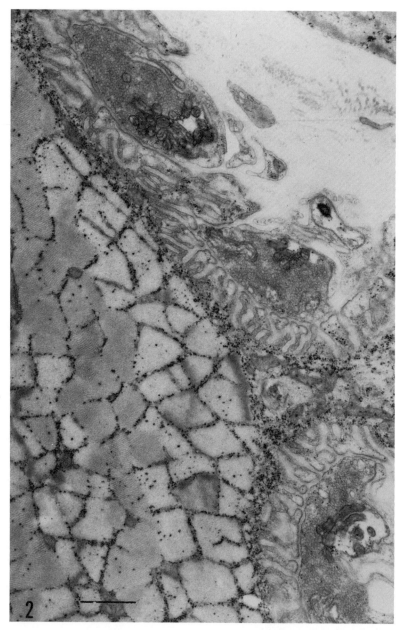

Fig. 2. Electron micrograph showing the extensive postjunctional sarcolemmal infolding under the nerve terminal of a twitch muscle fiber in the garter snake. The dark granules are glycogen. The line on the photograph indicates 1 μm.

Myoneural junctions differ from animal to animal in the size of the nerve terminal, the amount of arborization of the nerve terminal, and the extent and depth of postsynaptic sarcolemmal infolding. As an example, snake muscle fibers have intense sarcolemmal infolding (Hess, 1965), while the muscle fiber of the chicken is virtually devoid of folds under its robust motor end plate (Hess, 1967). There might be a relation between the extent of nerve terminal membrane and the extent of postsynaptic muscle fiber membrane with which it relates in order to produce an effective depolarization of the muscle fiber membrane. If the nerve terminal membrane is not extensive compared to the amount of membrane of the muscle fiber which it innervates, postjunctional folds are vigorous. If the nerve terminal membrane is extensive in amount in relation to the amount of muscle fiber membrane, the postjunctional folds are fewer. The postjunctional folds might well serve to allow the presynaptic membrane of the nerve to come into relation with a more extensive surface area of the postsynaptic membrane of the muscle fiber. Thus the very long muscle fibers of the snake have vigorous sarcolemmal folds under their individual nerve terminals, while the shorter fibers of the chicken do not need folds under their robust nerve endings.

3.2. Endings on Slow-Twitch and Rapid-Twitch Fibers

Attempts have been made to correlate the structure of muscle fibers with their physiology. In the case of slow-twitch and rapid-twitch fibers, this has been attempted thus far most frequently in mammals (Close, 1972). While only two types of physiological fiber have been found (slow twitch and rapid twitch), three morphological types of fiber have been proposed for mammals: red, white, and intermediate. Ultrastructural differences have been described in the neuromuscular junctions on these three fiber types (Padykula and Gauthier, 1970). In the red fiber, elliptical axonal endings contain only moderate numbers of vesicles, and the sarcolemmal folds are few and short. In the white fiber, the flat and elongated axonal endings have closely packed numerous vesicles and longer and more numerous folds under them. The neuromuscular junction of the intermediate fiber has features resembling each of the other two fiber types.

3.3. Endings on Slow Tonic Muscle Fibers

There are muscle fibers in frogs, reptiles, birds, and mammals that can undergo a contracture, rather than a contraction, after a nerve stimulus. These fibers have been called "slow tonic muscle fibers," in contrast to the ordinary twitch fiber (Hess, 1970). The neuromuscular junctions of the slow fibers in all vertebrates have distinct morphological characteristics which serve to differentiate them from the twitch fibers (Figs. 3 and 4).

A most distinctive characteristic of these slow fibers is that they have multiple nerve terminals, in contrast to the individual ending of a twitch fiber. These multiple endings are usually scattered variably along a muscle fiber and can be separated by very short distances of 10 μm in the cat extraocular muscles (Hess and Pilar, 1963) to long distances of over 1 mm in the frog (Hess, 1960). The chicken slow fiber is the only one that exhibits any regularity in the distribution of its multiple terminals, which are separated by fairly regular distances of about 250 μm in 1-week-old chicks to roughly 1000 μm in hens and roosters (Hess, 1961).

In addition to differences in distribution of the nerve terminals on slow as contrasted to twitch muscle fibers, there are also ultrastructural differences. The nerve ending on the slow fiber contains synaptic vesicles of the same size and shape as twitch fiber endings and is separated by a similarly sized synaptic cleft from its muscle fiber; in the synaptic cleft, the same amorphous basement membrane material occurs (Fig. 3). However, there are no postjunctional sarcolemmal infoldings on slow muscle fibers and hence no secondary synaptic clefts (Fig. 4). With what has been said above about the relation of extent of membranes of nerve terminal and postsynaptic muscle fiber, postjunctional sarcolemmal infoldings might not be expected to occur, since propagated action potentials can usually not be elicited from slow muscle fibers.

The extent of filament-free sole plate sarcoplasm is much less in slow than in twitch fibers and the myofilaments are much closer to the nerve terminals. Nuclei accumulation in the sole plate area is not marked, although nuclei do occur there even in slow fibers. The sole plate sarcoplasm of the slow fiber, like the twitch fiber, has many ribosomes, and mitochondria are also located there.

4. ELECTRIC ORGANS

Electric organs are found only in fish and are specialized for the production of an electrical field outside the body. Their structure and physiology have recently been extensively reviewed by Bennett (1971).

The organs differ in location and structure in different groups of fish. The cells generating the electric field are modified muscle fibers, usually flattened and called "electroplaques" or "electroplax." However, as suggested by Bennett (1971) and because all electroplax are not flattened, these cells are better called "electrocytes." In one group of fish, the modified muscle fibers

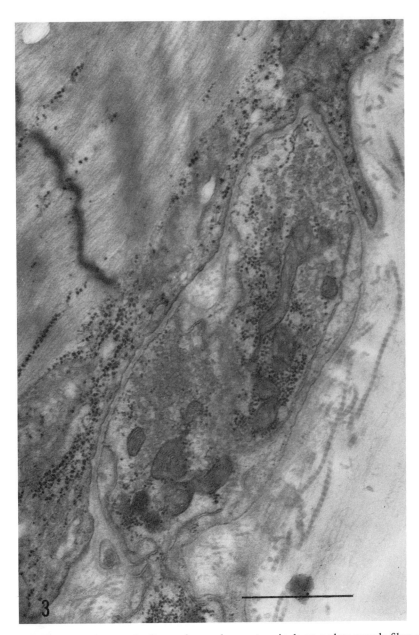

Fig. 3. Electron micrograph of one of several nerve terminals on a slow muscle fiber of the garter snake showing the terminal axonal organelles, the synaptic vesicles, and the amorphous substance in the space between nerve terminal and muscle fiber. The dark granules are glycogen. The line on the photograph indicates 1 μm.

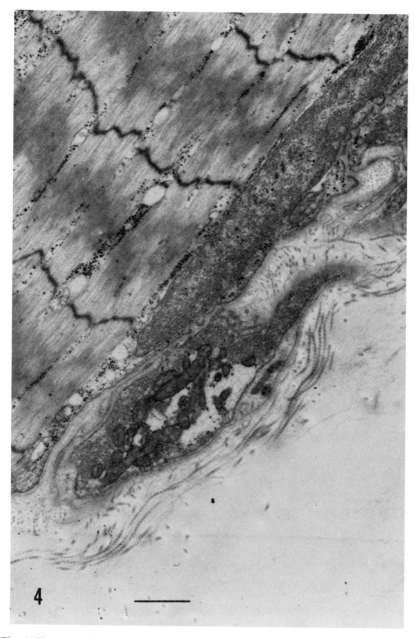

Fig. 4. Electron micrograph showing the virtual absence of postjunctional sarcolemmal infolding under one of several nerve terminals on a slow muscle fiber in the garter snake. The dark granules are glycogen. The line on the photograph indicates 1 μm.

are not present and the generating cells are formed from the nerve fibers themselves with altered and specialized nodes of Ranvier (Waxman *et al.*, 1972).

4.1. Electrocytes

Generally, the electrocytes are large flattened cells which form many layers of cells, sometimes several hundred, arranged in series one above the other. Electrocytes may also be disc shaped and send out protruding stalks that receive the nerve fiber. They can also be arranged in columns, with each column containing 100–200 cells in series. That electrocytes are indeed modified muscle fibers can be seen by study of their fine structure. Some are striated with or without Z lines and contain thick and/or thin filaments. These cells do not twitch and hence it is to be expected that the filaments are not well organized or oriented in the cells. Sarcoplasmic reticulum is usually lacking or very sparse. Depending on the location of the electric organ in the fish, electrocytes may originate from the eye, branchial, pectoral, axial, or tail musculature.

4.2. Innervation and Ultrastructure

Frequently, electrocytes have two surfaces: one receiving the nerve terminal and one away from the nerve endings. The surface away from the nerve ends usually has short processes or papillae protruding from it. This uninnervated surface usually has extensive invaginated folds which can branch and fuse with each other and form an extensive apparatus extending back into the cell. Ground substance material, on the membrane of the electrocyte, accompanies these infoldings into the cell throughout their varied and complex extensions. The innervated surface has many nerve terminals running along its border. These terminals contain synaptic vesicles and are embedded, in some forms quite markedly, in the electrocyte. The nerve terminal membrane is separated from the electrocyte membrane by a synaptic space in which ground substance of a moderate electron density lies. Postjunctional infoldings occur, but are not very frequent nor do they extend for long distances into the electrocyte. Hence the infoldings of the nerve-free surface of the electrocyte are much more extensive than those exhibited by the innervated face.

ACKNOWLEDGMENT

The author's efforts are supported by Research Grant NS–07662 from the National Institute of Neurological Diseases and Stroke, National Institutes of Health, U.S. Public Health Service.

5. REFERENCES

Bennett, M. V. L., 1971, Electric organs, in: *Fish Physiology*, Vol. 5: *Sensory Systems and Electric Organs* (W. S. Hoar and D. J. Randall, eds.), p. 347, Academic Press, New York.

Close, R. I., 1972, Dynamic properties of mammalian skeletal muscles, *Physiol. Rev.* **52**:129.

Coërs, C., 1967, Structure and organization of the myoneural junction, *Internat. Rev. Cytol.* **22**:239.

Couteaux, R., and Pécot-Dechavassine, M., 1970, Vésicules synaptiques et poches au niveau des "zones actives" de la jonction neuromusculaire, *Compt. Rend. Acad. Sci. Paris* **271**:2346.

Csillik, B., 1967, *Functional Structure of the Post-synaptic Membrane in the Myoneural Junction*, 156 pp., Akadémiai Kiadó, Hungarian Academy of Sciences, Budapest.

Hess, A., 1960, The structure of extrafusal muscle fibers in the frog and their innervation studied by the cholinesterase technique, *Am. J. Anat.* **107**:129.

Hess, A., 1961, Structural differences of fast and slow extrafusal muscle fibres and their nerve endings in chickens, *J. Physiol. Lond.* **157**:221.

Hess, A., 1965, The sarcoplasmic reticulum, the T system, and the motor terminals of slow and twitch muscle fibers in the garter snake, *J. Cell Biol.* **26**:467.

Hess, A., 1967, The structure of vertebrate slow and twitch muscle fibers, *Invest. Ophthalmol.* **6**:217.

Hess, A., 1970, Vertebrate slow muscle fibers, *Physiol. Rev.* **50**:40.

Hess, A., and Pilar, G., 1963, Slow fibres in the extracular muscles of the cat, *J. Physiol. Lond.* **169**:780.

Jones, S. F., and Kwanbunbumpen, S., 1970, The effects of nerve stimulation and hemicholinium on synaptic vesicles at the mammalian neuromuscular junction, *J. Physiol. Lond.* **207**:31.

Padykula, H. A., and Gauthier, G. F., 1970, The ultrastructure of the neuromuscular junctions of mammalian red, white, and intermediate skeletal muscle fibers, *J. Cell Biol.* **46**:27.

Robertson, J. D., 1960, Electron microscopy of the motor end-plate and the neuromuscular spindle, *Am. J. Phys. Med.* **39**:1.

Waxman, S. G., Pappas, G. D., and Bennett, M. V. L., 1972, Morphological correlates of functional differentiation of nodes of Ranvier along single fibers in the neurogenic electric organ of the knife fish *Sternarchus, J. Cell Biol.* **53**:210.

Zacks, S. I., 1964, *The Motor Endplate*, 321 pp., Saunders, Philadelphia.

Zacks, S. I., and Saito, A., 1969, Uptake of exogenous horseradish peroxidase by coated vesicles in mouse neuromuscular junctions, *J. Histochem. Cytochem.* **17**:161.

Chapter 5

The Peripheral Autonomic System

David M. Jacobowitz

Laboratory of Clinical Science
National Institute of Mental Health
Bethesda, Maryland, USA

1. ANATOMICAL CONSIDERATIONS: SYMPATHETIC AND PARASYMPATHETIC DIVISIONS

Classical anatomical and histochemical studies have established our general knowledge of the autonomic innervation of the various peripheral organs. The recent histofluorescent studies for catecholamine-containing structures (Falck, 1962; Norberg, 1967; Fuxe *et al.*, 1971) and the acetyl-cholinesterase (AChE) histochemical method for cholinergic nerves (Koelle and Friedenwald, 1949; Koelle, 1963) have opened up areas of study that were not possible with the conventional silver-staining techniques. Since 1962, a great deal of new and unusual information has accumulated in this highly specialized literature which is not yet generally appreciated. The nature of the localization of sympathetic nerves in the periphery has revealed the sites of action of the sympathetic neurotransmitter (norepinephrine).

In the present discourse, it will be assumed that the reader is generally familiar with the architectural arrangement of the autonomic nervous system (Mitchell, 1953). A less orthodox presentation of the autonomic nervous system derived from specific and sensitive histochemical methods for autonomic nerves will follow.

The sympathetic and parasympathetic divisions are two-neuron systems: preganglionic neurons emanate from the central nervous system and make synaptic contact within ganglia, from which postganglionic neurons emerge to

SYMPATHETIC DIVISION
(Thoracolumbar)

PARASYMPATHETIC DIVISION
(Craniosacral)

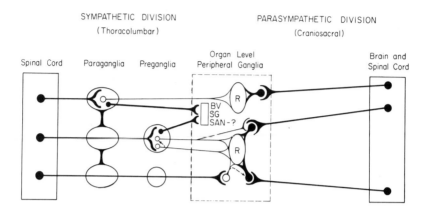

Fig. 1. Schematic representation of the autonomic nervous system. Filled circles (●) represent cholinergic cell bodies; open circles (○) represent adrenergic cell bodies. R, Receptor organ; BV, blood vessel; SG, sweat gland; SAN, SA node. Small dotted arrow indicates intraganglionic adrenergic system of fibers.

innervate peripheral organs (Fig. 1). In the sympathetic division, there are three classes of ganglia: (1) the paraganglia, located adjacent to the spinal cord; (2) the preganglia (e.g., celiac, inferior mesenteric); (3) the peripheral ganglia, usually located adjacent to or within the organ (e.g., bladder, secondary sex organs). The peripheral ganglia are frequently located in close proximity to the peripheral cholinergic neurons. In the parasympathetic division, the ganglia are generally located at the organ level.

Currently, the classical concept of dual innervation of autonomic end organs (smooth muscle, cardiac muscle, glands) must be revised to include more recently obtained information. The peripheral innervation can be classified into three patterns: (1) classical, dual adrenergic–cholinergic innervation, as found in certain vasculature (El-Badawi and Schenk, 1967; Bolme and Fuxe, 1970), salivary and mammary glands (Garrett, 1967; Norberg et al., 1969; Hebb and Linzell, 1970; Freitag and Engel, 1970), and the iris sphincter muscle (Laties and Jacobowitz, 1964; Ehinger, 1964); (2) adrenergic innervation to both the receptor muscle and the peripheral cholinergic ganglia contained within the organ, as observed in the heart (Jacobowitz, 1967); (3) an extensive adrenergic innervation located primarily at the level of the peripheral cholinergic ganglia, such as the Auerbach plexus ganglia within the gut (Norberg, 1964; Jacobowitz, 1965). Physiological studies indicating that an adrenergic inhibitory mechanism takes place primarily at the myenteric ganglia (Kewenter, 1965; Hulten, 1969) are, in effect, the first demonstration of sympathetic control at the organ level of an intermediate relay station, the parasympathetic ganglion (see also Chapter 9).

2. MORPHOLOGICAL OBSERVATIONS

2.1. Preganglionic Neurons

The neurons which give rise to the sympathetic preganglionic fibers are contained within the intermediolateral columns of the spinal cord and show heavy staining for AChE activity (Koelle, 1951). The analogous regions of the parasympathetic system located in the brain stem (Edinger-Westphal nucleus, dorsal motor nucleus of the vagus) contain AChE-stained cholinergic cell bodies (Koelle, 1954).

Numerous biochemical and histochemical studies following preganglionic denervation (Koelle, 1963) show that preganglionic axons, and particularly terminals which ramify in the ganglia, contain high concentrations of AChE (Fig. 2). The intricate arborization of the terminal preganglionic fibers is extremely complex; it is therefore essentially impossible to distinguish axo-

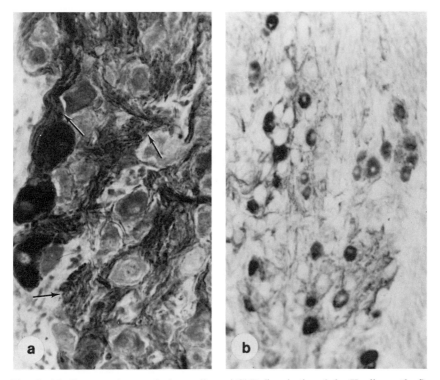

Fig. 2. (a) Cat superior cervical ganglion. AChE (incubation 3 h, Koelle method). Intense-staining cholinergic cell bodies and intraganglionic cholinergic processes (mostly preganglionic) (arrows). Cresyl violet counterstain. × 300. (b) Cat stellate ganglion. AChE (incubation 1 h, 10μm). Dense-staining cholinergic cell bodies and fibers. × 100.

dendritic from axosomatic contacts at the light microscopic level. At best, it can be said that the terminal fibers appear to be very fine varicose fibers which ramify in close proximity to the cell bodies (see Chapter 6).

2.2. Postganglionic Neurons

2.2.1. Ganglia

The ganglia are essentially intermediate relay stations that monitor electrical pulses emanating from the spinal cord, and thus are mediators between impulses from the central nervous system and peripheral organs. The sympathetic ganglia, located along the sympathetic chain (paravertebral ganglia) or within more peripherally located sites (prevertebral ganglia), spread information diffusely from the central nervous system to a number of organs. The histochemical demonstration of catecholamine in sympathetic ganglia gave support to previous investigators who proposed that catecholamines have a physiological role in modulation of transmission (see review by Volle, 1969).

The fact that ganglion cell bodies in the various sympathetic ganglia (paravertebral, prevertebral, and terminal ganglia) have variable intensities of fluorescence indicates the presence of different catecholamine concentrations (see reviews by Norberg and Hamberger, 1964; Norberg and Sjöqvist, 1966; Jacobowitz, 1970). The majority of the ganglion cells, however, generally exhibit a moderate fluorescence intensity (Figs. 3 and 4).* Frequently, the region surrounding the nucleus appears to contain a more intensely fluorescent ring of catecholamine which becomes less dense toward the periphery of the soma (Figs. 3 and 4). In any one ganglion, considerable variation in the size and shape of the cell bodies is observed; cell bodies of medium size predominate.

In addition to the fluorescent cells in sympathetic ganglia, there exists a small population of cholinergic cell bodies (Fig. 2) which are revealed by their heavy staining with the AChE method (Koelle, 1963). The number of the cells varies between approximately 1 and 10%, depending on the ganglion and species (Holmstedt and Sjöqvist, 1959); the cells are referred to as "cholinergic postganglionic sympathetic fibers" (anatomically sympathetic, physiologically cholinergic) and are said to innervate the vasodilator blood vessels and the sweat glands. However, the fact that stimulation of the stellate ganglion of the dog chronically treated with 6-hydroxydopamine (to destroy the adrenergic nerve terminals within the heart) resulted in slowing of the heart rate rather than cardioacceleration (personal observations) suggests a

---

* All photomicrographs of catecholamine fluorescence studies reproduced as figures in this chapter were cut at 14 μm unless noted otherwise.

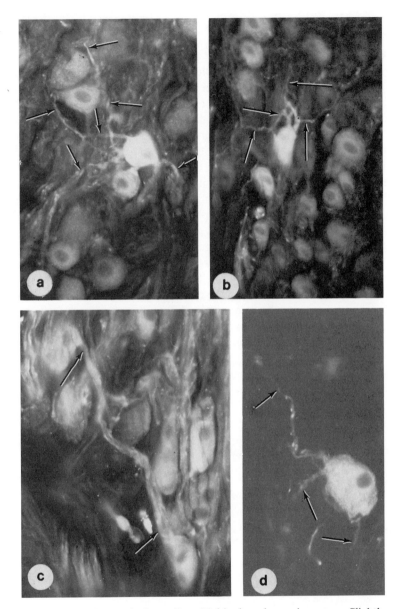

Fig. 3. (a) Cat superior cervical ganglion. Multipolar adrenergic neuron. Slightly over-exposed to enhance the fluorescent processes emanating from a single cell body (arrows). × 380. (b) Cat superior cervical ganglion. Multipolar neuron (20 μm). Note several bifurcating adrenergic processes (arrows) from an intense fluorescent cell body. × 240 (c) Rabbit superior cervical ganglion. Long smooth fluorescent process (arrows). × 380. (d) Dog stellate ganglion cell body with multiple processes (arrows). × 380.

possible contribution of stellate cholinergic nerves to the sinoauricular node (Fig. 1).

Occasionally, a variable number of fluorescent processes are observed to arise from the adrenergic cell bodies (Fig. 3). The processes are smooth (nonvaricose) and give the appearance of axons. Because the processes have no distinguishing characteristics such as size or intensity of fluorescence, it is impossible to distinguish axons from dendrites in sectioned ganglia. Because only a single axon is believed to emerge from the soma or from a dendrite (Cajal, 1911; DeCastro, 1932), it is probable that most of the observed fluorescent processes which emerge from the cell body are dendrites. The ramifying processes appear to be in close proximity to other ganglion cells, but no direct termination of the processes upon other cell bodies has ever been seen. In addition to the smooth axonal-like processes observed in the ganglia, the fluorescence technique has uncovered a system of adrenergic varicose terminals contained in the intercellular region in close proximity to the ganglion cells (Hamberger *et al.*, 1963; Norberg and Sjöqvist, 1966; Jacobowitz and Woodward, 1968; Jacobowitz, 1970). There is much variation in the density of the intraganglionic catecholamine-containing varicose fibers among the various sympathetic ganglia in one animal as well as among various species. In the cat superior cervical ganglion, there are comparatively few varicose fibers that are in close apposition with the perikarya (Fig. 4); in the rabbit or rat superior cervical ganglion, there are greater numbers of varicosities in proximity to the cell bodies suggesting possible synaptic contacts (Fig. 5). The rabbit superior cervical ganglion contains a greater density of varicose termi-

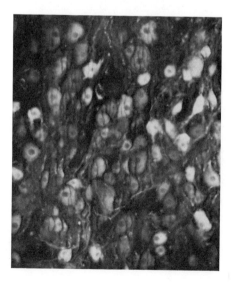

Fig. 4. Cat superior cervical ganglion. Relatively few pericellular adrenergic terminals (compare with Fig. 5). × 160.

Fig. 5. Cat celiac ganglion. Note numerous fine varicosities in close apposition to the cell bodies. × 160.

nals (Fig. 6) than does the cat superior cervical ganglion. Occasionally, basketlike pericellular arrangements are observed which envelop the entire cell body (Fig. 11). It appears that the adrenergic varicose terminals are of intraganglionic origin and emanate from the sympathetic ganglion cell population (Norberg *et al.*, 1966; Hamberger and Norberg, 1965*a*; Jacobowitz

Fig. 6. Rabbit superior cervical ganglion. Intercellular adrenergic varicosities in close proximity to the sympathetic ganglion cells. Note pericellular arrangement of varicosities surrounding the entire cell body (arrow). × 160.

and Woodward, 1968). It has been suggested that the intraganglionic system of adrenergic terminals may be derived from either interneurons (Norberg *et al.*, 1966), axonic collaterals (Norberg *et al.*, 1966; Jacobowitz and Woodward, 1968), or dendritic collaterals (Jacobowitz, 1970). Postganglionic denervation experiments would seem to rule out a predominantly interneuronal source for the intraganglionic terminals (Jacobowitz and Woodward, 1968). Whether they are axonic or dendritic collaterals remains to be demonstrated. Several classical neurohistologists have questioned the existence of axonic collaterals in autonomic ganglia (DeCastro, 1932). Because ganglion cells contain long dendritic processes which form terminal aborizations around other perikarya, it would be a reasonable presumption that the intraganglionic adrenergic terminal population may be at least partly derived from dendritic collaterals. A dendritic collateral system of varicosities may be derived from the smooth fluorescent processes that have been observed to emanate from cell bodies (Fig. 3). Electron microscopic studies of the superior cervical ganglia have revealed neurites containing dense core vesicles in synaptic contact with both dendrites and somata (Grillo, 1966). Furthermore, dendritic processes containing granular vesicles have been observed to arise from the perikaryon (Van Orden *et al.*, 1970). Whether a limited population of cell bodies is responsible for the intraganglionic adrenergic terminal varicosities remains to be elucidated.

The various possible anatomical arrangements of the intraganglionic adrenergic terminals are diagramatically outlined in Fig. 7. An axon and/or a dendritic collateral process is thought to terminate directly on, or more likely with, the short capsular dendrites of other soma. The possibility of a "feedback" synaptic arrangement on the preganglionic terminals is suggested.

Although most morphological studies on intraganglionic adrenergic terminals have been performed on pre- and paraganglia, peripheral sympathetic ganglia contained primarily in the genital organs also possess a network of fluorescent terminals (Owman and Sjöstrand, 1965; Owman *et al.*, 1967).

The parasympathetic ganglia are located directly on the periphery or within the organs. The majority of the cell bodies stain heavily for AChE (Fig. 8). The ganglia within the heart, lung, trachea, and gut are cholinergic; a mixed population of both cholinergic and adrenergic cell bodies is located within the urogenital viscera (Fig. 9) (Hamberger and Norberg, 1965*a*; Owman and Sjöstrand, 1965; El-Badawi and Schenk, 1966; Adham and Schenk, 1969). Glandular organs (lacrimal, submaxillary, sublingual, parotid) also contain cholinergic ganglia (Garrett, 1967).

The intraganglionic adrenergic terminals described above for sympathetic ganglia appear also to be present at least in some parasympathetic visceral ganglia. The most prominent system of monoamine-containing synaptic structures is found in cholinergic ganglia in the digestive tract (Nor-

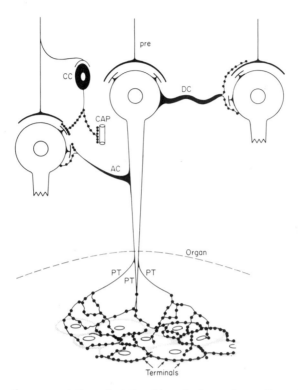

Fig. 7. Schematic representation of relationships of adrenergic ganglion cells with each other through an intraganglionic system of varicose terminals (dots) which emanate from dendritic collaterals (DC) and/or axonic collaterals (AC). These terminals are indicated to make synaptic contacts with short dendrites, the cell body, and preganglionic endings (pre). The chromaffin cell (CC) is suggested to innervate the cell body and possibly release catecholamines into the capillary (CAP) system of the ganglion. The autonomic ground plexus of terminal varicose fibers emanates from preterminal (PT) processes which emerge from the main axon.

berg, 1964; Jacobowitz, 1965; Jacobowitz and Nemir, 1969). The adrenergic nerves of the gut are derived from sympathetic preganglia (e.g., coeliac, inferior mesenteric) outside the digestive system and terminate in the proximity of the cholinergic ganglion cells of the myenteric plexus (Fig. 10). Electron microscopic studies have revealed the presence of adrenergic terminals in synaptic contact with the Auerbach plexus ganglion cell bodies (Gabella, 1971).

The parasympathetic ganglia in the heart are located mainly in the interatrial septum, close to the sinoauricular and atrioventricular nodes. Very fine adrenergic fibers are observed in close apposition to some of the cholinergic ganglion cells (Fig. 11). Similarly, varicose terminals have been observed

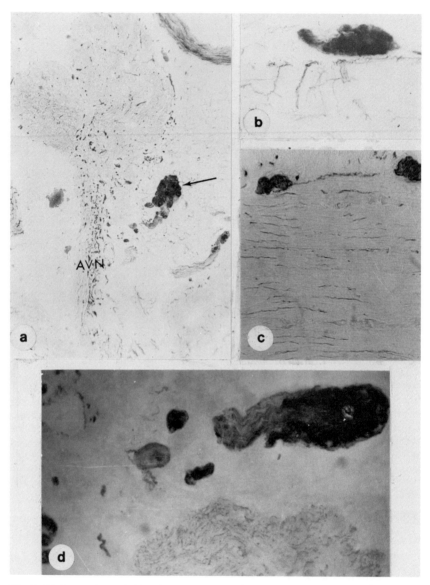

Fig. 8. (a) Rat atrium. AChE (incubation 1h, 20 μm). Dense-staining ganglion (arrow) close to the atrioventricular node (AVN) containing an abundant number of cholinergic fibers. × 40. (b) Dog trachea. AChE (incubation 2 h). Cholinergic ganglion with numerous dense-staining cell bodies. Cholinergic fibers on the muscle are also present. × 50. (c) Monkey colon. AChE (incubation 1 h). Cholinergic ganglia in the myenteric plexus and cholinergic nerves in the circular muscle region. × 135. (d) Dog bladder, trigone region. AChE (incubation 1 h). Dense-staining cholinergic ganglion next to the trigone muscle with an abundant number of cholinergic fibers. × 64.

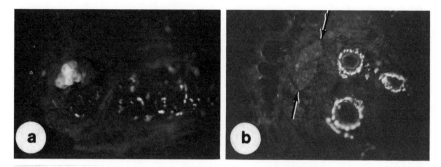

Fig. 9. (a) Guinea pig bladder. Fluorescent sympathetic ganglion cells in bladder near the ureteral junction. Adrenergic fibers are also observed. (b) Guinea pig bladder. Nonfluorescent cholinergic ganglion (arrows) next to three arteries surrounded by adrenergic nerves. × 100.

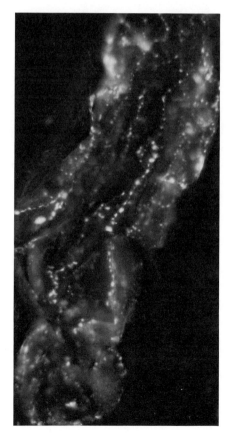

Fig. 10. Human rectosigmoid (7-year-old male). Adrenergic varicose terminals in Auerbach's plexus in proximity to non-fluorescent cholinergic ganglion cells. × 480.

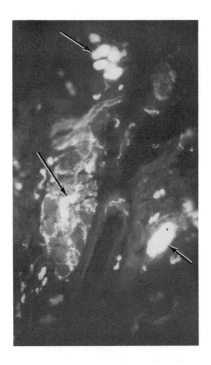

Fig. 11. Rat atrium. Nonfluorescent cholinergic ganglion containing an intraganglionic plexus of adrenergic fibers. Clusters of intense fluorescent chromaffin cells (arrows) within, or in close proximity to, the ganglion. × 160.

in anatomical proximity to cholinergic ganglia in the hilum region of the calf lung (personal observations) (Fig. 12), and comparatively few adrenergic synaptic-like structures were reported in the ciliary ganglion of the cat (Hamberger *et al.*, 1965). Currently, it is not known whether there exists an intraganglionic system of cholinergic terminals analogous to that described above for adrenergic ganglion cells.

The presence of the intraganglionic system of adrenergic terminal varicosities would suggest that the sympathetic transmitter has a physiological role in ganglionic transmission. Numerous studies have shown that catecholamines may influence functional activity within ganglia (Volle, 1969; Curtis, 1963). The existing overall evidence suggests that release of the adrenergic neurotransmitter would serve to modulate ganglionic transmission.

2.2.2. Autonomic Ground Plexus

The large smooth postganglionic axons that arise from ganglia course for various distances depending on their origin (para-, pre-, or peripheral ganglia). The axons enter an organ, usually via the vasculature; they ramify into smaller processes and finally, as Fig. 7 shows, enter the autonomic

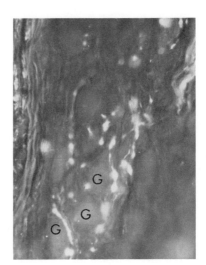

Fig. 12. Calf lung. Nonfluorescent cholinergic ganglion with varicose adrenergic fibers close to the cell bodies (G). × 405.

Fig. 13. Rat iris, adrenergic nerve plexus of terminal varicosities. × 170.

ground plexus where they become preterminal axons which give rise to fine anastomosing varicose fibers (Hillarp, 1946, 1959). The fluorescent character of the nonterminal adrenergic nerve trunks varies according to the organ and species studied. The classical rat iris flat preparation normally contains a few very smooth fluorescent preterminal processes (Fig. 13). In contrast, the heart possesses numerous preterminal nerve trunks which show moderate to intense fluorescence. There is a gradual transition of preterminal smooth nerve axons to varicose terminal fibers; both types of processes (preterminal and terminal) are occasionally observed within the same nerve trunk (Friedman *et al.*, 1968; Vogel *et al.*, 1969). The abundant varicose processes, which comprise the major portion of the autonomic ground plexus, constitute one to several fine fibers which run together for variable distances to form an anastomosing network in close proximity to the muscle (Fig. 14) or gland cells. The varicosities contain a high concentration of the transmitter; they are specialized structures for storage and release of the transmitter and are currently regarded as the physiological autonomic nerve terminals.

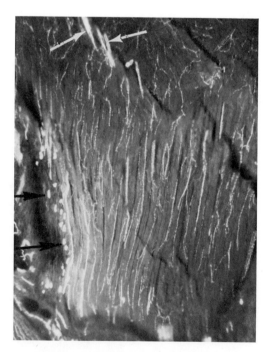

Fig. 14. Rat AV node. Network of adrenergic nerves close to the cardiac muscle. Preterminal nerve processes (white arrows) and yellow fluorescent, serotonin-containing mast cells in connective tissue (black arrows) are noted. × 70.

Table I. Classification of Comparative Density of Autonomic Nerves

	Adrenergic	Cholinergic	References
Cardiovascular			
SA and AV nodes	D[a]	D	Dahlström et al. (1965), James and Spence (1966), Nielsen and Owman (1968), Vogel et al. (1969)
Atrium	D	M–D	Holmstedt and Sjöqvist (1959), Jacobowitz et al. (1967), Mohr (1954)
Ventricle	M–D	S	Jacobowitz et al. (1967), James and Spence (1966), Koelle (1963), Vogel et al. (1969)
Conducting system (ventricles)	S	D	Gossrau (1971), Il'ina-Kakueva (1958), Vogel et al. (1969)
Digestive (intestine, stomach, esophagus)			
Muscle	S	D	Gerebtzoff and Bertrana (1957), Jacobowitz (1965), Jacobowitz and Nemir (1969), Koelle (1951), Norberg (1964)
Myenteric plexus	D	D	
Respiratory[b]			
Trachea	S	D	Dahlström et al. (1966), El-Bermani et al. (1970), Mohr (1955)
Bronchi	M–D	D	
Urogenital			
Ureter[b]	S-M	D	Dixon and Gosling (1971), El-Badawi and Schenk (1964), Wein et al. (1972)
Bladder[b]			
Body (dome, detrusor)	S	S	El-Badawi and Schenk (1966), Raezer et al. (1973)
Base (trigone, neck, sphincter)	D	D	
Uterus	M–D	M	Adham and Schenk (1969), Owman and Sjöberg (1966), Owman et al. (1967)
Vas deferens	D	S-D	Baumgarten et al. (1968), Jacobowitz and Koelle (1965), Norberg et al. (1967)
Ovary	M–D	S-M	Jacobowitz and Wallach (1967), Owman and Sjöberg (1966), Owman et al. (1967)

[a] D, = dense, M = moderate, S = sparse number of nerves.
[b] Personal observations in dog.

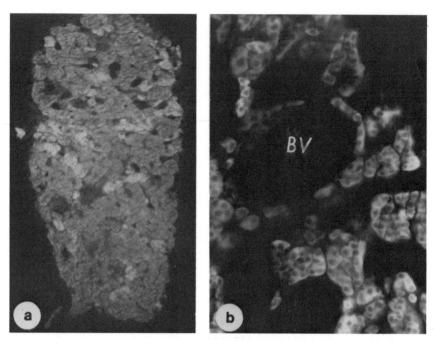

Fig. 15. Rat adrenal medulla (slightly underexposed). (a) Low-power view shows fewer clusters of cells with a greater intensity of catecholamine fluorescence indicating norepinephrine-containing islets. Most of the islets are epinephrine-containing islets. × 65. (b) High-power view of the chromaffin cell islets surrounding the blood vasculature (BV). × 270.

The cholinergic terminal plexus, as studied in the rat iris flat preparation, also appears to contain varicosities which ramify within the autonomic ground plexus along with the adrenergic nerves (Csillik and Koelle, 1965; Ehinger and Falck, 1966). From morphological observations of the close anatomical proximity of adrenergic and cholinergic nerves within the same nerve trunk of various muscles in several species (Jacobowitz and Koelle, 1965), it was suggested that an interaction might take place between the adjacent terminals. Earlier pharmacological studies led to the suggestion that adrenergic and cholinergic fibers interact within the atrium (Leaders, 1963). Similar conclusions were derived from electron microscopic studies whereby axoaxonal synaptic contacts were observed between cholinergic and adrenergic terminals in the iris, atrium, and pial arteries (Ehinger *et al.*, 1970; Nielsen *et al.*, 1971). Further studies are needed to elucidate the extent and physiological significance of what would appear to be a possible self-controlling mechanism to maintain autonomic neurotransmitter balance at the receptor level.

The autonomic smooth muscle neuroeffector sites show considerable variation in their content and distribution of adrenergic and cholinergic nerve fibers. It is difficult to make a general statement concerning the relative density of adrenergic and cholinergic nerves within an organ because of species variations. A classification can be made according to a comparative density of autonomic nerves within the terminal plexus. Three general groupings may be recognized within muscle effector sites: (1) abundant adrenergic and abundant cholinergic nerves; (2) abundant adrenergic and sparse cholinergic nerves; (3) abundant cholinergic and sparse adrenergic nerves (Table I). It is clear that a balanced dual innervation in terms of comparative numbers of adrenergic and cholinergic nerves within an organ can by no means be considered a good generalization. Furthermore, a greater number of nerves of one system should not be construed to mean a dominance of tone by that system.

2.3. Adrenal and Extra-adrenal Chromaffin Cells

The chromaffin cells of the adrenal medulla can be considered as modified sympathetic ganglion cells. Both cell types embryologically originate from neural crest elements (Yntema and Hammond, 1947). The adrenal medulla is

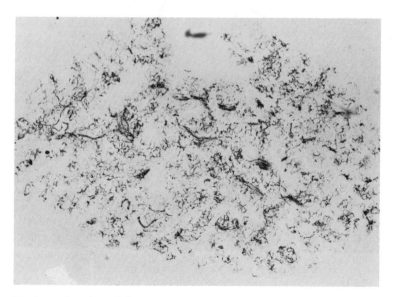

Fig. 16. Rat adrenal medulla. AChE (incubation 1 h, 20 μm). Dense network of preganglionic cholinergic terminals enveloping the chromaffin cells. × 65.

Fig. 17. Rat superior cervical ganglion containing two clusters of intense fluorescent chromaffin cells (arrows). × 170.

part of the sympathetic division of the autonomic nervous system. The chromaffin cells are small cells that lack processes and function through secretion of catecholamines directly into the circulation. They are conspicuously different from sympathetic ganglion cells because of their markedly greater intensity of fluorescence, cluster formation, and smallness of size (Fig. 15). The chromaffin cells, like ganglion cells, are innervated by a dense network of cholinergic terminals (Fig. 16).

In many of the autonomic ganglia, there exist populations of small intensely fluorescent cells that, by histofluorescence criteria, are identical to the chromaffin cells of the adrenal medulla (Jacobowitz, 1970). They are most prominent in preganglia (e.g., superior cervical, stellate, coeliac) and are usually found in cluster formation in variable numbers, shapes, and sizes (Fig. 17); they are also found in the cholinergic ganglia of the heart (Jacobowitz, 1967) (Fig. 18).

The extra-adrenal chromaffin-like cells have been referred to as "small intensely fluorescent cells" (SIF cells), "interneurons," or "small neurons." Positive chromaffin stains have been found in some, but not all, sympathetic ganglia (Coupland, 1965). Regardless of the chromaffin-staining qualities of these cells, the author prefers the use of the term "chromaffin cell" because of the striking morphological similarities with the adrenal chromaffin cells using histochemical fluorescence criteria.

The chromaffin cells are always found to be associated with a dense network of capillaries (Lempinen, 1964). In addition, the heart and para-ganglion chromaffin cells are innervated by cholinergic nerves (Jacobowitz, 1967; Jacobowitz, 1970). Fluorescent processes are frequently observed to emanate from chromaffin cell clusters (Fig. 19) and to be in close proximity to ganglion cell bodies. It is of interest that chromaffin cells of the adrenal medulla transplanted to the anterior chamber of a denervated rat eye were able to produce long varicose processes which were similar to the adrenergic ground plexus (Olson, 1970). Furthermore, a single long varicose process emanating from a chromaffin cell was identified in a crushed hypogastric ganglion preparation (Furness and Malmfors, 1971). The possibility therefore exists that extensive varicose processes derived from chromaffin cells permeate

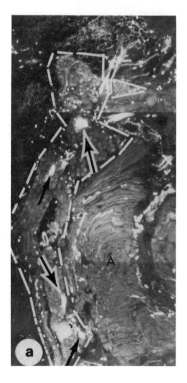

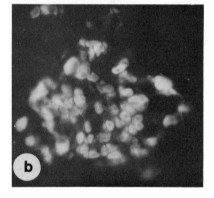

Fig. 18. Chromaffin cells of the heart. (a) Rat interatrial septum, montage. Note nonfluorescent cholinergic ganglia (white lines) containing clusters of chromaffin cells (arrows). Atrial muscle (A) with adrenergic fibers also present. × 35. (b) Owl monkey, AV node region. Large cluster of chromaffin cells. × 250.

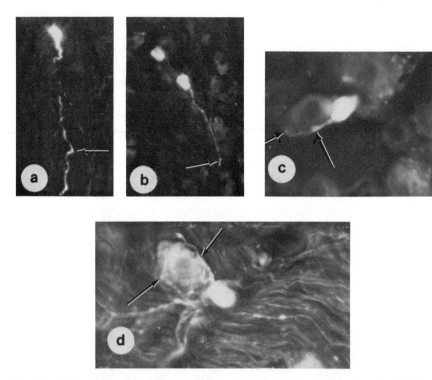

Fig. 19. (a) Dog heart, SA node region. Denervated by autotransplantation (17 days).
A chromaffin cell with a very long process (arrow). × 100. (b) Rat superior cervical
ganglion. Chromaffin cell with process (arrow) in close proximity to sympathetic
ganglion cell body. × 430. (c) Rat superior cervical ganglion (dexamethasone treated,
10 days old). Chromaffin cell with a long process (arrows) containing varicose-like
enlargements. × 270. (d) Cat superior cervical ganglion. A rare chromaffin-like cell with
multiple varicose-containing processes (arrows); two of the processes appear to engulf
a ganglion cell. × 400.

the ganglia and cannot be differentiated from the intraganglionic system of
adrenergic varicose processes which emanate from sympathetic ganglia.
Moreover, recent microspectrofluorometric evidence indicates that the
chromaffin cells of the ganglia contain dopamine (Björklund et al., 1970).
This is further supported by immunofluorescent (Fuxe et al., 1970) and electrophysiological (Kebabian and Greengard, 1971) evidence and would tend
to support the hypothesis that dopamine-containing chromaffin cells are
responsible for a postsynaptic inhibitory mechanism (P wave or slow IPSP)
(Libet, 1970). Figure 7 schematically indicates the possible action of the intraganglionic chromaffin cell, which is similar to the action suggested for the

chromaffin cells within the cardiac ganglia (Jacobowitz, 1967). The innervated chromaffin cells are thought to influence ganglionic transmission. The catecholamine (dopamine) could be released by the processes in close proximity to the ganglion cell bodies. Furthermore, the release of catecholamine into the capillaries could provide an additional route by which chromaffin cell products permeate the ganglion. Thus there is morphological evidence that chromaffin cells and intraganglionic adrenergic fibers could provide a modulatory influence on impulse transmission through the ganglion.

3. REFERENCES

Adham, N., and Schenk, E. A., 1969, Autonomic innervation of the rat vagina, cervix, and uterus and its cyclic variation, *Am. J. Obstet. Gynecol.* **104**:508.

Baumgarten, H. G., Falck, B., Holstein, A.-F., Owman, Ch., and Owman, T., 1968, Adrenergic innervation of the human testis, epididymis ductus deferens and prostate: A fluorescence microscopic and fluorimetric study, *Z. Zellforsch.* **90**:81.

Björklund, A., Cegrell, L., Falck, B., Ritzén, M., and Rosengren, E., 1970, Dopamine-containing cells in sympathetic ganglia, *Acta Physiol. Scand.* **78**:334.

Bolme, P., and Fuxe, K., 1970, Adrenergic and cholinergic nerve terminals in skeletal muscle vessels, *Acta Physiol. Scand.* **78**:52.

Cajal, R. S., 1911, *Histologie du Systeme Nerveux*, Maloine, Paris.

Coupland, R. E., 1965, *The Natural History of the Chromaffin Cell*, Longmans, London.

Csillik, B., and Koelle, G. B., 1965, Histochemistry of the adrenergic and the cholinergic autonomic innervation apparatus as represented by the rat iris, *Acta Histochem.* **22**:350.

Curtis, D., 1963, The pharmacology of central and peripheral inhibition, *Pharmacol. Rev.* **15**:333.

Dahlström, A., Fuxe, K., My-Tu, M., and Zetterstrom, B. E. M., 1965, Observations on adrenergic innervation of dog heart, *Am. J. Physiol.* **209**:689.

Dahlström, A., Fuxe, K., Hökfelt, T., and Norberg, K.-A., 1966, Adrenergic innervation of the bronchial muscle of the cat, *Acta Physiol. Scand.* **66**:507.

DeCastro, F., 1932, *Cytology and Cellular Pathology of the Nervous System* (W. Penfield, ed.), p. 317, Hoeber, New York.

Dixon, J. A., and Gosling, J. A., 1971, Histochemical and electron microscopic observations on the innervation of the upper segment of the mammalian ureter, *J. Anat.* **110**:57.

Ehinger, B., 1964, Adrenergic nerves to the eye and its adnexa in rabbit and guinea pig, *Acta Univ. Lundensis* **20**:1.

Ehinger, B., and Falck, B., 1966, Concomitant adrenergic and parasympathetic fibers in the rat iris, *Acta Physiol. Scand.* **67**:201.

Ehinger, B., Falck, B., and Sporrong, B., 1970, Possible axo-axonal synapses between peripheral adrenergic and cholinergic nerve terminals, *Z. Zellforsch.* **107**:508.

El-Badawi, A., and Schenk, E. A., 1966, Dual innervation of the mammalian urinary bladder: A histochemical study of the distribution of cholinergic and adrenergic nerves, *Am. J. Anat.* **119**:405.

El-Badawi, A., and Schenk, E. A., 1967, The distribution of cholinergic and adrenergic nerves in the mammalian epididymis: A comparative histochemical study, *Am. J. Anat.* **121**:1.

El-Badawi, A., and Schenk, E. A., 1969, Innervation of the abdominopelvic ureter in the cat, *Am. J. Anat.* **126**:103.

El-Bermani, A.-L., McNary, W. F., and Bradley, D. E., 1970, The distribution of acetyl-cholinesterase and catecholamine-containing nerves in the rat lung, *Anat. Rec.* **167**:205.

Falck, B., 1962, Observations on the possibilities for the cellular localization of mono-amines with a fluorescence method, *Acta Physiol. Scand.* **56**: Suppl. 197.

Freitag, P., and Engel, M. B., 1970, Autonomic innervation in rabbit salivary glands, *Anat. Rec.* **167**:87.

Friedman, W. F., Pool, P. E., Jacobowitz, D. M., Seagrens, S., and Braunwald, E., 1968, Sympathetic innervation of the developing mammalian heart: Biochemical and histo-chemical comparisons of fetal, neonatal and adult myocardium, *Circ. Res.* **29**:25.

Furness, J. B., and Malmfors, T., 1971, Aspects of the arrangement of the adrenergic innervation in guinea pigs as revealed by the fluorescence histochemical method applied to stretched, air-dried preparations, *Histochemie* **25**:297.

Fuxe, K., Goldstein, M., Hökfelt, T., and Joh, T. H., 1970, Immunohistochemical localization of dopamine-beta-hydroxylase in the peripheral and central nervous system, *Res. Commun. Chem. Pathol. Pharmacol.* **1**:627.

Fuxe, K., Hökfelt, T., Jonsson, G., and Ungerstedt, U., 1971, Fluorescence microscopy in neuroanatomy, in: *Contemporary Research Methods in Neuroanatomy*, pp. 275–314, Springer-Verlag, New York.

Gabella, G., 1971, Synapses of adrenergic fibers, *Experientia* **27**:280.

Garrett, J. R., 1967, The innervation of normal human submandibular and parotid salivary glands, *Arch. Oral Biol.* **12**:1417.

Gerebtzoff, M. A., and Bertrand, J., 1957, Gradients d'activite cholinesterasique dans la muquese du tube digestif, *Ann. Histochim.* **2**:149.

Gossrau, R., 1971, Histochemical fluorescence microscopical and experimental investi-gations on the impulse-conducting system of golden hamsters, mice and rats, *Histochemie* **26**:44.

Grillo, M., 1966, Electron microscopy of sympathetic tissues, *Pharmacol. Rev.* **18**:387.

Hamberger, B., and Norberg, K.-A., 1965a, Adrenergic synaptic terminals and nerve cells in bladder ganglia of the cat, *Internat. J. Neuropharmacol.* **4**:41.

Hamberger, B., and Norberg, K.-A., 1965b, Studies on some systems of adrenergic synaptic terminals in the abdominal ganglia of the cat, *Acta Physiol. Scand.* **65**:235.

Hamberger, B., Norberg, K.-A., and Sjöqvist, F., 1963, Evidence for adrenergic nerve terminals and synapses in sympathetic ganglia, *Internat. J. Neuropharmacol.* **2**:279.

Hamberger, B., Norberg, K.-A., and Ungerstedt, U., 1965, Adrenergic synaptic terminals in autonomic ganglia, *Acta Physiol. Scand.* **64**:285.

Hebb, C., and Linzell, J. L., 1970, Innervation of the mammary gland: A histochemical study in the rabbit, *Histochem. J.* **2**:491.

Hillarp, N.-A., 1946, Structure of the synapse of the peripheral innervation apparatus of the autonomic nervous system, *Acta Physiol. Scand.* **2**: Suppl. 4.

Hillarp, N.-A., 1959, The construction of functional organization of the autonomic innervation apparatus, *Acta Physiol. Scand.* **46**: Suppl. 157.

Holmes, R. L., 1957, Cholinesterase activity in the atrial wall of the dog and cat heart, *J. Physiol.* **137**:421.

Holmstedt, B., and Sjöqvist, F., 1959, Distribution of acetocholinesterase in the ganglion cells of various sympathetic ganglia, *Acta Physiol. Scand.* **47**:284.

Hulten, L., 1969, Extrinsic nervous control of colonic motility of blood flow, *Acta Physiol. Scand. Suppl.* **335**:1.

Il'ina-Kakueva, E. I., 1958, A histochemical study of the cholinesterase activity of the nerve cells and conducting system of the heart, *Bull. Exptl. Biol. Med.* **46**:1270.

Jacobowitz, D., 1965, Histochemical studies of the autonomic innervation of the gut, *J. Pharmacol. Exptl. Therap.* **149**:358.

Jacobowitz, D., 1967, Histochemical studies of the relationship of chromaffin cells and adrenergic nerve fibers to the cardiac ganglia of several species, *J. Pharmacol. Exptl. Therap.* **158**:227.

Jacobowitz, D., 1970, Catecholamine fluorescence studies of adrenergic neurons and chromaffin cells in sympathetic ganglia, *Fed. Proc.* **29**:1929.

Jacobowitz, D., and Koelle, G. B., 1965, Histochemical correlations of acetylcholinesterase and catecholamines in postganglionic autonomic nerves of the cat, rabbit and guinea pig, *J. Pharmacol. Exptl. Therap.* **148**:225.

Jacobowitz, D., and Nemir, P., 1969, The autonomic innervation of the esophagus of the dog, *J. Thorac. Cardiovasc. Surg.* **58**:678.

Jacobowitz, D., and Wallach, E. E., 1967, Histochemical and chemical studies of the autonomic innervation of the ovary, *Endocrinology* **81**:1132.

Jacobowitz, D., and Woodward, J. K., 1968, Adrenergic neurons in the cat superior cervical ganglion and cervical sympathetic nerve trunk: A histochemical study, *J. Pharmacol. Exptl. Therap.* **162**:213.

Jacobowitz, D., Cooper, T., and Barner, H. B., 1967, Histochemical and chemical studies of the localization of adrenergic and cholinergic nerves in normal and denervated cat hearts, *Circ. Res.* **20**:289.

James, T. N., and Spence, C. A., 1966, Distribution of cholinesterase within the sinus node and AV node of the human heart, *Anat. Rec.* **155**:151.

Kebabian, J. W., and Greengard, P., 1971, Dopamine-sensitive adenyl cyclase: Possible role in synaptic transmission, *Science* **174**:1346.

Kewenter, J., 1965, The vagal control of the jejunal and ileal motility and blood flow, *Acta Physiol. Scand. Suppl.* **251**:1.

Koelle, G. B., 1951, The elimination of enzymatic diffusion artifacts in the histochemical localization of cholinesterases and a survey of the cellular distributions, *J. Pharmacol. Exptl. Therap.* **103**:153.

Koelle, G. B., 1954, The histochemical localization of cholinesterases in the central nervous system of the rat, *J. Comp. Neurol.* **100**:211.

Koelle, G. B., 1955, The histochemical identification of acetylcholinesterase in cholinergic, adrenergic and sensory neurons, *J. Pharmacol. Exptl. Therap.* **114**:167.

Koelle, G. B., 1963, Cytological distributions and physiological functions of cholinesterases, in: *Cholinesterases and Anticholinesterase Agents* (*Heffter-Heubner Handbook of Experimental Pharmacology*, Suppl. 15), pp. 187–298, Springer-Verlag, Heidelberg.

Koelle, G. B., and Friedenwald, J. S., 1949, A histochemical method for localizing cholinesterase activity, *Proc. Soc. Exptl. Biol. Med.* **70**:617.

Laties, A., and Jacobowitz, D., 1964, A histochemical study of the adrenergic and cholinergic innervation of the anterior segment of the rabbit eye, *Invest. Ophthalmol.* **3**:592.

Leaders, F. E., 1963, Local cholinergic–adrenergic interaction mechanism for the biphasic chronotropic response to nerve stimulation, *J. Pharmacol. Exptl. Therap.* **142**:31.

Lempinen, M., 1964, Extra-adrenal chromaffin tissue of the rat and the effect of cortical hormones on it, *Acta Physiol. Scand.* **62**: Suppl. 231.

Libet, B., 1970, Generation of slow inhibition and excitatory postsynaptic potentials, *Fed. Proc.* **29**:1945.

Mitchell, G. A. G., 1953, *Anatomy of the Autonomic Nervous System*, Livingstone, Edinburgh.

Mohr, E., 1954, Localisation histochimique des cholinesterases du coeur, *Compt. Rend. Soc. Biol. (Paris)* **148**:629.

Mohr, E., 1955, Les cholinesterases dans l'appareil respiratoire, *Compt. Rend. Soc. Biol. (Paris)* **149**:828.

Nielsen, K. C., and Owman, Ch., 1968, Difference in cardiac adrenergic innervation between hibernators and non-hibernating mammals, *Acta Physiol. Scand. Suppl.* **316**:1.

Nielsen, K. C., Owman, Ch., and Sporrong, B., 1971, Ultrastructure of the autonomic innervation apparatus in the main pial arteries of rats and cats, *Brain Res.* **27**:25.

Norberg, K.-A., 1964, Adrenergic innervation of the intestinal wall studied by fluorescence microscopy, *Internat. J. Neuropharmacol.* **3**:374.

Norberg, K.-A., 1967, Transmitter histochemistry of the sympathetic adrenergic nervous system, *Brain Res.* **5**:125.

Norberg, K.-A., and Hamberger, B., 1964, The sympathetic adrenergic neuron, *Acta Physiol. Scand.* **63**: Suppl. 238.

Norberg, K.-A., and Sjöqvist, F., 1966, New possibilities for adrenergic modulation of ganglionic transmission, *Pharmacol. Rev.* **18**:743.

Norberg, K.-A., Ritzén, M., and Ungerstedt, U., 1966, Histochemical studies on a special catecholamine-containing cell type in sympathetic ganglia, *Acta Physiol. Scand.* **67**:260.

Norberg, K.-A, Risley, P. L., and Ungerstedt, U., 1967, Adrenergic innervation of the male reproductive ducts in some mammals. I. The distribution of adrenergic nerves, *Z. Zellforsch.* **76**:278.

Norberg, K.-A., Hökfelt, T., and Eneroth, C.-M., 1969, The autonomic innervation of human submandibular and parotid glands, *J. Neuro-Visceral Rel.* **31**:280.

Olson, L., 1970, Fluorescence histochemical evidence for axonal growth and secretion from transplanted adrenal medullary tissue, *Histochemie* **22**:1.

Owman, Ch., and Sjöberg, N.-O., 1966, Adrenergic nerves in the female genital tract of the rabbit with remarks on cholinesterase-containing structures, *Z. Zellforsch.* **74**:182.

Owman, Ch., and Sjöstrand, N.-O., 1965, Short adrenergic neurons and catecholamine-containing cells in vas deferens and accessory male genital glands of different mammals, *Z. Zellforsch.* **66**:300.

Owman, Ch., Rosengren, E., and Sjöberg, N.-O., 1967, Adrenergic innervation of the human female reproductive organs: A histochemical and chemical investigation, *Obstet. Glynecol.* **30**:763.

Raezer, D., Wein, A. J., Jacobowitz, D., Corriere, J. N., 1973, Autonomic innervation of canine urinary bladder. Cholinergic and adrenergic contributions and interaction of sympathetic and parasymphathetic nervous systems in bladder function, *Urology* **2**:211.

Van Orden, L. S., III, Burke, J. P., Geyer, M., and Lodoen, F., 1970, Localization of depletion-sensitive and depletion-resistant norepinephrine storage sites in autonomic ganglia, *J. Pharmacol. Exptl. Therap.* **174**:56.

Vogel, J., Jacobowitz, D., and Chidsey, C., 1969, The distribution of norepinephrine in the failing heart: Correlation of chemical analysis and fluorescent microscopy, *Circ. Res.* **24**:71.

Volle, R. L., 1969, Modification by drugs of synaptic mechanism in autonomic ganglia, *Pharmacol. Rev.* **18**:839.

Wein, A. J., Leoni, J. V., Schoenberg, H. W., and Jacobowitz, D., 1972, A study of the adrenergic nerves in the dog ureter, *J. Urol.* **108**:232.

Yntema, C. L., and Hammond, W. S., 1947, The development of the autonomic nervous system, *Biol. Rev.* **22**:344.

Chapter 6

Ultrastructure of Ganglionic Junctions

Margaret R. Matthews

Department of Human Anatomy
Oxford University
Oxford, England

1. GENERAL CONSIDERATIONS

The synapses of the peripheral autonomic ganglia of vertebrates have been studied with the electron microscope since the middle 1950s. Numerous descriptions of synaptic and other junctional specializations are available, for various ganglia and for various species. At their simplest, these ganglia are sites of synapse between preganglionic nerve fibers which arise from the central nervous system and postganglionic neurons whose axons leave the ganglia to terminate in relation to peripheral effectors (smooth muscle or gland cells). In keeping with the evidence that the transmitter substance liberated at the preganglionic nerve endings is acetylcholine (e.g., Dale, 1953; Hebb and Krnjevic, 1962), there has emerged a considerable degree of basic similarity of pre- to postganglionic synapses in a wide range of ganglia, particularly in the organelles of the preganglionic nerve terminals. There are, however, striking differences among various vertebrate groups and among various ganglia in the arrangement of these synapses in relation to the postganglionic neurons, which are revealed with some precision by the electron microscope. These differences are reflected in the function of the ganglia, influencing, for example, such questions as the security of transmission and the occurrence of convergence or divergence of preganglionic input.

   In addition to the synapse between pre- and postganglionic elements, intrinsic synaptic junctions have been demonstrated in certain sympathetic ganglia and in the enteric ganglia, and these may be the basis for local regulatory mechanisms such as inhibitory loops and sequential interactions. The enteric ganglia, moreover, have a multiplicity of inputs, and these also are beginning to be analyzed ultrastructurally.

Reviews on the morphology of synaptic junctions include those by Gray and Guillery (1966) and by Gray (1969, 1971). Much information on mammalian synapses is also given in a book by Peters *et al.* (1970) and in one edited by Pappas and Purpura (1973). An interesting hypothesis for the function of the dendritic spine has been put forward by Diamond *et al.* (1970).

2. SYMPATHETIC GANGLIA

2.1. Amphibia

One of the earliest investigations of the ultrastructure of synaptic junctions was made by De Robertis and Bennett (1955) in an abdominal sympathetic ganglion of the bullfrog, *Rana catesbiana* (and also in the nerve cord of the earthworm). This work was reported almost simultaneously with the early descriptions of synaptic structure in the central nervous system of the rat made by Palade and Palay (1954) and by Palay (1956). The major problems at this stage were to recognize the pre- and postsynaptic elements with the electron microscope, to define the relationships of the surface membranes in the synaptic region, and to identify features which might be correlated with the functional polarity of the synapse. In the frog sympathetic ganglion, the recognition of pre- and postsynaptic profiles was aided by the arrangement of the preganglionic nerve fiber at its termination. The neurons are known from light microscopy to be unipolar, and each receives the terminations of one or possibly two preganglionic nerve fibers, which are spirally wrapped around the axonal pole of the neuron (Fig. 1; e.g., Huber, 1900; Pick, 1963; Taxi, 1965). De Robertis and Bennett (1955) were able to recognize rounded presynaptic profiles applied to the cell surface. In these they identified mitochondria, which because of their known concentration within the "boutons terminaux" of light microscopy were a guide to the recognition of the presynaptic terminal profiles (Palade and Palay, 1954; Palay, 1956). The presynaptic profile but not the postsynaptic cytoplasm was found to contain many small vesicles, an ultrastructural demonstration of polarity at the synaptic junction. The precise interrelationships of the surface membranes at the junction were not clearly defined, but it appeared that the pre- and postsynaptic membranes lay in apposition, without the intervention of other cell processes (De Robertis and Bennett, 1955).

Over the succeeding few years, with the advantage of rapid improvements in technique, knowledge of the ultrastructure of synapses became much more complete (e.g., Palay, 1958; De Robertis, 1958). A series of studies of frog sympathetic ganglia (lumbar and other ganglia of *Rana esculenta*, also

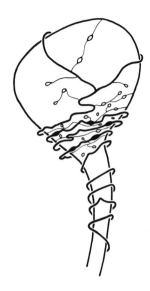

Fig. 1. Diagram of the spiral ending of a preganglionic nerve fiber upon a sympathetic neuron in the frog, with many boutons terminaux near the origin of the axon. From Taxi (1965). Contribution à l'étude des connexions des neurones moteurs du système nerveux autonome, Masson et Cie, Paris, *Ann. Sci. Nat. Zool.* 7:413.

in *Rana temporaria* and in toads) was made by Taxi (1961, 1964, 1965), who turned initially to the amphibian because he had found mammalian ganglia rather more complex in their synaptic arrangements (Taxi, 1957). Like De Robertis and Bennett, he used buffered osmium tetroxide for fixation. Guided by the new knowledge of synapses, and by the light microscopy (Fig. 1), he was readily able to identify presynaptic profiles, arranged in rows along and in contact with the surface of the neuron, especially near the axonal pole; some even lie upon the origin of its axon, as was observed also by Pick (1963). Taxi's diagram of these relationships is shown in Fig. 2. 20–25% of the neuronal surface may be covered by such contacts, close to the axonal pole (Hunt and Nelson, 1965; Nishi, Soeda and Koketsu, 1967). The whole complex of neuron and preganglionic axon, including the synaptic regions, is enveloped by Schwann or satellite cell cytoplasm. Such an arrangement is typical for most autonomic ganglia; i.e., all the intraganglionic nervous elements are enclosed within wrappings of Schwann cell (or neuronal satellite cell) cytoplasm which separates them from interstitial tissue spaces containing fine collagen fibers and intraganglionic blood vessels. The Schwann cell of the axon and the satellite cell of the neuron in these ganglia appear to be virtually indistinguishable anatomically and to have overlapping functions, in that the same cell frequently ensheathes both cell bodies, dendrites, and axons; they will in future be referred to mainly as Schwann cells, but with the proviso that Chamley *et al.*, (1972) have been able to distinguish between them in respect of their patterns of movement in tissue culture.

Around the origin of the axon in the frog ganglion (Fig. 2), the Schwann cell sheath is prolonged in the form of a hollow cone, from which slender

extensions project inward to support coils of the preganglionic axon (Yamamoto, 1963; Taxi, 1965). A similar frondlike or "tentaclelike" arrangement of
Schwann cell processes around the base of the axon has been noted in the toad
(Uchizono, 1964); it may have some electrically insulating function. The preterminal parts of the presynaptic fibers in the frog, although not myelinated,

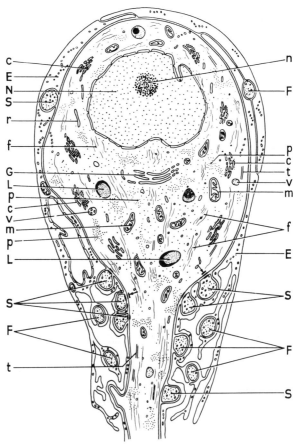

Fig. 2. Diagram of a frog sympathetic neuron and its satellite cell sheath. N, Nucleus;
n, nucleolus; c, Nissl body; P, free ribosomes; G, Golgi zone; r, smooth endoplasmic
reticulum; m, mitochondria; f, neurofilaments; t, microtubules; L, lysosomes (cytoplasmic dense bodies); v, multivesicular bodies; F, sections of spiral preganglionic nerve
fiber, some of which are giving synapses (S); arrows, subsynaptic bands; E, satellite cell
sheath with many vesicles of smooth endoplasmic reticulum: this sheath becomes divided
into two layers around the origin of the axon. From Taxi (1965). Contribution à l'étude
des connexions des neurones moteurs du système nerveux autonome, Masson et Cie,
Paris, *Ann. Sci. Nat. Zool.* 7:413.

may have a spiraling mesaxon or multiple layers of Schwann sheath (Pick, 1963), and the neuronal satellite sheath may similarly consist of several layers (Taxi, 1965). The toad sympathetic ganglion also shows these multiple wrappings ("loose myelin"; Uchizono, 1964). In the arrangement and character of synaptic junctions, the toad ganglion appears to closely resemble the frog ganglion (Uchizono, 1964; Taxi, 1965; Fujimoto, 1967), although sometimes the synaptic terminal profile may be deeply embedded in the cell soma (Uchizono, 1964). Fujimoto (1967), however, reported a new element in the toad: this was a type of small "granular" cell, located occasionally near to the larger blood vessels, which he regarded as analogous to the chromaffin cell of higher vertebrates.

2.1.1. Organelles of the Preganglionic Terminal Profile

Taxi (1961, 1964, 1965) and Pick (1963) showed that the presynaptic terminal profile in frog ganglia contains many small agranular vesicles of about 300–400 Å diameter, which cluster toward specialized denser regions of the apposed pre- and postsynaptic membranes (Fig. 3). In osmium-fixed material, these vesicles appear spherical. Small vesicles clustering toward a region of membrane specialization had been found to be typical of the synaptic junctions so far explored. Further away in the terminal profile, and in the immediate preterminal region of the presynaptic fiber, there lie a varying number of larger vesicles of about 800–1000 Å diameter with an electron-dense core of about 500 Å diameter and an electron-lucent halo. These are far less numerous than the small vesicles and are usually seen in association with a group of mitochondria. Occasionally one or more may be seen in contact with the presynaptic membrane (Hunt and Nelson, 1965). Taxi (1965) found that the cores of these dense-cored vesicles were not depleted by reserpine treatment, i.e., that they did not appear to be adrenergic. The presynaptic terminal profiles also usually contain some electron-dense granules of about 100 Å diameter, which are now known to represent glycogen granules (e.g., Pick, 1963, 1970). With the exception of the glycogen granules, which are seldom seen in mammals (e.g., De Ribaupierre, 1968), these organelles are typical of *preganglionic* terminal and preterminal profiles in sympathetic ganglia in general.

2.1.2. The Membrane Specialization

The region of synaptic membrane specialization (the "active zone") occupies only a part of the region of apposition of pre- and postsynaptic membranes. Sometimes there are two or more active zones of rather limited extent (Pick, 1963). Here, the membranes show a uniform interspacing (the

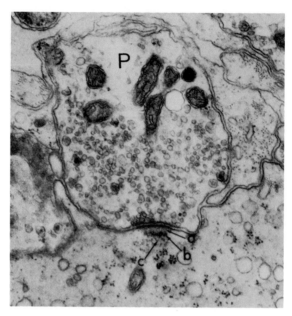

Fig. 3. Frog sympathetic ganglion. Synapse showing a subsynaptic band (b). The presynaptic profile (P) contains many small agranular vesicles, some larger dense-cored vesicles, and mitochondria. The postsynaptic cytoplasm is granular and more electron dense (a) between the subsynaptic band and the postsynaptic membrane specialization and (c) immediately deep to the subsynaptic band. × 26,000. From Taxi (1964). Étude de certaines synapses interneuronales du système nerveux autonome, *Acta Neuroveg.* **26**:360.

synaptic cleft) of about 200 Å and are slightly increased in density. Electron-dense material is apposed to the membranes in both pre- and postsynaptic cytoplasm, forming triangular dense projections on the presynaptic side, where the vesicles are clustered, and a continuous thicker layer on the postsynaptic side (Figs. 3 and 4). This is thus an asymmetrical type of synapse with respect to the associated dense material. Some moderately dense material is seen also between the membranes, in the synaptic cleft. The dense material which is associated with the membranes is not seen after fixation with permanganate (Yamamoto, 1963; Taxi, 1965), which preserves the membrane structure selectively. Taxi's diagram of this synapse is shown in Fig. 4.

2.1.3. The Postsynaptic Cytoplasm

In a proportion of *Rana esculenta* synapses (10–40%, Taxi, 1964; about 16%, Sotelo, 1968) there is found a subsynaptic band ("bandelette sous-synaptique") of dense material lying in the postsynaptic cytoplasm, parallel to the synaptic thickening but rather shorter (Figs. 3 and 4). The band may show discontinuities (Sotelo, 1968). It lies within a tapering web of slightly electron-dense cytoplasm (Figs. 3 and 4). Sometimes there are two or three subsynaptic bands, each less extensive than the first. Taxi (1965) also found this band in various other amphibia. Pick (1963), working with *Rana pipiens*, did not find subsynaptic bands but found that there was frequently a tapering subsynaptic web.

2.1.4. Nonsynaptic Attachment Plaques

In addition to synaptic zones, Sotelo (1968) noted occasional regions of increased density of the apposed membranes of pre- and postganglionic profiles, with a symmetrical arrangement of associated dense material in the underlying cytoplasm on either side, and without any clustering of vesicles toward either membrane. These attachment plaques, or desmosome-like regions, like the corresponding structures in epithelia, probably have a purely mechanical function.

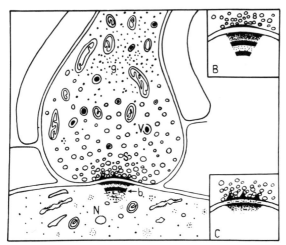

Fig. 4. Diagram of the pre- to postganglionic synapse in the frog sympathetic ganglion. S, Synaptic vesicles; g, dense particles (glycogen); V, larger dense-cored vesicles; b. subsynaptic band; N, ganglionic neuron. B: Diagram of a double subsynaptic band. C: Diagram of synaptic junction ("active zone") showing presynaptic dense projections and the content of the synaptic cleft. From Taxi (1965). Contribution a l'étude des connexions des neurones moteurs du système nerveux autonome, Masson et Cie, Paris, *Ann. Sci. Nat. Zool.* **7**:413.

2.1.5. Degeneration Studies

Taxi (1964) and Hunt and Nelson (1965) confirmed the preganglionic nature of the synaptic nerve endings in frog sympathetic ganglia by cutting the preganglionic nerve bundles and studying the effects in the ganglia. Taxi found that the presynaptic terminal profiles showed distinctive (degenerative) changes and became detached from the postsynaptic site between 2 and 4 days after he had cut the preganglionic nerve fibers. He reported that the postsynaptic membrane thickening and subsynaptic band persisted for about a day after the loss of the presynaptic profile. Sotelo (1968), extending Taxi's experiments, found that the postsynaptic membrane densities and dense bands could persist for at least 12 days after denervation, although by then they were becoming fewer. Hunt and Nelson (1965) studied ganglionic transmission as well as ultrastructure after a similar denervation and found that transmission failed progressively over the period 22–48 h postoperatively. They detected changes in fine structure of some of the nerve endings, interpreted as degenerative, already at 24 h, and observed that most of the endings became darkened and detached within the next few days, only a few altered terminal profiles persisting at 5 days postoperatively. No obvious changes were found in the postganglionic neurons.

2.2. Reptiles

In the cervical sympathetic ganglion of the turtle (Szentágothai, 1964), in contrast to the amphibian ganglion, the neurons are multipolar. Axosomatic synapses are relatively rare, and synapses are found more often upon the dendrites. Some are placed in the acute angle between the ganglion cell surface and the origin of a short intracapsular dendrite, but most lie on the longer dendrites at some distance from the cell bodies (Szentágothai, 1964). "Loose myelin" wrappings, i.e., multiple layers of Schwann cell cytoplasm, are found both on the preterminal regions of the preganglionic axons and enveloping the ganglion cell bodies. These wrappings end at the bases of the cell processes. The contents of the presynaptic terminal profiles are similar to those in the amphibia, i.e., many small (300–500 Å) agranular vesicles which cluster toward the synaptic membrane specialization, larger (1500–2500 Å) dense-cored vesicles and mitochondria farther away, and some glycogen. Commenting on the variation in numbers of dense-cored vesicles and their occasional absence, Szentágothai concluded nevertheless that there was no evidence to suggest more than a single population of synapses in terms of synaptic organelles: the differences found could be accounted for by such factors as variation in the plane of section.

The turtle, with its "loose myelin" wrappings and predominantly axo-dendritic synapses, represents a situation intermediate between that of the amphibian and the mammal.

2.3. Mammals

In mammalian sympathetic ganglia, the neurons are typically multipolar and the synaptic junctions are principally axodendritic. (A note of caution must be observed here: it is not always possible to distinguish axons from dendrites in the sympathetic ganglia, so it cannot be either excluded or confidently asserted that there may also be axoaxonic synapses.) The preganglionic synaptic endings are ultrastructurally very similar in organelle content to those in amphibia and the turtle, although on average smaller and with little or no glycogen. Perhaps because of a more rapid turnover of synaptic components in warm-blooded animals, the vesiculated synaptic profiles tend to show instead occasional cytoplasmic dense bodies or more rarely membranes encircling groups of vesicles (e.g., Elfvin 1963a,b); these suggest the occurrence of lytic processes. A few wrappings of "loose myelin" are sometimes seen on preterminal axons, but not on cell bodies.

There appear to be certain differences in structure between different ganglia of the sympathetic system, but much still remains to be explored.

2.3.1. Paravertebral Ganglia

Many studies have involved the superior cervical ganglion. In the smaller laboratory rodents, its relatively large size and relative accessibility make it convenient to work on. Its key position, supplying sympathetic postganglionic fibers to the entire head including the eye and the pineal gland, to much of the neck and in some species also to the heart, makes it, however, a rather specialized ganglion.

2.3.1a. Preganglionic Nerve Endings. Elfvin (1963a,b) made serial reconstructions of dendrites and of the predominantly axodendritic synapses in the cat superior cervical ganglion and showed that an unmyelinated preterminal axon (of diameter 0.1–0.3 μm) may be wrapped in spiral fashion around a dendrite, or run parallel with it, giving to it a number of *en passant* synapses from varicose enlargements. The intervaricose parts of the axon contain microtubules and neurofilaments. The varicosities contain organelles typical of preganglionic nerve endings (see above), and the synaptic membrane specializations are asymmetrical and do not occupy the whole of the region of contact between the synapsing profiles. Grillo (1965) found that in the rat the proportion occupied is 10–95%. Elfvin found that axosomatic synapses

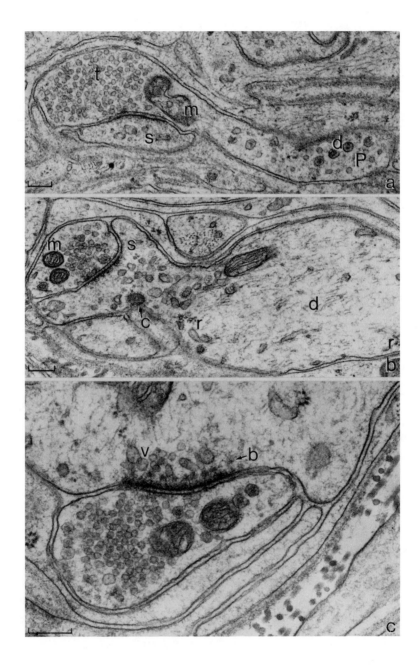

are rare; at these, the presynaptic axon profile may quite deeply indent the cell body. Elfvin (1963a,b) did not find other types of synapses; but Tamarind and Quilliam (1971) found a small proportion of synapses (3 in 79) which contained small dense-cored vesicles in addition to other types of vesicles (see 2.3. 1c below). In the rabbit ganglion, which otherwise resembled that of the cat, this proportion was higher (28 in 111). Lakos (1970) could not find any synapses remaining in the cat superior cervical ganglion at 18 days following preganglionic denervation and concluded that no interneurons are present in this ganglion.

In the superior cervical ganglion of the rat (von Forssmann, 1964; Taxi, 1965; Grillo, 1965, 1966; Tamarind and Quilliam, 1971) and also in rat thoracic ganglia (De Lemos and Pick, 1966; Pick, 1970), as in the cat, the synapses are principally axodendritic, and the great majority of the synaptic terminal profiles are of the type described above as being characteristic of preganglionic nerve endings (Fig. 5). Grillo (1965) found both small agranular vesicles and the larger (800–1000 Å) dense-cored vesicles in 82% of 185 synaptic bulbs taken at random; Tamarind and Quilliam (1971) obtained closely similar figures. Although in some instances the larger (800–1000 Å) dense-cored vesicles may not be seen in the terminal profile, they may be present in the preterminal region (Fig. 5a). The synaptic thickening is typically asymmetrical. The axodendritic synapses may lie either on the shafts of the dendrites or on spinelike projections from the dendrites (e.g., Fig. 5b,c; Grillo, 1965). These spines are usually short, often indented at the tip, and contain finely granular or fibrillar cytoplasm in which there may be a number of irregular vesicles or sacs of smooth endoplasmic reticulum (Fig. 5b; Matthews, unpublished observations). A spine apparatus of the type found in the mammalian cerebrum (Gray, 1959) has never been observed. In synapses upon dendritic shafts, there is sometimes seen a subsynaptic structure comprising a row of densities in the postsynaptic cytoplasm, linked with the synaptic thickening by finely fibrillar cytoplasm and having irregular vesicles associated with its deep aspect (Figs. 5c and 6b; Fig. 23 of Matthews and Raisman, 1969). This

---

Fig. 5. Axodendritic synapses of preganglionic type in rat superior cervical ganglion. Osmium fixation. Scale bars, 0.2 μm. a: Synaptic terminal profile (t), containing small agranular vesicles and a mitochondrion (m), in continuity with preterminal fiber (P) which contains a few agranular vesicles and larger dense-cored vesicles (d). The postsynaptic profile (s) has the character of a dendritic spine (*cf.* b). b: Synapse onto spine (s). of a dendrite (dendritic shaft, d). The spine is joined to the shaft by a narrower neck and contains irregular vesicles of smooth endoplasmic reticulum; it is indented by the presynaptic profile. m, Mitochondria in presynaptic profile; c, coated pit or vesicle in spine neck; r, clusters of ribosomes in dendritic shaft. c: Synapse onto dendritic shaft, showing a row of subsynaptic dense bodies (b). Irregular vesicles of smooth endoplasmic reticulum (v) are associated with its deep aspect.

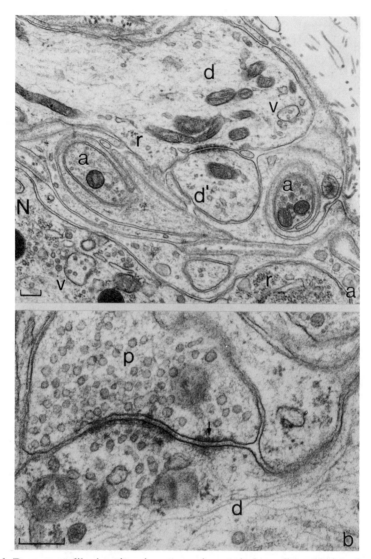

Fig. 6. Desmosome-like junctions in rat superior cervical ganglion. Osmium fixation. Scale bars, 0.2 μm. a: Symmetrical desmosome-like junction between a dendrite (d) and another profile, probably a dendrite (d'). Mitochondria approach closely to the junction, but there is no vesicle clustering on either side. r, Ribosomal clusters; v, multivesicular bodies; N, cell body of ganglionic neuron; a, preterminal axons. b: Synapse onto dendritic shaft (d) showing a symmetrical desmosome-like junction (arrow) in addition to the specialized synaptic region. Vesicles in the presynaptic profile (p) cluster toward the synaptic region but not toward the desmosome. The postsynaptic cytoplasm shows a row of subsynaptic dense bodies with associated vesicles.

in some ways resembles the "bandelette sous-synaptique" described by Taxi (1961, 1964, 1965). A few synapses from terminal profiles of preganglionic type are found upon the cell bodies (1% of 1473, Tamarind and Quilliam, 1971) or on short perikaryal spines (intracapsular pseudodendrites); these show an asymmetrical synaptic thickening. Preganglionic denervation of the superior cervical ganglion in the rat and cat leads to degeneration and disappearance of nerve endings of the type described here as preganglionic (Grillo, 1965, 1966; Clementi *et al.*, 1966; Quilliam and Tamarind, 1967; Hámori *et al.*, 1968; Lakos, 1970; Joó *et al.*, 1971).

2.3.1b. Desmosomelike Attachments. Elfvin (1963*a,b*), noted that in the cat superior cervical ganglion the insulation of nervous processes from each other by Schwann cytoplasm was relatively incomplete and that in addition to specialized synaptic contacts there were regions of apposition of dendrite with dendrite, or of dendrite with cell body, at which there might be localized

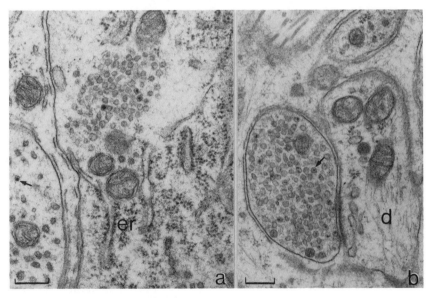

Fig. 7. Small dense-cored vesicles in rat superior cervical ganglion. Osmium fixation. Scale bars, 0.2 μm. a: Cluster of small vesicles, some with dense cores, near the surface of the cell body of a ganglionic neuron. e.r., Granular endoplasmic reticulum (Nissl substance); arrow, small dense-cored vesicle in adjacent profile, possibly dendrite. b: Synapse upon a dendritic shaft (d). The preterminal profile contains many small dense-cored (granular) vesicles (e.g., arrow), with agranular vesicles of the same size. (b, 6 days after section of preganglionic nerve fibers).

areas of symmetrical membrane specialization (having the character of attachment plaques, described above). Such relationships are also frequently seen in the superior cervical ganglion of rat and rabbit (Fig. 6a; Tamarind and Quilliam, 1971; Matthews, unpublished observations). More recently (Taxi *et al.*, 1969, rat superior cervical ganglion; Elfvin, 1971*a,b,c*, cat inferior mesenteric ganglion), it has been observed that these attachments may occur in close relationship to clusters of small vesicles, some with dense cores (this proportion depending partly on the fixative), which are found not far from the surface membranes of the postganglionic cell bodies and dendrites (Fig. 7a; Taxi, 1965; Grillo, 1966; Hökfelt, 1969; Matthews and Raisman, 1972). Elfvin (1971*a,b,c*) has suggested that there might be some form of inhibitory interaction here (Figs. 8a and 8b). (These groups of vesicles, apparently adrenergic, could moreover partly account for the adrenergic networks at the surface of the ganglion cell bodies and among the dendrites, which are visualized by fluorescence microscopy and which persist after preganglionic denervation; Norberg and Sjöqvist, 1966; Jacobowitz, 1970. Such networks are reported to be particularly well developed in the inferior mesenteric ganglion; see below.) Taxi *et al.* (1969) further noted appearances suggesting that the contents of the small dense-cored vesicles might at certain points be released into the intraganglionic tissue space, in rat ganglia a few days after preganglionic axotomy.

2.3.1c. Nerve Endings Containing Small Dense-Cored Vesicles. Cutting the preganglionic nerve fibers to the rat superior cervical ganglion and allowing several days or weeks for degeneration of axon terminals has revealed another scanty population of synaptic nerve endings, of a type reported by Grillo (1965) to be found occasionally in the normal ganglion, and found by Tamarind and Quilliam (1971) to constitute about 6% of normal synapses (4% in the cat, 25% in the rabbit). These are rounded profiles of medium size which contain both small agranular vesicles of about 300–600 Å diameter and a variable proportion of small dense-cored (granular) vesicles of about the same size (Fig. 7b). Tamarind and Quilliam (1971) observed that they may also contain larger dense-cored vesicles (800–1000 Å diameter). The presence of small dense-cored vesicles suggests that these endings are adrenergic (e.g., Wolfe *et al.*, 1964). They form synapses with asymmetrical thickenings upon dendrites in the ganglion (Grillo, 1966, 130 h postoperatively; Joó *et al.*, 1971, 5 weeks; Matthews, unpublished observations, 6 days). Lakos (1970, 18 days) also illustrates profiles of this type. The fact that these endings are seen quite early after the denervation, at a stage when few if any preganglionic fibers are likely to have regenerated and there are very few nerve endings in the ganglion, suggests that they could be of intraganglionic origin or that they are derived from some uninjured extraganglionic pathway.

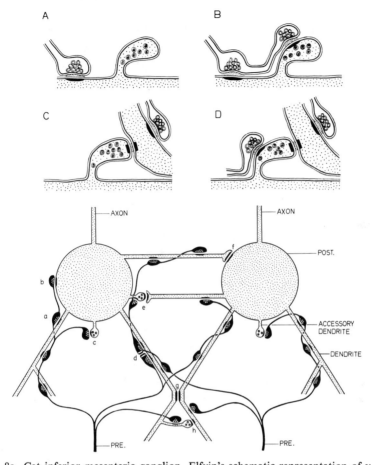

Fig. 8a. Cat inferior mesenteric ganglion. Elfvin's schematic representation of various types of relationships he observed between short cell processes (containing small dense-cored vesicles) from postganglionic neurons, the endings of preganglionic axons, and the dendrites of other postganglionic neurons. A, Axosomatic synapse close to short process; B, axon forming axosomatic synapse and synapse on adjacent short process; C, short process attached by desmosome-like junction to dendrite, which receives an axodendritic synapse; D, as C but synapse on short process in addition.

Fig. 8b. Cat inferior mesenteric ganglion. Elfvin's schematic diagram of the relationships he observed between preganglionic axons (PRE) and postganglionic neurons (POST). a, Axodendritic synapse; b, axosomatic synapse; c, synapse upon short process (accessory dendrite) containing dense-cored vesicles; d–h, symmetrical desmosome-like attachments: d, axoaxonic; f, dendrosomatic; g, dendrodendritic; e, h, between dendrites and accessory dendrites, the latter containing dense-cored vesicles and receiving synapses from pre-ganglionic axons. Elfvin suggests that these last sites may be points for inhibitory inter-action. From Elfvin (1971c) Ultrastructural studies on the synaptology of the inferior mesenteric ganglion of the cat. III. The structure and distribution of the axodendritic and dendrodeudritic contacts, *J. Ultrastruct. Res.* **37**:432.

Various intraganglionic possibilities have been suggested, e.g., that they may be dendrites of the postganglionic neurons, axon collaterals of the postganglionic neurons (although these neurons do not regularly form synaptic junctions of this type at their peripheral terminations) or axon terminals of some adrenergic interneuron. There is as yet, however, no certainty about the origin of these endings, nor whether their absolute incidence increases postoperatively.

2.3.1d. Small Granule-Containing Cells (Small Intensely Fluorescent Cells). Another component of the rat superior cervical ganglion is the small granule-containing cell (SG cell), which corresponds to the small intensely fluorescent cell (SIF cell) revealed in sympathetic ganglia by the Falck–Hillarp technique of formaldehyde-induced fluorescence for catecholamines (Eränkö and Härkönen, 1965). These cells have a number of short processes and contain many intracytoplasmic dense-cored vesicles, of diameter about 650–1200 Å or more. They were first described ultrastructurally by Siegrist et al. (1966) and by Grillo (1966), who found that they had Schwann cell sheaths and received axosomatic synapses, and soon afterward Williams (1967) reported that they formed outgoing synapses upon other profiles in the ganglion and therefore had the character of interneurons. Subsequent work has confirmed and added to these observations (Siegrist et al., 1968; Williams and Palay, 1969; Matthews and Raisman, 1969; Taxi et al., 1969). The cells are scattered in small clusters and larger groups in the rat superior cervical ganglion, seldom lying singly (about 30 groups or clusters in one ganglion, Matthews and Raisman, 1969). Eränkö and Eränkö (1971) have counted the SIF cells in single ganglia of three very young and five adult rats, and find from 372 to 986 such cells per ganglion. The cells are often associated with fenestrated blood vessels, and there are indications that the contents of their dense-cored vesicles could be liberated into the intraganglionic tissue spaces and might also enter these vessels (Siegrist et al., 1968; Matthews and Raisman, 1969). The cells receive axosomatic synapses from rounded terminal profiles which contain small agranular vesicles and some larger dense-cored vesicles, with mitochondria, like the typical preganglionic nerve endings (Grillo, 1966; Siegrist et al., 1968; Williams, 1967; Matthews and Raisman, 1969; Taxi et al., 1969). The region of vesicle clustering and synaptic specialization is, however, of very limited extent and may be multiple, and the membrane thickening is symmetrical, the postsynaptic thickening being quite inconspicuous (e.g., Matthews and Raisman, 1969). In addition, the ending frequently shows one or more desmosome-like attachment zones (e.g., Matthews and Ostberg, 1973).

Denervation experiments have indicated that these endings are preganglionic (Matthews, 1971; Matthews and Ostberg, 1973). There is strong evidence that transmission at these junctions is muscarinic (e.g., Libet, 1970);

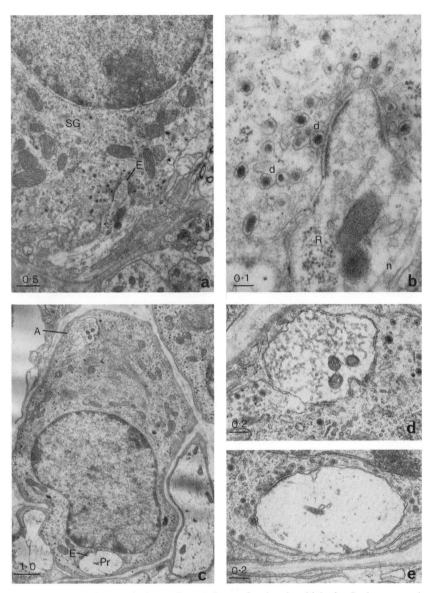

Fig. 9. Rat superior cervical ganglion. Primary fixation in aldehyde. Scales, μm. a,b:
Somatic efferent synapse (E) from a small granule-containing cell (SG) onto a spinelike
projection arising from a process containing microtubules (n) and ribosomes (R).
b shows detail of synaptic region. d, dense-cored vesicles of SG cell. c–e: SG cell receiving
an afferent (preganglionic) synapse at one pole of the soma and giving off a somatic
efferent synapse at the other. Both the afferent terminal profile (A) (shown in detail in d)
and the postsynaptic profile (Pr) (enlarged in e) deeply indent the body of the cell and are
partly covered by vesicle-free extensions of its cytoplasm. Note the flattening of vesicles
in the afferent presynaptic profile in d. From Matthews and Raisman (1969). The ultrastructure and somatic efferent synapses of small granule-containing cells in the superior
cervical ganglion, *J. Anat.* **105:255.**

i.e., they differ in this respect from the majority of pre- to postganglionic junctions, at which transmission is nicotinic. This might be correlated with the difference in the extent of the active synaptic zone and with the difference in postsynaptic membrane thickening in the two types of synapses.

Outgoing (efferent) synapses of a characteristic form (Fig. 9) are given by the SG cells, both from their processes and from the cell soma, to a variety of profiles (Williams, 1967; Siegrist et al., 1968; Williams and Palay, 1969; Matthews and Raisman, 1969). The synaptic thickening is distinctly asymmetrical, and the vesicle cluster includes the large dense-cored vesicles typical of the SG cell; agranular vesicles, if present, are few. The region of specialization may be quite extensive. These junctions seem to satisfy all the criteria of a synapse, as discussed by Matthews and Raisman (1969) (although the possession by the SG cells of other membrane specializations of a synaptoid or hemisynaptic nature has led Taxi et al., 1969, to question this view). Many of the postsynaptic profiles are small and difficult to identify, but some resemble dendritic spines, and others have the character of dendrites of the postganglionic neurons (Siegrist et al., 1968; Matthews and Raisman, 1969; Williams and Palay, 1969). Some contain many irregular agranular vesicles (e.g., Fig. 6 of Raisman and Matthews, 1972). An example of a soma-to-soma synapse from an SG cell to a postganglionic neuron, traced through serial sections, has been reported by Matthews and Nash (1970) (Fig. 10), and another, to a somatic spine, has been found by Yokota (1973). Taken with the preceding evidence, this serves to confirm that the SG cell may stand in an interneuronal relationship between the preganglionic axons and some at least of the postganglionic neurons. It does not exclude other possible functions or connections of these cells. The SG cells are not all of exactly the same character, even in the same ganglion (Siegrist et al., 1968; Matthews, 1971; Kanerva and Teräväinen, 1971; Watanabe, 1971). Figure 11 summarizes some of their ultrastructural characteristics, as found in the rat superior cervical ganglion (Matthews and Raisman, 1969), and compares the SG cell with the adrenal medullary chromaffin cell on the one hand and the sympathetic neuron on the other. It is not yet certainly established what catecholamine the SG cells contain, although this is probably dopamine (cf. Björklund et al., 1970; Eränkö and Eränkö, 1971), but it seems likely that they may be in some way involved in intraganglionic inhibitory mechanisms (see review by Libet, 1970).

There are thus in the present state of knowledge up to three possible anatomical substrates for catecholaminergic regulatory mechanisms in the mammalian sympathetic ganglion: the SG cells, the synaptic profiles containing small dense-cored vesicles (these appear more likely to be axon collaterals of the postganglionic neurons than to be derived from SG cells; e.g., Grillo, 1966), and the small dense-cored vesicles of the postganglionic cell bodies and

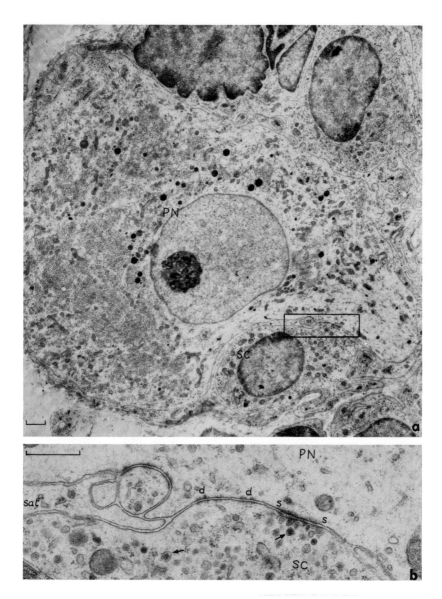

Fig. 10. a: Rat superior cervical ganglion. A small granule-containing cell (SC) forming a soma-to-soma efferent synapse upon a principal postganglionic neuron. Scale, 1 μm. b: Adjacent serial section, showing the region outlined in a. Scale, 0.5 μm. Sat, Satellite cell cytoplasm; d, desmosome-like attachment; s–s, region of synapse; arrows, dense-cored vesicles of SG cell. From Matthews and Nash (1970). An efferent synapse from a small granule-containing cell to a principal neurone in the superior cervical ganglion, *J. Physiol. Lond.* **210**:11P.

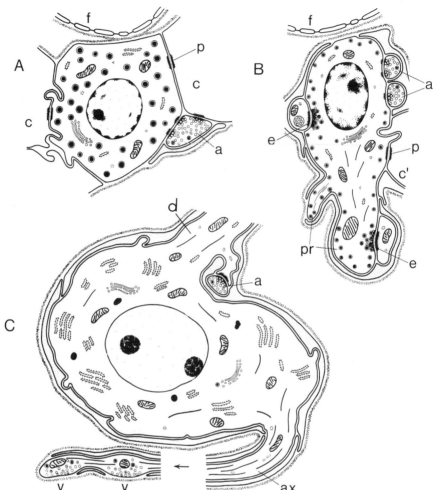

Fig. 11. Diagram comparing some features of an adrenal medullary chromaffin cell (A), a small granule-containing cell (B), and a principal sympathetic neuron (C). In the series A–C, the covering of satellite cytoplasm becomes progressively more extensive, while the distribution of intracytoplasmic dense-cored vesicles is progressively more restricted. Cell A, which secretes into the bloodstream, is freely related across basement membrane (coarse stippling) to fenestrated capillaries (f); and cell C, which directs the release of transmitter substance to its axon terminals, has a complete covering of satellite cytoplasm. Cell B, with efferent synapses (e) and cytoplasmic prolongations (pr) in addition to areas of cell surface free of satellite covering, appears to represent an intermediate cell type, exhibiting some of the features both of the neuron and of the chromaffin cell. a, Afferent synapses; p, attachment plaques; c, chromaffin cells adjacent to cell A; c′, small granule-containing cell adjacent to cell B; d, base of dendrite, ax, origin of axon, v, terminal varicosities of axon of cell C. From Matthews and Raisman (1969). The ultrastructure and somatic efferent synapses of small granule-containing cells in the superior cervical ganglion, *J. Anat.* **105**:255.

dendrites, perhaps acting via release of their contents at points of dendro-dendritic and dendrosomatic attachment (Elfvin, 1971a,b,c). These could well differ in importance in different ganglia, and for different pathways in the same ganglion.

2.3.2. Prevertebral Ganglia

Various features of the coeliac, inferior mesenteric, or hypogastric ganglia have been examined in several species (guinea pig: coeliac, Taxi, 1965; inferior mesenteric, Ostberg, 1970; hypogastric, Blackman et al., 1969; Watanabe, 1970, 1971; cat inferior mesenteric, Elfvin 1971a,b,c; rabbit inferior mesenteric, Elfvin, 1968). In addition, Kanerva and Teräväinen (1972) have studied the paracervical (uterine) ganglion of the rat. In these ganglia, although long extracapsular dendrites and axodendritic synapses are present; axosomatic synapses are not rare and may form the majority of the synapses (Taxi, 1965; Elfvin 1971a,b,c; Watanabe, 1970). Elfvin (1971a) has reconstructed an entire neuronal cell body and its associated synapses from serial sections. Many synapses are placed on short intracapsular projections from the cell bodies (somatic spines), and Blackman et al. (1969) found these synapses to be the most numerous. This situation is reminiscent of the arrangement described by Szentágothai (1964) in the turtle sympathetic ganglion.

The synaptic terminal profiles which have been observed are of a typical preganglionic (cholinergic) appearance. In addition to these, Watanabe (1970) found profiles in the hypogastric ganglion with the character of adrenergic terminal varicosities, i.e., containing many small vesicles of about 500 Å diameter, some with and some without a dense core, and a few larger dense-cored vesicles and mitochondria. These profiles were partly covered by Schwann cytoplasm, partly by basement membrane alone, and were not seen to form synapses. Watanabe proposed that these might account for the adrenergic pericellular network in this ganglion. Later (1971), he found a few such profiles rather deeply embedded in the ganglion cells, synapsing upon somatic spines.

SG cells have been found in the prevertebral ganglia. Many of these have larger granules (or dense-cored vesicles) than the SG cells typical of the rat superior cervical ganglion (e.g., 1250–2500 Å diameter). Watanabe (1971) distinguished four types, according to the character of their granules. Kanerva and Teräväinen (1972) confirmed two of these types in rat paracervical ganglion. They have not been found to give efferent synapses but might liberate the contents of their vesicles into the interstitial tissue space of the ganglion, or into related blood vessels (Elfvin, 1968; Blackman et al., 1969; Watanabe, 1970, 1971; Ostberg, 1970). In the guinea pig hypogastric ganglion, they tend to form a large group around the exit of the postganglionic axons (Blackman *et al.*, 1969).

In the cat inferior mesenteric ganglion, as described above, Elfvin (1971*a,b,c*) has proposed that the frequent desmosomelike junctions between the neurons and their dendrites may be sites of chemical interaction. These desmosome-like attachments could also be performing an important function in holding together or supporting the scaffolding of dendrites and cell bodies, upon which the varicosities of the preganglionic terminal axons are strung out. (These ganglia, like the superior cervical ganglion, are immediately related to major arteries, the pulsations of which must be powerfully transmitted through them.) The presence of numerous points of adhesion and adjoining regions of simple apposition of membranes clearly, however, offers scope for such interaction as Elfvin suggests.

2.4. Some Effects of Different Fixatives, of *in vitro* Manipulations, and of Stimulation

Bodian (1970) has noted that the small vesicles of peripheral cholinergic nerve endings may be flattened after aldehyde fixation, even though these endings are excitatory (*cf.* Uchizono, 1965; Bodian, 1966; Gray, 1971). This point is illustrated in the paper by Matthews and Raisman (1969) where axosomatic synaptic junctions upon SG cells are shown with flattened vesicles after aldehyde fixation and with round vesicles after osmium fixation (e.g., Fig. 9c). Valdivia (1971) has shown that the degree of flattening of synaptic vesicles of various kinds by aldehyde fixation depends on the osmolarity of the buffer used.

Many investigators have used buffered osmium tetroxide fixation (e.g., Palade, 1952) for sympathetic ganglia, because this appears to cause least shrinkage or distortion, but this may not so well preserve the dense cores of adrenergic vesicles as do aldehydes, or acrolein-dichromate (Woods, 1969), or permanganate fixation (Richardson, 1966; Hökfelt, 1969). Iwayama and Furness (1971) emphasize the value of incubation in oxygenated Krebs' solution, after excision and before fixing, for enhancing the cores of adrenergic vesicles. Pellegrino de Iraldi *et al.* (1971) report studies on the fixation of dense-cored vesicles and discuss the influence of different fixation schedules. Tamarind and Quilliam (1971) also describe the effects of several fixation procedures.

Investigating the effects of various experimental conditions on the rat superior cervical ganglion *in vitro*, Rouiller and his collaborators (Dolivo and Rouiller, 1969; Rouiller *et al.*, 1971; Rufener, Orci, and Rouiller, 1971) have found that the synapses are relatively resistant to anoxia and to hyperoxia, though rather rapidly susceptible to damage from lack of glucose at 37°C.

Under controlled conditions of experimental environment (either *in vivo* or *in vitro*) and of fixation, the agranular vesicles of the preganglionic nerve endings have been shown to become significantly fewer after prolonged preganglionic tetanic stimulation (rat superior cervical ganglion, Perri *et al.*, 1972; cat superior cervical ganglion, Birks, 1971; Friessen and Khatter, 1971; Pysh and Wiley, 1972, 1974). Párducz, Fehér, and Joó (1971) demonstrated an especially rapid and severe stimulation-induced depletion of synaptic vesicles in the cat ganglion following the administration of hemicholinium. These and the following observations have a bearing on the vesicle hypothesis of synaptic transmission, and on the question of release of transmitter from synaptic vesicles by exocytosis.

Quilliam and Tamarind (1973*a,b*) have found that in rat ganglia fixed within a few seconds after a period of tetanic preganglionic stimulation *in vitro* there are significantly more synaptic vesicles within a zone 0.25 μm wide adjacent to the presynaptic membrane than in unstimulated control ganglia and have suggested that this represents mobilization of synaptic vesicles preparatory to release of transmitter; this increase was prevented by the substitution of magnesium for calcium in the bathing solution. Pysh and Wiley (1972, 1974) observed that in preganglionically stimulated cat ganglia many of the synaptic endings, in addition to undergoing depletion of vesicles, became crescent-shaped or irregular in profile, extending their area of contact with dendrites and showing an increase in circumference though not in profile area; these alterations they attributed to increase of surface membrane by exocytosis of vesicles, and found that they were reversible during rest.

3. PARASYMPATHETIC GANGLIA

3.1. Ciliary Ganglion

The ultrastructure of the ciliary ganglion has been extensively investigated in birds (chick: De Lorenzo 1960, 1966; Hámori and Dyachkova, 1964; Hess, 1965; Takahashi and Hama, 1965; Taxi, 1965; Takahashi, 1967; Koenig, 1967; Hess *et al.*, 1969; pigeon: Szentágothai, 1964; Hess *et al.*, 1969; Landmesser and Pilar, 1972). Szentágothai (1964) has also examined the ciliary ganglion of the turtle.

The neurons are effectively unipolar. A single preganglionic fiber (from the oculomotor nerve) ends in relation to each neuron. In both chick and pigeon, the structure of the synapse varies according to age. Calyciform endings are present in early stages, and with increase of age there is an increasing proportion of brushlike or basketlike endings, as seen with the light microscope (Carpenter, 1911; von Lenhossek, 1911; Szentágothai, 1964). De Lorenzo (1960), examining the ultrastructure of the ganglion in chick embryos

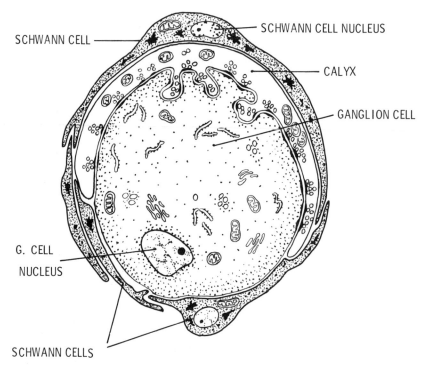

Fig. 12. Highly schematic drawing incorporating the principal fine structural details of calyciform endings in the ciliary ganglion of the chick, at late embryonic and newly hatched stages. Redrawn from De Lorenzo (1960).

and in newly hatched chicks, was able to identify both brushlike endings and calyces.

The single calyciform ending covers much of the ganglion cell surface (Fig. 12). Interdigitations of the calyx and the cell body may be present, increasing the area of apposed membranes. The calyx contains many small agranular vesicles of about 300–600 Å diameter, and these cluster toward a number of localized specializations of the apposed pre- and postsynaptic membranes, at which there is (asymmetrical) apposition of dense material, greater on the postsynaptic side. De Lorenzo (1960) found none of the larger (800–1000 Å) dense-cored vesicles which occur in sympathetic preganglionic endings (Szentágothai, 1964, found them very rarely). The calyx contains many mitochondria. The whole complex of calyx and neuron is covered by a sheath of Schwann cytoplasm, which may be multilayered, i.e., composed of "loose myelin."

Brushlike endings are similarly enveloped by "loose myelin" and consist of numerous bouton-like profiles with contents similar to those of the calyx, placed at the cell surface and on the axon hillock and separated from each other in places by glial tongues. In the adult (2 years), the endings are all of brush or basket form. Szentágothai (1964) described these in the adult pigeon: here many "intracapsular pseudodendrites" arise from the surface of the ganglion cell, including the axon hillock and initial segment of the axon, and

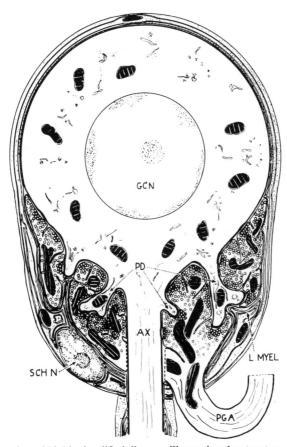

Fig. 13. Schematic and highly simplified diagram illustrating the structure of the so-called calyciform synapse in the avian and reptile ciliary ganglion. GCN, Ganglion cell nucleus; PD, pseudodendrites originating from synaptic region and axon hillock of the ganglion cell; AX, postganglionic axon; PGA, preganglionic axon; SCH N, nucleus of Schwann cell enveloping the ganglion cell and its synaptic cup, with loose myelin layers inside its plasma and some processes protruding into the synaptic cup. The synaptic terminal is no calyx, but a large number of individual terminal branches densely packed into calyciform shape and separated from each other by a system of extracellular clefts which reach the outer Schwann capsule. Pseudodendrites protrude into the synaptic cup and establish synaptic contacts also with terminals situated in its outer parts. From Szentágothai (1964). The structure of the autonomic interneuronal synapse, *Acta Neuroveg.* **26**:338.

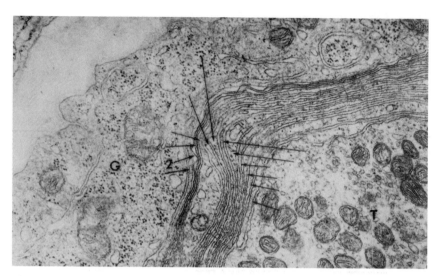

Fig. 14. Ciliary ganglion of (adult) chick. Wrappings of loose and semicompact myelin. The presynaptic terminal profile (T) is covered by many slender layers of Schwann cell cytoplasm (12 layers are indicated by arrows). G, Thick outer layer of Schwann cytoplasm. × 30,800. From Taxi (1965). Contribution à l'étude des connexions des neurones moteurs du système autonome, Masson et Cie, Paris, *Ann. Sci. Nat. Zool.* 7:413.

penetrate between the boutons. These pseudodendrites show a greater number of specialized synaptic zones than the cell body. Many desmosomelike contacts are seen between adjacent boutons, and also (in addition to synaptic contacts) between boutons and the cell body of the ganglion cell. Szentágothai's findings in the pigeon are illustrated in Fig. 13. In the turtle, he found that the situation is similar, except that there are more lamellae in the Schwann cell sheath and the pseudodendrites are smaller and fewer. Thus, as in the sympathetic ganglia, the warm-blooded species seems to have a greater emphasis on dendrites and a lesser tendency to multilayered Schwann wrappings.

Hámori and Dyachkova (1964) and Hess (1965) studied the change with age from calyx to brush form of the nerve terminals in the chick. The calyx begins to be subdivided immediately after hatching by clefts which penetrate it from the ganglion cell surface, and some of these are invaded by pseudodendrites put out from the neuron (Hámori and Dyachkova, 1964). "True" synaptic specializations are seen from 5 to 14 days after hatching. Hess (1965) noted a great increase in number and compactness of the lamellae of loose myelin (Schwann cell wrappings) between the 19-day embryo and the 4-day-old hatched chick, with only a slight increase between 4 days and adulthood (*cf.* Fig. 14). He found that at 6 months about half the neurons have calyces, while at 1–2 years virtually all have boutons. Calyces and loose myelin are confined to the neurons innervating the ciliary muscle, and only boutons are seen in relation to the smaller choroid neurons.

The findings of Takahashi and Hama (1965) in chicks of various ages from 10-day embryos to adults confirm the ultrastructure of the synaptic

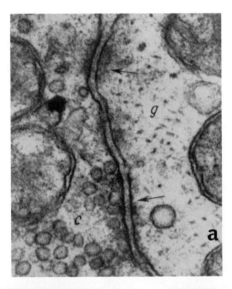

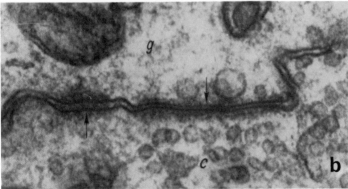

Fig. 15. a: Specialized junctions in ciliary ganglion of chick. A synaptic complex (lower arrow) and a desmosome-like structure (upper arrow) between a ciliary ganglion cell soma (g) and a calyx terminal (c). × 73,000. b: A close apposition or close junction (right-hand arrow) and a desmosome-like structure (left-hand arrow) between a ganglion cell soma (g) and a calyx terminal (c). × 78,000. From Takahashi and Hama (1965). Some observations on the fine structure of the synaptic area in the ciliary ganglion of the chick, *Z. Zellforsch.* **67**:174.

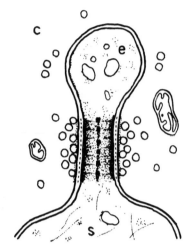

Fig. 16. Ciliary ganglion of chick. Schematic drawing of a special somatic spine synapse, as described in the text. c, Calyx terminal; s, ganglion cell soma; e, dilated end portion of spine. From Takahashi (1967). Special somatic synapses in the ciliary ganglion of the chick, *Z. Zellforsch.* **83**:70.

junction (Fig. 15) and the presence of attachment plaques (Fig. 15a, here shown between the synapsing profiles). They add an observation made also by De Lorenzo (1966), that there are occasional, localized areas (probably plaques) of close apposition between pre- and postsynaptic membranes (Fig. 15b). These are now termed "close junctions" or "gap junctions" (Gray, 1971). Here, the intermembrane interval is constant and is about 80 Å wide, not 200 Å–300 Å as at a conventional synapse or desmosome. No vesicles are accumulated in the immediately adjacent cytoplasm on either side of the gap junction, but there is a slight increase of dense material in this underlying cytoplasm. Takahashi and Hama (1965) found this type of junction rarely, in the calyx, from a few days after hatching to adulthood, but not earlier. De Lorenzo (1966) found it in 15 of 22 ganglion cells in which the plane of section passed through both the calyx and the axon hillock (out of 1000 cell profiles examined); it lay "between the terminal calyx and the axon hillock."

A further type of junction, a variant of the spine synapse, was reported later by Takahashi (1967) and by Koenig (1967) in the same ganglion. This is a synapse which forms a ring or cuff around the base of a short somatic spine (Fig. 16). A row of subsynaptic dense bodies occupies the core of the spine at the level of the synapse. This rather resembles a subsynaptic band; like the latter, it can persist after denervation (Koenig 1967). Synapses of this type have also been reported occasionally in the central nervous system.

Particular interest attached to the gap junctions at the time of their discovery because such junctions are known to be concerned with electrical rather than chemical transmission (e.g., Furshpan and Potter, 1959; Hama, 1966; Gray, 1971) and are important at certain invertebrate synapses. Examples in excitable tissues of vertebrates are found between cardiac muscle cells and between certain smooth muscle cells. In the avian ciliary ganglion, transmission is chemical at an early stage but becomes electrical for most of the neurons (those innervating the ciliary muscle) during developmental maturation (Martin and Pilar, 1963*a,b*). There would not, however, seem to be enough gap junctions to account for the electrical transmission. The large area of membrane apposition in the calyciform synapse of the immature ganglion would favor electrical transmission; paradoxically, however, the adult subdivision into boutons would favor chemical transmission. The "loose myelin" wrappings would assist electrical transmission by providing electrical insulation for the cell body and the nerve ending. In order to investigate the ultrastructural basis for the change in mode of transmission, Hess *et al.* (1969) compared the time course of the ultrastructural changes during development with the time course of the transition from chemical to electrical transmission in the pigeon and the chick. They found that the formation of the ensheathing lamellae of "loose myelin" was the change best correlated in time with the development of electrical transmission (Fig. 17). Landmesser and Pilar (1972) have recently extended these observations to

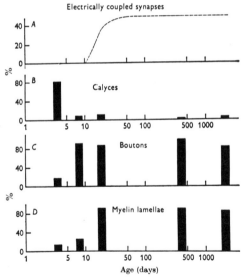

Fig. 17. Occurrence of calyces, boutons, and myelin lamellae in synaptic regions of pigeon ciliary ganglia. One hundred synapses from ganglia taken from 4-, 7-, and 16-day-old and 1- and 6-year-old birds were investigated by electron microscopy. The ordinates in bar graphs B, C, and D represent the percentage of each element. The relationship between the development of calyces, boutons, and myelin lamellae is compared to the appearance of electrically coupled synapses as shown in A. From Hess *et al.* (1969). Correlation between transmission and structure in avian ciliary ganglion synapses, *J. Physiol. Lond.* **202**:339.

earlier stages of development in the chick, finding that chemical transmission through the ganglion reaches 100% at a stage when there are few ultra-structurally identifiable synaptic contacts, with few vesicles. They describe the calyx as forming by probable coalescence of many terminal branches of a single axon, coupled with retraction of many fine processes put out by the developing neurons. They were not able to quantify gap junctions during development. A possible role for the gap junctions in the adult is suggested by De Lorenzo's observation that they lie at the base of the axon hillock. They could serve to increase the local resistance to current flow through the gap between the apposed membranes of the axon terminal and the cell body and help to ensure that the principal exchange of ions occurs across the membranes of the preterminal axon and the postganglionic axon hillock, which are both outside the sheath of "loose myelin." The function of the many, presumably cholinergic, agranular vesicles of the nerve terminal in the adult remains obscure.

3.2. Otic Ganglion

Reports on the ultrastructure of the otic ganglion in the adult rabbit (Dixon, 1966; Sangiacomo, 1969) show that it stands in sharp contrast to the highly specialized ciliary ganglion of the bird or reptile. The neurons are multipolar, having three or four short thin unbranched dendrites. They are enclosed in a continuous but not multilayered Schwann cell sheath. The synapses which they have been found to receive are mostly axodendritic; a few are axosomatic. The synaptic terminal profiles are of medium size and contain small agranular vesicles of 300–600 Å diameter, with a few larger dense-cored vesicles (1000–2500 Å) and mitochondria. The synaptic membrane cleft is about 300 Å wide, with asymmetrical membrane thickening. These nerve endings are therefore very like the preganglionic endings of sympathetic ganglia.

3.3. Ganglia of the Enteric Plexuses

The ultrastructure of the tiny ganglia of the enteric plexuses is relatively complex. Studies which have been made (principally in mammals) include those of Richardson (1958), Taxi (1958, 1965), Hager and Tafuri (1959), Tafuri (1964), Honjin et al. (1965), and more recently Baumgarten et al. (1970) and Gabella (1970, 1972). The earlier work has been reviewed by Schofield (1968); see also Burnstock (1969).

In Auerbach's (myenteric) plexus in the ileum or colon, the ganglia have a compact structure in which all cell membranes lie apposed, rather as in the neuropil of the central nervous system. They are devoid of connective tissue and also of blood vessels, and are ensheathed by basement membrane, across which all their nutrient exchanges must occur. The neurons are multipolar and receive both axodendritic and axosomatic synapses, predominantly the latter. Satellite (or "glial") cells send ensheathing processes among the neurons and the many fine unmyelinated nerve fibers within the ganglion, but there is extensive contact of nervous structures with each other and with the basement membrane. Symmetrical, desmosomelike junctions are frequently seen (Gabella, 1972). The following account of synaptic junctions is derived principally from Gabella's (1972) description of the myenteric plexus in the guinea-pig ileum.

Many vesiculated nerve endings lie immediately beneath the basement membrane and are apparently postganglionic endings, concerned in liberating transmitter substances toward the intestinal smooth muscle. They show a "hemisynaptic" clustering of agranular vesicles with dense material toward the basement membrane (or sometimes toward glial cells). The great majority of these profiles contain small round agranular vesicles of about 400–600 Å diameter with a variable number of mitochondria and in some cases a few larger dense-cored vesicles of 800–1000 Å diameter. These are thought to be cholinergic nerve endings, originating from the ganglion cells of the plexus. A smaller number of profiles having similar organelles form both axosomatic and axodendritic true synapses (with asymmetrical synaptic thickenings) within the ganglia, and these appear to be cholinergic preganglionic nerve endings.

Some of the nerve endings at the basement membrane are large and elongated and contain mostly flattened agranular vesicles, 500–700 Å long, with some larger dense-cored vesicles, mitochondria, and glycogen particles (glutaraldehyde fixation, Gabella, 1972). Occasional nerve endings of this type form synapses (with inconspicuous synaptic thickenings) upon the intraganglionic neurons, usually upon somatic spines. Gabella (1972) reported that these large nerve endings do not degenerate after the extrinsic nerves of the plexus are cut.

Two other types of nerve endings form synapses upon neurons within the plexus but are not found to have specialized endings at the basement membrane. One of these takes the form of chains of varicosities which contain a mixture of small agranular vesicles and small granular (dense-cored) vesicles, of about 400–600 Å diameter. A few larger dense-cored vesicles (of 800–1000 Å), mitochondria, and some glycogen granules are often seen; multivesicular bodies and lysosome-like structures may also be present. Profiles of this type are interpretable as adrenergic nerve terminals, and probably account for the uptake of ^{3}H-norepinephrine in the ganglia (Marks et al., 1962; Taxi and Droz, 1966). They form both axodendritic and axosomatic synapses, with asymmetrical thickenings, within the plexus. Several consecutive varicosities may synapse upon the same dendrite or upon a dendrite and the parent cell body. These are thought to represent specialized synaptic terminals of postganglionic sympathetic neurons, extrinsic to the plexus (Gabella, 1972).

The remaining type of synaptic nerve ending, similarly forming rows of varicosities, contains large dense-cored vesicles of an unusual kind ("heterogeneous granulated vesicles," Gabella, 1972). These are the "p-type" profiles of Baumgarten *et al.* (1970). They contain numerous vesicles of 900–1400 Å diameter, which have a finely granular interior of low to moderate electron density and either lack an electron-lucent halo or show a poorly defined one. These may be mixed with a few more typical dense-cored vesicles, of 800–1000 Å diameter. Small agranular vesicles are also present within the profile and form the vesicle cluster at the synapse, which has asymmetrical synaptic thickenings. Gabella (1972) found that these profiles formed axosomatic and axodendritic synapses in approximately equal numbers. He did not find them ending upon spines. In the colon, Baumgarten *et al.* (1970) found them the most frequent type of nerve ending inside the ganglia. These profiles may belong to intrinsic neurons of the plexuses. It is not known what may be contained within the unusual large dense-cored vesicles. Baumgarten *et al.* (1970) reported increased density of these vesicles after the administration of 5-hydroxydopamine, but Robinson *et al.* (1971) observed similar large dense-cored vesicles in presumed inhibitory nerve endings in toad lung and found that their appearance and incidence were not altered either by reserpine or by short-term application of 6-hydroxydopamine.

Convergence of several inputs on the neurons of Auerbach's plexus is indicated by Gabella's (1972) finding of up to three types of nerve endings synapsing upon the same neuron. Functionally, the enteric plexuses form an intricately integrated mechanism (e.g., Kottegoda, 1970), and a degree of anatomical complexity is therefore not surprising. It is advantageous that there exist such relatively well-marked distinguishing features, allowing the subdivision of the nerve endings into a number of classes, but these do not necessarily comprise all the different functional categories of endings within the plexus (*cf.* Gabella, 1972).

3.4. Cardiac Ganglion Cells

A recent study by McMahan and Kuffler (1971) of synapses upon the parasympathetic ganglion cells in the interatrial septum of the frog heart illustrates the value of precise determination of structure for the guidance and interpretation of electrophysiological and iontophoretic studies (Dennis *et al.*, 1971; Harris *et al.*, 1971) and the contributions which may be made by a range of techniques applied to the same situation.

Synaptic boutons were identified on the living neurons by interference microscopy for experimental studies, and this identification was confirmed and the synapses were studied by a number of light microscopic techniques and by electron microscopy. The synaptic arrangements resemble those in the frog sympathetic ganglion. The unipolar neurons are found each to receive up to 27 synapses from a single axon (sometimes two or three axons), coiled around the cell and ending as a spray or network of *en passant* varicosities and terminal boutons on the soma and on the proximal part of the axon. (Mean numbers of nine and 12 boutons per cell were found, by different methods, for large series of cells.) The endings are vagal and cholinergic and in ultrastructure are very similar to the preganglionic endings of the frog sympathetic ganglion, forming synapses of a similar type (see above). No other types of synapses were found on the neurons: sympathetic postganglionic axons (which reach the septum in company with the vagal preganglionic axons) end freely, as do the cholinergic axons of the ganglion cells, in chains of varicosities which lie at some little distance from the cardiac muscle cells, without close apposition of membranes.

4. SUMMARY AND COMMENT

It will be seen from this survey that studies of the ultrastructure of ganglionic junctions, beginning with the simpler ganglia, have established that certain characteristics are shared in common by known cholinergic preganglionic synapses (though they are not to be taken as exclusive to such synapses). These characteristics relate to the types and arrangement of the organelles of the cholinergic nerve endings. It has also been possible to distinguish probable adrenergic nerve endings (i.e., endings at which the transmitter is a catecholamine) by the presence of small granular vesicles, and these nerve endings have been seen to form apparently true synaptic junctions. Another apparently adrenergic synapse, involving in this case large dense-cored vesicles of a particular kind, is the efferent synapse of certain SG cells (SIF cells) of the sympathetic ganglion. With the possible exception of the ciliary ganglion, close or gap junctions do not seem to play a major part in ganglionic transmission in vertebrates.

These conclusions have been established only in conjunction with other studies, e.g., by determining the effects of denervation, and by correlation with the results of light microscopy and of pharmacological and electrophysiological studies. Application of these criteria for the identification of presynaptic profiles to the ganglia of the enteric plexuses has permitted the preliminary interpretation of the greater diversity of nerve endings which are found there.

The effect of a synaptic junction, however, depends not only on the nature of the transmitter action of the presynaptic nerve ending but also on the character, situation, and incidence of the receptor site on the postsynaptic neuron. Electron microscopy can show exactly how synapses are placed, whether on dendrites or the cell body or axon, and whether on spines, and can show the precise relationships of the membranes of the apposed profiles. Electron microscopy can also give information on the relative incidence of the various types of synapses, and even (e.g., by the more laborious method of serial reconstruction) on their absolute numbers. Additionally, it may become possible to correlate differences of receptor function with particular ultrastructural features, e.g., to find structural differences related to the distinction between nicotinic and muscarinic modes of transmission at cholinergic synapses. The patterns established so far should have predictive value, both for the interpretation of future ultrastructural studies and for the guidance of experiments involving other disciplines.

ACKNOWLEDGMENT

The author's own work in this field has been supported by a grant from the Medical Research Council of Great Britain.

5. REFERENCES

Baumgarten, H. G., Holstein, A.-F., and Owman, C., 1970, Auerbach's plexus of mammals and man: Electron microscopic identification of three different types of neuronal processes in myenteric ganglia of the large intestine from monkeys, guinea-pigs and man, Z. Zellforsch. Mikroskop. Anat. 106:376.

Birks, R. I., 1971, Effects of stimulation on synaptic vesicles in sympathetic ganglia, as shown by fixation in the presence of Mg^{2+}, J. Physiol. Lond. 216, 26P.

Björklund, A., Cegrell, L., Falck, B., Ritzén, M., and Rosengren, E., 1970, Dopamine-containing cells in sympathetic ganglia, Acta Physiol. Scand. 78:334.

Blackman, J. G., Crowcroft, P. J., Devine, C. E., Holman, M.'E., and Yonemura, K., 1969, Transmission from preganglionic fibres in the hypogastric nerve to peripheral ganglia of male guinea-pigs, J. Physiol. Lond. 201:723.

Bodian, D., 1966, Synaptic types on spinal motoneurons: An electron microscopic study, Johns Hopkins Hosp. Bull. 119:19.

Bodian, D., 1970, An electron microscopic characterization of classes of synaptic vesicles by means of controlled aldehyde fixation, J. Cell Biol. 44:115.

Burnstock, G., 1969, Evolution of the autonomic innervation of visceral and cardiovascular systems in vertebrates, Pharmacol. Revs. 21:247.

Carpenter, F. W., 1911, The ciliary ganglion of birds, Folia Neuro-biol. 5:738.

Chamley, J. H., Mark, G. E., and Burnstock, G., 1972, Sympathetic ganglia in culture. II. Accessory cells, Z. Zellforsch. mikrosk. Anat. 135, 315.

Clementi, F., Mantegazza, P., and Botturi, M., 1966, A pharmacologic and morphologic study on the nature of the dense-core granules present in the presynaptic endings of sympathetic ganglia, Internat. J. Neuropharmacol. 5:281.

Dale, H. H., 1953, Adventures in Physiology, The Wellcome Trust, London.

De Lemos, C., and Pick, J., 1966, The fine structure of thoracic sympathetic neurons in the adult rat, Z. Zellforsch. 71:189.

De Lorenzo, A. J., 1960, The fine structure of synapses in the ciliary ganglion of the chick, *J. Biophys. Biochem. Cytol.* **7**:31.

De Lorenzo, A. J., 1966, Electronmicroscopy: Tight junctions in synapses of the chick ciliary ganglion, *Science* **152**:76.

Dennis, M. J., Harris, A. J., and Kuffler, S. W., 1971, Synaptic transmission and its duplication by focally applied acetylcholine in parasympathetic neurons in the heart of the frog, *Proc. Roy. Soc. B* **177**:509.

De Ribaupierre, F., 1968, Localisation, synthèse et utilisation du glycogène dans le ganglion sympathique cervical du rat, *Brain Res.* **11**:42.

De Robertis, E., and Bennett, H. S., 1955, Some features of the submicroscopic morphology of synapses in frog and earthworm, *J. Biophys. Biochem. Cytol.* **1**:47.

De Robertis, E. D. P., 1958, Submicroscopic morphology and function of the synapse, *Exptl. Cell Res. Suppl.* **5**:347.

Diamond, J., Gray, E. G., and Yasargil, G. M., 1970, The function of the dendritic spine: An hypothesis, in: *Excitatory Synaptic Mechanisms* (P. Andersen and J. K. S. Jansen, eds.), pp. 213–222, Scand. Univ. Books, Oslo.

Dixon, J. S., 1966, The fine structure of parasympathetic nerve cells in the otic ganglia of the rabbit, *Anat. Rec.* **156**:239.

Dolivo, M., and Rouiller, C., 1969, Changes in ultrastructure and synaptic transmission in the sympathetic ganglion during various metabolic conditions, in: *Progress in Brain Research*, Vol. 31 (K. Akert and P. G. Waser, eds.), pp. 111–123, Elsevier, Amsterdam.

Elfvin, L.-G., 1963a, The ultrastructure of the superior cervical sympathetic ganglion of the cat. I. The structure of the ganglion cell processes as studied by serial sections, *J. Ultrastruct. Res.* **8**:403.

Elfvin, L.-G., 1963b, The ultrastructure of the superior cervical sympathetic ganglion of the cat. II. The structure of the preganglionic end fibres and the synapses as studied by serial sections, *J. Ultrastruct. Res.* **8**:441.

Elfvin, L.-G., 1968, A new granule-containing nerve cell in the inferior mesenteric ganglion of the rabbit, *J. Ultrastruct. Res.* **22**:37.

Elfvin, L.-G., 1971a, Ultrastructural studies on the synaptology of the inferior mesenteric ganglion of the cat. I. Observations on the cell surface of the postganglionic perikarya, *J. Ultrastruct. Res.* **37**:411.

Elfvin, L.-G., 1971b, Ultrastructural studies on the synaptology of the inferior mesenteric ganglion of the cat. II. Specialized serial neuronal contacts between preganglionic end fibers, *J. Ultrastruct. Res.* **37**:426.

Elfvin, L.-G., 1971c, Ultrastructural studies on the synaptology of the inferior mesenteric ganglion of the cat. III. The structure and distribution of the axodendritic and dendrodendritic contacts, *J. Ultrastruct. Res.* **37**:432.

Eränkö, O., and Eränkö, L., 1971, Small, intensely fluorescent granule-containing cells in the sympathetic ganglion of the rat, in: *Progress in Brain Research*, Vol. 34 (O. Eränkö, ed.), pp. 39–52, Elsevier, Amsterdam.

Eränkö, O., and Harkönen, M., 1965, Monoamine containing small cells in the superior cervical ganglion of the rat and an organ composed of them, *Acta Physiol. Scand.* **63**, 511.

Friessen, A. J. D., and Khatter, J. C., 1971, Effect of stimulation on synaptic vesicles in the superior cervical ganglion of the cat, *Experientia* **27**, 285.

Fujimoto, S., 1967, Some observations on the fine structure of the sympathetic ganglion of the toad *Bufo vulgaris japonicus*, *Arch. Histol. Jap.* **28**:313.

Furshpan, E. I., and Potter, D. D., 1959, Transmission at the giant motor synapses of the crayfish, *J. Physiol. Lond.* **145**:289.

Gabella, G., 1970, Synapses in the rat stomach and small intestine, *Experientia* **26**:619.

Gabella, G., 1972, Fine structure of the myenteric plexus in the guinea-pig ileum, *J. Anat.* **111**:69.

Gray, E. G., 1959, Axo-somatic and axo-dendritic synapses of the cerebral cortex: An electron microscopic study, *J. Anat.* **93**:420.

Gray, E. G., 1969, Electron microscopy of excitatory and inhibitory synapses: A brief review, in: *Progress in Brain Research*, Vol. 31 (K. Akert and P. G. Waser, eds.), pp. 141–156, Elsevier, Amsterdam.

Gray, E. G., 1971, The fine structural characterization of different types of synapses, in: *Progress in Brain Research*, Vol. 34 (O. Eränkö, ed.), pp. 149 160, Elsevier, Amsterdam.

Gray, E. G., and Guillery, R. W., 1966, Synaptic morphology in the normal and degenerating nervous system, *Internat. Rev. Cytol.* **19**:111.

Grillo, M. A., 1965, Synaptic morphology in the superior cervical ganglion of the rat before and after preganglionic denervation, *J. Cell Biol.* **27**:136A.

Grillo, M. A., 1966, Electron microscopy of sympathetic tissues, *Pharmacol. Rev.* **18**:387.

Hager, H., and Tafuri, W. L., 1959, Electron microscopic studies on the fine structure of the plexus myentericus (Auerbach) in the colon of the guinea-pig (*Cavia cobaya*), *Arch. Psychiat. Nervenkr.* **199**:437.

Hama, K., 1966, Studies on fine structure and function of synapses, in: *Progress in Brain Research*, Vol. 21A (T. Tokizane and J. P. Schadé, eds.), pp. 251–267, Elsevier, Amsterdam.

Hámori, J., and Dyachkova, L. N., 1964, Electron microscope studies on developmental differentiation of ciliary ganglion synapses in the chick, *Acta Biol. Acad. Sci. Hung.* **15**:213.

Hámori, J., Láng, E., and Simon, L., 1968, Experimental degeneration of the preganglionic fibers in the superior cervical ganglion of the cat: An electron microscope study, *Z. Zellforsch.* **90**:37.

Harris, A. J., Kuffler, S. W., and Dennis, M. J., 1971, Differential chemosensitivity of synaptic and extrasynaptic areas on the neuronal surface membrane in parasympathetic neurons of the frog, tested by microapplication of acetylcholine, *Proc. Roy. Soc. B* **177**:541.

Hebb, C. O., and Krnjevic, K., 1962, The physiological significance of acetylcholine, in: *Neurochemistry*, 2nd ed. (K. A. C. Elliott and J. H. Quastel, eds.), pp. 452–521, Charles C Thomas, Springfield, Ill.

Hess, A., 1965, Developmental changes in the structure of the synapse of the myelinated cell bodies of the chicken ciliary ganglion, *J. Cell Biol.* **25**(3) Part II:1.

Hess, A., Pilar, G., and Weakly, J. N., 1969, Correlation between transmission and structure in avian ciliary ganglion synapses, *J. Physiol. Lond.* **202**:339.

Hökfelt, T., 1969, Distribution of noradrenaline storing particles in peripheral adrenergic neurons as revealed by electron microscopy, *Acta Physiol. Scand.* **76**:427.

Honjin, R., Takahashi, A., Shimasaki, S., and Maruyama, H., 1965, Two types of synaptic nerve processes in the ganglia of Auerbach's plexus in mice, as revealed by electron microscopy, *J. Electronmicroscop.* **14**:43.

Huber, G. C., 1900, A contribution to the minute anatomy of the sympathetic ganglia of the different classes of vertebrates, *J. Morphol.* **16**:27.

Hunt, C. C., and Nelson, P. G., 1965, Structural and functional changes in the frog sympathetic ganglion following cutting of the presynaptic nerve fibres, *J. Physiol. Lond.* **177**:1.

Iwayama, T., and Furness, J. B., 1971, Enhancement of the granulation of adrenergic storage vesicles in drug-free solution, *J. Cell Biol.* **48**:699.

Jacobowitz, D., 1970, Catecholamine fluorescence studies of adrenergic neurones and chromaffin cells in sympathetic ganglia, *Fed. Proc.* **29**:1929.

Joó, F., Lever, J. D., Ivens, C., Mottram, D. R., and Presley, R., 1971, A fine structural and electron histochemical study of axon terminals in the rat superior cervical ganglion after acute and chronic preganglionic denervation, *J. Anat.* **110**:181.

Kanerva, L., and Teräväinen, H., 1972, Electron microscopy of the paracervical (Frankenhäuser) ganglion of the adult rat, *Z. Zellforsch. Mikroskop. Anat.* **129**:161.

Koenig, H.-L., 1967, Quelques particularités ultrastructurales des zones synaptiques dans le ganglion ciliaire du poulet, *Bull. Ass. Anat. Paris* **52**:711.

Kottegoda, S., 1970, Peristalsis of the small intestine, in: *Smooth Muscle* (E. Bülbring, A. F. Brading, A. W. Jones, and T. Tomita, eds.), pp. 525–541, Arnold, London.

Lakos, I., 1970, Ultrastructure of chronically denervated superior cervical ganglion in the cat and rat, *Acta Biol. Acad. Sci. Hung.* **21**:425.

Landmesser, L., and Pilar, G., 1972, The onset and development of transmission in the chick ciliary ganglion, *J. Physiol. Lond.* **222**:691.

Libet,, B., 1970, Generation of slow inhibitory and excitatory post-synaptic potentials, *Fed. Proc.* **29**:1945.

Marks, B. H., Samorajski, T., and Webster, E.-J., 1962, Radioautographic localization of norepinephrine-H^3 in the tissues of mice, *J. Pharmacol. Exptl. Therap.* **138**:376.

Martin, A. R., and Pilar, G., 1963a, Dual mode of synaptic transmission in the avian ciliary ganglion, *J. Physiol. Lond.* **168**:443.

Martin, A. R., and Pilar, G., 1963b, Transmission through the ciliary ganglion of the chick, *J. Physiol. Lond.* **168**:464.

Matthews, M. R., 1971, Evidence from degeneration experiments for the preganglionic origin of afferent fibres to the small granule-containing cells of the rat superior cervical ganglion, *J. Physiol. Lond.* **218**:95P.

Matthews, M. R., and Nash, J. R. G., 1970, An efferent synapse from a small granule-containing cell to a principal neurone in the superior cervical ganglion, *J. Physiol. Lond.* **210**:11P.

Matthews, M. R., and Ostberg, A., 1973, Effect of preganglionic nerve section upon the afferent innervation of the small granule-containing cells in the rat superior cervical ganglion, *Acta Physiol. Polonica* **24**:215.

Matthews, M. R., and Raisman, G., 1969, The ultrastructure and somatic efferent synapses of small granule-containing cells in the superior cervical ganglion, *J. Anat.* **105**:255.

McMahan, U. T., and Kuffler, S. W., 1971, Visual identification of synaptic boutons on living ganglion cells and of varicosities in postganglionic axons in the heart of the frog, *Proc. Roy. Soc. B* **177**:485.

Nishi, S., Soeda, H., and Koketsu, K., 1967, Release of acetylcholine from sympathetic preganglionic nerve terminals, *J. Neurophysiol.* **30**, 114.

Norberg, K.-A., and Sjöqvist, F., 1966, New possibilities for adrenergic modulation of ganglionic transmission, *Pharmacol. Rev.* **18**:743.

Ostberg, A., 1970, Granule-containing cells of the inferior mesenteric ganglion, *Proc. Aust. Physiol. Pharm. Soc.* **1**:72.

Palade, G. E., 1952, A study of fixation for electron microscopy, *J. Exptl. Med.* **95**:285.

Palade, G. E., and Palay, S. L., 1954, Electron microscope observations of interneuronal and neuromuscular synapses, *Anat. Rec.* **118**:335.

Palay, S. L., 1956, Synapses in the central nervous sytem, *J. Biophys. Biochem. Cytol. Suppl.* **2**:193.

Palay, S. L., 1958, The morphology of synapses in the central nervous system, *Exptl. Cell Res. Suppl.* **5**:275.

Pappas, G. D., and Purpura, D. P., eds, 1972, *Structure and Function of Synapses*, North-Holland Publishing Co., Amsterdam.

Párducz, Á., Fehér, O., and Joó, F., 1971, Effects of stimulation and hemicholinium (HC-3) on the fine structure of nerve endings in the superior cervical ganglion of the cat, *Brain Res.* **34**, 61.

Pellegrino de Iraldi, A., Gueudet, R., and Suburo, A. M., 1971, Differentiation between 5-hydroxytryptamine and catecholamines in synaptic vesicles, in: *Progress in Brain Research*, Vol. 34 (O. Eränkö, ed.), pp. 161–170, Elsevier, Amsterdam.

Perri, V., Sacchi, O., Raviola, E., and Raviola, G., 1972, Evaluation of the number and distribution of synaptic vesicles at cholinergic nerve-endings after sustained stimulation, *Brain Res.* **39**, 526.

Peters, A., Palay, S. L., and Webster, H. de F., 1970, *The Fine Structure of the Nervous System*, Hoeber, New York.

Pick, J., 1963, The submicroscopic organization of the sympathetic ganglion in the frog (*Rana pipiens*), *J. Comp. Neurol.* **120**:409.

Pick, J., 1970, The histology and fine structure of autonomic neurons, in: *The Autonomic Nervous System*, Chap. 5, pp. 103–185, Lipincott, Philadelphia.

Pysh, J. J., and Wiley, R. G., 1972, Morphologic alterations of synapses in electrically stimulated superior cervical ganglia of the cat, *Science, N.Y.*, **176**, 191.

Pysh, J. J., and Wiley, R. G., 1974, Synaptic vesicle depletion and recovery in cat superior cervical ganglion electrically stimulated *in vivo*, *J. Cell Biol.* **60**, 365.

Quilliam, J. P., and Tamarind, D. L., 1967, Ultrastructural changes in the superior cervical ganglion of the rat following preganglionic denervation, *J. Physiol. Lond.* **189**:13P.

Quilliam, J. P., and Tamarind, D. L., 1973a, Local vesicle populations in rat superior cervical ganglia and the vesicle hypothesis, *J. Neurocytol.* **2**, 59.

Quilliam, J. P., and Tamarind, D. L., 1973b, Some effects of preganglionic nerve stimulation on synaptic vesicle populations in the rat superior cervical ganglion, *J. Physiol. Lond.* **235**, 317.

Raisman, G., and Matthews, M. R., 1972, Degeneration and regeneration of synapses, in: *Structure and Function of Nervous Tissue*, Vol. IV (G. H. Bourne, ed.), pp. 61–104, Academic Press, New York.

Richardson, K. C., 1958, Electronmicroscopic observations on Auerbach's plexus in the rabbit, with special reference to the problem of smooth muscle innervation, *Am. J Anat.* **103**:99.

Richardson, K. C., 1966, Electron microscopic identification of autonomic nerve endings, *Nature, Lond.* **210**:756.

Robinson, P. M., McLean, J. R., and Burnstock, G., 1971, Ultrastructural identification of non-adrenergic inhibitory nerve fibers, *J. Pharmacol. Exptl. Therap.* **179**:149.

Rouiller, C., Nicolescu, P., Orci, L., and Rufener, C., 1971, The effect of anoxia on the ultrastructure of the superior cervical ganglion of the rat *in vitro*, *Virchows Arch. Abt. B. Zellpath.* **7**, 269.

Rufener, C., Orci, L., and Rouiller, C., 1971, The effect of hypoxia on the ultrastructure of the superior cervical ganglion of the rat *in vitro*, *Virchows Arch. Abt. B. Zellpath.* **7**, 293.

Sangiacomo, C. O., 1969, Submicroscopic organization of the otic ganglion of the adult rabbit, *Z. Zellforsch.* **95**:290.

Schofield, G. C., 1968, Anatomy of muscular and neural tissues in the alimentary canal, in: *Handbook of Physiology*, Vol. IV: *Motility*, Sect. 6: Alimentary Canal (C. F. Code, ed.), pp. 1579–1627, American Physiological Society, Washington, D.C.

Siegrist, G., De Ribaupierre, F. Dolivo, M., and Rouiller, C., 1966, Les cellules chromaffines des ganglions cervicaux supérieurs du rat, *J. Microscop.* **5**:791.

Siegrist, G., Dolivo, M., Dunant, Y., Foroglou-Kerameus, C., De Ribaupierre, F., and Rouiller, C., 1968, Ultrastructure and function of the chromaffin cells in the superior cervical ganglion of the rat, *J. Ultrastruct. Res.* **25**:381.

Sotelo, C., 1968, Permanence of postsynaptic specializations in the frog sympathetic ganglion cells after denervation, *Exptl. Brain Res.* **6**:294.

Szentágothai, J., 1964, The structure of the autonomic interneuronal synapse, *Acta Neuroveg.* **26**:338.

Tafuri, W. L., 1964, Ultrastructure of the vesicular component in the intramural nervous system of the guinea-pig's intestines, *Z. Naturforsch.* **19B**:622.

Takahashi, K., 1967, Special somatic spine synapses in the ciliary ganglion of the chick. *Z. Zellforsch.* **83**:70.

Takahashi, K., and Hama, K., 1965, Some observations on the fine structure of the synaptic area in the ciliary ganglion of the chick, *Z. Zellforsch.* **67**:174.

Tamarind, D. L., and Quilliam, J. P., 1971, Synaptic organization and other ultrastructural features of the superior cervical ganglion of the rat, kitten and rabbit, *Micron* **2**, 204.

Taxi, J., 1957, Étude au microscope électronique de ganglions sympathiques des mammifères, *Compt. Rend. Acad. Sci. Paris* **245**:564.

Taxi, J., 1958, Sur la structure du plexus d'Auerbach de la souris, étudié au microscope électronique, *Compt. Rend. Acad. Sci. Paris* **246**:1922.

Taxi, J., 1961, Étude de l'ultrastructure des zones synaptiques dans les ganglions sympathiques de la grenouille, *Compt. Rend. Acad. Sci. Paris* **252**:174.

Taxi, J., 1964, Étude de certaines synapses interneuronales du système nerveux autonome, *Acta Neuroveg,* **26**:360.

Taxi, J., 1965, Contribution a l'étude des connexions des neurones moteurs du système nerveux autonome, *Ann. Sci. Nat. Zool.* **7**:413.

Taxi, J., and Droz, B., 1966, Étude de l'incorporation de noradrénaline-^{3}H (NA-^{3}H) et de 5-hydroxytryptophane-^{3}H (5-HTP-^{3}H) dans les fibres nerveuses du canal déférent et de l'intestin, *Compt. Rend. Acad. Sci. Paris D* **263**:1237.

Taxi, J., Gautron, J., and L'Hermite, P., 1969, Données ultrastructurales sur une éventuelle modulation adrénergique de l'activité du ganglion cervical supérieur du rat, *Compt. Rend. Acad. Sci. Paris D* **269**:1281.

Uchizono, K., 1964, On different types of synaptic vesicles in the sympathetic ganglia of amphibia, *Jap. J. Physiol.* **14**:210.

Uchizono, K., 1965, Characteristics of excitatory and inhibitory synapses in the central nervous system of the cat, *Nature Lond.* **207**:642.

Valdivia, O., 1971, Methods of fixation and the morphology of synaptic vesicles, *J. Comp. Neurol.* **142**:257.

von Forssmann, W. G., 1964, Studien über den Feinbau des Ganglion cervicale superius der Ratte, *Acta Anat.* **59**:106.

von Lenhossek, M., 1911, Das Ganglion ciliare der Vögel, *Arch. Mikroskop. Anat.* **76**:745.

Watanabe, H., 1970, Adrenergic nerve endings in the peripheral autonomic ganglion, *Experientia* **26**:69.

Watanabe, H., 1971, Adrenergic nerve elements in the hypogastric ganglion of the guinea-pig, *Am. J. Anat.* **130**:305.

Williams, T. H., 1967, Electron microscopic evidence for an autonomic interneuron, *Nature Lond.* **214**:309.

Williams, T. H., and Palay, S. L., 1969, Ultrastructure of the small neurons in the superior cervical ganglion, *Brain Res.* **15**:17.

Wolfe, D. E., Potter, L. T., Richardson, K. C., and Axelrod, J., 1962, Localizing tritiated norepinephrine in sympathetic axons by electron microscopic autoradiography, *Science* **138**:440.

Woods, R. I., 1969, Acrylic aldehyde in sodium dichromate as a fixative for identifying catecholamine storage sites with the electron microscope, *J. Physiol. Lond.* **203**:35P.

Yamamoto, T., 1963, Some observations on the structure of the sympathetic ganglion of bullfrog, *J. Cell Biol.* **16**:159.

Yokota, R., 1973, The granule-containing cell somata in the superior cervical ganglion of the rat, as studied by a serial sampling method for electron microscopy, *Z. Zellforsch. mikrosk. Anat.* **141**, 331.

Junctional Transmission—Function

Chapter 7(i)

Neuromuscular Transmission— Presynaptic Factors

John I. Hubbard

Department of Physiology, Medical School
University of Otago
Dunedin, New Zealand

1. SYNTHESIS, STORAGE, AND RELEASE OF ACETYLCHOLINE

There is an enormous body of evidence indicating that ACh is synthesized and stored in, and released from, motor nerve terminals. Release of ACh from nerve terminals occurs spontaneously in multimolecular amounts (quanta) which can be detected by the resulting depolarization (m.e.p.p.) of the muscle membrane at the end plate. Nerve impulses accelerate quantal release. The quantal nature of release is currently thought to arise because ACh is stored in, and released from, the synaptic vesicles found in great number in nerve terminals (vesical hypothesis). Quantal release is then the release of the contents of vesicles into a synaptic cleft (reviewed by Martin, 1966; Hubbard, 1970, 1973).

1.1. Synthesis of ACh

It is now well established that ACh is synthesized in motoneurons and their axons but not in muscle. ACh derived from innervated muscles comes from the motor nerves, and the much smaller production of ACh in denervated muscles comes from the degenerating remnants of their nerves (Hebb *et al.*, 1964; Tucek, 1968).

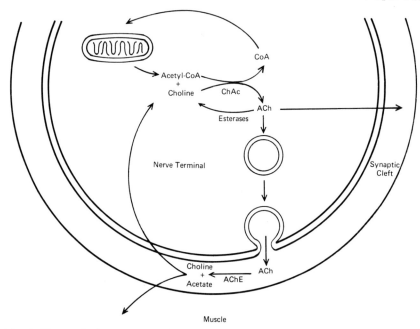

Fig. 1. The synthesis, storage, and release of ACh. Arrows indicate various metabolic cycles which interlock in the synthesis of ACh. Release of ACh into the synaptic cleft is indicated in quantal form from a vesicle and in nonquantal form (arrow). Choline uptake from the synaptic cleft by nerve terminals and muscles is indicated by arrows crossing the nerve terminal and muscle boundaries.

As Fig. 1 shows, ACh is synthesized by combination of choline and acetyl coenzyme A (acetyl CoA) catalyzed by the enzyme choline-*o*-acetyltransferase (ChAc, EC. 2.3.1.6) (Berg, 1965*a*,*b*), which is cytoplasmic and not associated with any particular subcellular organelle (Whittaker, 1965; Fonnum, 1968, 1970). This process takes place most actively in the region of motor nerve terminals (Hebb, 1963). In motoneurons, ChAc is at its highest concentration in the vicinity of motor nerve terminals (Hebb *et al.*, 1964; Potter, 1970) and it accumulates above and disappears below ligature sites on motor nerves (Hebb and Waites, 1956; Hebb and Silver, 1961; Tucek, 1968; Ekstrom and Emmelin, 1971). The findings are entirely consistent with formation in motoneuron bodies and transport to nerve terminals. Studies of the vagus and hypoglossal nerves indicate a passage time of about 10 days (Frizell *et al.*, 1970). Recent studies of isolated segments of the same nerves suggest, however, that a small fraction of ChAc is transported more rapidly (Fonnum *et al.*, 1973). Calculations based on this rapid transport suggest that the life span of the enzyme molecules in nerve terminals is 16–21 days.

There is still some uncertainty as to the source of the acetyl groups of

ACh. Acetyl CoA is formed from pyruvate in mitochondria (De Duve *et al.*, 1962) and cannot penetrate the mitochondrial membrane (Lowenstein, 1964). Two mechanisms for translocation of acetyl groups from mitochondria to the cytoplasm appear possible. One is that acetyl CoA is condensed with oxalo-acetate by citrate synthase (EC. 4.1.3.7.) to yield citrate. Citrate would diffuse to the cytoplasm, and extramitochondrial acetyl CoA could be formed from citrate through the action of ATP citrate lyase (EC. 4.1.3.8). Alternatively, intramitochondrial acetyl CoA would be hydrolyzed to acetate by acetyl CoA hydrolase (EC. 3.1.2.1.), and acetate upon transportation to the cytoplasm would be reconverted to acetyl CoA through the action of acetyl CoA synthetase (EC. 6.2.1.1.). Related studies of motor nerve endings have not been made, but in tissue slices, homogenates, and nerve-ending fractions of brain, citrate appeared a better source of acetyl groups for ACh than acetate (Bartley *et al.*, 1965; Tucek, 1967; Sollenberg and Sorbo, 1970). In rabbit brain *in vitro* (Tucek, 1967) and in rat brain *in vivo* upon intracisternal injection (Tucek and Cheng, 1970), acetate was the better source.

The store of choline in motor nerves is small, being sufficient to synthesize only about 8–9% of the total ACh store (Potter, 1970). The large amounts required for ACh synthesis in motor nerve terminals are derived, as Fig. 1 indicates, from sources outside nerve terminals by a carrier mechanism which can be inhibited by the drug α,α-dimethylethanolamino-4,4'-biacetophenone (hemicholinum-3, HC-3) and its analogs (Saekens and Stoll, 1965; Wallach *et al.*, 1967; Chang and Lee, 1970; Potter, 1970). The ultimate source of choline is presumably the plasma. In cats, dogs, rabbits, and man, the plasma choline concentration lies between 5 and 10 μM. Tests over a 6-month period in humans showed that plasma choline was maintained at a fairly constant level (Bligh, 1952).

Recent studies on the rat phrenic nerve–diaphragm preparation *in vitro* indicate that the phrenic nerve terminals have such an effective uptake system that nearly half the choline produced by ACh hydrolysis is regained (Potter, 1970). Most importantly, this uptake system is greatly accelerated by nerve stimulation. Indeed, so effective is the system that ACh synthesis could keep pace with release when the preparation was stimulated at a rate of 20 Hz for 5 min (Potter, 1970). As Fig. 1 indicates, some of the choline not taken up by nerve terminals is accumulated by muscle fibers which have a transport system similar to that found in terminals (Adamic, 1970; Chang and Lee, 1970).

ACh is probably not normally transported into nerve terminals. Rat motor nerve terminals, for instance, take up ACh only in the presence of eserine, a blocker of AChE action (Potter, 1970). The presence of eserine presumably allows the competition between ACh and choline for uptake sites to shift in favor of ACh.

1.2. Storage and Release

Exploration of the extent, lability, and nature of ACh stores has been a multidisciplinary pursuit. The ACh content of motor nerves and their terminals is substantial and does not normally change on nerve stimulation despite the release of ACh (Potter, 1970). There is thus an ACh store which is effectively replenished by synthetic mechanisms.

1.2.1. Releasable ACh and the Vesicle Hypothesis

If ACh synthesis is blocked by, for instance, using HC-3 to interfere with choline uptake, then the amount of ACh which can be released by stimulation of rat motor nerve terminals is limited to some 300,000 quanta, measured as m.e.p.p.'s or quantal content of e.p.p.'s (Elmqvist and Quastel, 1965a).

Several lines of evidence suggest that the quantal store of releasable ACh corresponds to the population of vesicles in nerve terminals. First, the number of vesicles in axon terminals at an end plate (about 3×10^5 in the frog, Birks et al., 1960) is about the same as the number of releasable quanta. Second, if frog nerve–muscle preparations in vitro are exposed to β-bungarotoxin (Chen and Lee, 1970) or to black widow spider venom or to hypo-osmotic solutions (Longnecker et al., 1970), a total of about 300,000 quanta is spontaneously released. After this, release stops. Electron microscopy of toxin, venom, and hypo-osmotically treated nerve terminals at this point shows them to be devoid of vesicles (Chen and Lee, 1970; Clark et al., 1972).

This would be very strong evidence for the identity of the vesicle and quantal stores if the reasons for vesicle disappearance were understood and were related to the release of ACh. Such evidence is available. As Fig. 2 shows, it is now thought that synaptic vesicles become part of the terminal membrane after release of their contents. They are then reformed, by membrane invagination, to appear as coated vesicles (Fig. 2) in nerve terminals. Coated vesicles fuse to form cisternae (Fig. 2) which bud off synaptic vesicles.

In part, this understanding has come about from a reappraisal of the coated or complex vesicle (Fig. 2). Such vesicles are formed by exocytosis in nerve and other cells (Roth and Porter, 1964; Nickel et al., 1967; Bunt, 1969; Nagasawa et al., 1970) and consist of a smooth-walled vesicle, apparently identical with the synaptic vesicle, surrounded by a shell (Fig. 3) formed of material arranged in a hexagonal array. This outer shell gives the appearance of bristles when cut in sections (Kaneseki and Kadota, 1969). The evidence (Heuser and Miledi, 1971; Heuser and Reese, 1972) that links coated vesicles, cisternae, and synaptic vesicles in the order illustrated in Fig. 2 comes from electron microscopy after labeling with the electron-dense stain horseradish peroxidase (HRP). Frog nerve–muscle preparations in vitro were incubated

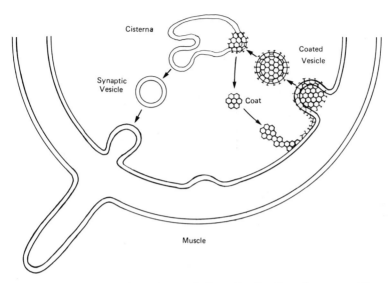

Fig. 2. The life history of vesicles. Arrows indicate the direction of movement (based on Heuser and Reese, 1972). Note that the diagram shows a nerve terminal lying in a groove in a muscle surface (primary groove) which has a secondary groove opposite a release site. The nerve terminal contains synaptic vesicles formed by outpouching from a cisterna, formed in its turn by fusion of coated vesicles (the coat is detached on fusion).

with HRP in conditions favoring ACh release, such as a raised bathing KCl concentration, and fixed after varying times of incubation. After short incubation times, there was a loss of synaptic vesicles, an increase in the membrane lining the synaptic cleft, and the appearance of HRP in complex vesicles forming the nerve terminal membrane. Fixation at later times showered HRP in cisternae in synaptic vesicles. It was possible to show that the HRP was later released from synaptic vesicles. These experiments were done at 0°C, and certain of the steps, particularly the formation of cisternae, are not prominent at higher temperatures, presumably because they then occur more quickly.

A mass of corollary evidence is available The fall in vesicle numbers during transmitter release (Hubbard and Kwanbunbumpen, 1968; Korneliussen et al., 1972), the increase in terminal membrane area found in preparations fixed during transmitter release (Heuser and Miledi, 1971; Clark et al., 1972), and the prominence of coated vesicles in such stimulated preparations (Csillik and Bense, 1971; Korneliussen et al., 1972) together with the ability of both synaptic and coated vesicles to apparently become labeled with HRP (Birks, 1966; Zacks and Saito, 1969) are all explained.

Direct evidence that vesicles or motor nerve terminals contain ACh has been difficult to obtain because nerve terminals are only a small part of a nerve–muscle preparation. Such subcellular fractionation experiments as have been done in nerve–muscle preparations (Potter, 1970; Whittaker, 1970) are compatible with ACh being both in vesicles and in the cytoplasm. Extensive experiments have been carried out with nerve terminals of the electric organ of *Torpedo* (Sheridan *et al.*, 1966; Israel *et al.*, 1968). When the fractionation experiments were carried out in media with the normal osmotic pressure of elasmobranch blood, it was found that the vesicle fraction contained no less than 80% of the ACh of the preparation (Israel *et al.*, 1968).

Similarly, the evidence that the amount of ACh in a quantum is congruent with the ACh content of vesicles is indirect and not definitive. The vesicles in motor nerve terminals have a featureless internal matrix and a 4- to 5-nm-thick wall (Birks *et al.*, 1960), and from electron microscopic examination of serial sections they appear to be spherical (Andersson-Cedergren, 1959). Their mean diameter in rat and mouse nerve terminals is about 45 nm (Andersson-Cedergren, 1959; Jones and Kwanbunbumpen, 1970), and their volume at rat terminals is $5.2 \times 10^4 \, nm^3$ (Jones and Kwanbunbumpen, 1970). If this volume contained a saturated solution of ACh, allowing for the wall thickness there would be 54,000 molecules (Canepa, 1964, and personal communication).

Direct estimates of the ACh content and the vesicle number in preparations of nerve terminals of electroplax suggest that vesicles there contain an ACh solution osmotic (0.4–0.5 M) with plasma (Sheridan *et al.*, 1966). Calculations of the ACh content of vesicles in rat motor nerve terminals based on the total ACh of nerve–muscle preparations and reasonable assumptions about the number of terminals and the percentage of terminal volume occupied by vesicles suggest a similar concentration in the smaller rat vesicles (Potter, 1970). There would then be about 4000 molecules in a rat vesicle.

Estimates of the number of ACh molecules in a quantum range between 10^5, which is the number which must be applied to imitate an m.e.p.p. (Miledi, 1961), and a few thousand, which follows from consideration of the membrane noise arising from the depolarization produced by individual ACh molecules. It is uncertain whether these elementary events arise from reaction of one ACh molecule or of more than one (Katz and Miledi, 1972). More accurate estimates have been made by measuring the amount of ACh released, per nerve impulse, from a nerve–muscle preparation; then, by dividing successively by the number of junctions and by the number of quanta released per impulse, one obtains the ACh content of a quantum. The best experiments have been made with the rat diaphragm, in which the number of junctions is known with some precision (Krnjević and Mitchell, 1961). Estimates of ACh release have progressively improved as experimenters have reduced both the stimulation rate and the number of nerve impulses, presumably because there was an increase in the percentage of impulses reaching axon terminals and releasing transmitter (Krnjević and Miledi, 1959). The estimates of release in molecules ACh/junctions/impulse have thus increased from 0.7–4.26 × 10^5 (Emmelin and MacIntosh, 1956; MacIntosh, 1959) to 14 × 10^5 (Straughan, 1960) to 90 × 10^5 (Krnjević and Mitchell, 1961). All the estimates quoted are for 38°C, and the last is for 1500 impulses at 2–5 Hz. Repetition of these experiments using radioactive ACh assay and collecting the ACh released by only 360 impulses at 2 Hz has given similar results (Potter, 1970).

These results depend on knowledge of the mean quantal release. Most authors have used a value of only 20 quanta per impulse (Krnjević and Mitchell, 1961), but more recent estimates made in the absence of d-tubocurarine are of the order of 100–300 quanta per impulse at stimulation rates of 2–5 Hz (Hubbard and Wilson, 1973). Using these higher figures with Potter's (1970) estimate of 4.2 ± 10^6 molecules of ACh per impulse per terminal for rat diaphragms in the absence of curare at 20°C, there are between 12,000 and 21,000 molecules of ACh per quantum, which can easily be packed into a vesicle.

It seems possible that ACh may be packed in vesicles together with proteins and ATP, which may play some part in ACh concentration. Recent studies of electroplaque vesicles show them to contain soluble proteins and ATP. Similar constituents in vertebrate vesicles may be inferred from the finding that ACh-binding acidic proteins and ATP are released, together with ACh, upon nerve stimulation of rat and mouse nerve–muscle preparations *in vitro* (Musick and Hubbard, 1972; Silinsky and Hubbard, 1973).

1.2.2. Divisions of the Releasable ACh

There is reason to believe that not all the 3 × 10^5 quanta in the releasable store have the same chance of release. This conclusion was first drawn from the finding that e.p.p. amplitude (which reflects e.p.p. quantal content) declines exponentially during nerve stimulation at frequencies greater than 0.1 Hz to reach a plateau amplitude, which is frequency dependent (Liley and North, 1953). The rate of stimulation can be increased to a frequency at which the quantal release per unit time is constant while the volley ouput is frequency dependent (Hubbard, 1963; Elmqvist and Quastel, 1965b; Capek et al., 1971). Similar experiments assaying ACh release directly indicate that during unphysiological rates of stimulation the amount of ACh released per impulse is not maintained but falls to a level at which the ouput per minute is constant (Potter, 1970). These observations can readily be explained using the model similar to that put forward by Birks and MacIntosh (1961) to explain release of ACh from ganglia (Fig. 3). There are a small (15–20%)

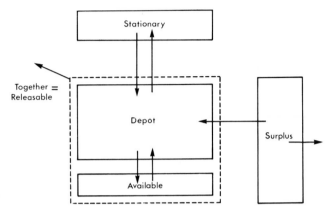

Fig. 3. The ACh stores in a motor nerve terminal. Arrows indicate the interchange of ACh between compartments or its movement into the synaptic cleft. "Stationary" indicates that part of the ACh is not released by nerve impulses. The releasable ACh (dotted box) is divided into a fraction immediately available for release and a larger fraction used when the available fraction is depleted. "Surplus" indicates the store that appears in the presence of anticholinesterases able to penetrate nerve terminal membranes.

immediately available fraction (Fig. 3) and a large depot fraction (Fig. 3), which can be mobilized more slowly.

The reason for putting these fractions in series, as Fig. 3 indicates rather than in parallel is the finding that the minute output of ACh in response to stimulation at high rates is maintained, but not the volley ouput (release per nerve impulse). There is no fall in the total ACh store under these conditions and there is no failure of the release mechanism, for the output of ACh/min can be maintained indefinitely (Potter, 1970). Under these conditions with the minute ouput independent of frequency of stimulation, there must be some process, independent of the spacing of volleys or of the rate of ACh synthesis, which limits ACh release. This is most simply explained as movement of ACh from the depot to the available fraction.

More recent findings which may be interpreted in terms of the model shown in Fig. 3 are that newly synthesized ACh, recognized by its labeling with radioactive choline, is released more than twice as rapidly as unlabeled, presumably preformed, ACh (Potter, 1970).

The morphological counterparts of the two fractions of releasable ACh (Fig. 3) are not yet known with certainty. As electron micrographs show, some vesicles are so close to the membrane that their contents could plausibly be released by a nerve impulse while others are at such a distance that Brownian movement could not possibly allow them to approach the membrane and release their contents within the available time (approximately 0.2 ms at

37°C, Hubbard and Schmidt, 1963). Accordingly, vesicles adjacent to the axon terminal have been proposed as morphological counterparts of the immediately available (Fig. 3) and newly synthesized store of ACh (reviewed by Hubbard, 1973). It is found that this population of vesicles does vary in magnitude with conditions of release, as would be expected from the model (Fig. 3). Under conditions in which the rate of release is slow (such as would be obtained by two- to tenfold acceleration of spontaneous frequency), electron micrographs showed that only vesicles close to the membrane were depleted; the rest of the vesicle population was not affected. When the rate of release was increased a hundredfold or more, both classes of vesicles were depleted (Hubbard and Kwanbunbumpen, 1968).

Recent experiments (Whittaker, 1971) with subcellular fractions from the *Torpedo* electric organ also suggest a two-compartment model of the releasable store. It was found that after exposure to radioactive choline and subsequent fractionation, two labeled fractions could be distinguished. The most highly labeled fraction contained vesicles and presynaptic membranes. These vesicles could correspond to the available fraction (Fig. 3) containing the most recently synthesized ACh. The other fraction, less highly labeled, was shown by electron microscopy to consist solely of vesicles. These vesicles presumably could form the depot (Fig. 3).

1.2.3. Stationary ACh

Assay of nerve–muscle preparations for ACh after HC-3 treatment and stimulation until release fails always reveals some remaining ACh. Generally, as Fig. 3 indicates, this is some 20% of the amount found in control preparations. As such assays have perforce to include intramuscular nerves as well as their terminals and these intramuscular nerves are thought to contain about 25% of the total ACh in an innervated rat diaphragm, it seems plausible to assume that most of the nonreleasable or stationary ACh is extraterminal, Potter (1970) has shown that all the ACh in rat diaphragm phrenic nerve preparations becomes equally labeled (with radioactive choline) upon being incubated for long times so that it must be assumed that terminal and extraterminal ACh are in dynamic equilibrium (arrows in Fig. 3).

1.2.4. Surplus ACh

An extra ACh compartment appears in the presence of anticholinesterases such as eserine, which can penetrate nerve terminals (Potter, 1970). Under these circumstances, the amount of ACh in nerve–muscle preparations can approximately double. When the eserine is withdrawn, this ACh, which as Fig. 3 indicates is termed "surplus," disappears, presumably because it is hydrolyzed by eserine-sensitive cholinesterases in the cytoplasm (Fig. 1). The amount of ACh released following brief nerve stimulation is not changed in the presence of surplus ACh, but the ACh release rate is better maintained during prolonged nerve stimulation when surplus ACh is present (Potter, 1970). These observations suggest that releasable and surplus stores are separate but that surplus ACh can contribute to the releasable store (Fig. 3, arrow). Presumably, the surplus ACh, formed in the presence of eserine, represents an enormous increase in cytoplasmic ACh due to inhibition of cytoplasmic esterases.

1.2.5. Sites of ACh Release

Anatomical and physiological evidence suggests that release sites are specialized areas and that release in quantal form occurs only at these sites. First, vesicles are not randomly arranged in motor nerve terminals but are aggregated in relation to densely staining structures in the terminal membrane which resemble cardboard egg containers. At frog motor nerve terminals, for instance, there are two parallel rows of three or four vesicles running in bands across terminal axons (Couteaux and Pécot-Dechavassine, 1970). Electron micrographs of frog and rat nerve terminals show accumulation of vesicles in these structures at approximately 0.7–1 μm intervals. Opposite each accumulation at rat, mouse, and frog terminals lies the opening of a fold in the muscle membrane (Birks et al., 1960; Hubbard and Kwanbunbumpen, 1968; Couteaux and Pécot-Dechavassine, 1970). Presumably, the recently discovered correlation of end plate size with number of quanta released from that end plate by nerve impulses has its source in this uniform spacing of presumed releasing sites (Kuno et al., 1971).

Second, reexamination of the mathematical character of quantal release, both spontaneous and in response to nerve impulses, has shown certain features which are most easily explicable in terms of release from a finite number of release sites, presumably the sites of vesicle aggregation. To a first approximation, spontaneous quantal release is a stochastic process of the Poisson type (Gage and Hubbard, 1965). Del Castillo and Katz (1956) suggested that such a process could arise from the random bombardment of a nerve terminal membrane by synaptic vesicles, each with a small probability of release. However, when the vesicle population is greatly depleted by nerve stimulation in the presence of HC-3 (Jones and Kwanbunbumpun, 1970), the process remains Poisson (Gage and Hubbard, 1965), which is surprising. An alternative also suggested by Del Castillo and Katz (1956) is that there are a finite number of release sites, each randomly active. Sophisticated computer analysis enables the testing of these alternatives. It is found that spontaneous quantal release deviates in one important respect from a Poisson process. A property of a Poisson process is that its mean and variance are the same. M.e.p.p. frequency at the rat neuromuscular junction, however, does not show this characteristic but deviates in the manner expected if spontaneous release were produced by a random phasing of the activity of a number of release sites (Hubbard and Jones, 1973). Computer simulation of such a situation shows that, as the number of sites increases, the approximation of the mean-to-variance curve to that expected for a Poisson process improves. It follows that if an increased rate of release brought more sites into action, the variance-to-mean ratio should approach unity. However, raising of the rate of release by the exhibition of an increased bathing $[K^+]_o$ at rat neuromuscular junctions *in vitro* showed no significant change in variance-to-mean ratio in each of five experiments, suggesting that the number of sites was unchanged and that activity at each site increased (Hubbard and Jones, 1973).

A similar argument for release sites also arises from consideration of quantal release evoked by nerve impulses. It has appeared anomalous that the number of quanta released by serial nerve impulses should form a Poisson series despite the large number of quanta released. It would be expected that as the probability of release increased—as happens when the $[Ca^{2+}]_o$ is raised (Hubbard *et al.*, 1971)—the release properties would be better described by binomial statistics rather than Poisson statistics. Very accurate determinations of the quantal content of e.p.p.'s recently made by Rahamimoff and his colleagues at the frog neuromuscular junction (Lermer, 1971, and personal communication) indicate indeed that, in the presence of $[Ca^{2+}]$ of 1.8 mM and above, binomial rather than the Poisson statistics do apply. The statistical properties of release can thus be completely explained by postulating the existence of release sites.

2. THE ACCELERATION OF RELEASE BY NERVE IMPULSES

ACh release by nerve impulses is most fruitfully considered as a transitory but powerful, Ca^{2+}-dependent acceleration of an ongoing process manifest as spontaneous release (Liley, 1956).

2.1. The Role of the Nerve Impulse

The nerve impulse not only initiates the acceleration of release, it is also, by virtue of its amplitude and time course, a potent determinant of the magnitude and time course of evoked release. These effects of a nerve impulse are summarized by the term "depolarization–secretion coupling."

2.1.4. The Time Interval between Depolarization and Secretion

Liley (1956) suggested that secretion followed depolarization in an "instantaneous" manner. The introduction of techniques for stimulation of and recording from motor nerve terminals *in vitro* (Hubbard and Schmidt, 1963; Katz and Miledi, 1965*a*) has enabled the testing of Liley's hypothesis, with decisive results. Transmitter release is not linked instantaneously to nerve terminal depolarization. For instance, depolarizing pulses of less than 0.4 ms duration applied to frog motor nerve terminals at 5°C evoke ACh release starting after the end of the pulse (Katz and Miledi, 1967*b*). Again, transmitter release by an action potential is prevented if a hyperpolarizing pulse is applied to a nerve terminal during the descending phase of that action potential (Katz and Miledi, 1967*b*).

When the probability of quantal release was greatly reduced, synaptic delays recorded at the same active end plate spot showed considerable fluctuation (Katz and Miledi, 1965*b*). Extracellular recording from a frog end plate at 20°C, for instance, showed a modal synaptic delay of 0.75 ms, but 50% of the delays were within ± 0.5 ms of the mode and the rest were spread out with apparent exponentially decaying probability for a further 3 ms. There are indications, indeed, that a small increase in the probability of quantal release persists for much longer after a nerve impulse. The probability of spontaneous appearance of a single quantum (m.e.p.p.) can be measured at various intervals after a nerve impulse and compared with measurements from similar time intervals before the nerve impulses. In agreement with the distribution of synaptic delays, such experiments reveal a maximum probability of release shortly after the impulse, but also a long tail, which decays over a 100-ms period. After two or more impulses, these effects appear to cumulate and become much more prominent (Hubbard, 1963.

Presumably, the finding (Katz and Miledi, 1967*b*; Benoit and Mambrini, 1970) that the magnitude of release increases in an S-shaped way as a depolarizing pulse applied to nerve terminals is lengthened (Fig. 4A) relates to this temporal dispersion of release. Katz and Miledi (1967*b*), for instance, have plausibly suggested that a long depolarization may be considered as the aggregate of the number of shorter depolarizations, each with an accelerating effect on release, which outlasts the provoking pulse and can sum with the effects of the following pulses.

Close examination of the events involved in synaptic delay has shown that the variation of synaptic delays is a property of the processes set in train during this interval. A powerful tool in this investigation has been the temperature dependence of synaptic delay. It has been known since 1923 (Samojloff, 1925) that the Q_{10} for stimulus–response intervals at neuromuscular junctions lies between 2 and 3. Reexamination shows that conduction in fine nerve terminals has a Q_{10} of 1.5–2, while the true synaptic delay has a Q_{10} greater than 3 (2–19°C). For instance, the minimum synaptic delay recorded extracellularly at a frog junction at one end plate spot varied between 7 ms (2.0°C) and 0.5 ms (20°C), while the temporal dispersion of transmitter release was also increased by lowering the temperature (Katz and Miledi, 1965d). The events following secretion—presumably diffusion of ACh across the synaptic cleft and ACh–receptor combination—do not have a high Q_{10}. Careful calculations (Del Castillo and Katz, 1955a; Eccles and Jaeger, 1957; Katz and Miledi, 1965b) indicate that at the frog end plate only about 50 μs of the true synaptic delay can be attributed to diffusion of ACh across the cleft and this process would not be expected to have a high Q_{10}. Further, when ACh is iontophoresed on the subsynaptic membrane an ACh potential develops with a latency of only 100–200 μs at 20°C or 170–300 μs at 2.5–6°C (Katz and Miledi, 1965d). The synaptic delay therefore has other components at frog junctions which take place after depolarization and before secretion and last between 0.25 ms (20°C) and 6.75 ms (2°C).

2.2. The Role of Ca^{2+}

Depolarization–secretion coupling is currently explained by the hypothesis that depolarization of nerve terminals permits the entry of Ca^{2+} and that this Ca influx in some as yet unexplained way accelerates transmitter release.

2.2.1. The Need for Ca^{2+} and the Timing of Ca Action

Recent reviews (e.g., Hubbard, 1970; Baker, 1972) have amply documented the absolute need for the presence of extracellular Ca^{2+} in a minimum concentration of about 10^{-4} M for any form of depolarization to release ACh from nerve terminals. This requirement is not connected with the propagation of action potentials into nerve terminals, for in the condition of Ca deprivation action potentials can still be recorded from nerve terminals even though these potentials release no ACh (Katz and Miledi, 1965c). Indeed, the requirement of Ca for action potential generation is some 10^3 times less than the Ca requirement for depolarization–secretion coupling (Frankenhaeuser, 1957).

These findings indicate a role for Ca^{2+} in the processes set in train by a nerve impulse. A clue to the nature of this action was given by the finding that Ca^{2+} must be present before depolarization of nerve terminals if this depolarization is to evoke secretion (Katz and Miledi, 1967c). In the most elegant of these experiments, nerve impulses were blocked by exposing frog sartorius preparations to TTX. Transmitter release was then effected by a brief depolarizing pulse applied directly to nerve terminals. The experiments were performed in the presence of a Ca-deficient medium so that the pulse only occasionally released transmitter. Calcium ions were applied electrophoretically, at varying intervals before and after depolarizing pulses. Release was accelerated only if the Ca^{2+} was applied before the depolarization. Calcium ions applied immediately after the depolarizing pulse did not influence release. Experimental difficulties prevented simultaneous application of Ca^{2+} and depolarization and limited the minimum interval to 50 μms.

2.2.1. Specificity for Ca^{2+}. The actions of Ca^{2+} in depolarization–secretion coupling appear specific, for only Sr^{2+} can replace Ca^{2+} sufficiently to allow release of transmitter by nerve impulses, and this action is about 100 times less effective than that of Ca at the same molar concentration (Dodge *et al.*, 1969; Meiri and Rahamimoff, 1971). The reported replacement of Ca^{2+} by Ba^{2+} (Blioch *et al.*, 1968) is a transient effect which can be explained by the depolarizing action of Ba^{2+} which allows calcium release from membrane (Laskowski and Thies, 1972).

2.2.2. The Acceleration of Calcium Action by Depolarization

As Fig. 5A indicates, m.e.p.p. frequency is accelerated by raising the bathing $[Ca^{2+}]$ (Boyd and Martin, 1956; Hubbard, 1961). However, the effect is small, there being only a five-fold increase in frequency for a thousandfold increase in extracellular $[Ca^{2+}]$. In the presence of a depolarization of nerve terminals (such as a nerve impulse), the effects of a change in extracellular $[Ca^{2+}]$ are powerfully increased (Del Castillo and Katz, 1954a; Jenkinson, 1957; Dodge and Rahamimoff, 1967; Hubbard *et al.*, 1968b). As Fig. 5B shows, when the $[Ca^{2+}]$ was increased over a thousandfold range there was a more than 10,000-fold increase in quantal release from rat phrenic nerve terminals.

The magnification of Ca action by depolarization, together with the finding that while Ca must be present before depolarization it acts after depolarization, is explained by the hypothesis that depolarization increases the Ca permeability of nerve terminals and that Ca^{2+} enters in proportion to the electrochemical gradient.

2.2.2a. Ca Entry. The evidence for Ca entry is drawn largely from experiments on squid giant axons and synapses, supplemented where possible by complementary experiments on nerve–muscle junctions.

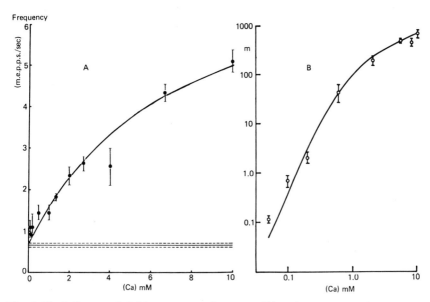

Fig. 5. The influence of Ca^{2+} on m.e.p.p. frequency (A) and e.p.p. quantal content (B) The bars on the points indicate $\pm$ SE of the mean frequency or quantal content (m). The horizontal line in A indicates the mean frequency in the presence of 10^{-5} M calcium, and the dotted lines above and below this line indicate $\pm$ SE of this mean value. The lines between the points in A and B are fitted according to the equation relating quantal release and $[Ca^{2+}]$ developed by Hubbard et al. (1968a,b), and the figures are from the same sources.

The first evidence that Ca uptake occurred, associated with depolarization, came from experiments in which squid giant axons were exposed to solutions containing ^{45}Ca. During stimulation such axons accumulated ^{45}Ca in their axoplasm in amounts roughly proportional to the external Ca concentration (Hodgkin and Keynes, 1957). The availability of the protein aequorin, which emits light in the presence of Ca^{2+}, enabled the time course of Ca entry to be analyzed using a voltage clamp (Baker et al., 1971). There were two phases of Ca entry associated with a depolarizing pulse—one with the time course of the Na channel, and like it blocked by TTX, and one with a time course very similar to that of the K channel. This channel was not blocked, however, by maneuvers which blocked the K channel, such as loading the axoplasm with TEA. It was affected by external concentrations of Mn or Mg which had little effect on the K current.

In view of the long-standing interest in Ca–Mg competition in the process of ACh release (Del Castillo and Katz, 1954a,b), it was natural to suppose that this second channel, if present in nerve terminals, was the link between depolarization and ACh release. Two characteristics of the channel gave further support to this hypothesis. First, Ca entry, as judged by the aequorin-emitted light, was maximum with a depolarizing pulse of about 80 mV.

A similar maximum was already known for transmitter release at the squid giant synapse in response to presynaptic depolarizing pulses (Katz and Miledi, 1970). Second, Ca^{2+} entry into the giant axon appeared to increase e-fold for a 6.3-mV depolarization. A similar relation had previously been derived for the Ca permeability of squid giant synapse presynaptic terminals, as a function of membrane potential (Katz and Miledi, 1970). Finally, it has been shown that nerve terminals of squid giant synapses, when loaded with aequorin and depolarized, emit light, presumably indicating Ca entry in a similar fashion to the axon (Llinas *et al.*, 1972).

There is probably some specialization of the Ca entry mechanism in nerve terminals when compared with the parent axon. This conclusion is based on experiments with giant synapses poisoned with TTX externally and TEA inside the nerve terminal. If the bathing fluid contains Ca, the terminal region will develop a regenerative response upon depolarization, dependent on external Ca and increasing in strength and duration as the Ca^{2+} concentration increases. Depolarizing pulses applied at successively greater distances from the terminal were correspondingly less effective (Katz and Miledi, 1969a) in evoking responses.

It may be inferred that motor nerve terminals have similar properties for spontaneous release and release by depolarizing pulses applied to frog motor nerve terminals both continue *in vitro* if the preparation is bathed in a medium consisting only of $CaCl_2$, while regenerative responses occur if the medium contains TEA, which implies that Ca^{2+} can enter motor nerve terminals (Katz and Miledi, 1969b). Other similarities with squid giant synapses come from studies of the effect of very large depolarizing pulses. If these pulses make the inside of a squid nerve terminal positive, release is blocked during the pulse and occurs when the pulse is turned off (Katz and Miledi, 1969a). An identical phenomenon occurs at frog motor nerve terminals depolarized with very large pulses (Katz and Miledi, 1967b). An associated phenomenon is the increase in the latency of release during a depolarizing pulse as its strength approaches the blocking strength. These phenomena are presently explained (Katz and Miledi, 1967b) by postulating that strong depolarization has two opposed effects on the entry of Ca^{2+} or a combined calcium receptor complex, CaX^+. Entry is facilitated by increasing the membrane permeability to the Ca^{2+} or CaX^+, but when the inside is positive the electrical field would tend to move more positively charged molecules, such as Ca^{2+} or CaX^+, out of the terminal. It is suggested (Katz and Miledi, 1967c) that the permeability effect would rise and decay with an appreciable time lag while the field effect would decay much more rapidly, allowing release after a strong pulse in proportion to the calcium entry after the field barrier was removed.

2.2.2b. Ca Permeability. A complete explanation of the effects of depolarization requires a knowledge of the dependence of Ca permeability on membrane potential. At present, such experiments can be carried out only by investigating the squid giant synapse at different levels of presynaptic membrane potential and in different $[Ca^{2+}]$. Katz and Miledi (1970) find that here, as at the neuromuscular junction (Fig. 5), there is a very steep relationship between the magnitude of the synaptic response and the ambient $[Ca^{2+}]$. As expected (Fig. 5B), the relationship was multiplied by depolarization so that a family of curves resulted relating release, $[Ca^{2+}]$, and presynaptic depolarization. For postsynaptic responses below 10–20 mV, it was found that all the slopes were parallel, suggesting a similar power relationship between $[Ca^{2+}]$ and release.

From such data, by making certain assumptions it is possible to calculate the Ca permeability of terminals (Katz and Miledi, 1970). Assuming that the Ca influx (m) is equal to $k[Ca]_o$, where k is a voltage- and time-dependent permeability coefficient and the postsynaptic responses (R) are the result of the activation of release by n Ca^{2+}, then the relationship between R and M will follow nth-power Michaelis–Menten kinetics with an initial slope for small values of M of

$$d(\log R)/d(\log M) = n$$

For a given depolarization (k constant)

$$d(\log R) \, d(\log [Ca]_o) = n$$

and for a constant $[Ca]_o$ and varying input voltage

$$d(\log R)/d(\log k) = n$$

where k varies as the nth root of R and may be derived from data relating the postsynaptic response to a range of presynaptic depolarizations in the presence of a constant $[Ca]_o$.

In Katz and Miledi's (1970) investigation, n was 2.7. Figure 6B shows k derived as the 2.7th root of the corresponding points in Fig. 6A (the postsynaptic response, R, in the presence of a constant $[Ca]_o$ of 2.75 mM). It will be noted that the permeability factor rises somewhat less steeply than the input–output curve and it appears to be reaching a maximum value close to an input depolarization of 80–100 mV. It is implicit in this approach that the steep relationship between $[Ca]_o$ and release is the result of Ca–receptor

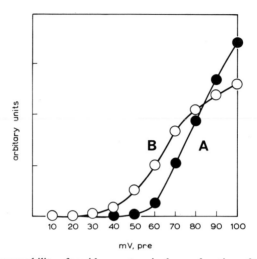

Fig. 6. Calcium permeability of squid nerve terminals as a function of terminal depolarization. Curve A: The postsynaptic responses to the range of depolarizations (abscissa) in the presence of a $[Ca^{2+}]$ of 2.75 mM. Curve B: The calcium permeability calculated from these data, as explained in the text, assuming an exponential rise of the curve to 50 mV (Katz and Miledi, 1970).

combination. The depolarization–dependent Ca permeability of the membrane is merely a gating mechanism.

Unlike k, n may be calculated for any junction where postsynaptic responses may be measured in the presence of a varying $[Ca]_o$. The assumption that release is activated by n Ca^{2+} has pitfalls. In the first place, the slopes are not whole numbers. While 2.7 was obtained at the squid synapse (Katz and Miledi, 1970), 3.78 was obtained from similar calculations at the frog neuromuscular junction (Dodge and Rahamimoff, 1967) and 2.6 at the rat junction (Hubbard *et al.*, 1968*b*). These fractional values may be explained as a failure to approach the limiting $[Ca^{2+}]$ (Dodge and Rahamimoff, 1967) or by combination of different numbers of ions (Werman, 1971). The 3.78 could result from a mixture of sites of combination with three or four Ca^{2+}; 2.6 from a mixture of sites combining with two or three ions. Second, schemes in which a receptor combines with whole numbers of Ca^{2+} (Dodge and Rahamimoff, 1967) or schemes in which there are several intermediate compounds with lesser numbers of Ca^{2+} (Hubbard *et al.*, 1968*b*) can equally well explain the results with evoked release (lines in Fig. 5B). Indeed, Quastel and his colleagues (Cooke *et al.*, 1973) have obtained equally good fits to the points in Fig. 5B on the basis that each Ca^{2+} entering nerve terminals independently multiplies release following combination with receptor sites.

2.2.3. Na–Ca Interaction

The Ca-dependent release process may normally be partially inactivated (Birks and Cohen, 1965; Colomo and Rahamimoff, 1968). The evidence for this conclusion is circumstantial and revolves around the finding that even a 50% reduction in extracellular [Na$^+$] has little or no effect on evoked ACh release (Birks and Cohen, 1965; Del Castillo and Katz, 1955b; Hutter and Kostial, 1955; Kelly, 1968), despite the expected fall in action potential amplitude (Hodgkin and Katz, 1949) which should reduce transmitter release (Katz and Miledi, 1967b). This apparent paradox has been resolved with the discovery that a reduction of the [Na$^+$]$_o$ by 50% or more increases evoked transmitter release if the [Ca^{2+}]$_o$ is simultaneously reduced (Birks and Cohen, 1965; Kelly, 1968, Colomo and Rahamimoff, 1968). Birks and Cohen (1965) suggested that this process operates at normal Ca concentrations and balances a depression brought about by a reduction of the presynaptic nerve action potential amplitude.

Direct evidence for the existence of a Na effect at normal Ca concentrations comes from the work of Gage and Quastel (1966) on m.e.p.p. frequency in rat diaphragm. They were able to demonstrate that even a 30% reduction of the [Na$^+$]$_o$ in the presence of normal [Ca^{2+}] caused a noticeable increase in m.e.p.p. frequency. When nerve terminals were depolarized by increasing the [K$^+$] of the bathing medium, this effect of Na withdrawal was markedly enhanced, to the extent that it gave quantitative support to the hypothesis that relief of Na–Ca competition compensated for a reduction of action potential amplitude.

2.2.4. Spontaneous Transmitter Release

The finding that evoked ACh release is a function of the [Ca^{2+}] at some intracellular nerve terminal site has implications for spontaneous release. Recent research on squid axons suggests that these tissues maintain a constant low internal [Ca^{2+}] due to the buffering action of mitochondria (Baker et al., 1971; Baker, 1972) and that axons take up Ca in proportion to the ambient [Ca^{2+}]. Such processes in motor nerve terminals could well account for the acceleration of m.e.p.p. frequency as the ambient extracellular [Ca^{2+}] is raised (Boyd and Martin, 1956; Hubbard, 1961) and the insensitivity of m.e.p.p. frequency to reduction of extracellular Ca below 10^{-5} M (Fig. 5A) (Hubbard, 1961; Hubbard et al., 1968b). Presumably, the insensitivity of the rate of spontaneous quantal release to a reduction of extracellular [Ca^{2+}] reflects the buffered steady state of intracellular Ca. As expected from this hypothesis, when drugs which inhibit mitochondrial phosphorylation are added to Ca-free solutions bathing rat or frog neuromuscular junctions, m.e.p.p. frequency is increased (Glagoleva et al., 1970).

2.3. After-Effects of Depolarization–Secretion Coupling

2.3.1. Facilitation and Post-tetanic Potentiation

As Fig. 7 shows, after a period of nerve stimulation, both the frequency of m.e.p.p.'s (Fig. 7B) and the quantal content of e.p.p.'s evoked by a testing nerve impulse may be increased (facilitation). Three types of e.p.p.

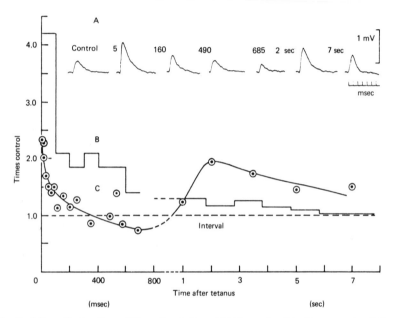

Fig. 7. After-effects of repetitive stimulation. (A) Records of testing e.p.p.'s elicited at the indicated interval (milliseconds or seconds) after the tetanus of 50 impulses at a frequency of 200 Hz. The records were selected to illustrate the average amplitude found in four to six trials at each interval. (C) The average amplitude plotted as a multiple of the control e.p.p. amplitude found in the absence of tetanic stimulation. This control amplitude was measured repeatedly after two or three intervals had been assessed and was remarkably constant throughout the experiment. In this and other experiments, the amplitude of testing e.p.p.'s was potentiated at intervals up to 400 ms after the tetanus, was depressed at longer intervals up to 1 s, and thereafter was potentiated again. (B) The probability of m.e.p.p. occurrence after 50 impulses at 200 Hz as a multiple of the control probability. This probability was calculated for 100-ms periods for the first 700 ms after the tetanus and thereafter for 1-s periods. The control m.e.p.p. probability and e.p.p. amplitude are shown by the same interrupted line. Note the break in the abscissal scale between 800 ms and 1 s and the similar breaks in the graphs. The e.p.p. and m.e.p.p. results are not from the same junction, but are representative of seven experiments in which e.p.p. amplitudes were successfully measured and four experiments in which m.e.p.p. frequency was assessed. The [Mg$^+$] was 11 mmolar and the temperature 37°C for all these experiments (Hubbard, 1963).

facilitation are evident in this figure. At short (milliseconds) intervals, there is a marked facilitation (Fig. 7A, 5 ms) which rapidly decays (Eccles, *et al.*, 1941; Lundberg and Quilisch, 1953; Katz and Miledi, 1968*a*). At slightly longer intervals (Fig. 7A, 160 ms), the facilitation is still evident but is decaying (Fig. 7C) more slowly. Careful analysis indicates that two processes, with different time courses, are involved (Mallart and Martin, 1967). At much longer intervals after the conditioning nerve impulses (Fig. 5A, 2 s, and Fig. 7C, 1–7 s), another form of facilitation—post-tetanic potentiation—is evident (Feng, 1941; Liley and North, 1953). The first two forms of facilitation are often not seen if the conditioning nerve impulse has released more than a few hundred quanta. Depression of the amplitude and quantal content of e.p.p.'s is then found (Eccles *et al.*, 1941; Lundberg and Quilisch, 1953; Liley and North, 1953; Takeuchi, 1958; Thies, 1965; Betz, 1970). Post-tetanic potentiation is, however, still evident (Liley and North, 1953; Hubbard, 1963).

The mechanisms involved are still obscure. The facilitatory and depressor phenomena effected by nerve impulses are elicited if the conditioning stimuli are applied directly to terminals in tetrodotoxin-poisoned preparations, indicating that depolarization *per se* rather than Na entry is the initiating event (Katz and Miledi, 1968*a*; Betz, 1970; Weinrich, 1971). Further, facilitation is still seen if the conditioning nerve impulses release no transmitter (Del Castillo and Katz, 1954*c*; Hubbard, 1963), from which it may be concluded that the events between depolarization and secretion are involved. It is clear, too, that the facilitation of e.p.p. amplitude and m.e.p.p. frequency, seen immediately after repetitive nerve stimulation, develops during the period of stimulation and thereafter rapidly decays (Hubbard, 1963). These facts are presently explained by the hypothesis that a small fraction of the Ca^{2+} entering as the result of a nerve impulse may still be present and effective in release when the next impulse arrives, so potentiating the effect of this impulse. The hypothesis has been supported by experiments in which the amount of calcium entering with the first or second of a pair of impulses was experimentally varied (Katz and Miledi, 1968*a*; Rahamimoff, 1968). The removal of this residual calcium appears to be enhanced as the ambient temperature is raised; however, the process is not immediately dependent on metabolism (Hubbard *et al.*, 1971).

The smaller facilitation which succeeds this primary facilitation has been associated with the increase in amplitude of action potentials recorded from nerve terminals during this period (Hubbard and Schmidt, 1963).

Post-tetanic potentiation was attributed by Gage and Hubbard (1966), after an exhaustive investigation, to an accumulation of intracellular membrane calcium during the conditioning activity. More recent investigations have provided strong evidence that post-tetanic potentiation is indeed connected with accumulation of calcium. It is known, for instance, that the duration and magnitude of the process are determined by the number of tetanic stimuli and the extracellular $[Ca^{2+}]$ during the period of stimulation (Liley and North, 1953; Rosenthal, 1969; Weinrich, 1971). The shortening of the duration of the process as the temperature is raised (Rosenthal, 1969) may be attributed to a temperature-enhanced decay of the calcium store, as presumably occurs for primary facilitation (Hubbard et al., 1971). The facilitations found immediately after stimulation and post-tetanic potentiation appear to be quantitative variants of the same process (Hubbard et al., 1971).

2.3.2. Depression

The depression of the quantal content of an e.p.p. elicited by a testing stimulus after stimulation if the conditioning stimuli have released more than a few hundred quanta is currently unexplained. Recently, some depression of release has even been reported after release of only a few quanta (Rahamimoff and Yaari, 1973). There are indications that both the available ACh (Fig. 3) and the probability of release of individual quanta are reduced during depression (Betz, 1970; Christensen and Martin, 1970). Complicated time courses of facilitation and depression may be found after high-frequency stimulation in curarized preparations due to the coexistence of the various forms of facilitation and depression (Hubbard, 1963; Mallart and Martin, 1968).

5. REFERENCES

Adamic, S., 1970, Accumulation of acetylcholine by the rat diaphragm, Biochem. Pharmacol. 19:2445.

Andersson-Cedergren, E., 1959, Ultra-structure of motor end-plate and sarcoplasmic components of mouse skeletal muscle fibre as revealed by three dimensional reconstructions from serial sections, J. Ultrastruct. Res. 1:1.

Baker, P. F., 1972, Transport and metabolism of calcium ions in nerve, Progr. Biophys. Mol. Biol. 24:177.

Baker, P. F., Hodgkin, A. L., and Ridgway, E. B., 1971, Depolarization and calcium entry in squid giant axons, J. Physiol. Lond. 218:709.

Bartley, J., Abraham, S., and Chaikoff, I. L., 1965, Concerning the form in which acetyl units produced in mitochondria are transferred to the site of de novo fatty acid synthesis in the cell, Biochem. Biophys. Res. Commun. 19:770.

Benoit, P. R., and Mambrini, J., 1970, Modification of transmitter release by ions which prolong the presynaptic action potential, J. Physiol. Lond. 210:681.

Berg, P., 1956a, Acyl adrenylates: An enzyme mechanism of acetate activation, J. Biol. Chem. 222:991.

Berg, P., 1956b, Acyl adrenylates: The synthesis and properties of adrenyl acetate, J. Biol. Chem. 222:1015.

Betz, W. J., 1970, Depression of transmitter release at neuromuscular junction of the frog, J. Physiol. 206:629.

Birks, R. I., 1966, The fine structure of motor nerve endings at frog myoneural junctions, *Ann. N.Y. Acad. Sci.* **135**:8.

Birks, R. L., and Cohen, M. W., 1965, Effects of sodium on transmitter release from frog motor nerve terminals, in: *Muscle* (W. M. Paul, E. E. David, C. M. Kay, and G. Monckton, eds.), pp. 403–420, Pergamon Press, Oxford.

Birks, R., and MacIntosh, F. C., 1961, Acetylcholine metabolism of a sympathetic ganglion, *Can. J. Biochem. Physiol.* **39**:787.

Birks, R., Huxley, H. E., and Katz, B., 1960, The fine structure of the neuromuscular junction of the frog, *J. Physiol. Lond* **150**:134.

Bligh, J., 1952, The level of free choline in plasma, *J. Physiol. Lond.* **117**:234.

Blioch, Z. L., Glagoleva, I. M., Liberman, E. A., and Nenashev, V. A., 1968, A study of the mechanism of quantal transmitter release at a chemical synapse, *J. Physiol. Lond.* **199**:11.

Boyd, I. A., and Martin, A. R., 1956, Spontaneous subthreshold activity at mammalian neuromuscular junctions, *J. Physiol. Lond.* **132**:61.

Braun, M., and Schmidt, R. F., 1966, Potential changes recorded from the frog motor nerve terminal during its activation, *Pflügers Arch. Ges. Physiol.* **287**:56.

Bunt, A. H., 1969, Formation of coated and synaptic vesicles within neurosecretory axon terminals of the crustacean sinus gland, *J. Ultrastruct. Res.* **28**:411.

Capek, R., Esplin, D. W., and Salehmoghaddam, S., 1971, Rates of transmitter turnover at the frog neuromuscular junction estimated by electrophysiological techniques, *J. Neurophysiol.* **34**:831.

Canepa, F. G., 1964, Acetylcholine quanta, *Nature* **201**:184.

Chang, C. C., and Lee, C., 1970, Studies on the [^{3}H]choline uptake in rat phrenic nerve–diaphragm preparations, *Neuropharmacology* **9**:223.

Chen, I. L., and Lee, C. Y., 1970, Ultrastructural changes in the motor nerve terminals caused by β bungarotoxin, *Virchows Arch. Abt. B. Zellpathol* **6**:318.

Christensen, B. N., and Martin, A. R., 1970, Estimates of probability of transmitter release at the mammalian neuromuscular junction. *J. Physiol. Lond.* **210**:933.

Clark, A. W., Hurlbut, W. P., and Mauro, A., 1972, Changes in the fine structure of the neuromuscular junction of the frog caused by black widow spider venom, *J. Cell Biol.* **52**:1.

Colomo, F., and Rahamimoff, R., 1968, Interaction between sodium and calcium ions in the process of transmitter release at the neuromuscular junction, *J. Physiol. Lond.* **198**:203.

Cooke, J. D., Okamoto, K., and Quastel, D. N. J., 1973, The role of calcium in depolarization–secretion coupling at the motor nerve terminal, *J. Physiol.* **228**:459.

Couteaux, R., and Pécot-Dechavassine, M., 1970, Vesicles synaptiques et poches an niveau des "zones actives" de la jonction neuromusculaire, *Compt. Rend. Acad. Sci.* **271**:2346.

Csillik, B., and Bense, S., 1971, Function dependent alterations in the distribution of synaptic vesicles, *Acta Biol. Acad. Sci. Hung.* **22**:131.

De Duve, C., Wattiaux, R., and Baudhuin, P., 1962, Distribution of enzymes between subcellular fractions in animal tissues, in: *Advances in Enzymology*, Vol. 24 (R. F. Nord, ed.), pp. 192–358, Interscience, New York.

Del Castillo, J., and Katz, B., 1954a, Quantal components of the endplate potential, *J. Physiol.* **124**:560.

Del Castillo, J., and Katz, B., 1954b, Changes in endplate activity produced by presynaptic polarization, *J. Physiol. Lond.* **124**:586.

Del Castillo, J., and Katz, B., 1954c, Statistical factors involved in neuromuscular facilitation and depression, *J. Physiol. Lond.* **124**:574.

Del Castillo, J., and Katz, B., 1955a, On the localization of acetylcholine receptors, *J. Physiol. Lond.* **128**:157.

Del Castillo, J., and Katz, B., 1955b, Local activity at a depolarized nerve–muscle junction, *J. Physiol. Lond.* **128**:396.

Del Castillo, J., and Katz, B., 1956, Biophysical aspects of neuromuscular transmission, *Progr. Biophys. Biophys. Chem.* **6**:121.

Dodge, F. A., Jr., and Rahamimoff, R., 1967, Co-operative action of calcium ions in transmitter release at the neuromuscular junction, *J. Physiol. Lond.* **193**:419.

Dodge, F. A., Jr., Miledi, R., and Rahamimoff, R., 1969, Strontium and quantal release of transmitter at the neuromuscular junction, *J. Physiol. Lond.* **200**:267.

Eccles, J. C., and Jaeger, J. C., 1957, The relationship between the mode of operation and the dimensions of the junctional regions at synapses and motor end-organs, *Proc. Roy. Soc. Sci. B* **148**:38.

Eccles, J. C., Katz, B., and Kuffler, S. W., 1941, Nature of the "end-plate potential" in curarized muscle, *J. Neurophysiol.* **4**:363.

Ekstrom, J., and Emmelin, N., 1971, Movement of choline acetyltransferase in axons disconnected from their cell bodies, *J. Physiol. Lond.* **216**:247.

Elmqvist, D., and Quastel, D. M. J., 1965a, Presynaptic action of hemicholinum at the neuromuscular junction, *J. Physiol. Lond.* **167**:463.

Elmqvist, D., and Quastel, D. M. J., 1965b, A quantitative study of end-plate potentials in isolated human muscle, *J. Physiol. Lond.* **178**:505.

Emmelin, H., and MacIntosh, F. C., 1956, The release of acetylcholine from perfused sympathetic ganglia and skeletal muscle, *J. Physiol. Lond.* **131**:477.

Feng, T. P., 1941, Studies on the neuromuscular junction. XXVI. The changes of the end-plate potential during and after the prolonged stimulation, *Chin. J. Physiol.* **16**:341.

Fonnum, F., 1968, Choline acetyltransferase binding to and release from membranes, *Biochem. J.* **109**:389.

Fonnum, F., 1970, Surface charge of choline acetyltransferase from different species, *J. Neurochem.* **17**:1095.

Fonnum, F., Frizell, M., and Sjöstrand, J., 1973, Transport, turnover and distribution of choline acetyltransferase and acetylcholinesterase in the vagus and hypoglossal nerves of the rabbit, *J. Neurochem.* **21**:1109.

Frankenhaeuser, B., 1957, The effect of calcium on the myelinated nerve fibre, *J. Physiol. Lond.* **137**:245.

Frizell, M., Hasselgren, P. O., and Sjöstrand, J., 1970, Axoplasmic transport of acetyl-cholinesterase and choline acetyltransferase in the vagus and hypoglossal nerve of the rabbit, *Exptl. Brain. Res.* **10**:526.

Gage, P. W., and Hubbard, J. I., 1965, Evidence for a Poisson distribution of miniature end-plate potentials and some implications, *Nature* **208**:395.

Gage, P. W., and Hubbard, J. I., 1966, An investigation of the post-tetanic potentiation of end-plate potentials at a mammalian neuromuscular junction, *J. Physiol. Lond.* **184**:353.

Gage, P. W., and Quastel, D. M. J., 1966, Competition between sodium and calcium ions in transmitter release at a mammalian neuromuscular junction, *J. Physiol. Lond.* **185**:95.

Glagoleva, I. M., Liberman, E. A., and Khashaev, Z. Kh.-M., 1970, Effect of uncouplers of oxidative phosphorylation on output of acetylcholine from nerve endings, *Biofizika* **15**:76.

Hagiwara, S., and Saito, N., 1959, Voltage–current relations in nerve cell membrane of *Onechidium verruculatum, J. Physiol. Lond.* **148**:161.

Hagiwara, S., and Tasaki, I., 1958, A study of the mechanism of impulse transmission across the giant synapse of the squid, *J. Physiol. Lond.* **143**:114.

Hebb, C., 1963, Formation, storage and liberation of acetylcholine, in: *Cholinesterases and Anticholinesterase Agents* (G. B. Koelle, ed.), pp. 55–88, Springer-Verlag, Berlin.

Hebb, C. O., and Silver, A., 1961, Gradient of choline acetylase activity, *Nature* **189**:123.

Hebb, C. O., and Waites, G. M. H., 1956, Choline acetylase in antero- and retrograde degeneration of a cholinergic nerve, *J. Physiol. Lond.* **132**:667.

Hebb, C. O., Krnjevíc, K., and Silver, A., 1964, Acetylcholine and choline acetyltransferase in the diaphragm of the rat, *J. Physiol. Lond.* **171**:504.

Heuser, J., and Miledi, R., 1971, Effect of lanthanum ions on function and structure of frog neuromuscular junctions, *Proc. Roy. Soc. Lond. B.* **179**:247.

Heuser, J., and Reese, T. S., 1972, Stimulation induced uptake and release of peroxidase from synaptic vesicles in frog neuromuscular junctions, *Anat. Rec.* **172**:329.

Hodgkin, A. L., and Katz, B. J., 1949, The effect of sodium ions on the electrical activity of the giant axon of the squid, *J. Physiol. Lond.* **108**:37.

Hodgkin, A. L., and Keynes, R. D., 1957, Movement of labelled calcium in squid giant axons, *J. Physiol. Lond.* **138**:253.

Hubbard, J. I., 1961, The effect of calcium and magnesium on the spontaneous release of transmitter from mammalian motor nerve endings, *J. Physiol. Lond.* **159**:507.

Hubbard, J. I., 1963, Repetitive stimulation at the mammalian neuromuscular junction and the mobilization of transmitter, *J. Physiol. Lond.* **169**:641.

Hubbard, J. I., 1970, Mechanism of transmitter release, *Progr. Biophys. Mol. Biol.* **21**:33.

Hubbard, J. I., 1973, Microphysiology of vertebrate neuromuscular transmission, *Physiol. Rev.* **53**:674.

Hubbard, J. I., and Jones, S., 1973, Spontaneous quantal transmitter release: A statistical analysis and some implications, *J. Physiol. Lond.* **232**:1.

Hubbard, J. I., and Kwanbunbumpen, S., 1968, Evidence for the vesicle hypothesis, *J. Physiol. Lond.* **194**:407.

Hubbard, J. I., and Schmidt, R. F., 1963, An electrophysiological investigation of mammalian motor nerve terminals, *J. Physiol. London.* **166**:145.

Hubbard, J. I., and Wilson, D. F., 1973, Neuromuscular transmission in a mammalian preparation in the absence of blocking drugs and the effect of D-tubocurarine, *J. Physiol. Lond.* **228**:307.

Hubbard, J. I., Jones, S. F., and Landau, E. M., 1968a, On the mechanism by which calcium and magnesium affect the spontaneous release of transmitter from mammalian motor nerve terminals, *J. Physiol. Lond.* **194**:355.

Hubbard, J. I., Jones, S. F., and Landau, E. M., 1968b, On the mechanism by which calcium and magnesium affect the release of transmitter by nerve impulses, *J. Physiol. Lond.* **196**:75.

Hubbard, J. I., Jones, S. F., and Landau, E. M., 1971, The effect of temperature change upon transmitter release, facilitation and post-tetanic potentiation, *J. Physiol. Lond.* **216**:591.

Hutter, O. F., and Kostial, K., 1955, The relationship of sodium ions to the release of acetylcholine, *J. Physiol. Lond.* **129**:159.

Israel, M., Gautron, J., and Lesbats, B., 1968, Isolement des vésicules synaptiques de l'organe électrique de la Torpille et localization de l'acetylcholine à leur niveau, *Compt. Rend. Hebd. Seanc. Acad. Sci. Paris* **266**:273.

Jenkinson, D. H., 1957, The nature of the antagonism between calcium and magnesium ions at the neuromuscular junction, *J. Physiol. Lond.* **138**:438.

Jones, S. F., and Kwanbunbumpen, S., 1970, The effects of nerve stimulation and hemicholinium on synaptic vesicles at the mammalian neuromuscular junction, *J. Physiol. Lond.* **207**:31.

Kanaseki, T., and Kadota, K., 1969, The vesicle in a "basket": A morphological study of the coated vesicle fraction isolated from the nerve endings of the guinea pig brain with special reference to the mechanism of membrane movements, *J. Cell Biol.* **42**:202.

Kao, C. T., 1966, Tetrodotoxin, saxitoxin and their significance in the study of excitation phenomena, *Pharmacol. Rev.* **18**:997.

Katz, B., and Miledi, R., 1965a, Propagation of electric activity in motor nerve terminals, *Proc. Roy. Soc. Lond. B* **161**:453.

Katz, B., and Miledi, R., 1965b, The measurement of synaptic delay, and the time course of acetylcholine release at the neuromuscular junction, *Proc. Roy. Soc. Lond. B* **161**:483.

Katz, B., and Miledi, R., 1965c, The effect of calcium on acetylcholine release from motor nerve endings, *Proc. Roy. Soc. Lond. B* **161**:496.

Katz, B., and Miledi, R., 1965d, The effect of temperature on the synaptic delay at the neuromuscular junction, *J. Physiol. Lond.* **181**:656.

Katz, B., and Miledi, R., 1967a, Tetrodotoxin and neuromuscular transmission, *Proc. Roy. Soc. Lond. B* **167**:8.

Katz, B., and Miledi, R., 1967b, The release of acetylcholine from nerve endings by graded electric pulses, *Proc. Roy. Soc. Lond. B* **167**:23.

Katz, B., and Miledi, R., 1967c, The timing of calcium action during neuromuscular transmission, *J. Physiol. Lond.* **189**:535.

Katz, B., and Miledi, R., 1968a, The role of calcium in neuromuscular facilitation, *J. Physiol. Lond.* **195**:481.

Katz, B., and Miledi, R., 1968b, The effect of local blockage of motor nerve terminals, *J. Physiol. Lond.* **199**:729.

Katz, B., and Miledi, R., 1969a, Tetrodotoxin-resistant electric activity in presynaptic terminals, *J. Physiol. Lond.* **203**:459.

Katz, B., and Miledi, R., 1969b, Spontaneous and evoked activity of motor nerve endings in calcium Ringer, *J. Physiol. Lond.* **203**:689.

Katz, B., and Miledi, R., 1970, A further study of the role of calcium in synaptic transmission, *J. Physiol. Lond.* **207**:789.

Katz, B., and Miledi, R., 1972, The statistical nature of the acetylcholine potential and its molecular components, *J. Physiol. Lond.* **224**:665.

Kelly, J. S., 1968, The antagonism of Ca^{++} by Na^+ and other monovalent ions at the frog neuromuscular junction, *Quart. J. Exptl. Physiol.* **53**:239.

Korneliussen, H., Barstad, J. A. B., and Lilleheil, G., 1972, Vesicle hypothesis, effect of nerve stimulation on the synaptic vesicles of motor endplates, *Experientia* **28**:1055.

Krnjević, K., and Miledi, R., 1959, Presynaptic failure of neuro-muscular propagation in rats, *J. Physiol. Lond.* **149**:1.

Krnjević, K., and Mitchell, J. F., 1961, The release of acetylcholine in the isolated rat diaphragm, *J. Physiol. Lond.* **155**:246.

Kuba, K., and Tomita, T., 1972, Effect of noradrenaline on miniature end-plate potentials and on end-plate potential, *J. Theoret. Biol.* **36**:81.

Kuno, M., Turkanis, S. A., and Weakley, J. N., 1971, Correlation between nerve terminal size and transmitter release at the neuromuscular junction of the frog, *J. Physiol. Lond.* **213**:545.

Landau, E. M., 1969, The interaction of presynaptic polarization with calcium and magnesium in modifying spontaneous transmitter release from mammalian motor nerve terminals, *J. Physiol. Lond.* **203**:281.

Laskowski, M. B., and Thies, R., 1972, Interaction between clacium and barium on the spontaneous release of transmitter from mammalian motor nerve terminals, *Internat. J. Neurosci.* **4**:11.

Lermer, H., 1971, Estimation of quantal content in detubulated nerve–muscle preparation, in: *Proceedings of the Twenty-fifth International Congress of Physiology*, Vol. 9, German Physiological Society, Munich, p. 344.

Liley, A. W., 1956, The effects of presynaptic polarization on the spontaneous activity at the mammalian neuromuscular junction, *J. Physiol. Lond.* **134**:427.

Liley, A. W., and North, K. A. K, 1953, An electrical investigation of effects of repetitive stimulation on mammalian neuromuscular junction, *J. Neuro-Physiol.* **16**:509.

Llinas, R., Blinks, J. R., and Nicholson, C., 1972, Calcium transient in presynaptic terminals of squid giant synapse: Detection with aequorin, *Science N. Y.* **176**:1127.

Longenecker, H. E., Hurlbut, W. P., Mauro, A., and Clark, A. W., 1970, Effects of black widow spider venom on the frog neuromuscular junctions: Effects on endplate potential, miniature endplate potential and nerve terminal spike, *Nature* **225**:701.

Lowenstein, J. M., 1964, in: *Oxygen in the Animal Organism* (F. Duhens and E. Neil, Eds.), p. 163, Pergamon Press, Oxford.

Lundberg, A., and Quilisch, H., 1953, Presynaptic potentiation and depression of neuromuscular transmission in frog and rat, *Acta Physiol. Scand.* **30**: Suppl. III.

MacIntosh, F. C., 1959, Formation, storage, and release of acetylcholine at nerve endings, *Can. J. Biochem. Physiol.* **37**:343.

Mallart, A., and Martin, A. R., 1967, An analysis of facilitation of transmitter release at the neuromuscular junction of the frog, *J. Physiol. Lond.* **193**:679.

Mallart, A., and Martin, A. R., 1968, The relation between quantum content and facilitation at the neuromuscular junction of the frog, *J. Physiol. Lond.* **196**:593.

Martin, A. R., 1955, A further study of the statistical composition of end-plate potential, *J. Physiol. Lond.* **130**:114.

Martin, A. R., 1966, Quantal nature of synaptic transmission, *Physiol. Rev.* **46**:51.

Meiri, U., and Rahamimoff, R., 1971, Activation of transmitter· release by strontium and calcium ions at the neuromuscular junction, *J. Physiol. Lond.* **215**:709.

Miledi, R., 1961, From nerve to muscle, *Discovery* **22**:442.

Mitchell, J. F., and Silver, A., 1963, The spontaneous release of acetylcholine from the denervated hemidiaphragm of the rat, *J. Physiol. Lond.* **165**:117.

Musick, J., and Hubbard, J. I., 1972, Release of protein from mouse motor nerve terminals, *Nature* **237**:279.

Nagasawa, J., Douglas, W. W., and Schulz, R. A., 1970, Ultrastructural evidence of secretion by exocytosis and of a synaptic vesicle formation in posterior pituitary glands, *Nature* **227**:407.

Nickel, E., Vogel, A., and Waser, P. G., 1967, "Coated vesicles" in der Umgebung der neuro muskularen Synapsen, *Z. Zellforsch. Mikroskop. Anat.* **78**:261.

Potter, L. T., 1970, Synthesis, storage and release of [^{14}C] acetylcholine in isolated rat diaphragm muscles, *J. Physiol. Lond.* **206**:145.

Rahamimoff, R., 1968, A dual effect of calcium ions on neuromuscular facilitation, *J. Physiol. Lond.* **195**:471.

Rahamimoff, R., and Yaari, Y., 1973, Delayed release of transmitter at the frog neuromuscular junction, *J. Physiol. Lond.* **228**:241.

Rosenthal, J., 1969, Post-tetanic potentiation at the neuromuscular junction of the frog, *J. Physiol. Lond.* **203**:121.

Roth, T. F., and Porter, K. R., 1964, Yolk protein uptake in the oocyte of the mosquito *Aedes aegypti* L., *J. Cell Biol.* **20**:313.

Saekens, T. K., and Stoll, W. R., 1965, Radiochemical determination of choline and acetylcholine flux from isolated tissue, *J. Pharmacol. Exptl. Therap.* **147**:336.

Samojloff, A., 1925, Zur Frage des Überganges der Erregung vom motorischen Nerven auf der quergestreiften Muskel, *Pflügers Arch. Ges. Physiol.* **208**:508.

Sheridan, M. N., Whittaker, V. P., and Israel, M., 1966, The subcellular fractionation of the electric organ of *Torpedo*, *Z. Zellforsch. Mikroskop. Anat.* **74**:291.

Silinsky, E., and Hubbard, J. I., 1973, Release of ATP from rat notor nerve terminals, *Nature* **243**:404.

Sollenberg, J., and Sorbo, B., 1970, On the origin of the acetylcholine in brain studied with a differential labelling technique using ^3H-^{14}C-mixed labelled glucose and acetate, *J. Neurochem.* **17**:201.

Straughan, D. W., 1960, The release of acetylcholine from mammalian motor nerve endings, *Brit. J. Pharmacol.* **15**:417.

Takeuchi, A., 1958, The long-lasting depression in neuromuscular transmission of frog, *Jap. J. Physiol.* **8**:102.

Takeuchi, A., and Takeuchi, N., 1962, Electrical changes in the pre- and postsynaptic axons of the giant synapse of *Loligo*, *J. Gen. Physiol.* **45**:1181.

Thies, R. E., 1965, Neuromuscular depression and apparent depletion of transmitter in mammalian muscle, *J. Neurophysiol.* **28**:427.

Tucek, S., 1967, Observations on the subcellular distribution of choline acetyltransferase in the brain tissue of mammals and comparison of acetylcholine synthesis from acetate and citrate in homogenates and nerve ending fractions, *J. Neurochem.* **14**:519.

Tucek, S., 1968, Motor nerve and the activity of choline acetyltransferase in the skeletal muscle, *Biochim. Biophys. Acta* **170**:457.

Tucek, S., and Cheng, S.-C., 1970, Precursors of acetyl groups in acetylcholine in the brain *in vivo*, *Biochim. Biophys. Acta* **208**:538.

Wallach, M. B., Goldberg, A. M., and Shideman, F. E., 1967, The synthesis of labelled acetylcholine by the isolated cat heart and its release by vagal stimulation, *Internat. J. Neuropharmacol.* **6**:317.

Weinrich, D., 1971, Ionic mechanism of post-tetanic potentiation at neuromuscular junction of frog, *J. Physiol. Lond.* **212**:431.

Werman, R., 1971, The number of receptors for calcium ions at the nerve terminals of one endplate, *Comp. Gen. Pharmacol.* **2**:129.

Whittaker, V. P., 1965, The application of subcellular fractionation techniques to the study of brain function, *Progr. Biophys. Mol. Biol.* **15**:39.

Whittaker, V. P., 1970, The vesicle hypothesis, in: *Excitatory Synaptic Mechanisms* (P. Anderson and J. K. S. Jansen, eds.), pp. 66–76, Universitetforslaget, Oslo.

Whittaker, V. P., 1971, Origin and function of synaptic vesicles, *Ann. N. Y. Acad. Sci.* **183**:21.

Zacks, S. I., and Saito, A., 1969, Uptake of exogenous horseradish peroxidase by coated vesicles in mouse neuromuscular junctions, *J. Histochem. Cytochem.* **17**:161.

Chapter 7(ii)

Neuromuscular Transmission—The Transmitter–Receptor Combination

Mohyee E. Eldefrawi

Section of Neurobiology and Behavior
Cornell University
Ithaca, New York, USA

1. INTRODUCTION

Our understanding of neuromuscular transmission has improved greatly since the classic experiments of Claude Bernard (1856) showing that injection of curare produced paralysis in frog leg muscle and that the curare-poisoned leg muscle could not be stimulated electrically via its nerve, but was fully sensitive to direct electrical stimulation. Almost 50 years later, Langley (1906) demonstrated that nicotine stimulated skeletal muscles and its action was blocked by curare, and introduced the term "receptive substance" to define the site of action of these drugs. Evidence of cholinergic transmission at the neuromuscular junctions of skeletal muscles was obtained by Dale *et al.* (1936), who recovered ACh from the perfusate of neuromuscular preparations following nerve stimulation and produced twitchlike contraction in the muscle following close arterial injection of ACh. Until recently, the notion of the ACh-receptor was essentially an operational term, but opinions differed as to its precise nature. The advent of improved electrophysiological techniques, such as the microelectrode (which made intracellular recording possible) and iontophoresis (with which the amount of applied agent was controlled) as well as voltage clamp techniques, helped accumulate data essential for the models of neuromuscular transmission.

The electric organs of the electric ray, *Torpedo* sp., or the electric eel, *Electrophorus electricus*, are specialized tissues for the production of electric current and are believed to be derived from embryonic muscle tissue in which the contractile elements have vanished. Studies on rows of electroplax and later on the monocellular preparation of *Electrophorus* electroplax, established the nicotinic cholinergic nature of their synaptic transmission (Feldberg and Fessard, 1942; Keynes and Martins-Ferreira, 1953) and thereby their similar pharmacology to skeletal neuromuscular junctions. In addition, these electric tissues were found to be rich sources of acetylcholine (ACh) (40–100 μg tissue in *Torpedo*) and acetylcholinesterase (AChE) (Nachmansohn and Lederer, 1939; Feldberg and Fessard, 1942). Since these tissues are purely nicotinic cholinergic, as opposed to brain tissue which has mixed receptors, electric organs became the choice tissues for the isolation and purification of ACh-receptors. Only during the past 3 years have there been concentrated and successful efforts to identify and isolate ACh-receptors (Changeux *et al.*, 1971; Eldefrawi *et al.*, 1971d, 1972; Karlin *et al.*, 1971; Miledi *et al.*, 1971; Raftery *et al.*, 1971; Hall, 1972; Karlsson *et al.*, 1972; O'Brien *et al.*, 1972; Olsen *et al.*, 1972; Schmidt and Raftery, 1973; Klett *et al.*, 1973; Eldefrawi and Eldefrawi, 1973a).

In this chapter, I shall use the term "ACh-receptor" to designate specifically the macromolecule(s) present in the postsynaptic membrane of muscle or electroplax, which bears recognition site(s) for ACh, the binding of which triggers depolarization of the postsynaptic membrane. Attempts will be made to contrast and compare the *in situ* physiological and pharmacological observations with the recent *in vitro* discoveries.

2. MOLECULAR BASIS OF CHEMOELECTRIC TRANSDUCTION

Acetylcholine acts as the messenger between presynaptic nerve endings and postsynaptic membranes in skeletal neuromuscular junctions and electric organs. Acetylcholine is recognized and bound by highly specialized receptors on the normally polarized postsynaptic membrane, and this triggers the chain of events that lead to membrane depolarization. AChE is also located in the postsynaptic membrane, and it recognizes, binds, and hydrolyzes ACh, thus ending its role as a transmitter [see Chapter 7(iii)].

Our knowledge of the molecular events and the quantitative aspects of end plate currents induced by transmitter–receptor combinations is not clear, and many assumptions are made. Nevertheless, the latest works of Katz and Miledi (1970, 1971) provide us with more information to formulate a working hypothesis. They found that the end plate depolarization produced by a steady dose of ACh was accompanied by a significant increase in voltage noise across the membrane. They suggested that this "noise" arises from statistical variation of high-frequency collisions between ACh molecules and end plate receptors and also that each collision or several collisions open a single ionic channel for an average duration of 1 ms and cause a depolarization equivalent to 0.22 μV (at 22°C).

If one makes the assumptions that a single transmitter–receptor occupation opens one ionic channel of an average constant size and duration and that voltage change is proportional to conductance, one may calculate that a miniature end plate potential (m.e.p.p.), which results from a small depolarization of about 0.5 mV, would require about 1.5×10^3 transmitter–receptor occupations (Table I). Accordingly, the number of ACh molecules released per quantum should be in excess of 1.5×10^3. The available estimates from iontophoretic data range from 10^3 to 10^5 (Katz, 1971), with an average of 10^4 ACh molecules. Fatt and Katz (1952) found that these randomly recurring m.e.p.p.'s occur in the absence of any form of stimulation and arise from spontaneous discharge of a multimolecular quantum of ACh from the nerve ending. Each m.e.p.p. is highly localized and involves only a very small portion of the synaptic axon surface, successive discharges forming a random sequence in temporal as well as in spatial distribution along the motor nerve ending.

When several hundred quanta of ACh are released from the presynaptic nerve ending within a millisecond, which occurs as a result of nerve stimulation, an end plate potential (e.p.p.) is produced. This depolarization rises above the firing threshold of the muscle fiber and initiates a propagating wave of

Table I. Suggested Relationship Between the Number of Transmitter–Receptor Interactions and the Physiological Response

Physiological response	Estimated number of ACh molecules released	Average depolarization (mV)	Membrane conductance (mho)	Estimated number of opened ionic channels
Noise	1	0.00022^a	10^{-10a}	1^a
m.e.p.p.	10^{4b}	0.5^c	$1 - 2 \times 10^{-7d}$	1.5×10^{3g}
e.p.p.	3×10^{6e}	50.0^b	5×10^{-5f}	5×10^{5g}

[a] From Katz and Miledi (1971).
[b] An average value from Katz (1971).
[c] From Fatt and Katz (1952).
[d] From Takeuchi and Takeuchi (1960).
[e] From Potter (1970).
[f] Calculated from Ginsborg (1967).
[g] Calculated on the assumption that there is a linear relationship between membrane conductance and the number of opened channels, and that the opening of a single channel causes a conductance change equal to 10^{-10} mho.

membrane excitation. The e.p.p. differs from the m.e.p.p. only in amplitude (e.p.p. is often more than 50 mV) and represents the statistical fusion of quantal components identical with the m.e.p.p.'s within the same short time interval (Katz, 1971). In effect, the e.p.p. arises when a much higher portion of the ACh-receptor sites are affected almost simultaneously (about 1 ms), leading to a depolarization of about 50 mV and the opening of 5×10^5 ionic channels (Table I).

The affinity of ACh for its receptor may be determined directly from the formula $K_A = 1/[A]_{50}$, where K_A is the association or affinity constant and $[A]_{50}$ is the activator concentration which gives half maximal response; and the dissociation constant $K_D = 1/K_A = [A]_{50}$. Using the electrophysiologically obtained figures relating the concentration of applied ACh to the observed response, apparent K_D values for ACh can be obtained. These range from 0.05 μM in smooth muscles (Burgen, 1965; Sastry and Cheng, 1972) to 0.1 μM in skeletal muscles (Jenkinson, 1960) to 9 μM in *Electrophorus* electroplax (calculated from Bartels and Nachmansohn, 1965). The dissociation constant for ACh determined directly by *in vitro* measurement of the binding of ^{3}H-ACh to the majority of the ACh-receptors of *Torpedo* electroplax varies according to the condition of the receptor and is calculated as 0.068, 0.22, and 2 μM for the membrane-bound, Lubrol-solubilized, and highly purified ACh-receptors, respectively (Eldefrawi *et al.*, 1971a, 1972; Eldefrawi and Eldefrawi, 1973a). Theoretically, the ACh molecule could bind to the receptor site with an electrostatic bond ($\simeq 7$ kcal) through its quaternary ammonium group, a hydrogen bond ($\simeq 3$ kcal) through its carbonyl oxygen, a dipole–dipole interaction ($\simeq 1$ kcal) through the carbonyl carbon, plus several hydrophobic bonds (each 0.6 kcal) through various methyl groups (Fig. 1). The average free energy supplied in these reactions would be in the neighborhood of 12.5 kcal/mole. Such a ΔF is sufficient to give a dissociation constant in the nanomolar range. In fact, it was recently observed that ACh binds to the purified ACh-receptor at such low concentrations with a Hill coefficient of 1.6, indicating positive cooperativity (Eldefrawi and Eldefrawi, 1973b).

ACh_receptor

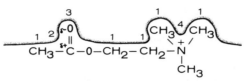

Fig. 1. Bonds that may be involved in the binding of ACh to its receptor. 1, Hydrophobic bonds; 2, dipolar interactions; 3, hydrogen bond; 4, electrostatic bond.

The effect of ACh on neuromuscular transmission is dependent on the concentration of ACh within the synaptic cleft, which is in turn dependent on the number of ACh molecules released per impulse and the volume of the cleft. Krnjevic and Mitchell (1961) estimated the number of ACh molecules released per nerve impulse to be 6×10^6 molecules, and more recently Potter (1970) reported a value of 3×10^6 molecules released per impulse per end plate of the rat diaphragm. By utilizing Potter's value and the cleft volumes calculated for various end plates, and assuming that the released ACh follows a square pulse with no leakage or hydrolysis and becomes uniformly distributed within the cleft, the concentration of ACh in the cleft would range from 6.3 to 25 μM (Table II).

Eccles (1966) suggested that in the brief time during an m.e.p.p. (1–2 ms), the quantum of ACh can diffuse to only 10–20 μm^2 of postsynaptic surface, which when compared to the total calculated area of the postsynaptic surface (Table II) would constitute only a very small portion (0.1–0.5%) of it. The ratio of the area of the postsynaptic membrane affected in an m.e.p.p. to that in an e.p.p. (in which presumably all the postsynaptic membrane is affected) is similar to the ratio of ACh molecules released in each case (0.3%) (Table I). Therefore, the ACh concentration at the postsynaptic membrane following the spontaneous discharge of a single quantum leading to m.e.p.p. is similar to that after a nerve impulse leading to an e.p.p. This suggests the presence of a single population of ACh-receptor sites, occupation of a small portion of which leads to m.e.p.p., while occupation of a larger portion leads to an e.p.p.

Acetylcholinesterase in the end plate should be capable of hydrolyzing almost all of the ACh released from the presynapse, within the brief period of

Table II. Calculated Postsynaptic Membrane Area, Cleft Volume, and the Concentration of ACh Prevailing in the End Plate Necessary for Production of an E.p.p. in Different Tissues

Tissue and animal	Postsynaptic membrane area[a] (μm^2)	Cleft volume[a] (μ^3m)	Estimated ACh concentration[b] (μM)
Mouse diaphragm	3000	200	25
Mouse sternomastoid	9000	800	6.3
Rat diaphragm	7000	450	11
Rat sternomastoid	9000	800	6.3

[a] From Salpeter and Eldefrawi (1973).
[b] Assuming the release of 3×10^6 ACh molecules/nerve impulse calculated for an end plate of rat diaphragm (Potter, 1970).

the opening of ion gates (probably 1–2 ms); otherwise, one would observe sustained depolarization resulting from secondary receptor occupation. The turnover number for purified AChE from *Electrophorus* electroplax was given as 7.6–8.8 $\times$ 10^5 molecules/catalytic site/minute at 25°C (Rosenberry *et al.*, 1972), or an average of 13.7 molecules/catalytic site/millisecond at the optimum ACh concentration of 2.7 mM. However, the concentration of ACh in the cleft during transmission is 11 μM. At this low concentration, the rate of hydrolysis should be lower than the maximal rate according to the Michaelis–Menten kinetics. Using the Ellman *et al.* (1961) method for determining hydrolysis of acetylthiocholine by AChE from *Electrophorus* electroplax and a substrate concentration of 10 μM, a hydrolysis rate equivalent to 2% of the maximum was observed (Lewis and Eldefrawi, unpublished). Therefore, if the AChE in the end plate were in solution, then the 1.7 $\times$ 10^7 AChE active sites per rat diaphragm end plate (Salpeter *et al.*, 1972) are capable of hydrolyzing 4.7 $\times$ 10^6 molecules of ACh in 1 ms, which is 1.5 times the amount of ACh released per nerve impulse.

Depolarization of the postsynaptic membrane is caused by the opening of ionic channels, which is triggered by transmitter–receptor combination. This allows simultaneous net fluxes of Na^+ and K^+ along their electrochemical gradients (i.e., Na^+ inward and K^+ outward). There may also be increases in permeability to other ions such as Ca^{2+}, but these play only a minor role under physiological conditions (Takeuchi and Takeuchi, 1960).

Most of the evidence for the opening of the channels comes from measurement of changes in electrical potential across membranes, but some information is also available from measurement of the flux of radioactive ions through membranes. Jenkinson and Nicholls (1961) showed that application of ACh to a chronically denervated rat diaphragm, already completely depolarized in K^+-enriched solution, increased the rates of influx and efflux of $^{42}K^+$, $^{24}Na^+$, $^{45}Ca^{2+}$, while the movement of $^{36}Cl^-$ was virtually unchanged. These results agree well with those of Takeuchi and Takeuchi (1959, 1960), who used the voltage-clamp technique on the frog neuromuscular junction and showed that the bathing concentrations of Na^+ and K^+ but not Cl^- directly affected the equilibrium potential for the end plate current. This property of excitable membranes is modified in subcellular fragments from *Electrophorus* electroplax (Kasai and Changeux, 1971*a,b,c*). Application of the activator carbamylcholine to the microsacs formed from the innervated membranes increased the efflux of $^{24}Na^+$, $^{42}K^+$, or $^{45}Ca^{2+}$, and the increase of Na efflux was inhibited by *d*-tubocurarine. Yet, the conductance calculated from the Na flux-rate was five orders of magnitude smaller than that calculated by Katz and Miledi (1972) to occur in an end plate.

The mechanism by which the combination of ACh with ACh-receptor opens the ionic channels is still unknown. Nachmansohn (1955) proposed two decades ago that a conformational change occurs in ACh-receptor as a result of binding of ACh, and this may initiate the sequence of reactions resulting in increased permeability. The findings, from the monocellular preparation of *Electrophorus* electroplax, that the maximum extent of depolarization can vary widely depending on the ligand studied and that certain inhibitors abolish in varying degrees the ability of different ligands to trigger depolarization have been interpreted in terms of a simple and quantitative molecular mechanism based on the state function of the allosteric model (Edelstein, 1972). Changeux *et al.* (1969) added the suggestion that the recognition sites for ACh (on the receptor) and for the inorganic cations (on the ionophore, which transports them passively along their electrochemical gradient) are topographically distinct.

The mechanism of chemoelectric transduction is not understood. It is conceivable that the ACh-receptor is coupled directly to an ionophore or indirectly by means of an enzyme, which amplifies the message by producing a second messenger in a manner analogous to coupling of hormone receptors with nucleotide cyclases. In fact, several recent reports suggest that the muscarinic ACh-receptor is coupled to guanyl cyclase, since application of ACh or agonists to brain increases the cellular levels of cyclic GMP (Illiano *et al.*, 1973).

Another alternative takes into account the possible role played by structured water. In liquid water, various numbers of water molecules may become tightly bound together by hydrogen bonding and form areas of short-lived (10^{-10}–10^{-11} s) clusters of water molecules (Nemethy and Scheraga, 1962). Hydrogen bonding is considerably facilitated by a hydrophobic environment, so that around hydrophobic areas there may be several layers of tightly bound water molecules. It is possible that the conformation of receptor in the resting state is maintained under the pressure of surrounding structured water molecules and binding of ACh to ACh-receptor causes disturbances in the structure of water which lead to a conformational change in the ACh-receptor and possibly in the ionophore, thus opening ionic channels. In other words, the transduction function of the postjunctional membrane might be directly controlled by making and breaking of structured water and under the influence of transmitter–receptor interactions.

An approach that may resolve these differences and yield information on the mechanism of transduction is the use of artificial membranes after incorporation of pure ACh-receptor. It has been possible to impart excitability to phospholipid membranes (of the Muller–Rubin type) by incorporation of AChE, which then responded to application of ACh, but also to *d*-tubocurarine (Del Castillo *et al.*, 1967). A better preparation for such studies may be the unilamellar vesicles made from phospholipids, where actual flux of radioactive ions can be measured (Kimelberg and Papahadjopoulos, 1971).

3. PHARMACOLOGY

Drugs which react with ACh-receptor and affect transmission are classified either as activators (or agonists), if they cause depolarization of the postsynaptic membrane, or as blockers (or antagonists), if they block the depolarization caused by ACh or its agonists. A few drugs called "depolarizing
blockers" bridge the gap between the two main classes. Long before ACh was
recognized as the neurotransmitter at neuromuscular junctions, ACh-receptors
were classified into muscarinic and nicotinic types. The first is present in
junctions of smooth muscles and is activated by muscarine and inhibited by
atropine, the second is present in junctions of skeletal muscles and electric
organs and is activated by nicotine and inhibited by d-tubocurarine.

The fact that ACh binds to both muscarinic and nicotinic ACh-receptors,
AChE, choline acetyltransferase, and storage proteins indicates that there are
similarities among the active sites of these macromolecules. Since the action of
many drugs is attributable to their having structural similarities to the
neurotransmitter, it is not strange to find a cholinergic drug with more than
one site of action, with the primary target usually being the macromolecule
for which it has the highest affinity. For example, hemicholinium-3, whose
ultimate effect is the reduction of ACh released from the presynaptic nerve
ending (possibly through blockade of choline transport at the presynaptic
membrane or competition with ACh binding at its storage site), is also known
to block ACh-receptors (Bertolini *et al.*, 1967). Another example is the
organophosphate inhibitors of AChE, which have very high affinities for the
enzyme and irreversibly phosphorylate its active site ($K_i = 0.01$–0.1 μM)
(O'Brien, 1960); thereby activating neuromuscular transmission by prolonging
the high concentration of ACh in the synapse. Yet recently they have been
shown to act on the ACh-receptor, but reversibly and only at high drug
concentrations (above 0.1 mM) (Bartels and Nachmansohn, 1969; Eldefrawi
et al., 1971*b*). By analogy, classification of drugs into muscarinic and nicotinic groups is dependent on their affinities for the two kinds of ACh-receptors.
For example, the well-known blocker of the ACh-receptor of muscarinic
junctions, atropine ($K_D = 0.001$ μM, Paton and Rang, 1966), has also been
shown to block ACh-receptors of skeletal muscle at 0.2 mM (Johnson and
Parsons, 1972). In addition to ACh, muscarone is known to have high affinity
for both kinds of receptors (Pauling and Petcher, 1972).

An interesting group of toxic compounds which bind to nicotinic neuromuscular ACh-receptors are the neurotoxins of snake venoms, such as
α-bungarotoxin from the krait, *Bungarus multicinctus*, and the neurotoxin
from the cobra, *Naja naja* (Lee, 1972). These toxins are basic polypeptides
(mol. wt. 7000–8000), and they seem to bind to the nicotinic ACh-receptor
with very high affinities, so that, from a pharmacological point of view, their

binding is considered irreversible. These toxins are considered highly specific for the ACh-receptor; however, they have been found to bind irreversibly to the sarcoplasm when present at high concentrations (Porter *et al.*, 1973). The neurotoxins have been isotopically labeled and have become widely used in tagging the ACh-receptor during its isolation and purification (Miledi *et al.*, 1971; Berg *et al.*, 1972; Raftery *et al.*, 1971; Meunier *et al.*, 1972). The neuro-toxin from cobra has also been covalently attached to solid support (e.g., Sepharose 4B) and used to selectively adsorb the ACh-receptor from among other proteins. The receptor is then desorbed by high concentrations of carbamylcholine, and a highly purified ACh-receptor is obtained (Karlsson *et al.*, 1972; Eldefrawi and Eldefrawi, 1973).

To correlate and quantitate the concentration of an activator with its observed effect on the postsynaptic membrane, several hypotheses were proposed. Clark (1933) suggested that drug–receptor interactions obeyed a simple Langmuir relationship of the form $Kx = Y/100 - Y$, where x is the concentration of activator and Y is the percentage of maximal response. This "occupation theory" predicts that response is linearly proportional to the percentage of receptor sites occupied, that maximal response requires occu-pation of all receptor sites, and that the different response elicited by equal concentrations of activators is dependent on their affinities for the receptor. This hypothesis does not account for the different maximal responses generated by different activators. Therefore, Ariens (1954) added the concept of "in-trinsic activity," which is the ability of the activator to produce a response, a quality inherent in each activator molecule.

The "occupation theory" was also modified by Stephenson (1956), who suggested that maximal response produced by an activator does not require occupation of 100% of the receptor sites and that response is a function of the number of sites occupied as well as the activator "efficacy" (a term similar to Ariens' "intrinsic activity"). Assuming that one receptor controls one channel, the occupation of only 5×10^5 receptor sites would be required to produce an e.p.p. (Table I), which is less than 1% of the number of receptor sites in an end plate. Since it is estimated that 3×10^6 ACh molecules are released per impulse (Potter, 1970), a maximum of 10% of the available ACh-receptor sites might be occupied, if each ACh molecule interacts with only one ACh-receptor site before it is hydrolyzed.

We can examine "efficacy" or "intrinsic activity" in view of the recent findings of Katz and Miledi (1971, 1972) that carbamylcholine opens the ionic channels for a shorter duration than ACh (0.3–0.4 ms compared to 1.2 ms), which they suggest may be due to a larger dissociation rate constant for carbamylcholine. In that context, "intrinsic activity" or "efficacy" would be an inherent property of the affinity of the activator for the receptor. In fact, we found during our *in vitro* binding studies that while K_D of ACh for 90% of

ACh-receptor sites in *Torpedo* electroplax was 0.068 μM (Eldefrawi *et al.*, 1971*a*), the affinity of carbamylcholine was lower, so that its dissociation constant, calculated by inhibition of ACh-binding (K_i) (Fig. 2), was 1.1 μM. Supporting evidence is the finding that a higher concentration of carbamylcholine than ACh is needed to produce a similar response in the monocellular preparation of *Electrophorus* electroplax (Bartels and Nachmansohn, 1969).

Another hypothesis of drug–receptor interaction is that of Paton (1961), called the "rate theory." It states that drug effects are not related to the proportion of receptor sites occupied, but are proportional to the rate of drug–receptor interaction, each ACh-receptor association providing one "quantum of excitation." Thus whereas "occupation theory" proposes that the effect of the activator increases with the increase in number of receptor sites occupied until equilibrium is reached, the "rate theory" proposes that maximum effect is reached directly after application (because all receptor sites are free) and then the effect fades to a steady-state response. According to the discussion presented above, the level of excitation is dependent on the rate of drug–receptor interaction and also on the proportion of receptor sites occupied. The "rate theory" also assumes that activators and antagonists bind to the same receptor sites and predicts higher affinities for antagonists. However,

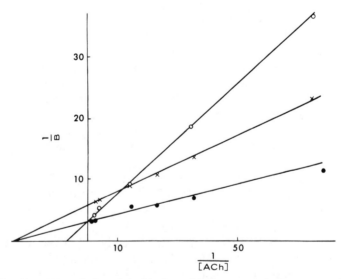

Fig. 2. Double reciprocal plot of the binding of ACh to a particulate preparation from *Torpedo* electroplax in the absence (●) or presence of 1 μM carbamylcholine (×) or 1 μM *d*-tubocurarine (○). *B*, Nanomoles bound per gram of electroplax; ACh concentration is in μM. Blockade of ACh binding by carbamylcholine is competitive, whereas that by *d*-tubocurarine is noncompetitive at the concentrations used.

recent findings from *in vitro* binding studies on membrane-bound or highly purified ACh-receptor suggest that whereas ACh and agonists bind to the active site, antagonists bind to a different site (Eldefrawi and Eldefrawi, unpublished). Inhibition of ^{3}H-ACh binding to *Torpedo* ACh-receptors shows that dimethyl *d*-tubocurarine is a noncompetitive antagonist of ACh at the concentrations used (Fig. 2).

It is clear that many physicochemical processes may contribute to the observed depolarization effect, and it is possible that a combination of hypotheses may be required to explain drug action. With the possibility of the existence of more than one kind of binding site on the ACh-receptor, the situation is even more complicated. This is another of the problems that will be resolved now that pure ACh-receptors are available.

Several laboratories have isolated a highly purified ACh-receptor from electric tissues (Karlsson *et al.*, 1972; Olsen *et al.*, 1972; Schmidt and Raftery, 1973; Klett *et al.*, 1973; Eldefrawi and Eldefrawi, 1973*a*); however, a major problem has been its *in vitro* identification. Once a cholinergic tissue is homogenized, one loses the usual means for identification of ACh-receptors (i.e., the effect of drugs on depolarization of membranes or muscle contraction). A successful way to identify ACh-receptors in subcellular fractions is to study their binding of cholinergic ligands. However, binding of such ligands, by itself, is insufficient for the identification, because macromolecules other than ACh-receptors (e.g., acidic mucopolysaccharide or albumin) can bind some cholinergic ligands. Ligands such as ACh or muscarone do not bind to as many macromolecules as does *d*-tubocurarine or decamethonium (Eldefrawi *et al.*, 1971*c*). One should explore the characteristics of the *in vitro* binding and compare them with the physiological effects. If the effect of a drug on an ACh-receptor is reversible, its *in vitro* binding to it should also be reversible. Furthermore, drugs with *in situ* effects on ACh-receptors (whether agonists or antagonists) would be expected to interfere with their *in vitro* binding of cholinergic ligands. Such a "drug profile" of solubilized ACh-receptors of *Torpedo* electroplax is shown in Table III. In general, the more effective a drug is on nicotinic ACh-receptors *in situ*, the better it is in blocking ACh binding. Thus the nicotinic drugs as well as α-bungarotoxin and cobra toxin are highly effective at low concentrations, and so are the anticholinesterases at 1 mM. The muscarinic drugs (the last six in the table) are either ineffective or have little effect, and the noncholinergic ones are without any effect. Thus this test tube pharmacological approach indicates that the ACh-receptor preserves its drug specificity even after detachment from the membrane, and the same has been observed for the highly purified ACh-receptor from *Torpedo* electroplax (Eldefrawi and Eldefrawi, 1973).

It is generally difficult to determine physiologically whether a nondepolarizing blocking drug acts by (1) interference with transmitter–receptor combination by direct competition for the receptor site, (2) changing of receptor properties through binding to an allosteric site, or (3) interference with permeability changes through binding to the ionophore. Biochemically, it is easier to determine the site of action of such drugs. Even though studies on the

Table III. Blockade of Binding of ACh (at 0.1 μM) to the Lubrol-Solubilized AChR from *Torpedo* Electroplax by Different Drugs [a]

Drug (10 μM)	Percent blockade of ACh binding $\pm$ SE	Significance (P)
Butyrylcholine	91 $\pm$ 37	0.01
Carbamylcholine	74 $\pm$ 16	0.01
Benzoylcholine	12 $\pm$ 3	0.05
Choline	6 $\pm$ 1	N.S.
Succinylcholine	75 $\pm$ 19	0.01
Decamethonium	54 $\pm$ 8	0.01
Hexamethonium	12 $\pm$ 1	0.01
d-Tubocurarine	60 $\pm$ 6	0.01
Gallamine	32 $\pm$ 5	0.01
Nicotine	41 $\pm$ 7	0.01
Anabasine	19 $\pm$ 3	0.01
Hemicholinium-3	19 $\pm$ 2	0.01
Eserine (1 mM)	30 $\pm$ 6	0.01
Neostigmine (1mM)	82 $\pm$ 20	0.01
Pyridostigmine (1 mM)	20 $\pm$ 2	0.01
Edrophonium (1 mM)	100 $\pm$ 25	0.01
Paraoxon (1 mM)	15 $\pm$ 2	0.01
α-Bungarotoxin (0.1 μM)[b]	99 $\pm$ 12	0.01
Cobra toxin (1 μM)[b]	98 $\pm$ 10	0.01
L(+)-Muscarine	4 $\pm$ 2	N.S.
Areocoline	3 $\pm$ 1	N.S.
Pilocarpine	12 $\pm$ 1	0.05
Atropine	10 $\pm$ 1	0.05
Scopolamine	1 $\pm$ 0.2	N.S.
Acetyl-β-methylcholine	9 $\pm$ 2	0.05

Data from Eldefrawi *et al.* (1972).

[a] Binding of ^{3}H-ACh was measured by equilibrium dialysis in the absence or presence of different drugs in the dialysis medium. Among the stimulants, strychnine blocked 25 $\pm$ 3% of ACh binding, but amphetamine, metamphetamine, caffeine, and picrotoxin had no effect. Dibenamine was the only adrenergic drug which blocked ACh binding significantly (14 $\pm$ 2%). Ineffective adrenergic ligands were epinephrine, norepinephrine, dopamine, L-dopa, and ergotamine. No blocking was observed by local anesthetics (procaine, piperocaine, tetracaine, codeine), hypnotics (sodium diethyl barbital), or hallucinogens (d-LSD-25, mescaline hemisulfate). Other ineffective compounds were serotonin, histamine, glutamate, glutamine, and γ-aminobutyrate.

[b] These neurotoxins were added to the AChR preparation 30 min before the start of equilibrium dialysis.

action of various drugs on the binding of transmitter to receptor in solution have allowed us to do quantitative studies that were lacking in physiological experiments, full realization of the various molecular interactions between ACh-receptors and cholinergic drugs is now feasible on the purified ACh-receptor.

4. CHEMICAL NATURE OF THE ACETYLCHOLINE RECEPTOR

Several years ago, Nachmansohn (1955) suggested that the ACh-receptor is a protein on the assumption that only proteins have the ability to "recognize" specific molecules. Until a highly purified ACh-receptor was isolated, evidence on its chemical nature accumulated from two different lines of research. Whenever modification of a certain chemical group affected depolarization of the postsynaptic membrane *in situ*, it was possible to suggest the presence in the ACh-receptor of such groups. The other line was the *in vitro* studies on binding of ACh to ACh-receptor and the effect of different chemical treatments of the tissue preparation on its binding.

The proteinaceous nature of ACh-receptors was established when it was shown that several protein-modifying reagents affected the response of neuromuscular and electroplax preparations. Thus the blockade of response to depolarizing drugs in *Electrophorus* electroplax (Karlin and Bartels, 1966) and chick biventer cervicis muscle (Rang and Ritter, 1969), following treatment with 1,4-dithiothreitol, demonstrates the presence of disulfide bond(s). Similarly, blockade of response in *Electrophorus* electroplax following treatment with *p*-chloromercuribenzoate and *p*-(trimethylammonium)benzene diazonium fluoroborate indicates the presence of sulfhydryl groups as well as amino acid side-chains susceptible to diazotization (Karlin and Bartels, 1966; Changeux *et al.*, 1969). Incubation of the membrane preparation of ACh-receptor from *Torpedo* electroplax with each of these three reagents also inhibits ACh binding (Eldefrawi and Eldefrawi, 1972). Evidence for the presence of carboxyl groups in ACh-receptors is provided by the *in situ* effect of carbodiimide in frog sartorius muscle (Edwards *et al.*, 1970).

Strong support for the proteinaceous nature of ACh-receptor comes from its sensitivity to the action of proteolytic enzymes such as trypsin and chymotrypsin on the solubilized and highly purified ACh-receptor (Eldefrawi *et al.*, 1972; Eldefrawi and Eldefrawi, 1973a). The possible involvement of a phospholipid component is also suggested, based on the effect of phospholipase A treatment on binding of ACh by its receptor (Eldefrawi *et al.*, 1972).

Not only can we prove that ACh-receptor is a protein, but now that a highly purified ACh-receptor is available its amino acid content is obtainable (Table IV), and soon their sequence will be determined. The amino acid composition of ACh-receptor is similar to that of AChE, a macromolecule which has been suspected by some of playing the role of the ACh-receptor (see O'Brien *et al.*, 1972). The AChE and ACh-receptor are similar in many aspects, such as their presence in the same subcellular fractions at similar concentrations [e.g., 7.2×10^3 sites/μm^2 of rat diaphragm for the ACh-receptor as judged by α-bungarotoxin binding and 2.5×10^3 sites/μm^2 of the same end plate for AChE (Salpeter and Eldefrawi, 1973)]. Also, they both bind ACh and other cholinergic ligands such as decamethonium, curare, galla-mine, and atropine (Belleau *et al.*, 1970; Kato *et al.*, 1970, 1972; Belleau and DiTullio, 1971; Roufogalis and Quist, 1972). The use of affinity chromatography or adsorption has recently resulted in separation of ACh-receptor from

Table IV. Amino Acid Composition of the Highly Purified ACh-Receptor from *Torpedo* **Electroplax (Eldefrawi and Eldefrawi, 1973a) and Comparison with Those Calculated from Previously Reported Values for AChE from** *Electrophorus*

Amino acid	ACh-receptor (mole %)	AChE (mole %)		
		Leuzinger and Baker (1967)	Dudai *et al.* (1972)	Rosenberry *et al.* (1972)
Lysine	6.1	4.3	4.8	4.6
Histidine	2.1	2.3	2.1	2.3
Arginine	3.5	5.4	5.0	5.2
Aspartic acid	11.8	10.8	12.6	13.1
Threonine	6.3	4.3	4.1	4.5
Serine	7.1	6.9	6.8	6.8
Glutamic acid	10.7	9.4	11.1	10.4
Proline	6.2	8.1	7	5.9
Glycine	6.4	7.7	8.8	8.7
Alanine	6.0	5.5	7.4	6.2
Half cystine	2.0	1.1	0.9	1.6
Valine	5.5	7.0	6.9	7.1
Methionine	1.7	3.0	1.3	2.7
Isoleucine	5.2	3.7	4.0	3.8
Leucine	9.3	9.0	8.2	8.6
Tyrosine	3.6	3.8	2.9	3.6
Phenylalanine	4.4	5.3	5.1	5.3
Tryptophan	2.1	2.0	—	2.0
Hexosamine	0[a]	1.6	1.3	—

[a] The ACh-receptor preparation contained 1 mole of carbohydrates per 10,000 daltons of protein. Since an equal concentration was found in a blank (1% Triton in Ringer) and in a bovine serum albumin preparation, both subjected to the same affinity adsorption procedure, it was concluded that the source of these high concentrations of carbohydrates was the Sepharose used in the purification protocol, and that if hexosamine were present in the ACh-receptor molecule its presence might be masked by this large amount of carbohydrates.

AChE, so that in one preparation from such a procedure there remains only one catalytic site of AChE for every 20,000 receptor ACh-binding sites (Eldefrawi and Eldefrawi, 1973a).

There appear to be more similarities than there are differences in the amino acid composition of ACh-receptor and AChE (Table IV). The basic amino acids make up approximately 12 mole % of either macromolecule, but the ACh-receptor has about 35% more lysine and 44% less arginine than AChE. There are approximately equal amounts of glutamic and aspartic acids, which make up about 20–23 mole % of either macromolecule, a fact that would account for the low isoelectric points of the two macromolecules, 4.5–4.8 for ACh-receptor (Eldefrawi and Eldefrawi, 1972, 1973a; Raftery et al., 1971). The ACh-receptor has a higher percent of threonine, half cystine, and isoleucine, and less of glycine and valine.

5. DESENSITIZATION

A phenomenon of great interest in neuromuscular transmission is the inactivation or desensitization of the end plate receptors of the muscle (Axelsson and Thesleff, 1958; Katz and Thesleff, 1957; Rang and Ritter, 1970) or electroplax (Bennett et al., 1961) by high dosages of ACh or other activators, or by sustained application of low depolarizing doses (causing 0.5–1 mV depolarization) (Katz and Thesleff, 1957). The muscle recovers its activity seconds after withdrawal of the high dosage or cessation of stimulation. In some physiological studies, different cholinergic drugs are used to prevent mechanical movement of the muscle or inhibit AChE (Otsuka et al., 1962). Such drugs have been shown to have more than one target; e.g., curare not only blocks the ACh-receptor, but it was also found to inhibit the soluble and activate the membrane-bound AChE (Ehrenpreis et al., 1971), as well as act presynaptically (Hubbard et al., 1969). Anti-AChE were found to block the ACh-receptor when applied at high concentrations (Bartels and Nachmansohn, 1969). Such multiple effects of drugs complicate the interpretations of the results obtained.

Katz and Thesleff (1957) proposed the following scheme to explain the mechanism of desensitization:

$$\begin{array}{ccc} ACh + R & \underset{(fast)}{\rightleftharpoons} & RACh \\ (slow)\,k_2 \uparrow & & \downarrow k_1\,(slow) \\ ACh + R' & \underset{(fast)}{\rightleftharpoons} & R'ACh \end{array}$$

They proposed that the occupied ACh-receptor (R) changes its conformation to an inactive form (R'), thereby causing desensitization, but they did not suggest how this change in conformation is brought about.

In the course of our studies of ^{3}H-ACh binding to *Torpedo* cholinergic receptors, we observed that binding reached saturation at 1 μM, and at higher concentrations there was a reduction in total ACh binding (Eldefrawi and O'Brien, 1971). This autoinhibition was reversible upon removal of excess ACh. Therefore, we suggested that this autoinhibitory effect of high transmitter concentration may be due to ACh binding to regulatory sites on the receptor molecule, which causes the receptor macromolecule to change conformation and in the process reject the ACh molecules bound to a larger number of active sites. On the other hand, the observed decrease in affinity of the purified ACh-receptor of *Torpedo* for ACh at high concentrations, due possibly to negative cooperativity (Eldefrawi and Eldefrawi, 1973*b*), represents a more likely basis for desensitization. If so, binding of ACh to the regulatory sites on the ACh-receptor would represent the molecular mechanism underlying the conformational change proposed by Katz and Thesleff.

ACKNOWLEDGMENTS

Experimental work reported herein from this laboratory was supported by U.S.P.H.S. grants NS 09144 and GM 07804. I am grateful to Drs. R. D. O'Brien, T. Podleski, A. T. Eldefrawi, and W. Thompson as well as S. Seifert for their valuable comments which helped in the preparation of this chapter.

6. REFERENCES

Ariens, E. J., 1954, Affinity and intrinsic activity in the theory of competitive inhibition. Part I. Problems and theory, *Arch. Int. Pharmacodyn.* **99**:32.

Axelsson, J., and Thesleff, S., 1958, The "desensitizing" effect of acetylcholine on the mammalian motor end-plate, *Acta Physiol. Scand.* **43**:15.

Bartels, E., and Nachmansohn, D., 1965, Molecular structure determining the action of local anesthetics on the acetylcholine receptor, *Biochem. Z.* **342**:359.

Bartels, E., and Nachmansohn, D., 1969, Organophosphate inhibitors of acetylcholine-receptor and -esterase tested on the electroplax, *Arch. Biochem. Biophys.* **133**:1.

Belleau, B., and DiTullio, V., 1971, Specific labelling of the curare binding sites of acetyl-cholinesterase and some properties of the modified enzyme, *Can. J. Biochem.* **49**:1131.

Belleau, B., DiTullio, V., and Tsai, Y.-H., 1970, Kinetic effects of leptocurares on the methanesulfonylation of acetylcholinesterase: A correlation with pharmacodynamic properties, *Mol. Pharmacol.* **6**:41.

Bennett, M. V. L., Wurzel, M., and Grundfest, H., 1961, The electrophysiology of electric organs of marine electric fishes, *J. Gen. Physiol.* **44**:757.

Berg, D. K., Kelly, R. B., Sargent, P. B., Williamson, P., and Hall, Z. W., 1972, Binding of a α-bungarotoxin to acetylcholine receptors in mammalian muscle, *Proc. Natl. Acad. Sci. USA* **69**:147.

Bernard, C., 1856, Analyse physiologique des propriétés des systèmes musculaire et nerveux au moyen du curare, *Compt. Rend. Hebd. Séanc. Acad. Sci. Paris* **43**:825.

Bertolini, A., Greggia, A., and Ferrari, W., 1967, Atropine-like properties of hemicholinium-3, *Life Sci.* **6**:537.

Burgen, A. S. V., 1965, The role of ionic interaction at the muscarinic receptor, *Brit. J. Pharmacol.* **25**:4.

Changeux, J.-P., Podleski, T., and Meunier, J.-C., 1969, On some structural analogies between acetylcholinesterase and the macromolecular receptor of acetylcholine, *J. Gen. Physiol.* **54**:225S.

Changeux, J.-P., Meunier, J.-C., and Huchet, M., 1971, Studies on the cholinergic receptor protein of *Electrophorus electricus*, *Mol. Pharmacol.* **7**:538.

Clark, A. J., 1933, *The Mode of Action of Drugs on Cells*, Arnold, London.

Dale, H. H., Feldberg, W., and Vogt, M., 1936, Release of acetylcholine at voluntary motor nerve endings, *J. Physiol. Lond.* **86**:353.

Del Castillo, J., Rodriguez, A., and Romero, C. A., 1967, Pharmacological studies on an artificial transmitter–receptor system, *Ann. N.Y. Acad. Sci.* **144**:803.

Dudai, Y., Silman, I., Kalderon, N., and Blumberg, S., 1972, Purification by affinity chromatography of acetylcholinesterase from electric organ tissue of the electric eel subsequent to tryptic treatment, *Biochim. Biophys. Acta* **268**:138.

Eccles, J. C., 1966, The ionic mechanisms of excitatory and inhibitory synaptic action, *Ann. N.Y. Acad. Sci.* **137**:473.

Edelstein, S. J., 1972, An allosteric mechanism for the acetylcholine receptor, *Biochem. Biophys. Res. Commun.* **48**:1160.

Edwards, C., Bunch, W., Marfey, P., Marois, R., and Van Meter, D., 1970, Studies on the chemical properties of the acetylcholine receptor site of the frog neuromuscular junction, *J. Membrane Biol.* **2**:119.

Ehrenpreis, S., Hehir, R. M., and Mittag, J. W., 1971, Assay and properties of essential (junctional) cholinesterases of the rat diaphragm, in: *Cholinergic Ligand Interactions* (D. Triggle, J. Moran, and E. Barnard, eds.), p. 67, Academic Press, New York.

Eldefrawi, M. E., and Eldefrawi, A. T., 1972, Characterization and partial purification of the acetylcholine receptor from *Torpedo* electroplax, *Proc. Natl. Acad. Sci. USA* **69**:1776.

Eldefrawi, M. E., and Eldefrawi, A. T., 1973a, High recovery purification and molecular properties of the acetylcholine receptor from *Torpedo* electroplax, *Arch. Biochem. Biophys.* **159**:362.

Eldefrawi, M. E., and Eldefrawi, A. T., 1973b, Cooperativities in the binding of acetylcholine to its receptor, *Biochem. Pharmacol.* **22**:3145.

Eldefrawi, M. E., and O'Brien, R. D., 1971, Autoinhibition of acetylcholine binding to *Torpedo* electroplax; a possible molecular mechanism for desensitization, *Proc. Natl. Acad. Sci. USA* **68**:2006.

Eldefrawi, M. E., Britten, A. G., and Eldefrawi, A. T., 1971a, Acetylcholine binding to *Torpedo* electroplax: Relationship to acetylcholine receptors, *Science* **173**:338.

Eldefrawi, M. E., Britten, A. G., and O'Brien, R. D., 1971b, Action of organophosphates on binding of cholinergic ligands, *Pesticide Biochem. Physiol.* **1**:101.

Eldefrawi, M. E., Eldefrawi, A. T., and O'Brien, R. D., 1971c, Binding sites for cholinergic ligands in a particulate fraction of *Electrophorus* electroplax, *Proc. Natl. Acad. Sci. USA* **68**:1047.

Eldefrawi, M. E., Eldefrawi, A. T., Gilmour, L. P., and O'Brien, R. D., 1971d, Multiple affinities for binding of cholinergic ligands to a particulate fraction of *Torpedo* electroplax, *Mol. Pharmacol.* **7**:420.

Eldefrawi, M. E., Eldefrawi, A. T., Seifert, S., and O'Brien, R. D., 1972, Properties of

Lubrol-solubilized acetylcholine receptor from *Torpedo* electroplax, *Arch. Biochem. Biophys.* **150**:210.

Ellman, G. L., Courtney, K. D., Andres, V., Jr., Featherstone, R. M., 1961, A new and rapid colorimetric determination of acetylcholinesterase activity, *Biochem. Pharmacol.* **7**:88.

Fatt, P., and Katz, B., 1952, Spontaneous subthreshold activity at motor nerve endings, *J. Physiol.* **117**:109.

Feldberg, W., and Fessard, A., 1942, The cholinergic nature of the nerves to the electric organ of the *Torpedo* (*Torpedo marmorata*), *J. Physiol.* **101**:200.

Ginsborg, B. L., 1967, Ion movements in junctional transmission, *Pharmacol. Rev.* **19**:289.

Hall, Z. W., 1972, Release of neurotransmitters and their interaction with receptors, *Ann. Rev. Biochem.* **41**:925.

Hubbard, J. I., Wilson, D. F., and Miyamoto, M., 1969, Reduction of transmitter release by D-tubocurarine, *Nature Lond.* **223**:531.

Illiano, G., Tell, G. P. E., Siegel, M. I., and Cuatrecasas, P., 1973, Guanosine 3′:5′-cyclic monophosphate and the action of insulin, *Proc. Nat. Acad. Sci. USA* **70**:2443.

Jenkinson, D. H., 1960, The antagonism between tubocurarine and substances which depolarize the motor end-plate, *J. Physiol.* **152**:309.

Jenkinson, D. H., and Nicholls, J. G., 1961, Contractures and permeability changes produced by acetylcholine in depolarized denervated muscle, *J. Physiol.* **159**:111.

Johnson, E. W., and Parsons, R. L., 1972, Characteristics of postjunctional carbamylcholine receptor activation and inhibition, *Am. J. Physiol.* **222**:793.

Karlin, A., and Bartels, E., 1966, Effects of blocking sulfhydryl groups and of reducing disulfide bonds on the acetylcholine-activated permeability system of the electroplax, *Biochim. Biophys. Acta* **126**:525.

Karlin, A., Prives, J., Deal, W., and Winnik, M., 1971, Affinity labeling of the acetylcholine receptor in the electroplax, *J. Mol. Biol.* **61**:175.

Karlsson, E., Heilbronn, E., and Widlung, L., 1972, Isolation of the nicotinic acetylcholine receptor by biospecific chromatography on insolubilized *Naja naja* neurotoxin, *FEBS Letters* **28**:107.

Kasai, M., and Changeux, J.-P., 1971*a*, *In vitro* excitation of purified membrane fragments by cholinergic agonists. I. Pharmacological properties of the excitable membrane fragments, *J. Membrane Biol.* **6**:1.

Kasai, M., and Changeux, J.-P., 1971*b*, *In vitro* excitation of purified membrane fragments by cholinergic agonists. II. The permeability change caused by cholinergic agonists, *J. Membrane Biol.* **6**:24.

Kasai, M., and Changeux, J.-P., 1971*c*, *In vitro* excitation of purified membrane fragments by cholinergic agonists III. *J. Membrane Biol.* **6**:58.

Kato, G., Yong, J., and Ihnat, M., 1970, NMR studies of the interaction of eserine and atropine with acetylcholinesterase, *Biochem. Biophys. Res. Commun.* **40**:15.

Kato, G., Tan, E., and Yung, J., 1972, Allosteric properties of acetylcholinesterase, *Nature New Biol.* **236**:185.

Katz, B., 1971, Quantal mechanism of neural transmitter release, *Science* **173**:123.

Katz, B., and Miledi, R., 1970, Membrane noise produced by acetylcholine, *Nature* **226**:962.

Katz, B., and Miledi, R., 1971, Further observations on acetylcholine noise, *Nature New Biol.* **232**:124.

Katz, B., and Miledi, R., 1972, The statistical nature of the acetylcholine potential and its molecular component, *J. Physiol.* **224**:665.

Katz, B., and Thesleff, S., 1957, A study of the "desensitization" produced by acetylcholine at the motor end-plate, *J. Physiol.* **138**:63.

Keynes, R. D., and Martins-Ferreira, H., 1953, Membrane potentials in the electroplates of the electric eel, *J. Physiol.* **119**:315.

Kimelberg, H. K., and Papahadjopoulos, D., 1971, Interactions of basic proteins with phospholipid membranes, *J. Biol. Chem.* **246**:1142.

Klett, R. P., Fulpius, B. W., Cooper, D., Smith, M., Reich, E., and Possani, L. D., 1973, The acetylcholine receptor. I. Purification and characterization of a macromolecule isolated from *Electrophorus electricus*, *J. Biol. Chem.* **248**:6841.

Krnjevic, K., and Mitchell, J. F., 1961, The release of acetylcholine in the isolated rat diaphragm, *J. Physiol.* **155**:246.

Langley, J. N., 1906, On the reaction of cells and of nerve endings to certain poisons, chiefly as regards the reaction of striated muscles to nicotine and curare, *J. Physiol.* **20**:223.

Lee, C. Y., 1972, Chemistry and pharmacology of polypeptide toxins in snake venoms, *Ann. Rev. Pharmacol.* **12**:265.

Leuzinger, W., and Baker, A. L., 1967, Acetylcholinesterase. I. Large-scale purification, homogeneity, and amino acid analysis, *Proc. Natl. Acad. Sci. USA* **57**:446.

Meunier, J.-C., Olsen, R. W., Menez, A., Fromageot, P., Boquet, P., and Changeux, J.-P., 1972, Some physical properties of the cholinergic receptor protein from *Electrophorus electricus* revealed by a tritiated α-toxin from *Naja nigrocollis* venom, *Biochemistry* **11**:1200.

Miledi, R., and Potter, L. T., 1971, Acetylcholine receptors in muscle fibers, *Nature* **233**:599.

Miledi, R., Molinoff, P., and Potter, L. T., 1971, Isolation of the cholinergic receptor protein of *Torpedo* electric tissue, *Nature* **229**:554.

Nachmansohn, D., 1955, Metabolism and function of the nerve cell, *Harvey Lect.* (1953/1954) **49**:57.

Nachmansohn, D., and Lederer, E., 1939, Sur la biochemie de la cholinesterase, *Bull. Soc. Chim. Biol. (Paris)* **21**:797.

Nemethy, G., and Scheraga, H. A., 1962, Structure of water and hydrophobic bonding in proteins. I. A model of thermodynamic properties of liquid water, *J. Chem. Phys.* **36**:3382.

O'Brien, R. D., 1960, *Toxic Phosphorus Esters*, 434 pp., Academic Press, New York.

O'Brien, R. D., Eldefrawi, M. E., and Eldefrawi, A. T., 1972, Isolation of acetylcholine receptors, *Ann. Rev. Pharmacol.* **12**:19.

Olsen, R. W., Meunier, J.-C., and Changeux, J.-P., 1972, Progress in the purification of the cholinergic receptor protein from *Electrophorus electricus* by affinity chromatography, *FEBS Letters* **28**:96.

Otsuka, M., Endo, M., and Nonomura, Y., 1962, Presynaptic nature of neuromuscular depression, *Jap. J. Physiol.* **12**:573.

Paton, W. D. M., 1961, A theory of drug action based on the rate of drug–receptor combination, *Proc. Roy. Soc. Lond. B* **154**:21.

Paton, W. D. M., and Rang, H. P., 1966, The uptake of atropine and related drugs by intestinal smooth muscle of the guinea-pig in relation to acetylcholine receptor, *Proc. Roy. Soc. Lond. B* **163**:2.

Pauling, P., and Petcher, T. J., 1972, Muscarone: An enigma resolved? *Nature New Biol.* **236**:112.

Porter, C. W., Chiu, T. H., Wieckowski, J., and Barnard, E. A., 1973, Types and locations of cholinergic receptor-like molecules in muscle fiber, *Nature New Biol.* **241**:3.

Potter, L. T., 1970, Synthesis, storage and release of C^{14} acetylcholine in isolated rat diaphragm muscles, *J. Physiol.* **206**:145.

Raftery, M. A., Schmidt, J., Clark, D. G., and Wolcott, R. G., 1971, Demonstration of a specific α-bungarotoxin binding component in *Electrophorus electricus* electroplax membranes, *Biochem. Biophys. Res. Commun.* **45**:1622.

Rang, H. P., and Ritter, J. M., 1969, Disulphide bond reduction in nicotinic receptors, *Brit. J. Pharmacol.* **37**:538P.

Rang, H. P., and Ritter, J. M., 1970, On the mechanism of desensitization of cholinergic receptors, *Mol. Pharmacol.* **6**:357.

Rosenberry, T. L., Chang, H. W., and Chen, Y. T., 1972, Purification of acetylcholinesterase by affinity chromatography and determination of active site stoichiometry, *J. Biol. Chem.* **247**:1555.

Roufogalis, B. D., and Quist, E. E., 1972, Relative binding sites of pharmacologically active ligands on bovine erythrocyte acetylcholinesterase, *Mol. Pharmacol.* **8**:41.

Salpeter, M. M., and Eldefrawi, M. E., 1973, Sizes of end-plate compartments, densities of ACh-receptor and other quantitative aspects of neuromuscular transmission, *J. Histochem. Cytochem.* **21**:769.

Salpeter, M. M., Plattner, H., and Rogers, A. W., 1972, Quantitative assay of esterases in end plate of mouse diaphragm by E. M. autoradiography, *J. Histochem. Cytochem.* **20**:1059.

Sastry, B. V. R., and Cheng, C., 1972, Dissociation constants of D- and L-lactoylcholines and related compounds at cholinergic receptors, *J. Pharmacol. Exptl. Therap.* **180**:326.

Schmidt, J., and Raftery, M. A., 1973, Purification of acetylcholine receptors from *Torpedo californica* electroplax by affinity chromatography, *Biochemistry* **12**:852.

Stephenson, R. P., 1956, A modification of receptor theory, *Brit. J. Pharmacol. Chemotherap.* **11**:379.

Takeuchi, A., and Takeuchi, N., 1959, Active phase of frog's end-plate potential, *J. Neurophysiol.* **22**:395.

Takeuchi, A., and Takeuchi, N., 1960, On the permeability of end-plate membrane during the action of transmitter, *J. Physiol.* **154**:52.

Chapter 7(iii)

Neuromuscular Transmission— Enzymatic Destruction of Acetylcholine

Eric A. Barnard

Departments of Biochemistry and Biochemical Pharmacology
State University of New York, Buffalo, New York, USA

1. LOCATION AND MEASUREMENT OF CHOLINESTERASES AT THE JUNCTION

The action of acetylcholine (ACh) at peripheral junctions was postulated, from an early stage of its study, to be terminated by its destruction by a specific enzyme (Dale, 1914; Loewi and Navratil, 1926; Eccles, 1937; Marnay and Nachmansohn, 1938). Two main classes of ChE* in nervous tissue have since been described in detail, AChE and BuChE; however, this should be regarded as a broad classification only, since a variety of closely related types actually occur in various sources (Augustinsson, 1963; Usdin, 1970). Both classes split ACh, but AChE does so at a much faster rate than it splits choline esters of butyric or higher acids. BuChE cleaves a wide range of choline esters, with butyrylcholine hydrolysis the fastest. A convenient practical distinction is the high capacity of AChE, but not of BuChE, to hydrolyze acetyl-β-methyl-choline. Both types also act, more slowly, on some noncholine esters, but ChE enzymes are also distinguished from nonspecific carboxylic esterases by the inhibition of ChE by eserine at 10^{-5} M concentration. These distinctions,

---

* Nonstandard abbreviations: ChE, cholinesterase (all types); AChE, acetylcholinesterase; BuChE, butyrylcholinesterase; DFP, diisopropyl fluorophosphate; EM, electron microscope; PAM, pyridine-2-aldoxime methiodide; BW 284C51, 1:5-bis (4-allyl-methylammonium phenyl)-pentane-3-one diiodide.

and their complications and species differences, are reviewed in detail by Augustinsson (1963) and Usdin (1970).

A high concentration of AChE in muscle and peripheral nerve is revealed by biochemical assay of homogenates of these tissues (Ord and Thompson, 1950; Nachmansohn, 1959; Augustinsson, 1963). This approach does not, however, demonstrate the relationship of AChE to the synaptic junctions. For this, several methods possessing high spatial resolution have been used:

1.1. Histochemical Staining

Histochemical staining employs the deposition of some visible product of AChE activity (reviewed by Koelle, 1963). These staining methods (with newer modifications, Karnovsky and Roots, 1964) have established that a high local concentration of AChE is characteristic of all skeletal muscle junctions in vertebrates. There are also a number of versions of these methods used at the EM level, the most recent of which demonstrate a localization of end plate AChE at the junctional membranes. This occurs, in most reports, throughout the secondary infoldings of the postsynaptic membrane, as well as, often, along the presynaptic membrane (Karnovsky, 1964; Davis and Koelle, 1967; Davis et al., 1972). The precise ultrastructural location seen may, however, be influenced by diffusion and selective adsorption of the reaction product. This must account for the differences in this distribution seen with some of these methods, including additional apparent AChE sites at axonal vesicles (Barrnett, 1962; Miledi, 1964) or subneural sarcoplasm (Teräväinen, 1967). Whether AChE is actually on the external surface of the synaptic membrane or in the cleft, or both, is in dispute in the conclusions of these various studies.

By the use of parallel EM methods, BuChE has been reported to be in low concentration at the same membrane sites as AChE, but also to be in or on teloglial Schwann cells (Davis and Koelle, 1967; Teräväinen, 1967; Davis et al., 1972). Unfortunately, none of the histochemical methods can be used quantitatively.

1.2. Microchemical Methods

In the microchemical approach, enzymatic activity is measured after the synaptic structure, e.g., a motor end plate or ganglionic synapse, has been isolated, either by sectioning of a frozen layer (Couteaux and Nachmansohn, 1940; Lowry et al., 1954; Guth et al., 1964) or by microdissection (Brzin and Zajicek, 1958). Exquisitely sensitive assays, such as those of Cartesian micro-diver gasimetry (Giacobini and Holmstedt, 1960; Brzin and Zeuthen, 1961) or fluorometry (Guilbault et al., 1968) or use of a radioactive substrate

(Buckley and Heaton, 1968; Koslow and Giacobini, 1969), can permit quantitation of AChE down to the single synapse level. However, considerable fluctuation between replicate specimens has been found in the microdiver measurements on motor end plates (Giacobini and Holmstedt, 1960; Brzin and Zeuthen, 1961). An interesting new possibility is interference microscopy of the enzyme reaction product (Barter *et al.*, 1956) applied to the AChE of single cells (Wieckowski, 1971), which also is quantitative and is very reproducible. A valuable method is microspectrophotometric assay of AChE in groups of microdissected motor end plates, or muscle membranes, which has been used to determine absolute activities, specificities, and enzyme kinetics of the synaptic enzyme (Buckley and Nowell, 1966; Namba and Grob, 1968, 1970; Jedrzejczyk and Barnard, 1974). All of the microchemical methods agree in showing quantitatively a very high local concentration of AChE at the motor end plate and a low concentration elsewhere in the muscle. The minute volume of end plates compared to the whole muscle, however, leads to the situation that 80% of the total ChE activity of the rat tibialis, for example, is outside the end plates (Namba and Grob, 1968). Some of the actual ChE activities that have been measured in end plates are shown in Table I.

1.3. Assay of External AChE

Ehrenpreis and coworkers have reported evidence that in an intact tissue such as a whole muscle, the AChE measurable by hydrolysis of bath-applied radioactive substrate is due to extracellular, membrane-bound, junctional enzyme (Mittag *et al.*, 1971; Ehrenpreis *et al.*, 1971; Mittag and Patrick, 1969). In rat diaphragm, again 80% of the total AChE activity (measured on acetyl-1-^{14}C-β-methylcholine) activity was found to be inaccessible in the intact state, and hence at non–end plate sites (Mittag *et al.*, 1971).

1.4. Radioautographic Methods

Radioactive DFP has been used to label ChE at end plates, under conditions conferring the required specificity on its reaction; radioautography then can provide relative (if ^{3}H is used) or absolute (if ^{32}P and β-track counting are used) measurements of the enzymatic active centers per end plate (Barnard and Ostrowski, 1961; Rogers *et al.*, 1969; Barnard, 1970). This method combines accurate quantitation with high spatial resolution (extending to the EM level, Budd, 1970) and is applicable to intact junctions. AChE has been distinguished (Rogers *et al.*, 1969) by the reactivation of its DFP-

Table I. Kinetic Constants for ACh Hydrolysis per End Plate

Muscle	Conditions	K_m (mM)	Rate of hydrolysis (molecules/msec/end plate)		Reference
			At $(S) = 3-4$ mM	V_{max}	
Rat intercostal	37°C, pH 7.5	3.1	2.7×10^8	4.9×10^8	Namba and Grob (1968)
Human intercostal		4.1	1.2×10^8	2.5×10^8	Namba and Grob (1970)
Rat diaphragm	30°C, pH 7.4	1.1	7.8×10^7	9.7×10^7	Mittag et al. (1971)
(Solubilized)[a]	37°C, pH 7.0	0.2	4.9×10^8		Hall (1973)
Mouse diaphragm	25°C, pH 7.4			2.9×10^7	Brzin and Zajicek (1958)
Mouse gastrocnemius				6.0×10^7	
Rabbit gastrocnemius				3.7×10^8	Brzin and Majcen-Tkacev (1963)
Rat rectus abdominus				3.5×10^8	Giacobini and Holmstedt (1960)
Rat extraocular, twitch	23°C, pH 7.0		1.3×10^7		Buckley and Heaton (1968)
tonic			0.3×10^7		
Guinea pig extraocular, twitch			2.3×10^7		
tonic			0.3×10^7		

[a] Both diaphragm and leg muscles were used. The AChE form (16 S sedimentation constant) characteristic of the end-plate-containing zone showed substrate inhibition at (ACh) $> 10^{-3}$ M; the K_m was calculated from data at lower concentrations.

Table II. Types of DFP-Reactive Sites at Skeletal Muscle End Plates[a]

| | ChE type | | | |
Characteristic	I (AChE)	II (BuChE)	III	Non-ChE
A.				
Eserine (10^{-5} M) binding	+	+	+	−
PAM reactivation after DFP reaction	+	−	−	−
Ethopropazine (3×10^{-5} M) binding	−	+	−	−
BW 284C51 (3×10^{-5} M) binding	+	−	Partial	−
B.				
Acetylthiocholine hydrolysis	+	~ 0	−	−
Butyrylthiocholine hydrolysis	−	+	−	−
Proportion[b]	35%	0–5%	$\sim 30\%$	30%

[a] For set B, the enzyme in microdissected sternomastoid (mouse) end plates was assayed by a microspectrophotometric method, with characterization of the component responsible by use, in parallel, of the treatments listed in A (Jedrzejczyk and Barnard, 1974).
[b] Percentage of the total DFP-reactive sites at each end plate, in mouse and rat muscles. These proportions are quite different in different species (Barnard et al., 1971a).

blocked sites by the AChE-specific reagent, PAM, and by its affinity (measured by protection from DFP) for the bis-quaternary Burroughs Wellcome (Austin and Berry, 1953) inhibitor BW 284C51; BuChE was characterized by its affinity for ethopropazine (Table II). These methods can yield, therefore, the numbers of active centers of each of the classes of ChE-like molecules at individual synapses (Fig. 1). At the ultrastructural level, the same methods applied in the EM have indicated (in mouse skeletal muscle) the location of AChE to be primarily on the postsynaptic membrane (Fig. 2), although the EM radioautography does not distinguish this from the synaptic cleft and folds (Salpeter, 1967, 1969). The number of AChE active centers per unit area of synaptic membrane can then be determined by grain counting in relation to membrane profiles, and is about $2500/\mu m^2$ in mouse motor end plates or $9000/\mu m^2$ for total DFP-reactive sites (Salpeter et al., 1972; Porter et al., 1973)

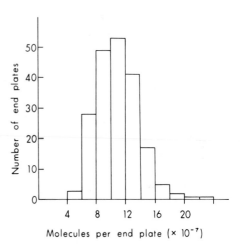

Fig. 1. Histogram showing the relatively uniform distribution of DFP-
reactive sites per end plate in the
population (200 end plates) of white
fibers of the sternomastoid muscle of
the rat (approximately 300 g body
weight). The standard error of the
mean is only 2% of the mean. The
values for AChE active center numbers are 35% of these values. From
^{32}P-DFP track-counting data of J.
Wieckowski and E. A. Barnard.

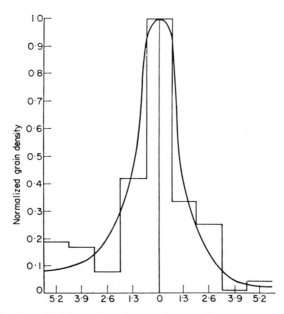

Fig. 2. Distribution of AChE active centers across the synaptic junction of the sternomastoid muscle fiber of the mouse. ^{3}H-DFP labeling, with a PAM treatment sequence to
obtain specificity for AChE, was used. The grain distribution in the EM radioautograms
is plotted relative to distance (in units of 1600 Å), measured from the postsynaptic membrane as origin. The maximum grain density has been set as 1.0. The curve shows the
theoretical spread of grains from a line source following the contours of the postsynaptic
membrane. From Salpeter (1969).

2. AMOUNTS AND TYPES OF CHOLINESTERASE AT THE JUNCTIONS

The number of active centers of AChE per motor end plate has been determined (Table III) in a variety of muscle types in vertebrates (Rogers et al., 1969; Barnard et al., 1971a). Of the end plate sites that react with DFP rapidly and to a plateau value, the proportion that possess the properties of AChE (Table II) varies considerably among species (but appears to be constant within a species), being, e.g., about 35% in mouse and rat muscles but 60% in chicken muscles (Barnard et al., 1971a). However, only this fraction hydrolyzes ACh at a significant rate, as judged by the total abolition of that activity in rat muscle end plate membranes by $1–5 \times 10^{-6}$ M BW 284C51 and similar AChE inhibitors (Namba and Grob, 1968; Hall, 1973). Similarly, the activity of microdissected mouse sternomastoid end plates on acetylthiocholine is, after blockade by DFP, restored quantitatively by PAM reactivation (Jedrzejczyk and Barnard, 1974). The BuChE and the other unidentified type of ChE-like site (type III, Table II), which, therefore, appear to be ineffective on ACh, are of unknown function. In mammalian intestinal smooth muscle junctions, too, Mittag and Patrick (1969) have given evidence that the enzyme

Table III. Numbers of Active Centers of AChE and of ChE-like Sites at the Motor End Plate in Various Muscle Types[a]

Species	Muscle	Predominant fiber type	ChE (total)	AChE
			Active sites per end plate	
Mouse	Diaphragm	Red	2.1×10^7	1.1×10^7
Rat	Diaphragm	Red	4.6×10^7	2.2×10^7
Rat	Intercostal	Red	5.1×10^7	2.5×10^7
Mouse	Sternomastoid	White	6.8×10^7	3.4×10^7
Rat	Sternomastoid	White	6.9×10^7	3.5×10^7
Chicken	Posterior latissimus dorsi	Twitch[b]	2.0×10^7	1.4×10^7
	Anterior latissimus dorsi	Tonic	1.6×10^7	1.0×10^7
Mouse	Extraocular	Twitch[b]	4.0×10^7	2.0×10^7
	Extraocular	Tonic	0.8×10^7	0.4×10^7
Monkey (rhesus)	Sphincter ani	Tonic	1.9×10^7	0.4×10^7

[a] From ^{32}P-DFP track-counting measurements (Barnard et al., 1971a).
[b] Not classifiable in the same three categories as the usual mammalian twitch muscles: these fibers appear white, but are poor in postjunctional membrane folds (Hess, 1967).

cleaving ^{14}C-butyrylcholine is essentially inactive on ^{14}C-ACh, in contrast to the well-known BuChE of mammalian serum. Whether this holds true for the ChE types at end plates in all muscles in vertebrates has yet to be established.

Vertebrate skeletal muscle fibers are classified as twitch or tonic (slow) fibers (Peachey and Huxley, 1962; Hess, 1967), the latter (rare in mammals) being multiply innervated and responding with a prolonged contracture instead of a rapid twitch. The twitch fibers can be divided into red, white, and intermediate types (Gauthier and Padykula, 1966; Guth et al., 1970; Peter et al., 1972). Subclasses of these have been distinguished (Schiaffino et al., 1970), and the types themselves are variable with functional demands (Guth and Yellin, 1971), but generally the form of the neuromuscular junction is determined by one of these fiber types (Padykula and Gauthier, 1970). The white fibers have the most, and the red fibers the least, postsynaptic membrane per junction. The white fiber end plates have also been reported to contain many more presynaptic vesicles (Padykula and Gauthier, 1970). In a reasonably homogeneous muscle such as the white sternomastoid of the rat, the content of ChE (or AChE) molecules per end plate is found to be uniform, within the experimental error of measurements (Fig. 1). When different muscle types are compared (Barnard et al., 1971a), a correlation is found between the end plate content of ChE-like sites and muscle fiber size (Fig. 3). Most mammalian twitch muscles are of mixed fiber categories, so that this correlation can be made only with the predominant type in a given muscle. The white fibers are found to have a higher content of these sites than the red (Table III). Mammalian tonic muscle fibers, which are much smaller in diameter and have very small end plates, have distinctly less of the enzyme at each end plate (Table III). This overall correlation with fiber type and size suggests that

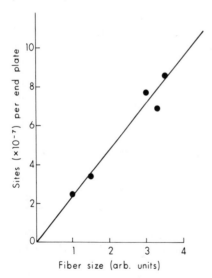

Fig. 3. Increase with muscle fiber diameter of DFP-reactive sites per end plate (or AChE sites, if the values are multiplied by 0.35). Each point represents the mean content for the end plate from a given rat muscle type, plotted against the mean diameter (in arbitrary relative units) of the same group of fibers. From data of J. Wieckowski and E. A. Barnard, on five muscle types from the rat.

there is a constant density of the ChE molecules on the postsynaptic membrane in all of these junctions: as the muscle fiber diameter increases, or is changed from red to white, the postsynaptic membrane surface increases and more ChE is accommodated.

3. REQUIREMENT FOR AChE IN IMPULSE TRANSMISSION

A direct requirement for AChE in limiting the action of ACh at the skeletal neuromuscular junction is inferred from (1) the high local concentration (Tables I and III) of AChE in or close to (Fig. 2) the postsynaptic membrane there, and (2) the effects of anticholinesterases in modifying impulse transmission. A direct relationship between a measured inhibition of synaptic AChE by an anticholinesterase and modification of rapid e.p.p. propagation needs, however, to be demonstrated before such a requirement is established. Important questions here are (1) is all of the AChE at the junction required for normal transmission at physiological rates? (2) is there a simple relationship between inhibition of AChE molecules and the inducibility and form of the e.p.p.? (3) does the rest of the ChE complement (Table II) play a role? (4) is the quantitative role of AChE the same at all nicotinic junctions? (5) is there a definite molecular or steric relationship between AChE and the ACh receptor? Evidence, not always yet definitive, has become available in recent years on these questions.

The effects of cholinesterase inhibitors on the observable parameters of neuromuscular transmission have been extensively documented and interpreted (see the comprehensive review by Werner and Kuperman, 1963). Characteristically, an effective but submaximal dose potentiates the muscle response to nerve stimulation (Fig. 4) or to ACh application, and it frequently produces spontaneous repeated contractions involving whole motor units (fasciculation). Further anticholinesterase treatment depresses transmission,

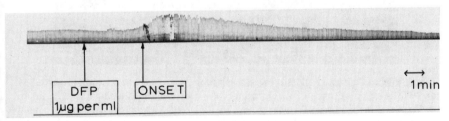

Fig. 4. Response of nerve–muscle preparation to treatment with an irreversible anticholinesterase. The isometric contractions of the rat diaphragm at 37°C, in response to nerve stimulation at 12/min, are potentiated during the initial phase of the reaction of DFP at the end plates; as the reaction proceeds, this potentiation disappears. By parallel radioautographic determination (using ³H-DFP) on these fibers, it was shown that at the onset point for the potentiation, 65% of the AChE active centers are blocked. From Barnard and Wieckowski (1970).

an effect which increases with stimulus frequency. The phase of potentiation is associated with repetitive antidromic discharges in the motor neurons, attributed to a depolarization of the presynaptic terminal (Werner, 1961; Barstad, 1962; Hubbard *et al.*, 1965). Increase of amplitude of m.e.p.p.'s is also produced in this phase (Fig. 5). All of these effects can be produced in appropriate conditions by graded doses of ACh, and all of them can be explained in terms of an increased synaptic concentration of ACh. However, the direct pre- or postsynaptic actions of many anticholinesterases (Werner and Kuperman, 1963; Blaber and Christ, 1967) could interfere in such experiments. These can be examined by pretreatment with an excess of another anticholinesterase or by stimulation by an agonist resistant to ChE (e.g., carbachol), when (Katz and Thesleff, 1957; Goldsmith, 1963) any direct actions of the anticholinesterase present are seen (Fig. 5). Probably, all of the

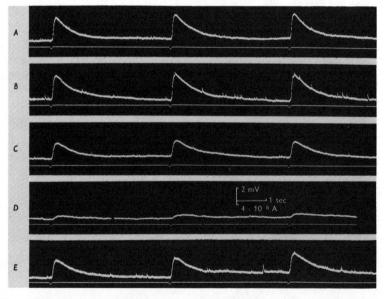

Fig. 5. Effect of an anticholinesterase (edrophonium) on the depolarization produced by an AChE-resistant drug, carbachol. Intracellular recording from a single position in an end plate of the curarized frog sartorius, 20°C. Current applied through the carbachol micropipette is indicated by the downward deflections in the lower trace in each record. In A, the muscle was in Ringer's solution; B, in 10 μg/ml edrophonium solution; C, 30 μg/ml edrophonium; D, 100 μg/ml edrophonium; E, Ringer's solution again. The m.e.p.p.'s are seen as small upward deflections; note that they become more pronounced in B and E. Edrophonium at 10 μg/ml, ineffective on the carbachol potential here, would give a large initial increase in the e.p.p. or an ACh potential. At higher concentrations, edrophonium has a separate curare-like action, as seen in C and D, which is (E) reversible. From Goldsmith (1963).

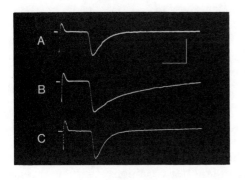

Fig. 6. Direct assessment of AChE inhibition, by using an irreversible anticholinesterase, with subsequent removal of unreacted reagent, and measurement of changes in the end plate current. The effects of DFP, and their reversal by PAM, are shown for the voltage-clamped, glycerol-treated frog sartorius muscle, at 25°C. (A) Control, showing the end plate current. (B) After complete DFP inhibition and washing. (C) After reversal of the blockade by treatment with PAM (10^{-3} M, 20 min) and washing. The horizontal bar represents 3 ms, and the vertical bar represents 3×10^{-7} A. The holding potential for A, B, and C was -90 mV. No curare was used. Note the great prolongation of the decay phase after blockade (the mean ratio of the half-decay times for end plates in A compared to B was about 3) and also the complete return after reactivation of AChE alone by PAM. Note also that in preparation C there will still remain the blockade by DFP of all of the non-AChE ChE-type sites (see Table II) but that the synaptic response is completely normal. From experiments of K. Kuba, E. X. Albuquerque, and E. A. Barnard. Similar data have also been obtained on the voltage-clamped rat end plate.

reversible anticholinesterases have, as would be expected from evidence for molecular similarities in AChE and the ACh-receptor, direct pre- or post-synaptic actions to some extent, but usually these are found to be minor at the enzyme-inhibitory concentrations used (Fig. 5B; *cf.* Werner and Kuperman, 1963). However, certain of them, e.g., in the ambenomium series (Karczmar, 1967; Blaber and Christ, 1967), do exhibit there considerable nonclassical activities. All such difficulties can be avoided by the use of an irreversible inhibitor such as DFP, followed by washout to avoid the extraneous effects of organophosphates, the latter side-reactions always being reversible (van der Meer and Meeter, 1956; Groblewski *et al.*, 1956; Werner and Kuperman, 1963), as is illustrated in Fig. 6B, where a pure anticholinesterase effect is demonstrated.

A direct assessment of anticholinesterase action is provided by the change produced in the e.p.p.: its amplitude is increased and the decay is much prolonged (Eccles and MacFarlane, 1949; Fatt and Katz, 1951; Kuba and Tomita, 1971). These increases are unambiguously seen in the end plate current as measured in voltage-clamp experiments (Fig. 6), notably in its partly exponential decay phase (Takeuchi and Takeuchi, 1959; Magleby and Stevens, 1972*a*). The usual interpretation of these facts (*cf.* Eccles, 1964; p. 48; Werman, 1969) has been that the time course of the end plate current denotes the changes in ACh concentration at the receptor sites. The change in total concentration, $c(t)$, of ACh after an interval t is expressed by a conservation equation:

$$\overline{V}\frac{dc(t)}{dt} = \underbrace{f(t)}_{\text{release}} - \underbrace{\int_0^t G(t-\tau)c(\tau)\,d\tau}_{\text{diffusion}} - \underbrace{k_E c(t)}_{\text{hydrolysis}} \tag{1}$$

where $\overline{V}$ is the volume of the cleft (assumed to be without a gradient in ACh), the function $f(t)$ describes the release of ACh from the nerve terminal, a complex function G describes the diffusional loss of ACh with respect to time τ, and the third term on the right-hand side represents the AChE hydrolysis using a first-order rate constant (for conditions far below enzyme saturation by substrate) (Magleby and Stevens, 1972b). The observed simple exponential decay of the end plate conductance is then accounted for by the hydrolysis and diffusion terms in equation (1). The rate of ACh release, $f(t)$, is too rapid to affect the ACh disappearance, being at least ten times faster than the observed end plate current decay (Katz and Miledi, 1965). The role of AChE in the normal decline would be measurable by the effect of low levels of anticholinesterase in reducing the last term in equation (1).

The diffusion term in equation (1) can only be calculated approximately, due to the complex geometry of the end plate. Eccles and Jaeger (1958) showed that the diffusional loss of transmitter has a half time of 2 ms, from a long strip (4μm in width) approximating the motor end plate contacts. They deduced that, for the usual types of neuromuscular junction geometry, simple diffusion of ACh could account for the observed course of cessation of its action in the anticholinesterase-poisoned preparation, indicating that AChE activity is normally important. The half-decay time of the end plate current for the amphibian (Takeuchi and Takeuchi, 1959) and mammalian (Gage and Armstrong, 1968; Albuquerque and Adler, 1974) end plates is on the order of 1 ms or less (at 25°C), and in all cases these times are prolonged by anticholinesterase treatment (cf. Fig. 6). In glycerol-treated frog sartorius fibers (at 20°C), the maximal prolongation by neostigmine is 2.2-fold (Magleby and Stevens, 1972a), over a considerable range of clamped membrane potential. This, and the heightened amplitude of the end plate current, suggest that in the normal end plate the diffusion and hydrolysis contributions are of the same order of magnitude. In mammalian fast fiber end plates, with their large extent of folding and higher ChE content (Table III), the contribution of hydrolysis is probably greater. The diffusion of ACh when near the receptors is not free, however; for example, Katz and Miledi (1973) found, from the effect of partial curare blockade on the frog miniature end plate current, that 66% of the local ACh is reversibly bound to receptors, and only 34% was free to diffuse, when AChE is all blocked. Mechanical pressure by a micro-electrode halved the current decay rate, due to obstruction of this diffusion, whereas when AChE was not blocked, this effect was insignificant, showing that the hydrolysis term normally dominates the diffusion term in the receptor zone.

This type of interpretation has been contested by Magleby and Stevens (1972a,b), on the basis of the observed voltage dependence of the end plate current, which was attributed by these authors to conformational changes in the ACh-receptor complex, which are held to be rate-limiting. This would mean that the ACh diffusion (equation 1) is rapid and that any reduction in the hydrolysis by AChE is insignificant in prolonging end plate current. That the latter prolongation is actually observed with anticholinesterases is then explained by some other, direct effect of those agents on the receptors. This view is, however, in opposition to a great deal of other evidence noted above; further, it is opposed by the observation that the same prolongation is obtained when the anticholinesterase is an irreversible one which is subsequently washed out, in conditions such that only the AChE is reacted (Fig. 6). That a number of anticholinesterases do actually inhibit AChE in the end plates has been demonstrated by the use of the *in situ* analytical methods enumerated earlier. Also, Potter (1970) has shown that there is 97% inhibition of ^{3}H-ACh hydrolysis in diaphragm treated with 3×10^{-5} M eserine or neostigmine.

With the irreversible anticholinesterase DFP, receptor activity can become affected reversibly, i.e. when the DFP (10^{-3} M) is maintained in the medium, apparently by blockade of its ionic conductance system (Kuba et al., 1974) or by uncoupling of the latter from the activated receptor (Kuba et al., 1973). When the excess DFP is removed, a marked prolongation of the current is observed that is attributable to simple anticholinesterase action, as in Fig. 6. However, in general, the relationship between the end plate current amplitude and the local concentration of ACh is *not* the direct one noted earlier, since some of the effects produced by AChE blockade last much longer than predicted thus (Magleby and Stevens, 1972b; Kuba et al., 1973, 1974). Computer simulations with various assumed rate constants for the terms in equation (1) and in receptor-ACh complexing (Kordas, 1972) show that the lifetime of ACh in the cleft *could* be much shorter than that of the activated receptor complex. The latter should be the direct determinant of the end-plate current, and conformational changes in it and the linked ion conductance modulator could reasonably explain the observed rates. Hence, hydrolysis by AChE normally operates to keep the ACh concentration less than rate-limiting for the decline of the end plate current. When the AChE is blocked (and in the absence of extraneous reversible effects of the blocker), the increased local ACh concentration must prolong the decline of the current, the various effects seen in this phase (Magleby and Stevens, 1972a; Kuba et al., 1973, 1974) being presumably determined also by buffering of ACh levels by receptor binding (Katz and Miledi, 1973), by locally restricted diffusion zones, and by the excess of receptors over ACh molecules (see below).

Considering question (1) above, i.e., the quantitative requirement for end plate AChE, the degree of inhibition of the enzyme activity by irreversible (organophosphate) anticholinesterases has been measured at twitch potentiation (70–80% inhibition) and at later stages of blockade in the rat diaphragm, by Barstad (1956, 1960), van der Meer and Meeter (1956), and Barnes and Duff (1953). However, the enzyme activity on ACh was measured in muscle homogenates, where, as we have seen, only a minor fraction is due to the end plate AChE. A direct correlation with the end plate AChE has been made by the radioautographic method (Barnard and Wieckowski, 1970). It was found in rat sternomastoid and diaphragm muscles (Fig. 4) that twitch potentiation commences when 65% of the AChE sites have been blocked. Concurrent data have been obtained by the assay of surface AChE (Mittag et al., 1971). Failure to sustain tetani during 120/s stimulation occurred at 80% blockade of AChE, or at 90% and above at lower frequencies of indirect stimulation (Barnard and Wieckowski, 1970). Therefore, at least 20% of the AChE active centers are essential, to avoid the synaptic accumulation of ACh sufficient to prevent independent transmission of impulses at 8 ms (or shorter) intervals.

It also has been established that in end plates in which all the non-AChE DFP-reactive sites (including BuChE) are blocked (i.e., after DFP treatment and PAM reactivation), all of the responses remain normal. This can be shown by the end plate current time course (Fig. 6) and by the complete return to normal of the tetanic response (Barnard and Wieckowski, 1970) in muscles in this state. In a quantitative study of this (Kuba et al., 1973, 1974), in end plates where all of the non-AChE sites were blocked by DFP (as shown by autoradiographic analysis) and the AChE sites were all reactivated, the amplitude and decay-time course of the end plate current were normal. (The decay was less voltage sensitive than in the normal, but this is thought to be due to incomplete wash-out of the 10^{-2} M PAM used finally.) Hence, answering question (3) above, these non-AChE sites, although comprising 65% of the DFP-reactive sites, are not involved at all in transmission processes.

4. RELATION OF AChE TO ACh-RECEPTORS

The possible existence in a single macromolecule of the active centers of AChE and the ACh-receptor has been much debated (for reviews, see Ehrenpreis, 1967; O'Brien et al., 1972). However, from electroplax a physical separation has been made of the receptor macromolecule (as recognized by α-bungarotoxin or ACh binding) and AChE (De Robertis and Fiszer de Plazas, 1970; Meunier et al., 1971). In motor end plates, the DFP-reactive sites were shown to be distinct from the ACh-receptor sites (as recognized by α-bungarotoxin binding) by the independent labeling of either, but the numbers of these two types were found equal at each end plate in a variety of muscles (Barnard *et al.*, 1971*b*, 1972). Hence (*cf.* Table II) the active center ratio AChE:ACh-receptor is 0.3–0.5 in various species. In electroplax, this ratio has been found to be approximately 1.0 (Kasai and Changeux, 1971; Miledi *et al.*, 1971) or, by reversible ligand binding, 0.3 (O'Brien *et al.*, 1970).

Collagenase or certain other proteases can detach AChE selectively from vertebrate muscle end plates (Albuquerque *et al.*, 1968; Hall and Kelly, 1971; Betz and Sakmann, 1971). The receptor system was reported to be left functionally intact in the membrane, and the half-decay times of the e.p.p. and m.e.p.p. were increased about 1.6 times. After such proteolytic deletion of AChE, Albuquerque *et al.* (1968) showed that the synaptic response to ACh, now prolonged, cannot be further potentiated by anticholinesterases (Fig. 7), in line with the interpretations discussed above. The proteolytic digestion simultaneously removes the synaptic surface coat, an extracellular layer in the synaptic cleft detected by various methods as synaptic cleft substance (Pfenninger, 1971), synaptic material (Bloom and Aghajanian, 1968), intersynaptic filaments (De Robertis *et al.*, 1967), or ectolemma (Betz and Sakmann, 1971). This layer contains protein (Bloom and Aghajanian, 1968; Pfenninger, 1971) and carbohydrate (Rambourg and Leblond, 1967) material and has been suggested as connecting the two synaptic membranes by polyionic binding (Pfenninger, 1971). We can hypothesize models for this system (Fig. 8), taking into account the high density of ACh-receptors in the post-synaptic membrane, about 9,000/μm^2 (Barnard *et al.*, 1971*b*; Porter *et al.*,

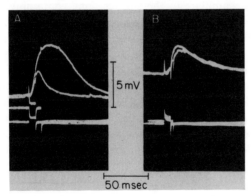

Fig. 7. Effect of proteolytic deletion of AChE on the course of the potential due to micro-iontophoretically applied ACh at the end plate of frog sartorius muscle. Record A (upper tracing) shows the potentiation of an ACh potential by a preceding edrophonium pulse. Record B (upper tracing) shows the failure of edrophonium to potentiate the effect of ACh in the protease-modified end plate. Both records are superimposed tracings showing the effect of ACh alone and the response following edrophonium. The currents releasing ACh and edrophonium, respectively, are monitored in the lower tracings. The duration of the ACh pulse was 10 ms, and for edrophonium it was 70 ms. From Albuquerque *et al.* (1968).

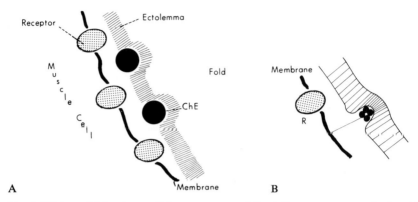

Fig. 8. (A) A model for the possible arrangement of the ACh-receptor system in the post-synaptic membrane and of the ChE molecules (both active AChE and the inactive sub-units of unknown significance) in the cleft substance (ectolemma). (B) In an alternative scheme, the ChE complex is attached by projecting protein chains to the membrane, at intervals between each receptor in a lattice. ACh on its outward path is protected from AChE by the embedded situation of the enzyme in the cleft substance.

1973). The ACh-receptors lie in the membrane in a lattice, their centers about 100 Å apart. The ChE-like sites, which include the AChE active centers, are bound in the cleft substance, either randomly or in a complementary lattice, facing the receptor layer. ACh molecules pass readily through the porous cleft substance, but have an increased chance of collision with an AChE active center once they accumulate in the surface zone containing receptors. The "silent" ChE-like sites (Table 2) may be on subunits inactivated toward polar ligands by the attachment of the AChE complex to the cleft substance. The non-ChE esterase is probably not in this system and appears to be in part in the terminal axon and the glial cells (Davis *et al.*, 1972). The AChE is probably (from its observed distribution, Fig. 2) close to the postsynaptic side; this could be achieved either by binding of it on one face of the doubly layered (Pfenninger, 1971) cleft substance (Fig. 8A) or by attachment to collagen-like chains projecting from the postsynaptic membrane (Fig. 8B), like the glyco-protein chain projections from the erythrocyte surface (Marchesi *et al.*, 1972). Either of these models could explain the means of positioning the AChE lattice, the protease sensitivity, the avoidance of destruction of ACh on its out-ward journey, and the means of insuring that, when diffusion is inadequate, no significant number of ACh molecules can survive in the vicinity of the receptors.

5. QUANTITATIVE RELATION OF AChE TO ACh AT THE END PLATE

The number of ACh molecules released in one impulse has been esti-mated by several methods (see Chapter 7(i)) and varies with muscle fiber type and size: in the rat diaphragm at 37°C, recent estimates (for maximal release at low frequencies of stimulation) are 3–9 × 10⁶ molecules per end plate. The amount of ACh which arrives at the receptor-bearing surfaces must be less than this, and we can take 6 × 10⁶ molecules as the maximum there in any impulse. This quantity decays to a negligible level within an interval [from observation of the mammalian end plate current at 37°C (Albuquerque and Adler, 1974)] of about 1 ms. This period is shorter still at positive membrane potentials (Magleby and Stevens, 1972a), and, as noted above, the lifetime of the ACh is likely to be even less than that of the conductance change. There are 2 × 10⁷ active centers of AChE at this end plate (Table III). Hence the enzyme exceeds the substrate in amount. However, so short is the time available for action that this is not a large excess.

The numbers of ACh molecules that are hydrolyzed in 1 ms by the enzyme within mammalian end plates, and its K_m value, have been measured using the microchemical and the external AChE methods discussed previously (Table I). Correcting the values approximately to 37°C, pH 7.4, and an arbitrary ACh concentration of 4 mM, the maximum value would be about 2 × 10⁸ ACh molecules (or 3 × 10⁸ at saturation with substrate) for the rat diaphragm and intercostal end plates, which are (Table III) about equivalent in AChE content. These values measured in end plates *in vitro* were determined for a constant high ACh concentration, whereas this must, by definition, decay very steeply through the interval of end plate current decline. Hence the amount of ACh that can be destroyed must be very much less. To evaluate the hydrolysis term in equation (1), we can estimate the maximum concentrations of AChE and of ACh in the synapse as follows: The density of AChE active centers found by EM radioautography (Salpeter et al., 1972) over the zone of cleft and junctional folds is 30,000/μm³, i.e., 5 × 10⁻⁵ M, when taken as an average over the whole zone possibly accessible to ACh. The highest possible "effective" concentration of the AChE can be deduced from its surface density and the overlying depth of the folds and cleft (Barnard and Rogers, 1967); this gives, with the recent value (Salpeter et al., 1972) of 2400 AChE molecules/μm² of the synaptic surface, a maximum of 2 × 10⁻⁴ M. Since there are, as seen above, not more than 6 molecules of ACh per 20 AChE active centers at the rat diaphragm end plate, the *maximum* concentration attained by ACh in the cleft and folds is, assuming rapid mixing, 1.5 × 10⁻⁵ M, and probably (due to diffusion and hydrolysis) is below this.

A simple linear relationship of hydrolysis rate v to ACh concentration (S) for (S) < K_m, has been used to predict (Salpeter and Eldefrawi, 1972), taking $K_m = 5 × 10^{-4}$ M and (S) = 10^{-5} M, that v during an impulse is 2% of the theoretical maximal rate. This method gives $v = 6 × 10^6$ ACh molecules/msec here, i.e., about the maximum number to be dealt with (see above). But this calculation considerably overestimates the rate attainable, since (S) declines rapidly toward zero during the process under consideration. We should, therefore, integrate the Michaelis equation for this case (Barnard and Rogers, 1967). We use the turnover number of 8×10^5 min^{-1}, derived from the mean V_{max} value (Table I) and the AChE active center number (Table III). This turnover number coincides with that of the electroplax AChE (at 25°C) (Rosenberry et al., 1972), suggesting that all of the AChE is, indeed, effective when V_{max} for the whole end plate is measured. If the AChE concentration is taken as the above-derived maximum level of 2×10^{-4} M, and if $K_m > 1 \times 10^{-3}$ M (as observed in situ: Table I), 20% or more of the ACh will remain after 0.6 msec. If the K_m value for solubilized AChE from the end plate zone, 2×10^{-4} M (Table I), is taken, then only 0.03% remains after 0.6 msec. Since the efficiency is so sensitive to the values of K_m and of the local AChE concentration, its exact level remains uncertain at present; but it seems likely, on the considerations noted here, that the AChE is capable of destroying most of the available ACh in the required time, but is not present in great functional excess. It seems highly probable that AChE molecules are positioned in the vicinity of all the receptors, as in the model of Fig. 8, for efficiency. In fact, it has recently been shown by EM autoradiographic analysis that AChE is fairly uniformly distributed over the entire postsynaptic region, whereas the receptors are mostly concentrated at or near the tips of the folds (Barnard et al., 1974; Albuquerque et al., 1974). As noted (p. 202) the EM cytochemical evidence also indicates, qualitatively, that AChE occurs throughout the secondary folds.

The action of AChE must be considerably aided by removal of ACh by diffusion, as discussed previously. AChE action is likely to be more important than diffusion deep in the folds, where escape of ACh will be slower. The above-noted occurrence of much AChE, but few receptors, in the lower parts of folds, is thus understandable. The role of diffusion will differ in different types of nerve ending: red fibers of mammals (Padykula and Gauthier, 1970) and various twitch fibers of birds (Hess, 1967), for example, have few and shallow junctional folds. The lower AChE content in these end plates (Table III) is consistent with the idea that its density (per μm^2 synaptic membrane) remains approximately constant in all end plates. In a given type of fiber, the quantum content increases with the size of the end plate (Kuno et al., 1971), as does the AChE content. The extreme case is provided by the tonic fibers of vertebrates, in which transmitter action is required to persist for much longer times (Hess and Pilar, 1964; Orkand, 1963). These have virtually no postjunctional folds (Hess, 1967) and, correspondingly, very low amounts of AChE (Tables I and III). Diffusion can account for almost all of the ACh decay in this case. A test of this interpretation has been provided by the experimental innervation of frog sartorius twitch fibers by the preganglionic nerve fibers of the vagus, when functional junctions form that are devoid of AChE and of synaptic gutters or teloglial enclosures

(Landmesser, 1972). The half-decay time of the e.p.p. was thereby increased from 3 ms (with the normal innervation) to 7–17 ms, and the latter time, unlike the former, was not extended by neostigmine or eserine application. This shows that, with an imperfectly contacting synaptic surface, diffusion of ACh is sufficient for impulse transmission but not for the rapid trains of impulses that control normal twitch muscle fibers *in vivo*. For the latter function, a strategic synaptic distribution of AChE is essential.

ACKNOWLEDGMENT

Work in the author's laboratory referred to here was supported by National institutes of Health Grant GM-11754.

6. REFERENCES

Albuquerque, E. X., and Adler, M., 1974, unpublished observations.

Albuquerque, E. X., Barnard, E. A., Porter, C. W., and Warnick, J. E., 1974, The density of acetylcholine receptors and their sensitivity in the postsynaptic membrane of muscle endplates, *Proc. Nat. Acad. Sci. U.S.A.* (in press).

Albuquerque, E. X., Sokoll, M. D., Sonesson, B., and Thesleff, S., 1968, Studies on the nature of the cholinergic receptor, *Europ. J. Pharmacol.* **4**:40.

Augustinsson, K.-B., 1963, Classification and comparative enzymology of the cholinesterases, and methods for their determination, in: *Handbuch der Experimentellen Pharmakologie*, Vol. 15 (G. B. Koelle, ed.), pp. 89–128, Springer-Verlag, Berlin.

Austin, L., and Berry, W. K., 1953, Two competitive inhibitors of cholinesterase, *Biochem. J.* **54**:695.

Barnard, E. A., 1970, Location and measurement of enzymes in single cells by isotopic methods. I. Principles and light microscope applications, *Internat. Rev. Cytol.* **29**:213.

Barnard, E. A., Dolly, O. J., Porter, C. W., and Albuquerque, E. X., 1974, The acetylcholine receptor and the ionic conductance modulation system. *Fed. Proc.* (in press).

Barnard, E. A., and Ostrowski, K., 1961, Application of isotopically-labelled specific inhibitors as a method in enzyme cytochemistry, *Exptl. Cell Res.* **25**:465.

Barnard, E. A., and Rogers, A. W., 1967, Determination of the number, distribution and some *in situ* properties of cholinesterase molecules in the motor endplate, using labelled inhibitor methods, *Ann. N.Y. Acad. Sci.* **144**:584.

Barnard, E. A., and Wieckowski, J., 1970, The autoradiographic approach to receptor systems and its application to some components of cholinergic junctions, in: *Fundamental Concepts in Drug–Receptor Interactions* (J. F. Danielli, J. F. Moran, and D. J. Triggle, eds.), pp. 229–242, Academic Press, New York.

Barnard, E. A., Rymaszewska, T., and Wieckowski, J., 1971a, Cholinesterases at individual neuromuscular junctions, in: *Cholinergic Ligand Interactions* (D. J. Triggle, J. F. Moran, and E. A. Barnard, eds.), ppl 175–200, Academic Press, New York.

Barnard, E. A., Wieckowski, J., and Chiu, T. H., 1971b, Cholinergic receptor molecules and cholinesterase molecules at skeletal muscle junctions, *Nature* **234**:207.

Barnard, E. A., Chiu, T. H., Jedrejczyk, J. Porter, C. W., and Wieckowski, J., 1972, Acetylcholine receptor and cholinesterase molecules of vertebrate skeletal muscles and their nerve junctions, in: *Drug Receptors* (H. P. Rang, ed.) pp. 225–240, Macmillan, London.

Barnes, J. M., and Duff, J. I., 1953, The role of cholinesterase at the myoneural junction, *Brit. J. Pharmacol.* **8**:334.

Barnett, R. J., 1962, The fine structural localization of acetylcholinesterase at the myoneural junction, *J. Cell Biol.* **12**:247.

Barstad, J. A. B., 1956, The effect of di-isopropylfluorophosphate on the neuromuscular transmission and the the importance of cholinesterase for the transmission of single impulses, *Arch. Int. Pharmacodyn.* **107**:21.

Barstad, J. A. B., 1960, Cholinesterase inhibition and the effect of anticholinesterases on indirectly evoked single and tetanic muscle contractions in the phrenic nerve–diaphragm preparation from the rat, *Arch. Int. Pharmacodyn.* **128**:143.

Barstad, J. A. B., 1962, Presynaptic effect of the neuromuscular transmitter, *Experientia* **18**:579.

Barter, R., Danielli, J. F., and Davies, H. G., 1956, A quantitative cytochemical method for estimating alkaline phosphatase activity, *Proc. Roy. Soc. Lond. B* **144**:412.

Bergmann, R. A., Ueno, H., Morizono, R., Hanker, J. S., and Seligman, A. M., 1967, Ultrastructural demonstration of acetylcholinesterase activity of motor endplates via osmophilic diazothioethers, *Histochemie* **11**:1.

Betz, W., and Sakmann, B., 1971, "Disjunction" of frog neuromuscular synapses by treatment with proteolytic enzymes, *Nature* **232**:94.

Blaber, L. C., and Christ, D. D., 1967, The action of facilitatory drugs in the isolated tenuissimus muscle of the cat, *Internat. J. Neuropharmacol.* **6**:473.

Bloom, F. E., and Aghajanian, G. K., 1968, Fine structural and cytochemical analysis of the staining of synaptic junctions with phosphotungstic acid, *J. Ultrastruct. Res.* **22**:361.

Brzin, M., and Majcen-Tkacev, Z., 1963, Cholinesterase in denervated endplates and muscle fibers, *J. Cell Biol.* **19**:349.

Brzin, M., and Zajicek, J., 1958, Quantitative determination of cholinesterase activity in individual endplates of normal and denervated gastrocnemius, *Nature* **181**:626.

Brzin, M., and Zeuthen, E., 1961, Quantitative evaluation of the thiocholine method for cholinesterase as applied to single endplates from mouse gastrocnemius muscle, *Compt. Rend. Lab. Carlsberg* **32**:139.

Buckley, G. A., and Heaton, J., 1968, A quantitative study of cholinesterases in myoneural junctions from rat and guinea-pig extraocular muscles, *J. Physiol.* **199**:743.

Buckley, G. A., and Nowell, P. T., 1966, Micro-colorimetric determination of cholinesterase activity of motor endplates in the rat diaphragm, *J. Pharm. Pharmacol.* **18**:146S (Suppl.).

Budd, G. C., 1970, Location and measurement of enzymes in single cells by isotopic methods. Part II. Electron microscope applications, *Internat. Rev. Cytol.* **29**:244.

Couteaux, R., and Nachmansohn, D., 1940, Changes of cholinesterase at endplates of voluntary muscle following section of sciatic nerve, *Proc. Soc. Exptl. Biol.* **43**:177.

Dale, H. H., 1914, The action of certain esters and ethers of choline, and their relation to muscarine, *J. Pharmacol. Exptl. Therap.* **6**:147.

Davis, D. A., Wasserkrug, H. L., Heyman, I. A., Padmanabhan, K. C., Seligman, G. A., Plapinger, R. E., and Seligman, A. M., 1972, Comparison of ultrastructural cholinesterase demonstration in the motor endplate with α-acetylthiol-*m*-toluenediazonium ion and 3-acetoxy-5-indolediazonium ion, *J. Histochem. Cytochem.* **20**:161.

Davis, R., and Koelle, G. B., 1967, Electron microscopic localization of acetylcholinesterase and nonspecific cholinesterase at the neuromuscular junction by the gold–thiocholine and gold–thiolacetic acid methods, *J. Cell Biol.* **34**:157.

De Robertis, E., and Fiszer de Plazas, S., 1970, Acetylcholinesterase and acetylcholine proteolipid receptor: Two different components of electroplax membranes, *Biochim. Biophys. Acta* **219**:388.

De Robertis, E., Azcurra, J. M., and Fiszer, S., 1967, Ultrastructure and cholinergic binding capacity of junctional complexes isolated from rat brain, *Brain Res.* **5**:45.

Eccles, J. C., 1937, Synaptic and neuro-muscular transmission, *Physiol. Rev.* **17**:538.

Eccles, J. C., 1964, *The Physiology of Synapses*, Academic Press, New York.

Eccles, J. C., and Jaeger, J. C., 1958, The relationship between the mode of operation and the dimensions of the junctional regions at synapses and motor end-organs, *Proc. Roy. Soc. Lond. B* **48**:38.

Eccles, J. C., and MacFarlane, W. V., 1949, Actions of anticholinesterases on endplate potential of frog muscle, *J. Neurophysiol.* **12**:59.

Ehrenpreis, S., 1967, Possible nature of the cholinergic receptor, *Ann. N.Y. Acad. Sci.* **144**:720.

Ehrenpreis, S., Hehir, R. M., and Mittag, T. W., 1971, Assay and properties of essential (junctional) cholinesterases of the rat diaphragm, in: *Cholinergic Ligand Interactions* (D. J. Triggle, J. F. Moran, and E. A. Barnard, eds.), pp. 67–81, Academic Press, New York.

Fatt, P., and Katz, B., 1951, An analysis of the endplate potential recorded with an intracellular electrode, *J. Physiol.* **115**:320.

Gage, A. W., and Armstrong, C. M., 1968, Miniature endplate currents in voltage-clamped muscle fibre, *Nature* **218**:363.

Gauthier, G. F., and Padykula, H. A., 1966, Cytological studies of fiber types in skeletal muscle: A comparative study of the mammalian diaphragm, *J. Cell Biol.* **28**:333.

Giacobini, E., and Holmstedt, B., 1960, Cholinesterase in muscles: A histochemical and microgasometric study, *Acta Pharmacol. Toxicol.* **17**:94.

Goldsmith, T. H., 1963, Rates of action of bath-applied drugs at the neuromuscular junction of the frog, *J. Physiol.* **165**:368.

Groblewski, G. E., McNamara, B. P., and Wills, J. H., 1956, Stimulation of denervated muscle by DFP and related compounds, *J. Pharmacol. Exptl. Therap.* **118**:116.

Guilbault, G. G., Sadar, M. H., Glazer, R., and Skou, C., 1968, *N*-Methyl indoxyl esters as substrates for cholinesterase, *Anal. Letters* **1**:365.

Guth, L., Albers, R. W., and Brown, W. C., 1964, Quantitative changes in cholinesterase activity of denervated muscle fibers and sole plates, *Exptl. Neurol.* **10**:236.

Guth, L., and Yellin, H., 1971, The dynamic nature of the so-called "fiber types" of mammalian skeletal muscle, *Exptl. Neurol.* **31**:277.

Guth, L., Samaha, F. J., and Albers, R. W., 1970, The neural regulation of some phenotypic differences between the fiber types of mammalian skeletal muscle, *Exptl. Neurol.* **26**:126.

Hall, Z. W., 1973, Multiple forms of acetylcholinesterase and their distribution in endplate and non-endplate regions of rat diaphragm muscle, *J. Neurobiol.* **4**:343.

Hall, Z. W., and Kelly, R. B., 1971, Enzymatic detachment of acetylcholinesterase from muscle, *Nature* **232**:62.

Hess, A., 1967, The structure of vertebrate slow and twitch muscle fibers, *Invest. Ophthalmol.* **6**:217.

Hess, A., and Pilar, G., 1964, Slow fibres in the extraocular muscles of the cat, *J. Physiol.* **169**:780.

Hubbard, J. I., Schmidt, R. F., and Yokuta, T., 1965, The effect of acetylcholine upon mammalian motor nerve terminals, *J. Physiol.* **181**:810.

Jedrzejczyk, J., and Barnard, E. A., 1974, in preparation.

Karczmar, A. G., 1967, Neuromuscular pharmacology, *Ann. Rev. Pharmacol.* **7**:241.

Karnovsky, M. J., 1964, The localization of cholinesterase activity in rat cardiac muscle by electron microscopy, *J. Cell Biol.* **23**:217.

Karnovsky, M. J., and Roots, L., 1964, A "direct-coloring" thiocholine method for cholinesterases, *J. Histochem. Cytochem.* **12**:219.

Kasai, M., and Changeux, J.-P., 1971, *In vitro* excitation of purified membrane fragments by cholinergic agonists. III. Comparison of the dose–response curves to decamethonium with the corresponding curves of decamethonium to the cholinergic receptor, *J. Membrane Biol.* **6**:58.

Katz, B., and Miledi, R., 1965, The measurement of synaptic delay and the time course of acetylcholine release at the neuromuscular junction, *Proc. Roy. Soc. Lond. B* **161**:483.

Katz, B., and Miledi, R., 1973, The binding of acetylcholine to receptors and its removal from the synaptic cleft, *J. Physiol.* **231**:549.

Katz, B., and Thesleff, S., 1957, The interaction between edrophonium (tensilon) and acetylcholine at the motor endplate, *Brit. J. Pharmacol.* **12**:260.

Koelle, G. B., 1963, Cytological distributions and physiological functions of cholinesterases, in: *Handbuch der Experimentellen Pharmacologie*, Vol. 15 (G. B. Koelle, ed.), pp. 187–298, Springer-Verlag, Berlin.

Kordas, M., 1972, An attempt at an analysis of the factors determining the time course of the end-plate current, *J. Physiol.* **224**:317.

Koslow, S. H., and Giacobini, E., 1969, An isotopic micromethod for the measurement of cholinesterase activity in individual cells, *J. Neurochem.* **16**:1523.

Kuba, K., Albuquerque, E. X., and Barnard, E. A., 1973, Diisopropylfluorophosphate: Suppression of the ionic conductance of the cholinergic receptor, *Science* **181**:853.

Kuba, K., Albuquerque, E. X., and Barnard, E. A., 1974, A study of the irreversible cholinesterase inhibitor, diisopropylfluorophosphate, on the time course of endplate currents in frog sartorius muscle, *J. Pharmacol. Exptl. Ther.* **189**:499.

Kuba, K., and Tomita, T., 1971, Effect of prostigmine on the time-course of the endplate potential in the rat diaphragm, *J. Physiol.* **213**:533.

Kuno, M., Tarkonis, S. A., and Weakly, J. N., 1971, Correlation between nerve terminal size and transmitter release at the neuromuscular junction of the frog, *J. Physiol.* **213**:545.

Landmesser, L., 1972, Pharmacological properties, cholinesterase activity and anatomy of nerve–muscle junctions in vagus-innervated frog sartorius, *J. Physiol.* **220**:243.

Loewi, O., and Navratil, E., 1926, Über humorale Übertragborkeit der Herznervenwirkung. X. Über das schicksal des Vagusstoffes, *Pflügers Arch. Ges. Physiol.* **214**:678.

Lowry, O. H., Roberts, N. R., Wu, M.-L., Hixon, W. S., and Crawford, D. J., 1954, The quantitative histochemistry of brain. II. Enzyme measurements, *J. Biol. Chem.* **207**:19.

Magleby, K. L., and Stevens, C. F., 1972a, The effect of voltage on the time course of endplate currents, *J. Physiol.* **223**:151.

Magleby, K. L., and Stevens, C. F., 1972b, A quantitative description of endplate currents, *J. Physiol.* **223**:173.

Marchesi, V. T., Tillack, T. W., Jackson, R. L., Segrest, J. P., and Scott, R. E., 1972, Chemical characterization and surface orientation of the major glycoprotein of the human erythrocyte membrane, *Proc. Natl. Acad. Sci. USA* **69**:1445.

Marnay, A., and Nachmansohn, D., 1938, Cholinesterase in voluntary muscle, *J. Physiol.* **92**:37.

Meeter, E., 1958, The relation between endplate depolarisation and the repetitive response elicited in the isolated rat phrenic nerve–diaphragm preparation by DFP, *J. Physiol.* **144**:38.

Meunier, J.-C., Huchet, M., Boquet, P., and Changeux, J.-P., 1971, Séparation de la protéine receptrice de l'acétylcholine et de l'acétylcholinesterase, *Compt. Rend. Acad. Sci. Paris* **272**:117D.

Miledi, R., 1964, Electron microscopical localization of products from histochemical reactions used to detect cholinesterase in muscle, *Nature* 204:293.

Miledi, R., Molinoff, P., and Potter, L. T., 1971, Isolation of the cholinergic receptor protein of *Torpedo* electric tissue, *Nature* 229:554.

Mittag, T. W., and Patrick, P., 1969, Properties of cholinesterases (ChE) in intact guinea pig ileum *in vitro*, *Fed. Proc.* 28:292.

Mittag, T. W., Ehrenpreis, S., and Hehir, R. M., 1971, Functional acetylcholinesterase of rat diaphragm muscle, *Biochem. Pharmacol.* 20:2263.

Nachmansohn, D., 1959, *Chemical and Molecular Basis of Nerve Activity*, Academic Press, New York.

Namba, T., and Grob, D., 1968, Cholinesterase activity of the motor endplate in isolated muscle membrane, *J. Neurochem.* 15:1445.

Namba, T., and Grob, D., 1970, Cholinesterase activity of motor end plate in human skeletal muscle, *J. Clin. Invest.* 49:936.

O'Brien, R. D., Gilmour, L. P., and Eldefrawi, M. E., 1970, A muscarine-binding material in electroplax and its relation to the acetylcholine receptor. II. Dialysis assay, *Proc. Natl. Acad. Sci. USA* 65:438.

O'Brien, R. D., Eldefrawi, M. E., and Eldefrawi, A. T., 1972, Isolation of acetylcholine receptors, *Ann. Rev. Pharmacol.* 12:19.

Ord, M. G., and Thompson, R. H. S., 1950, The distribution of cholinesterase types in mammalian tissues, *Biochem. J.* 46:346.

Orkand, R. K., 1963, A further study of electrical responses in slow and twitch muscle fibres of the frog, *J. Physiol.* 167:181.

Padykula, H. A., and Gauthier, G. F., 1970, The ultrastructure of the neuromuscular junctions of mammalian red, white and intermediate skeletal muscle fibers, *J. Cell Biol.* 46:27.

Peachey, L. D., and Luxley, A. F., 1962, Structural identification of twitch and slow striated muscle fibers of the frog, *J. Cell Biol.* 13:177.

Peter, J. B., Barnard, R. J., Edgerton, V. R., Gillespie, C. A., and Stempel, K. E., 1972, Metabolic profiles of three fiber types of skeletal muscle in guinea pigs and rabbits, *Biochemistry* 11:2627.

Pfenninger, K. H., 1971, The cytochemistry of synaptic densities. II. Proteinaceous components and mechanism of synaptic connectivity, *J. Ultrastruct. Res.* 35:451.

Porter, C. W., Chiu, T. H., Wieckowski, J., and Barnard, E. A., 1973, Types and locations of cholinergic receptor-like molecules in muscle fibers, *Nature New Biology* 241:3.

Porter, C. W., Barnard, E. A., and Chiu, T. H., 1973, The ultrastructural localization and quantitation of cholinergic receptors at the mouse motor endplate, *J. Membrane Biol.* 14:383.

Potter, L. H., 1970, Synthesis, storage and release of [^{14}C]acetylcholine in isolated rat diaphragm muscles, *J. Physiol.* 206:145.

Rambourg, A., and Leblond, C. P., 1967, Electron microscope observations on the carbohydrate-rich cell coat present at the surface of cells in the rat, *J. Cell Biol.* 32:27.

Rogers, A. W., Darzynkiewicz, Z., Salpeter, M. M., Ostrowski, K., and Barnard, E. A., 1969, Quantitative studies on enzymes in structures in striated muscles by labeled inhibitor methods. I. The number of acetylcholinesterase molecules and of other DFP-reactive sites at motor endplates, measured radioautographically, *J. Cell Biol.* 41:865.

Rosenberry, T. L., Chang, H. W., and Chen, Y. T., 1972, Purification of acetylcholinesterase by affinity chromatography and determination of active site stoichiometry, *J. Biol. Chem.* 247:1555.

Salpeter, M. M., 1967, Electronmicroscope radioautography as a quantitative tool in enzyme cytochemistry. I. The distribution of acetylcholinesterase at motor endplates of a vertebrate twitch muscle, *J. Cell Biol.* **32**:379.

Salpeter, M. M., 1969, Electron microscope radioautography as a quantitative tool in enzyme cytochemistry. II. The distribution of DFP-reactive sites at motor endplates of a vertebrate twitch muscle, *J. Cell Biol.* **42**:122.

Salpeter, M. M., Plattner, H., and Rogers, A. W., 1972, Quantitative assay of esterases in end plates of mouse diaphragm by electron microscope autoradiography. *J. Histochem. Cytochem.* **20**:1059.

Salpeter, M. M., and Eldefrawi, M. E., 1973, Sizes of end plate compartments, densities of acetylcholine receptor and other quantitative aspects of neuromuscular transmission, *J. Histochem. Cytochem.* **21**:769.

Schiaffino, S., Hanzlikova, V., and Pierobon, S., 1970, Relations between structure and function in rat skeletal muscle fibers, *J. Cell Biol.* **47**:107.

Silver, A., 1963, A histochemical investigation of cholinesterases at neuromuscular junctions in mammalian and avian muscle, *J. Physiol.* **169**:386.

Takeuchi, A., and Takeuchi, N., 1959, Active phase of frog's endplate potential, *J. Neurophysiol.* **22**:395.

Teräväinen, H., 1967, Electron microscopic localization of cholinesterase in the rat myoneural junction, *Histochemie* **10**:266.

Usdin, E., 1970, Reactions of cholinesterases with substrates, inhibitors and reactivators, in: *Anticholinesterase Agents*, Vol. I (A. G. Karczmar, ed.), pp. 47–354, Pergamon, Oxford.

van der Meer, C., and Meeter, E., 1956, The mechanism of action of anticholinesterases. II. The effect of diisopropylfluorophosphorate (DFP) on the isolated rat phrenic nerve–diaphragm preparation. A. Irreversible effects, *Acta Physiol. Pharmacol. Neerl.* **4**:454.

Werman, R., 1969, An electrophysiological approach to drug–receptor mechanisms, *Comp. Biochem. Physiol.* **30**:997.

Werner, G., 1961, Antidromic activity in motor nerves and its relation to a generated event in nerve terminals, *J. Neurophysiol.* **24**:401.

Werner, G., and Kuperman, A. S., 1963, Actions at the neuromuscular junction, in: *Handbuch der Experimentellen Pharmakologie*, Vol. 15 (G. B. Koelle, ed.), pp. 570–678, Springer-Verlag, Berlin.

Wieckowski, J., 1971, Interferometric measurements of acetylcholinesterase activity in rat megokaryocytes, *J. Histochem. Cytochem.* **19**:712.

Chapter 8

Ganglionic Transmission

Syogoro Nishi

Neurophysiology Laboratory, Department of Pharmacology
Loyola University Medical Center
Maywood, Illinois, USA

1. INTRODUCTION

The sympathetic ganglion, particularly the superior cervical ganglion, has long been studied as a prototype of autonomic ganglia and a monosynaptic model of the nervous system. Along with the accumulation of new experimental knowledge, however, the prevailing concept that the ganglion forms a simple excitatory synapse has been challenged. First, electrophysiological and pharmacological investigations revealed that the ganglion cells are endowed with two types (nicotinic and muscarinic) of cholinergic excitatory postsynaptic sites (Eccles and Libet, 1961; Volle, 1962; Volle and Koelle, 1961) as well as an adrenergic inhibitory postsynaptic site (Eccles and Libet, 1961). The inhibitory system in the ganglion has been postulated to be disynaptic and mediated by the intraganglionic chromaffin cells, which liberate an adrenergic substance (Eccles and Libet, 1961); this hypothesis, based on physiological observations, has found support in the electron microscopic finding of synaptic junctions between chromaffin cells and principal ganglion cells (Matthews and Raisman, 1969). Second, the sympathetic ganglion cells of some vertebrates are also endowed with a noncholinergic excitatory postsynaptic site which generates an extremely prolonged excitatory postsynaptic potential (e.p.s.p.) lasting for several minutes (Nishi and Koketsu, 1968a; Alkadhi and McIsaac, 1971; Chen, 1971). Finally, cholinoceptive (Koketsu and Nishi, 1968; Ginsborg, 1971) as well as adrenoceptive (Nishi, 1970;

Christ and Nishi, 1971a,b) sites at the preganglionic nerve terminals, which directly and indirectly influence the liberation of transmitter, have been reported. Thus the small seemingly simple structure of the sympathetic ganglion conceals functional and structural complexities not previously considered (see also Chapter 6).

In contrast to the recent advance in the study of sympathetic ganglia, the neurons in parasympathetic ganglia have been scarcely investigated, and most of their functions are very poorly understood. This is because the majority of parasympathetic ganglion cells are scattered diffusely throughout the effector organs; there are only a few anatomically recognizable parasympathetic ganglia (the ciliary, mandibular, otic, and sphenopalatine), and these are not readily accessible for electrical recording. In addition, synaptic transmission at both the parasympathetic ganglia and the neuroeffector junctions is cholinergic. Drugs possessing a cholinomimetic or cholinolytic property may therefore influence both junctional sites, thereby complicating the analysis of ganglionic function with pharmacological agents.

2. RESPONSE OF AUTONOMIC GANGLIA TO PREGANGLIONIC VOLLEYS

It is generally accepted that the transmission of impulses at ganglionic synapses is chemical and that the principal transmitter is acetylcholine (ACh). However, there is an exception; some avian ganglia have both chemical and electrical transmission (Martin and Pilar, 1963a,b).

Upon arrival of an impulse, the small unmyelinated terminal boutons of preganglionic nerve fibers liberate packets of ACh from their storage sites. Although the process leading to liberation of ACh is understood in only a rudimentary way, it is well known that the entry of minute amounts of Ca ions is indispensable to the excitation–liberation coupling (Katz and Miledi, 1966, 1967). The liberated ACh diffuses across the synaptic cleft in a few microseconds (Eccles and Jaeger, 1958) and impinges upon the subsynaptic membrane of the ganglion cells. The resulting interaction between ACh and the receptor sites greatly increases the ionic permeability of the subsynaptic membrane, and gives rise to a local and graded depolarization of the cell membrane. The amplitude of this depolarization (e.p.s.p.) is dependent on the amount of liberated ACh and the number of individual synapses activated. As the synapses of mammalian autonomic neurons are mainly of axodendritic type (Elfvin, 1963a,b), the e.p.s.p. spreads electrotonically along the dendrites to the soma, where an all-or-none, propagating impulse is generated as soon as the tonically spreading e.p.s.p. is large enough to excite the soma membrane. The impulse generated at the soma is conducted along the axon to the postganglionic nerve terminals.

2.1. Response of Normal Ganglia

In response to a preganglionic volley, the autonomic ganglion produces a complex wave form with three components (Bishop and Heinbecker, 1932; Brown, 1934; Eccles, 1935a,b,c, 1937). The first component is a spike potential with a single peak or multiple peaks, and this is followed by a slow negative potential lasting 50–100 ms. This long-lasting negative potential is followed, in turn, by a longer-lasting positive wave form of approximately 500 ms. The initial spike response represents a compound action potential of ganglion cells, and the second (negative) and third (positive) components represent, respectively, the late portion of the synaptic potential and the afterhyperpolarization of the action potential.

The shape of the initial component is determined mainly by the pattern of innervation of the ganglion cells. For example, the spike response of the superior cervical ganglion of the cat consists of four discrete peaks due to the presence of four different groups (S_1–S_4) of preganglionic fibers differing in conduction velocity (Eccles, 1935a). S_1–S_3 groups belong to the B nerve fibers and S_4 to the C fibers. In contrast to the superior cervical ganglion, the stellate ganglion of the cat receives only one main fiber type belonging to the B group (Bronk, 1939; Larrabee and Posternak, 1952); as a consequence, the electrical response of this ganglion to a preganglionic volley is much simpler than that of the superior cervical ganglion. The lumbar sympathetic ganglion of the cat shows compound fast and slow spikes in response to a single volley, indicating that its preganglionic trunk contains a variety of B and C fibers (Obrador and Odoriz, 1936). The response of the cat inferior splanchnic nerve stimulation is similar to that of the stellate ganglion (Lloyd, 1937, 1939). The ciliary ganglion (parasympathetic) of the cat shows a fast and a compound slow spike in response to a single volley (Whitteridge, 1937). This ganglion consists of a large number of B-type neurons which have myelinated axons and a small number of C-type neurons which have unmyelinated axons. The B neurons are innervated exclusively by preganglionic B fibers, while the C neurons are innervated by preganglionic C fibers (Nishi and Christ, 1971). Such a characteristic pattern of innervation of the ciliary ganglion is quite similar to that of the amphibian sympathetic ganglia (Nishi, et al., 1965).

2.2. Response of Curarized Ganglia

2.2.1. Negative (N), Late Negative (LN), and Positive (P) Waves

Blockade of ganglionic transmission is produced by relatively low concentrations of hexamethonium, d-tubocurarine, β-erythroidine, or related substances. Under such conditions, the ganglionic spike is replaced by a

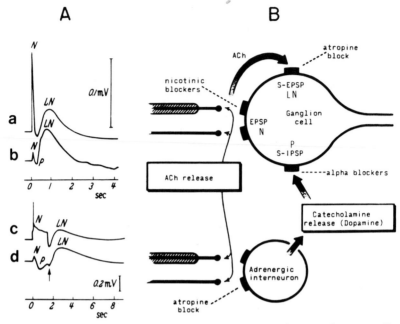

Fig. 1. (A) Postganglionic potentials (N, LN, and P waves) set up by preganglionic volleys and recorded between the ganglion and the postganglionic trunk of the isolated superior cervical ganglion of the rabbit. (a,b) Potentials evoked by single preganglionic volleys in the presence of *d*-tubocurarine, 2.5×10^{-5} M (a) and 8×10^{-5} M (b). (c,d) Similar responses but with repetitive stimulation (20 Hz) in the presence of *d*-tubocurarine, 1.6×10^{-5} M (c) and 8×10^{-5} M (d). The end of the tetanus is marked by the arrow. From Eccles (1952). (B) Schema for synaptic mediation of N, LN (slow e.p.s.p.), and P (slow i.p.s.p.) waves. From Libet (1970), modified from Eccles and Libet (1961); N, LN, and P added by the present author.

prolonged local potential—a subthreshold e.p.s.p. (N wave). Recording from a curarized superior cervical ganglion of the rabbit on a slow time base (Fig. 1A,a) reveals that the N wave of about 100 ms duration is followed, after a slight positivity (P wave), by a later negative potential (LN wave) more than 2 s in duration (Eccles, 1952). At a deeper level of curarization, the N wave is greatly depressed but the LN wave is increased (Fig. 1A,b). These slow P and LN waves are distinctly larger and more definite following a tetanic train of preganglionic volleys (Fig. 1A,c,d) than after a single volley. The P and LN waves become concurrent during the tetanus, while the LN wave is dominant after the tetanus.

According to Eccles and Libet (1961), the P wave is sensitive to the frequency rather than to the total number of the preganglionic volleys which elicit it; it becomes maximal with 40–60 Hz tetani. In contrast, the post-tetanically observed LN wave increases significantly in amplitude and duration mainly with increase in the total number of volleys, and shows relatively little change with increase in frequency above 6 or 10 Hz.

2.2.2. Synaptic Meditation of LN and P Waves

Pharmacological investigations reveal distinctive properties for the N, LN, and P waves (Eccles and Libet, 1961). Botulinum toxin, which has the selective action of depressing the release of ACh from cholinergic nerve terminals (Burgen et al., 1948), depresses the N, P, and LN waves without any definite distinction. Atropine in low concentrations abolishes the LN wave and strongly depresses the P potential, with little effect on the N wave. Dibenamine, an α-adrenergic blocking agent, preferentially depresses the P wave.

Based on these findings, Eccles and Libet (1961) proposed the following hypothesis to describe the synaptic origins of the ganglionic responses (Fig. 1B): The ACh liberated from the presynaptic fiber reacts with subsynaptic sites (N) to elicit the primary depolarizing synaptic response, the N wave. When this ACh diffuses away from the primary subsynaptic regions, it is thought to become bound to LN receptor sites and generate a slowly rising and long-lasting depolarization, the LN wave. The binding of ACh at LN receptor sites is relatively insensitive to curariform agents, but it is highly sensitive to blockade by atropine. The chromaffin cells in the ganglion receive preganglionic fibers which also release ACh, and their postsynaptic sites are also very sensitive to atropine block, rather than to curariform agents. Upon adequate excitation by the released ACh, the chromaffin cell secretes an adrenergic substance. The diffusing adrenergic substance encounters P receptor sites on ganglion cells in the vicinity. This interaction results in hyperpolarization of the ganglion cell membrane—the P wave. The action of the adrenergic substance at the P receptor sites is prevented by dibenamine. Eccles and Libet (1961) suggested originally that the adrenergic substance was epinephrine, but Libet (1970) has produced pharmacological evidence suggesting that dopamine is the mediator of the P wave (see below).

The N, LN, and P waves have been recorded from a number of sympathetic ganglia, including the lumbar sympathetic ganglia of the bullfrog (Libet et al., 1968; Nishi and Koketsu, 1968a; Tosaka et al., 1968), the superior cervical ganglion of the turtle (Laporte and Lorente de Nó, 1950), rat, rabbit, and cat (Dunant and Dolivo, 1967; Eccles and Libet, 1961; Libet, 1967), and the stellate and coeliac ganglia of the cat (Libet, 1964, 1967). In contrast, the ciliary ganglion (parasympathetic) of the cat exhibits an N wave and a very small LN wave but no detectable P wave (Nishi and Christ, unpublished observations). It is not yet known, however, if this is true for other parasympathetic ganglia.

2.3. Slow Ganglionic Responses and Afterdischarges

It has long been known that repetitive stimulation of mammalian sympathetic preganglionic fibers is followed by a prolonged postganglionic afterdischarge (Bronk, 1939; Eccles, 1944; Larrabee and Bronk, 1947). According to Emmelin and MacIntosh (1956), the afterdischarge of ganglia perfused with media containing anticholinesterase drugs was blocked by small doses of procaine but not by hexamethonium or *d*-tubocurarine. Takeshige and Volle (1962, 1963, 1964*a*) have shown that similar afterdischarges are extremely sensitive to blockade by atropine. Treatment of the ganglia with anticholinesterase agents without applying preganglionic stimulation also evokes a persistent postganglionic firing that is sensitive to blockade by a small dose of atropine and is unaffected by ganglionic blocking doses of hexamethonium (Takeshige and Volle, 1962, 1963; Volle, 1962; Volle and Koelle, 1961). It is also known that the ACh-depolarization of ganglia remaining after curarization can be eliminated by the addition of atropine (Takeshige and Volle, 1964*b*). These experimental facts indicate that the afterdischarge following repetitive preganglionic stimulation and the drug-induced long-lasting firing of mammalian sympathetic ganglia mainly depend on the atropine-sensitive cholinoceptive site.

Nishi and Koketsu (1966, 1968*a*) studied the afterdischarge of the isolated bullfrog sympathetic ganglia with regard to its physiological and pharmocological nature and its relation to the slow postsynaptic potentials. They found that under normal conditions the afterdischarge of postganglionic fibers is elicited only when the preganglionic fibers are stimulated with a train of supramaximal pulses of relatively high frequency (50 Hz). The afterdischarge is enhanced and prolonged after nicotinization or curarization of the ganglion. The weak appearance of the afterdischarge in the physiological condition is ascribed to the presence of a prolonged post-tetanic hyperpolarization which suppresses the triggering potentials. The afterdischarge elicited by tetanic B nerve stimulation in the presence of nicotine or *d*-tubocurarine is relatively short-lived (less than 1 min) and can be abolished by addition of atropine. However, the afterdischarge triggered by tetanic B and C nerve stimulation is sustained for a much longer period (up to several minutes) and cannot be completely blocked by atropine in a high concentration. Its initial part is eliminated while its later part remains unaffected when atropine or ACh is added. Thus it is evident that the afterdischarge has two different components. The component which is sensitive to atropine is termed the "early afterdischarge" (e.a.d.), and that which is insensitive to atropine and ACh is termed the "late afterdischarge" (l.a.d.). Recording of the deeply nicotinized or curarized ganglia with a sucrose-gap method (Kosterlitz *et al.*, 1968) reveals that tetanic presynaptic B nerve stimulation produces only an atropine-sensitive slow depolarization (LN wave), while tetanic presynaptic B and C nerve stimulation induces a large LN wave followed by an extremely long-lasting slow depolarization which is insensitive to atropine. The atropine-insensitive slow depolarization is termed the "late late negative" (LLN) wave. It is concluded that the e.a.d. and l.a.d. are respectively triggered by the LN response and the LLN response and that the LLN wave is generated at a specific postsynaptic site in response to a noncholinergic transmitter substance which is released when the preganglionic stimulation is strong enough to stimulate the C fibers.

The existence of a similar noncholinergic postsynaptic response in the mammalian superior cervical ganglion has recently been reported by Alkadhi and McIsaac (1971) and Chen (1971).

3. ELECTRICAL CONSTANTS OF GANGLION CELL MEMBRANE

Since Eccles (1955) introduced the intracellular microelectrode technique to the study of autonomic neurons, information regarding the electrophysiological properties of the ganglion cell membrane has progressively accumulated. Table I summarizes the membrane constants of amphibian and mammalian sympathetic ganglion cells.

The resting membrane potential of ganglion cells measured with conventional intracellular microelectrodes is normally -45 to -60 mV, although the values reported range from -40 to -110 mV, as seen in the table. The large range is probably due to artifacts, principally the injurious effects and/or tip-potentials of microelectrodes. The small size of ganglion cells makes intracellular recording for long intervals difficult. Not surprisingly, no systematic analysis of the resting membrane potential has so far been carried out.

In contrast to the simple unipolar feature of amphibian sympathetic ganglion cells, mammalian autonomic neurons of both the sympathetic and parasympathetic systems are multipolar, with varying numbers of processes. Because of this geometrical complexity, determination of their passive electrical characteristics requires special techniques. As Rall (1959, 1960) pointed out, the current intracellularly applied to a multipolar neuron passes across not only the soma membrane but also the membranes of the axon and the dendritic tree. The current flowing along each of these different paths is determined by a combination of electrical and geometrical factors. The latter include the size of the neuron soma, the size and taper of all its cellular processes, and also the number of dendrites and the extent of their branching. It is therefore desirable in the determination of membrane properties to obtain the exact geometrical features of each neuron from which passive electrical transients are recorded. Iontophoretic injection of a fluorescent dye (procion yellow M4RS, Stretton and Kravitz, 1968) into the ganglion cell cytoplasm

Table I. Electrical Membrane Properties of Sympathetic Ganglion Cells[a]

Ganglion	Soma diameter (μm)	R.p. (mV)	R_N (MΩ)	τ (ms)	R_m (Ωcm²)	C_m (μF/cm²)	Reference
Lumbar							
Frog	22–32	55–75	12–24	7.2–13	235–738	14–40	Nishi and Koketsu (1960)
	37.5–47.5	48 ± 8.8	100 ± 46	10–12		4.9	Hunt and Nelson (1965)
Toad							
B cells	30–40	65	7.2–15	6–10	265–754	13–26	Nishi et al. (1965)
C cells	14–20	40–65	14–18	6–7	111–188	32–63	
Pelvic							
Guinea pig	20–30	40–70	40–150	5–200	2000–10000	2–5	Blackman et al. (1969)
Thoracic							
Guinea pig	31[b] and 19[c]	50–70	19–186	6–14	1000	10	Blackman and Purves (1969)
Superior cervical							
Rat	4.4[d]	45–90	39.4 ± 3.2	2.7 ± 0.3	1800	1.6	Perri et al. (1970)
Guinea pig	5.6[d]	45–90	40.6 ± 4.3	4.4 ± 0.5	2300	2.1	
Rabbit	<70	40–110		2.8–7.7			Erulkar and Woodward (~968)
Cat		57 ± 2.0	15.5 ± 2.2	8.5–10	500–3200	3–17	Skok (1965)

[a] R.p., Resting membrane potential; R_N, total neuron resistance; τ, membrane time constant; R_m and C_m, resistance and capacitance for a unit area of membrane, respectively. Resting membrane potentials are negative in polarity but expressed as positive.
[b] Major diameter.
[c] Minor diameter.
[d] Surface area, × 10⁻⁵ cm².

Table II. Matching Geometrical and Electrophysiological Data on Mammalian Ganglion Cells and Motoneurons[a]

Neuron	Soma surface area (μm^2)	Dendrites Number	Dendrites Length (μm)	R_N (MΩ)	R_m (Ω cm^2)	ρ	τ (ms)	C_m ($\mu F/cm^2$)	λ (μm)	l/λ
Superior cervical ganglion cells (rabbit)	2,900	14	180	32.4	4640	4.5	11.5	2.5	490	0.38
Ciliary ganglion cells (cat)	4,400	15	200	18.5	3320	3.3	6.1	2.1	425	0.46
Spinal motoneurons (cat)	144,690[b]	—	—	1.9	1770 ~ 2520	9.3 ~ 12.7	5.2	2.1 ~ 2.9	—	1.4

[a] R_N, Total neuron resistance; R_m, resistance across a unit area of membrane; ρ, ratio of combined dendritic input conductance to soma membrane conductance; τ, membrane time constant; C_m, capacitance for a unit area of membrane; λ, space constant of dendrite; l, length of dendrite; l/λ, electrotonic length of dendrite.
[b] Surface area of soma and dendrites.

through the intercellular recording electrode is a desirable procedure for this purpose (Nishi and Christ, 1971). This intracellular recording and staining method permits the fairly precise measurement of electrical and geometrical parameters of single neurons which is required to determine the electrical membrane properties.

Table II summarizes the passive membrane constants obtained by this method from the superior cervical ganglion cells of the rabbit and the ciliary ganglion cells of the cat. Calculations were all based on the mathematical formulas established by Rall (1959, 1960) for determination of membrane constants of multipolar neurons. For comparison, the membrane constants of cat spinal motoneurons measured recently by Barrett and Crill (1971) with a similar dye injection technique are also shown. It can be seen that although the total neuron resistance (R_N) of the autonomic neurons is approximately ten times or more that of the motoneurons, the specific resistance (R_m) of autonomic neurons is only about twice that of the motoneurons. The difference in the total neuron resistance is therefore mainly attributable to the difference in the total effective surface area. The dendritic-to-soma conductance ratio (ρ) for autonomic neurons appeared to be about 3–5 compared with 9–13 for motoneurons. This implies that in the autonomic neurons approximately one-fourth to one-sixth of the total current applied to the soma passes through the soma membrane and the rest flows through the dendrite and axon membrane, while in motoneurons only one-tenth to one-fourteenth of the total current applied to the soma passes through the soma membrane and the rest goes to the cellular processes. The average space constants of the cervical and ciliary neuron dendrites were estimated to be about 490 and 430 μm, respectively. These values are much greater than the actual length of the dendrites, and the electrotonic lengths of the cervical and ciliary neuron dendrites are only 0.38 and 0.46, respectively. These data evidently suggest that the synaptic potentials of autonomic neuron dendrites can influence the soma membrane potential more effectively than those of motoneuron dendrites.

4. ACTION POTENTIALS OF SINGLE GANGLION CELLS

4.1. Response to Antidromic Stimulation

When an antidromic impulse is propagated into a ganglion cell, it sets up an action potential with a sharp rising phase and a relatively slow falling phase, followed by a long-lasting afterhyperpolarization. By recording with a fast time base, the antidromic spike of many autonomic neurons reveals an inflection on the rising phase at approximately 30–40 mV from the resting potential (Fig. 2A). The spike can be fractionated in an all-or-none manner

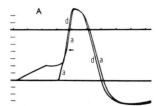 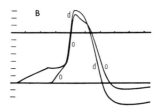

Fig. 2. Comparison of antidromic, orthodromic, and direct responses obtained from a frog sympathetic ganglion cell. (A) Tracings of antidromic (*a*) and direct (*d*) responses. The arrow indicates the height of inflection on the rising phase of the antidromic response. (B) Tracings of orthodromic (*o*) and direct (*d*) responses. Time mark on zero lines, 1 ms; each division of vertical columns, 10 mV. From Nishi and Koketsu (1960).

at the point of inflection when an antidromic response is evoked a few milliseconds after a conditioning response or during an artificial hyperpolarization of the cell membrane (Nishi and Koketsu, 1960).

From the geometrical standpoint, the most difficult point for antidromic propagation of an impulse would probably be the axon–soma junction (Coombs *et al.*, 1957*a*). Therefore, the inflection on the rising phase of the full spike could be attributed to a delay in the invasion process at the axon–soma junction (Nishi and Koketsu, 1960). Similarly, the isolation of the small spike could indicate a blockade of antidromic conduction at the axon–soma junction, and the small spike could be the rapid depolarization of the soma (and the proximal dendritic membrane in case of mammalian neurons) produced by the current flowing into the proximal axon. Evidence that the full spike occurs when the small spike reaches the level of inflection indicates that the threshold level for the firing of the soma membrane is equal to the height of the inflection (Nishi and Koketsu, 1960).

In the B-type neurons, which are the major constituent of the amphibian sympathetic ganglion (Nishi *et al.*, 1965) and the mammalian ciliary ganglion (Nishi and Christ, 1971), strong hyperpolarization of the cell membrane results in a further all-or-none type of separation of the isolated small spike, leaving a very small spike. This is clearly indicative of the segmental myelination of the B neuron axons. The isolated very small spike may correspond to the action potential of the first Ranvier node (Nishi *et al.*, 1965). In the C-type neurons, which are the major constituent of the mammalian sympathetic ganglion, the isolated small spike behaves quite differently under applied hyperpolarization (Nishi *et al.*, 1965). This isolated small spike cannot be fractioned in the all-or-none fashion. Instead, increasing hyperpolarization always brings about a gradual decrease in the height of the isolated small spike. The difference in the mode of separation of the antidromic response can be used as a criterion for differentiating the B- and the C-type neurons, particularly when their axonal conduction velocities cannot be correctly measured or fall in a similar range.

4.2. Response to Direct Intracellular Stimulation

The size and time course of spike potentials evoked by intracellular direct stimulation are similar to those elicited by an antidromic impulse. However, the threshold depolarization for spike initiation (about 25 mV from the resting potential) is clearly lower than the height of the inflection (40 mV) on the rising phase of the antidromic response, as seen in Fig. 2A. This difference is commonly seen in amphibian sympathetic neurons and suggests that direct intracellular stimulation may initially evoke the action potential of the axon hillock and the proximal part of the axon where the threshold may be lower, as has been proposed for spinal motoneurons (Araki and Otani, 1955; Fatt, 1957; Fuortes *et al.*, 1957; Coombs *et al.*, 1957*a,b*). In the mammalian sympathetic neurons, the difference in excitability between the soma membrane and its vicinity has not been clearly established (Eccles, 1963). In these neurons, it is likely that the depolarization registered in the cell body excites the soma membrane directly. On the other hand, in the mammalian ciliary neurons the mode of spike generation is quite similar to that in the amphibian sympathetic neurons (Nishi and Christ, 1971).

Autonomic ganglion cells fire repetitively in response to a strong continuous cathodal current. In amphibian B neurons, the frequency of discharge increases in proportion to the intensity of applied current until it reaches a maximum frequency of 40–70 Hz. On the other hand, the amphibian C neurons show a marked accommodation to the cathodal current. In the majority of C neurons, a strong cathodal current elicits only two or three responses, and those following the initial response are usually abortive, merging into a decremental oscillation. Some C neurons, however, can generate impulses for a considerable period of time, although generally not exceeding 150 ms—the maximum frequency of discharge being 20–40 Hz. Unlike the amphibian C neurons, the mammalian ganglion cells are able to maintain a high rate of firing almost indefinitely during continuous depolarization (Blackman and Purves, 1969). Their maximum frequency of discharge has been reported to be 80 Hz (Blackman and Purves, 1969) or as high as 150–170 Hz (Crowcroft and Szurszewski, 1971).

4.3. Response to Orthodromic Stimulation

Figure 3 shows a series of orthodromic responses of a rabbit superior cervical ganglion cell induced by a single stimulus of varying intensity. The spike response is preceded by an initial depolarization phase (fast e.p.s.p.)

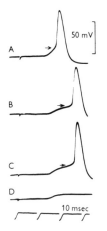

Fig. 3. Intracellular records from a rabbit superior cervical ganglion cell. (A) The action potential in response to a maximal single preganglionic volley. (B,C,D) The responses when the stimulus strength is progressively reduced. Arrows indicate the level of depolarization at which the spike arises. From Eccles (1955).

which forms a step at about 15 mV from the resting potential (A–C). Gradual reduction of the strength of stimulus causes a progressive slowing of the rising phase of the synaptic potential, a delayed onset of spike initiation (B, C), and finally a lowering of the synaptic potential below the threshold level for generating a spike (D). These alterations of synaptic potential indicate that a single ganglion cell is innervated by several presynaptic fibers differing in threshold of firing. Indeed, a maximal presynaptic stimulation applied away from the ganglion induces multiple synaptic potentials due to the difference in conduction time of each innervating fiber, and lowering of stimulus strength reduces the number of synaptic potentials (*cf.* Erulkar and Woodward, 1968).

Comparison of the orthodromic response and the direct response obtained from the same cell in a frog ganglion is shown in Fig. 2B. The peak of the orthodromic response is slightly lower than that of the direct response. This is probably due to the fact that the activated synaptic membrane short-circuits the active neuronal membrane (Fatt and Katz, 1951; Nishi and Koketsu, 1960). The threshold level for the initiation of the orthodromic response is practically identical to that for the direct response, but always 10–20 mV lower than the inflection of the antidromic response. Furthermore, the orthodromic response occasionally shows an inflection on its rising phase at the same level as that of the antidromic response. Such evidence suggests that the spike responses evoked by a synaptic potential and a directly applied current are identical in their initiation process. A similar mode of spike generation was also found in both B and C neurons of the cat ciliary ganglion (Nishi and Christ, 1971). In the rabbit superior cervical ganglion cells, however, the synaptically evoked spike seems to arise anywhere from the soma–dendritic membrane and not specifically from the axon hillock and/or the proximal part of the axon (Eccles, 1963).

Although mammalian ganglion cells are able to fire at a high rate (80–170 Hz) in response to direct intracellular stimulation (Blackman and Purves, 1969; Crowcroft and Szurszewski, 1971), they are incapable of responding with such a high rate to repetitive preganglionic stimulation. For instance, the superior cervical ganglion cells of the rabbit respond faithfully to preganglionic volleys at 35 Hz or less; these cells show at most only abortive spike responses except for the first full spike when stimulus frequencies are greater than 35 Hz (Eccles, 1955). However, even at a frequency of 160 Hz, a small synaptic potential appears following each preganglionic volley, indicating that some preganglionic fibers are capable of responding to this frequency (Eccles, 1955).

4.4. Ionic Requirement for Generation of Action Potential

The amphibian sympathetic ganglion cells have a remarkable characteristic; they are capable of producing action potentials not only in Ringer's fluid but also in media in which Na ions are totally replaced by either Ba, Sr, or Ca (Koketsu and Nishi, 1969). In contrast, the mammalian autonomic neurons (rabbit superior cervical ganglion cells, Tashiro and Nishi, 1972) are inexcitable in a Na-free Ca or Sr medium but can produce an action potential in a Na-free Ba medium. The preganglionic fibers also have this property (Greengard and Straub, 1959). This difference between amphibian and mammalian neurons might imply that along with the phylogenic evolution of the animal, the autonomic ganglion cell membrane alters its physicochemical properties.

5. NATURE AND ELECTROGENESIS OF POSTSYNAPTIC POTENTIALS

5.1. The "Fast" Excitatory Postsynaptic Potential

The ordinary e.p.s.p. of ganglion cells, which resembles in many respects the end plate potential of skeletal muscle, is now referred to as the "fast" e.p.s.p. in order to differentiate it from the "slow" e.p.s.p.'s (see below) of ganglion cells. The fast e.p.s.p. plays the major role in impulse transmission at the ganglion, while all other ganglionic postsynaptic potentials are secondary in this respect, serving as synaptic modulators of the ganglion cell excitability.

5.1.1. Synaptic Delay

Classical experiments showed that the synaptic delay for the fast e.p.s.p. in the mammalian sympathetic ganglia is 1–2 ms (Brown, 1934) or 0.5–4 ms

(Eccles, 1936). These values were obtained from the estimated arrival time of an impulse at the presynaptic nerve terminals and the onset time of the post-synaptic depolarization. A recent experiment on single superior cervical ganglion cells of the rabbit (Christ and Nishi, 1971b) showed that the synaptic delay measured between the time of direct stimulation of presynaptic ter-minals and the onset of the fast e.p.s.p. is 1.5–2.0 ms. The values obtained with a similar method from toad B and C sympathetic ganglion cells are 1.6 and 2.6 ms, respectively (Nishi and Soeda, unpublished observations).

5.1.2. Time Course

The fast e.p.s.p. recorded from the surface (N wave) of curarized mam-malian sympathetic ganglia shows a peak time of about 10 ms and a half-decay time of 60–90 ms (Eccles, 1943). The time course is much slower than that of the intracellularly recorded fast e.p.s.p., which shows a peak time of about 4 ms and a half-decay time of about 4 ms (Eccles, 1955). The slowness of the surface records is probably due to summation and fusion of the fast e.p.s.p.'s dispersed temporally by the difference in conduction velocity of presynaptic fibers. Perri et al. (1970) reported that the average time constant of decay of the fast e.p.s.p. is 6.7 ms in rat superior cervical neurons, and the corres-ponding value is 8.5 ms in guinea pig superior cervical neurons. They found that the time constant of e.p.s.p. decay is much longer than the time constant of an electrotonic potential, the difference being 148% in the rat and 93% in the guinea pig.

Because of the much simpler geometrical features of amphibian sym-pathetic neurons, which are spherical and devoid of dendrites, comparison of the e.p.s.p. and membrane time constant can be made more accurately in these neurons than in mammalian neurons (Nishi and Kokestu, 1960; Nishi et al., 1965). In toad sympathetic ganglion cells, the fast e.p.s.p. declines with an exponential time course having an average time constant of 10.4 ms for the B neurons and 13.9 ms for the C neurons. These values are 1.3 (B neurons) to 2 times (C neurons) larger than the membrane constants, suggesting that the decay of the fast e.p.s.p. is slowed down by a residual transmitter action.

5.1.3. Ionic Mechanism

It has been suggested that the chemical transmitter (ACh) liberated from the motor nerve terminals produces a marked increase in the ionic perme-ability of the end plate membrane. Consequently, the membrane potential of the activated end plate is driven toward a new "equilibrium" potential

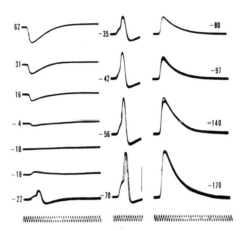

Fig. 4. A series of fast e.p.s.p.'s set up in a frog sympathetic ganglion cell. Membrane potential was changed from the resting level (−70 mV) by steady current through the recording microelectrode, the actual potential being indicated in millivolts on each record. Action potentials are evoked by the synaptic potentials at membrane potentials between −22 mV and −70 mV. Calibration, 50 mV; time mark, 1000 Hz. From Nishi and Koketsu (1960).

(Fatt and Katz, 1951). The action of the synaptic transmitter (ACh) on the nicotinic postsynaptic site of sympathetic ganglion cells is essentially similar to that on the end plate membrane, as illustrated in Fig. 4. In this figure, a series of fast e.p.s.p.'s in a frog sympathetic ganglion cell was set up at various levels of membrane potential. It is seen that the e.p.s.p. is nullified or even reversed when the membrane potential is held at strongly depolarized levels. Moreover, the e.p.s.p. is greatly increased when the membrane is hyperpolarized above the resting potential of −70 mV. There is an approximately linear relationship of the e.p.s.p. amplitude to the membrane potential; the e.p.s.p. is zero at −10 mV, which is thus the equilibrium potential for the ionic mechanism that produces it. The mean value of this equilibrium potential for frog sympathetic ganglion cells is −14 mV (range −8 to −20 mV). Similar experiments on the fast e.p.s.p.'s of toad sympathetic ganglion cells indicate that the equilibrium potential is about −10 mV for B neurons and −6 mV for C neurons. The fast e.p.s.p. of rabbit superior cervical ganglion cells shows the equilibrium potential of −15 mV to −10 mV (Nishi and Tashiro, unpublished observations). A much lower value (−30 mV) has been reported for cat superior cervical ganglion cells (Skok, 1968).

In amphibian sympathetic ganglion cells, the equilibrium potential of the fast e.p.s.p. is not altered when the perfusing Ringer's fluid is changed to a Cl-free solution (Nishi and Koketsu, 1967; Koketsu, 1969). A decrease in the external Na concentration shifts the equilibrium potential toward the resting potential. An increase or decrease in the K concentration shifts the equilibrium potential toward zero or the resting potential level, respectively. These results imply that the fast e.p.s.p. is generated by an increased Na and K conductance of the subsynaptic membrane, as in the case of the end plate potential (Takeuchi and Takeuchi, 1960).

5.1.4. Quantal Liberation of ACh and the Fast E.p.s.p.'s

Miniature fast e.p.s.p.'s appear spontaneously and randomly in both amphibian (Blackman et al., 1963; Hunt and Nelson, 1965; Nishi and Koketsu, 1960) and mammalian sympathetic ganglion cells (Blackman et al., 1969; Nishi and Christ, 1971). The size of these potentials is usually about 1 mV or less, with a frequency that varies considerably (0.05–10 Hz) in different cells. Hunt and Nelson (1965) estimated that in frog sympathetic ganglion cells the maximum shunt conductance of the subsynaptic membrane (G_s) during a miniature e.p.s.p. is approximately 1.7×10^{-9} mho. Nishi et al. (1967) estimated that in toad sympathetic ganglion cells the average G_s during a miniature e.p.s.p. is 6.6×10^{-9} mho for B neurons and 2.5×10^{-9} mho for C neurons, and that the average G_s during an evoked e.p.s.p. is 0.85×10^{-6} mho for B neurons and 0.2×10^{-6} mho for C neurons. From these values, the quantal content of an evoked e.p.s.p. can be calculated as 130 for B neurons and 80 for C neurons. Using bioassay of the liberated ACh from the toad sympathetic ganglia, Nishi et al. (1967) estimated that a single preganglionic volley releases approximately 2.6×10^{-16} g of ACh per ganglion cell. Comparison of this ACh output and the quantal content of an evoked e.p.s.p. suggested that a single quantum of transmitter contains 8000–12,000 molecules of ACh. If a sympathetic vesicle represents a quantum, these estimates indicate that the ACh in the sympathetic synaptic vesicles may be stored hypertonically, for if the transmitter is present in the vesicles as an isotonic solution of an ACh salt there would be about 6000 molecules in a spherical vesicle about 50 nm in diameter.

From electron microscopic observations of ganglionic synapses, Nishi et al. (1967) estimated that there are about 55 synaptic knobs on a B neuron and about 15 knobs on a C neuron of the toad. By dividing the quantal content of an e.p.s.p. by the number of synaptic knobs on a single cell, it appears that a single knob on a B neuron would liberate at least 2 quanta of transmitter per impulse, and a single knob on a C neuron about 5 quanta. Provided that the synaptic cleft is a cylinder 20 nm in height and 3 μm in diameter, the maximum concentration of liberated ACh in a cleft, per impulse, in the presence of an anticholinesterase would be 2.3×10^{-4} M for B neurons and 8.4×10^{-4} M for C neurons.

5.2. The "Slow" Excitatory Postsynaptic Potential

Using intracellular recording in curarized ganglia of both frog and rabbit, Tosaka and Libet (1965) and Libet and Tosaka (1966) showed that the LN wave is in fact a depolarizing postsynaptic response. It was also demonstrated that an atropine-sensitive facilitation of orthodromic discharges of ganglion cells roughly matched the time course and amplitude of the LN response (Libet, 1964). The LN wave has since been referred to as the "slow excitatory postsynaptic potential" (slow e.p.s.p.) (Libet, 1967).

The slow e.p.s.p. can be recorded from the majority of neurons in the rabbit superior cervical ganglion and from the majority of B and C neurons in the bullfrog sympathetic ganglia. In the case of the latter preparation, the preganglionic B nerve alone should be stimulated to record the slow e.p.s.p., since the slow e.p.s.p. as well as the late slow e.p.s.p. (the intracellular counterpart of the LLN wave; see below) would be evoked when both the preganglionic B and C nerves were stimulated (Nishi and Koketsu, 1968a) (Fig. 5).

The slow e.p.s.p. has a latency of 100–400 ms and may last more than 20 s after a tetanic (10–50 Hz) train of stimuli lasting for 1–5 s (Libet, 1967; Libet et al., 1968; Nishi and Koketsu, 1968a) (Fig. 5a). This large synaptic delay had been explained earlier (Eccles and Libet, 1961; Libet, 1967) by the concept that the liberated ACh might take a long time to diffuse to the

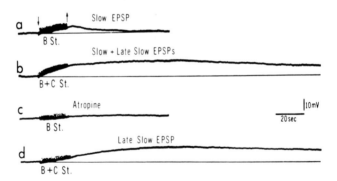

Fig. 5. Slow and late slow e.p.s.p.'s of a nicotinized bullfrog sympathetic ganglion cell. Tetanic (10 Hz for 20 s) stimulation of the preganglionic B fibers causes a short-lasting slow depolarization (slow e.p.s.p.) of the soma membrane (a). In contrast, tetanic stimulation of the preganglionic B and C fibers induces a long-lasting slow depolarization (slow plus late slow e.p.s.p.'s) (b). After addition of atropine (0.014 mM) to the perfusing solution, tetanic stimulation of the preganglionic B fibers elicits no appreciable potential change (c) whereas tetanic stimulation of B and C fibers still induces a long-lasting depolarization (late slow e.p.s.p.) but with a marked depression in its initial portion due to the disappearance of the slow e.p.s.p. (d). From Nishi and Koketsu (1968a).

muscarinic (LN) postsynaptic sites on the ganglion cell. However, with the iontophoretic application of ACh to the very close vicinity of a ganglion cell, Koketsu *et al.* (1968) have shown that there is a similar time lag for the onset of the atropine-sensitive slow depolarization (slow ACh-potential) of the ganglion cell. This implies that the large synaptic delay of the slow e.p.s.p. is due mainly to a postsynaptic process underlying the initiation of the slow e.p.s.p. The amplitude of the slow e.p.s.p. varies considerably (5–25 mV) from cell to cell in both frog and rabbit ganglia, indicating that the area occupied by the muscarinic postsynaptic receptors also differs between individual cells.

The slow e.p.s.p. does not behave like a postsynaptic depolarization generated by an increased ion permeability. Libet and Kobayashi (1968, 1969; see also Kobayashi and Libet, 1968, 1970) found no decrease in membrane resistance during the slow e.p.s.p. in frog or rabbit ganglion cells. Actually, there is an increase in membrane resistance in the frog ganglion cells. Similarly, the depolarization elicited by the muscarinic action of ACh is accompanied by no appreciable change in membrane resistance in curarized rabbit cells and by an increase in membrane resistance in nicotinized frog cells (Libet and Kobayashi, 1969; Kobayashi and Libet, 1970). The effect of membrane potential on the slow e.p.s.p. is also unusual. In frog ganglion cells, the slow e.p.s.p. is enhanced by moderate depolarization of 10–20 mV, and it is depressed by moder hyperpolarization of 10–20 mV (Kobayashi and Libet, 1968; Libet and Kobayashi, 1968), the reverse of the findings for the fast e.p.s.p. In contrast to the slow e.p.s.p. in frog cells, the slow e.p.s.p. in rabbit cells is depressed by depolarization and enhanced by moderate hyperpolarization of 10–15 mV. However, even in these cells stronger hyperpolarization of 20–30 mV depresses and abolishes the slow e.p.s.p. even though the fast e.p.s.p. is appropriately enhanced under these conditions (Kobayashi and Libet, 1968).

Nishi *et al.* (1969) found that in frog ganglia the effect of membrane potential on the slow e.p.s.p. differs considerably from cell to cell. For example, hyperpolarization of the cell membrane (by approximately 30 mV) causes either a decrease, an increase, or even no change in size of the slow e.p.s.p. depending on the individual cell. However, the membrane current associated with the slow e.p.s.p. (slow e.p.s.c.), which can be obtained by a manually controlled voltage-clamp method (cf. Nishi *et al.*, 1969), is decreased during hyperpolarization and increased during depolarization (10–15 mV) in most cells. The increase of membrane resistance during the slow e.p.s.p. is found only when the cell membrane is depolarized. Nishi *et al.* (1969) also found that the size of the slow e.p.s.p. and e.p.s.c. is not appreciably altered when the external K concentration is reduced to one-tenth or the external NaCl concentration is lowered to one-half.

Kobayashi and Libet (1968) showed that metabolic inhibitors such as dinitrophenol, azide, and anoxia all preferentially depress the slow e.p.s.p. They also demonstrated that the slow e.p.s.p. is not specifically depressed by ouabain, K-free Ringer's, or Cl-free Ringer's, or by iontophoretic reduction of the intracellular Cl ions. Kobayashi and Libet then proposed that the slow e.p.s.p. was generated by a metabolically based electrogenic mechanism but not an electrogenic Na–K pump or a Cl pump.

An alternative hypothesis, that the slow e.p.s.p. is due to a synaptic inactivation of K conductance of the postsynaptic membrane, was suggested by Weight and Votava (1970). Their conclusion was based on the following results (Weight and Votava, 1970): First, the size of the slow e.p.s.p. in frog ganglion cells varies inversely with membrane potential. Second, the slow e.p.s.p. reverses from a depolarization to a hyperpolarization at a membrane potential close to the K equilibrium potential. Third, a significant decrease in membrane conductance is also found during the slow e.p.s.p. This hypothesis is simple and attractive; however, it requires further clarification, particularly with regard to two points. One is that, as Kobayashi and Libet (1970) described, hyperpolarization reverses only the initial portion of the slow e.p.s.p. Although it is reported that the B neurons, which Weight and Votava used, do not show the slow i.p.s.p. (Tosaka et al., 1968), there is still a possibility that the reversal could be due to an unmasking of the slow i.p.s.p., which is known to be augmented by hyperpolarization (Koketsu and Nishi, 1967; Nishi and Koketsu, 1968b). The other point is that a partial or total removal of the external K does not significantly affect the size of a slow e.p.s.p. (Kobayashi and Libet, 1968; Nishi et al. 1969). According to Weight and Votava's hypothesis, the slow e.p.s.p. should be augmented under such conditions.

5.3. The "Late Slow" Excitatory Postsynaptic Potential

As mentioned in section 2.3, frog sympathetic ganglia treated with nicotine (or d-tubocurarine) and atropine are still able to produce an extremely long-lasting slow depolarization (LLN wave) in response to repetitive stimulation of preganglionic B and C nerves (Nishi and Koketsu, 1968a) (Fig. 5c). Several experimental facts support a synaptic origin of the LLN wave. The response can be recorded intracellularly from both B and C ganglion cells. The response in the presence of nicotine (or d-tubocurarine) and atropine is induced without any detectable preceding potential that could act as its generator. The response is reversibly abolished by Ca-free Ringer's. The response, as will be mentioned below, is accompanied by an increased membrane conductance. For these reasons and because of its delayed onset (1–5 s) and extremely prolonged time course (5–10 min), the response has been referred to as the "late slow e.p.s.p." (Nishi and Koketsu, 1968a).

Unlike the slow e.p.s.p., the late slow e.p.s.p. is always accompanied by a decrease in membrane resistance. This can be seen even when the late slow e.p.s.p. is nullified by delivering an anodal counter-current through the intracellular recording electrode, indicating that the reduction of membrane resistance is not due to the membrane depolarization (Nishi, 1972). The membrane current associated with the late slow e.p.s.p. (late slow e.p.s.c.) is enhanced when the membrane potential is increased and depressed when the membrane potential is decreased: the relationship between the amplitude of the late slow e.p.s.c. and membrane potential is almost linear, and the equilibrium potential obtained by extrapolation is approximately -35 mV. This level is not significantly altered by total replacement of the external Cl ions with glutamate ions, while it is shifted to the level of approximately -45 mV by reducing the external K concentration to one-tenth or by reducing the external NaCl concentration to one-half. The results suggest that the late slow e.p.s.p. is produced by a slow and sustained permeability increase of the noncholinergic receptor membrane to Na and K ions (Nishi, 1972).

5.4. The "Slow" Inhibitory Postsynaptic Potential

Intracellular recordings from curarized ganglia of both frog and rabbit have validated the hypothesis that the P wave is a hyperpolarizing postsynaptic potential, which can be generated in the absence of any cell discharge (Libet and Tosaka, 1966). The P wave has therefore been referred to as the "slow i.p.s.p." Although the depressant action of the slow i.p.s.p. on the excitability of mammalian ganglion cells has not been clearly shown, it has been demonstrated in frog sympathetic ganglia that a marked inhibition of afterdischarge occurs at the same time as the generation of the P wave (Koketsu and Nishi, 1967). The slow i.p.s.p. (cf. Fig. 6) induced by a train of preganglionic stimuli (10–40 Hz for 1 s) shows a synaptic delay of 30–100 ms, amplitude of 2–8 mV (with intracellular recording) and duration of 10–30 s; a single orthodromic volley elicits a very small or hardly detectable slow i.p.s.p. (Eccles and Libet, 1961; Libet, 1967, 1970; Libet et al., 1968; Nishi and Koketsu, 1968b).

Like the slow e.p.s.p., the slow i.p.s.p. does not behave as one would expect for an i.p.s.p. generated by an increased postsynaptic permeability to ions (Kobayashi and Libet, 1968; Koketsu and Nishi, 1967; Nishi and Koketsu, 1968b). The slow i.p.s.p. recorded from the surface of nicotinized frog ganglia is diminished and eventually abolished by depolarization, whereas it is markedly enhanced by moderate hyperpolarization. When the applied hyperpolarization is strong enough to nullify or reverse the afterhyperpolarization of a ganglionic action potential, the slow i.p.s.p. tends to decrease. A much stronger hyperpolarization eventually abolishes the slow

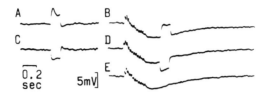

Fig. 6. Membrane resistance during slow i.p.s.p. Records from a rabbit ganglion cell, resting potential − 52 mV, in the presence of *d*-tubocurarine (20 μg/ml). (A,C) Responses of membrane potential to equal depolarizing (A) and hyperpolarizing (C) short current pulses in the resting cell. (B,D) Similar pulses delivered during the slow i.p.s.p. produced by a 0.3 s train of preganglionic stimuli at 40 Hz. (E) As in B and D but without the current pulse. The slow i.p.s.p. begins to develop after the start of the train. Note the small summated fast e.p.s.p.'s during the stimulus train, superimposed on the initial part of the slow i.p.s.p. From Kobayashi and Libet, (1968).

i.p.s.p. but cannot reverse the polarity of the response (Koketsu and Nishi, 1967; Nishi and Koketsu, 1968*b*). In curarized rabbit ganglion cells (Kobayashi and Libet, 1968), the slow i.p.s.p. is decreased in amplitude by progressive reduction of membrane potential and is nullified by a 20-mV depolarization. On the other hand, the amplitude of the slow i.p.s.p. is increased by moderate hyperpolarization of 10–30 mV, although further hyperpolarization consistently produces a decrease in amplitude and the i.p.s.p. can usually be nullified by hyperpolarizations somewhat greater than 30 mV. It should be pointed out that no alteration in membrane conductance is detected during the slow i.p.s.p. in both frog and rabbit ganglion cells (Kobayashi and Libet, 1968; Nishi and Koketsu, 1968*c*) (Fig. 6).

Koketsu and Nishi (1967) and Nishi and Koketsu (1968*b*) found in nicotinized frog sympathetic ganglia that alteration of the external Cl has little effect on the slow i.p.s.p. but also reported that the slow i.p.s.p. is depressed or abolished by ouabain, low temperature, or the removal of the external K ions and is enhanced markedly after loading the ganglia with Na. On the basis of these results, they suggested that the slow i.p.s.p. is due to the synaptic activation of an electrogenic Na pump. Kobayashi and Libet (1968), on the other hand, reported that removal of the extracellular K does not depress the slow i.p.s.p., and further the depressant action of ouabain on the slow i.p.s.p. is not specific because there is also depression of the fast e.p.s.p. (Kobayashi and Libet, 1968). From all the experiments so far carried out, it is evident that the slow i.p.s.p. is not generated by an increased ionic permeability; whether it is the result of a Na pump or some other active process is yet to be elucidated.

The hypothesis of an intervening adrenergic step in mediating the slow i.p.s.p. (Eccles and Libet, 1961; see Section 2.3) is linked to the observations that epinephrine exerts an inhibitory action on sympathetic ganglion cells (Marrazzi, 1939; Lundberg, 1952) and that the chromaffin cells in the ganglion probably are responsible for the output of epinephrine produced by preganglionic volleys (Bülbring, 1944). It has been shown that norepinephrine and epinephrine do elicit hyperpolarizing responses in mammalian sympathetic ganglia (De Groat and Volle, 1966; Libet and Kobayashi, 1968, 1969), and recent histological evidence is consistent with the disynaptic hypothesis of Eccles and Libet (1961). Matthews and Raisman (1969) demonstrated that the chromaffin-like cells make efferent synaptic contacts with the dendrites and somata of ganglion cells and that they also make afferent synaptic contracts with presynaptic boutons filled with nongranulated vesicles.

Libet (1970) has shown more recently that dopamine can elicit hyperpolarizing responses in mammalian sympathetic ganglia as effectively as norepinephrine and epinephrine and that dopamine is the only catecholamine able to restore the slow i.p.s.p. of the ganglia in which catecholamines of chromaffin cells were believed to be depleted by bethanechol. He found, moreover, the incubation of ganglia with diethyldithiocarbamate, which inhibits the enzymatic conversion of dopamine to norepinephrine, specifically enhances the slow i.p.s.p. On the basis of these findings, Libet (1970) proposed that dopamine is probably the major if not the exclusive second transmitter in the disynaptic sequence that physiologically mediates the slow i.p.s.p.

6. CHOLINERGIC AND ADRENERGIC RECEPTORS AT PREGANGLIONIC NERVE TERMINALS

6.1. Cholinergic Receptor Site

When an anticholinerterase is applied to the superior cervical ganglion of the cat by close-arterial injection, it evokes a prolonged postganglionic discharge (Takeshige and Volle, 1962; Volle, 1962; Volle and Koelle, 1961). Because this discharge does not occur in the chronically denervated ganglion and since acetylcholinerterase is located on presynaptic nerve terminals of the ganglion (Koelle and Koelle, 1959), it was suggested that this discharge is initiated by the action of ACh liberated from the preganglionic nerve terminals (Koelle, 1961, 1962; Volle and Koelle, 1961). The rat superior cervical ganglion infected with pseudorabies shows periodic bursts of impulse discharge (Dempsher et al., 1955; Dempsher and Riker, 1957). Dempsher and Riker (1957) suggested that the virus-induced impulses have their origin in the synaptic endings and that ACh plays a role in the genesis and spread of this periodic activity over both pre- and postganglionic trunks.

With the sucrose-gap technique, Koketsu and Nishi (1968) have shown that ACh, either liberated by nerve impulses or applied directly, causes a transient depolarization of the intraganglionic portion of the preganglionic nerve in the sympathetic chain of the bullfrog. This depolarization is accompanied by an attenuation of the preganglionic action potentials. A similar presynaptic depolarization also occurs in the superior cervical ganglion of the rat when ACh is directly applied (Koketsu and Nishi, 1968). In both bullfrog and rat ganglia, the presynaptic ACh-depolarization is depressed or abolished by d-tubocurarine or nicotine but is unaffected by atropine. From these results, Koketsu and Nishi (1968) suggested that the terminal region of the preganglionic nerve is endowed with a nicotinic receptor site. This idea has been supported by the recent findings of Nishi (1970) and Ginsborg (1971); Nishi (1970) showed that the endogenous and exogenous ACh does indeed cause a temporary reduction of the threshold (presumably by depolarization) of preganglionic nerve terminals in bullfrog sympathetic ganglia. Ginsborg (1971) showed that ACh and also carbachol transiently depress or even abolish the action potentials recorded extracellularly from individual preganglionic nerve terminals in frog sympathetic ganglia.

It should be pointed out, however, that ACh applied iontophoretically to the presynaptic nerve terminals does not consistently evoke miniature e.p.s.p.'s except in a few eserinized cells (Nishi, 1970). Furthermore, according to Collier et al. (1969) only high concentrations of ACh are capable of releasing labeled endogenous ACh from the cat superior cervical ganglion, and the amount of ACh thus released is markedly less than that liberated by nerve stimulation.

Although the physiological significance of the presynaptic nicotinic receptors is as yet unclear, it seems likely that the receptors serve as a site of negative feedback; liberation of ACh from the presynaptic nerve terminals would inhibit itself by virtue of its depolarizing action.

6.2. Adrenergic Receptor Site

Catecholamines have long been known to depress ganglionic transmission (cf. Curtis, 1963; Trendelenburg, 1961). Lundberg (1952) suggested that epinephrine hyperpolarizes the postsynaptic membrane, but this change in membrane potential is not always present when transmission is depressed by this drug. Contrary to their general blocking action, an enhancement of transmission has also been found when lower doses of adrenergic substances were administered (Bülbring, 1944; Bülbring and Burn, 1942; Malméjac, 1955; Trendelenburg, 1956). Furthermore, blocking doses of catecholamines have been observed to potentiate the ganglionic responses to ACh (Kewitz and Reinert, 1952; Konzett, 1950). Costa et al. (1961) showed that ganglionic transmission is enhanced following administration of dibenamine or after depletion of ganglionic catecholamines with reserpine. Recent experiments of

De Groat and Volle (1966) disclosed that sympathetic ganglia contain two pharmacologically distinct adrenoceptive sites; one, which is blocked by α-adrenergic blocking agents, mediates catecholamine-induced inhibition and ganglionic hyperpolarization, and the other, which is blocked by β-adrenergic blocking agents, mediates catecholamine-evoked facilitation and ganglionic depolarization.

Although the slow i.p.s.p., which, as mentioned before, is meditated by a catecholamine, effectively counteracts the slow e.p.s.p.'s and depresses the afterdischarges of ganglion cells (Koketsu and Nishi, 1967; Nishi and Koketsu, 1968a), it is generally too small to suppress the fast e.p.s.p. which plays the major role in ganglionic transmission. Furthermore, the slow i.p.s.p. is not generated by increases in ionic conductance of the postsynaptic membrane (Kobayashi and Libet, 1968; Nishi and Koketsu, 1968c). This unusual characteristic of the slow i.p.s.p. may imply that it has a lesser inhibitory capacity that the ordinary i.p.s.p.'s in other neurons such as spinal motoneurons. Even if exogenously applied epinephrine acts at the same sites that generate the slow i.p.s.p., the resulting hyperpolarization may possibly be too weak to account for the epinephrine-induced depression of ganglionic transmission. Indeed, Christ and Nishi (1971a) and Nishi (1970) have reported that epinephrine does not significantly hyperpolarize the ganglion cell membrane in concentrations which block transmission. They reached the conclusion that epinephrine blockade is primarily caused by a decrease in transmitter output and that this action of epinephrine is exerted through an α-adrenoceptive site at the presynaptic nerve terminals. Their concept is based on the following results obtained from the isolated rabbit superior cervical ganglion by means of the intracellular microelectrode method: First, epinephrine decreases the amplitude of fast e.p.s.p.'s without noticeably affecting the resting membrane potential or conductance, and it does not affect the postsynaptic depolarization induced by iontophoretic application of ACh. Second, epinephrine decreases the frequency of miniature e.p.s.p.'s and quantal content of evoked e.p.s.p.'s without affecting the quantal size. These actions of epinephrine are completely antagonized by α-adrenergic blocking agents but not affected by all the β-blockers. This observed presynaptic depressant action of epinephrine is consistent with the earlier observations of Birks and MacIntosh (1961) and Paton and Thompson (1953), who showed that epinephrine reduces the ACh output from sympathetic ganglia.

A more recent analysis of its action (Christ and Nishi, 1971b) indicates that epinephrine does not appreciably change the probability of quantal release nor does it affect the excitability of the terminal membrane. What appears most likely at present is that epinephrine reversibly decreases the number of quanta of transmitter immediately available for release. Although the mechanism of this action of epinephrine cannot be directly proved, it seems certain that the presynaptic nerve terminals are endowed with an α-adrenoceptive site. These sites may subserve a function of presynaptic inhibition, so long as catecholamines in the intraganglionic chromaffin cells or in the blood plasma can effectively reach them.

ACKNOWLEDGMENTS

Most of the investigations carried out in the author's laboratory were supported by NIH Research Grant NS06672 and NSF Research Grant GB 30360. The manuscript was kindly revised by Drs. R. A. North and J. P. Gallagher.

7. REFERENCES

Alkadhi, K. A., and McIsaac, R. J., 1971, Non-nicotinic ganglionic transmission during partial ganglionic blockade with chlorisondamine, *Fed. Proc.* **30**:655

Araki, T., and Otani, T., 1955, Response of single motoneurons to direct stimulation in toad's spinal cord, *J. Neurophysiol.* **18**:472.

Barrett, J. N., and Crill, W. E., 1971, Specific membrane resistivity of dye-injected cat motoneurons, *Brain Res.* **28**:556.

Birks, R., and MacIntosh, F. C., 1961, Acetylcholine metabolism of a sympathetic ganglion, *Can. J. Biochem. Physiol.* **39**:787.

Bishop, G. H., and Heinbecker, P., 1932, A functional analysis of the cervical sympathetic nerve supply to the eye, *Am. J. Physiol.* **100**:519.

Blackman, J. G., and Purves, R. D., 1969, Intracellular recordings from ganglia of the thoracic sympathetic chain of the guinea-pig, *J. Physiol. Lond.* **203**:173.

Blackman, J. G., Ginsborg, B. L., and Ray, C., 1963, Spontaneous synaptic activity in sympathetic ganglion cells of the frog, *J. Physiol. Lond.* **167**:389.

Blackman, J. G., Crowcroft, P. J., Devine, C. E., Holman, M. E., and Yonemura, K., 1969, Transmission from preganglionic fibres in the hypogastric nerve to peripheral ganglia of male guinea-pigs, *J. Physiol. Lond.* **201**:723.

Bronk, D. W., 1939, Synaptic mechanisms in sympathetic ganglia, *J. Neurophysiol.* **2**:380.

Brown, G. L., 1934, Conduction in the cervical sympathetic, *J. Physiol. Lond.* **81**:228.

Bülbring, E., 1944, The action of adrenaline on transmission in the superior cervical ganglion, *J. Physiol. Lond.* **103**:55.

Bülbring, E., and Burn, J. H., 1942, An action of adrenaline on transmission in sympathetic ganglia which may play a part in shock, *J. Physiol. Lond.* **101**:289.

Burgen, A. S. V., Dickens, F., and Zatman, L. J., 1948, The action of botulinum toxin on the neuromuscular junction, *J. Physiol. Lond.* **109**:10.

Chen, S. S., 1971, Transmission in superior cervical ganglion of the dog after cholinergic suppression, *Am. J. Physiol.* **221**:209.

Christ, D. D., and Nishi, S., 1971a, Site of adrenaline blockade in the superior cervical ganglion of the rabbit, *J. Physiol. Lond.* **213**:107.

Christ, D. D., and Nishi, S., 1971b, Effects of adrenaline on nerve terminals in the superior cervical ganglion of the rabbit, *Brit. J. Pharmacol.* **41**:331.

Collier, B., Vickerson, F. H. L., and Varma, D. R., 1969, Effect of acetylcholine (ACh) on transmitter release in cat superior cervical ganglion, *Fed. Proc.* **28**:670.

Coombs, J. S., Curtis, D. R., and Eccles, J. C., 1957a, The interpretation of spike potentials of motoneurones, *J. Physiol. Lond.* **139**:198.

Coombs, J. S., Curtis, D. R., and Eccles, J. C., 1957b, The generation of impulses in motoneurones, *J. Physiol. Lond.* **139**:232.

Costa, E., Revzin, A. M., Kuntzman, R., Spector, S., and Brodie, B. B., 1961, Role for ganglionic norepinephrine in sympathetic synaptic transmission, *Science N.Y.* **133**:1822.

Crowcroft, P. J., and Szurszewski, J. H., 1971, A study of the inferior mesenteric and pelvic ganglion of guinea-pigs with intracellular electrodes, *J. Physiol. Lond.* **219**:421.

Curtis, D. R., 1963, The pharmacology of central and peripheral inhibition, *Pharmacol. Rev.* **15**:333.

De Groat, W. C., and Volle, R. L., 1966, The actions of the catecholamines on transmission in the superior cervical ganglion of the cat, *J. Pharmacol. Exptl. Therap.* **154**:1.

Dempsher, J., and Riker, W. K., 1957, The role of acetylcholine in virus-infected sympathetic ganglia, *J. Physiol. Lond.* **139**:145.

Dempsher, J., Larrabee, M. G., Bang, F. B., and Bodian, D., 1955, Physiological changes in sympathetic ganglia infected with pseudorabies virus, *Am. J. Physiol.* **182**:203.

Dunant, Y., and Dolivo, M., 1967, Relations entre les potentiels synaptiques lents et l'excitabilite du ganglion sympathique chez le rat, *J. Physiol. Paris* **59**:281.

Eccles, J. C., 1935a, Facilitation and inhibition in the superior cervical ganglion, *J. Physiol. Lond.* **85**:207.

Eccles, J. C., 1935b, Slow potential waves in the superior cervical ganglion, *J. Physiol. Lond.* **85**:464.

Eccles, J. C., 1935c, The action potential of the superior cervical ganglion, *J. Physiol. Lond.* **85**:179.

Eccles, J. C., 1936, Synaptic and neuromuscular transmission, *Ergebn. Physiol.* **38**:339.

Eccles, J. C., 1937, Synaptic and neuromuscular transmission, *Physiol. Rev.* **17**:538.

Eccles, J. C., 1943, Synaptic potentials and transmission in sympathetic ganglion, *J. Physiol. Lond.* **101**:465.

Eccles, J. C., 1944, The nature of synaptic transmission in a sympathetic ganglion, *J. Physiol. Lond.* **103**:27.

Eccles, J. C., and Jaeger, J. C., 1958, The relationship between the mode of operation and the dimensions of the junctional regions at synapses and motor end-organs, *Proc. Roy. Soc. Lond. B* **148**:38.

Eccles, R. M., 1952, Responses of isolated curarized sympathetic ganglia, *J. Physiol. Lond.* **117**:196.

Eccles, R. M., 1955, Intracellular potentials recorded from a mammalian sympathetic ganglion, *J. Physiol. Lond.* **130**:572.

Eccles, R. M., 1963, Orthodromic activation of single ganglion cells, *J. Physiol. Lond.* **165**:387.

Eccles, R. M., and Libet, B., 1961, Origin and blockade of the synaptic responses of curarized sympathetic ganglia, *J. Physiol. Lond.* **157**:484.

Elfvin, L. G., 1963a, The ultrastructure of the superior cervical sympathetic ganglion of the cat. I. The structure of the ganglion cell processes as studied by serial sections, *J. Ultrastruct. Res.* **8**:403.

Elfvin, L. G., 1963b, The ultrastructure of the superior cervical sympathetic ganglion of the cat. II. The structure of the preganglionic end fibres and the synapses as studied by serial sections, *J. Ultrastruct. Res.* **8**:441.

Emmelin, N., and MacIntosh, F. C., 1956, The release of acetylcholine from perfused sympathetic ganglia and skeletal muscles, *J. Physiol. Lond.* **131**:477.

Erulkar, S. D., and Woodward, J. K., 1968, Intracellular recording from mammalian superior cervical ganglion *in situ, J. Physiol. Lond.* **199**:189.

Fatt, P., 1957, Sequence of events in synaptic activation of a motoneurone, *J. Neurophysiol.* **20**:61.

Fatt, P., and Katz, B., 1951, An analysis of the end-plate potential recorded with an intracellular electrode, *J. Physiol. Lond.* **115**:320.

Fuortes, M. G. F., Frank, K., and Becker, M. D., 1957, Steps in the production of motoneuron spikes, *J. Gen. Physiol.* **40**:735.

Ginsborg, B. L., 1971, On the presynaptic acetylcholine receptors in sympathetic ganglia of the frog, *J. Physiol. Lond.* **216**:237.

Greengard, P., and Straub, R. W., 1959, Restoration by barium of action potentials in sodium-deprived mammalian B and C fibres, *J. Physiol. Lond.* **145**:562.

Hunt, C. C., and Nelson, P. G., 1965, Structural and functional changes in the frog sympathetic ganglion following cutting of the presynaptic nerve fibres, *J. Physiol. Lond.* **177**:1.

Katz, B., and Miledi, R., 1966, Input–output relation of a single synapse, *Nature Lond.* **212**:1242.

Katz, B., and Miledi, R., 1967, The release of acetylcholine from nerve endings by graded electric pulses, *Proc. Roy. Soc. Lond. B* **167**:23.

Kewitz, H., and Reinert, H., 1952, Prüfung pharmakologischer Wirkungen am oberen sympatischen Halsganglion bei verschiedenen Erregungzuständen, *Arch. Exptl. Pathol. Pharm.* **215**:547.

Kobayashi, H., and Libet, B., 1968, Generation of slow postsynaptic potentials without increases in ionic conductance, *Proc. Natl. Acad. Sci. USA* **60**:1304.

Kobayashi, H., and Libet, B., 1970, Actions of noradrenaline and acetylcholine on sympathetic ganglion cells, *J. Physiol. Lond.* **208**:353.

Koelle, G. B., 1961, A proposed dual neurohumoral role of acetylcholine: Its functions at the pre- and post-synaptic sites, *Nature Lond.* **190**:208.

Koelle, G. B., 1962, A new general concept of the neurohumoral functions of acetylcholine and acetylcholinesterase, *J. Pharm. Pharmacol.* **14**:65.

Koelle, W. A., and Koelle, G. B., 1959, The location of external or functional acetylcholinesterase at the synapses of autonomic ganglia, *J. Pharmacol. Exptl. Therap.* **126**:1.

Koketsu, K., 1969, Cholinergic synaptic potentials and the underlying ionic mechanisms, *Fed. Proc.* **28**:101.

Koketsu, K., and Nishi, S., 1967, Characteristics of the slow inhibitory postsynaptic potential of bullfrog sympathetic ganglion cells, *Life Sci.* **6**:1827.

Koketsu, K., and Nishi, S., 1968, Cholinergic receptors at sympathetic preganglionic nerve terminals, *J. Physiol. Lond.* **196**:293.

Koketsu, K., and Nishi, S., 1969, Calcium and action potentials of bullfrog sympathetic ganglion cells, *J. Gen. Physiol.* **53**:608.

Koketsu, K., Nishi, S., and Soeda, H., 1968, Acetylcholine-potential of sympathetic ganglion cell membrane, *Life Sci.* **7**:741.

Konzett, H., 1950, Sympathicomimetica und Sympathicolytica am isoliert durchströmten Ganglien cervicale superius der Katze, *Helv. Physiol. Pharmacol. Acta* **8**:245.

Kosterlitz, H. W., Lees, G. M., and Wallis, D. I., 1968, Resintg and action potentials recorded by the sucrose-gap method in the superior cervical ganglion of the rabbit, *J. Physiol. Lond.* **195**:39.

Laporte, Y., and Lorente de Nó, R., 1950, Potential changes evoked in a curarized sympathetic ganglion by presynaptic volleys of impulses, *J. Cell. Comp. Physiol.* **35**:61 (Suppl. 1).

Larrabee, M. G., and Bronk, D. W., 1947, Prolonged facilitation of synaptic excitation in sympathetic ganglia, *J. Neurophysiol.* **10**:139.

Larrabee, M. G., and Posternak, J. M., 1952, Selective action of anesthetics in synapses and axons in mammalian sympathetic ganglia, *J. Neurophysiol.* **15**:91.

Libet, B., 1964, Slow synaptic responses and excitatory changes in sympathetic ganglia *J. Physiol. Lond.* **174**:1.

Libet, B., 1967, Long latent periods and further analysis of slow synaptic responses in sympathetic ganglia, *J. Neurophysiol.* **30**:494.

Libet, B., 1970, Generation of slow inhibitory and excitatory postsynaptic potentials, *Fed. Proc.* **29**:1945.

Libet, B., and Kobayashi, H., 1968, Electrogenesis of slow postsynaptic potentials in sympathetic ganglion cells, *Fed. Proc.* **27**:750.

Libet, B., and Kobayashi, H., 1969, Generation of adrenergic and cholinergic potentials in sympathetic ganglion cells, *Science N. Y.* **164**:1530.

Libet, B., and Tosaka, T., 1956, Slow postsynaptic potentials recorded intracellularly in sympathetic ganglia, *Fed. Proc.* **25**:270.

Libet, B., Chichibu, S., and Tosaka, T., 1968, Slow synaptic responses and excitability in sympathetic ganglia of the bullfrog, *J. Neurophysiol.* **31**:383.

Lloyd, D. P. C., 1937, The transmission of impulses through the inferior mesenteric ganglia, *J. Physiol. Lond.* **91**:296.

Lloyd, D. P. C., 1939, The excitability states of inferior mesenteric ganglion cells following preganglionic activation, *J. Physiol. Lond.* **95**:464.

Lundberg, A., 1952, Adrenaline and transmission in the sympathetic ganglion of the cat, *Acta. Physiol. Scand.* **26**:252.

Malméjac, J., 1955, Action of adrenaline on synaptic transmission and on adrenal medullary secretion, *J. Physiol. Lond.* **130**:497.

Marazzi, A. S., 1939, Adrenergic inhibition at sympathetic synapses, *Am. J. Physiol.* **127**:738.

Martin, A. R., and Pilar, G., 1963a, Dual mode of synaptic transmission in the avian ciliary ganglion, *J. Physiol. Lond.* **168**:443.

Martin, A. R., and Pilar, G., 1963b, Transmission through the ciliary ganglion of the chick, *J. Physiol. Lond.* **168**:464.

Matthews, M. R., and Raisman, G., 1969, The ultrastructure and somatic efferent synapses of small granule-containing cells in the superior cervical ganglion, *J. Anat.* **105**:255.

Nishi, S., 1970, Cholinergic and adrenergic receptors at sympathetic preganglionic nerve terminals, *Fed. Proc.* **29**:1957.

Nishi, S., 1972, Electrogenesis of muscarinic and noncholinergic slow EPSP's of amphibian sympathetic ganglion cells, in: *Interneuronal Transmission in the Autonomic Nervous System* (P. Kostyuk, ed.), pp. 112–135, Naukova Dumka, Kiev, USSR (in Russian).

Nishi, S., and Christ, D. D., 1971, Electrophysiological and anatomical properties of mammalian parasympathetic ganglion cells, *Proc. Internat. Union Physiol. Sci.* **9**:421.

Nishi, S., and Koketsu, K., 1960, Electrical properties and activities of single sympathetic neurons in frogs, *J. Cell. Comp. Physiol.* **55**:15.

Nishi, S., and Koketsu, K., 1966, Late after-discharge of sympathetic postganglionic fibers, *Life Sci.* **5**:1991.

Nishi, S., and Koketsu, K., 1967, Excitatory and inhibitory postsynaptic potentials of amphibian sympathetic ganglion cells, *Fed. Proc.* **26**:329.

Nishi, S., and Koketsu, K., 1968a, Early and late after-discharges of amphibian sympathetic ganglion cells, *J. Neurophysiol.* **31**:109.

Nishi, S., and Koketsu, K., 1968b, Analysis of slow inhibitory postsynaptic potential of bullfrog sympathetic ganglion, *J. Neurophysiol.* **31**:717.

Nishi, S., and Koketsu, K., 1968c, Underlying mechanisms of ganglionic slow IPSP and post-tetanic hyperpolarization of pre- and postganglionic elements, *Proc. Internat. Union Sci.* **7**:321.

Nishi, S., Soeda, H., and Koketsu, K., 1965, Studies on sympathetic B and C neurons and patterns of preganglionic innervation, *J. Cell. Comp. Physiol.* **66**:19.

Nishi, S., Soeda, H., and Koketsu, K., 1967, Release of acetylcholine from sympathetic ganglionic nerve terminals, *J. Neurophysiol.* **30**:114.

Nishi, S., Soeda, H., and Koketsu, K., 1969, Unusual nature of ganglionic slow EPSP studied by a voltage clamp method, *Life Sci.* **8**:33.

Obrador, S., and Odoriz, J. B., 1936, Transmission through a lumbar sympathetic ganglion, *J. Physiol. Lond.* **86**:269.

Paton, W. D. M., and Thompson, J. W., 1953, The mechanism of action of adrenaline on the superior cervical ganglion of the cat, *Internat. Physiol. Congr.* **19**:664.

Perri, V., Sacchi, O., and Casella, C., 1970, Electrical properties of the sympathetic neurons in the rat and guinea-pig superior cervical ganglion, *Pflügers Arch. Ges. Physiol.* **314**:40.

Rall, W., 1959, Branching dendritic trees and motoneuron membrane resistivity, *Exptl. Neurol.* **1**:491.

Rall, W., 1960, Membrane potential transients and membrane time constant of motoneurons, *Exptl. Neurol.* **2**:503.

Skok, V., 1968, The electrophysiology of cat's superior cervical sympathetic ganglion neurons, *Proc. Internat. Union Physiol. Sci.* **7**:403.

Stretton, A. O. W., and Kravitz, E. A., 1968, Neuronal geometry: Determination with a technique of intracellular dye injection, *Science N.Y.* **162**:132.

Takeshige, C., and Volle, R. L., 1962, Bimodal response of sympathetic ganglia to acetylcholine following eserine or repetitive preganglionic stimulation, *J. Pharmacol. Exptl. Therap.* **138**:66.

Takeshige, C., and Volle, R. L., 1963, Asynchronous postganglionic firing from the cat superior cervical sympathetic ganglion treated with neostigmin, *Brit. J. Pharmacol.* **20**:214.

Takeshige, C., and Volle, R. L., 1964a, Modification of ganglionic responses to cholinomimetic drugs following preganglionic stimulation, anticholinesterase agents, and pilocarpine, *J. Pharmacol. Exptl. Therap.* **146**:335.

Takeshige, C., and Volle, R. L., 1964b, A comparison of the ganglion potentials and block produced by acetylcholine and tetraethylammonium, *Brit. J. Pharmacol.* **23**:80.

Takeuchi, A., and Takeuchi, N., 1960, On the permeability of the end-plate membrane during the action of transmitter, *J. Physiol. Lond.* **154**:52.

Tashiro, N., and Nishi, S., 1972, Effects of alkali-earth cations on sympathetic ganglion cells of the rabbit, *Life Sci.* **11**:941.

Tosaka, T., and Libet, B., 1965, Slow postsynaptic potentials recorded intracellularly in sympathetic ganglia of frog, *Proc. Internat. Union Physiol. Sci.* **4**:386.

Tosaka, T., Chichibu, S., and Libet, B., 1968, Intracellular analysis of slow inhibitory and excitatory postsynaptic potentials in sympathetic ganglia of the frog, *J. Neurophysiol.* **31**:396.

Trendelenburg, U., 1956, Modification of transmission through the superior cervical ganglion of the cat, *J. Physiol. Lond.* **132**:529.

Trendelenburg, U., 1961, Pharmacology of autonomic ganglia, *Ann. Rev. Pharmacol.* **1**:219.

Volle, R. L., 1962, The actions of several ganglion blocking agents on the postganglionic discharge induced by diisopropyl phosphorofluoridate (DFP) in sympathetic ganglia, *J. Pharmacol. Exptl. Therap.* **135**:45.

Volle, R. L., and Koelle, G. B., 1961, The physiological role of acetylcholinesterase (AChE) in sympathetic ganglia, *J. Pharmacol. Exptl. Therap.* **133**:223.

Weight, F. F., and Votava, J., 1970, Slow synaptic excitation in sympathetic ganglion cells: Evidence for synaptic inactivation of potassium conductance, *Science N.Y.* **170**:755.

Whitteridge, D., 1937, The transmission of impulses through the ciliary ganglion, *J. Physiol. Lond.* **89**:99.

Chapter 9

Function of Autonomic Ganglia

J. G. Blackman

Department of Pharmacology
University of Otago Medical School
Dunedin, New Zealand

1. INTRODUCTION

Integration of autonomic nervous activity is very largely carried out within the central nervous system (see Ingram, 1960). This being so, it is not unreasonable to conclude with the authors of one text (Davson and Eggleton, 1968) that integration in autonomic ganglia is a "very minor matter." Indeed, in many accounts of the autonomic nervous sytem it is assumed that the ganglia merely pass on unmodified the impulses they receive from preganglionic nerve cells, and for practical purposes this view seems to serve very well. Studies of the past 40 years, commencing with those of Eccles in the 1930s, do not, however, support this simplistic view of ganglionic function. It will be shown that, as a result of their anatomical connections (see Chapter 6) and synaptic properties (see Chapter 8), autonomic ganglia are capable of several different kinds of activity each reflecting a particular function.

2. GANGLIA AS COORDINATING CENTERS

2.1. The Relay Hypothesis of Ganglionic Function

We owe a great deal to Langley, who around the turn of the century delineated the main pathways of the autonomic nervous system. Langley established the existence of synapses within the ganglia and determined the functional connections of their neurons. He did not speculate as to how ganglionic synapses might affect impulse traffic. His view, as far as can be judged from his writing, was that the ganglion acted simply as a relay, in the sense that received impulses were passed on from the central nervous system to the periphery: he had no need of a more explicit hypothesis.

Langley did consider the question of the possible "automatism" of autonomic ganglia, that is, the possibility that ganglion cells maintain tonic activity independently of the central nervous system (Langley, 1900). He rejected the hypothesis, for ganglia severed from connection with the spinal cord sustained only slight, if any, tonic activity.

Langley also considered and rejected the hypothesis that ganglion cells can form the efferent limb of peripheral reflex arcs. He believed that such examples as he had examined were "pseudoreflexes" (axon reflexes) resulting from the retrograde activation of a preganglionic fiber back to a point of branching whence impulses were conducted orthodromically.

Langley applied these strictures to the two main divisions of the autonomic nervous sytem only. He left open the question of autonomous activity in the ganglion cells of the enteric nervous system—Langley usefully distinguished the ganglionated plexuses of the gut from the rest of the autonomic nervous system by this term.

2.2. Development of a Stochastic Hypothesis

Early evidence that more fibers leave a ganglion than enter it led Langley (1903) to conclude that probably all preganglionic fibers divide to supply two or more ganglionic neurons. He did not, therefore, subscribe to the view that ganglia function as relays in the simple one-to-one fashion made explicit in Fig. 1A. It is, nevertheless, hard to exclude the possibility that this arrangement does sometimes occur.

2.2.1. Branching and Distributive Function

Simple counting reveals that nerve cells in ganglia outnumber the preganglionic fibers which supply them. Billingsley and Ranson (1918) reported a "pre:post" ratio of 1:32 in a cat superior cervical ganglion, but nonmyelinated fibers in the cervical sympathetic trunk were not included in their count. More reliable counts by Ebbesson (1968) show that ratios for the superior cervical ganglion can vary from 1:28 in the squirrel monkey to 1:196 in man. In the ciliary ganglion of the cat, the ratio is approximately 1:2 (Wolf, 1941). Provided that the ratio exceeds 1:1, we must conclude that preganglionic fibers branch to supply more than one ganglion cell (Fig. 1B). Autonomic ganglia may thus function as distributing centers.

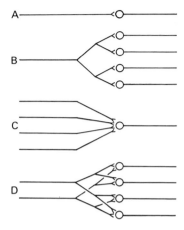

Fig. 1. Relationship between preganglionic fibers (left) and postganglionic neurons (right). Further description is given in the text.

The pre:post ratio cannot, however, be taken as a direct measure of the extent of branching of preganglionic fibers; the occurrence of convergence affects the calculation. It is not possible, therefore, to justify general conclusions about the relative distributive functions of autonomic ganglia on the basis of pre:post ratios alone.

2.2.2. Convergence and Integrative Function

Eccles (1935a) obtained evidence of convergence in the superior cervical ganglion of the cat in the following way: He recorded postganglionic electrical responses to stimulation of two natural divisions (ansa subclavia) of the preganglionic trunk. Stimuli could be so adjusted that when applied to either division alone they produced no postganglionic response but when applied simultaneously to both divisions they did. This could only mean that there were cells in the ganglion which received more than one preganglionic fiber. An impulse in any such fiber produced only subthreshold excitation, but impulses simultaneously converging on a cell from several preganglionic fibers produced responses which summed to fire it. Direct evidence of such spatial summation is readily obtained, as Fig. 2 shows, from a single ganglion cell with an intracellular microelectrode (Purves, 1968).

Wherever convergence (Fig. 1C) is demonstrated, a principal condition for integrative activity is fulfilled. Eccles (1935b) concluded "that the superior cervical ganglion must be regarded as a coordinating center as well as a transmitting and distributing station." The ganglion is thus not simply a collection of relays.

To the extent that authors describing the detailed properties and responses of autonomic ganglia have in mind a particular model, it is likely that

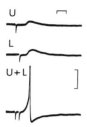

Fig. 2. Spatial summation in a ganglion cell of the thoracic para-vertebral chain of the guinea pig. Subliminal responses to stimu-lation of sympathetic chain above (U) and below (L) sum to discharge the cell (U + L). Intracellular recording. Calibration, 20 mV, 10 ms. From Purves (1968).

they subscribe to one incorporating the features established above (but see Haefely, 1972; Skok, 1973).

Anatomically, this means that a ganglion may be represented as a set of branched preganglionic fibers converging on a set of neurons more numerous than the fibers supplying them (Fig. 1D).

Physiologically, it means that an impulse will be propagated toward the periphery only when responses to convergent impulses sum to threshold and fire the cell. The primary event is a subthreshold excitatory synaptic potential (e.p.s.p.). Without exception, it appears to be caused by acetylcholine released from preganglionic endings on soma and dendrites.

Natural activity in this model may be pictured as follows (Fig. 3): Five convergent fibers are shown to be active. It is assumed that impulses arrive at irregular intervals as a result of some stochastic process and that three or four synaptic potentials must sum to fire the cell. Blackman and Purves (1969) found that ganglion cells of the guinea pig thoracic sympathetic chain, for

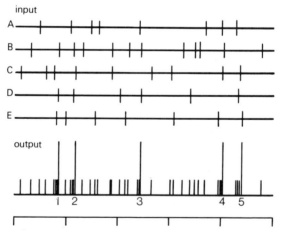

Fig. 3. Stochastic model of activity in a ganglion cell. Input consists of 42 impulses occurring at "random" intervals in five preganglionic fibers. Output consists of five action potentials (1-5) triggered by summation of synaptic potentials. Time scale in seconds.

example, were fired only when three or four preganglionic fibers were activated synchronously. The output can be seen to be but a fraction of the total input. Moreover, we can guess, without subjecting the model to detailed analysis, that the output frequency is likely to be determined by the average of the input frequencies. The effectiveness of summation to threshold will depend on the influence of a number of factors, which will be discussed briefly later.

This stochastic model of hypothetical ganglionic activity was early expounded by Bronk (1939). It does not immediately offer a description of ganglionic function. Its functional significance must remain obscure as long as we can postulate nothing about the central origin of the convergent preganglionic fibers, the patterns of impulse activity which they convey, and the afferent influences which evoke or modify that activity.

We must now ask whether this general view of the ganglion and the activity which it sustains is consistent with observation.

3. EXPERIMENTAL EVIDENCE

The most direct way of observing ganglionic activity and obtaining evidence of ganglionic function is to impale single cells of autonomic ganglia *in situ* in the living animal. Most studies have been less direct. Some have been aimed at discovering mechanisms which might be evoked to influence ganglionic transmission. Others have been aimed at determining patterns of innervation of autonomic ganglia. All these results bear to a greater or lesser degree on the question of the function of autonomic ganglia.

3.1. Observed Patterns of Innervation

3.1.1. Single Innervation

Ganglion cells which receive only one preganglionic fiber obviously do not conform to the orthodox view of the ganglion presented in the previous section. Cells are presumed to be singly innervated when finely graded preganglionic stimuli evoke all-or-nothing responses only. In favorable cases, microscopic methods also may provide unequivocal evidence of single innervation.

Single innervation has been demonstrated physiologically in both sympathetic and parasympathetic ganglia, notably in the sympathetic chain of the frog and toad (Nishi and Koketsu, 1960; Blackman *et al.*, 1963*a*; Nishi *et al.*, 1965), in the interatrial septum of frog heart (McMahan and Kuffler, 1971; Dennis *et al.*, 1971), in ciliary ganglia of birds (Martin and Pilar, 1963), and in the pelvic plexus ganglia of the male guinea pig (Blackman, *et al.*, 1969; Crowcroft and Szurszewski, 1971). Since the response of such cells to preganglionic stimulation is generally a suprathreshold synaptic potential, it appears that they have a simple relay function. The possible significance of this is worth examining in a little more detail.

Within the avian ciliary ganglion, for example, there are two distinct populations of cells (Marwitt *et al.*, 1971), each singly innervated. One group gives rise to axons forming the ciliary nerve, which innervates the iris and ciliary body. Axons of the other group form the choroid nerve, which inner-vates the smooth muscle coat of the choroid. Synapses on the ciliary cells transmit by a dual mechanism, electrical and chemical. Synapses on the choroid cells transmit by a chemical mechanism only. Both populations of cells are thus distinct anatomically and physiologically. Their function within the ganglion, however, can hardly be more than to relay and presumably distribute preganglionic activity unmodified to distinct destinations: evidently, transactions in these ganglia are adequately performed without the benefit of a convergent input.

In ganglia of the toad sympathetic chain, two populations of cells can be identified, also. Not all these cells are singly innervated, however. The two classes of neurons, sB and sC, give rise to axons having the characteristics of B and C fibers, respectively (Nishi *et al.*, 1965; Honma, 1970). The sB cells are innervated by a single B fiber, the sC cells by one or more C fibers. The sympathetic outflow is thus divided into faster and more slowly conducting pathways. They appear to differ functionally also. Thus there is evidence that the sB neurons of the tenth ganglion innervate the toxic glands of the skin and that the sC neurons innervate the blood vessels of the lower limb (Honma, 1970).

This is tenuous enough evidence upon which to speculate, but it does suggest a simple hypothesis of ganglionic function which may be stated as follows: Fiber paths which must intermittently mediate an emergency response, as in a toxic gland, will be as well served by a simple relay connec-tion as by any other. Fiber paths which, on the other hand, are normally concerned with continuous homeostatic regulation, as of blood vessels, may respond more appropriately if they can coordinate impulse activity in con-vergent pathways. The presence of both single and multiple innervation of cells in the pelvic plexus ganglia of the male guinea pig is not inconsistent with this view, for whether there be one preganglionic fiber or more supplying the cell, most appear to be able to initiate an action potential (see Fig. 9 in Crowcroft and Szurszewski, 1971). As Haefely (1972) has noted in relation to the singly innervated cells, activation of these fiber paths, which presumably supply the vas deferens, "is continuous, but occurs in relatively rare bursts." In these circumstances, a simple relay secures the required "fail-safe" transmission.

3.1.2. Multiple Innervation

Neurons in autonomic ganglia most commonly receive more than one preganglionic fiber. In consequence, evoked synaptic activity recorded in a single cell can be graded according to stimulus strength: the amplitude and maximum rate of rise of synaptic potentials increase and additional synaptic potentials of different latency may appear in an all-or-nothing fashion as the

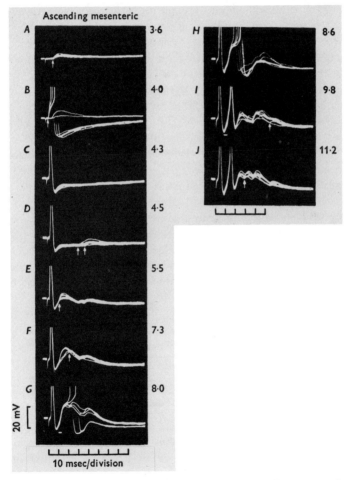

Fig. 4. Effect of increasing strength of stimulus (A–J) to ascending mesenteric nerve on synaptic response in a cell of the inferior mesenteric ganglion of the guinea pig. Intracellular recording. Each trace consists of six successive responses to stimulation of constant strength. Numbers indicate stimulus strength. Arrows indicate synaptic response due to recruitment of additional fiber or fibers. From Crowcroft and Szurszewski (1971).

preganglionic stimulus strength is increased (Fig. 4). Grading has been observed in most mammalian sympathetic ganglia.

3.1.2.a. The Extent of Convergence. The exact number of fibers supplying a cell cannot usually be determined with any certainty by grading. Insufficiently different stimulus thresholds, "quantal fluctuation" of amplitude of the synaptic potential, facilitation, and unfavorable latency may all obscure evidence of "all-or-nothing" recruitment of successive fibers. The occurrence of *en passant* branches will add to the counting error, also. Nevertheless, some minimum estimates of the number of fibers supplying a cell have been made. For example, at least a dozen fibers, perhaps double that number, supply cells of the thoracic paravertebral sympathetic ganglia of the guinea pig (Blackman and Purves, 1969), while in the inferior mesenteric ganglion of the guinea pig some 40 fibers, derived variously from the colonic, ascending mesenteric, hypogastric, and splanchnic nerves, appear to converge on each cell (Crowcroft and Szurszewski, 1971). In the cat superior cervical ganglion, the number of convergent fibers has been estimated at 25–30 (Crowcroft, personal communication), but not more than five fibers supply cells of the pelvic plexus ganglia of the guinea pig (Crowcroft and Szurszewski, 1971). It is evident from these and other examples that the extent of convergence is likely to range widely from ganglion to ganglion, and between cells in a given ganglion, and it presumably reflects differences in the character of the integrative activity which they sustain. The conduction velocities of fibers converging on a cell may vary widely also. Skok (1973) has observed that since these are likely to have their own functional significance "their convergence may mean that there is an interaction in the ganglion between functionally different pathways."

3.1.2.b. Convergence and Dispersion of Activity. Where there is multiple innervation, the average number of cells supplied by each preganglionic fiber must be much larger than is indicated by the pre:post ratio of fibers to neurons.

If the ratio of fibers to neurons is $1:x$, and the average number of fibers converging on each neuron is y, it follows that each fiber supplies an average of xy cells. Given typical estimates of x and y, it can be seen that a single fiber may supply many hundreds of cells. Thus the dispersion of preganglionic activity within the ganglion can be very large. It does not follow, however, that functional dispersion by the ganglion is equally large; indeed, output activity may be quite discrete.

3.1.2.c. Convergence and Discrete Regulation. Figure 5 shows preganglionic fibers and postganglionic neurons arranged to form a "selection

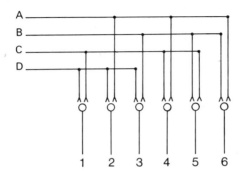

Fig. 5. "Selection matrix." Each cell (1–6) is selectively discharged by synchronous arrival of an impulse in each of the appropriate pair of preganglionic fibers (A–D). Note "pre:-post" ratio = 1:1.5, convergence = 2, each fiber has 1.5 × 2 = 3 branches.

matrix." If both fibers supplying a cell must be activated to fire it, discrete regulation of postganglionic activity can be achieved by selecting the appropriate pair of fibers. More complex arrangements are easily devised. Skok (1973) has noted the economy of such arrangements for selectively discharging postganglionic neurons. It should not be overlooked that there are fewer incoming fibers than cells and that fibers are branched, yet dispersion of activity is not a necessary consequence.

We do not know whether any autonomic ganglia work in this way. We may observe that discrete regulation of effector cells normally requires appropriately distributed sensory innervation to form a control loop. As far as centrally mediated reflexes are concerned, the autonomic nervous system does not appear to be generously endowed with afferent pathways exhibiting the discrete distribution required. It is true that a peripheral region supplied by sympathetic fibers from a given white ramus generally lies within the region supplied by sensory fibers from that ramus (see Langley, 1900), but within the region there is probably little localization of distribution, for stimulation of a few efferent fibers seems to evoke responses as widely distributed as stimulation of many fibers (Bishop and Heinbecker, 1932).

Selective activation of ganglionic neurons also requires more or less simultaneous arrival of impulses in the appropriate convergent fibers. This must be achieved despite the possibility of marked differences in conduction velocity and fiber length and a large random component in at least some preganglionic activity (Mannard and Polosa, 1973).

3.1.2.d. Relay Fibers and Disperse Discharge. Crowcroft and Szurszewski (1971) have reported the occurrence of relay fibers (fibers which alone discharge the cell) in the convergent input to cells of the inferior mesenteric ganglion and pelvic plexus of the guinea pig. They suggest that the function of these fibers "is to make a direct connection between the central nervous system and the effector organ involved." The extent to which relay fibers are distributed to cells which are otherwise supplied by fibers causing sub-threshold excitation only is not known. Were they to occur more generally in sympathetic ganglia, and particularly if they were derived from a few highly branched preganglionic neurons, they would provide an economical means of achieving the widespread discharge of the sympathetic system which is characteristic of the "fight-or-flight" reaction.

3.2. Ganglionic Activity and Factors Influencing It

Bronk (1939) looked forward to the day when direct observations of activity in single ganglion cells would be made. The technical difficulties in the way of achieving this object were then insurmountable. Only recently have they been overcome, notably by Skok and coworkers, who have recorded natural activity in single cells of several different mammalian ganglia *in situ*.

3.2.1. Natural Activity in Mammalian Ganglion Cells

A full discussion of Skok's important work in this field may be found in the English edition of his book (Skok, 1973).

3.2.1.a. Natural Activity in a Sympathetic Ganglion. Figure 6 shows intracellularly recorded tonic activity in three neurons in the superior cervical ganglion of the anesthetized rabbit (Mirgorodsky and Skok, 1969). Tonic activity was not observed in all cells. Activity consisted of e.p.s.p.'s which in 80% of the 133 active neurons studied were accompanied by less frequently occurring action potentials. Fast i.p.s.p.'s were not seen. Spikes discharged irregularly in bursts or singly (Fig. 6C,D), or in bursts related to breathing (Fig. 6A) or, as in a few neurons only, to the heart rate. The mean frequency of occurrence of spikes for all the discharging cells was 3.4 Hz. The highest frequency of bursts was 32 Hz.

It is not obvious from the record that spikes arise from chance summation of irregularly occurring subthreshold synaptic potentials (compare Fig. 3). Indeed, the unstepped and rapid rate of rise of most synaptic potentials evoking spikes, the reduced amplitude of these spikes, and the absence of afterhyperpolarization, are all consistent with brief but intense transmitter action such as might be evoked by the discharge of single preganglionic fibers (relay fibers). However, an alternative explanation favored by Skok (1973) is that these spikes arise from the highly synchronous discharge of many preganglionic fibers. This explanation is supported by the evidence that

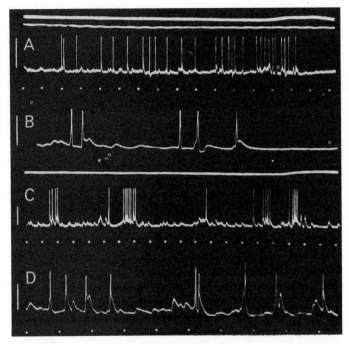

Fig. 6. Intracellular recording of tonic activity in three neurons of the superior cervical ganglion of the rabbit. (A) Upper trace, respiration with upward movement indicating inspiration; middle trace, blood pressure; lower trace, intracellularly recorded potentials. (B) Same cell as A, but potentials recorded on faster-moving film. (C) Upper trace, respiration; lower trace, intracellular potentials (second cell). (D) Intracellular potentials (third cell). Time mark on each record, 0.5 ms; calibration, 50 mV. From Mirgorodsky and Skok (1969).

selective conduction block of the low-threshold higher-velocity group of fibers supplying the cells markedly reduces and in some cases abolishes natural synaptic activity (Fig. 7). These fibers, therefore, carry most and sometimes all the natural activity observed under these conditions.

It is remarkable that the discharge of these ganglion cells should be achieved by such precisely timed summation. We can only suppose that equally precise mechanisms control the discharge of the selected preganglionic neurons within the spinal cord.

3.2.1.b. Natural Activity in a Parasympathetic Ganglion. Intracellular recording has revealed tonic activity in the majority of cells in the ciliary ganglion of the anesthetized cat (Melnitchenko and Skok, 1970). In contrast

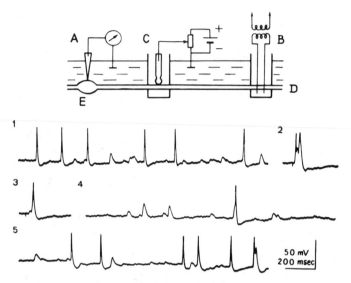

Fig. 7. Effect of partial conduction block in cervical sympathetic nerve on tonic activity in a neuron of the superior cervical ganglion of the rabbit. Intracellular recording. 1, Background tonic activity recorded (A) from the ganglion (E). 2, Response to single supramaximal stimulus (B) applied to cervical sympathetic nerve (D). 3,4, The same as 2 and 1, respectively, but recorded during passage of constant current at C causing partial conduction block in cervical sympathetic nerve. 5, Tonic activity recorded after constant current is switched off. Distance between electrodes A and B is 45 mm. From Mirgorodsky and Skok (1970).

to the large amount of subthreshold activity observed in the sympathetic neurons, spike activity predominated in the parasympathetic neurons. Two-thirds of the 66 active cells studied were discharged by every e.p.s.p. that occurred, and in the remainder only a minority of synaptic potentials were ineffective. No fast i.p.s.p.'s were seen.

Figure 8A shows the increase in synaptic activity which was evoked reflexly in a cell by illuminating the eye; Fig. 8B shows reflex inhibition in another cell—such cells probably supply the dilator muscle of the pupil (Melnitchenko and Skok, 1970).

As in the superior cervical ganglion, the discharge of cells is not obviously due to the chance summation of irregularly evoked synaptic potentials. Reflex inhibition of synaptic activity (Fig. 8B) caused the synaptic step to become more prominent—it could be graded—presumably because the number of preganglionic fibers contributing to the response had been reduced. Thus spike activity again appears to be due to the highly synchronous discharge of a number of preganglionic fibers.

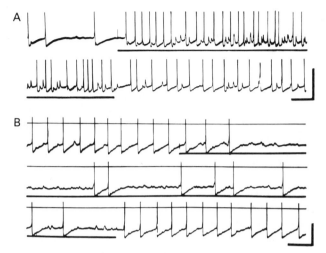

Fig. 8. Tonic activity in two neurons (A,B) of the ciliary ganglion of the cat, and responses to illumination of the eye. Intracellular recording. Solid bar beneath each record indicates illumination of eye. Only beginning and end of each record are shown (3.8s omitted in A; 2.0 s omitted in B between middle and lower traces). Calibration, 50 mV, 0.2 s. Adapted from Melnitchenko and Skok (1970).

Inhibition of spike activity was not obviously due to hyperpolarization or other mechanisms acting directly at membrane level; it is evidently of central location and due to suppression of the synchronous preganglionic volleys (Melnitchenko and Skok, 1970).

We may wonder that transmission, which in the ciliary ganglia of birds is achieved by the discharge of a single fiber supplying each cell, should, in the mammal, be achieved by a more complex mechanism requiring such remarkably precise control. The mammalian arrangement, however, permits unique activation of selected neurons by a minimum of preganglionic fibers.

3.2.1.c. Transmission of Reflexly Evoked Activity. The high safety factor for transmission of natural activity by the mechanism described above leaves little room for modification by local ganglionic influence. Not surprisingly, therefore, reflexly evoked natural activity appears to be transmitted with little modification by the ganglion. Thus Sato and Schmidt (1971), in experiments on the superior cervical ganglion of the anesthetized cat, observed that patterns of postganglionic discharge evoked by stimulation of various muscle and cutaneous afferent nerves were closely similar to preganglionic patterns of discharge. The ganglion seemed to act simply as a relay station. More subtle events may have escaped observation, however, for under the conditions of their experiments, in which a mass reflex discharge was evoked, activity in individual pathways could not be observed, and, moreover, synchronous activity would have been preferentially recorded.

3.2.2. Natural Preganglionic Activity

It was assumed in the stochastic model of ganglionic activity illustrated in Fig. 3 that impulses in the convergent preganglionic fibers would occur in an irregular if not strictly random sequence. In view of the evidence that cells of some ganglia are discharged naturally by so "unnatural" a form of stimulation as a synchronous preganglionic volley (see Perry, 1957), it is of interest to consider the patterns of natural activity that may be observed in single preganglionic neurons.

Polosa (1968) and Mannard and Polosa (1973) have recorded activity in single identified cervical sympathetic preganglionic neurons in the upper thoracic cord of the cat. Their results are, therefore, particularly relevant to observations of natural activity in cells of the superior cervical ganglion.

Of the preganglionic units identified in the cord, rather more than 20% exhibited "spontaneous" activity. Most activity was "irregular," but in other neurons firing was "regular" or rhythmic (Polosa, 1968). An analysis of these patterns in the sympathetic neurons supplying the cervical nerve (Mannard and Polosa, 1973) has shown that irregular firing is characterized by a unimodal distribution of interspike intervals corresponding to a mean recurrence frequency of about 2 Hz. In most cases, the frequency distribution of intervals longer than the modal interval was exponential and therefore consistent with a Poisson process of spike generation—we need not be concerned here with the mechanisms determining this behavior.

As far as a ganglion cell is concerned, however, such spike activity will appear to be random and unpredictable. The irregular subthreshold activity detected by Mirgorodsky and Skok (1969, 1970) in cells of the superior cervical ganglion probably reflects this sort of preganglionic activity, but the pattern of discharge of cells is clearly not the result of chance summation of such randomly occurring synaptic activity.

Preganglionic fibers also showed rhythmic patterns of firing. These discharges were often related to the rate of breathing or to the heart beat. They presumably generate the similarly rhythmic activity detected by Mirgorodsky and Skok (1969, 1970) in a proportion of sympathetic ganglion cells. Significantly, these rhythms are not seen in the parasympathetic fibers supplying cells of the ciliary ganglion (Melnitchenko and Skok, 1970).

This limited discussion perhaps allows one conclusion: that the prediction of activity in a ganglionic neuron requires more than a statistical knowledge of activity in single preganglionic neurons—a simple stochastic model is likely to be inadequate.

3.2.3. Factors Affecting Summation in Ganglion Cells

In many ganglia, but not all, the primary event leading to discharge of the cells is the summation of synaptic potentials. Successful summation to threshold depends in the first instance on the temporal pattern of arrival of preganglionic impulses, but also to a variably determined extent on many secondary events that affect transmitter release or cell excitability.

Greatest interest has been taken in the slow depolarizing and hyperpolarizing afterpotentials which can be evoked by presynaptic stimulation (Eccles and Libet, 1961). These are postulated to "modulate" transmission, but whether they are evoked during natural ganglionic activity is undecided (see Skok, 1973). We can expect their influence to be greatest when summation to threshold is achieved with little margin for safety, for example, when it has the characteristics of a stochastic process (cf. Redman and Lampard, 1968; Lampard and Redman, 1969).

These slow synaptic phenomena have been fully described in this volume (Chapter 8) and elsewhere (see Koketsu, 1969; Libet, 1970; Nishi, 1970; Haefely, 1972).

Other phenomena likely to influence the outcome of summation are the obligatory consequence of synaptic activity: facilitation and depression, quantal fluctuation of transmitter output, and afterhyperpolarization.

Both facilitation and depression of transmitter output have been observed in single cells of mammalian sympathetic ganglia (Blackman and Purves, 1969; Sacchi and Perri, 1971; Bennett and McLachlan, 1972). Facilitation is of particular interest, for it is evoked at repetition rates greater than 0.1 Hz and has a time constant of decay of more than 10 s (McLachlan, 1973). Facilitation is likely, therefore, to be a constantly fluctuating factor in determining the output of transmitter during normal activity in a ganglion.

The mean size of the unit quantum in mammalian ganglia is generally large (0.6–3.0 mV, Blackman and Purves, 1969; Sacchi and Perri, 1971; Christ and Nishi, 1971). Random fluctuations in the quantum content of synaptic potentials will for a Poisson process of release be large also, and must add a significant random component to the summation process, particularly when the safety factor for discharge is not high.

Epinephrine reduces the quantal release of transmitter in the ganglion (Christ and Nishi, 1971) and it has been suggested, therefore, that epinephrine or other catecholamines either released locally from the innervated small granule-containing cells or circulating in the blood may modulate normal transmission.

The principal secondary event affecting cell membrane excitability is the afterhyperpolarization component of the action potential, a phase of recovery from enhanced permeability to K^+ (Blackman et al., 1963b;

Kosterlitz *et al.*, 1968) with a total duration of several hundreds of milliseconds. Since the equilibrium potential of the conductance increase is more negative than the spike threshold, inhibition of firing must occur. This has been observed (Crowcroft and Szurszewski, 1971).

It will be evident from what has been said above that when a cell is discharged with a high safety factor, as for example by a single fiber releasing a large amount of acetylcholine or by many convergent fibers acting synchronously, the influence of these secondary events is likely to be insignificant

3.3. Relative Autonomy of Ganglia

The reflex responses that can be evoked in segments of gut completely isolated from the central nervous system are witness to the relative autonomy of the ganglia of the intramural enteric plexuses. These ganglia may not be autonomous to the extent that they fire spontaneously and act as centers in their own right, but they undoubtedly take part in local reflexes. Their behavior is in contrast to that of the paravertebral ganglia, which are not known to act independently of the central nervous system.

The prevertebral ganglia, however, have long been suspected of such clandestine activity. Direct evidence that the inferior mesenteric ganglion takes part in peripheral reflexes has been obtained recently (Crowcroft *et al.*, 1971). The discussion below is confined to this example.

3.3.1. A Peripheral Ganglionic Reflex

Crowcroft and Szurszewski (1971) showed that the lumbar colonic nerves contain fibers which excite the neurons of the inferior mesenteric ganglion by the release of acetylcholine. These fibers have their origin in the cell wall of the distal colon and form the afferent limb of a peripheral reflex arc, the efferent limb of which is the postganglionic adrenergic neuron.

Thus, in an isolated preparation consisting of the inferior mesenteric ganglion attached by means of the colonic nerves to a segment of the distal colon, continuous electrical activity was recorded from cells of the ganglion (Crowcroft *et al.*, 1971). The activity consisted of e.p.s.p.'s (Fig. 9A,B), or e.p.s.p.'s and action potentials (Fig. 9C,D,E). Spikes were due either to summation or to "an individual synaptic potential." It is of interest to compare this form of natural activity with that in Figs. 6, 7, and 8. Its character, except when relay fibers are active, conforms more closely to that of the stochastic model.

Cutting the colonic nerve connection to the ganglion immediately and irreversibly abolished activity. Distension of the colon increased the frequency of synaptic activity. Conversely, synaptic activity was decreased by applying norepinephrine to the colon or by repetitively stimulating the neurons of the ganglion.

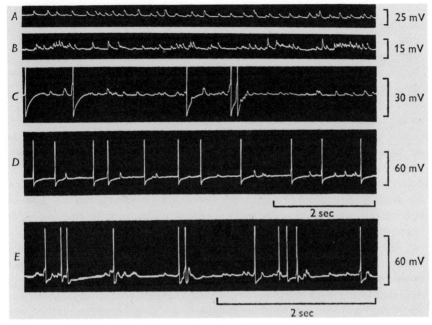

Fig. 9. Patterns of synaptic activity recorded from neurons of the inferior mesenteric ganglion of the guinea pig in five isolated preparations each consisting of the ganglion attached via the lumbar colonic nerves to a segment of distal colon. The pattern in C is the most frequently observed. The time base in D applies to A–D. From Crowcroft *et al.* (1971).

These observations show that enteric cholinergic neurons, many of which may be driven by other enteric cholinergic neurons, innervate the adrenergic neurons of the inferior mesenteric ganglion and thereby form a feedback loop.

This ganglion, therefore, has a function in part independent of the central nervous system.

4. CONCLUSIONS

Such limited evidence as has been examined shows that ganglia of the autonomic nervous system are capable of distinctly different kinds of activity —no one model adequately describes their behavior. Thus, at one extreme, cells innervated singly by branched fibers which always evoke a discharge are merely series elements of the final path for dispersion of preganglionic activity. Such ganglia function as simple relays. At the other extreme, and more commonly, the branched preganglionic fibers converge in greater or smaller number on the neurons. Here, the ganglion neurons represent the final *common* path.

A simple stochastic model based on this latter arrangement (Bronk, 1939) assumes random or otherwise irregular arrival of impulses in convergent fibers. Discharge of the cell depends, therefore, on the chance summation of subthreshold synaptic potentials. This is a form of temporal integration (Beacham and Perl, 1964) in which, theoretically, no one cell of the population has a greater chance of being discharged than another.

In contrast, the synchronous arrival of impulses in particular combinations of preganglionic fibers may uniquely obtain the discharge of selected cells of the population. The highly synchronous activity which appears to be the cause of firing in cells of the mammalian superior cervical and ciliary ganglia *in situ* may be evidence of just such selective discharge. This facility does not preclude mass discharge of the cell population by sufficiently synchronous activity in all preganglionic fibers. Mass discharge might, however, be achieved independently and more economically by impulses in a few highly branched relay fibers supplying the population.

Ultimately, the part played by each ganglion in the autonomic nervous system is determined by the temporal and spatial pattern of discharge evoked in its neurons. That pattern cannot be predicted by a model ignoring the origin of convergent preganglionic fibers, the patterns of impulse activity which they convey, and the afferent influences which determine that activity. The relative autonomy of those ganglia which participate in peripheral reflexes emphasizes the fact that ganglia are not merely a system of efferent neurons but part of a complex and as yet imperfectly understood series of control loops.

Perhaps more than has been suspected, ganglia may be specialized to mediate one or more of several different kinds of autonomic activity: widespread discharge, as in "fight-or-flight" emergencies; intermittent, more local discharge, serving special functions such as reproduction; regional or more discrete continuous regulation, as in homeostasis; and local reflex regulation, as in the gastrointestinal tract.

ACKNOWLEDGMENTS

The author is indebted to Dr. R. D. Purves, whose collaboration in earlier studies has contributed much to the development of ideas expressed in this essay. The author's work in this field is supported by a Project Grant from the Medical Research Council of New Zealand.

5. REFERENCES

Beacham, W. S., and Perl, E. R., 1964, Characteristics of a spinal sympathetic reflex, *J. Physiol. Lond.* **173**:431.

Bennett, M. R., and McLachlan, E. M., 1972, An electrophysiological analysis of the storage of acetylcholine in preganglionic nerve terminals, *J. Physiol. Lond.* **221**:657.

Billingsley, P. R., and Ranson, S. W., 1918, On the number of nerve cells in the ganglion cervicale superius and of nerve fibers in the cephalic end of the truncus sympathicus in the cat and on the numerical relations of preganglionic and postganglionic neurones, *J. Comp. Neurol.* **29**:359.

Bishop, G. H., and Heinbecker, P., 1932, A functional analysis of the cervical sympathetic nerve supply to the eye, *Am. J. Physiol.* **100**:519.

Blackman, J. G., and Purves, R. D., 1969, Intracellular recordings from ganglia of the thoracic sympathetic chain of the guinea-pig, *J. Physiol. Lond.* **203**:173.

Blackman, J. G., Ginsborg, B. L., and Ray, C., 1963a, Synaptic transmission in the sympathetic ganglion of the frog, *J. Physiol.* **167**:355.

Blackman, J. G., Ginsborg, B. L., and Ray, C., 1963b, Some effects of changes in ionic concentration on the action potential of sympathetic ganglion cells in the frog, *J. Physiol. Lond.* **167**:374.

Blackman, J. G., Crowcroft, P. J., Devine, C. E., Holman, M. E., and Yonemura, K., 1969, Transmission from preganglionic fibers in the hypogastric nerve to peripheral ganglia of male guinea-pigs, *J. Physiol. Lond.* **201**:723.

Bronk, D. W., 1939, Synaptic mechanisms in sympathetic ganglia, *J. Neurophysiol.* **2**:380.

Christ, D. D., and Nishi, S., 1971, Site of adrenergic blockade in the superior cervical ganglion of the rabbit, *J. Physiol. Lond.* **213**:107.

Crowcroft, P. J., and Szurszewski, J. H., 1971, A study of the inferior mesenteric and pelvic ganglia of guinea-pigs with intracellular electrodes, *J. Physiol. Lond.* **219**:421.

Crowcroft, P. J., Holman, M. E., and Szurszewski, J. H., 1971, Excitatory input from the distal colon to the inferior mesenteric ganglion in the guinea-pig, *J. Physiol. Lond.* **219**:443.

Davson, H., and Eggleton, M. G., (eds.), 1968, *Principles of Human Physiology*, 14th ed., p. 1161, Churchill, London.

Dennis, M. J., Harris, A. J., and Kuffler, S. W., 1971, Synaptic transmission and its duplication by focally applied acetylcholine in parasympathetic neurons in the heart of the frog, *Proc. Roy. Soc. Lond. B* **177**:509.

Ebbesson, S. O. E., 1968, Quantitative studies of superior cervical sympathetic ganglia in a variety of primates including man. I. The ratio of preganglionic fibers to ganglionic neurons, *J. Morphol.* **124**:117.

Eccles, J. C., 1935a, The action potential of the superior cervical ganglion, *J. Physiol. Lond.* **85**:179.

Eccles, J. C., 1935b, Facilitation and inhibition in the superior cervical ganglion, *J. Physiol. Lond.* **85**:207.

Eccles, R. M., and Libet, B., 1961, Origin and blockade of the synaptic responses of curarized sympathetic ganglia, *J. Physiol. Lond.* **157**:484.

Haefely, W., 1972, Electrophysiology of the adrenergic neuron, in: *Handbook of Experimental Pharmacology*, Vol. 33 (H. Blaschko and E. Muscholl, eds.), pp. 661–725, Springer-Verlag, Berlin.

Honma, S., 1970, Functional differentiation in sB and sC neurons of toad sympathetic ganglia, *Jap. J. Physiol.* **20**:281.

Ingram, W. R., 1960, Central autonomic mechanisms, in: *Handbook of Physiology*, Section I: *Neurophysiology*, Vol. II (H. W. Magoun, ed.), pp. 951–978, American Physiological Society, Washington, D.C.

Koketsu, K., 1969, Cholinergic synaptic potentials and the underlying ionic mechanisms, *Fed. Proc.* **28**:101.

Kosterlitz, H. W., Lees, G. M., and Wallis, D. I., 1968, Resting and action potentials recorded by the sucrose-gap method in the superior cervical ganglion of the rabbit, *J. Physiol. Lond.* **195**:39.

Lampard, D. G., and Redman, S. J., 1969, Stochastic stimulation for the pharmacological study of monosynaptic spinal reflexes, *Europ. J. Pharmacol.* **5**:141.

Langley, J. N., 1900, The sympathetic and other related systems of nerves, in: *Text Book of Physiology*, Vol. 2 (E. A. Shäfer, ed.), pp. 616–696, Pentland, Edinburgh.

Langley, J. N., 1903, The autonomic nervous system, *Brain* **25**:1.

Libet, B., 1970, Generation of slow inhibitory and excitatory postsynaptic potentials, *Fed. Proc.* **29**:1945.

Mannard, A., and Polosa, C., 1973, Analysis of background firing of single sympathetic preganglionic neurons of cat cervical nerve, *J. Neurophysiol.* **36**:398.

Martin, A. R., and Pilar, G., 1963, Dual mode of synaptic transmission in the avian ciliary ganglion, *J. Physiol. Lond.* **168**:443.

Marwitt, R., Pilar, G., and Weakly, J. N., 1971, Characterization of two ganglion cell populations in avian ciliary ganglia, *Brain Res.* **25**:317.

McLachlan, E. M., 1973, The release of acetycholine from preganglionic nerve terminals by short trains of impulses, *Proc. Aust. Physiol. Pharmacol. Soc.* **4**:67.

McMahan, U. J., and Kuffler, S. W., 1971, Visual identification of synaptic boutons on living ganglion cells and of varicosities in postganglionic axons in the heart of the frog, *Proc. Roy. Soc. Lond.* B **177**:485.

Melnitchenko, L. V., and Skok, V. I., 1970, Natural electrical activity in mammalian parasympathetic ganglion neurones, *Brain Res.* **23**:277.

Mirgorodsky, V. N., and Skok, V. I., 1969, Intracellular potentials recorded from a tonically active mammalian sympathetic ganglion, *Brain Res.* **15**:570.

Mirgorodsky, V. N., and Skok, C. I., 1970, The role of different preganglionic fibers in tonic activity of the mammalian sympathetic ganglion, *Brain Res.* **22**:262.

Nishi, S., 1970, Cholinergic and adrenergic receptors at sympathetic preganglionic nerve terminals, *Fed. Proc.* **29**:1957.

Nishi, S., and Koketsu, K., 1960, Electrical properties and activities of single sympathetic neurons in frogs, *J. Cell. Comp. Physiol.* **55**:15.

Nishi, S., Soeda, H., and Koketsu, K., 1965, Studies on sympathetic B and C neurons and patterns of preganglionic innervation, *J. Cell. Comp. Physiol.* **66**:19.

Perry, W. L. M., 1957, Transmission in autonomic ganglia, *Brit. Med. Bull.* **13**:220.

Polosa, C., 1968, Spontaneous activity of sympathetic preganglionic neurons, *Can. J. Physiol. Pharmacol.* **46**:887.

Purves, R. D., 1968, Intracellular recording from mammalian sympathetic ganglia, Thesis (B. Med. Sci.), University of Otago, Dunedin, New Zealand.

Redman, S. J., and Lampard, D. G., 1968, Monosynaptic stochastic stimulation of cat, spinal motoneurons. I. Response of motoneurons to sustained stimulation, *J. Neurophysiol.* **31**:485.

Sacchi, O., and Perri, V., 1971, Quantal release of acetylcholine from the nerve endings of the guinea-pig superior cervical ganglion, *Pflügers Arch. Ges. Physiol.* **329**:207.

Sato, A., and Schmidt, R. F., 1971, Ganglionic transmission of somatically induced sympathetic reflexes, *Pflügers Arch. Ges Physiol.* **326**:240.

Skok, V. I., 1973, *Physiology of Autonomic Ganglia*, Igaku Shoin, Tokyo.

Wolf, G. A., 1941, The ratio of preganglionic neurons to postganglionic neurons in the visceral nervous system, *J. Comp. Neurol.* **75**:235.

Chapter 10

Peripheral Autonomic Transmission

Geoffrey Burnstock and Christopher Bell

Department of Zoology
University of Melbourne
Victoria, Australia

1. INTRODUCTION

Understanding of transmission at the autonomic neuroeffector junction has lagged behind knowledge of transmission at the skeletal neuromuscular junction, largely because the relationship of the complex "autonomic ground plexuse" (Hillarp, 1949) to effector cells was difficult to determine with light microscopy and whole organ pharmacology. Some valiant attempts to resolve autonomic transmission mechanisms were made on the basis of external electrode recording (e.g., Eccles and Magladery, 1937; Bozler, 1948; Rosenblueth, 1950), but it was not until membrane potential changes were recorded in single cells during stimulation of autonomic nerves (Burnstock and Holman, 1960; see Holman, 1970), and the precise relationships of nerve fibers to single muscle cells were determined with the electron microscope (Caesar *et al.*, 1957; see Burnstock, 1970), that there was a real opportunity to resolve the mechanism of autonomic neuromuscular transmission.

Before considering details of transmission, it is necessary to define the morphology of the autonomic neuromuscular junction (see Chaper 5). This is important because, unlike the skeletal neuromuscular system, where the end plate potentials recorded in individual striated muscle cells are due to the discrete release of transmitter at well-defined motor end plates (see Katz, 1966), the junction potentials recorded in individual smooth muscle cells are the result of transmitter released *en passage* from a large and variable number of varicosities in the terminal regions of one or more nerves and of the spread of electrical activity from neighboring smooth muscle cells across low-resistance pathways (see Bennett and Burnstock, 1968; Burnstock and Iwayama, 1971).

The process of transmission from adrenergic nerves to smooth muscle will be considered first since this system has been explored at the greatest depth, and further sections will deal with cholinergic and purinergic transmission.

For detailed treatment of the biochemistry and pharmacology of autonomic transmission, the reader is referred to review papers in Acheson (1966), Goodman and Gilman (1970), Bacq (1970), Blaschko and Smith (1971), and Blaschko and Muscholl (1972).

2. DEFINITION OF THE AUTONOMIC NEUROMUSCULAR JUNCTION

2.1. Relation of Nerve Fibers to Muscle Effector Bundles

Electron microscope and histochemical studies of the relationship of individual nerves to single smooth muscle cells combined with electrophysiological studies of transmission have allowed a model of the sympathetic neuromuscular junction to be proposed (Burnstock and Iwayama, 1971) (Fig. 1). The essential features of this model are that (1) transmitter is released *en passage* from large numbers of terminal varicosities (Fig. 2); (2) the effector is the muscle bundle rather than the single smooth muscle cell, and individual cells within muscle effector bundles are connected by low-resistance pathways, represented by nexuses (Dewey and Barr, 1962), which allow electrotonic spread of activity within the effector bundle (Fig. 3); (3) in most organs, some, but not all, muscle cells are directly innervated; (4) the cells adjoining "directly innervated cells" are coupled electrotonically to them so that excitatory junction potentials can be recorded (these cells have been termed "coupled cells"); (5) when the muscle cells in an area of an effector bundle become depolarized in this way, an all-or-none action potential is initiated which propagates through the tissue. Thus, in some tissues, many cells (called "indirectly coupled cells") are neither directly innervated nor coupled, yet contract on stimulation of the nerves supplying the organ. It is unlikely that all three cell types described in this model are different in structure and properties. On the contrary, it seems likely that many cells might play the role of a "directly innervated," "coupled," or "indirectly coupled" cell at different times during the normal physiological pattern of nervous control of the organ.

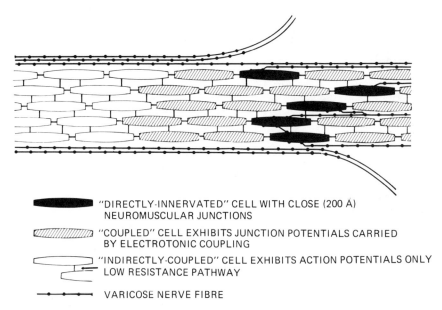

"DIRECTLY-INNERVATED" CELL WITH CLOSE (200 Å)
NEUROMUSCULAR JUNCTIONS

"COUPLED" CELL EXHIBITS JUNCTION POTENTIALS CARRIED
BY ELECTROTONIC COUPLING

"INDIRECTLY-COUPLED" CELL EXHIBITS ACTION POTENTIALS ONLY
LOW RESISTANCE PATHWAY

VARICOSE NERVE FIBRE

Fig. 1. Schematic representation of autonomic innervation of smooth muscle. For explanation, see text. From Burnstock and Iwayama (1971).

There is considerable variation in the density of innervation of smooth muscle in different systems (see Burnstock, 1970). For example, all the muscle cells of the mouse and rat vas deferens (Fig. 4) and probably some other organs appear to be "directly innervated" with at least one and probably up to six close neuromuscular junctions. In other organs such as the urinary bladder, nictitating membrane, guinea pig vas deferens, and dog retractor penis, about one-third of the muscle cells appear to be directly innervated, so that only a small proportion of "indirectly coupled" cells are present. Finally,

Fig. 2. Scanning electron micrograph of varicosities (arrows) in a single nerve fiber growing in a culture of newborn guinea pig sympathetic ganglia. From Burnstock (1974a).

in organs such as the ureter, uterus and many arteries (Fig. 5), only a small proportion of muscle cells are directly innervated, so that a large number of cells are indirectly coupled and are activated via a well-developed nexus system which allows rapid spread of activity between muscle cells.

2.2. Relation of Nerve Fibers to Individual Smooth Muscle Cells

2.2.1. Junctional Cleft

The varicosities in the terminal regions of autonomic neurons in most tissues have a diameter of between 0.5 and 2 μm compared to intervaricosity diameters of 0.1–0.5 μm (see Burnstock, 1970). Varicosities occur at irregular intervals of about 3–5 μm and are a genetically determined feature of adrenergic nerves, since they appear in culture in the absence of effector muscle (Chamley et al., 1972) (Fig. 2). Varicosities are packed with mitochondria and

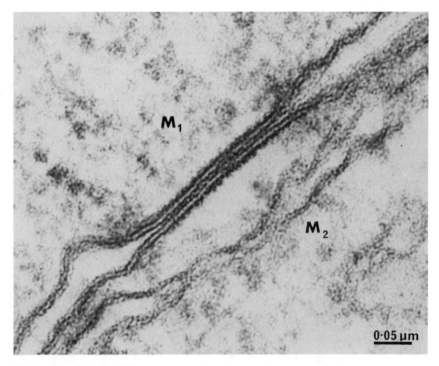

Fig. 3. "Gap junction" between two cultured smooth muscle cells (M$_1$ and M$_2$) from embryo chicken gizzard. From Campbell et al. (1971).

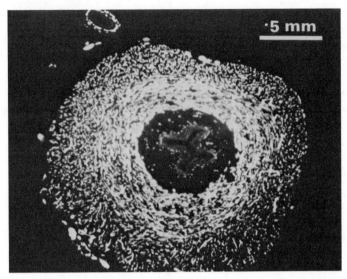

Fig. 4. Fluorescence histochemical demonstration of adrenergic nerve fibers. Rat vas deferens T.S. Note dense innervation of muscle coats. Courtesy of J. R. McLean, Department of Zoology, University of Melbourne.

vesicles of various kinds, while intervaricosities usually contain predominantly neurofibrils or neurofilaments.

Physiological and histochemical evidence for *en passage* release of noradrenaline (NA) from varicosities has been presented (see Bennett and Burnstock, 1968). Furthermore, it has recently been reported that short areas of varicosity membranes (about 0.1 μm) are thickened and associated with clusters of vesicles, suggesting that they may represent transmitter release sites by analogy with other synapses (McMahan and Kuffler, 1971). In pre-terminal axons or the proximal portions of terminal axons, vesicles are usually aggregated in the central regions of axon profiles (Rogers and Burnstock, 1966). Varicosities show considerable variation in the number of vesicles they contain. This does not appear to depend on their proximity to smooth muscle cells. Consecutive varicosities from the same neuron appear to have a comparable vesicle density (Fillenz, 1971). It has been calculated that each nerve varicosity contains approximately 1000–2000 vesicles (Dählström *et al.*, 1966), compared to a figure of about 300 obtained from vesicle counts in serial sections of rat iris (Hökfelt, 1969). It is possible that the variation in vesicle size and density between different neurons might reflect different levels of activity (see Geffen and Livett, 1971).

The relationship of individual adrenergic nerve varicosities to "directly innervated" smooth muscle cells varies in different organs (see Burnstock and

Iwayama, 1971). Nerve–muscle separation in the regions of closest apposition in the vas deferens and sphincter pupillae is about 150–200 Å (Fig. 6). Nerve profiles in the vas deferens occasionally penetrate and perhaps terminate deep inside smooth muscle cells (Watanabe, 1969; Furness and Iwayama, 1971). From an electron microscopic analysis of semiserial sections (Merrillees, 1968) combined with an electrophysiological study of the neuroenvironment of single muscle cells in the vas deferens, it was concluded that transmitter released from varicosities farther than about 1000 Å away would be unlikely to have a significant effect on muscle cells (Bennett and Merrillees, 1966). This conclusion was supported by the results of an entirely different approach, namely, acetylcholinesterase (AChE) staining (Robinson, 1969). In this study, about 15–20% of the axon profiles in the guinea pig vas deferens showed heavy positive staining for AChE but only muscle membranes within 1200 Å of these profiles showed matching AChE staining. Furthermore, Schwann cell processes intervened between muscle and nerve membranes in 80% of all the cases where nerves were separated from muscle by greater than 1100 Å. In the

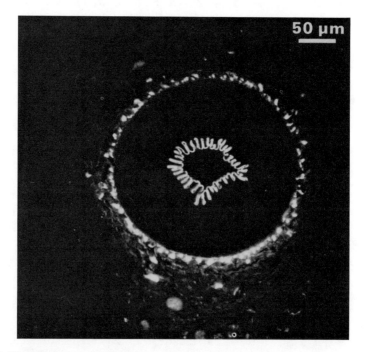

Fig. 5. Fluorescence histochemical demonstration of adrenergic nerve fibers. Rabbit ear artery T.S. Note restriction of adrenergic fibers to adventitial–medial border. From Burnstock *et al.* (1972*a*).

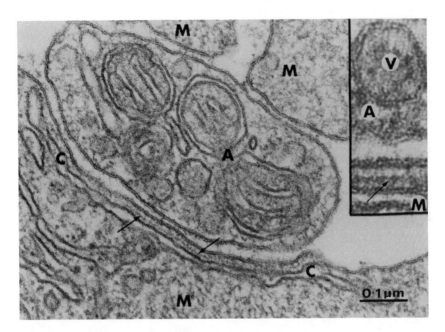

Fig. 6. Synaptic cleft and postsynaptic specialization in guinea pig sphincter pupillae. Note the subsurface cisterna (C) beneath the plasma membrane of the muscle cell (M) in the close-contact (within 200 Å) area between the naked axon (A) and the muscle cell. The cytoplasmic zone between the muscle cell membrane and the distal membrane of the cisterna is consistent in width (150–170 Å) and contains a continuous electron-dense intermediate layer (arrow). Inset is a high-power electron micrograph showing the organized cytoplasmic zone containing the intermediate layer (arrow) about 40 Å thick between the plasma membrane of muscle cell (M) and the distal membrane of the cisterna. The intermediate layer is about 80 Å apart from the plasma membrane and about 40 Å from the distal cisternal membrane. A, Terminal axon; V, synaptic vesicle. From Uehara and Burnstock (1972).

circular muscle coat in some regions of the gut of some species, many examples of close (150–200 Å) apposition of nerve and muscle membranes have also been reported (see Burnstock, 1970). In contrast, the closest apposition between adrenergic nerves and smooth muscle cells in most blood vessels, where the adrenergic nerves are confined to the adventitial–medial border and rarely penetrate the smooth muscle coat, is about 500–800 Å (see Burnstock *et al.*, 1970*b*) (Fig. 7) and transmission appears to be effective across neuromuscular separations up to at least 10,000 Å (Bell, 1969*a*). In the longitudinal muscle coat of the alimentary tract, the closest approach of intramural nerve varicosities to muscle cells appears to be of the order of 1000 Å (see Bennett and Burnstock, 1968).

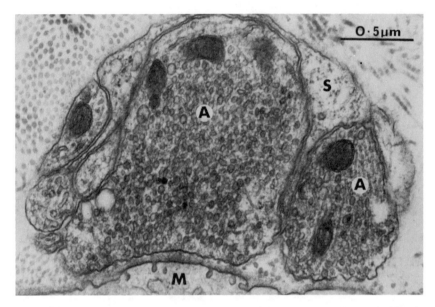

Fig. 7. Relation of axons (A) and smooth muscle (M) at the adventitial–medial border of the anterior cerebral artery of the rat. Note the relatively wide junctional cleft of about 800 Å. S, Schwann cells. From Burnstock *et al.* (1970*b*).

2.2.2. Postjunctional Specialization

A number of authors have examined the question of postjunctional specialization of smooth muscle membranes in the regions of closest apposition with terminal varicosities of adrenergic nerves (see Uehara and Burnstock, 1972).

Areas of increased density of the postsynaptic muscle membrane have been reported, but this appears to be a rare feature. Aggregates of micropinocytotic vesicles and smooth muscle membranes apposed to nerve varicosities in the gut, vas deferens, and some blood vessels have also been reported (Fig. 7). Perhaps the most convincing autonomic postsynaptic specialization described is subsynaptic cisternae at close (about 200 Å) neuromuscular junctions in the vas deferens. In comparable postsynaptic structures in the guinea pig sphincter pupillae, an eccentrically placed electron-dense structure about 40–60 Å thick is interposed between the subsynaptic cisternae and the postsynaptic membrane; filamentous elements traverse the space between the muscle membrane and the distal membrane of the cisternae (Fig. 6).

3. ADRENERGIC TRANSMISSION

3.1. Introduction

Current views (see Geffen and Livett, 1971; Blaschko and Smith, 1971; Blaschko and Muscholl, 1972) concerning the process of synthesis, storage, release, and inactivation of NA at the adrenergic neuromuscular junction are summarized in Fig. 8. All the enzymes involved in the synthesis and breakdown of NA [tyrosine hydroxylase, dopa decarboxylase, dopamine-β-hydroxylase, monoamine oxidase (MAO), and probably some catechol-O-methyl transferase (COMT)] are present throughout the adrenergic neuron. Tyrosine hydroxylase forms the rate-limit step in NA synthesis, and control is mediated by feedback inhibition of its activity by an extravesicular pool of NA which rapidly equilibrates with vesicular stores. NA is stored in granular vesicles together with chromogranin and dopamine-β-hydroxylase. During transmission, it is released into the junctional cleft, probably by a process of "partial exocytosis." Following its action on the postsynaptic muscle membrane, NA is inactivated largely by reuptake into the nerves, where it is either reincorporated into vesicular stores or degraded by MAO. Some NA is taken up by

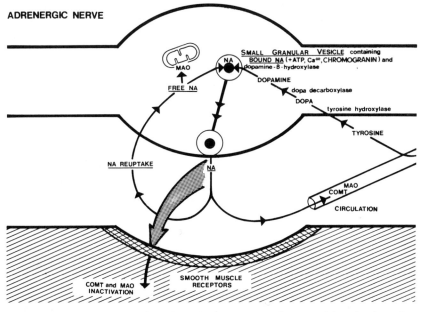

Fig. 8. Schematic representation of synthesis, storage, release, and inactivation of autonomic neurotransmitters at adrenergic neuromuscular junction. From Burnstock (1972).

smooth muscle cells and inactivated by intracellular MAO or COMT, while any NA that leaks away into the circulation is inactivated by the same enzymes largely in the liver or kidney.

The hypothesis that intra-axonal ACh might play a part in the release of NA from postganglionic adrenergic nerve fibers was first proposed by Burn and Rand (1959) and has been the subject of considerable controversy since then (see, for example, Burn and Rand, 1965; Ferry, 1966; Campbell, 1970). The possibility has also been considered that release of ACh from cholinergic terminals, shown to be in close relation to the terminal varicosities of adrenergic nerves, could lead to the release of NA (Burn and Rand, 1962; Burn, 1968).

3.2. Structure of Adrenergic Neurons and Storage of Noradrenaline

3.2.1. Structure and Distribution

In a typical sympathetic neuron, the cell body has a diameter of about 30 μm and a single axon about 1 μm in diameter extends for up to 10 cm before it branches and forms a varicose terminal network. The extent and degree of branching of terminal varicose fibers and the relationship of varicosities to smooth muscle cells are variable depending on the organ. The terminal regions of "long adrenergic neurons" (i.e., those with their cell bodies in the pre- or paravertebral ganglia) appear to be extensive and usually branch. For example, sympathetic nerves supplying the iris give rise to a highly branched terminal system estimated to be equivalent to 10–30 cm in length with as many as 30,000 varicosities (Malmfors, 1968). The proportion of transmitter synthesized in the perikaryon appears to be low compared to transmitter synthesized in terminal varicosities.

The term "short adrenergic neuron" was introduced by Owman and Sjöstrand (1965) to apply to those whose cell bodies are located close to target organ. For example, neurons in the hypogastric ganglion have shorter processes (see Swedin, 1971) and appear to branch rarely except when free of Schwann cell investment in the last few microns (Merrillees, 1968). NA turnover is low in short, relative to long, adrenergic neurons (see Geffen and Livett, 1971). Short adrenergic neurons are less sensitive to β-methylparatyrosine, 6-hydroxydopamine, reserpine, and immunosympathectomy than long adrenergic neurons (see Iversen et al., 1966; Malmfors and Sachs, 1968; Swedin, 1971). However, they are more sensitive to guanethidine (Burnstock et al., 1971).

Intramural adrenergic neurons in visceral organs such as the intestine (Costa et al., 1971; Ehinger and Falck, 1970), urinary bladder (Hamberger and Norberg, 1965; McLean and Burnstock, 1967), and urethra (Owman *et al.*, 1971) appear to contain low levels of NA and often need to be "loaded" by various methods in order to be detected by the fluorescence histochemical method (Read and Burnstock, 1969; Costa *et al.*, 1971). Similarly, adrenergic neurons in the ciliary ganglion are claimed to contain low catecholamine levels (Ehinger and Falck, 1970). These neurons may be sufficiently different from both "long" and "short" adrenergic neurons to represent a third group.

Cells exhibiting exceptionally high fluorescence of monoamines, generally greater than that seen in adrenergic neurons, have been shown to be widely distributed in the body, particularly in relation to blood vessels and sympathetic ganglia (see Eränkö and Eränkö, 1971). These were termed "small intensely fluorescent cells" (SIF cells) by Norberg *et al.* (1966). Many recent workers favor the possibility that they are interneurons with properties intermediate between those of adrenergic neurons and chromaffin cells.

Thus there appears to be wide variation in structure, storage, and turnover of NA in different catecholamine-containing neurons. There is no evidence to suggest that there are qualitative differences in the transmission process, but careful comparative studies of the electrophysiology of transmission from the different types of neurons described above are desirable.

3.2.2. Noradrenaline Storage Vesicles

NA is not distributed evenly throughout the neuron. Rough estimations, based largely on fluorescent histochemistry and chemical assay of tissue NA content, suggest that the cell body contains NA at a concentration of 10–100 μg/g, compared to about 100–500 μg/g in preterminal axons and 1000–10,000 μg/g in the terminal varicosities (see Geffen and Livett, 1971). Estimates of the NA content of single varicosities in different tissues are in good agreement: 4–6 × 10^{-15} g for rat iris and vas deferens (Dählström *et al.*, 1966), 10^{-14} g for rabbit pulmonary artery (calculated from Bevan *et al.*, 1969), and 3.4 × 10^{-14} g for guinea pig uterine artery (Bell and Vogt, 1971).

It is generally agreed that most of the NA in terminal varicosities is contained in granular vesicles (see Hökfelt, 1969; Geffen and Livett, 1971; Blaschko and Smith, 1971). The vesicular composition of adult adrenergic nerves is as follows: 80–85% small (300–500 Å) granular vesicles; 2–3% large (600–1200 Å) granular vesicles; 10–15% small (300–500 Å) agranular vesicles (Bloom and Barrnett, 1966; Geffen and Ostberg, 1969; Yamauchi and Burnstock, 1969) (see Fig. 9a,b).

While NA is stored in both small and large granular vesicles (see Tranzer and Thoenen, 1968; Furness *et al.*, 1970), there is evidence that only the large granular vesicles contain dopamine-β-hydroxylase as well as NA (Chubb *et al.*, 1970), suggesting that small and large granular vesicles may play different roles.

Individual small granular vesicles have been estimated to store about 15,000 molecules of NA (Folkow *et al.*, 1968). However, there is considerable variation in the NA content of vesicles (Fillenz and Howe, 1971). The agranular vesicles present in adrenergic nerves are unlikely to represent vesicles containing ACh (see Burn and Rand, 1965), since loading the nerves with NA in the presence of the MAO inhibitor nialamide leads to an increase in the percentage of small granular vesicles (Tranzer and Thoenen, 1967).

3.3. Electrophysiology of Adrenergic Transmission

3.3.1. Excitatory Junction Potentials

In the first application of electrophysiological methods to adrenergic junctions, Burnstock and Holman (1960, 1961) recorded excitatory junction potentials (e.j.p.'s) in single smooth muscle cells of the guinea pig vas deferens in response to stimulation of the hypogastric nerves. When the depolarization produced by a single e.j.p. or by a train of e.j.p.'s reaches a critical level, an action potential is initiated and contraction occurs (Figs. 10 and 12). Excitatory junction potentials of similar time course have subsequently been recorded also in dog retractor penis (Orlov, 1962) and various arteries (Speden, 1964, 1967; Bell, 1969*b*). The e.j.p.'s recorded in arterial smooth muscle had maximum amplitudes considerably lower than those recorded in the vas deferens. This difference may be due to the neuromuscular relationship in the two tissues; the minimum separation of nerve and muscle membranes is of the order of 200 Å in the guinea pig vas deferens compared to about 800 Å

Fig. 9. Intra-axonal structure of various autonomic nerves. (a) Cholinergic (C) and noradrenergic (N) nerve profiles in the circular muscle coat of the vas deferens of a rat treated for 30 min with 5-OHDA (50 mg/kg). Note that *both* small and large granular vesicles in the adrenergic profile have taken up the drug, but not the agranular or large granular vesicles in the cholinergic profile. Osmium fixation. × 38,000. (b) Adrenergic axon profile in Auerbach's plexus of chicken gizzard. In this case, large granular vesicles (which take up 5- and 6-OHDA) are predominant. Note halo between intravesicular, granular, and limiting vesicle membrane. Osmium fixation. × 42,000. (c) Nonadrenergic, noncholinergic axon profile (asterisk) in large intestine of toad, treated for 45 min with 6-OHDA (100 mg/kg). The large opaque vesicles (characterized by granulation *throughout* the vesicle) contained in these nerves do not take up 6-OHDA. Note also the cholinergic nerve profile (C). Glutaraldehyde–osmium fixation. × 48,000. (d) Nerve profile (S) probably representing the terminal portion of a sensory nerve fiber in the mucosa of the finch ureter. Note the aggregation of small mitochondria, absence of vesicles, and Schwann cell investment. The other axons (C) are probably cholinergic. Osmium fixation. × 48,000. From Burnstock and Iwayama (1971).

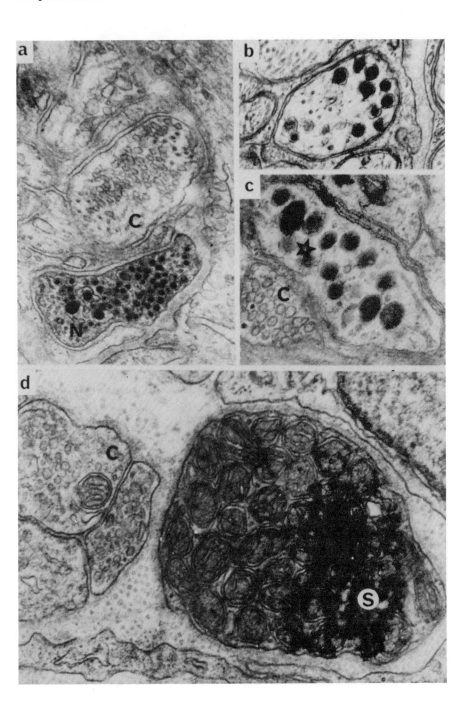

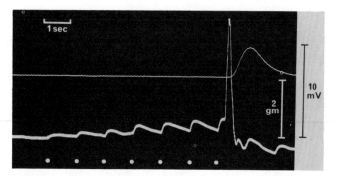

Fig. 10. Electrophysiology of transmission at adrenergic excitatory neuromuscular junctions in the guinea pig vas deferens. Excitatory junction potentials in response to repetitive stimulation of postganglionic sympathetic nerves (white dots). Upper trace, tension; lower trace, electrical activity, recorded extracellularly by the sucrose-gap method. Note both summation and facilitation of successive junction potentials. At a critical depolarization threshold, an action potential is initiated which results in contraction.

in arteries (see Section 3.2). Despite the differences in e.j.p. amplitude between these preparations, their time course is comparable; this suggests that the time taken for NA diffusion across the neuromuscular gap is not a significant factor in determining time course of postjunctional events.

Qualitative and quantitative differences in the mechanism of adrenergic nervous control of blood vessels are emerging (see Somlyo and Somlyo, 1968a, b; Holman, 1969; Speden, 1970; Bevan et al., 1971). In view of the wide variation in pattern of adrenergic innervation of different-sized vessels in different places and in different species (see Somlyo and Somlyo, 1968a,b; 1970; Burnstock et al., 1970b), this is not altogether surprising. In many vessels, intermuscle fiber spread of excitation appears to play an essential role in the transmission process (Holman, 1969; Bell, 1969b; Burnstock et al., 1970b; Johansson and Ljung, 1971), and in these vessels direct transmitter action is probably limited to the outermost muscle cells of the medial coat

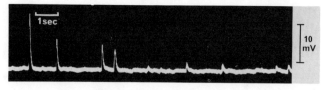

Fig. 11. Microelectrode recording of spontaneous junction potentials in single smooth muscle cells. From Burnstock and Holman (1962).

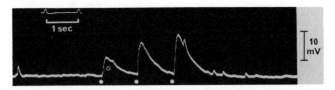

Fig. 12. Comparison of the time course of excitatory junction potentials in response to nerve stimulation (white dots) and spontaneous junction potentials. Note also post-stimulation potentiation of spontaneous discharge. From Burnstock and Holman (1964).

(see, e.g., Bell, 1969b). In others, muscle coupling seems to be unimportant and transmitter may act on individual muscle cells throughout the media (Gerova et al., 1967; Bevan et al., 1971), either by depolarization or possibly by direct activation of the contractile apparatus (Somlyo and Somlyo, 1968a,b; Su and Bevan, 1966; Bohr and Uchida, 1969).

In the absence of nerve stimulation, spontaneous depolarizations, with a shorter time course than the e.j.p., occur at random intervals (Figs. 11 and 12). Since the occurrence of these potentials is reduced by reserpine or post-synaptic adrenoceptor blocking agents, they probably represent the spontaneous release of packets of NA from the nerves (see Burnstock and Holman, 1966).

Facilitation of successive e.j.p.'s in response to repetitive nerve stimulation occurs and appears to be due to increased release of NA with each stimulus, rather than to increased postsynaptic sensitivity (Burnstock et al., 1964b) (Fig. 10). Enhancement of spontaneous release of NA follows nerve stimulation (Burnstock and Holman, 1966). These results suggest that the mechanism of storage and release of NA from sympathetic nerves is comparable to the release of ACh at the motor end plate (Katz, 1969). However, there are some notable differences from skeletal neuromuscular transmission. For example as Table I shows, the time course of the e.j.p. is very long (100–1000 ms) and there is a long, but variable, delay time for the appearance of e.j.p.'s following nerve stimulation in different cells (minimum 6 ms). Reduction of the number of nerve fibers stimulated leads to a general reduction in amplitude of e.j.p.'s in all cells penetrated rather than complete loss of e.j.p.'s in localized areas (Burnstock and Holman, 1961). Further, the amplitude of e.j.p.'s in the majority of cells in the vas deferens is unaffected by depolarizing and by hyperpolarizing currents (Bennett and Merrillees, 1966). These differences from the classical transmission characteristics known for the skeletal neuromuscular junction have been explained in terms of the model of the autonomic neuromuscular junction outlined in Section 2, which emphasizes electrotonic coupling of activity between neighboring cells within

Table I. Temporal Characteristics of Adrenergic Junction Potentials, Compared with Those of Transmission at the Skeletal Neuromuscular Junction

Tissue	Stimulus site[a]	Minimum latency (ms)	Rise time (ms)	Duration (ms)	Reference
Guinea pig vas deferens	Preg.	20	15–20 (half rise time)	1000	Burnstock and Holman (1961)
Mouse vas deferens	Postg. (T/M)	6	40	500	Kuriyama (1963)
	Postg. (T/M)	10	10–20	100–250	Holman (1970)
	Postg. (T/M)	5	28–34	—	Furness (1970a)
Rat vas deferens	Postg. (T/M)	10	10–20	~150	Holman (1970)
Cat nictitating membrane[b]	Postg.	20	50–80	500	Eccles and Magladery (1937)
Rabbit ear and mesenteric arteries	Postg. (T/M)	12	70–100	500–1000	Speden (1967)
Guinea pig uterine artery	Postg. (T/M)	20	—	900–1000	Bell (1969b)
Rat skeletal neuromuscular junction	—	0.2	0.6	2–3	Boyd and Martin (1956)

[a] Preg., preganglionic; postg., postganglionic; T/M, transmural.
[b] Extracellular recording.

muscle effector bundles and *en passage* release of transmitter from extensive terminal varicose nerve fibers.

In a study of synaptic delay in the mouse vas deferens, Furness (1970*a*) plotted latency against distance and obtained the delay for zero distance by extrapolation. A minimum latency of 5.1 ms was recorded when micro-electrodes were placed within 100–300 μm of the cathodal stimulating electrode, of which 0.1–0.7 ms was calculated to be due to the nerve conduction time. Thus it was concluded that there was a synaptic delay of 4–5 ms for this tissue, with a conduction velocity of 0.46–0.6 ms, in the terminal regions of the adrenergic nerve fibers. Whether the long delay time of the e.j.p. is due largely to presynaptic or postsynaptic factors is not yet known (see Holman, 1970 and p. 302). It seems unlikely to represent the time required for transmitter to diffuse from nerve terminals to the effector sites (Furness, 1970*a*; Bell and Vogt, 1971).

The reasons for the long time course of the e.j.p., or for that matter all autonomic junction potentials, need further exploration. It seems unlikely, according to calculations made from measurements taken from semiserial

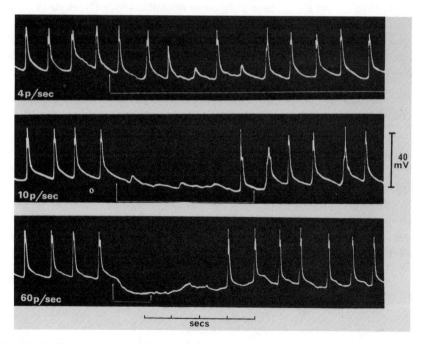

Fig. 13. Inhibitory hyperpolarizations at different frequencies of stimulation of the peri-vascular inhibitory nerves recorded in single smooth muscle cells of the guinea pig taenia coli. Nerves stimulated for the period indicated by the arrows. From Bennett *et al.* (1966a).

electron microscope sections of autonomic neuromuscular junctions, that the long time course is due to asynchronous release of transmitter from the varicosities as a result of slow conduction of the action potential along the terminal regions of the nerves, or to the time for diffusion of transmitter from the varicosities to the muscle cells (Bennett and Burnstock, 1968; Furness, 1970a). Two further possibilities remain: that the time course of the junction potential is determined by the rate of inactivation of the neurotransmitter or that it is determined by the electrical properties of the smooth muscle effector bundle. Furness (1970a) argues against the first possibility for the vas deferens largely on the grounds that there is a striking decrease in decay time of the e.j.p. when the potassium concentration is increased and that high potassium would, if anything, reduce the rate of uptake of NA released from the nerve (Bogdanski and Brodie, 1969). The explanation for the long time course of junction potentials most favored at the present time is that it is determined largely by the passive electrical properties of smooth muscle (Bennett and Burnstock, 1968; Holman, 1970; Furness, 1970a). However, the long decay time of the e.j.p. in the guinea pig vas deferens compared to that of the externally evoked electrotonic potentials indicates that transmitter action may persist throughout the e.j.p. in this tissue (Tomita, 1967; Holman, 1970).

In the frog arrested sinus venosus, del Castillo and Katz (1955a) described "graded subthreshold depolarizations" in response to single impulses to sympathetic nerves. These events either decayed locally or initiated action potentials and contraction.

3.3.2. Hyperpolarizations

Inhibitory junction potentials in response to stimulation of adrenergic nerves supplying smooth muscle of the gastrointestinal tract have *not* been recorded. In the gut, repetitive nerve stimulation rates of 5 Hz or more are necessary to produce an overall hyperpolarization of the membrane of smooth muscle cells leading to inhibition of spike activity and relaxation (Gillespie, 1962; Bennett et al., 1966a; Furness, 1969a; Bennett, 1969b) (Fig. 13). The explanation for this difference from adrenergic excitatory transmission may be that adrenergic innervation is sparse in most regions of the gut and that inhibition is largely the result of overflow of NA from adrenergic nerves that innervate enteric neurons and blood vessels (see Norberg, 1964; Read and Burnstock, 1969; Furness and Burnstock, 1974). The main inhibitory autonomic nerve supply to gut muscle appears to be by nonadrenergic ("purinergic") nerves (see Section 5).

Hyperpolarizing secretory potentials have been reported in feline salivary acinar cells in response to repetitive stimulation of sympathetic nerves (Lundberg, 1955, 1958; Creed and Wilson, 1969). These responses differed from the secretory potentials evoked by parasympathetic stimulation (see Section 4.3) in that they exhibited longer latencies and were not seen in response to single impulses.

3.3.3. Release of Noradrenaline

While the mechanism of secretion of adrenal catecholamines seems likely to be by a process of exocytosis (de Robertis and Ferreira, 1957; Douglas, 1968; Kirschner and Kirschner, 1971), release of NA from adrenergic nerve terminals by exocytosis is still not clearly established (see Geffen et al., 1970; Banks and Helle, 1971; Smith, 1971; De Potter, 1971). Chromagranin A and dopamine-β-hydroxylase have been shown to be released from perfused spleen together with NA during stimulation of adrenergic nerves, while enzymes such as dopa decarboxylase located outside the vesicles were not. However, the amount of protein relative to catecholamines released from nerve terminals is much lower than that released from adrenal medullary cells. Furthermore, there is evidence to suggest that ATP is contained in adrenergic nerve vesicles in a substantially lower ratio to catecholamines than found in adrenal medullary granules (see De Potter, 1971), and there has still been no clear demonstration that ATP is released together with NA from adrenergic nerves (Stjärne et al., 1970, but see Su et al., 1971).

As in the adrenal medulla (see Douglas, 1968; Kirschner and Kirschner, 1971), the release of NA from adrenergic nerves is dependent on the presence of Ca^{2+} in the extracellular fluid (see Smith, 1971). Output of NA from perfused rabbit heart, cat spleen, or colon following adrenergic nerve stimulation is strongly reduced in Ca-free media (Huković and Muscholl, 1962; Kirpekar and Misu, 1967). It seems likely by analogy with the skeletal neuromuscular junction (Katz, 1969) that when an impulse reaches the nerve terminals, Ca enters the terminals and provides the essential link in "stimulus secretion coupling" (see Douglas, 1968) for NA release into the synaptic cleft. It is possible that Ca neutralizes net negative charges on the vesicle and nerve membranes, allowing them to coalesce, but it has been suggested that a metabolic process is more likely to be involved (Iversen and Callingham, 1970).

While there is electrophysiological evidence for packaged release of NA from adrenergic terminals, it is still not possible to say whether or not the packages are quantal (see Holman, 1970; Katz, 1971). According to standard statistical tests, spontaneous e.j.p.'s recorded in the vas deferens show a skew distribution and appear with random amplitude, although there was some hint of grouped discharges of two or three comparably sized spontaneous e.j.p.'s at intervals of 10 min or more (Burnstock and Holman, 1962). The complication, however, is that junction potentials recorded in single muscle cells cannot be used for the analysis of transmitter released from individual varicosities, since electrical coupling of activity from neighboring muscle cells occurs and transmitter reaching a muscle cell is released at various distances from successive varicosities from one or more nerves.

Calculations based on the quantity of NA released during periarterial nervous stimulation led Bell and Vogt (1971) to propose that in the guinea pig uterine artery the peak postjunctional concentration of NA during transmission is of the order of 4×10^{-4} M. Using pharmacological techniques, Ljung (1969) calculated a peak postjunctional NA concentration during transmission to the rat portal vein of 2×10^{-5} M. In contrast, Bevan et al. (1971) using the rabbit pulmonary artery, where the neuromuscular gap is much greater than those in the other two tissues, derived a peak figure of about 6×10^{-9} M.

On the basis of estimates of the quantity of NA released with a single impulse from vasomotor nerves and of the vesicular content of NA, it has been calculated for some vascular tissues either that only part of the NA store in a vesicle is released with any single impulse or that one impulse releases transmitter from only a fraction of the total varicosities (Folkow et al., 1968; Bevan et al., 1969). On the other hand, the estimates of NA release made by Bell and Vogt (1971) are compatible with total discharge of the contents of one or two vesicles from every varicosity with one impulse. On the basis of dopamine-β-hydroxylase measurements rather than NA, De Potter and Chubb (1971) concluded that it is likely that the entire NA store of each vesicle is released when it discharged.

3.4. Ionic Basis of the Action of Catecholamines on the Postjunctional Membrane

Catecholamines act on smooth muscle systems supplied by inhibitory sympathetic nerves by producing hyperpolarization of the muscle membrane, resulting in reduction or cessation of spike activity and relaxation (Bülbring, 1957; Burnstock, 1958b; Bülbring and Kuriyama, 1963). There has been considerable debate about the mechanism of action of catecholamines on the postsynaptic muscle "receptors" in producing this action (see Burnstock et al., 1963b; Setekleiv, 1970; Tomita, 1970; Kuriyama, 1970; Axelsson, 1971). Although adrenaline has been shown to increase both K and Cl conductance in intestinal smooth muscle, Na and Ca permeability changes as well as metabolic processes also seem to be involved. One theory, first put forward by Burnstock (1958b), was that catecholamines cause hyperpolarization by stimulating an electrogenic Na pump. A considerable body of evidence has been put forward in support of this hypothesis (see Bülbring and Kuriyama, 1963; Holman, 1970; Goodford, 1970), but it seems unlikely to be the only action of catecholamines. Another hypothesis (Bülbring and

Tomita, 1969; Kuriyama, 1970) is that catecholamines act on Ca-binding sites in the smooth muscle membrane. It has been proposed that Ca bound to the inner membrane controls K conductivity, while Ca bound to the outer membrane controls Na conductivity (Brading et al., 1969). Thus increased Ca at inner sites increases K conductance and hyperpolarization, while decreased Ca at outer sites increases Na conductance (Tomita, 1970).

When catecholamines are applied to pig esophagus or dog retractor penis, which are innervated by excitatory sympathetic nerves, they produce depolarization and initiation or increase in frequency of spike activity, which is indistinguishable from the excitatory action of ACh on smooth muscle (Burnstock, 1960 and see Section 4.4). However, in a recent study of the estrogen-dominated guinea pig uterus, it has been suggested that whereas depolarization by ACh is due to an increase in Na permeability, depolarization by catecholamines is due to an increase in Cl permeability (Szurszewski and Bülbring, 1973).

It is usually assumed that drugs applied directly to isolated smooth muscles act uniformly on the membrane surface of all the cells. This assumption might be questioned on several grounds. For example, by analogy with the skeletal neuromuscular junction, it seems likely that the sensitivity of the smooth muscle membrane in the regions of apposition with axon varicosities may be considerable higher than in the membrane of the rest of the cell. In organs with multiple innervation such as the gut, recording from single muscle cells in response to cholinergic, adrenergic, and purinergic nerve stimulation has shown that some cells respond to all three nerve types, some to two, some to one, and some to none (see Section 5.2). These findings imply differential sensitivity of different smooth muscle cells to transmitter action, as well as the possibility of differential sensitivity of different areas of the smooth muscle membrane of individual cells.

In 1948, Ahlqvist introduced the concept of α- and β-adrenoceptors based on the relative potencies of noradrenaline, adrenaline, and isoprenaline, and this has been followed in principle, but with some modification, to the present time. The most recent development is that several subtypes of β-adrenoceptors are now recognized (see Raper and McCulloch, 1971). For the most part, α-adrenoceptors mediate excitation, while β-adrenoceptors mediate inhibition, but this is by no means always true. Some responses to catecholamines appear to be mediated by a mixture of both α- and β-adrenoceptors (e.g., intestinal inhibition). It is not known whether both α- and β-adrenoceptors are located on the smooth muscle membrane of single cells or are confined to different cells within the organ; iontophoretic application of small amounts of catecholamines to smooth muscle systems with their narrow extracellular spacing has proved to be a technical near impossibility.

The suggestion has been made in recent years that the β-adrenoceptor is represented by adenyl cyclase, which results in increased production of cyclic AMP in the postsynaptic cell following adrenergic nerve stimulation (see Robison *et al.*, 1971).

3.5. Summary

1. A model of synthesis, storage, release, and inactivation of NA at adrenergic neuromuscular junctions is presented.
2. The structure of adrenergic neurons is described, and differences in form, NA turnover, and sensitivity to drugs between long and short adrenergic nerves, intramural adrenergic nerves, and SIF cells are emphasized.
3. NA is stored in granular vesicles in terminal varicosities together with chromagranin and dopamine-β-hydroxylase.
4. Excitatory junction potentials (e.j.p.'s) appear in smooth muscle cells, in response to single pulses to the adrenergic nerves supplying the vas deferens, retractor penis, and various arteries. E.j.p.'s sum and facilitate with repetitive stimulation.
5. Spontaneous e.j.p.'s appear at random intervals and appear to represent the spontaneous release of packets of NA.
6. The reasons for the long latency and time course of e.j.p.'s are discussed.
7. Inhibitory hyperpolarizations occur in smooth muscle of the gut in response to repetitive stimulation (5 Hz or more) of adrenergic nerves and may result largely from overflow of NA from adrenergic nerves which innervate enteric neurons and blood vessels.
8. The mechanism of release of NA from adrenergic nerves and estimations of the amounts of NA released per single impulse are discussed and related to the question of packaged release from granular vesicles.
9. The ionic basis of the action of catecholamines on postsynaptic smooth muscle "receptors" is discussed.

4. CHOLINERGIC TRANSMISSION

4.1. Introduction

Current views regarding the synthesis, storage, release, and metabolism of acetylcholine (ACh) are summarized in Fig. 14. Synthesis of the ACh by choline acetyltransferase occurs both in the neuron body and in the peripheral terminal axon. The ACh is stored in electron-transparent "agranular" vesicles, 300–600 Å in diameter, and released into the junctional cleft probably by a process of partial exocytosis. Inactivation of ACh following its interaction with the postjunctional receptors is due in the main to local

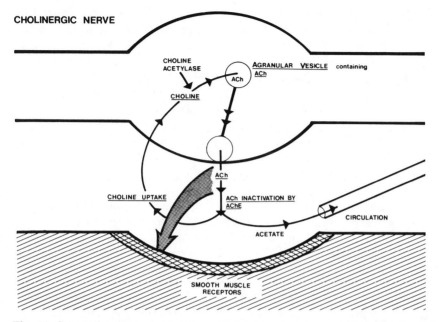

Fig. 14. Schematic representation of synthesis, storage, release, and inactivation of autonomic neurotransmitters at cholinergic neuromuscular junction. From Burnstock (1972).

hydrolysis by postjunctionally situated acetylcholinesterase (AChE), although a small fraction of ACh may diffuse away from the junctional cleft to be hydrolyzed by cholinesterases elsewhere in the effector tissue or in the circulation. Reuptake of ACh itself into the nerve terminals does not occur. However, choline produced by ACh hydrolysis is actively resorbed and may be important in maintaining continued transmitter synthesis. For more detailed accounts of these processes, the reader is referred to Ehrenpreis (1967), Collier and MacIntosh (1969), Potter (1970), and Phillis (1970).

It must be emphasized that although there are now ample grounds for concluding that cholinergic axons contain predominantly agranular vesicles (see Burnstock, 1970), there is no proof that all axons with this characteristic are cholinergic. In contrast to the capacity of adrenergic vesicles to concentrate electron-opaque NA analogs, no specific technique so far exists by which the ACh content of the vesicles can be characterized in a tissue section.

4.2. Localization of Acetylcholinesterase

Histochemical localization of AChE has been widely used for the identification of cholinergic nerves on the basis that such nerves contain high levels of this enzyme relative to other nerve types (see Koelle, 1963) (Fig. 15). Although AChE activity can also be demonstrated in noncholinergic nerves (Koelle, 1969) and in nonnervous tissue (Gerebtzoff, 1959; Koelle, 1963), assessment of the results of numerous studies employing combinations of histochemical techniques for localization of AChE and of NA and electron microscopic investigations indicate that AChE-positivity can be employed as a criterion of cholinergic function provided that the reaction intensity is similar to that of known cholinergic elements from the same animal (for instance, motor end plates or the visceromotor neurones of Auerbach's plexus). However, the possibility of a positive reaction in noncholinergic axons when staining is prolonged means that reports of AChE-positivity in the absence of such controls must be viewed with some reservation.

Histochemical studies of the fine-structural relationships between cholinergic axons and smooth muscle cells have been performed on the bladder of the toad and on the uterine artery and vas deferens of the guinea pig. In these tissues, it was noted that where an AChE-positive axon profile lay close to a muscle cell, without the interposition of other cell types, reaction

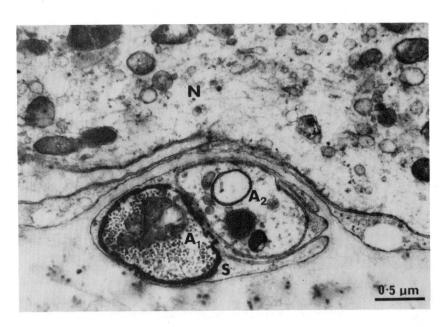

Fig. 15. Nerve bundle enclosed in Schwann cell (S) stained for acetylcholinesterase. One axon, A_1 (presumably cholinergic), exhibits reaction product of the histochemical process around its outer membrane. The adjacent axon, A_2 (presumably noncholinergic), is unstained. N, Cell body of sympathetic ganglion. From Burnstock and Robinson (1967).

product was also present on the adjacent area of the muscle cell membrane (Robinson and Bell, 1967; Bell, 1969a; Robinson, 1969). Where the axon was completely surrounded by Schwann cell, or in the case of the artery studied where the external elastic lamina separated axon and muscle, no postsynaptic staining occurred. Staining was absent from the muscle membrane in areas remote from axons. Several pieces of evidence were presented in these studies to suggest that the postsynaptic staining was not due to diffusion either of AChE or of reaction product from the axons, and it appears likely that it represents a true primary site for AChE activity. In the vas deferens, postsynaptic staining was associated only with axons lying within about 1100 Å of a muscle cell, approximating the maximal distance over which transmission has been predicted to be effective in this tissue (see Section 2.2). In the uterine artery, postsynaptic AChE was seen consistently in tissues from pregnant animals, at which time the cholinergic vasomotor nerves are functional (Bell, 1968), but was sparse or absent in tissues from nonpregnant animals, when the arterial muscle is insensitive to ACh.

Thus it seems that the association of postsynaptic AChE with an adjacent AChE-positive axon can be regarded as a criterion for a functional cholinergic synapse. As the most likely function for this muscle-bound AChE is destruction of neurally liberated ACh, its restriction to a small area of membrane opposite the axon suggests that transmitter action is also spatially restricted (Bell, 1969a). As yet, there is no way of knowing whether this region is truly analogous to the skeletal neuromuscular junction in terms of an increased local density of receptors for transmitter. Histochemical studies of the relationship between cholinergic axons and their effectors in the guinea pig heart (Hirano and Ogawa, 1967) and the rat salivary gland (Hand, 1970; Bogart, 1971) also demonstrated the absence of appreciable AChE activity from areas of effector cell membranes remote from axonal contact.

4.3. Electrophysiology of Cholinergic Transmission

4.3.1. Excitatory Junction Potentials

4.3.1a. Smooth Muscle. Stimulation of excitatory cholinergic nerves to intestinal smooth muscle characteristically produces excitatory junction potentials (e.j.p.'s) associated with each stimulating pulse (Fig. 16). In various preparations, the time course of the e.j.p. varies somewhat but is of the order of 500–1000 ms duration, similar to that seen with adrenergic e.j.p.'s in the guinea pig vas deferens (*cf.* Tables I and II). However, both the latency and the rate of rise of the cholinergic e.j.p. have been generally found to be rather greater than those seen with adrenergic transmission (Fig. 16). Although two recent reports have claimed minimum latencies of as low as 15–20 ms during

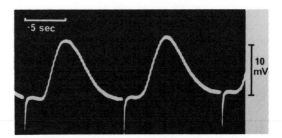

Fig. 16. Cholinergic excitatory junction potentials (e.j.p.'s) recorded from a muscle cell of the guinea pig colon during repetitive stimulation of the pelvic nerve. From Furness (1969a).

stimulation of intramural cholinergic nerves in guinea pig intestine (Hidaka and Kuriyama, 1969; Furness, 1970b), in most tissues latencies of 70 ms or greater have been observed (Table II). While the rise times of adrenergic e.j.p.'s vary between 10 and 100 ms, those of cholinergic e.j.p.'s have never been reported as less than 100 ms and may be as long as 250 ms. Where latencies have been compared in the same tissue employing both preganglionic and transmural stimulation, at least 200 ms can be accounted for by nervous conduction and ganglionic transmission (Gillespie, 1968; Bennett, 1969b). However, stimulation of purely postganglionic fibers in the presence of ganglion-blocking agents still evokes e.j.p.'s with minimum latencies of 70 ms or more in some tissues (Bennett, 1969b; Ohashi, 1971). Investigation of the changes of latency of e.j.p.'s with increasing distance between stimulating and recording sites in the chick esophagus has indicated that conduction time is unlikely to account for more than about 25 ms of the 90 ms latency in this tissue (Ohashi, 1971). As with adrenergic e.j.p.'s, diffusion is unlikely to be a significant factor. The most likely explanation is that there is a considerable delay at cholinergic junctions in the rate of ACh interaction with the post-

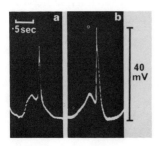

Fig. 17. Stimulus-evoked (a) and spontaneous (b) e.j.p.'s recorded from muscle cells of the guinea pig taenia coli. Both e.j.p.'s are associated with action potential firing in the cells. From Bennett (1966b).

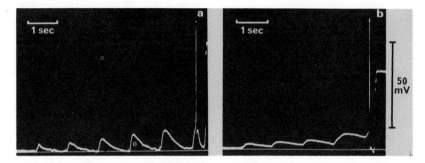

Fig. 18. E.j.p.'s recorded from muscle cells of the guinea pig vas deferens during post-ganglionic nerve stimulation (a) under control conditions and (b) in the presence of physostigmine, 5×10^{-6} g/ml. Note the increase in decay time of the e.j.p.'s following cholinesterase inhibition, resulting in summation of successive e.j.p.'s. From Bell (1967).

synaptic receptors (Purves, 1974). Similar arguments can be put forward regarding the relatively slow rate of rise of cholinergic e.j.p.'s.

During repetitive low-frequency stimulation of cholinergic nerves supplying intestinal muscle cells, facilitation of successive e.j.p.'s has been seen in rabbit colon (Gillespie, 1962), guinea pig jejunum (Kuriyama *et al.*, 1967) and taenia coli (Burnstock *et al.*, 1964*a*), and avian gizzard (Bennett, 1969*b*) and esophagus (Ohashi, 1971). The character of this facilitation is similar to that seen with adrenergic transmission to the vas deferens, with progressive enhancement of amplitude of successive e.j.p.'s up to a stable peak level without alteration of e.j.p. time course (see Section 3.3). As suggested for adrenergic e.j.p.'s (see Section 3.3), the process of facilitation probably represents a presynaptic increase in the recruitment of transmitter for release with successive pulses, similar to the situation at the skeletal motor end plate (del Castillo and Katz, 1954).

In the guinea pig taenia coli, repetitive stimulation of the intramural cholinergic nerves with sufficiently high-voltage pulses at 1 Hz causes action potentials to arise from the peak of each e.j.p. At higher frequencies of

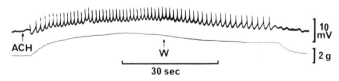

Fig. 19. Depolarization, action potential discharge, and contraction (W) initiated by application of ACh to the isolated taenia coli of the guinea pig (sucrose-gap recording). From Bülbring and Burnstock (1960).

Table II. Temporal Characteristics of Cholinergic Junction Potentials and Secretory Potentials

Tissue	Stimulus site[a]	Minimum latency (ms)	Rise time (ms)	Duration (ms)	Reference
Rabbit colon	Preg.	400	~250	~600	Gillespie (1962, 1968)
	T/M	220	150–200	~1000	Furness (1969a, 1970b)
Guinea pig colon	Preg.	100			
	T/M	15			
Guinea pig stomach	Preg.	150	200	400–500	Beani et al (1971)
Guinea pig taenia coli	T/M	100	100–200	500–800	Bennett (1966b)
Chick gizzard	Preg.	≤350	—	430–1300	Bennett (1969b)
	T/M	90			
Pigeon gizzard	Preg.	≤250	—	430–900	Bennett (1969b)
	T/M	70			
Chick esophagus[b]	T/M	90	150–250	600–1200	Ohashi (1971)
Rabbit bladder	Postg.	35–65	~100	>400 <1000	Ursillo (1961)
Guinea pig jejunum	T/M	20	—	—	Hidaka and Kuriyama (1969)
Cat submandibular gland	Preg.	180	~500	~900	Creed and Wilson (1969)
Possum submandibular gland	Preg.	150	—	—	Creed and McDonald (1968)
	Postg.	130			
Frog sinus venosus	Preg.	~500	1000–1500	5000–7000	del Castillo and Katz (1955b)

[a] Preg., preganglionic; Postg., postganglionic; T/M, transmural.
[b] Extracellular recording.

stimulation, however, this activity is not maintained. Rather, the muscle membrane repolarizes, probably due to increased membrane stability caused by concurrent activation of intramural inhibitory fibers (Bennett, 1966a). In rabbit colon, Gillespie (1962) was able to produce cholinergic nervous activation without concurrent inhibitory effects and noted that action potentials were initiated by e.j.p.'s in response to stimulation at frequencies up to several Hz. As stimulation frequency was increased, successive e.j.p.'s summated to a progressively greater extent, and above about 6 Hz the muscle membrane remained depolarized by about 25 mV. Under these conditions, action potential firing was no longer seen but mechanical tension was maintained.

In the guinea pig vas deferens, there are pharmacological and morphological data to indicate the presence of a small percentage of cholinergic excitatory nerves in the predominantly adrenergic population (Birmingham, 1966; Bell, 1967; Bell and McLean, 1967; Robinson, 1969). Although the use of autonomic drugs in combination with electrophysiological recording has supported this view (see below), it appears that few if any cells are innervated only by cholinergic fibers. It is therefore not possible to characterize the cholinergic e.j.p. in this tissue.

Two types of spontaneous excitatory events have been described in intestinal muscles. The first of these resembles the miniature spontaneous e.j.p. discharge seen in the retractor penis and vas deferens (see Section 3.3), which appears to be due to random spontaneous release of transmitter from the axons. Events of similar appearance have been described in the gizzard of chick and pigeon in a small percentage of cells impaled (Bennett, 1969b). They were not seen in preparations treated with hyoscine and can be presumed to represent spontaneous ACh discharge. The absence of such spontaneous e.j.p.'s from other intestinal tissues examined probably reflects the lack of close apposition between axonal and muscle membranes.

The second type of spontaneous event which has been reported is similar in time course to the potential change evoked by a nervous stimulating pulse (Fig. 17). Depolarizations of this type have been observed in guinea pig taenia coli and colon (Bennett, 1966a; Furness, 1969a) and in avian gizzard (Bennett, 1969b). The temporal similarity of these events to stimulus-evoked potential changes suggests that they are due to spontaneous nervous impulse activity rather than to passive leakage of transmitter from the axons. This is supported by their absence from gizzard preparations in which the neurons of Auerbach's plexus were removed (Bennett, 1969a).

In some preparations of intestinal smooth muscle, spontaneous slow rhythmic oscillations of membrane potential occur, spontaneous action potential firing occurring in bursts only at the peaks of depolarization. In the guinea pig jejunum, Kuriyama et al. (1967) reported that this pattern of activity was seen only in tissue segments in which Auerbach's plexus was intact and that blockade of nervous conduction with low concentrations of tetrodotoxin changed the pattern of spontaneous activity to one of regular action potential discharge with no preceding slow depolarization. This slow phenomenon might therefore also be related to spontaneous activity of the cholinergic nerves.

In the avian gizzard and guinea pig vas deferens, exposure to anticholinesterase drugs in concentrations higher than 10^{-6} g/ml caused an increase in the time course of decay of e.j.p.'s (Bell, 1967; Bennett, 1969a). There is reason to believe that this effect was due to prolongation of the action of transmitter rather than to a direct effect of the drugs used; in the vas deferens, where the cholinergic innervation is sparse, prolongation was seen only in 25% of cells examined (Fig. 18). In the gizzard, recording from single cells before and after application of cholinesterase inhibitors revealed an increase in e.j.p. amplitude. These results suggest that both the magnitude and the time course of ACh action on the smooth muscle cell membrane are controlled in part by AChE activity. In the guinea pig jejunum, application of high concentrations of neostigmine has been reported to greatly increase the amplitude and time course of the "prepotential" associated with spontaneous action potential firing (Kuriyama et al., 1967).

4.3.1b. Glands. Excitatory cholinergic transmission has also been studied in the acinar cells of cat and possum salivary glands (Lundberg, 1955, 1958; Creed and Wilson, 1969; Creed and McDonald, 1968) and of mouse pancreas (Dean and Matthews, 1968). Excitatory transmission to feline salivary secretory cells is represented by a hyperpolarizing secretory potential which is in some ways similar to the cholinergic e.j.p. of intestinal muscle, having a latency of 180–400 ms and a time course of about 900 ms and exhibiting facilitation with repetitive low-frequency stimulation. However, the rate of rise of the secretory potential is slower than that of the e.j.p., representing more than half the total time course of potential change. In the salivary gland of the Australian possum, the latency of secretory potentials is shorter (Table II) and repetitive stimulation at 1 Hz causes depression rather than facilitation of successive potentials. It may also be noted that in the cat, the latency of secretory potentials showed a direct relation to stimulation frequency over the range 1–8 Hz, while in the possum no such change was noted.

Stimulation of secretomotor cholinergic nerves to the cells of mouse pancreas produces depolarization. The only published record of transmission in the pancreas is concerned with nervous stimulation at 10 Hz, and it is therefore not possible to know whether discrete secretory potentials are evoked with single pulses.

Discharges of spontaneous depolarizing events resembling spontaneous e.j.p.'s have been recorded from pancreatic acinar cells (Dean and Matthews,

1968), while Lundberg (1958) has reported the existence of spontaneous hyperpolarizations resembling secretory potentials in the cells of feline salivary gland. This author suggested that such events represented spontaneous firing of postganglionic cholinergic neurons rather than passive transmitter leakage.

4.3.2. Inhibitory Events

The only inhibitory cholinergic neuroeffector system which has been extensively studied using electrophysiological techniques is the vagal innervation to cardiac conducting tissue. Repetitive vagal stimulation leads to hyperpolarization of the effector cell with cessation of spontaneous action potential discharge (Hutter and Trautwein, 1956; Cranefield and Hoffman, 1958; West and Toda, 1967). Only one report exists of inhibitory responses to single vagal stimuli, in the arrested sinus venosus of the frog (del Castillo and Katz, 1955b). Here stimulation evoked a hyperpolarization which had a latency similar to that recorded at other muscarinic junctions during preganglionic stimulation (0.4 s) but an extremely long time course, with rise and fall times on the other of 1.5 and 5.5 s, i.e., about ten times as long as junction potentials recorded elsewhere.

Preliminary observations on transmission from cholinergic dilator nerves to smooth muscle cells in the guinea pig uterine artery have indicated that the mechanical dilator response to nerve stimulation may not be accompanied by any alteration in membrane potential (Bell, 1969b). It is possible that in this situation dilation is accomplished by inhibition of the initiation or spread of excitatory events within the muscle.

4.4. Ionic Basis of the Action of ACh on the Postjunctional Membrane

ACh depolarizes intestinal smooth muscle, resulting in spike discharge and contraction (Fig. 19). From studies with ACh and carbachol (see Kuriyama, 1970; Bolton, 1972), it appears that both Na and K conductance of the muscle membrane increased during depolarization. Ca conductance is also increased but it is not established whether this is a primary factor in eliciting membrane activation. Cholinergic agonists may also increase muscle membrane Cl conductance, although this effect appears to be small in certain tissues and could reflect passive Cl movement secondary to cation fluxes (see Casteels, 1971).

The hyperpolarizing action of ACh in cardiac conducting tissue appears to be associated with a specific rise in membrane K conductance, with no effect on Cl conductance (Hutter, 1957; Trautwein and Dudel, 1958; Woodbury, 1962).

4.5. Summary

1. Postganglionic cholinergic autonomic axons can be distinguished by the relatively high AChE-reactivity of their axolemma.
2. Functional synapses between such axons and effector cells appear to be characterized by AChE activity on the immediately adjacent effector cell membrane.
3. Excitatory junction potentials evoked by cholinergic nervous activation differ from those evoked by adrenergic nervous activation in exhibiting generally slower rates of rise and longer latencies.
4. In smooth muscle, cholinergic excitation is associated with increases in conductance for Na, K, and perhaps Ca ions. In cardiac muscle, cholinergic inhibition is associated with an increase in K conductance.

5. PURINERGIC TRANSMISSION

5.1. Introduction

It is now well established that there are intramural inhibitory neurons which are neither adrenergic nor cholinergic in the alimentary tract of a wide range of vertebrate species (see Burnstock, 1969, 1972).

The cell bodies of nonadrenergic inhibitory neurons are located in Auerbach's plexus throughout the gut in mammals, but are limited to the stomach in lower vertebrates. In the stomach of all groups, they are controlled by preganglionic parasympathetic fibers running in the vagus nerves; in the mammalian large intestine, they are controlled by intramural cholinergic nerves, but appear to be without extrinsic nerve connections except in the distal rectum. Terminal varicosities of nonadrenergic inhibitory nerves appear to be characterized by a predominance of large vesicles (Burnstock and Iwayama, 1971). These have been termed "large opaque vesicles" (LOV) (Burnstock, 1972), in order to distinguish them from the "large granular vesicles" (LGV) found in small numbers in both adrenergic and cholinergic nerves, which are smaller and characterized by a prominent electron-transparent halo between the dense granule and vesicle membrane (cf. Fig. 9a,b,c).

Evidence has been presented which suggests that the principal active substance released by these nerves is a purine nucleotide (Burnstock et al., 1970a, 1972b; Satchell and Burnstock, 1971; Su et al., 1971; Satchell Lynch et al., 1972), and they have therefore been tentatively called "purinergic" (Burnstock, 1971). The broad criteria required to satisfy the establishment of a neurotransmitter (see, e.g., Eccles, 1964) appear to be satisfied, including evidence for (1) synthesis and storage of ATP in the nerves, (2) release of ATP from the nerves when they are stimulated, (3) exogenously applied ATP mimicking the action of nerve-released transmitter, (4) the presence of enzymes which inactivate ATP, and (5) drugs which produce similar blocking or potentiating effects on the response to exogenously applied ATP and nerve stimulation.

Knowledge of purinergic neurons is in its infancy, in contrast to the voluminous literature on the biochemistry, electrophysiology, and pharmacology of transmission and morphology and adrenergic and cholinergic nerves. Nevertheless, certain features of purinergic nerves are already clearly established, and by analogy with the pathways known for adrenergic and cholinergic systems (Figs. 8 and 14), a tentative model of the synthesis, storage, release, and inactivation of ATP during purinergic nerve transmission has been proposed (Burnstock, 1972) (Fig. 20). It is hoped that this will provide a framework for and stimulus to further studies in this field.

Some studies have been made of the physiological role of purinergic nerves supplying the alimentary tract (Burnstock and Costa, 1973). Since the fluorescence histochemical method for localizing monoamines has been applied to gut preparations, it has been recognized that adrenergic nerves do *not* form the major inhibitory pathway to the gut muscle as was accepted as

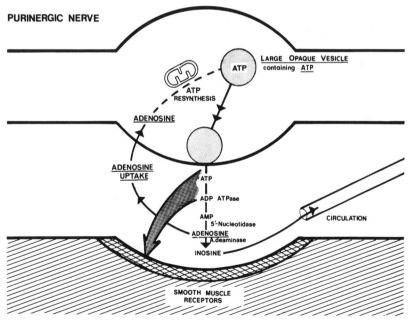

Fig. 20. Schematic representation of synthesis, storage, release, and inactivation of autonomic neurotransmitters at "purinergic" neuromuscular junction. From Burnstock (1972).

the classical concept for many years. Rather, most adrenergic nerves form terminal networks about ganglion cells in the enteric plexuses (Norberg, 1964; Read and Burnstock, 1968; Costa and Gabella, 1971) and are concerned largely with modulation of local reflex activity (see Furness and Costa, 1972). Thus purinergic rather than adrenergic nerves are the main antagonistic inhibitory system to cholinergic excitatory nerves in propulsive gut motility. Purinergic nerves are probably concerned in the phase of "descending inhibition" of peristalsis (Bayliss and Starling, 1899; Holman and Hughes, 1965; Crema, 1970), which is unaffected by sympathetic denervation (Crema et al., 1970). The powerful rebound contractions following the relaxation of the intestine produced by activation of purinergic nerves could provide an appropriate mechanism for assisting the passage of boluses further down the intestine during peristaltic propagation. Purinergic nerves have also been implicated in the mechanism of "receptive relaxation" of the stomach (Jansson, 1969a,b; Ohga et al., 1970) and reflex relaxation of the anal sphincter (Garrett and Howard, 1972) and of the esophagogastric junction (Code and Schlegel, 1968).

In addition to purinergic neurons in the gut wall, fibers which are neither adrenergic nor cholinergic have been shown to supply a variety of other organs. ATP mimics the nerve-mediated responses of these preparations whether they produce contraction or relaxation. However, it is not yet known whether any, some, or all of these nerves are purinergic.

5.2. Electrophysiology of Purinergic Transmission

Most studies of the electrophysiology of purinergic nerve transmission have been carried out on the taenia coli of the guinea pig (see Bennett and Burnstock, 1968; Holman, 1970), but inhibitory junction potentials have also been recorded in the longitudinal muscle of the guinea pig jejunum (Kuriyama et al., 1967; Hidaka and Kuriyama, 1969), in longitudinal and circular muscle of the guinea pig and rabbit colon (Furness, 1969a,b), in chicken and pigeon gizzard (Bennett, 1969a,b, 1970), in guinea pig stomach (Kuriyama et al., 1970; Beani et al., 1971; Beck and Osa, 1971), and in pig and sheep intestine (Furness, unpublished observations).

5.2.1. Inhibitory Junction Potentials

Stimulation of intramural purinergic nerves with *single pulses* of short duration (less than 0.3 ms) produces transient hyperpolarizations or inhibitory junction potentials (i.j.p.'s) of up to 25 mV in single smooth muscle cells of the gut (see Burnstock, 1972) (Fig. 21d). I.j.p.'s have also been recorded in the stomach in response to stimulation of vagal nerves (Bennett, 1969b, 1970;

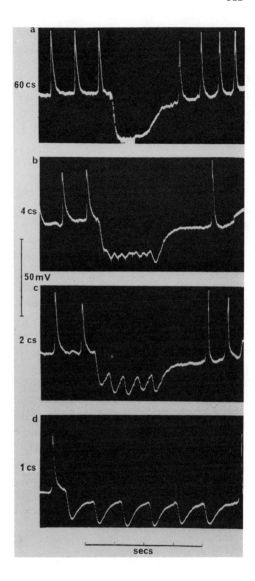

Fig. 21. Inhibitory junction potentials in response to "purinergic" nerve stimulation. Effect of stimulating across the taenia coli with repetitive pulses of maximal strength at different frequencies. Note the increase in amplitude of the action potential after the i.j.p. in (b), (c), and (d) and the increased rate of firing after the i.j.p. in (a) and (c). From Bennett *et al.* (1966*b*).

Beani *et al.*, 1971). I.j.p.'s are unaffected by adrenergic neuron blocking agents or sympathetic denervation, but are abolished by tetrodotoxin.

Repetitive stimulation of purinergic nerves results in summation of individual i.j.p.'s and prolonged hyperpolarization of up to 50 mV (Fig. 21a,b,c). There may be some facilitation of the first two or three i.j.p.'s in a train (Furness, 1969*a*). The amplitude of i.j.p.'s in response to single stimuli can be graded with increasing strength of stimulation up to a maximum of about 25 mV, whereas the maximum amplitude reached during repetitive stimulation is about 50 mV. The time taken to reach maximum hyperpolarization during repetitive stimulation at 10 Hz or more is slightly shorter than that of the rise time of a single i.j.p.; when maximum hyperpolarization is reached, the response begins to decay in spite of continuing stimulation. At stimulation frequencies of 30 Hz or more, relaxation is rarely maintained for more than about 15 s, and even at 5–10 Hz (Burnstock *et al.*, 1966) it begins to weaken after more than 20–30 s.

The latency of the i.j.p. in response to postganglionic stimulation of the intramural purinergic nerves in the gut of various species is long (about 45–80 ms) relative to the latencies of adrenergic e.j.p.'s recorded in nonintestinal smooth muscle (about 6–20 ms). This long latency, however, appears to be comparable to that of cholinergic e.j.p.'s (see Section 4.3). The basis of the long latency of the responses of smooth muscle to autonomic nerves in general is discussed in Sections 3.3 and 4.3. In the taenia coli, measurements of the increase in latency of the i.j.p. at increasing distances between stimulating and recording electrodes implied a conduction velocity of 10–20 cm/s in the terminal regions of purinergic nerves (Bülbring and Tomita, 1967).

The time course of the i.j.p. appears to be comparable, or perhaps slightly longer, than that of cholinergic e.j.p.'s recorded in the gut, but considerably longer than that of some adrenergic e.j.p.'s (see Tables II and III). The rise time of the i.j.p. is about 150–250 ms; the decay time to half maximum is 200–400 ms and is approximately exponential, while the total duration of the i.j.p. is of the order of 1 s. Since the maximum rate of spontaneously firing action potentials in the taenia coli is about 1 Hz (Burnstock, 1958*a*; Holman, 1958; Jenkinson and Morton, 1965), an i.j.p. lasting for about 1 s would be necessary to inhibit spike initiation and bring about relaxation.

Spontaneous hyperpolarizations with about the same time course and amplitude as i.j.p.'s have been observed on rare occasions in mammalian preparations (Bennett *et al.*, 1966*a*; Furness, 1969*a*) and appear in trains in the longitudinal coat of carp stomach (Ito and Kuriyama, 1971). They may represent the spontaneous release of packages of transmitter from terminal regions of nerves, but it seems more likely that they are the result of nerve impulses generated spontaneously in purinergic neurons in the myenteric ganglia. It is interesting in this respect that bursts of spontaneous electrical activity have been recorded from single ganglion cells in Auerbach's plexus (Yokoyama, 1966; Wood, 1970).

A characteristic feature of the responses to stimulation of purinergic nerves is the rebound excitation which follows the main inhibitory response (Burnstock *et al.*, 1963*a*; Bennett, 1966*a*; Campbell, 1966; Furness, 1971). Rebound excitation usually occurs at the end of stimulation, but may also "break through" during a period of repetitive stimulation, especially at high

Table III. Temporal Characteristics of Noncholinergic, Nonadrenergic "Purinergic" Inhibitory Junction Potentials

Tissue	Stimulus site[a]	Minimum latency (ms)	Rise time (ms)	Duration (ms)	Reference
Guinea pig taenia coli	T/M	80	200–500	1000	Bennett et al. (1966b)
	T/M	140	200–300	—	Bülbring and Tomita (1967)
Rabbit colon	T/M	80	150–250	800–1200	Furness (1969a)
Guinea pig colon	T/M	45	150–250	800–1300	Furness (1969a)
Pigeon gizzard	T/M	70		500–1500	Bennett (1969b)
Chick gizzard	T/M	75		400–1500	Bennett (1969b)
Guinea pig jejunum	T/M	50	120–280	<1000	Kuriyama et al. (1967)
Guinea pig stomach	Preg.	150	200–300	1000–1800	Beani et al. (1971)

[a] Preg., preganglionic; T/M, transmural.

frequency. The electrical activity associated with rebound contractions consists of depolarization following cessation of the hyperpolarization produced by purinergic inhibitory nerve stimulation (see Fig. 21a,c). The membrane potential usually depolarizes beyond its original level, with the result that the frequency of spike discharge, and therefore contraction, is greater than that seen before nerve stimulation. In preparations where there are no spontaneous spikes and associated contractions, stimulation of the inhibitory purinergic nerves still produces hyperpolarization. Since this is followed by rebound depolarization and subsequent initiation of spike activity, the result is to produce contraction rather than relaxation. The mechanism of rebound excitation is not understood.

5.2.2. Postsynaptic Action of Transmitter

Studies have been made of the ionic basis of the i.j.p. (Bennett et al., 1963; Bennett, 1966c; Hidaka and Kuriyama, 1969; Tomita and Watanabe, 1973). The results of varying the ionic composition of the bathing solution show that both nerve-released transmitter and exogenously applied ATP cause a specific increase in K conductance; i.e., the equilibrium potential for transmitter action is approximately the same as the K equilibrium potential (E_k). No evidence was found for increase in anion conductance. Determinations of the increase in membrane conductance in response to purinergic nerve stimulation are complicated by the low-resistance pathways between cells. Low $[Ca]_o$ and high $[Mg]_o$ have been reported to have no effect on the i.j.p. (Hidaka and Kuriyama, 1969); this surprising observation needs further exploration.

5.2.3. Interaction of Purinergic with Cholinergic and Adrenergic Responses in Single Cells

In the absence of specific blocking agents, the response of most smooth muscle cells of the taenia coli to transmural stimulation appears to be a mixture of inhibitory and excitatory junction potentials. It is interesting in this respect that "multiaxonal junctions," where groups of up to seven axons lie in close apposition with single muscle cells, have been described in the circular coat of the intestine (Brettschneider, 1962; Rogers and Burnstock, 1966). Only small groups of cells are encountered which receive a predominantly cholinergic excitatory innervation (Bennett, 1966b). Occasionally, cells are found which respond to transmural stimulation with a diphasic response consisting of depolarization followed by hyperpolarization. In the presence of atropine, i.j.p.'s in response to single pulses can be seen in consistent form and amplitude in the majority of cells (Bennett et al., 1966b).

Stimulation of the pelvic nerves in rabbit and guinea pig evokes e.j.p.'s in most cells of the longitudinal muscle coat of the colon (Gillespie, 1962, 1968; Furness, 1969a), but transmural stimulation produces e.j.p.'s in only about 5% of the cells, i.j.p.'s being recorded in the remainder (Furness, 1969a). It seems likely therefore that cholinergic nerves innervate all the muscle cells, but that when transmural stimulating electrodes are used the i.j.p. dominates the response. This conclusion has been supported by experiments with the guinea pig colon in which the interaction of e.j.p.'s and i.j.p.'s in individual smooth muscle cells was studied during extrinsic stimulation of cholinergic nerves and transmural stimulation of purinergic nerves (Furness, 1969a). It was shown that the i.j.p. was capable of obliterating the e.j.p., but the reverse situation was never observed. This suggests that the conductance change underlying the i.j.p. may be considerably greater than that of the e.j.p. The possibility of occlusion at a ganglionic level, as suggested by the hypothesis of Kottegoda (1969), seems unlikely, since stimulation of intrinsic inhibitory nerves by transmural electrodes is largely postganglionic (Furness, 1969a).

Studies of the interaction of nerve-mediated excitation and inhibition of single smooth muscle cells have also been carried out in the avian (chick and pigeon) gizzard (Bennett, 1970) and in guinea pig stomach (Beani et al., 1971). In contrast to the situation in the colon (Furness, 1969a), the e.j.p. appeared to dominate the i.j.p. in most muscle cells of the guinea pig stomach when both cholinergic and purinergic nerves were stimulated together (Beani et al., 1971). This difference may be accounted for in terms of the smaller amplitude of i.j.p.'s evoked by preganglionic nerve stimulation in the stomach. Some cells in the guinea pig stomach receive only vagal inhibitory innervation; other cells are innervated solely by cholinergic excitatory nerves (Beani et al., 1971). In the avian gizzard, transmural stimulation frequently evoked an e.j.p. followed by an i.j.p. in the same cell (Bennett, 1970). Cells were encountered which responded to stimulation of the vagus nerve with an e.j.p. and to perivascular nerve stimulation with an i.j.p.; other cells showed the opposite responses. E.j.p.'s evoked in the same cell by both vagal and perivascular stimulation summed with each other. Some cells responded with i.j.p.'s to both vagal and perivascular stimulation.

5.3. Summary

1. Inhibitory junction potentials (i.j.p.'s) have been recorded in single smooth muscle cells in both the circular and the longitudinal muscle coats of the gut in response to stimulation of enteric nerves.
2. I.j.p.'s persist in the presence of atropine and adrenergic neuron blocking agents or after degeneration of sympathetic adrenergic nerves but are abolished when nerve conduction is blocked by tetro-

dotoxin. Evidence has been presented that the transmitter released from these nerves is a purine nucleotide, so they have been tentatively termed "purinergic."

3. Repetitive stimulation of purinergic nerves results in summation of individual i.j.p.'s and hyperpolarizations of up to 50 mV; there may be facilitation of the first two or three i.j.p.'s in a train.

4. A feature of purinergic transmission is the rapid decay of the response to repetitive nerve stimulation; the amplitude of response is rarely maintained for more than 20–30 s even at physiological frequencies of 5–10 Hz. This is in marked contrast to the inhibitory response of the intestine to adrenergic nerves.

5. The latency of the i.j.p. in response to stimulation of postganglionic purinergic nerves is about 45–80 ms.

6. The time course of i.j.p.'s recorded in smooth muscle of the gut has a rise time of 150–250 ms and a total duration of 800–1200 ms.

7. Spontaneous i.j.p.'s occur, but mostly only in low-frequency trains.

8. A characteristic feature of the response to stimulation of purinergic nerves is rebound depolarization associated with spikes and contraction, following the main inhibitory response. Consequently, in low-tone preparations, particularly those with little or no spontaneous spike activity, stimulation of inhibitory purinergic nerves can result in long latency contraction rather than relaxation.

9. There is evidence that the transmitter released from purinergic nerves acts by producing a specific increase in K^+ conductance as does exogenously applied ATP.

10. Studies of the interaction of responses of single muscle cells to stimulation of enteric, intrinsic, and extrinsic nerves suggest that most cells receive both cholinergic excitatory and purinergic inhibitory innervation.

6. CONCLUSIONS

The work carried out in the last decade has established that transmission from autonomic nerves to effector organs is essentially comparable to that established earlier for other neuroeffector synapses. There are well-defined junction potentials which exhibit such features as summation and facilitation, and miniature potentials which represent spontaneous release of transmitter.

The marked differences in latency and time course of junction potentials from those recorded in skeletal muscle may be explained in terms of the equivalent circuit of muscle effector bundles and probably also to some extent by the contribution of transmitter released from many varicosities at variable distances. Very little is known about the distribution of "receptors" in smooth muscle membrane, largely because technical problems make iontophoretic studies extremely difficult.

It seems likely that only a limited amount of further information on autonomic transmission will be readily obtained using intact tissues. More complete elucidation of the processes involved may come from studies of cell and organ maturation during ontogenesis and in *in vitro* cultures. An area of current interest, in common with studies of other peripheral synaptic mechanisms, is toward long-term rather than short-term mechanisms of interaction between nerves and muscles (see Burnstock, 1974*b*).

7. REFERENCES

Acheson, G. H. (ed.), 1966, Second symposium on catecholamines, *Pharmacol. Rev.* **18**:1.

Ahlqvist, R. P., 1948, A study of the adrenotropic receptors, *Am. J. Physiol.* **153**:586.

Axelsson, J., 1971, Catecholamine functions, *Ann. Rev. Physiol.* **33**:1.

Bacq, Z. M., (ed.), 1970, Synaptic vesicles, specific granules, autopharmacology, in: *Fundamentals of Biochemical Pharmacology*, Pergamon Press, Oxford and New York.

Banks, P., and Helle, K. B., 1971, Chromogranins in sympathetic nerves, *Phil. Trans. Roy. Soc. Lond. Ser. B* **261**:305.

Bayliss, W. M., and Starling, E. H., 1899, The movement and innervation of the small intestine, *J. Physiol. Lond.* **24**:99.

Beani, L., Bianchi, C., and Crema, A., 1971, Vagal non-adrenergic inhibition of guinea-pig stomach, *J. Physiol. Lond.* **217**:259.

Beck, C. S., and Osa, T., 1971, Membrane activity in guinea-pig gastric sling muscle: A nerve-dependent phenomenon, *Am. J. Physiol.* **220**:1397.

Bell, C., 1967, An electrophysiological study of the effects of atropine and physostigmine on transmission to the guinea-pig vas deferens, *J. Physiol. Lond.* **189**:31.

Bell, C., 1968, Dual vasoconstrictor and vasodilator innervation of the uterine artery supply in the guinea-pig, *Circ. Res.* **23**:279.

Bell, C., 1969*a*, Fine structural localization of acetylcholinesterase at a cholinergic vasodilator nerve–arterial smooth muscle synapse, *Circ. Res.* **24**:61.

Bell, C., 1969*b*, Transmission from vasoconstrictor and vasodilator nerves to single smooth muscle cells of the guinea-pig uterine artery, *J. Physiol. Lond.* **205**:695.

Bell, C., and McLean, J. R., 1967, Localization of norepinephrine and acetylcholinesterase in separate neurons supplying the guinea-pig vas deferens, *J. Pharmacol. Exptl. Therap.* **157**:69.

Bell, C., and Vogt, M., 1971, Release of endogenous noradrenaline from an isolated muscular artery, *J. Physiol. Lond.* **215**:509.

Bennett, M. R., 1966*a*, Rebound excitation of the smooth muscle cells of the guinea-pig taenia coli after stimulation of intramural inhibitory nerves, *J. Physiol. Lond.* **185**:124.

Bennett, M. R., 1966*b*, Transmission from intramural excitatory nerves to the smooth muscle cells of the guinea-pig taenia coli, *J. Physiol. Lond.* **185**:132.

Bennett, M. R., 1966*c*, Model of the membrane of smooth muscle cells of the guinea-pig taenia coli muscle during transmission from inhibitory and excitatory nerves, *Nature Lond.* **211**:1149.

Bennett, M. R., and Burnstock, G., 1968, Electrophysiology of the innervation of intestinal smooth muscle, in: *Handbook of Physiology*, Section 6: *Alimentary Canal*, Vol. IV: *Motility*, pp. 1709–1732, American Physiological Society, Washington, D.C.

Bennett, M. R., and Merrillees, N. C. R., 1966, An analysis of the transmission of excitation from autonomic nerves to smooth muscle, *J. Physiol. Lond.* **185**:520.

Bennett, M. R., Burnstock, G., and Holman, M. E., 1963, The effect of potassium and chloride ions on the inhibitory potential recorded in the guinea-pig taenia coli, *J. Physiol. Lond.* **169**:33.

Bennett, M. R., Burnstock, G., and Holman, M. E., 1966a, Transmission from perivascular inhibitory nerves to the smooth muscle of the guinea-pig taenia coli, *J. Physiol. Lond.* **182**:527.

Bennett, M. R., Burnstock, G., and Holman, M. E., 1966b, Transmission from intramural inhibitory nerves to the smooth muscle of the guinea-pig taenia coli, *J. Physiol. Lond.* **182**:541.

Bennett, T., 1969a, The effects of hyoscine and anticholinesterases on cholinergic transmission to the smooth muscle cells of the avian gizzard, *Brit. J. Pharmacol.* **37**:585.

Bennett, T., 1969b, Nerve-mediated excitation and inhibition of the smooth muscle cells of the avian gizzard, *J. Physiol. Lond.* **204**:669.

Bennett, T., 1970, Interaction of nerve-mediated excitation and inhibition of single smooth muscle cells of the avian gizzard, *Comp. Biochem. Physiol.* **32**:669.

Bevan, J. A., Chesher, G. B., and Su, C., 1969, Release of adrenergic transmitter from terminal nerve plexus in artery, *Agents & Actions* **1**:20.

Bevan, J. A., Nedergaard, O. A., Osher, J. V., Su, C., Török, J., and Verity, M. A., 1971, On the mechanism of neuromuscular transmission in blood vessels, in: *Proceedings of the Fourth International Congress of Pharmacology* (July 1969, Basel), Vol. 2, pp. 7–23, Schwabe, Basel.

Birmingham, A. T., 1966, The potentiation by anticholinesterase drugs on the responses of the guinea-pig isolated vas deferens to alternate preganglionic and postganglionic stimulation, *Brit. J. Pharmacol. Chemotherap.* **27**:145.

Blaschko, H., and Muscholl, E. (eds.), 1972, *Catecholamines*, Springer Verlag, Berlin, Heidleberg, New York.

Blaschko, H. K. F., and Smith, A. D., 1971, A discussion on subcellular and macromolecular aspects of synaptic transmission, *Phil. Trans. Roy. Soc. Lond. Ser. B* **261**:273.

Bloom, F. E., and Barrnett, R. J., 1966, Fine structural localization of noradrenaline in vesicles of autonomic nerve endings, *Nature Lond.* **210**:599.

Bogart, B. I., 1971, The fine structural localization of acetylcholinesterase activity in the rat parotid and sublingual glands, *Am. J. Anat.* **132**:259.

Bogdanski, D. F., and Brodie, B. B., 1969, The effects of inorganic ions on the storage and uptake of H^3-norepinephrine by rat heart slices, *J. Pharmacol. Exptl. Therap.* **165**:181.

Bohr, D. H., and Uchida, E., 1969, Activation of vascular smooth muscle, in: *The Pulmonary Circulation and Interstitial Space* (A. P. Fishman and H. H. Hecht, eds.), pp. 133–145, University of Chicago Press, Chicago and London.

Bolton, T. B., 1972, The depolarizing action of ACh or carbachol in intestinal smooth muscle, *J. Physiol. Lond.* **220**:647.

Boyd, I. A., and Martin, A. R., 1956, The end-plate potential in mammalian muscle, *J. Physiol. Lond.* **132**:74.

Bozler, E., 1948, Conduction, automacity and tonus of visceral muscles, *Experientia* **4**:213.

Brading, A. F., Bülbring, E., and Tomita, T., 1969, The effect of temperature on the membrane conductance of the smooth muscle of the guinea-pig taenia coli, *J. Physiol. Lond.* **200**:621.

Brettschneider, H., 1962, Elektronenmikroskopische Untersuchungen über die Innervation der glatten Muskulatur des Darmes, *Z. Mikroskop.-anat. Forsch.* **68**:333.

Bülbring, E., 1957, Changes in configuration of spontaneously discharged spike potentials from smooth muscle of the guinea-pig taenia coli: The effect of electrotonic currents and of adrenaline, acetylcholine and histamine, *J. Physiol. Lond.* **135**:412.

Bülbring, E., and Burnstock, G., 1960, Membrane potential changes associated with tachyphylaxis and potentiation of the response to stimulating drugs in smooth muscle, *Brit. J. Pharmacol.* **15**:611.

Bülbring, E., and Kuriyama, H., 1963, The effect of adrenaline on the smooth muscle of the guinea-pig taenia coli in relation to the degree of stretch, *J. Physiol. Lond.* **169**:198.

Bülbring, E., and Tomita, T., 1967, Properties of the inhibitory potential of smooth muscle as observed in the response to field stimulation of the guinea-pig taenia coli, *J. Physiol. Lond.* **189**:299.

Bülbring, E., and Tomita, T., 1969, Effect of calcium, barium and manganese on the action of adrenaline in the smooth muscle of the guinea-pig taenia coli, *Proc. Roy. Soc. B* **182**:121.

Burn, J. H., 1968, The mechanism of the release of noradrenaline, in: *Adrenergic Neurotransmission* (G. E. W. Wolstenholme and M. O'Connor, eds.), pp. 16–25, Ciba Foundation, Study Group No. 33, J. & A. Churchill, London.

Burn, J. H., and Rand, M. J., 1959, Sympathetic postganglionic mechanism, *Nature Lond.* **184**:163.

Burn, J. H., and Rand, M. J., 1962, A new interpretation of the adrenergic nerve fibre, in: *Advances in Pharmacology*, Vol. 1 (S. Garattini and P. A. Shore, eds.), pp. 2–30, Academic Press, London.

Burn, J. H., and Rand, M. J., 1965, Acetylcholine in adrenergic transmission, *Ann. Rev. Pharmacol.* **5**:163.

Burnstock, G., 1958a, The effects of acetylcholine on membrane potential, spike frequency, conduction velocity and excitability in the taenia coli of the guinea-pig, *J. Physiol. Lond.* **143**:165.

Burnstock, G., 1958b, The action of adrenaline on excitability and membrane potential in the taenia coli of the guinea-pig and the effect of DNP on this action and on the action of acetylcholine, *J. Physiol. Lond.* **143**:183.

Burnstock, G., 1960, Membrane potential changes associated with stimulation of smooth muscle by adrenalin, *Nature Lond.* **186**:727.

Burnstock, G., 1969, Evolution of the autonomic innervation of visceral and cardiovascular systems in vertebrates, *Pharmacol. Rev.* **21**:247.

Burnstock, G., 1970, Structure of smooth muscle and its innervation, in: *Smooth Muscle* (E. Bülbring, A. F. Brading, A. W. Jones, and T. Tomita, eds.), pp. 1–69, E. Arnold, London.

Burnstock, G., 1971, Neural nomenclature, *Nature Lond.* **229**:282.

Burnstock, G., 1972, Purinergic nerves, *Pharmacol. Rev.* **24**:509.

Burnstock, G., 1974a, Electron microscopy: Vesicles, synaptic gaps, pharmacological agents in: *Methods in Pharmacology* Section IA3, Vol. III: *Smooth Muscle* (E. E. Daniel and D. M. Paton, eds.), Appleton-Century-Crofts.

Burnstock, G., and Costa, M., 1973, Inhibitory innervation of the gut, *Gastroent.* **64:** 141.

Burnstock, G., 1974b, Degeneration and orientated growth of autonomic nerves in relation to smooth muscle in joint cultures and anterior eye chamber transplants, In "Dynamics of Degeneration and Growth in Neurons," Pergamon Press, Oxford, in press.

Burnstock, G., and Holman, M. E., 1960, Autonomic nerve–smooth muscle transmission, *Nature Lond.* **187:** 951.

Burnstock, G., and Holman, M. E., 1961, The transmission of excitation from autonomic nerve to smooth muscle, *J. Physiol. Lond.* **155:** 115.

Burnstock, G., and Holman, M. E., 1962, Spontaneous potentials at sympathetic nerve endings in smooth muscle, *J. Physiol. Lond.* **160:** 446.

Burnstock, G., and Holman, M. E., 1964, An electrophysiological investigation of the actions of some autonomic blocking drugs on transmission in the guinea-pig vas deferens, *Brit. J. Pharmacol.* **23:** 600.

Burnstock, G., and Holman, M. E., 1966, Junction potentials at adrenergic synapses, *Pharmacol. Rev.* **18:** 481.

Burnstock, G., and Iwayama, T., 1971, Fine structural identification of autonomic nerves and their relation to smooth muscle, in: *Progress in Brain Research*, Vol. 34: *Histochemistry of Nervous Transmission* (O. Eränkö, ed.), pp. 389–404, Elsevier, Amsterdam.

Burnstock, G., and Robinson, P. M., 1967, Localization of catecholamines and acetylcholinesterase in autonomic nerves, in: American Heart Association Monograph No. 17, *Circ. Res.* **21:** 43 (Suppl. 3).

Burnstock, G., Campbell, G., Bennet, M., and Holman, M. E., 1963a, The effects of drugs on the transmission of inhibition from autonomic nerves to the smooth muscle of the guinea-pig taenia coli, *Biochem. Pharmacol. Suppl.* **12:** 134.

Burnstock, G., Holman, M. E., and Prosser, C. L., 1963b, Electrophysiology of smooth muscle, *Physiol. Rev.* **43:** 482.

Burnstock, G., Campbell, G., Bennett, M., and Holman, M. E., 1964a, Innervation of the guinea-pig taenia coli: Are there intrinsic inhibitory nerves which are distinct from sympathetic nerves? *Internat. J. Neuropharmacol.* **3:** 163.

Burnstock, G., Holman, M. E., and Kuriyama, H., 1964b, Facilitation of transmission from autonomic nerve to smooth muscle of guinea-pig vas deferens, *J. Physiol. Lond.* **172:** 31.

Burnstock, G., Campbell, G., and Rand, M. J., 1966, The inhibitory innervation of the taenia of the guinea-pig caecum, *J. Physiol. Lond.* **182:** 504.

Burnstock, G., Campbell, G., Satchell, D. G., and Smythe, A., 1970a, Evidence that adenosine triphosphate or a related nucleotide is the transmitter substance released by non-adrenergic inhibitory nerves in the gut, *Brit. J. Pharmacol.* **40:** 668.

Burnstock, G., Gannon, B. J., and Iwayama, T., 1970b, Sympathetic innervation of vascular smooth muscle in normal and hypertensive animals, in: Symposium on Hypertensive Mechanisms, *Circ. Res. Suppl.* **27:** 5.

Burnstock, G., Evans, B., Gannon, B. J., Heath, J., and James, V., 1971, A new method for destroying adrenergic nerves in adult animals using guanethidine, *Brit. J. Pharmacol.* **43:** 295.

Burnstock, G., McCulloch, M., Story, D., and Wright, M., 1972a, Factors affecting the extraneuronal inactivation of noradrenaline in cardiac and smooth muscle, *Brit. J. Pharmacol.* **46:** 243.

Burnstock, G., Satchell, D. G., and Smythe, A., 1972b, A comparison of the excitatory and inhibitory effects of non-adrenergic, non-cholinergic nerve stimulation and exogenously applied ATP on a variety of smooth muscle preparations from different vertebrate species, *Brit. J. Pharmacol.* **46**:234.

Caesar, R., Edwards, G. A., and Ruska, H., 1957, Architecture and nerve supply of mammalian smooth muscle tissue, *J. Biophys. Biochem. Cytol.* **3**:867.

Campbell, G., 1966, Nerve-mediated excitation of the taenia of the guinea-pig caecum, *J. Physiol. Lond.* **185**:148.

Campbell, G., 1970, Autonomic nervous supply to effector tissues, in: *Smooth Muscle* (E. Bülbring, A. F. Brading. A. W. Jones, and T. Tomita, eds.), pp. 451–495, Edward Arnold, London.

Campbell, G. R., Uehara, Y., Mark, G., and Burnstock, G., 1971, Fine structure of smooth muscle cells grown in tissue culture, *J. Cell Biol.* **49**:21.

Casteels, R., 1971, The distribution of chloride ions in the smooth muscle cells of the guinea-pig's taenia coli, *J. Physiol. Lond.* **214**:225.

Chamley, J. H., Mark, G. E., Campbell, G. R., and Burnstock, G., 1972, Sympathetic ganglia in culture. I. Neurons, *Z. Zellforsch.* **135**:287.

Chubb, I. W., de Potter, W. P., and de Schaepdryver, A. F., 1970, Evidence for two types of noradrenaline storage particles in dog spleen, *Nature Lond.* **228**:1203.

Code, C. F., and Schegel, J. F., 1968, Motor action of the esophagus and its sphincters, in: *Handbook of Physiology*, Section 6: *Alimentary Canal*, Vol. IV, pp. 1821–1839, American Physiological Society, Washington D.C.

Collier, B., and MacIntosh, F. C., 1969, The source of choline for acetylcholine synthesis in a sympathetic ganglion, *Can. J. Phys. Pharm.* **47**:127.

Costa, M., and Gabella, G., 1971, Adrenergic innervation of the alimentary canal, *Z. Zellforsch.* **122**:357.

Costa, M. Furness J. B. and Gabella G. 1971 Catecholamine containing nerve cells in the mammalian myenteric plexus *Histochemie* **25**:103.

Cranefield P. F. and Hoffman B. F. 1958 Electrophysiology of simple cardiac cells. *Physiol. Rev.* **38**:41.

Creed K. E. and McDonald I. R. 1968 Salivary secretory potentials in a marsupial (Trichosurus vulpecula) *Aust. J. Exptl. Biol. Med. Sci.* **46**:17.

Creed K. E. and Wilson J. A. F. 1969 The latency of responses of secretory acinar cells to nerve stimulation in submaxillary gland of the cat *Aust. J. Exptl. Biol. Med. Sci.* **47**:135

Crema A. 1970 On the polarity of the peristaltic reflex in the colon, in: *Smooth Muscle* (E. Bülbring, A. F. Brading, A. W. Jones, and T. Tomita, eds.), pp. 542–548, Edward Arnold, London.

Crema, A., Frigo, G. M., and Lecchini, S., 1970, A pharmacological analysis of the peristaltic reflex in the isolated colon of the guinea-pig or cat, *Brit. J. Pharmacol.* **39**:334.

Dählström, A., Häggendal, J., and Hökfelt, T., 1966, The noradrenaline content of the varicosities of sympathetic adrenergic nerve terminals in the rat, *Acta Physiol. Scand.* **67**:289.

Dean, P. M., and Matthews, E. K., 1968, Miniature depolarization potentials in pancreatic acinar cells, *J. Physiol. Lond.* **198**:90.

del Castillo, J., and Katz, B., 1954, Quantal components of the end-plate potential, *J. Physiol. Lond.* **124**:560.

del Castillo, J., and Katz, B., 1955a, Effects of vagal and sympathetic nerve impulses on the membrane potential of the frog's heart, *J. Physiol. Lond.* **129**:48.

del Castillo, J., and Katz, B., 1955b, Production of membrane potential changes in the frog's heart by inhibitory nerve impulses, *Nature Lond.* **175**:1035.

De Potter, W. P., 1971, Noradrenaline storage particles in splenic nerve, *Phil. Trans. Roy. Soc. Lond. Ser. B* **261**:313.

De Potter, W. P., and Chubb, I. W., 1971, The turnover rate of noradrenergic vesicles, *Biochem. J.* **125**:375

de Robertis, E., and Ferreira, A. V., 1957, Submicroscopic changes of the nerve endings in the adrenal medulla after stimulation of the splanchnic nerve, *J. Biophys. Biochem. Cytol.* **3**:611.

Dewey, M. M., and Barr, L., 1962, Intercellular connection between smooth muscle cells: The nexus, *Science N.Y.* **137**:670.

Douglas, W. W., 1968, Stimulus–secretion coupling: The concept and clues from chromaffin and other cells, *Brit. J. Pharmacol.* **34**:451.

Eccles, J. C., 1964, *The Physiology of Synapses*, Springer-Verlag, Berlin.

Eccles, J. C., and Magladery, J. W., 1937, The excitation and response of smooth muscle, *J. Physiol. Lond.* **90**:31.

Ehinger, B., and Falck, B., 1970, Uptake of some catecholamines and their precursors into neurons of the rat ciliary ganglion, *Acta Physiol. Scand.* **78**:132.

Ehrenpreis, S. (ed.), 1967, Cholinergic mechanisms, *Ann. N.Y. Acad. Sci.* **144**:383.

Eränkö, O., and Eränkö, L., 1971, Small, intensely fluorescent granule-containing cells in the sympathetic ganglion of the rat, in: *Histochemistry of Nervous Transmission*, Vol. 34 (O. Eränkö, ed.), pp. 39–51, Elsevier, Amsterdam, London, New York.

Ferry, C. B., 1966, Cholinergic link hypothesis in adrenergic neuroeffector transmission, *Physiol. Rev.* **46**:420.

Fillenz, M., 1971, Fine structure of noradrenaline storage vesicles in nerve terminals of the rat vas deferens, *Phil. Trans. Roy. Soc. Lond. Ser. B* **261**:319.

Fillenz, M., and Howe, P. R. C., 1971, Increase in the vesicular noradrenaline of nerve terminals, *J. Physiol. Lond.* **217**:27.

Folkow, B., Häggendal, J., and Lisander, B., 1968, Extent of release and elimination of noradrenaline at peripheral adrenergic nerve terminals, *Acta Physiol. Scand.* **72**:1 (Suppl. 307).

Furness, J. B., 1969a, An electrophysiological study of the innervation of the smooth muscle of the colon, *J. Physiol. Lond.* **205**:549.

Furness, J. B., 1969b, The presence of inhibitory fibres in the colon after sympathetic denervation, *Europ. J. Pharmacol.* **6**:349.

Furness, J. B., 1970a, The effect of external potassium ion concentration on autonomic neuro-muscular transmission, *Pflügers Arch. Ges. Physiol. Menschen Tiere* **317**:310.

Furness, J. B., 1970b, An examination of nerve-mediated hyoscine resistant excitation of the guinea-pig colon, *J. Physiol. Lond.* **207**:803.

Furness, J. B., Secondary excitation of intestinal smooth muscle, *Brit. J. Pharmacol.* **41**:213.

Furness, J. B., and Burnstock, G., 1974, The role of circulating catecholamines in the gastrointestinal tract, in: *Handbook of Physiology: Endocrinology* (H. Blaschko and A. D. Smith, eds.), American Physiological Society, Washington, D.C. (in press).

Furness, J. B., and Costa, M., 1973, The nervous release and the action of substances which affect intestinal muscle through neither adrenoceptors nor cholinoceptors, in: Recent Developments in Vertebrate Smooth Muscle Physiology, *Phil. Trans. Roy. Soc.* **265**:123.

Furness, J. B., and Iwayama, T., 1971, Terminal axons ensheathed in smooth muscle cells of the vas deferens, *Z. Zellforsch.* **113**:259.

Furness, J. B., Campbell, G. R., Gillard, S. M., Malmfors, T., and Burnstock, G., 1970,

Cellular studies of sympathetic denervation produced by 6-hydroxydopamine in the vas deferens, *J. Pharmacol. Exptl. Therap.* **174**:111.

Garrett, J. R., and Howard, E. R., 1972, Effect of rectal distension on the internal anal sphincter of cats, *J. Physiol. Lond.* **222**:85.

Geffen, L. B., and Livett, B. G., 1971, Synaptic vesicles in sympathetic neurons, *Physiol. Rev.* **51**:98.

Geffen, L. B., and Ostberg, A., 1969, Distribution of granular vesicles in normal and constricted sympathetic neurones, *J. Physiol. Lond.* **204**:583.

Geffen, L. B., Livett, B. G., and Rush, R. A., 1970, Immunohistochemical localization of chromogranins in sheep sympathetic neurones and their release by nerve impulse, in: *Bayer-Symposium*, Vol. II, pp. 58–72. Springer Verlag, Berlin.

Gerebtzoff, M. A., 1959 *Cholinesterases: A Histochemical Contribution to the Solution of Some Functional Problems*, Pergamon Press, London.

Gerova, M., Gero, J., and Dolezel, S., 1967, Mechanisms of sympathetic regulation of arterial smooth muscle, *Experientia* **23**:639.

Gillespie, J. S., 1962, The electrical and mechanical responses of intestinal smooth muscle cells to stimulation of their extrinsic parasympathetic nerves, *J. Physiol. Lond.* **162**:76.

Gillespie, J. S., 1968, Electrical activity in the colon, in: *Handbook of Physiology*, Section 6: *Alimentary Canal*, Vol. IV: *Motility* (C. F. Code, ed.), pp. 2093–2120, American physiological Society, Washington, D. C.

Goodford, P. J., 1970, Ionic interactions in smooth muscle, in: *Smooth Muscle* (E. Bülbring, A. F. Brading, A. W. Jones, and T. Tomita, eds.), pp. 100–121, Edward Arnold, London.

Goodman, L. S., and Gilman, A. (eds.), 1970, *The Pharmacological Basis of Therapeutics*, 4th ed., Macmillan, New York.

Hamberger, B., and Norberg, K.-A., 1965, Studies on some systems of adrenergic synaptic terminals in the abdominal ganglia of the cat, *Acta Physiol. Scand.* **65**:235.

Hand, A. R., 1970, Nerve–acinar cell relationships in the rat parotid gland, *J. Cell Biol.* **47**:540.

Hidaka, T., and Kuriyama, H., 1969, Responses of the smooth muscle cell membrane of the guinea-pig jejunum elicited to the field stimulation, *J. Gen. Physiol.* **53**:471.

Hillarp, N.-Å., 1949, The functional organization of the peripheral autonomic innervation, *Acta Physiol. Scand.* **17**:120.

Hirano, H., and Ogawa, K., 1967, Ultrastructural localization of cholinesterase activity in nerve endings in the guinea-pig heart, *J. Electronmicroscop.* **16**:313.

Hökfelt, T., 1969, Distribution of noradrenaline storing particles in peripheral adrenergic neurons as revealed by electron microscopy, *Acta Physiol. Scand.* **76**:427.

Holman, M. E., 1958, Membrane potentials recorded with high-resistance microelectrodes and the effects of changes in ionic environment on the electrical and mechanical activity of the smooth muscle of the taenia coli of the guinea-pig, *J. Physiol. Lond.* **141**:464.

Holman, M. E., 1969, Electrophysiology of vascular smooth muscle, *Ergebn. Physiol.* **61**:137.

Holman, M. E., 1970, Junction potentials in smooth muscle, in: *Smooth Muscle* (E. Bülbring, A. F. Brading. A. W. Jones, and T. Tomita, eds.), pp. 244–288, Edward Arnold, London.

Holman, M. E., and Hughes, J. R., 1965, An inhibitory component of the response to distension of rat ileum, *Nature Lond.* **207**:641.

Huković, S., and Muscholl, E., 1962, Die Noradrenalin-Abgabe aus dem isolierten Kaninchenherzen bei sympathischer Nervenreizung und ihre pharmakologische Beeinflussung, *Naunyn-Schmiedeberg's Arch. Exptl. Pathol. Pharmakol.* **244**:81.

Hutter, O. F., 1957, Mode of action of autonomic transmitters on the heart, *Brit. Med. Bull.* **13**:176.

Hutter, O. F., and Trautwein, W., 1956, Vagal and sympathetic effects on the pacemaker fibers in the sinus venosus of the heart, *J. Gen. Physiol.* **39**:715.

Ito, Y., and Kuriyama, H., 1971, Nervous control of the motility of the alimentary canal of the silver carp, *J. Exptl. Biol.* **55**:469.

Iversen, L. L., and Callingham, B. A., 1970, Adrenergic transmission, in *Synaptic Vesicles, Specific Granules, Autopharmacology*, pp. 253–305, reprinted from *Fundamentals of Biochemical Pharmacology*, (Z. M. Bacq, ed. , pp. 221–365, Pergamon Press, Oxford and New York.

Iversen, L. L., Glowinski, J., and Axelrod, J., 1966, The physiologic disposition and metabolism of norepinephrine in immunosympathectomized animals, *J. Pharmacol. Exptl. Therap.* **151**:273.

Jansson, G., 1969a, Vaso-vagal reflex relaxation of the stomach in the cat, *Acta Physiol. Scand.* **75**:245.

Jansson, G., 1969b, Extrinsic nervous control of gastric motility: An experimental study in the cat, *Acta Physiol. Scand. Suppl.* **326**:1.

Jenkinson, D. H., and Morton, I. K. M., 1965, Effects of noradrenaline and isoprenaline on the permeability of depolarized intestinal smooth muscle to inorganic ions, *Nature Lond.* **205**:505.

Johansson, B., and Ljung, B., 1971, The neuroeffector system of a propagating vascular smooth muscle, in: *Proceedings of the Fourth International Congress of Pharmacology* (July 1969, Basel), Vol. II, pp. 23–28, Schwabe, Basel.

Katz, B., 1966, *Nerve, Muscle and Synapse*, McGraw-Hill, New York.

Katz, B., 1969, *The Release of Neural Transmitter Substances*, University Press, Liverpool.

Katz, B., 1971, Quantal mechanism of neural transmitter release, *Science* **173**:123.

Kirpekar, S. M., and Misu, Y., 1967, Release of noradrenaline by splenic nerve stimulation and its dependence on calcium, *J. Physiol. Lond.* **188**:219.

Kirshner, N., and Kirshner, A. G., 1971, Chromogranin A, dopamine-β-hydroxylase and secretion from the adrenal medulla, *Phil. Trans. Roy. Soc. Lond. Ser. B* **261**:279.

Koelle, G. B., 1963, Cytological distributions and physiological functions of cholinesterases, in: *Handbuch der Experimentellen Pharmakologie; Cholinesterases and Anticholinesterase Agents* (G. B. Koelle, ed. , Suppl. 15, pp. 187–298, Springer-Verlag, Berlin.

Koelle, G. B., 1969, Significance of acetylcholinesterase in central synaptic transmission, *Fed. Proc.* **28**:95.

Kottegoda, S. R., 1969, An analysis of possible nervous mechanisms involved in the peristaltic reflex, *J. Physiol. Lond.* **200**:687.

Kuriyama, H., 1963, Electrophysiological observations on the motor innervation of the smooth muscle cells in the guinea-pig vas deferens, *J. Physiol. Lond.* **169**:213.

Kuriyama, H., 1970, Effects of ions and drugs on the electrical activity of smooth muscle, in: *Smooth Muscle* (E. Bülbring, A. F. Brading, A. W. Jones, and T. Tomita, eds.), pp. 366–395, Edward Arnold, London.

Kuriyama, H., Osa, T., and Toida, N., 1967, Nervous factors influencing the membrane activity of intestinal smooth muscle, *J. Physiol. Lond.* **191**:257.

Kuriyama, H., Osa, T., and Tasaki, H., 1970, Electrophysiological studies of the antrum muscle fibres of the guinea-pig stomach, *J. Gen. Physiol.* **55**:48.

Ljung, B., 1969, Local transmitter concentrations in vascular smooth muscle during vasoconstrictor nerve activity, *Acta Physiol. Scand.* **77**:212.

Lundberg, A., 1955, The electrophysiology of the submaxillary gland of the cat, *Acta Physiol. Scand.* **35**:1.

Lundberg, A., 1958, Electrophysiology of salivary glands, *Physiol. Rev.* **38**:21.

Malmfors, T., 1968, Histochemical studies of adrenergic transmission, in: *Adrenergic Neurotransmission*, pp. 26–36, CIBA Foundation Study Group, Churchill, London.

Malmfors, T., and Sachs, Ch., 1968, Degeneration of adrenergic nerves produced by 6-hydroxydopamine, *Europ. J. Pharmacol.* **3**:89.

McLean, J. R., and Burnstock, G., 1967, Innervation of the urinary bladder of the sleepy lizard (*Trachysaurus rugosus*). I. Fluorescent histochemical localization of catecholamines, *Comp. Biochem. Physiol.* **20**:667.

McMahon, U. J., and Kuffler, S. W., 1971, Visual identification of synaptic boutons on living ganglion cells and of varicosities in postganglionic axons in the heart of the frog, *Proc. Roy. Soc. Lond. B* **177**:485.

Merrillees, N. C. R., 1968, The nervous environment of individual smooth muscle cells of the guinea-pig vas deferens, *J. Cell Biol.* **37**:794.

Norberg, K.-A., 1964, Adrenergic innervation of the intestinal wall studied by fluorescence microscopy, *Internat. J. Neuropharmacol.* **3**:379.

Norberg, K.-A., Ritzen, M., and Ungerstedt, U., 1966, Histochemical studies on a special catecholamine-containing cell type in sympathetic ganglia, *Acta Physiol. Scand.* **67**:260.

Ohashi, H., 1971, An electrophysiological study of transmission from intramura excitatory nerves to the smooth muscle cells of the chicken oesophagus, *Jap. J. Pharmacol.* **21**:585.

Ohga, A., Nakazato, Y., and Saito, K., 1970, Considerations of the efferent nervous mechanism of the vago-vagal reflex relaxation of the stomach in the dog, *Jap. J. Pharmacol.* **20**:116.

Orlov, R. S., 1962, On impulse transmission from motor sympathetic nerve to smooth muscle, *Fiziol. Zh. SSSR* **48**:342.

Owman, Ch., and Sjöstrand, N. O., 1965, Short adrenergic neurons and catecholamine-containing cells in vas deferens and accessory male genital glands of different mammals, *Z. Zellforsch.* **66**:300.

Owman, Ch., Owman, T., and Sjöberg, N.-O., 1971, Short adrenergic neurons innervating the female urethra of the cat, *Experientia* **27**:313.

Phillis, J. W., 1970, *The Pharmacology of Synapses*, Pergamon Press, Oxford.

Potter, L. T., 1970, Synthesis, storage and release of (^{14}C) acetylcholine in isolated rat diaphragm muscles, *J. Physiol. Lond.* **206**:145.

Purves, R. D., 1974, Muscarinic excitation: a microelectrophoretic study of cultured smooth muscle cells, *Brit. J. Pharmacol.* (in press).

Raper, C., and McCulloch, M. W., 1971, Adrenoreceptor classification, *Med. J. Aust.* **2**:1331.

Read, J. B., and Burnstock, G., 1968, Comparative histochemical studies of adrenergic nerves in the enteric plexuses of vertebrate large intestine, *Comp. Biochem. Physiol.* **27**:505.

Read, J. B., and Burnstock, G., 1969, Adrenergic innervation of the gut, *Histochemie* **17**:263.

Robinson, P. M., 1969, A cholinergic component in the innervation of the longitudinal smooth muscle of the guinea-pig vas deferens: The fine structural localization of acetylcholinesterase, *J. Cell Biol.* **41**:462.

Robinson, P. M., and Bell, C., 1967, The localization of acetylcholinesterase at the autonomic neuromuscular junction, *J. Cell Biol.* **33**:C93.

Robison, G. A., Butcher, R. W., and Sutherland, E. W. (eds.), 1971, *Cyclic AMP*,
Academic Press, London.

Rogers, D. C., and Burnstock, G., 1966, Multiaxonal autonomic junctions in intestinal
smooth muscle of the toad (*Bufo marinus*), *J. Comp. Neurol.* **126**:625.

Rosenblueth, A., 1950, *The Transmission of Nerve Impulses at Neuroeffector Junctions
and Peripheral Synapses*, Technology Press, New York.

Satchell, D. G., and Burnstock, G., 1971, Quantitative studies of the release of purine
compounds following stimulation of non-adrenergic inhibitory nerves in the stomach, *Biochem. Pharmacol.* **20**:1694.

Satchell, D. G., Lynch, A., Bourke, P. M., and Burnstock, G., 1972, Potentiation of the
effects of exogenously applied ATP and purinergic nerve stimulation on the guinea-
pig taenia coli by dipyridamole and hexobendine, *Europ. J. Pharmacol.* **19**:343.

Setekleiv, J., 1970, Effect of drugs on ion distribution and flux in smooth muscle, in:
Smooth Muscle (E. Bülbring, A. F. Brading. A. W. Jones, and T. Tomita, eds.),
pp. 343–365, Edward Arnold, London.

Smith, A. D., 1971, Secretion of proteins (chromogranin A and dopamine β-hydroxylase)
from a sympathetic neuron, *Phil. Trans. Roy. Soc. Lond. Ser. B* **261**:363.

Somlyo, A. P., and Somlyo, A. V., 1968a, Vascular smooth muscle. I. Normal structure
pathology, biochemistry and biophysics, *Pharmacol. Rev.* **20**:197.

Somlyo, A. P., and Somlyo, A. V., 1968b, Electromechanical and pharmacological
coupling in vascular smooth muscle, *J. Pharmacol. Exptl. Therap.* **159**:129.

Somlyo, A. P., and Somlyo, A. V., 1970, Vascular smooth muscle. II. Pharmacology of
normal and hypertensive vessels, *Pharmacol. Rev.* **22**:249.

Speden, R. N., 1964, Electrical activity of single smooth muscle cells of the mesenteric
artery produced by splanchnic nerve stimulation of the guinea-pig, *Nature Lond.*
202:193.

Speden, R. N., 1967, Adrenergic transmission in small arteries, *Nature Lond.* **216**:289.

Speden, R. N., 1970, Excitation of vascular smooth muscle, in: *Smooth Muscle* (E. Büll-
bring, A. F. Brading. A. W. Jones, and T. Tomita, eds.), pp. 558–588, Edward
Arnold, London.

Stjärne, L. S., Hedquist, P., and Lagercrantz, H., 1970, Catecholamines and adenosine
nucleotides material in effluent from stimulated adrenal medulla and spleen: A
study of the exocytosis hypothesis for hormone secretion and neurotransmitter
release, *Biochem. Pharmacol.* **19**:1147.

Su, C., and Bevan, J. A., 1966, Electrical and mechanical responses of pulmonary artery
muscle to neural and chemical stimulation, *Bibl. Anat.* **8**:30.

Su, C., Bevan, J., and Burnstock, G., 1971, (^{3}H) Adenosine triphosphate: Release during
stimulation of enteric nerves, *Science N.Y.* **173**:337.

Swedin, G., 1971, Studies on neurotransmission mechanisms in the rat and guinea-pig
vas deferens, *Acta Physiol. Scand.* **369**:1.

Szurszewski, J. H., and Bülbring, E., 1973, The stimulant actions of acetylcholine and
catecholamines on the uterus, in: Recent Developments in Vertebrate Smooth
Muscle Physiology, *Phil. Trans. Roy. Soc.* **265**:149.

Tomita, T., 1967, Current spread in the smooth muscle of the guinea-pig vas deferens,
J. Physiol. Lond **189**:163.

Tomita, T., 1970, Electrical properties of mammalian smooth muscle, in: *Smooth
Muscle* (E. Bülbring, A. F. Brading, A. W. Jones, and T. Tomita, eds.), pp. 197–243,
Edward Arnold, London.

Tomita, T., and Watanabe, H., 1973, A comparison of the effects of adenosine triphosphate with noradrenaline and with the inhibitory potential of the guinea-pig taenia coli, *J. Physiol. Lond.* **231**:167.

Tranzer, J. P., and Thoenen, H., 1967, Significance of "empty vesicles" in postganglionic sympathetic nerve terminals, *Experientia* **23**:123.

Tranzer, J. P., and Thoenen, H., 1968, Various types of amine-storing vesicles in peripheral adrenergic nerve terminals, *Experientia* **24**:484.

Trautwein, W., and Dudel, J., 1958, Zum Mechanismus der Membranwirkung des Acetylcholin an der Herzmuskelfaser, *Pflügers Arch. Ges. Physiol.* **266**:324.

Uehara, Y., and Burnstock, G., 1972, Postsynaptic specialization of smooth muscle at close neuromuscular junctions in the guinea-pig sphincter pupillae, *J. Cell Biol.* **53**:849.

Ursillo, R. C., 1961, Electrical activity of the isolated nerve–urinary bladder strip preparation of the rabbit, *Am. J. Physiol.* **210**:408.

Watanabe, H., 1969, Electron microscopic observations on the innervation of smooth muscle in the guinea-pig vas deferens, *Acta Anat. Nippon* **44**:189.

West, T. C., and Toda, N., 1967, Response of the A-V node of the rabbit to stimulation of intracardiac cholinergic nerves, *Circ. Res.* **20**:18.

Wood, J. D., 1970, Electrical activity from single neurons in Auerbach's plexus, *Am. J. Physiol.* **219**:159.

Woodbury, J. W., 1962, Cellular electrophysiology of the heart, in: *Handbook of Physiology*, Section 2, Vol. 1: *Circulation*, pp. 237–286, American Physiological Society, Washington, D.C.

Yamauchi, A., and and Burnstock, G., 1969, Post-natal development of the innervation of the mouse vas deferens: A fine structural study, *J. Anat. Lond.* **104**:17.

Yokoyama, S., 1966, Aktionpotentiale der Ganglienzelle des Auerbachschen Plexus im Kaninchendunndarm, *Pflügers. Arch. Ges. Physiol.* **288**:95.

Chapter 11

"Trophic" Functions

Lloyd Guth

Laboratory of Neurochemistry
National Institute of Neurological Diseases and Stroke, NIH
Public Health Service, Department of Health, Education, and Welfare
Bethesda, Maryland, USA

1. INTRODUCTION

The concept of neurotrophic function is an old one indeed. For over half a century, the term "trophic" has been used to describe a variety of phenomena whose mechanisms are not yet understood. However, it eventually became clear that the term "trophic" had to be either defined better or discarded, and in 1968, at a meeting called to address itself to this very issue, it was agreed that for scientific as well as historical reasons this undeniably vague term should be retained (Guth, 1969). Several of the phenomena to which it has been applied, *viz.*, the neural regulation of differentiation of vertebrate taste buds, the neural regulation of amphibian limb regeneration, and the neural regulation of certain physiological and metabolic properties of mammalian muscles, all have in common certain features which fit the following definition of "neurotrophic" effects: "interactions between nerves and other cells which initiate or control molecular modification in the other cell" (Guth, 1969). Trophic influences can thus be distinguished operationally from other neurophysiological phenomena by the long-term nature of their effects even though the fundamental mechanisms that are responsible for these effects are not yet known.

In the following pages, I will document experiments that have led to the aforementioned definition. Since every important aspect of this subject has been reviewed within the past few years, the bibliographical citations will refer primarily to these references rather than the original works. This will permit the casual reader to peruse this chapter unencumbered by excessive parenthetical bibliographical citations, will enable the interested student to locate a complete treatise on any aspect of the subject, and will indicate where the specialist can find a complete bibliography.

2. REGULATION OF TASTE BUDS*

It is now almost 100 years since the discovery that taste buds disappear when the gustatory nerve is severed. This observation, made on rabbits, was subsequently verified for other mammals as well as for most vertebrates, and in many of these studies the histopathology of denervated taste buds was rather fully described. The taste bud is a flask-shaped organ in which the taste cells reside; the latter were originally categorized as gustatory or sustentacular, although the morphological evidence for this physiological distinction was not convincing and was rendered even more questionable with the recent demonstration that taste buds undergo continual cell renewal. Like all epithelia, the cells of the taste bud have a life cycle of several days length, and they are replaced by newly differentiated cells of the germinal epithelium. The subject of cell types is still far from solved, however. For example, ultrastructural studies by Murray and his colleagues and by others (reviewed by Murray, 1971) revealed that the buds of the rabbit's foliate papilla contain at least three distinct cell types, although there are cells intermediate in appearance between these three categories. Experimental studies led Murray to conclude that they are not various stages in the life history of a single cell type. For example, denervation produced degeneration of type II cells consistently, but only rarely did the type I and III cells degenerate. Of course, a given cell line that is undergoing a changing life history could be more susceptible to denervation at one stage than another, and Murray (1971) correctly warns that the evidence is not conclusive, although it does seem plausible that there are "three entirely independent cell lines, each originating from the basal cell, and presumably each carrying out a unique function within the taste bud." Following reinnervation of the denervated taste bud, all three types reappeared simultaneously rather than sequentially, and, furthermore, following administration of tritiated thymidine, the label appeared first in the undifferentiated basal (germinative) cells and later in all three differentiated types of cells of the taste bud simultaneously.

The evidence for a trophic or neurohumoral regulation of taste buds derived initially from studies of taste buds on the catfish barbel. The rate of

---

* The references for statements not documented by a specific citation will be found in the review by Guth (1971).

disappearance of denervated taste buds is temperature dependent; it doubles with every 10°C increment in temperature, in apparent agreement with Van't Hoff's law for chemical reactions. Also, the taste buds persist for a longer time if the nerve is transected far from the barbel rather than near to it. Finally, electrical stimulation of the peripheral stump of the transected nerve hastens the disappearance of taste buds. These observations led to the interpretation that the nerve possesses some nourishing or trophic factor that is gradually used up after denervation.

Of course, two conditions must be satisfied for this hypothesis. One is that the transport of trophic neurohumor, by axoplasmic flow, must continue in the distal segment of the transected nerve. A study by Ochs and Ranish (1969) has proved that the fast transport system continues to function in axons that have been disconnected from their perikaryon. Second, the degenerating nerve fibers must remain in some degree of continuity with the taste buds. This has been shown by light microscopical study not yet by electron microscopy in the catfish. There are obviously insufficient data available to prove the neurohumoral hypothesis; hence the theory is placed at the beginning of the chapter to serve as a paradigm against which all the experimental evidence can be considered.

Regardless of the mechanism responsible for the maintenance of the taste bud, the neural influence cannot be questioned. First of all, the taste buds are maintained only if the taste cells and the neuronal perikaryon are in contiguity via the peripheral nerve; transection of the sensory fibers peripheral to the ganglion results in disappearance of the taste buds, whereas transection central to the ganglion is without effect on taste buds. However, the "trophic influence" of the neuronal cell body has no physiological polarity. Zalewski (1969) found that the taste buds reappeared when the circumvallate papilla was reinnervated with either the central processes or the peripheral processes of the gustatory ganglion cells; thus the sensory ganglion's axons and dendrites are equally capable of transmitting the trophic message.

As might be expected of any biological system, this neural influence does not operate independently of either humoral factors or epithelial influences. Administration of testosterone to normal male rats induces the formation of taste buds in lingual regions that are normally devoid of them. This hormonal effect is nerve dependent; testosterone does not induce taste buds in denervated tongues or in tongues that have been reinnervated by nongustatory nerves. Furthermore, gustatory nerves will not case taste buds to form in nongustatory epithelia. Zalewski (1972) transplanted the vagal ganglion and epithelial tissue simultaneously to the anterior chamber of a rat's eye. The ganglion cells survived provided that the immune response was minimized by the use of inbred strains of experimental animals. Nerve fibers regenerated from the ganglion to the epithelium, but taste buds appeared only if the epithelium was lingual in origin; combinations of gustatory ganglion and cutaneous epithelium consistently failed to elicit the reappearance of taste buds.

In summary, taste cells normally undergo a life cycle during which they differentiate from newly divided indifferent basal cells, mature into taste or supporting cells, grow old, and die. Since taste buds degenerate and disappear when their nerve supply is interrupted, and they reappear when the nerve regenerates, it seems likely that the nerve regulates the differentiation of the taste cell, enabling the newly divided basal cells to differentiate into taste or supporting cells rather than into ordinary squamous epithelium. This "trophic" influence is specific to gustatory neurons, but it is quantitatively modified by extrinsic hormonal factors and requires a specific gustatory epithelium for its full expression.

3. REGULATION OF AMPHIBIAN LIMB REGENERATION*

Amputation of a limb is followed by regeneration of the lost extremity in certain lower vertebrates. It occurs completely and rapidly in larval and adult urodeles and in larval anurans, but this regenerative capacity is either diminished or absent in adult anurans, reptiles, birds, and mammals. The salamander has been used very extensively for the study of limb regeneration, and the histopathology of limb regeneration has been fully described in this species. Immediately after amputation, there is a short period of tissue destruction; during this time, phagocytes migrate into the amputation stump and remove necrotic tissue and cellular debris. Mononuclear mesenchymatous cells accumulate in this region as a result of the dedifferentiation of some of the surviving cells and constitute the blastema from which regeneration proceeds. These cells divide and differentiate, giving rise ultimately to a fully formed normal appendage. The nervous system plays a paramount role in this regeneration process. It has long been known that regeneration of the amputated limb does not occur if the regional nerves are transected before or shortly after amputation; the systematic investigations by Singer subsequently clarified the quantitative and qualitative aspects of this relationship between nerve and periphery. Sensory nerves are more potent in stimulating limb regeneration, but motor nerves are fully effective provided there are a sufficient number of them in the blastema. Reflex nervous connections with the central nervous system are unimportant; regeneration proceeds when the central processes of the sensory ganglion are interrupted or when isolated

---

* This subject was comprehensively reviewed by Singer in 1952 and by Thornton in 1968 and 1970; the reader is referred to these works for a complete bibliography. Bibliographic citations will be indicated only for those works that are not included in these review articles.

sensory ganglia or fragments of CNS tissue are implanted locally into the otherwise denervated regeneration stump. Thus, except for the absence of modality specificity, the interaction between nerve and regenerating limb is similar to that between nerve and taste bud. Although there is little qualitative specificity in the trophic neural effect, there is a rather rigid quantitative neural requirement. Regeneration proceeds only if the number of nerve fibers in the amputation blastema exceeds a certain threshold. This threshold appears to be similar for larval and adult animals (although there is indeed some conflicting evidence on this point); regeneration can even be induced in the young adult frog (a species which does not ordinarily regenerate severed limbs) provided that a sufficient number of nerve fibers are diverted to the amputation site. The threshold level is not so much a question of the number of nerve fibers as of the total amount of neuroplasm in contact with the peripheral tissues. *Xenopus*, an anuran which can regenerate amputated limbs, has a small number of very large fibers, whereas *Rana*, an anuran which does not exhibit limb regeneration, has a large number of small-caliber nerve fibers. However, quantitative calculations revealed that the total amount of neuroplasm in contact with the peripheral tissues is considerably greater for *Xenopus* than for *Rana*.

The nerve is essential only in the earlier stages of limb regeneration. Once regeneration has proceeded in an innervated limb bud for 9 days or more, it will continue even if the nerve is then transected. However, regeneration ceases and regressive changes ensue if the denervation is performed earlier.

The chemical mechanism by which the nerve initiates and maintains the early stages of limb regeneration is not known. It is apparently unrelated to the known chemical transmitters; the infusion of transmitter substances or blocking agents (e.g., acetylcholine, atropine, procaine, tetraethyl ammonium hydroxide, and botulinum toxin) produced no effect on limb regeneration that could be attributed to their pharmacological activity.

The "aneurogenic limb" is one very important and instructive exception to the rule that an intact nerve supply is a prerequisite for limb regeneration. If the neural tube is extirpated in very young embryos of *Ambystoma*, the limbs that form subsequently lack any innervation and have been called "aneurogenic limbs." These limbs are fully formed, although they are functionless. Such limbs, which have developed in the absence of neural influences and which remain uninnervated, will regenerate after amputation and are thus independent of any neurotrophic requirement. However, these limbs become nerve dependent after exposure to neural tissues. For example, when aneurogenic limbs were grafted to a normal animal and allowed to become innervated by the host's brachial nerves, they became nerve dependent within 10–13 days. The grafted aneurogenic limbs regenerated if amputated and denervated less than 10 days postoperatively, but regeneration did not ensue if the amputation and denervation were performed 13 days after transplantation. Furthermore, if transplanted aneurogenic limbs which had been allowed to become innervated and "nerve dependent" were then denervated and maintained in this state for 40 days or more, their condition of "nerve dependence" was reversed, and they again became capable of regenerating in the absence of innervation.

It is thus clear that the neurotrophic control of limb regeneration can best be described as an interaction between nerve and blastema. Dresden (1969) reported reduction in synthesis of DNA, RNA, and protein by denervated blastemas in comparison with innervated ones, and he suggested that the nerve directly regulates protein synthesis. Lebowitz and Singer (1970) showed that the uptake of radioactive leucine by denervated blastemas is less than that by innervated blastemas. They were able to ameliorate this effect of denervation by infusing nerve extracts into the denervated blastemas. These results suggest the intriguing possibility that the nerve's effect may be relatively nonspecific; perhaps the nerve merely stimulates protein synthesis sufficiently to enable differentiation to proceed. The ability of the aneurogenic limbs to regenerate in the absence of innervation, the importance of a threshold number of nerve fibers for regeneration, and the lack of any qualitative specificity of the neural requirement are observations consistent with this hypothesis. Singer has even suggested that trophic substances may be elaborated by nonneural cells during early embryonic development. The *trophic* influence becomes *neurotrophic* later in development, possibly because the nerve then inhibits the production of trophic agents by nonneural tissues. Such a hypothesis is plausible, although the available evidence is insufficient to prove it. In other words, we cannot be certain whether the nerve restricts the production of trophic substance by nonneural tissues, whether the nerve alters the tissue's requirements for such substances, or whether both occur.

If the nerve secretes some relatively nonspecific growth-promoting agent, one might expect the blastema's response to be hormone dependent. Unfortunately, this possibility has not yet been investigated systematically. It is known that regeneration cannot proceed normally in the absence of normal pituitary and thyroid function and that growth hormone and/or prolactin seem to be the most likely active pituitary principles. However, the one hormone most closely related to protein synthesis, testosterone, has never been assayed for regeneration-promoting activity. Such a study would be important inasmuch as testosterone enhances the neurotrophic influence on mammalian taste buds and because it stimulates protein synthesis in muscle (Florini, 1970).

The problem of the neurotrophic mechanism can be approached experimentally in various ways. The denervation studies demonstrated the importance of the neural influence, and the experiments on aneurogenic limbs revealed that this neural factor was not the sole determinant of regenerative capacity. The more recent studies designed to elucidate the chemical nature of the neurotrophic substance (whether it be related to neural transmitters or hormones) have revealed that the nerve regulates the synthesis of DNA, RNA, and protein. Experiments are now being performed to determine more precisely the site of action of the neural influence. The blastema is, of course, a complex organ composed of a variety of tissues and cell types of which any or all may be neurally regulated. If the mesoderm of an aneurogenic limb is replaced by the mesoderm from an innervated one, regeneration will occur, but regeneration fails in the aneurogenic limb if the wound epithelium is replaced by that from a normal (nonaneurogenic) animal. As Thornton (1968) points out, "these data would allow speculation that aneurogenic limb skin possesses regeneration-promoting capacities which are lacking in corresponding mesodermal tissues . . . [and that it is] possible to separate the epidermal and mesodermal components throughout limb regeneration and analyze the enzymic, nucleic acid, and protein changes which occur in them." There are now sufficient data to begin a systematic and coordinated biochemical investigation into the neural, epithelial, mesodermal, and hormonal mechanisms which, by their interaction, determine the regenerative capacity of the amphibian limb.

4. REGULATION OF PHYSIOLOGICAL AND METABOLIC PROPERTIES OF MUSCLE

In the motor system, the nerve impulse and the neurotrophic influence both travel centrifugally from the perikaryon. For this reason, it is difficult to distinguish between the effects of these two kinds of influences, and as a result we cannot be absolutely certain that extrafusal muscle fibers are neurotrophically regulated. Furthermore, in the absence of either impulse transmission or muscular activity (as induced by denervation or disuse, respectively), the muscle atrophies profoundly, and it becomes difficult to evaluate trophic influences under such pathological conditions. The present state of our knowledge is therefore unsatisfactory, and a coherent story cannot yet be written. There are several mechanisms by which nerve might influence the muscle; these include the quantal release of ACh (m.e.p.p.s), the impulse-directed release of ACh (e.p.p.s), and the programming of muscular activity. In addition, studies on the regulation of the resting membrane potential (r.m.p.), the acetylcholine (ACh) sensitivity, and the cholinesterase (ChE) activity seem to indicate the existence of a neurotrophic influence.

4.1. Resting Membrane Potential

By an exquisite analysis of changes in the properties of denervated muscle fibers, Albuquerque *et al.* (1971) observed a decrease in the r.m.p.

about 2 h after denervation. This partial depolarization preceded the changes in miniature end plate potentials (m.e.p.p.s) ACh sensitivity, and membrane resistance. Since the change in r.m.p. occurred before any change in m.e.p.p.s, it was concluded that the quantal release of ACh plays no direct role in maintaining the r.m.p. Furthermore, these authors showed that when the nerve was cut near to the muscle the decrease in r.m.p. occurred sooner than when the nerve was cut far from it. Since impulse transmission and contractile activity cease immediately upon denervation, regardless of the level of the lesion, it was concluded that the r.m.p. is independent of these phenomena. The importance of this experiment cannot be overemphasized. Other changes in muscle have been related to the level of the lesion (reviewed by Guth, 1968). The breakdown of sole plates, onset of proteolytic activity, loss of glycogen, decrease in ACh transferase activity, and failure of impulse transmission all occur sooner when the nerve is cut near to rather than far from the muscle. However, none of these changes occurs prior to the disappearance of m.e.p.p.s. The fact that a decrease in r.m.p. is the first change seen in denervated muscle and the finding that this change is related to the level of the lesion together constitute evidence sufficient to postulate that the r.m.p. is regulated neurotrophically, i.e., by a process unrelated to any known physiological mechanism.

In their discussion of these results, the authors make the important suggestion that the nerve may control the r.m.p. by regulating the activity of the electrogenic sodium pump; they also speculate that a decrease in intracellular potassium concentration in the denervated muscle could result in a redistribution of potassium to protein-synthesizing sites. The redistribution of this ion could account for alterations in protein synthesis that produce changes in sarcoplasmic and myofibrillar proteins.

4.2. Acetylcholine Sensitivity

In the normal muscle fiber, the highest sensitivity to applied ACh is found at the motor end-plate. Following denervation, the ACh sensitivity gradually spreads centrifugally from this "junctional" region as a result of the formation of extrajunctional receptors. A similar spread of ACh sensitivity is found in muscles poisoned with botulinum toxin. Since the major pharmacological action of botulinum toxin is prevention of the release of ACh, it has been suggested that ACh release regulates the ACh sensitivity of the muscle fiber, and, furthermore, since muscles poisoned with botulinum toxin undergo an atrophy that is almost indistinguishable from that produced by denervation, Drachman suggested that ACh may be the only "neurotrophic agent" (quoted in Guth, 1969). However, recent evidence makes this view untenable. A spread of sensitivity in the presence of normal quantal release of ACh is found in muscles whose contractile activity has been blocked by diphtheria toxin or a local nerve anesthetic (Lømo and Rosenthal, 1972); the spread of sensitivity occurring under these conditions or during denervation can be reduced by electrical stimulation of the muscle (Lømo and Rosenthal, 1972; Drachman and Witzke, 1972). The effect of the electrical stimulation in these experiments cannot be ascribed solely to impulse-directed release of ACh but probably to an effect on protein metabolism, since the spread of sensitivity in denervated muscle can be prevented by the administration of inhibitors of RNA and protein synthesis (Fambrough, 1970). In the absence of any influence of ACh on proteosynthesis, we must look elsewhere for the neural mechanisms responsible for the synthesis of the extrajunctional receptors. In this regard, the aforementioned speculation by Albuquerque *et al.* (1971) on the role of potassium shifts in protein synthesis in denervated muscle may provide an important clue for further research.

Miledi has provided other evidence militating against a direct participation of ACh in the control of ACh sensitivity (quoted in Guth, 1969). Addition of ACh to cultures of denervated muscle did not retard or prevent the development of supersensitivity. Furthermore, during reinnervation of denervated muscle, the ACh sensitivity often returns to normal before functional reinnervation occurs; this finding is incompatible with the possibility of direct influence of e.p.p.s on the restoration of normal ACh sensitivity.

4.3. Cholinesterase Activity

The nerve is to a large part responsible for regulating the ChE activity of the muscle fiber (see Guth, 1969, for complete review). It induces the formation of ChE in newly formed sole plates of embryonic or adult muscle. In adult muscle, junctional ChE activity decreases by 50% within 3 days after denervation, and, in the absence of reinnervation, it persists at this reduced level. The available evidence indicates that the nerve regulates the synthesis of this enzyme. In one study, DFP, an irreversible inhibitor of ChE was administered. This drug eliminates all junctional ChE activity and the subsequent gradual reappearance of ChE activity interpreted as resulting from newly synthesized enzyme. Such *de novo* synthesis occurred in normally innervated muscles that had been poisoned with DFP but not in denervated ones. There is also considerable evidence that the neural release of ACh is unrelated to the regulation of ChE activity of the muscle. Strömblad (1960) observed that botulinum toxin (which prevents release of ACh) does not cause as severe a loss of muscle ChE activity as does denervation. Furthermore, the influence of muscular activity is not significant, since little change in ChE activity occurs during tenotomy or immobilization. Finally, extracts of nervous tissue have been shown to be effective in inducing increased ChE activity in muscle cultures *in vitro* (Lentz, 1971). Sensory ganglia, ganglia separated from the muscle by Millipore filter, and homogenates of nervous tissue produced the greatest increases in ChE activity of the cultured muscle fibers. These observations provide evidence of a neurotrophic control of ChE activity.

4.4. The Role of ACh Release

The studies on r.m.p., ACh sensitivity, and ChE activity indicate that there is a trophic influence of nerve on muscle that cannot be explained by any known physiological mechanism. However, numerous experiments have shown that the elimination of ACh release (by the intramuscular application of botulinum toxin) produces effects similar to denervation. Drachman (see Guth, 1968) initially concluded that ACh is probably the trophic agent or, at the very least, mediates the trophic influences. The recent study by Albuquerque *et al.* (1972) has proved this view false. These authors applied a silastic cuff containing colchicine or vinblastine to the nerves supplying certain hindlimb muscles in the rat. Three to five days later, these muscles developed a decreased r.m.p. and, subsequently, extrajunctional ACh sensitivity. Despite these changes that are normally attributed to denervation, there was no significant alteration in m.e.p.p.s, nerve transmission across the site of the cuff was unimpaired, and the muscle's response to indirect stimulation was essentially normal. Electron microscopic examination showed that the drugs had caused a disruption of the axoplasm and microtubules without substantially affecting the axolemma. The authors concluded that the drugs had elicited these denervation-like changes by interfering with the release of some neural factor or factors other than the ACh.

As regards the role of ACh, one can only suggest that transmitter release and muscular activity exert a general life-conferring influence on muscle. In the absence of this influence, the muscle fiber exhibits pathological changes, undergoes atrophy, and may even die. But there are more subtle and equally important influences that cannot be demonstrated in the absence of ACh release, because under these conditions the muscle fiber is dying. The experiments on the effects of botulinum toxin are therefore not really relevant to the question of trophic nerve function.

4.5. The Dynamic Nature of the Muscle Fiber

4.5.1. Effect of Cross-Reinnervation

The subject of the dynamic nature of the muscle fiber has been comprehensively reviewed by Close (1972). The experiments of Buller, Eccles, and

Eccles, performed more than a decade ago, showed that the nerve regulates the isometric contraction time of muscle and that this physiological property of muscle can be altered even during adult life. These authors reinnervated a fast muscle by a nerve that normally supplies a slow one, and reinnervated a slow muscle by a nerve that normally innervates a fast one; they found that the isometric contraction time of the fast muscle became longer and that of the slow muscle became shorter. Subsequently, Close showed that the intrinsic speed of shortening of the sarcomere is modified by these cross-reinnervation procedures, and he therefore suggested that the basic properties of the myosin molecule must be neurally controlled. This suggestion was verified biochemically by Samaha, Guth, and Albers and by Bárány and Close. Their experiments showed that myosins of slow and fast muscle are qualitatively different and that these differences in the structure of the molecule are neurally regulated (i.e., they are reversed by cross-reinnervation).

The observations of qualitative changes in cross-reinnervated muscle have a special significance; they indicate a control over the type of protein manufactured by the cell. The amount of protein within a cell is controlled by the relative rates of synthesis and degradation; these are processes which can be controlled in a variety of ways. However, whether a cell will or will not make a certain protein is a decision that is determined by gene action, and it has therefore been suggested that one of the trophic influences of the nervous system is the regulation of gene expression in the muscle cell.

Cross-reinnervation does produce characteristic quantitative changes in many properties of the muscle fiber; slow and fast muscles differ in level of ATPase activity, glycogen content, potassium concentration, soluble protein components, enzymes of carbohydrate metabolism, and lactic dehydrogenase isozymes. All of these properties exhibit a complete or partial reversal following cross-reinnervation. However, since quantitative changes can be accomplished in a variety of ways, these studies have limited importance to the problem of trophic function.

4.5.2. Influence of Exercise

It is obvious that muscle tissue is of profound evolutionary significance for the survival of a species. Certain animals have muscles which adapt them for brief periods of running at great speeds, whereas other animals run more slowly but with greater endurance. Furthermore, different muscles of an animal are functionally specialized (e.g., for tonic or phasic activity). Certainly the structure of a muscle is influenced by the nature of its activity; the type of exercise performed is thus responsible for the development of some of these specific properties of muscle.

The influence of exercise on histochemical, biochemical, and physiological properties of muscle has been summarized by Peter (1971). A program
of standardized training (such as swimming or running on a motor-driven
treadmill) results in histochemical and biochemical changes reflecting increased
endurance, *viz.*, an increased activity of those sarcoplasmic enzymes that are
responsible for the oxidative capacity of the muscle. Although this type of
exercise did not produce any alteration in the actomyosin ATPase activity,
compensatory hypertrophy of the soleus (produced by excision of the
synergistic gastrocnemius and plantaris muscles) resulted in a decreased
ATPase activity as determined histochemically (Guth and Yellin, 1971).
Conversely, denervation of antagonistic muscles to the soleus (by transection
of the common peroneal nerve) produced increased ATPase activity in many
fibers, this conversion being accompanied by a physiological speeding of the
muscle (Guth and Wells, 1972). Although these experiments are not true
"exercise studies," they do reveal that alterations in myofibrillar proteins and
speed of contraction can be accomplished by procedures other than cross-
reinnervation.

4.6. Plasticity of the Motor Unit

Histochemical studies have revealed that most mammalian muscles are
composed of three kinds of muscle fibers. When individual muscle fibers are
examined for their actomyosin ATPase and oxidative enzyme activities, the
fibers can be assigned to the classes indicated in Table I. The physiological
properties of each of these fiber types have been determined by stimulating
individual motor neurons intracellularly and recording the histochemical and
physiological properties of the muscle fibers they innervate (Burke *et al.*,
1971). As indicated in the table, this study showed that the ATPase activity is
inversely proportional to the isometric contraction time and is presumably
directly proportional to the speed of shortening; the oxidative activity is
indicative of the fatiguability of the muscle fiber. Furthermore, this study
proved that the motor unit is histochemically and physiologically homogene-

Table I. Histochemical and Physiological Characteristics of the Three General Classes of Muscle Fibers

Denotation	ATPase activity	Oxidative activity	Presumed speed of shortening	Fatiguability
S	Low	High	Slow	Fatigue resistant
FF	High	Low	Fast	Fast fatiguing
FR	High	High	Fast	Fatigue resistant

ous; i.e., every muscle fiber innervated by the same neuron is histochemically and physiologically identical. The physiological and biochemical changes occurring in muscle after cross-reinnervation are demonstrative of the plasticity of the motor unit, and the changes seen following exercise indicate that this plasticity plays an important physiological role throughout adult life. Furthermore, since the motor unit is homogeneous, changes observed in the muscle fibers are indicative of changes in the motor neuron. Whether these changes represent changes in pattern of activation, trophic function, or both is a question that has not yet been studied experimentally.

5. MECHANISMS OF NEURAL REGULATION

What are the features common to the neurotrophic influence on taste buds, limb regeneration, and muscle? In each case, the nerve regulates cellular proteins either quantitatively or qualitatively: in the taste bud, it controls the differentiation of the basal cell into the taste cell; in the blastema of the amputated limb, it stimulates protein synthesis and initiates differentiation; in muscle, it prevents the formation of extrajunctional receptors, induces ChE activity, and determines the nature of the myosin molecule. The nerve not only stimulates protein synthesis nonspecifically but also exerts a qualitative influence on the type of protein synthesized; this has led to the suggestion of a neural influence on gene expression as being one of the major aspects of neurotrophic function. Of course, this is merely a hypothesis which requires direct experimental verification.

A second feature of this neural influence on gene expression is that, like any embryonic induction, it requires the active participation of the end organ. In other words, it represents an interaction between the appropriate tissue (at the proper stage of development), the nerve, and extrinsic hormonal factors. The neurotrophic influence of the gustatory nerve can elicit taste bud formation in gustatory epithelium only, regeneration in the aneurogenic limb occurs only if the wound epithelium derives from an aneurogenic limb, and in muscle the trophic influence interacts with the physiological conditions under which the muscle happens to be functioning. The nature of the work being performed by the muscle (weightbearing vs. nonweightbearing), the frequency of use (phasic vs. tonic), and the degree of stretch to which the muscle is subjected can all influence the physiological and metabolic properties of the muscle fiber directly and by interacting with neurotrophic influences.

The hormonal factors can best be categorized as nonspecific influences on the end organ. Administration of testosterone permits taste buds to appear in regions of gustatory epithelium where they are not normally found. But this effect requires the specific participation of the appropriate nerve and the appropriate epithelium. This hormone exerts an equally nonspecific effect on muscle. Florini (1970) administered testosterone in a dosage sufficient to produce a 60% increase in RNA and protein synthesis. Despite this stimulation of protein metabolism, he found no qualitative alterations in the muscle proteins, and he therefore concluded that the effects of the hormone involve increased expression of previously active genes (or activation of redundant genes).

It is apparent that there are features common to the neural regulation of these three diverse systems, and it follows that it is appropriate to group these influences as "neurotrophic." As a result of numerous studies, especially those of the past decade, these influences now seem less mysterious and more amenable to experimental investigation.

6. REFERENCES

Albuquerque, E. X., Schuh, F. T., and Kauffman, F. C., 1971, Early membrane depolarization of the fast mammalian muscle after denervation, *Pflügers Arch. Ges. Physiol.* **328**:36.

Albuquerque, E. X., Warnick, J. E., Tasse, J. R., and Sansone, F. M., 1972, Effects of vinblastine and colchicine on neural regulation of the fast and slow skeletal muscles of the rat, *Exptl. Neurol.* **37**:607.

Burke, R. E., Levine, D. N., Zajac, F. E., Tsairis, P., and Engel, W. K., 1971, Mammalian motor units: Physiological–histochemical correlation in three types in cat gastrocnemius, *Science* **174**:709.

Close, R. I., 1972, Dynamic properties of mammalian skeletal muscles, *Physiol. Rev.* **52**:129.

Drachman, D. B., and Witzke, F., 1972, Trophic regulation of acetylcholine sensitivity of muscle: Effect of electrical stimulation, *Science* **176**:514.

Dresden, M. H., 1969, Denervation effects on newt limb regeneration: DNA, RNA, and protein synthesis, *Develop. Biol.* **19**:311.

Fambrough, D. M., 1970, Acetylcholine sensitivity of muscle fiber membranes: Mechanism of regulation by motoneurons, *Science* **168**:372.

Florini, J. R., 1970, Effects of testosterone on qualitative pattern of protein synthesis in skeletal muscle, *Biochemistry* **9**:909.

Guth, L., 1968, "Trophic" influences of nerve on muscle, *Physiol. Rev.* **48**:645.

Guth, L., 1969, "Trophic" effects of vertebrate neurons, *Neurosci. Res. Prog. Bull.* **7**:1.

Guth, L., 1971, Degeneration and regeneration of taste buds, in: *Handbook of Sensory Physiology*, Vol. 4: *Chemical Senses*, Part 2: *Taste* (L. M. Beidler, ed.), pp. 63–74, Springer-Verlag, Berlin, Heidelberg, New York.

Guth, L., and Wells, J. B., 1972, Physiological and histochemical properties of the soleus muscle after denervation of its antagonists, *Exptl. Neurol.* **36**:463.

Guth, L., and Yellin, H., 1971, The dynamic nature of the so-called "fiber types" of mammalian skeletal muscle, *Exptl. Neurol.* **31**:277.

Lebowitz, P., and Singer, M., 1970, Neurotrophic control of protein synthesis in the regenerating limb of the newt, *Triturus*, *Nature* **225**:824.

Lentz, T. L., 1971, Nerve trophic function: *In vitro* assay of effects of nerve tissue on muscle cholinesterase activity, *Science* **171**:187.

Lømo, T., and Rosenthal, J., 1972, Control of ACh sensitivity by muscle activity, *J. Physiol.* **221**:493.

Murray, R. G., 1971, Ultrastructure of taste receptors, in: *Handbook of Sensory Physiology*, Vol. 4: *Chemical Senses*, Part 2: *Taste* (L. M. Beidler, ed.), pp. 31–50, Springer-Verlag, Berlin, Heidelberg, New York.

Ochs, S., and Ranish, N., 1969, Characteristics of the fast transport system in mammalian nerve fibers, *J. Neurobiol.* **1**:247.

Peter, J. B., 1971, Histochemical, biochemical, and physiological studies of skeletal muscle and its adaptation to exercise, in: *Contractility of Muscle Cells and Related Processes* (R. J. Podolsky, ed.), pp. 161–173, Prentice-Hall, Englewood Cliffs, N.J.

Singer, M., 1952, The influence of the nerve in regeneration of the amphibian extremity, *Quart. Rev. Biol.* **27**:169.

Strömblad, B. C. R., 1960, Cholinesterase activity in skeletal muscle after botulinum toxin, *Experientia* **16**:458.

Thornton, C. S., 1968, Amphibian limb regeneration, *Advan. Morphogenet.* **7**:205.

Thornton, C. S., 1970, Amphibian limb regeneration and its relation to nerves, *Am. Zoologist* **10**:113.

Zalewski, A. A., 1969, Regeneration of taste buds after reinnervation by peripheral or central fibers of vagal ganglia, *Exptl. Neurol.* **25**:429.

Zalewski, A. A., 1972, Regeneration of taste buds after transplantation of tongue and ganglia grafts to the anterior chamber of the eye, *Exptl. Neurol.* **35**:519

Receptors—Structure and Function

Cutaneous Receptors

Ainsley Iggo

Department of Veterinary Physiology
University of Edinburgh
Edinburgh, Scotland

1. INTRODUCTION

The skin is richly innervated with axons of afferent nerve fibers, estimates of the numbers ranging around 1 million. The density of innervation is, however, quite variable; most of the afferent fibers terminate in the face or the extremities, with relatively few supplying the dorsal surface of the trunk. The structure of the skin of the face and extremities, as well as the degree of specialization of the receptors, is also more complex. Glabrous or hairless skin occurs at these places, and complex hair follicles (sinus hairs) are present in the face of many mammals. Structural features of glabrous skin, in addition to the thickening of the epidermis, are a regular epidermal ridge formation, associated with uniformly organized nerve supply, and the presence of complex encapsulated sensory receptors in regular arrays and with sweat glands. Hairy skin, in contrast, has as its dominant feature hair follicles of several kinds often arrayed in regular patterns. In hairy skin, the majority of the sensory receptors are integral parts of the hair follicles or other organized, but less numerous, receptors, and most afferent nerve fibers end either in the hair follicles or close to the basal layer of the epidermis. Some nerves penetrate the basement membrane of the epithelium to end closer to the skin surface, but these are found in highly specialized skin, such as Eimer's organs in the snout of the mole. Nerves ending within the basement membrane of the epidermis include the distinctive Merkel disc, which is associated with

Merkel's cell. Nonmyelinated fibers and specialized small myelinated axons also end on the epidermal side of the basement membrane, or close to it (Cauna, 1969). As a general feature, sensory receptors do not penetrate deeply into the epidermis, and when they are present the epidermis itself may be thickened and specialized. Many receptors lie just beneath the basement membrane or within 100–200 μm of it, although isolated larger receptor structures such as the Pacinian corpuscle and Ruffini ending, may be more deeply located in the corium.

In the older literature, two plexuses of nerves were described in the skin, a superficial and a deep. The plexuses were nerves containing many axons. The deep one can now be identified as a branching nerve network carrying fibers to be distributed to the superficial plexus; the latter, lying close to the epidermis, contains axons being distributed to the nerve terminals. Neither of these plexuses is a receptor. Some of the older histological methods (silver staining, osmication), in skilled and experienced hands capable of yielding exact information about the axons, often failed to reveal the nerve endings, as is now clear from electron microscopic studies. For these technical reasons, the older work could not establish the actual relation of the superficial plexus to the receptors, although the structure of encapsulated receptors was sometimes described with great accuracy (Ruffini, 1894). It can now be stated that the superficial plexus is distributing axons to subepidermal and basal-epidermal receptors of several kinds and that it does not form a syncitium.

The deep plexus is in its turn derived from still deeper nerves that arise from cutaneous branches of mixed or cutaneous nerves. These larger nerves usually run for some distance as distinct nerve fascicles in the subcutaneous tissue and contain both afferent (dorsal root) and efferent (sympathetic) nerve fibers. The cutaneous nerves may also include fascicles that supply articular joints. For example, the saphenous nerve when it leaves the femoral nerve includes axons which leave it in a separate fascicle to supply the posterior aspect of the knee joint. All the cutaneous nerves, except the trigeminal, eventually join major mixed nerves (i.e., nerves supplying both muscle and skin and containing motor and sensory fibers) derived from cranial or spinal nerves, and these latter eventually form the dorsal (afferent) and ventral (efferent) spinal roots. From an experimental viewpoint, therefore, it is possible to work on nerves containing exclusively cutaneous fibers only in the periphery, and even at such places the nerves may contain joint afferents and will always include sympathetic axons. The dorsal roots are always mixed with cutaneous, muscular, and visceral components, as also are the dorsal root (and cranial nerve) ganglia.

In the account that follows, the morphological characteristics of the skin nerve supply will be treated systematically, working from the center outward to the receptors, and the physiological characteristics by working in from the periphery.

2. MORPHOLOGY OF CUTANEOUS NERVES

The cutaneous nerves contain axons with cell bodies in the dorsal root ganglia, but impulses traveling centripetally from the skin do not always invade the ganglion cells, especially at high discharge frequencies (Dun, 1955). The axons vary in diameter from a maximum of 20 μm to a minimum of 0.2 μm. The range of diameters varies according to (1) the destination of the nerve (in general, the largest axons are in nerves supplying the extremities and face) and (2) the species (large animals such as the ox have larger axons than small animals such as the rabbit). Electron microscopy has greatly increased the accuracy of axonal diameter measurement by leading to improved methods of fixation of the tissues, by reducing errors of mensuration, and by making visible what was previously in doubt. The myelinated axons, from about 1 to 20 μm in diameter, usually show a bimodal distribution of axonal diameters with one peak at 7–8 μm and a second peak at 2–4 μm. This latter peak shows considerable species variation. In nonprimate mammals, there is a single peak at 3 μm, whereas in primates there are two peaks, one between 3 and 4 μm and the other about 2 μm. This larger number of the smallest myelinated axons in primate cutaneous nerves is related to the kinds of receptors present.

Two systems of classification are used for the fiber spectrum of peripheral nerves—the older one was introduced by the St. Louis School (Erlanger, Gasser, and Bishop) and is based on shape of the compound action potential recorded from the nerve trunk, A, B, and C waves representing A, the myelinated somatic axons, B, the myelinated autonomic efferents in visceral nerves (subsequently abandoned when most of the myelinated axons in visceral nerves were found to be afferent), and C, the nonmyelinated axons, including both dorsal root afferent and autonomic efferent axons. The A wave was subdivided into α, β, γ, and δ components which subsequently reduced to α and δ; the β and γ waves were attributed to artifacts (Gasser, 1960). The actual configuration of the compound action potential depends on the relative proportions of axons of different diameter, as do the peak conduction velocities of the two components (in muscle nerve the maximal conduction velocity is 120 m/s compared to 80–90 in a cutaneous nerve such as the saphenous). In primates where there is such a prominent peak of axons of less than 2 μm diameter that the δ wave may have two peaks, the second is sometimes referred to as "post-δ." Hursh (1939) and later Gasser and others have attempted to provide a generally applicable factor for converting the conduction velocities to axonal diameters. Hursh's experimental method limited him to studying the largest axons, and he found that the best fit was given by a factor of 6 (i.e., conduction velocity in m/s = axon diameter in μm $\times$ 6). The smaller myelinated axons were later found to give a better fit for a factor of 4 or 5. The nonmyelinated (C) axons of dorsal root origin require a factor of 1.7 (Gasser, 1955).

The second major classification is based on axonal diameter distributions in muscle nerves of the cat (Lloyd, 1943). Four groups were made: I, II, and III for the myelinated axons and IV for the nonmyelinated. The boundaries were set at I $>$ 12 μm, II = 6–12 μm, III = 1–6 μm, and IV $<$ 1 μm (nonmyelinated). The same classification has been used for cutaneous nerves, with the following correspondences: group I, absent; group II, 6–12 + μm $\equiv$ Aα; group III, 1–6 μm $\equiv$ Aδ; and group IV $\equiv$ C. The fit is least satisfactory for the group III, Aδ category. The majority of skin nerve Aδ fibers conduct at less than 24 m/s, and inspection of fiber diameter distributions, such as that of Dyck *et al.* (1972), shows that the natural boundary lies between 4 and 5 μm. With a minor adjustment of the boundary of groups II and III, placing it at 5 μm rather than 6 μm and, for converting diameter to conduction velocity, using the factor of 5 for these small fibers rather than 6, a very good fit can be obtained. As will become evident later, this boundary between groups II and III (Aα and Aδ) also has a physiological significance.

The nonmyelinated (C) fibers, comprising both afferent somatic and efferent autonomic fibers, also exhibit a range of axonal diameters. Gasser's discovery that these axons do not travel separately from each other in the peripheral nerves, as is the case for myelinated axons which have personal Schwann cells, but instead share a Schwann cell among as many as 20 axons, raised the possibility that the axons discharge impulses synchronously; i.e., all the axons in a common Schwann bundle discharge impulses at the same time. In both compound action potential (Gasser, 1955) and single unit (Iggo, 1958) studies, this has been shown not normally to be so. There is some indication, however, that circumstances might arise where synchronization could occur, e.g., in the waves of potential, much larger than can be attributed to single unit activity, that may be recorded from visceral nerves.

2.1. Uniformity of Cutaneous Axons

The axons supplying the skin do not divide after leaving the dorsal root ganglion until they are near their termination in the skin, nor is there any evidence for conspicuous systematic longitudinal changes in axonal diameter in the majority of the axons. Some of the largest myelinated axons, which supply morphologically specialized receptors, do not divide until they reach the receptor itself (e.g., Ruffini endings, Pacinian corpuscles), whereas others may bifurcate several millimeters before their entry into organized receptors

(Merkel *Tastflecken*, touch spots) where the branches further subdivide to innervate individual Merkel cells (*Tastzellen*). On the other hand, the group II and III myelinated axons in innervating hair follicles branch much more extensively in the deep cutaneous plexuses, since an individual stem axon can supply as many as 50 follicles in an area of 50 cm². The smallest myelinated and the nonmyelinated axons, like some of the large myelinated axons, do not branch, since the physiological evidence establishes that an individual axon supplies a very restricted area of skin (up to 3 by 2 mm) and may supply only a single small spot (less than 1 mm²).

There is one special class of axons, most common in primate hairy skin, that shows clear evidence of tapering. These are axons which in the proximal half of their length have conduction velocities of about 4–6 m/s (corresponding to diameters of 1 μm) but are more slowly conducting in the periphery—about 1 m/s (Iggo and Ogawa, 1971). The simplest explanation is that the axons are myelinated proximally but lack a myelin sheath in the periphery. Similar axons have also been found in a visceral nerve (vagus, Iggo, 1958). This apparent loss of myelin was not due to the division of the axon into two surviving branches, since each axon supplied only one small receptive field.

2.2. Relative Numbers of Myelinated and Nonmyelinated Axons

Although the largest myelinated axons occupy most of the cross-sectional area of a peripheral cutaneous nerve and also dominate the compound action potential, they are numerically fewest. The group III (Aδ) are the most abundant myelinated axons, outnumbering the group II by at least 2:1. The total population of myelinated fibers is, however, greatly outnumbered (4:1 or 5:1) by the nonmyelinated axons (somatic afferent and autonomic efferent). Dyck *et al.* (1972) reported an average ratio of 4.6C:1A in nine healthy human sural nerves. This value depends on the location of the tissues innervated. The lingual nerve supply to the epithelium of the tongue, for example, contains few nonmyelinated axons. The nerves supplying the extremities, especially glabrous skin, also contain relatively few nonmyelinated axons in contrast to the more proximal part of the limbs supplied by the saphenous nerve. Finally, the ratio is species dependent. Larger animals have relatively few nonmyelinated axons.

3. MORPHOLOGY OF CUTANEOUS RECEPTORS

Cutaneous receptors can be divided into two major kinds on the basis of their structure—corpuscular and noncorpuscular. The former can be further divided into encapsulated receptors, which are in the dermis, and nonencapsulated, which have an epidermal location.

3.1. Encapsulated Receptors

The capsule, formed from nonnervous tissue, completely invests the nerve ending and usually takes the form of lamellation, which is most conspicuous in Pacini, Herbst, and Golgi–Mazzoni receptors, but may have only four or five layers, as in the Ruffini ending. The disposition of the nerve endings also varies from the relatively simple inner core of the Pacinian corpuscle to the extensive brushlike inner spindle of the Ruffini ending or the interleaved internal cross-lamination of the Meissner corpuscle. The encapsulated receptors also contain capillaries and venules, which may have a sympathetic nerve supply. The encapsulated receptors are innervated by myelinated axons, the majority of which are group II, although Cunningham and Fitzgerald (1972) have recently reported that simple encapsulated receptors in the mouse have axons of 2–3 μm diameter. In addition to the main afferent axon, some encapsulated receptors also receive a nonmyelinated nerve supply (Timofeef, 1896), which in electron microscopic preparations is seen to contain several nonmyelinated axons with an as yet undefined function. Each corpuscle is supplied by a single myelinated axon, which may be one of several branches of the stem axon, all supplying similar corpuscles. The myelination of the axon is continued up to or within the capsule, where the nerve forms the terminal characteristic of the given receptor. This terminal arborization represents a physiological specialization of the afferent nerve, since it is the region in which receptor or generator potentials arise. The function of the encasing tissue has been investigated systematically only for the Pacinian corpuscle, where Loewenstein was able to dissect away most of the lamellae without impairing the capacity of the nerve terminal to transduce applied mechanical displacements into nerve impulses, via the intermediary generator potentials. In the Pacinian corpuscles, the lamellae act as high-pass mechanical filters, allowing only the rapid mechanical transients to travel to the core of the receptor. Loewenstein did not succeed in removing all the nonnervous tissue from the decapsulated Pacinian core, and subsequent ultrastructural studies (Quilliam, 1966; Andres, 1969) indicated that the nerve terminal in his experiments was still in contact with adjacent tissue, which may have contributed to the initiation of the generator potential.

3.1.1. The Pacinian Corpuscle

The basic structure of the encapsulated receptors is illustrated by the Pacinian corpuscle (Pacini, 1840), described elsewhere in this volume by Hunt (Chapter 13). The nerve terminal forms the core of the receptor and at the fine-structural level can be seen to have small protrusions of its membrane that may enter clefts in the encapsulating nonnervous tissue, rather than with the closely attached adjacent enveloping cell membranes. It is presumed, though there is no direct evidence, that these processes are actively involved in the transduction of mechanical to electrical energy, via a change in membrane permeability. The axon becomes myelinated within the core of the receptor so that all the nerve fiber outside the encapsulated receptor is myelinated. There is physiological evidence (Diamond *et al.*, 1956) that the impulse is set up in the terminal node of Ranvier, not in the unmyelinated terminal of the axon. The lamellae, which make up the greater part of the receptor, are nonnervous.

3.1.2. The Ruffini Ending

The Ruffini ending (Ruffini, 1894) is very differently organized. The capsule is very thinly lamellated, similar to a perineural sheath, and surrounds a fluid-filled space at the center of which is the receptor core. This is composed of the nerve terminals, of connective tissue, and of cells giving rise to thin membranes that divide the space between the capsule and core into compartments. In cat skin, the receptors are from 0.5 to 2 mm in length and about 150 μm in diameter equatorially tapering to 30 μm at the poles (Chambers *et al.*, 1972). Similar receptors are found in or near diarthrodial joints. The receptors are innervated by myelinated axons, with fibers ranging from 7 to 12 μm, that do not branch unless they are close to the receptors, when a single axon may subdivide to supply several receptors. The fiber may enter the receptor at one pole or at the equator and is myelinated until it enters the receptor core. Distal to the last myelin lamellae is a clublike expansion of axoplasm from which numerous branches up to 200 μm long emerge. These ramify throughout the core of the receptor, to give the typical bushy appearance depicted by Ruffini. The branches are accompanied by endoneural cells and also have direct contact with the collagenous fibrils of the central core. The terminal ramifications of the nerve fiber have, on their surfaces, numerous thornlike processes about 0.2–1.0 μm in diameter, which lack the usual cell organelles and contain thin filaments and vesicles. The collagen fibrils with which these spurs are in contact derive from collagen fibers that in turn are in continuity, via the poles of the receptor, with the connective tissue of the corium (Fig. 1). By this means, the receptor terminals in the core of the receptor can be affected by tension transmitted through the connective tissue of the corium of the skin. No specialized transducer cells, other than the nerve terminal, have been seen in electron microscopic studies of the receptor, so that the neuron itself must function as the mechanoelectric transducer, is as also the case with the Pacinian corpuscle.

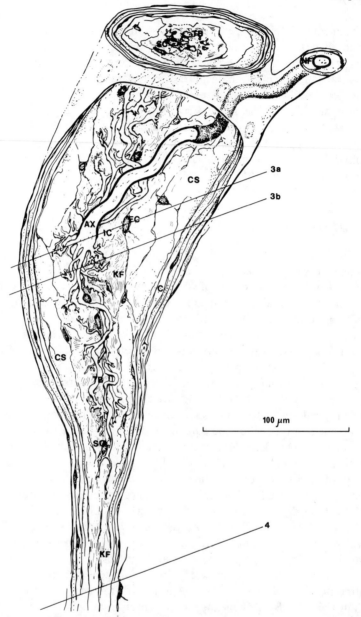

Fig. 1. Structure of a Ruffini ending in cat hairy skin, based on serial semithin and ultra-thin sections. The myelinated nerve fiber enters the middle of the receptor and breaks up into terminal branches and filaments that make contact with collagenous fibrils. A cross-sectional view of the upper part of the receptor shows the intracapsular structure. AX, Axon; C, capsule; CS, endoneural capsule space; EC, endoneural cell; IC, inner core; KF, collagenous fibrils; NF, myelinated nerve fiber; SC Schwann cell; TB, terminal rami-fications of axon. From Chambers *et al.* (1972).

3.1.3. Meissner Corpuscle

Meissner corpuscles (Wagner and Meissner, 1852) are found in the papillary ridges of glabrous skin in primates, also have a thick lamellated capsule, are circular to oval in cross-section, 20–40 μm in diameter, and up to 150 μm long in adult human skin (Cauna, 1966). The internal structure reveals a cross-lamination of flattened laminar cells interleaved with terminal nerve endings (Fig. 2) to form a column. The intercellular substance is distinctive, with a fibrillar structure in which the fine fibrils are arranged in small bundles bound together by dense material. The nonnervous laminar cells contain flattened nuclei and, as is commonly the case in receptors, pinocytotic

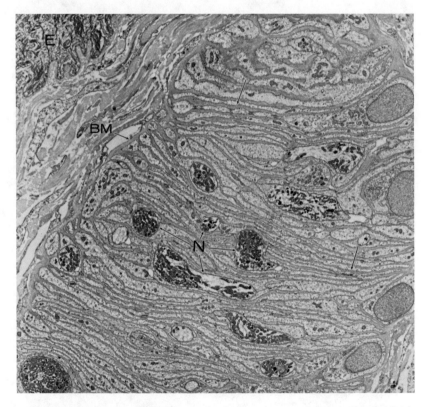

Fig. 2. Fine structure of a Meissner corpuscle from human glabrous digital skin, in a longitudinal section of the superficial part of the corpuscle. The laminar cells (lighter bands) are separated from one another by an intercellular substance (darker bands). The latter exhibits periodic structure in certain planes or orientation (unlabeled arrows). The nerve endings (N), packed with mitochondria, are interleaved with the laminar cells. BM, Basement membrane of the corpuscle continuous with the intercellular substance; E, epidermis. Hairless digital skin, 21-year-old female. ×1320 From Cauna (1966).

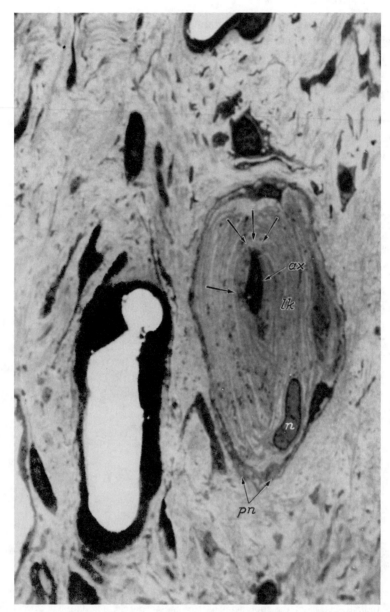

Fig. 3. A Golgi–Mazzoni corpuscle from the inner hair bulge of a cat sinus hair. The axonal ending (ax) is in strong contrast to the nonnervous lamellar cell (lk) and a lamellar-cell nucleus (n). The perineural sheath (pn) surrounds the whole corpuscle. From Andres (1966).

vesicles aligned along the cell membrane. These latter presumably have a nutritive function. The nerve terminals, densely packed with mitochondria, are in close apposition to the laminar cell membranes. They are derived from myelinated fibers that retain their myelination until they are close to the corpuscle. Within the receptor, the nerve fibers are fine until they expand to form the terminals. According to Cauna (1966), several myelinated fibers innervate one Meissner corpuscle, but it is not clear whether they are branches of a single fiber nor whether a single nerve fiber can innervate several corpuscles.

3.1.4. Golgi–Mazzoni Corpuscle

The existence of the Golgi–Mazzoni corpuscle as a morphologically distinct entity has been in doubt, but once again electron microscopy has helped to resolve the problem. The Golgi–Mazzoni corpuscles are in the subcutaneous connective tissue of human fingers (Ruffini, 1905) and originally were considered to be variants of the Pacinian corpuscle. Andres (1966) described Golgi–Mazzoni corpuscles in electron microscopic preparations of facial sinus hairs. The corpuscles have a very simple perineural sheath capsule and numerous Schwann cell lamellae (Fig. 3), but with a much simpler organization than the Pacinian corpuscle. The nerve fiber terminal has an axial location in the corpuscle and a simple cylindrical structure and the usual accumulation of mitochondria. Other authors classify an apparently similar receptor, also with a dermal location, as "simple encapsulated corpuscles" (Polacek, 1966), and the lamellated receptor in the dermis at the base of Eimer's organ may also be a Golgi–Mazzoni receptor.

3.1.5. Krause End Bulb

There is still uncertainty about the Krause end bulb (*Endkolb*, Krause, 1860). Originally, it was reported as occurring most frequently toward the extremities and in the more superficial layers of the dermis. In light microscope preparations, it is evident as an encapsulated swelling (Jänig, 1971) on myelinated nerve fibers. The terminals of the nerve may ramify within the capsule. Jänig (1971) considers the receptors in the dermal papillae of the footpads in nonprimate mammals to be Krause end bulbs and equates the structure with Winkelmann's "mammalian end organ."

3.1.6. Grandry Corpuscle

Grandry corpuscles (Grandry, 1869) are present in the bill of the duck, especially the distal end, and occupy a superficial position in the dermis, often adjacent to Herbst corpuscles (Fig. 4). The spherical corpuscle (30–80 μm

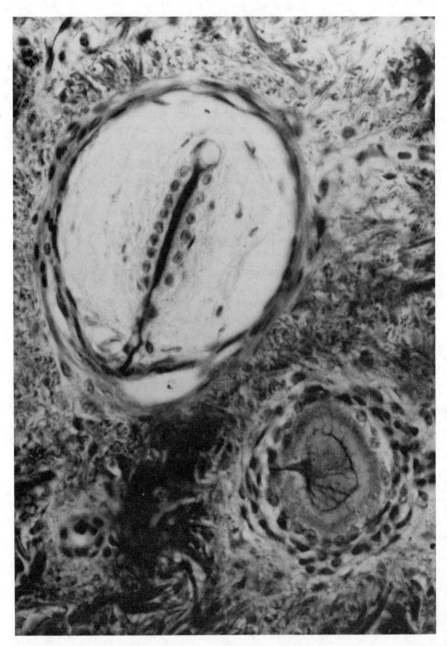

Fig. 4. Herbst corpuscle (upper left) and Grandry corpuscle (lower right) in the skin of the bill of a duck. The Herbst corpuscle has a thick cellular capsule, an outer lamellated core, and an inner core containing the nerve terminal flanked by two rows of nuclei. The Grandry corpuscle has a thick-walled cellular capsule and a fan-shaped nerve terminal disc. This nerve terminal is sandwiched between two large satellite cells (evident as a filamentous and granular groundwork). × 680. From Quilliam (1966).

diameter) has a thick capsule of interdigitating cellular processes. The single large myelinated nerve fiber does not lose its myelin sheath and Schwann cell sheath until it enters the corpuscle. The terminal of the nerve forms a thin disk, 1–3 μm thick and 20–50 μm in diameter, packed with mitochondria. There are signs of structurally specialized connections between the nerve terminal and the pair of nonnervous satellite cells. These latter are large and contain spherical nuclei, mitochondria, and dense osmiophilic granules with membranes. The satellite cells send finger-like or rodlike processes into the capsule and from the base of these, bundles of filaments pass into the satellite cell cytoplasm (Quilliam, 1966). A rather similar structural feature is present in Merkel cells, and it is possible that these specialized satellite cells may have a mechanoelectric transducer function.

3.1.7. Herbst Corpuscle

The Herbst corpuscle (Herbst, 1848) is a lamellated corpuscle (60–100 μm) sometimes confused with the Pacinian corpuscle, although the latter is up to 1000 times larger. It is found in the skin of the bill of wading and aquatic birds and in the palate and tongue of these and other birds, as well as near the feathers and interosseus membranes (a location in which Pacinian corpuscles are found in mammals, see Hunt, Chapter 13).

The lamellation is similar to that of Pacinian corpuscle, with an outer capsule and an inner core containing the axial nerve terminal (Fig. 4). A distinctive and consistent feature is the presence of twin rows of six to ten satellite cells (and their nuclei). The corpuscle is supplied by a single myelinated fiber (up to 20 μm in diameter) which loses its myelin after entry to the corpuscle and forms a single straight terminal (60 μm long).

3.2. Unencapsulated Corpuscular Receptors

There are several sensory structures innervated by myelinated afferent fibers but in which there is no evident encapsulation. These sense organs are associated with epidermis and dermis which is structurally modified. It is a matter of debate whether such specialized organs should be termed "corpuscular." It can also be questioned whether there is any valid reason to regard the distinctive and special innervation of hair as noncorpuscular.

3.2.1. Epithelial Cell–Neurite Complexes

Although epithelial cell–neurite complexes form highly organized receptor structures, they lack an enveloping capsule and so cannot properly be classed as encapsulated receptors. Their name (Munger, 1971) adequately describes them. The Merkel "touch spot" receptor and Eimer's organ are the best-known examples of corpuscular receptors incorporating these complexes.

   3.2.1a. Merkel's Touch Spot. The unit of the Merkel "touch spot" (*Tastfleck*, Merkel, 1880) is the Merkel tactile cell and associated nerve disc (Merkel disc—*Tastmeniscen* or hederiform ending) located in the basal layer of the epidermis on the epidermal side of the basement membrane. These receptors (Fig. 5) were first described by Merkel in 1880 in vertebrate animals and have since then been repeatedly reported. The technical difficulties of fixing and staining neural tissue led to a vigorous controversy regarding both their existence and their structure, and it was not until electron microscopic techniques were used, in association with greatly improved tissue fixation procedures, that the controversy was resolved in favor of Merkel's original description. Cauna (1962) first published an electron micrograph of a Merkel tactile cell, to be followed by Munger (1965), Andres (1966), and others. The

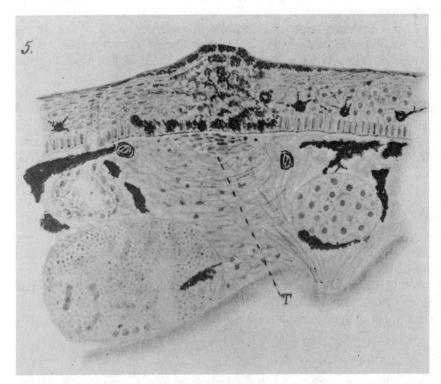

Fig. 5. An original drawing by Merkel of a "touch spot" (*Tastfleck*) in the skin of the leg of the frog. The epidermis is thickened and pigmented in the region overlying the nerve terminals (T), and there is a conspicuous dome. From Merkel (1880).

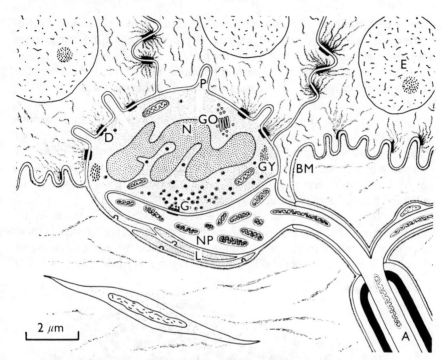

Fig. 6. A diagram showing the detailed structure of a Merkel tactile cell and its associated nerve plate or disc in hairy skin of the cat. A, Myelinated axon; BM, basement
membrane; D, desmosome; E, epithelial cell nucleus; G, granular vesicles in the tactile
cell near its junction with the nerve plate, NP; GO, Golgi apparatus; GY, glycogen;
L, lamellae underlying nerve plate; P, cytoplasmic processes from the tactile cell. From
Iggo and Muir (1969).

essential details of the structure are shown in Fig. 6. The tactile cell is almost
spherical in shape, with its superficial hemisphere embedded in the epidermis
and its lower half bulging out into the dermis. A plate- or disclike expansion
of the nerve invaginates the tactile cell deep to its single, remarkably poly-
lobulated nucleus. There are desmosodal plaques between the superficial
surface of tactile cell and adjacent epidermal cells, but the recognizable fibrils
radiating from them penetrate the tactile cell cytoplasm only a short distance.
Clusters of electron-dense particles with a compound structure—presumably
glycogen granules—are present at the poles of the nucleus. Numerous spherical
granules, consisting of a dense homogeneous core surrounded by a membranous envelope, are concentrated in the cytoplasm between the nucleus
and the nerve plate. Another distinctive feature of the Merkel cell (Andres,
1966; Iggo and Muir, 1969) is the presence on its superficial half of rod- or

finger-like cylindrical (1.5 μm long by 0.3 μm diameter) processes that fill corresponding indentations in the adjacent epidermal cells. Similar processes are present in the Grandry cell. The nerve plate (8–10 μm diameter and 1–3 μm thick) is an expansion of a branch of the afferent nerve fiber and lies parallel to the elongated nucleus of the tactile cell and the skin surface. It contains numerous mitochondria.

A common location for these tactile cells in both hairy and glabrous skin is at the base of the epidermis, which as described below may be thickened (Fig. 7). In glabrous skin, there are rete pegs (projections of the epidermis into the subjacent dermis) in which the Merkel cells may be embedded so as not to lie at the innermost epidermal margin, although the structure of the cells may not otherwise be different (Halata, 1970).

The "touch spots," of which the individual Merkel cells are component units, have been rediscovered and renamed many times since Merkel's (1880) description of them in the frog. Figure 7 shows the basic organization of one of these receptors in hair skin of the cat (Iggo and Muir, 1969). A single

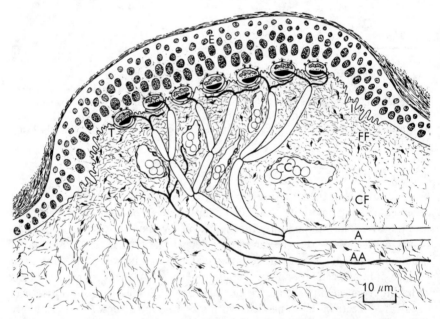

Fig. 7. A diagram of the structure of a Merkel "touch spot" (touch corpuscle) as seen in light microscope sections. A, Single myelinated axon; AA, nonmyelinated axons (accessory fiber of Timofeef); E, thickened epidermis; FF and CF, fine and coarse bundles of collagen fibers; I, extensive indentations of the dermis by the dermis; T, tactile cell and its associated nerve plate or disc (see Fig. 6); C, capillary. From Iggo and Muir (1969).

myelinated fiber (7–12 μm in diameter) approaches the receptor through the dermis and in the dense dermal core of the receptor breaks up into many finer myelinated branches that lose their myelin sheaths about 10 μm from the epidermodermal junction. The "touch spot" in the cat appears as a dome-shaped elevation of the epidermis, 0.1–0.4 mm in diameter, often, though not necessarily, in association with a large hair ("tylotrich," Straile, 1960). There is no encapsulation of the receptor as for the other corpuscular receptors, presumably because of its epidermal location. Instead, the epidermis is thickened (Fig. 7) and the dermal core of the dome contains very fine collagen bundles and a convoluted plexus of capillaries. The basement membrane of the dome shows extensive folding, especially around its perimeter, and these folds may serve to anchor the receptor and insulate the receptor terminals from indirect mechanical stimuli.

3.2.1b. Eimer's Organ. Eimer's organ (Eimer, 1871), a complex epidermal receptor, is found in abundance in the snout of the mole (*Talpa europaea*) and contains at its base Merkel cells and in the subjacent dermis a lightly encapsulated receptor (termed "innominate" by Quilliam, 1966) (Andres, 1969; Halata, 1972). The epidermis in Eimer's organ is greatly thickened and contains nerve terminals (70 μm long by 1 μm diameter) that ascend vertically from the basement membrane toward the stratum spinosum and end with spiny protrusions in the stratum granulosum, within a few microns of the skin surface. As Fig. 8 shows, there is a central terminal surrounded by an array of 20–40 similar filaments, separated by a slender central column of epidermal cells (about 10–15 μm in radius) and surrounded by peripheral cells. The nerve terminals appear to be embedded in the cytoplasmic perimeter of the central columnar cells. Whether all the terminals derive from a single afferent nerve fiber is uncertain. The nerve fibers arise from a plexus in the dermis, and the penetrating fibers lose their Schwann cell sheaths at the basement membrane, with the Schwann cells "fusing" with the epidermal cells. The nerve terminals in the epidermis are invested by the central columnar cells and thus are not "naked" or "free" (Halata, 1972).

3.2.1c. Cold Receptors. The morphology of cold receptors has long excited interest, but it was only by the combination of electrophysiology and electron microscopy that identified cold receptors were found (Andres and Hensel, 1971). The receptor in the cat's nose is an "epithelial cell–neurite complex" of a less distinctive kind than the Merkel cell system. The small myelinated axon approaches the dermoepidermal junction and loses its myelin sheath close to the junction, which it then penetrates to form an interdigitating

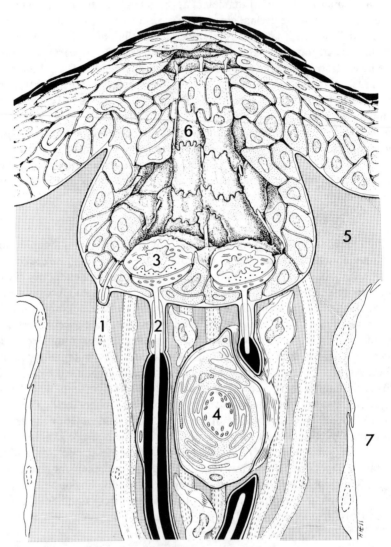

Fig. 8. Semischematic diagram of Eimer's organ from the hairless snout of the mole (*Talpa europaea*). There are several hundreds of these in the skin of the snout. The epidermis is greatly thickened and contains Merkel cells and discs (3) at its base innervated by myelinated axons (2). There are vertically oriented nerve fibers (1) running up to the epidermal surface to end with knoblike thickenings in the stratum spinosum. These nerve fibers penetrate through epidermal cells that form a central pillar (6). Beneath the Eimer's organ is a lamellated corpuscle (4) (equivalent to a Golgi–Mazzoni receptor). The epidermal peg that penetrates the corium is bound to it by a network of collagen (5) surrounded by a capillary (7). From Halata (1972).

bulblike protrusion into the basal epidermal zone. The expansion of the nerve terminal has a clearer appearance in the electron micrograph than the epidermal cells. Fuller details of this receptor are to be published by Hensel (1972).

This list of corpuscular receptors, although comprehensive, is not exhaustive, and reference to the anatomical literature will reveal the true confusion surrounding the subject. In the physiological section of this chapter, an attempt will be made to give the functional significance of many of the receptors described above.

3.3. Noncorpuscular Receptors

3.3.1. Terminals of Nonmyelinated Axons

The terminals of nonmyelinated axons are of interest partly because of the association of nonmyelinated fibers with pain but principally because the nonmyelinated fibers form the great majority of cutaneous afferent fibers. The classical view is that they are "free nerve endings" in both the epidermis and the dermis. Attempts to identify the terminals of nonmyelinated axons in electron micrographs have established the great difficulty of distinguishing the fine nerve tissue from other cellular elements and of recognizing the terminals when present. A recent study by Cauna (1969) showed that the nonmyelinated fibers in the skin of the external ear of the rat branch extensively in the superficial dermis of hairy skin to form a horizontal layer which avoids the regions of the hair follicles and does not extend into the dermal papillae adjacent to hair follicles. An ending, in Cauna's (1969) view, usually consists of several axonal terminals ensheathed by a single Schwann cell and surrounded by basement membrane. Branches of these axons are seen in the dermis, with sheaths derived from the Schwann cell of the bundle of axons (i.e., the terminals are not naked). Other collaterals enter the epidermis, and lose their Schwann cell sheath when they do so. The basement membrane, however, becomes continuous with that of the epidermis. These intraepidermal endings of the nonmyelinated fiber travels toward the stratum corneum of the epidermis in invaginations of epidermal cells, without being exposed directly to the intercellular spaces, so that these endings are not naked (Fig. 9). No specialization of the associated epidermal cells is evident (Cauna, 1969). The cytoplasm of the nerve terminals lacks any conspicuous morphological specialization, containing a few mitochondria but no granules. As will be made clear later in this chapter, the nonmyelinated axons are functionally specialized, but it has not yet proved possible to relate the physiological specificity to any morphological characteristics.

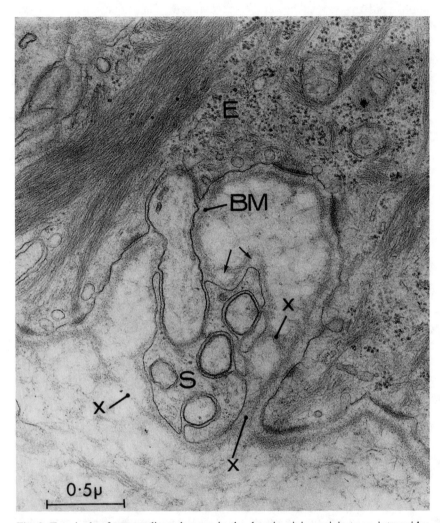

Fig. 9. Terminals of nonmyelinated axons in the dermis, giving origin to an intraepider-mal nerve ending in the rat. S, Schwann sheath containing four nonmyelinated axons, one of which enters the epidermis (E). The basement membrane (BM) of the nerve becomes continuous with that of the epidermis. x, Strands of basement membrane material be-tween the nerve ending and the epidermis. From Cauna (1969).

3.3.2. *Afferent Innervation of Hair Follicles*

The hair follicles provide a different kind of receptor arrangement in which the afferent nerve terminals bear a particular relation to the follicle rather than to the dermis or epidermis. The myelinated afferent nerve fibers which innervate them are distinct and separate from those which innervate other receptors, although the fibers may run in common nerves in the dermal plexuses; i.e., individual afferent fibers innervate only one kind of receptor terminal.

3.3.2a. Pelage Hairs. Several degrees of complexity are found from the simple whorl of endings in the smallest pelage hairs (the down hairs), through the palisade array of terminals oriented longitudinally in the smaller guard hairs and the basketwork arrangement of the larger guard hairs (monotrichs) in which the fine nerve fibers have a radial as well as a longitudinal orientation, to the more complex tylotrich follicle (with conspicuous vascular sinus) and rich nerve supply (Straile, 1960), and finally to the elaborate sinus hair follicles (Andres, 1966) in which the sinus, with a very rich vascular supply, is much larger even than the tylotrich follicle, is firmly encapsulated, and has an abundant myelinated nerve supply which innervates encapsulated corpuscles and epithelial cell–neurite complexes and hair-follicle type lanceolate terminals within the sinus body.

Electron microscopic studies show that the sensory nerve terminals in the follicle, which are derived from myelinated fibers, are elongated, thin (1.0–1.5 μm), mitochondria-rich filaments (Fig. 10). In the fine single hairs of the rat ear (Cauna, 1969) and fine hairs in the face of the mouse (Yamamoto, 1966), they run as a palisade encircling in a crescent the epithelian root sheath of the hair. The abundant mitochondria are large (0.25–0.5 μm in diameter), and other cell inclusions are vesicles (400–800 Å in diameter) and glycogen granules. Each terminal filament is enclosed by Schwann cell processes, with two regularly oriented gaps, one facing the hair and the other the corium. On the hair side, the gap dimension is uniformly about 0.1 μm and the terminal is at this point apposed to the epithelian root sheath.

In hairy skin of the body surface, there is a similar structural arrangement of the nerve terminals. The conspicuous basketwork appearance of the nerve terminals in the large guard hairs and the tylotrichs may result only from a larger number of nerve fibers supplying the follicle with, as a consequence, more circularly arranged fiber branches that still give rise to longitudinally oriented nerve terminals.

3.3.2b. The Sinus Hairs. The sinus hairs, in contrast, have a much more complex nerve supply. At least 100 myelinated axons enter a single sinus hair follicle. The structural homology of sinus and other hair follicles has caused great confusion in the literature, but a recent reappraisal of the evidence (see Gottschaldt *et al.*, 1972) establishes that they are both morphologically and functionally distinct. The sinus hairs include vibrissae and other facial sinus hairs which are present in nonprimate mammals including aquatic species,

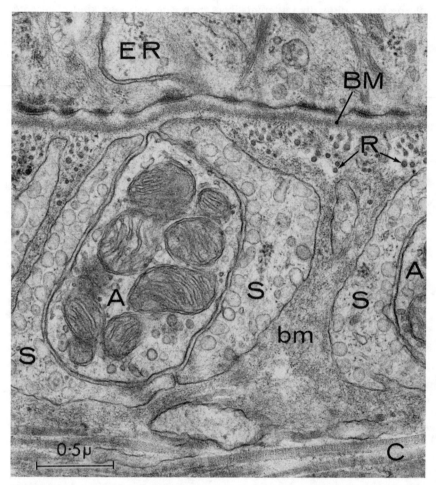

Fig. 10. Electron migrograph of nerve terminal in a hair follicle from the ear of a rat. The fine nerve filaments (A) run parallel to, and encircle, the hair and epithelial root sheath and are therefore termed "palisade endings" (correspond in position to the "straight lanceolate" endings of Fig. 11). They are apposed to the basement membrane (BM) of the epithelial root sheath (ER), with flattened processes of the encasing Schwann cells (S) making contact with the basement membrane on one side. On the opposite side, the Schwann cell processes are in contact with the collagen (C) of the corium. The Schwann cells are embedded in basement membrane material (bm). (R), fine collagen fibers aligned parallel to the long axis of the hair. From Cauna (1969).

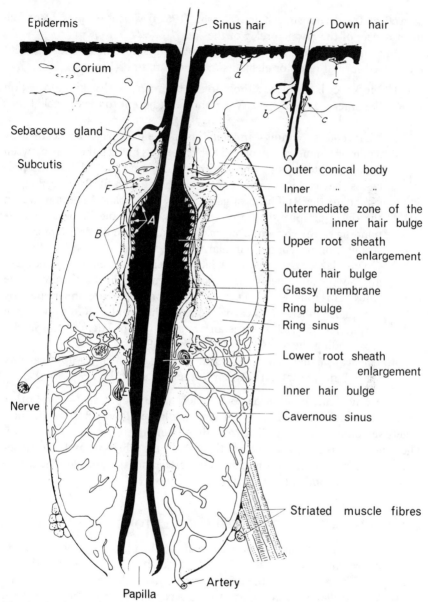

Epidermis   Sinus hair   Down hair

Corium

Sebaceous gland

Subcutis

Outer conical body

Inner   "   "

Intermediate zone of the
                inner hair bulge

Upper root sheath
                enlargement

Outer hair bulge

Glassy membrane

Ring bulge

Ring sinus

Lower root sheath
                enlargement

Inner hair bulge

Cavernous sinus

Nerve

Striated muscle fibres

Papilla   Artery

Fig. 11. Semischematic diagram of a sinus hair from the upper lip of a rat. The nerve terminals are found in several typical places. A, Merkel cells and discs on the epithelial root sheath side of the glassy membrane, in the superior enlargement of the root sheath. B, "straight lanceolate" endings in the corium abutting the opposite side of the glassy membrane. C, "Branched lanceolate" endings in the inferior enlargement of the root sheath. D, "Circular lanceolate" endings in the inner conus. E, Lamellated (Golgi–Mazzoni) corpuscles. F, Free nerve endings. From Andres (1966).

as well as the carpal sinus hairs (Nilsson, 1969a) which are present on the inner aspect of the lower foreleg of the cat.

In a thorough electron microscopic study of sinus hairs, Andres (1966) recognized several receptor elements in the cat and rat (Fig. 11):

1. Merkel cells, similar to those found elsewhere in the skin, located on the inner side of the glassy membrane, adjacent to the epithelial root sheath.

2. "Lanceolate" endings, in which the nerve terminal is ensheathed by a pair of symmetrically placed Schwann cells but at either side between these satellite cells has projections which bear special spurlike processes that make intimate contact with collagen fibrils, in a manner similar to the Ruffini terminals. These "lanceolate" endings are on the outer peripheral side of the glassy membrane in tissue corresponding to the corium of normal skin, and three kinds are present—straight, branched, and circular.

3. Golgi–Mazzoni corpuscles, which are encapsulated and lamellated and lie above or below the lanceolate endings in the corium of the sinus hair follicles in the face. The corpuscles are innervated by myelinated fibers. The carpal hairs do not contain Golgi–Mazzoni corpuscles; instead, there is an accumulation of Pacinian corpuscles surrounding the sinus body (Nilsson, 1969b).

4. Unencapsulated endings, present in the rat, which do not bear any special morphological relation to the hair shaft.

The sinus hair, in addition to this rich nerve supply, has several other structural modifications (Fig. 11). There is a large blood sinus which completely surrounds the hair follicle root, thus insulating it from adjacent tissue. The sinus body is highly motile, particularly in the vibrissae, and this movement results from the insertion of striated muscle into the capsule. The carpal sinus hairs are supplied by smooth muscle.

4. PHYSIOLOGY OF CUTANEOUS RECEPTORS

Various methods have been used to study the physiology of peripheral cutaneous receptor mechanisms. The most direct is to record electrically, from either the receptor or the afferent nerve fiber, the responses to quantitatively controlled stimuli applied to the receptor or skin. There are three major kinds of afferent units—mechanoreceptors, thermoreceptors, and nociceptors—defined according to their "selective sensitivity" as tested by their responses to peripheral stimuli. Alternative terms are "peripheral specificity" and "biophysical specificity." There are no necessary implications for sensory function in this classification, although it would seem most reasonable to assume that mechanoreceptors contribute the primary afferent information in the perception of touch/pressure, etc. Indeed, the organization of spinal pathways and their afferent input provides strong support for this hypothesis.

4.1. Cutaneous Mechanoreceptors

Cutaneous mechanoreceptors respond to touch or mechanical displacement of the skin by stimulators at skin temperature, conditions in which there is no change in the skin temperature, and thus are considered to be responding solely and directly to their physical distortion. Some can also be excited by a change in temperature, but this is a "spurious thermoreceptor" response.

Electrophysiological recording shows that the duration of the discharge of impulses from cutaneous mechanoreceptors in response to a standardized ramp and plateau mechanical displacement depends on the kind of mechanoreceptor. Some receptors lack any discharge in the absence of a stimulus and respond with only one impulse, regardless of ramp velocity or plateau duration. At the other extreme are mechanoreceptors that carry a resting discharge, in the absence of any applied stimulus, which is enhanced by the stimulus, continues throughout the mechanical stimulus, and, after a brief pause, returns to the resting value on withdrawal of the stimulus. Various terms have been used to describe this variety of responses; the earlier was "adaptation," used by Adrian (1928). The short-lasting response was called "rapidly adapting" and the long-lasting one "slowly adapting."

Advances in our knowledge of the physiology of the receptors revealed a deficiency in this classification as it became established that some afferent units respond only during the application of the stimulus, i.e., while the velocity is changing, whereas other units respond both to changing velocity and to static displacement. The terms "velocity detectors" and (steady) "displacement detectors" were therefore introduced (Brown and Iggo, 1967). Because very high velocities of displacement are required to excite some mechanoreceptors (e.g., Pacinian corpuscles), they have been termed "acceleration detectors."

Several factors appear to determine the functional characteristics of a receptor discharge. One is the duration of the generator or receptor potential in response to a standard stimulus. In the lamellated encapsulated mechanoreceptors (e.g., Pacini corpuscle, Herbst corpuscle), the lamellation acts as a high-pass mechanical filter (Loewenstein and Skalak, 1966) and limits the duration of action of the mechanical forces acting on the receptor terminals. The desheathed receptor core, however, is capable of responding for perhaps 10 ms to a square-wave mechanical displacement. Nevertheless, only a single orthodromic impulse is set up at the spike initiation zone of the receptor.

The special characteristics of this zone (Edwards and Ottoson, 1958; Ringham, 1971) may be important in determining, at least in part, the discharge pattern in afferent fibers. Nakajima and Onodera (1969) found that the peripheral sensory neuron of the crayfish stretch receptors, of which there are fast- and slow-adapting types, responds with short and long trains of orthodromic impulses in response to a sustained electrically induced depolarization of the peripherally located cell body. The short as well as the long discharge type can both, however, produce a long-lasting generator potential to a sustained stretch of the muscle. The spike initiation zone is therefore operating to increase the functional differentiation of the otherwise similar (though not identical) receptors. The number of spike initiation sites can influence the afferent discharge in another way—by determining the *pattern* of discharge (Iggo and Muir, 1969; Chambers *et al.*, 1972). Mechanoreceptors with a single site of spike initiation (e.g., SA II) produce a steady stream of spikes with regular intervals, whereas multiple generation sites (e.g., SA I) can lead to an irregular stream of intervals, in which the interval distribution may be semi-Poisson (i.e., interval lengths randomly distributed). The significance of these various patterns for information transfer is not known, and they may arise simply because of the organization of the receptors.

4.1.1. Mechanical Sensitivity

The cutaneous mechanoreceptors are characterized by remarkably high sensitivity to mechanical displacement. In hairy skin, where the epidermis is thin the threshold identation for epidermally located receptors (SA I) is only 1 μm. Similar values have been found for Pacinian corpuscles. The threshold is affected by the location of the receptor, and for the dermal receptors the presence of intervening tissue between deforming stimulus at the skin surface and the receptor may increase the threshold displacement severalfold. There are also wide regional differences, and receptors in the glabrous skin of the face, hands, and feet which are insulated mechanically by the overlying thick epidermis have higher thresholds on average. There is some compensation provided by the much denser innervation of the skin in these tactually important regions, and by the smaller receptive fields of individual afferent fibers. In addition, there may, in hairy skin, be specialization of the hair. Sinus hairs, in contrast to other hairs on the body surface, are found only on the face or inner aspects of the forelegs of many mammals. Individual afferent fibers supply only one hair, each follicle receives many afferent fibers, and, finally, the sinus hairs project further from the body surface than the normal pelage hairs among which they are embedded. All these modifications lead to improved tactual acuity.

The various cutaneous mechanoreceptors may also have functional mechanical insulation—thus the Merkel "touch spot" receptors, although they are in the epidermis just 30–40 μm from the skin surface in hairy skin, are excited easily only by direct contact of the mechanical probe with the slightly elevated dome of the receptor. Adjacent skin is insensitive. This specialization is due to the presence of mechanical insulation or tissue that prevents adjacent or subjacent skin displacement from affecting the transducers. In contrast, the Pacinian corpuscle, although it has a highly developed structure, is sensitive to mechanical vibrations transmitted over long distances through the tissues, especially the bones. The sinus hair Golgi–Mazzoni receptor (functionally similar to the Pacini receptor) responds very rigorously to vibration of the sinus hair but is indifferent to vibration even of adjacent skin. This difference can be attributed to the insulation provided by a large vascular sinus which is typical of the sinus hair follicle and which completely surrounds the receptor structures within it.

In the same way that the cutaneous receptors can be classified according to their morphology, they can also be classified functionally, and, in several instances, the functional units have been identified with morphologically distinct receptors.

4.1.2. Rapidly Adapting Mechanoreceptors (Velocity or Acceleration Detectors)

4.1.2a. Pacinian Corpuscle. The Pacinian corpuscle is a high-frequency detector; it is described in detail in Chapter 13 of this volume.

4.1.2b. High-Frequency Detectors. Other afferent units which are excited only by relatively high-frequency alternation of the mechanical stimulus are found in sinus hairs in mammals and in the skin of birds. They possess a tuning curve with maximum sensitivity at stimulus frequencies between 400 and 800 Hz and are not excited by steadily maintained, nonoscillating pressure. The Golgi–Mazzoni corpuscle in the sinus hair follicle is probably the transducer for high-frequency mechanical oscillations (Gottschaldt *et al.*, 1972). The vibration-sensitive receptors in periosteal tissue of the jaw identified as "Golgi–Mazzoni receptors" by Sakada and Aida (1971) also respond to vibratory mechanical stimulators and to vibration of masticatory muscles, teeth, and jaws.

In birds, a rapidly adapting or velocity detector response can be recorded from nerves supplying the hindlimbs, the feathers, and the bill. The maximum sensitivity to mechanical stimulation is at frequencies of 400–800 Hz when the threshold displacement is less than 1 μm (Dorward, 1970; Dorward and McIntyre, 1971). These units are readily excited by tapping the leg, wings, or bill of the bird, and the receptors have been identified as Herbst corpuscles.

The general principle that emerges from the above results is that lamellated receptors are vibration detectors. The lamellation does not have a protective function; it acts as a filter for low-frequency mechanical displacements enabling the receptors to respond only to high-frequency stimuli.

4.1.2c. Hair Follicle Receptors. Movement of the hairs on the body surface is an effective stimulus for the discharge of impulses in cutaneous afferent fibers. The hairs can be classified into several kinds, and the following account is limited to hairs on the body and limb surfaces, excluding the specialized tactile hairs ("sinus hairs") which will be considered later.

The rapidly adapting hair follicle afferent units are excited only by moving stimulators; i.e., they are "phasic" or "velocity detectors." The general general response, under strictly controlled conditions, is for a discharge of impulses to occur only during the movement of a single hair or a group of hairs (Fig. 12). The interspike interval during movement of a hair is related to the velocity (Brown and Iggo, 1967) and appears to be fairly uniform for any given velocity over limited angles of deflection. The discharge frequency can theoretically, therefore, provide unambiguous information about move-

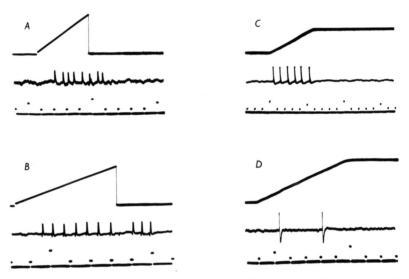

Fig. 12. Discharge in rapidly adapting hair follicle afferent units in the cat, evoked by moving single hairs and recorded from the saphenous nerve. In each record, the upper trace shows the movement of the hair and the lower trace the discharge in a single fiber. There is a discharge only during constant velocity movement of the hair, and in A and B an off-discharge (two spikes in A, three in B). Time marks at 1-ms intervals in all records. The kinds of afferent unit are (A) type D, (B) type T, (C) type G_2 (D) type G_1. From Brown and Iggo (1967).

ment velocity. However, it is unlikely, in the normal course of events for hair to be moved with the necessary precision, and a second factor to be considered is the receptive field for individual afferent fibers supplying hair follicles. Normally the receptive field is large, involving at least several hairs and maybe several hundred. The discharge in the afferent fiber can therefore arise from many places in the receptive field and will be affected by interaction between impulses initiated at several points in the field by a moving stimulus. Individual follicles, in addition, are innervated by many afferent fibers, with receptive fields that are not necessarily coincident. The receptive fields are usually much larger on the trunk and proximal limbs than they are at the extremities or in the face. The latter is, however, a special case since in many species there is a very dense afferent innervation of the perioral skin of the face.

Recent detailed electrophysiological studies on the hair follicle afferent units have led to a system of classification based partly on hair follicle structure and partly on the functional characteristics of the afferent units (Brown and Iggo, 1967). Three major categories and several minor subdivisions are at present formed: type T, type G (G_1 plus G_2), and type D. In all cases, the afferent fibers are myelinated.

The normal pelage hairs of the cat and rabbit can be classed into three groups:

1. The least common hairs (1–2%) have a symmetrical follicle, are circular, and contain a central medulla. When associated with a vascular sinus, they have been termed "tylotrichs" (Straile, 1960). Each of these large, long hairs emerges singly from a follicle.
2. The second and more common hairs (12%) are the "guard hairs" that emerge singly or in pairs from follicles, are long, straight, or slightly curved, and form the overhair or top hair. In the cat, their diameters range from 45 to 110 μm (mean 78).
3. The third type of hair, the "down hairs" (underhair, wool), are thin (32 μm diameter), short, and wavy and form the undercoat in the cat and rabbit. They are the most numerous (86%).

The diversity of hair in the mammals, induced by natural and artificial selection, presents many problems when a classification of hairs is attempted, and the system above is that used for the purpose of physiological classification of the afferent fibers. There are numerous alternatives (see, e.g., Straile and Mann, 1972).

In the following classification of afferent units, the following factors are taken into account: (1) kind of hair follicle (down, guard, or tylotrich), (2) size and kind of the receptive field, (3) mechanical sensitivity of the afferent unit, and (4) diameter of the afferent fiber.

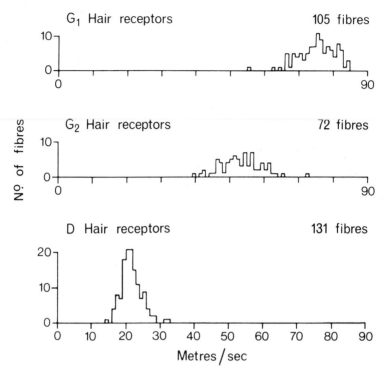

Fig. 13, Conduction velocities of type G_1, G_2, and D hair unit afferent fibers in the cat. The G_1 and G_2 are in the Aα range and D is in the Aδ range. From Burgess *et al.* (1968).

Type G Units: Type G units are excited when individual guard hairs are deflected (Fig. 12) in any direction from the normal resting position but not by movement of down hairs (Brown and Iggo, 1967). A high-frequency burst of impulses can be evoked by brushing the fur. Such a stimulus will excite the hairs both while they are being deflected and when they spring back to their resting position, at which they may also show a damped oscillation. The stimulus situation is therefore complex. The receptive fields are large, especially on the proximal parts of the limbs and on the trunk, and may range from 0.5 to 6.00 cm² in the cat. Within such large fields, there may be 500 guard hairs, although only a limited number may be innervated by a single afferent fiber. The mechanical thresholds, tested as in Fig. 12, are not uniform within the group. Two distinct subsets can be recognized—G_1, with high critical slopes and a low-frequency discharge (these units may respond only when the hair is released after it has been deflected), and G_2, with low critical slopes which typically discharge a stream of impulses during displacement of a hair (Fig. 12C). Burgess *et al.* (1968) recognize an intermediate guard hair unit, with critical slopes that lie between those for G_1 and G_2. The afferent fibers for type G are myelinated, with mean conduction velocities of 54.3 m/s in the cat and 28.9 m/s in the rabbit (Brown and Iggo, 1967), corresponding to the Aα group or group II (6–12 μm) of the Lloyd system. Burgess *et al* (1968) separated the G_1 and G_2 into two groups; G_1 had the faster-conducting axons, 75 m/s compared with 53 m/s for G_2 (Fig. 13).

Type T Units: Type T afferent units respond in a manner similar to type G but differ from them in that the hair follicles involved are the tylotrichs. In the rabbit, in which the tylotrichs are more conspicuous than in the cat, receptive fields vary from 0.25 to 6.00 cm² area, but only very few tylotrichs are involved for any given afferent unit (2–7, mean 4.7). This small number of hairs innervated by individual afferent fibers is a distinctive feature of the organization of the type T units. Because each follicle receives multiple innervation, any individual follicle can be a component of several overlapping receptive fields.

Type T units are velocity detectors and do not respond during steady fixed displacement of a hair. Some units have very low critical slopes, whereas others are high (Brown and Iggo, 1967), and, as with type G, there may be two subsets (T_1 and T_2).

The nerve fibers are myelinated, with relatively high conduction velocities (mean 68.2 m/s in cat and 35.6 m/s in rabbit), and the axons are significantly larger than for type G units (Table I).

Type D Units: Movement of individual down hairs or small clusters of down hairs does not excite G or T units, but can excite very sensitive mechano-receptors (Fig. 12A). Individual receptive fields range from 0.5 to 6.5 cm² in cat and rabbit, and carefully controlled movement of any down hairs in the field appears to be effective, as also is movement of guard hairs. Because of this ready excitation by down hair movements, the units were called "type D" by Brown and Iggo (1967). The critical slopes are low (less than 1 μm/ms) and mechanical sensitivity high, so that lightly resting a hand-held stimulus probe among the hairs is sufficient to set up an irregular discharge of impulses. Type D units can also discharge in synchrony with the arterial pulse because of their high sensitivity. A stream of air directed across the receptive field is a particularly effective stimulus.

The afferent fibers are myelinated, with mean conduction velocities of 17.9 m/s and 9.0 m/s in the cat and rabbit. Similar units in the monkey have a mean velocity of 14 m/s. In each case, this velocity is in the Aδ range and very few of the axons overlap the type G units (Fig. 13). These type D units are therefore a homogeneous and distinctive group. They comprise the majority of the δ fibers in the saphenous nerve of cat and rabbit (about 80%, Brown and Iggo, 1967) and the remainder innervate nociceptors (Burgess and Perl, 1967). In the primate, although the δ fibers also innervate type D units

Table I. Number and Percentage of Cutaneous Afferent Units with Myelinated Axons in the Saphenous Nerve of Cat and Rabbit and the Conduction Velocities of the Axons^a

Type of unit	Location of receptor	Number of units		Conduction velocities (m/s)			
				Cat		Rabbit	
		Cat	Rabbit	Range	Mean ± SE	Range	Mean ± SE
Rapidly adapting							
Hair follicle Type D	Down hair follicles	90 (18.0%)	91 (33.6%)	15–24	17.9 ± 0.23	5–16	9.0 ± 0.2
Hair follicle Type G	Guard hair follicles	207 (41.2%)	45 (16.6%)	18–93	54.3 ± 0.88	7–52	28.9 ± 14.4
Hair follicle Type T	Tylotrich follicles	25 (5.0%)	42 (15.5%)	44–72	68.0 ± 2.72	8–53	35.6 ± 17.0
Slowly adapting							
Type I (touch corpuscle)	Epidermis	113 (22.6%)	77 (28.4%)	33–95	57.2 ± 0.99	16–96	47.3 ± 1.77
Type II	Dermis	43 (8.6%)	9 (3.3%)	20–100	53.6 ± 2.21	24–45	31.4 ± 2.40
Unclassified (including nociceptors)		23 (4.6%)	7 (2.6%)				
Total		501 (100%)	271 (100%)				

^{a} Type T units in the cat have conduction velocities significantly higher than types G, I, and II ($P < 0.001$). Type D units have significantly slower axons ($P < 0.001$) than all other types. Type I units in the rabbit have conduction velocities significantly higher ($P < 0.001$) than the next fastest group (type T), and the type T are significantly faster ($P < 0.005$) than type G.

and nociceptors, there is in addition a slow δ group that innervates thermo-receptors and nociceptors.

4.1.2d. Field Receptors. Units reported by Burgess *et al.* (1968) with afferent fibers in the sural nerve of the cat could be excited by rapid move-ments of the hair or skin, and were commonest in the hairy skin of the foot and toepad. They were classified separately from the G units because of their relative insensitivity to movement of the hair tips, even though they were otherwise similar, in conduction velocity, receptive field organization, and critical slopes. Some were reported to adapt more slowly than type G units.

4.1.3. Slowly Adapting Mechanoreceptors (Displacement Detectors)
Slowly adapting mechanoreceptors are the other major group of mam-malian cutaneous mechanoreceptors, in which the characteristic response is a discharge of impulses during both the dynamic and static phases of mechani-cal stimulation of the skin (Fig. 14). They are found in most regions of the body, and their responses may be influenced by the tissues in which they are

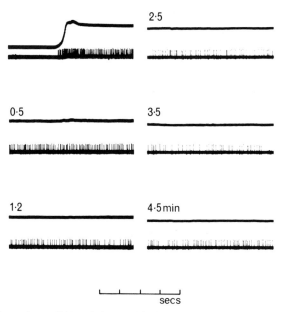

Fig. 14. Discharge in an SAI unit in cat skin in response to the application and main-tenance of steady indentation of the skin. The records were taken at the time indicated (in minutes). There are both a dynamic and a static response, and the discharge displays both adaptation and the characteristic irregularity of interspike intervals. From Iggo (1963*a*).

Table II. Comparison of the Properties of Slowly Adapting Type I and Type II Cutaneous Mechanoreceptors

Similarities

1. Slowly adapting. The discharge to maintained mechanical stimulus lasts for several minutes, at least.
2. Respond to vertical displacement of the skin—with dynamic and static components.
3. The dynamic response has both velocity and displacement components.
4. Found in cat, rabbit (Tapper, 1965; Brown and Iggo, 1967; Burgess *et al.*, 1968), and monkey (Iggo, 1963*b*; Perl, 1968; Harrington and Merzenich, 1970), and units with similar properties exist in man (Boman and Hensel, 1960; Vallbo and Hagbarth, 1968; Knibestöl and Vallbo, 1970).
5. Innervated by myelinated axons, conduction velocities ranging from 20 to 100 m/s (mean 57 and 54 in cat, 47 and 31 in rabbit, Brown and Iggo, 1967).

Differences

SAI	SAII
1. Irregular discharges to maintained stimulus. Coefficient of variation > 0.50.	1. Regular discharge to maintained stimulus. Coefficient of variation < 0.30.
2. Does not respond to stretching, unless severe and prolonged[a].	2. Responds readily to stretching of the skin.
3. Capable of high-frequency discharge to all effective stimuli. Smallest ISI < 1.0 ms (> 1000 Hz).	3. Generally low-frequency response to all effective stimuli. Smallest ISI 1.3 ms (800 Hz).
4. Resting discharge unusual.	4. Usually has a resting discharge.
5. Distinct dome on surface of the skin (cat).	5. No evident surface feature.
6. From 1 to 5 receptors per axon. These may be scattered over an area of 25 cm².	6. One receptor per axon.
7. Receptor terminals are Merkel discs associated with Merkel cells.	7. Receptor is Ruffini ending.

[a] SAI units in the skin covering the dorsum of the hand in monkey (Iggo and Ogawa. 1971) are more readily excited by stretching the skin than those described previously.

located. In particular, the response in glabrous skin may be abbreviated by the mechanical properties of the thickened, cornified epidermis.

As Table II indicates, in hairy skin there are two kinds of slowly adapting mechanoreceptors, types I and II (SAI and SAII) (see Iggo and Muir, 1969; Chambers *et al.*, 1972, for details).

4.1.3a. Slowly Adapting Type I (SAI) Mechanoreceptors. In the cat, small domelike elevations of the hairy skin are innervated by large myelinated afferent fibers. When a mechanical probe touches the surface of such a dome and remains in contact with it, a stream of impulses is conducted centrally along the afferent fiber. Contact with adjacent skin is usually ineffective, as also is stretching of the skin.

The spotlike receptive fields have been known for some time (Franken-haeuser, 1949; Maruhashi *et al.*, 1952), and in later work their association with the domes was established (Iggo, 1963*a*). The first morphological description of the domes was given by Merkel (1880) in frog skin, who called them "touch spots" (*Tastflecken*), although at that time he had no positive means of establishing their excitation by touch. Subsequently these structures and their component Merkel cells have been reported many times in various species from frog to man and given a bewildering variety of names (e.g., *Haarscheibe*, Pinkus, 1904; "tactile pad," Tapper, 1965; "touch corpuscle," Iggo, 1963*a*). The organized receptor together with its afferent neuron forms an afferent unit, and it is this entity which is an SAI unit. Similar afferent units have been reported in rat, rabbit, monkey, baboon, man, and reptiles. In mammals, they are often, though not necessarily, associated with distinctive hairs (tylotrichs).

The SAI unit rarely carries a resting discharge in the absence of a maintained stimulus. The threshold for a response is a mechanical displacement of as little as 1 μm, and the discharge continues for at least several minutes when suprathreshold stimuli are used. The "static" component of the afferent discharge is strictly related to the size of the mechanical displacement by a power function relationship ($R = KS^n$) Werner and Mountcastle, 1965; Tapper, 1965). The receptors also respond to the dynamic component of the stimulus, but, unlike the rapidly adapting units, the response has both a velocity and an amplitude component (Iggo and Muir, 1969) so that during a given constant velocity displacement, the interspike interval decreases progressively, in contrast to the hair follicle units in which it remains more or less constant. The discharge continues when the given amplitude of discharge is reached, but the frequency declines; i.e., the unit adapts (Fig. 14). The rate of adaptation is not uniform and can be described accurately by an expression containing three time constants. Under constant displacement, the units may eventually adapt to silence, but the total time during which a discharge is present varies from tens of seconds to minutes and depends partly on the intensity of mechanical indentation.

Discharge Pattern: A very characteristic, and indeed diagnostic, feature of the SAI units is that the interspike intervals are quite variable in their lengths, even early in the phase of adaptation, but particularly when the frequency has declined after adaptation. The interval distribution in an interspike interval histogram containing several hundred intervals (Fig. 15A), is Poisson with a dead time, implying that, apart from a refractory period effect which limits the number of short intervals, there is a random distribution of interspike intervals. This pattern of discharge has been attributed to the presence of multiple spike generation sites in the receptors, which contain 50–100 individual Merkel cells and discs (Iggo and Muir, 1969).

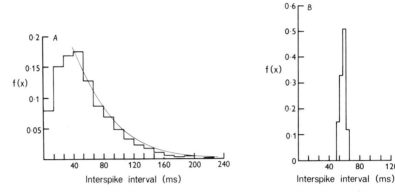

Fig. 15. (A) Frequency distribution of interspike intervals for the adapted discharge of an SAI unit, for 1460 intervals. The theoretical curve for Poisson distribution, $f(x) = \rho e^{-\rho x}$, is drawn as a continuous line. Coefficient of variation, 0.63. (B) Distribution of intervals for the adapted discharge of an SAII unit, with a mean frequency similar to the SAI in A. The coefficient of variation for this Gaussian distribution was 0.05. From Iggo and Muir (1969).

Temperature Sensitivity: The SAI units can be excited to discharge impulses, or an existing discharge can be modified, by altering skin temperatures (Hunt and McIntyre, 1960a; Iggo and Muir, 1969). Temperatures above about 45°C and below 15°C suppress the response to mechanical stimulation. The maximum discharge at given constant skin temperatures occurs in the range 30–40°C. A consistent feature is the initiation of a discharge when the skin is cooled quickly. These thermal responses can be misleading, and the units have been termed "spurious thermoreceptors" (Iggo, 1969). The afferent fibers project centrally into mechanoreceptive tracts.

4.1.3b. Slowly Adapting Type II (SAII) Mechanoreceptors. The other main type of slowly adapting cutaneous mechanoreceptor is less well known and has only recently been identified with certainty as a distinctive unit, to which the name "slowly adapting type II mechanoreceptor" (SAII) has been given (Iggo, 1966; Chambers *et al.*, 1972). Each SAII unit can be excited at threshold from a single spot on the skin, but, in contrast to the SAI, they often carry a resting discharge and are easily excited by stretching the skin. The sensitive skin spot, again in contrast to the SAI, has no distinctive surface feature by which it can be recognized. This has increased the difficulty of identifying the morphological substrate of the unit, but recent work (Chambers *et al.*, 1972) indicates that it is the Ruffini ending which is situated intradermally. The SAII units have now been found in cat, rabbit, monkey (Iggo, 1963b; Harrington and Merzenich, 1970), baboon, man

(Knibestöl and Vallbo, 1970), and reptiles (Kenton *et al.*, 1971) as have the SAI, and appear to be a general feature of hairy and, probably, glabrous skin.

Resting Discharge: The SAII units in cat hairy skin often carry a resting discharge. The interspike intervals are remarkably uniform in length, with a small coefficient of variation (Chambers *et al.*, 1972). This resting discharge can be altered by vertical indentation of the skin near the receptor, by stretching the skin, and, to a lesser extent, by altering skin temperature.

Mechanical Stimulation: When the skin is indented at constant velocity, the frequency of discharge increases smoothly from the resting value. The interspike intervals are related to both velocity and amplitude of indentation, and the relation between stimulus and response can be described equally well by a power function or an exponential function. The discharge declines (adapts) when a given indentation is maintained, and, as with the SAI, the rate of decline in discharge frequency can be described by an expression containing at least three time constants. The static discharge after adaptation, in contrast to the SAI, can be sustained at a nearly constant frequency for hours, by which time it has become effectively nonadapting (Fig. 16).

Discharge Pattern: The interspike intervals in the SAII discharge are uniform in length, under static conditions. The interval distribution of the adapted discharge is Gaussian (normal), in sharp contrast to the Poisson distribution of SAI intervals. This difference in pattern can be used as an aid to the identification of the slowly adapting mechanoreceptors, in the first-order fibers (Fig. 15B). The origin of the differences is probably the morphology of the receptors. In the SAII receptor (Ruffini ending), there is probably a single spike initiation zone that integrates the generator currents from all of the receptor terminals, which under static conditions would be expected to have a relatively constant mean amplitude. The SAI receptor (Merkel touch spot), on the other hand, has 50–100 individual nerve terminals each borne on a branch of the myelinated afferent fiber so that there is the possibility of many spike initiation sites, which if they acted independently would generate a Poisson spike interval distribution (Chambers *et al.*, 1972).

Thermal Sensitivity: The SAII, like the SAI, are excited by a fall in skin temperature and temporarily depressed by a rise. The adapted discharge also exhibits a temperature dependence. Because of their resting discharge, this temperature dependence is more conspicuous in the SAII than in the SAI.

4.1.4. Receptors in Glabrous Skin

Glabrous or hairless skin is found on the volar aspect of the feet of mammals, the extent varying from the footpads of carnivores to the whole plantar surface of the feet and hands in primates. The face is the other major

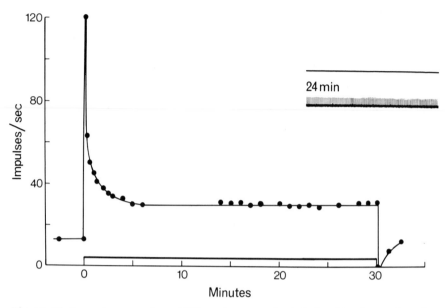

Fig. 16. Discharge frequency in an SAII mechanoreceptor in hairy skin of a monkey. A steady indentation of the skin was applied to the skin at zero time and removed 30 min later. After a period of adaptation lasting about 5 min, there was a continuous adapted discharge. After removal of the stimulus (indicated by bar at bottom of graph), there was a silent period followed by a progressive recovery of the original resting discharge. From Iggo (1963b).

region where glabrous skin is present, and again there principally the snout and perioral regions. Glabrous skin has a highly organized and densely packed afferent nerve supply, which hinders the ready identification of the receptors for individual afferent units.

4.1.4a. Rapidly Adapting Glabrous Units. A typical response of rapidly adapting glabrous units is the discharge of a burst of impulses when a smooth mechanical probe is drawn across the ridged skin and no discharge to a fixed steady indentation of glabrous skin of the monkey hand (Iggo, 1963b). The receptive fields are about 10 mm^2 in the palm and 3.7 mm^2 on the distal phalanx (Talbot *et al.*, 1968), thus covering several ridges. The receptors are probably Meissner corpuscles, and the afferent fibers are 5–12 μm in diameter. In response to sinusoidal stimulation, maximal sensitivity is at 30–40 Hz, in contrast to Pacinian corpuscles for which maximum sensitivity is at 200–300 Hz. Most units respond only to sudden indentation of the skin, but some, like some type T and G units, give a continuous discharge at low velocities of indentation.

Human glabrous skin contains similar rapidly adapting units (Knibestöl and Vallbo, 1970). Critical slopes are 0.1–9.0 newton/s, and the receptive fields (10–620 mm^2) are larger than in the monkey hand.

In the nonprimate animals, the glabrous skin of the footpad contains rapidly adapting endings (Jänig, 1971) innervated by fast-conducting axons (55 m/s) and responding only to moving stimuli. The region of minimal thresholds extends over several ridges, and according to Jänig, the receptors are the encapsulated endings homologous with Krause end bulbs (Winkelmann's "mammalian end organ") present in the dermal papillae of the upper dermis.

The other kind of rapidly adapting response from the footpads follows high frequencies in the manner typical of Pacinian corpuscles, which are present in the subcutaneous tissue. Pacinian corpuscles are also present deep to the glabrous skin in man and there too exhibit the same high-frequency sensitivity (Knibestöl and Vallbo, 1970).

4.1.4b. Slowly Adapting Glabrous Units. The slowly adapting afferent units in glabrous skin differ from those in hairy skin by their lower average sensitivity to mechanical stimulation and the shorter duration of discharge of some of them to a sustained indentation of the skin. These differences are at least partly due to the thick epidermis of glabrous skin. The kinds of glabrous skin slowly adapting mechanoreceptors should be considered in the light of the results from hairy skin, which have established two distinct types, and Knibestöl and Vallbo's (1970) analysis of human cutaneous mechanoreceptors in glabrous skin. The characteristic differences in discharge pattern of the SAI and SAII as well as the receptive field properties and presence or absence of resting discharge are all helpful indices. A reassessment of published data leads to the conclusion that glabrous slowly adapting units are also present in two basic types.

Glabrous SAI Mechanoreceptors: Glabrous SAI mechanoreceptors form the majority. They do not carry a resting discharge, are not excited by stretching the skin, have a high dynamic sensitivity, and give a discharge (with irregular interspike intervals) that is sustained for many seconds in man, monkey, and footpad of the cat (these last units often carry a low-frequency resting discharge of less than 1/s, Jänig *et al.*, 1968). The afferent fibers are myelinated (greater than 6 μm in diameter). When interspike interval histograms are generated, they are Poisson or semi-Poisson. The receptors are probably Merkel receptors which are present at the base of the epidermis or in epidermal pegs in all glabrous skin studied (Miller *et al.*, 1958; Mountcastle *et al.*, 1969; Jänig, 1971; Halata, 1970). Strong support for this view comes from the characteristics of the SAI in hairy skin and their established termination in Merkel touch spots.

Glabrous SAII Mechanoreceptors: Glabrous SAII mechanoreceptors are a much less common type of mechanoreceptor, to judge from published reports, not all of which attempted to distinguish the two classes of slowly adapting units. These units often carry a resting discharge, with regular interspike intervals, are excited both by indentation and stretching of the skin (Knibestöl and Vallbo, 1970), have large myelinated fibers, give a very well sustained discharge on constant indentation of the skin, and have directional sensitivity of skin stretch. The receptive fields extend over several epidermal ridges, in contrast to the glabrous SAI, which may exhibit maximal sensitivity on a single surface ridge (probably overlying the intermediate epidermal papilla, or rete peg, containing Merkel cells below). Ruffini endings in glabrous skin are located in the dermis (Ruffini, 1894) and so will have a less localized point of maximal sensitivity on the surface (the tactile field of Iggo, 1963*b*).

4.1.5. Cutaneous Mechanoreceptors with Nonmyelinated Afferent Fibers

The majority (about 50%) of cutaneous nonmyelinated afferent fibers supplying hairy skin end peripherally in sensitive mechanoreceptors (Iggo, 1960; Bessou *et al.*, 1971).

The receptive fields in hairy skin are small, typically oval, 2.3 by 1–2 mm. Within such a field, the mechanical sensitivity is fairly uniform. A mechanical indentation of the skin will cause a dynamic and a static discharge (Fig. 17), in the cat linearly proportional to skin indentation (Iggo and Kornhuber, 1968). The discharge is highly sensitive to the rate at which the mechanical stimulus is applied, and at low intensities there is summation within the receptive field so that a weak ineffective stimulus at one point may cause a discharge if the same indentation is applied over a larger area (Iggo and Kornhuber, 1968). Such a response indicates summation of depolarization within the terminal arborization of the single afferent unit and presumably

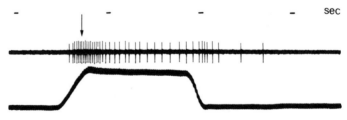

Fig. 17. The response of a C-mechanoreceptor to indentation of the hairy skin in the cat with a probe (tip diameter 0.25 mm). The lower trace indicates the force applied and the upper trace the discharge in a single C-mechanoreceptor unit. From Iggo (1960).

accounts for the greater efficacy of a slowly moving mechanical stimulus reported by Bessou *et al.* (1971).

The discharge evoked by a mechanical stimulus persists beyond the end of the "dynamic" component of the movement and can continue to decline with a time constant of 20–30 s during steady maintenance of the stimulus. The discharge does, however, eventually disappear, in contrast to the SAI and SAII mechanoreceptors in hairy skin in which the discharge will continue for many minutes. The C-mechanoreceptors thus fail to respond to long-continued steady indentation, although in appropriate circumstances they can give an accurate transform of stimulus intensity (Fig. 18).

The C-mechanoreceptors, unlike mechanoreceptors with myelinated fibers, are markedly affected by repeated mechanical or thermal stimulation. Skin that has been untouched for 30 min generates a vigorous discharge in C-mechanoreceptors when the hair is stroked, whereas after vigorous stroking of the skin for, say, 20 s, the receptors may become totally unresponsive (Iggo, 1960). Recovery from such unresponsive receptors may take 8 min, and normally a consistent response is obtained if intervals of 3–4 min are allowed between stimuli (Iggo, 1960; Iggo and Kornhuber, 1968; Bessou *et al.*, 1971; Hahn, 1971). This reduced responsiveness is restricted to the activated part of the receptive field. It does not affect adjacent regions, from which a normal mechanically evoked response can still be obtained. The unresponsiveness is apparently restricted to the active nerve terminals since C axons in peripheral nerves can carry impulses to rates up to 300/s without evident fatigue, compared with maximal rates of 100/s in response to natural stimulation (Franz and Iggo, 1968), and the unconditioned parts of the receptive field can still evoke an afferent discharge.

The sensitive C-mechanoreceptors can be excited by a fall (but not a rise) in skin temperature, provided it is sufficiently rapid, and in this respect are similar to slowly adapting myelinated mechanoreceptors (Iggo, 1960). There is an interaction between the mechanical and thermal stimuli, which Hahn (1971) has examined in detail. He compared the effect of decreased responsiveness to mechanical test following a thermal stimulus (and *vice versa*) to test for the interaction and found by this method that although cross-depression occurred it was less than that following conditioning by the same modality.

4.1.5a. Afterdischarge. A characteristic feature of the sensitive C-mechanoreceptors (Zotterman, 1939; Iggo, 1966; Bessou *et al.*, 1971) is that the nervous discharge may continue at a low frequency for several seconds after a stroke of the skin. It is not conspicuous after the skin has been indented by a small probe (Fig. 19), although it can still occur (Iggo, 1960), nor is it elicitable during the period of reduced excitability following vigorous

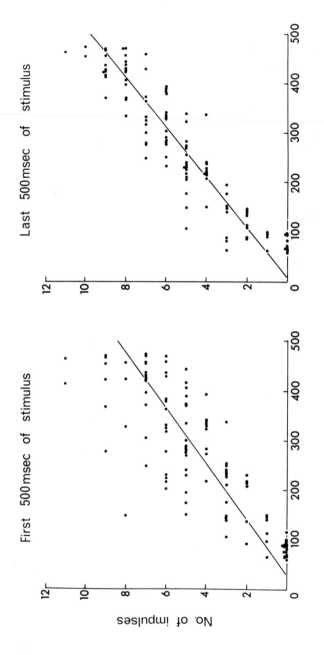

Fig. 18. The stimulus–response curve for a single C-mechanoreceptor in hairy skin to indentation with a time course similar to that in Fig. 17, using a random intensity series. Courtesy of H. H. Kornhuber and A. Iggo.

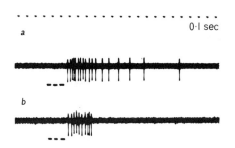

Fig. 19. The "afterdischarge" of a C-mechanoreceptor in cat hairy skin, in response (a) to a brief stroke of the skin and (b) to brief vertical indentation of the skin with a small probe. The dashed lines indicate the duration of the stimulus. After allowing for conduction delay in the afferent fiber, the response in (b) lasts for a time equal to the actual stimulus, whereas in (a) it long outlasts the stimulus. From Iggo (1960).

natural activation of a receptor. This "afterdischarge" is not an "off-discharge." With a ramp–plateau–ramp mechanical stimulus, there is a discharge during both directions of movement and, of even greater interest, a discharge during the slow removal of a probe which has been left on the skin for some minutes (during which time the static response has adapted to silence). The C-mechanoreceptors are thus bidirectional in response, in contrast to SAI and SAII receptors, and part of the "afterdischarge" may arise from excitation of the nerve terminals when the skin is returning to its original position. Microscopic observation of the skin has shown that the C-mechanoreceptor "afterdischarge" following a stroke of the skin occurs at the same time as small restorative movements of the skin.

4.1.5b. C-Mechanoreceptors in Glabrous Skin. None of the investigations of C-mechanoreceptors reports their presence in any numbers in glabrous skin, in cat or monkey.

4.1.6. Sinus Hairs

The sinus hair follicles are very richly innervated, and there have been several electrophysiological studies that establish their differences from ordinary pelage hairs (Fitzgerald, 1940; Zucker and Welker, 1969; Gottschaldt et al., 1972). There are four kinds of afferent units, with myelinated afferent fibers, supplying the facial sinus hairs (including vibrissae of the cat); two are slowly adapting and two are rapidly adapting. The slowly adapting units have characteristics that homologize them with the SAI and SAII of the skin (Gottschaldt et al., 1972). Those corresponding to SAI are directionally sensitive, whereas those corresponding to SAII have a positional, not a directional, sensitivity. The parallels with epidermal SAI and dermal SAII units extend also to the morphological substrate—Gottschaldt et al. (1972) propose that the sinus hair SAI innervate Merkel discs and the SAII terminate in "branched" and "circular" lanceolate endings within the sinus follicle.

The rapidly adapting units are also of two kinds, one responding to high-frequency mechanical stimuli (peak sensitivity at 500–600 Hz). These units are considered to end in the small Golgi–Mazzoni corpuscles in the follicles. The other units respond to lower-velocity stimuli (similar to type G units) and do not carry a resting discharge. They may terminate in the "straight" lanceolate endings which abut the glossy membrane in the follicle.

4.2. Cutaneous Thermoreceptors

Cutaneous thermoreceptors form a distinctive class of cutaneous afferent units, although for several decades there was sustained controversy regarding their independent existence. Electrophysiological evidence for "cold" receptors was first provided for afferent units in the tongue (Hensel and Zotterman, 1951), and only later was their existence in the skin established (Boman, 1958; Iggo, 1959; Hensel et al., 1960).

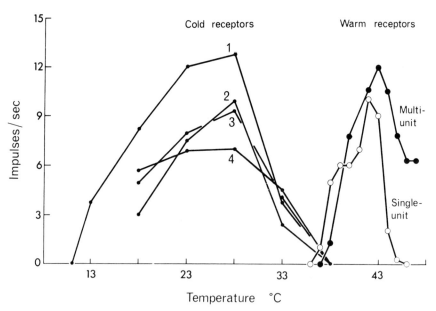

Fig. 20. Static sensitivity curves for "cold" and "warm" thermoreceptors in scrotal skin of a rat, recorded from single units dissected from the scrotal nerve. Each point was the mean discharge recorded after the skin had been held at the given temperature for at least 3 min. From Iggo (1959).

The general functional properties of thermoreceptors can be defined electrophysiologically as follows:

1. Maintained discharge of impulses at constant skin temperatures, the frequency of which depends on skin temperature (static response) (Fig. 20).
2. A rise (or fall) of the frequency of discharge during a change of skin temperature (dynamic response)—for cold receptors (Fig. 21), the frequency increases for a fall in temperature, within certain limits, and *vice versa* for warm receptors.
3. Insensitivity to nonthermal stimuli (especially marked in primates).
4. Threshold sensitivity similar to human perceptual thresholds for temperature changes in the skin.
5. Small receptive fields, with each afferent fiber supplying usually one, and occasionally two, adjacent, small receptive spots (less than 1 mm^2) in hairy or glabrous skin.
6. Afferent fibers with conduction velocities less than 20 m/s (Aδ fibers, group III) and in some species as low as 0.4 m/s (Table III).

These functional characteristics distinguish the sensitive thermoreceptors from the "spurious" thermoreceptors (Iggo, 1969) which usually turn out to be SAI and, particularly, SAII mechanoreceptors.

4.2.1. Cold Receptors

The static discharge is temperature dependent, with the characteristic bell-shaped curves of Fig. 20. For each unit, there is a narrow range of temperatures for which the discharge frequency is maximal. Two populations of thermoreceptors exist, with maxima on either side of deep body temperature and minimal activity at an intervening temperature. In addition to these sensitive cold and warm thermoreceptors, there is another population of units which are active only at higher and/or lower temperatures—at noxious temperatures. These latter units are also more readily excited by mechanical and chemical stimuli than the true thermoreceptors and are considered separately in Section 4.3.

The dynamic discharge in response to changing skin temperatures also occurs over a limited range, which is, however, wider than the static range. There is also a maximal dynamic sensitivity at about the same temperature as the static peak (Iggo, 1969).

For thermoreceptors that discharge a steady stream of impulses, there is an ambiguity in the information since the same frequency of discharge can occur at widely different temperatures, as in Fig. 20. This kind of discharge is characteristic of cold and warm receptors in the hairy skin (except the face)

Table III. Conduction Velocities of Single Cold and Warm fibers in Peripheral Nerves in Several Species

Species	Nerve	Receptive field	Cold fibers[a] Myelinated (m/s)	Cold fibers[a] Nonmyelinated (m/s)	Warm fibers,[a] nonmyelinated (m/s)	Reference
Monkey	Saphenous *M. mulatta*	Hairy skin, leg, and foot dorsum	6.3 ± 2.5 (8)	0.7 ± 0.3 (6)	0.7 ± 0.2 (9)	Hensel and Iggo (1971)
	Radial *S. sciureus*	Hairy skin, hand	8.0 ± 3.0 (16)			Perl (1968)
	Musculocutaneous *C. aethiops*	Hairy skin, arm	5.2 ± 1.8 (5)	0.6 (1)		Iggo (1969)
	Median *C. aethiops*	Glabrous skin, hand	10.7 ± 3.0 (5)			Iggo (1969)
Cat	Saphenous	Hairy skin, leg		1.0 (3)	0.8 (1)	Hensel *et al* (1960)
	Posterior femoral cutaneous	Hairy skin, leg		0.8–1.1 (8)	0.8 (2)	Bessou and Perl (1969)
	Plantar	Glabrous skin, footpad	5.0–6.8 (3)		1.1 (1)	Burgess and Perl (1971)
		Hairy skin, leg		1.0 (1)		
Dog	Dorsal root ganglion	Hairy skin, tail		1.3–1.4 (2)	0.8–1.2 (5)	Burgess (1971)
	Saphenous	Hairy skin, leg			0.4–0.6 (2)	Iriuchijima and Zotterman (1960)
	Infraorbital	Hairy and marginal skin, face	14 (3)			Iggo (1969)
Rat	Saphenous	Hairy skin		0.9 ± 0.1 (6)	1.0 ± 0.2 (7)	Iriuchijima and Zotterman (1960)

[a] Number of units indicated in parentheses.

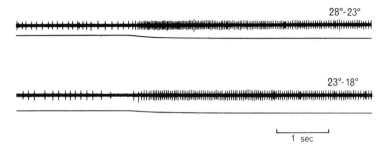

Fig. 21. Discharge in the afferent fiber of cold receptor in scrotal skin of a rat. In each pair of records, the upper trace shows the discharge in the nerve strand and the lower trace shows the skin temperature. At the start of each record, the temperature had been held at 28°C and 23°C, respectively, for at least 3 min, before the sudden fall of 5°C. From Iggo (1969).

of nonprimate mammals. Primate cold receptors and nonprimate orofacial cold receptors have a distinctive grouped discharge which is particularly prominent in the primates. The discharge is in groups of two to seven or more impulses; both the presence of groups and the number of impulses in a group are temperature dependent (Iggo, 1969), as illustrated in Fig. 22, which shows the discharge in a monkey cold receptor during progressive lowering of skin temperature, i.e., under dynamic conditions. Under static thermal conditions,

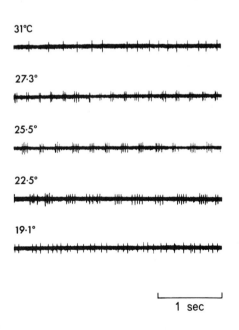

Fig. 22. The discharge of impulses in a cold fiber during continuous cooling of the receptive field (in hairy skin of monkey) at 0.3°C/s. The records are excerpts from a continuous strip record during which the skin was cooled from 42°C to 15°C, at each of which temperatures there was no "static" discharge. From Iggo and Iggo (1971).

the grouped discharge in monkey cold receptors is present below 32°C. The cold receptors in the face and tongue of the cat and dog may also show a grouped discharge, originally reported for lingual cold receptors by Hensel and Zotterman (1951) and Dodt (1952).

The primate cold receptors show a greater complexity of response in that (1) the peak static discharge frequency is higher, (2) the static discharge is invariably grouped in bursts over the midpart of the temperature range, (3) there are more impulses in each burst than for nonprimate thermoreceptors, (4) the majority of the cold receptors have myelinated axons (up to 3 μm in diameter), and (5) the peak frequency of discharge during dynamic thermal stimulation is as high as 200 Hz.

The presence of the grouped discharge may be utilized to diminish the ambiguity of the discharge, since temperatures on either side of the peak sensitivity are more likely to set up distinctive patterns of discharge in these afferent fibers than for the regularly discharging units in Figs. 20 and 21.

4.2.2. Warm Receptors

The cutaneous warm receptors in all mammals have a maximal static response at temperatures above deep body temperature (Fig. 20). The discharge is in a regular stream or, especially at the higher temperatures, may become irregular without, however, developing the grouped discharge seen in some cold receptors. Their general characteristics are the converse of those of the cold receptors. They become more active, or are excited, when skin temperatures are rising. As Fig. 20 shows, the maximal activity occurs over a narrower temperature range than for the cold fibers, and in the monkey there is some evidence for two kinds of warm units, with maxima at 40–42°C and above 45°C, respectively (Hensel and Iggo, 1971).

From these results, it is evident that at temperatures between 30 and 40°C both cold and warm units will be active, and from the dynamic properties of the thermoreceptors the relative balance of activity will depend on both the rate and the direction of temperature changes.

4.3. Nociceptors

The third major class of cutaneous receptors are the nociceptors, which in Sherrington's original definition are "non-selective . . . in that they are excited by physical and chemical stimuli of diverse kind" and "the stimulus . . . must . . . possess in order to stimulate them the quality of tending to do immediate harm to the skin" (Sherrington, 1906). In addition, the reflexes they arouse are (1) prepotent, (2) protective, and (3) imperative, and, in addition, activity in the nociceptors will, in man, normally give rise to pain.

Normally, in physiological experiments, the peripheral nociceptors are identified by their thresholds for mechanical and thermal stimuli, with the effects of chemicals sometimes helping but more usually hindering the process. If a single afferent unit, in electrophysiological experiments, has an elevated threshold for thermal or mechanical stimuli and fails to be excited by any low-intensity stimulus, it is defined as a "nociceptor." A methodological problem is that the sensitive thermoreceptors sometimes can be excited by a severe mechanical stimulus, and *vice versa*, for the sensitive mechano-receptors, i.e., the "specific" receptors, are not absolutely specific in a biophysical sense of responding exclusively to one form of energy (for this reason, the term "selective sensitivity" is preferable to "specificity"). Insufficiently careful testing of single unit preparations in the electrophysiological study of cutaneous receptor mechanisms may succeed only in confusing the issue because of these effects. The gradual technical improvements in recording, stimulation, and analysis have in the past two decades established the "nociceptors" as a distinctive class and have in addition brought to light differences among units in the general class that require a further subdivision into at least two subgroups, each of which is capable of further subdivision. These two groups are the "mechanical" nociceptors, excited most effectively by high-intensity mechanical stimuli, and the "thermal" nociceptors, which are excited in addition by high and/or low skin temperatures. There are in addition the excitatory responses to chemicals, some of which are noxious or cause pain. There is as yet insufficient information to decide exactly how they act or what their role is in the process of excitation, in particular whether they act as essential intermediaries in the chain of excitatory events or whether they merely have an ancillary function.

Painful stimuli can be divided arbitrarily into three categories: (1) physical injury of mechanical or thermal origin, such as pinprick or from pressure or high temperature; (2) inflammation of the tissues which may follow physical injury, but may also arise from local tissue reactions to chemicals, e.g., toxins; and (3) ischemia, which arises from impairment of the normal blood supply (pain can readily be elicited from ischemic human muscle).

The electrophysiological analysis of "pain receptors" or nociceptors depends on the use of a battery of tests to insure that thresholds to a spectrum of stimuli are measured. The recognition of a separate nociceptor class depends partly on the now secure evidence for "specific" or "selectively sensitive" mechano- and thermoreceptors, as already discussed. The essential distinguishing characteristics of the "nociceptors" as a class are the following:

1. High threshold for the appropriate stimulus—especially mechanical or thermal—in contrast to the "specific" mechanoreceptors and thermoreceptors.

2. Relatively small receptive fields in skin, muscle, and viscera.
3. Persistent discharge for a suprathreshold stimulus, so that they give continued information about the presence of high-intensity stimuli (particularly the muscle nociceptors).
4. Small-diameter afferent fibers in most cases, and especially for the units responding to high skin temperatures.

4.3.1. Mechanical Nociceptors

About 20% of the small myelinated (Aδ) fibers (conduction velocity less than 24 m/s) in the saphenous and sural nerves in the monkey, cat, and rabbit are excited only if a severe mechanical stimulus (such as pricking or squeezing) is delivered to the skin, and not by high or low skin temperatures. The discharge appears soon after the stimulus is applied and is stimulus-locked; i.e., it does not outlast the stimulus nor, since it is initiated so quickly, can it involve an inflammatory reaction. The receptive fields of these myelinated units can be as large as 2 cm^2 (Burgess and Perl, 1967).

Nonmyelinated axons also innervate "mechanical" nociceptors which respond to pinprick or mechanical distortion but not to thermal stimuli. They number about 20% of the afferent C fibers supplying the skin. Their receptive fields are smaller (2 by 3 mm) than those of the myelinated mechanical nociceptors (Iggo, 1960; Bessou and Perl, 1969).

The typical response of a mechanical nociceptor to stimulation of the skin with a sharp-pointed probe is shown in Fig. 23. There is a brisk response

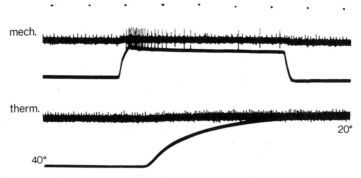

Fig. 23. Nonmyelinated mechanical nociceptor in hairy skin of a monkey arm, showing the response (large spikes in the uppermost trace) to pressing of the skin with a sharp, pointed probe (force indicated on the second trace) and the lack of response to very rapid cooling of the skin from 40°C to 20°C (there was also a lack of response to heating the skin). The small spikes in the records are from an unrelated unit. From Iggo (1963*b*).

during insertion of the pin, followed by an irregular discharge. Firm pressure with forceps causes a similar discharge which may be better sustained. Frequent repetition of the stimulus leads to an inexcitability of the receptor from which there is a slow recovery lasting several minutes, as was described for the sensitive C-mechanoreceptors.

The morphology of the mechanical nociceptors is unknown, but a well-established view is that they are not encapsulated. Those with nonmyelinated axons may have endings of the simple kind described by Cauna (1969), and there certainly is physiological evidence that they end in or close to the epidermis.

4.3.2. Thermal Nociceptors

High-intensity (burning) thermal stimuli will excite a discharge of impulses in small afferent fibers (Zotterman, 1939), and single unit studies (Iggo, 1959; Hensel *et al.*, 1960) have established that, in the cat and monkey, the axons are nonmyelinated. Characteristic responses are shown in Fig. 24. There is a short latency of response, indicating a direct action of the high temperature on the receptor, rather than via an inflammatory reaction. Repeated heating will depress the response, but if an interval of 3 min is allowed a uniform response is established (Iggo, 1959). Following initial stimulation of a previously untested unit, there may be an enhancement of the response and a lowering of threshold (corresponding to hyperalgesia) by as much as 5°C (Bessou and Perl, 1969).

The "thermal" nociceptors can be excited by severe mechanical stimuli at intensities that excite the mechanical nociceptors. Bessou and Perl (1969) use the term "polymodal" for these nociceptors, since they can also be excited by acids, etc., placed on the skin. The receptive fields for thermal and mechanical stimuli are coincident, so that they are presumably exciting the same terminals. The enhancement induced by thermal stimuli (see above) is accompanied by hypersensitivity to mechanical stimulation, and both thresholds, according to Bessou and Perl (1969), can remain lowered for several hours. This change may depend on inflammatory responses.

Low temperatures (less than 20°C) can also excite nociceptors. Some are excited more vigorously by high temperatures, but others appear to be excited only by low temperatures (Iggo, 1959).

In nonprimate animals, most of the cutaneous thermal nociceptors have nonmyelinated axons. In primate hairy and glabrous skin of the extremities, some of the thermal nociceptors have thin myelinated axons (Iggo and Ogawa, 1971) with conduction velocities up to 7 m/s. The receptive field characteristics and physiological responses are otherwise similar to those with nonmyelinated axons.

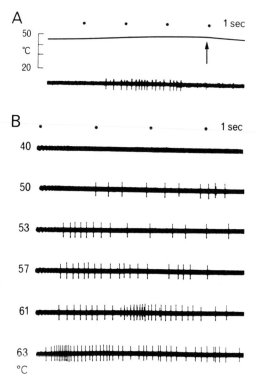

Fig. 24. The responses of two "thermal nociceptors" in hairy skin of the cat with non-myelinated afferent fibers to heating the skin. (A) Radiant heat was used, and the skin temperature is indicated by the upper trace (calibration scale at right-hand side)—threshold was 44–46°C. (B) Each record was obtained when a metal rod, at the indicated temperatures, was placed on the skin—threshold was less than 50°C and the response increased in intensity at higher temperatures. From Iggo (1959).

4.3.3. "Double Pain"

When a noxious stimulus (pinprick or brief contact with a sufficiently hot object) is delivered to the arm or leg of a conscious human subject, the pain can be experienced as two distinct sensations, separated by as long as 1 s (Lewis, 1942). The existence, or mechanism, of "double pain" or "fast" and "slow" pain has been a fruitful field for controversy. The new information on rapidly and slowly conducting afferent fibers innervating nociceptors provides a rational basis for resolving the conflicts, since the fast pain could be conducted in myelinated fibers and slow pain in nonmyelinated fibers, as suggested long ago by Zotterman (1933). Confirmation of the involvement of fast- and slow-conducting axons in the double pain has come from Dyson and

Brindley (1966), who used differential compressive block of the sciatic nerve in conscious man, combined with natural and electrical stimulation, to show the separate contributions of myelinated and nonmyelinated fibers to the perception of pain.

4.3.4. Chemical Excitants of Pain

The involvement of chemicals in the genesis of pain is well known, and the cantharidin blister-base technique of Armstrong *et al.* (1953) established that many chemicals will cause pain. The "chemoreceptor" view of pain receptors was vigorously promoted by Lim (1968) on the grounds that bradykinin and related kinins (2) cause pain on intra-arterial injection and (2) are destroyed so rapidly by kinase in the blood, so that (3) the nociceptors must have a paravascular location in order for these chemicals to act. In fact, the kinins can modify the action of afferent fibers and receptors with encapsulated endings that are not in the walls of blood vessels so that the conclusion is invalid and Lim's hypothesis has to be rejected on this ground.

There are several biological chemicals (the amines—histamine, 5-HT, and ACh; polypeptides, especially bradykinin and kallidin; the prostaglandins) which will evoke pain from both superficial and deep tissues. Electrophysiological methods have been used to test the effects of K ions, ACh, histamine, 5-HT, bradykinin, ATP, and lactic acid. K ions and ACh have

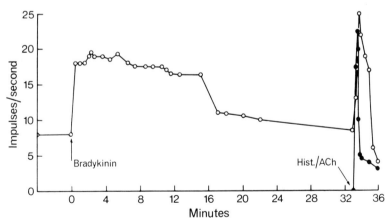

Fig. 25. The effect of the retrograde close-arterial injection of 400 μg impure bradykinin, followed after 30 min by a mixture of histamine (10 μg) and ACh (24 μg), on the discharge of a fine nerve strand dissected from the saphenous nerve of a cat. Both injections enhanced the resting discharge in an SAII mechanoreceptor (○), whereas only the latter injection excited nonmyelinated fibers in the same strand (●). From Iggo (1962).

an almost immediate and brief action with a latency of a few seconds, whereas the other amines and the bradykinins act with a latency of at least 20 s and have a persistent effect that can last 60 min. The effect is not exclusively excitatory but can be bi- or triphasic, with alternating periods of excitation and depression (Fig. 25). The action is not specific for nociceptors, and the slowly adapting mechanoreceptors (SAII) can also be excited. The experiments so far reported (Fjällbrant and Iggo, 1961) therefore fail to provide a satisfactory test for the hypothesis that the tested chemicals have an exclusively nociceptive action, and the mechanisms underlying inflammatory and chemically induced pain remain to be elucidated.

5. REFERENCES

Adrian, E. D., 1928, The basis of sensation, in: *The Action of Sense Organs*, p. 122, Christofers, London.

Andres, K. H., 1966, Über die Feinstruktur der Rezeptoren an Sinushaaren, *Z. Zellforsch.* **75**:339.

Andres, K. H., 1969, Zur Ultrastruktur verschiedener Mechanorezeptoren von höheren Wirbeltieren, *Anat. Anz.* **124**:551.

Andres, K. H., and Hensel, H., 1971, Personal communication.

Armstrong, D., Dry, R. M. L., Keele, C. A., and Markham, J. W., 1953, Observations on chemical excitants of pain, *J. Physiol.* **120**:326.

Bessou, P., and Perl, E. R., 1969, Response of cutaneous sensory units with unmyelinated fibers to noxious stimuli, *J. Neurophysiol.* **32**:1025.

Bessou, P., Burgess, P. R., Perl, E. R., and Taylor, C. B., 1971, Dynamic properties of mechanoreceptors with unmyelinated (C) fibers, *J. Neurophysiol.* **34**:116.

Boman, K. K. A., 1958, Elektrophysiologische Untersuchungen über die Thermorezeptoren der Gesichtshaut, *Acta Physiol. Scand.* **44**:1.

Boman, K. K. A., and Hensel, H., 1960, Afferent impulses in cutaneous sensory nerves in conscious human subjects, *J. Neurophysiol.* **23**:564.

Brown, A. G., and Iggo, A., 1967, A quantitative study of cutaneous receptors and afferent fibres in the cat and rabbit, *J. Physiol.* **193**:707.

Burgess, P. R., 1971, Unpublished data; quoted in Hensel and Iggo (1971).

Burgess, P. R., and Perl, E. R., 1967, Myelinated afferent fibres responding specifically to noxious stimulation of the skin, *J. Physiol.* **190**:541.

Burgess, P. R., and Perl, E. R., 1971, Unpublished data; quoted in Hensel and Iggo (1971).

Burgess, P. R., Petit, D., and Warren, R. M., 1968, Receptor types in cat hairy skin supplied by myelinated fibers, *J. Neurophysiol.* **31**:833.

Cauna, N., 1962, Functional significance of the submicroscopical, histochemical and microscopical organization of the cutaneous receptor organs, *Anat. Anz.* **111**:181.

Cauna, N., 1966, Fine structure of the receptor organs and its probable functional significance, in: *Touch, Heat and Pain* (A. V. S. de Reuck and J. Knight, eds.), p. 117, Churchill, London.

Cauna, N., 1969, The fine morphology of the sensory receptor organs in the auricle of the rat, *J. Comp. Neurol.* **136**:81.

Chambers, M. R., Andres, K. H., von Duering, M. and Iggo, A., 1972, The structure and function of the slowly adapting type II mechanoreceptor in hairy skin, *Quart. J. Exptl. Physiol.* **57**:417.

Cunningham, F. O., and Fitzgerald, M. J. T., 1972, Encapsulated nerve endings in hairy skin, *J. Anat.* **112**:93.

Diamond, J., Gray, J. A. B., and Sato, M., 1956, The site of initiation of impulses in Pacinian corpuscles, *J. Physiol.* **133**:54.

Dodt, E., 1952, The behaviour of thermoceptors at low and high temperatures with special reference to Ebbecke's temperature phenomena, *Acta Physiol. Scand.* **27**:295.

Dorward, P. K., 1970, Response characteristics of muscle afferent in the domestic duck, *J. Physiol.* **211**:1.

Dorward, P. K., and McIntyre, A. K., 1971, Responses of vibration-sensitive receptors in the interosseous region of the duck's hind limb, *J. Physiol.* **219**:77.

Dun, F. T., 1955, The delay and blockage of sensory impulses in the dorsal roof ganglion, *J. Physiol.* **127**:252.

Dyck, P. J., Lambert, E. H., and Nicholas, P. C., 1972, Quantitative measurement of sensation related to compound action potential and number and sizes of myelinated and unmyelinated fibres of the sural nerve in health, Friedreich's ataxia, hereditary sensory neuropathy, and tabes dorsalis, in: *Handbook of Electroencephalography and Clinical Neurophysiology*, Vol. 9, pp. 83–118, Elsevier, Amsterdam.

Dyson, C., and Brindley, G. S., 1966, Strength–duration curves for the production of cutaneous pain by electrical stimuli, *Clin. Sci.* **30**:237.

Edwards, C., and Ottoson, D., 1958, The site of impulse initiation in a nerve cell of a crustacean stretch receptor, *J. Physiol.* **143**:138.

Eimer, T., 1871, Die Schnauze des Maulwurfs als Tastwerkzeug, *Arch. Mikroskop. Anat.* **7**:181.

Fitzgerald, O. J., 1940, Discharges from the sensory organs of the cat's vibrissae and the modifications in their activity by ions, *J. Physiol.* **98**:163.

Fjällbrant, N., and Iggo, A., 1961, The effect of histamine, 5-hydroxytryptamine and acetylcholine on cutaneous afferent fibres, *J. Physiol.* **156**:578.

Frankenhaeuser, B., 1949, Impulses from a cutaneous receptor with slow adaptation and low mechanical threshold, *Acta Physiol. Scand.* **18**:68.

Franz, D. N., and Iggo, A., 1968, Conduction failure in myelinated and non-myelinated axons at low temperatures, *J. Physiol.* **199**:319

Gasser, H. S., 1955, Properties of dorsal root unmedullated fibers on the two sides of the ganglion, *J. Gen. Physiol.* **38**:709.

Gasser, H. S., 1960, Effect of the method of leading on the recording of the nerve fibre spectrum, *J. Gen. Physiol.* **43**:927.

Gottschaldt, K.-M., Iggo, A., and Young, D. W., 1972, Electrophysiology of the afferent innervation of sinus hairs, including vibrissae, of the cat, *J. Physiol.* **222**:60.

Grandry, M., 1869, *J. Anat. Physiol. Paris* **6**:390.

Hahn, J. F., 1971, Thermal–mechanical stimulus interactions in low-threshold C-fibre mechanoreceptors of cat, *Exptl. Neurol.* **33**:607.

Halata, Z., 1970, Zu den Nervenendigungen (Merkelsche Endigungen) in der haarlosen Nasenhaut der Katze, *Z. Zellforsch.* **106**:50.

Halata, Z., 1972, Innervation der unbehaarten Nasenhaut des Maulwurfs (*Talpa europaea*). 1. Intraepidermale Nervenendigungen, *Z. Zellforsch.* **125**:108.

Harrington, T., and Merzenich, M. M., 1970, Neural coding in the sense of touch: Human sensations of skin indentation compared with the responses of slowly adapting mechanoreceptive afferents innervating the hairy skin of monkeys, *Exptl. Brain Res.* **10**:251.

Hensel, H., 1972, Cutaneous thermoreceptors, in: *Somatosensory System*, Springer-Verlag, Heidelberg.

Hensel, H., and Iggo, A., 1971, Analysis of cutaneous warm and cold fibres in primates, *Pflügers Arch. Ges. Physiol.* **329**:1.

Hensel, H., and Zotterman, Y., 1951, Quantitative Beziehungen zwischen der Entladung einzelner Kältefasern und der Temperatur, *Acta Physiol. Scand.* **23**:291.

Hensel, H., Iggo, A., and Witt, I., 1960, A quantitative study of sensitive thermoreceptors with C afferent fibres, *J. Physiol.* **153**:113.

Herbst, G. E. F., 1848, *Die Pacinischen Körper und ihre Bedeutung*, Badenhoech und Ruprecht, Göttingen.

Hunt, C. C., and McIntyre, A. K., 1960a, Properties of cutaneous touch receptors in cat, *J. Physiol.* **153**:88.

Hunt, C. C., and McIntyre, A. K., 1960b, An analysis of fibre diameter and receptor characteristics of myelinated cutaneous afferent fibres in cat, *J. Physiol.* **153**:99.

Hursh, J. B., 1939, Conduction velocity and diameter of nerve fibres, *Am. J. Physiol.* **127**:131.

Iggo, A., 1958, Single C fibres from cutaneous receptors, *J. Physiol.* **143**:47.

Iggo, A., 1959, Cutaneous heat and cold receptors with slowly-conducting (C) afferent fibres, *Quart. J. Exptl. Physiol.* **44**:362.

Iggo, A., 1960, Cutaneous mechanoreceptors with afferent C fibres, *J. Physiol.* **152**:337.

Iggo, A., 1962, Non-myelinated visceral, muscular and cutaneous afferent fibres and pain, in: *The Assessment of Pain in Man and Animals* (C. A. Keele and R. Smith, eds.), pp. 74–88, Livingstone, London.

Iggo, A., 1963a, New specific sensory structures in hairy skin, *Acta Neuroveg.* **24**:175.

Iggo, A., 1963b, An electrophysiological analysis of afferent fibres in primate skin, *Acta Neuroveg.* **24**:225.

Iggo, A., 1966, Cutaneous receptors with a high sensitivity to mechanical displacement, in: *Touch, Heat and Pain*, (A. V. S. de Reuck and J. Knight, eds.), pp. 237–256, Churchill, London.

Iggo, A., 1969, Cutaneous thermoreceptors in primates and sub-primates, *J. Physiol.* **200**:403.

Iggo, A., and Iggo, B. J., 1971, Impulse coding in primate cutaneous thermoreceptors in dynamic thermal conditions, *J. Physiol. Paris* **63**:287.

Iggo, A., and Kornhuber, H. H., 1968, A quantitative analysis of nonmyelinated cutaneous mechanoreceptors, *J. Physiol.* **198**:113.

Iggo, A., and Muir, A. R., 1969, The structure and function of a slowly adapting touch corpuscle in hairy skin, *J. Physiol.* **200**:763.

Iggo, A., and Ogawa, H., 1971, Primate cutaneous thermal nociceptors, *J. Physiol.* **216**:77.

Iriuchijima, J., and Zotterman, Y., 1960, The specificity of afferent cutaneous C fibres in mammals, *Acta Physiol. Scand.* **49**:267.

Jänig, W., 1971, Morphology of rapidly and slowly adapting mechanoreceptors in the hairless skin of the cat's hind foot, *Brain Res.* **28**:217.

Jänig, W., Schmidt, R. F., and Zimmerman, M., 1968, Single unit responses and total afferent outflow from the cat's foot pad upon mechanical stimulation, *Exptl. Brain Res.* **6**:116.

Kenton, B., Kruger, L., and Woo, M., 1971, Two classes of slowly adapting mechanoreceptor fibres in reptile cutaneous nerve, *J. Physiol.* **212**:21.

Knibestöl, M., and Vallbo, A. B., 1970, Single unit analysis of mechanoreceptor activity from the human glabrous skin, *Acta Physiol. Scand.* **80**:178.

Krause, W., 1860, *Die terminalen Körperchen der einfachen sensiblen Nerven*, Hahn'sche Hofbuch-Handlung, Hanover.

Lewis, T., 1942, *Pain*, Macmillan, New York.

Lim, R. K. S., 1968, Neuropharmacology of pain and analgesia, in: *Proceedings of the Third International Pharmacological Meeting*, Vol. 9, pp. 169–217, Pergamon Press, Oxford and New York.

Lloyd, D. P. C., 1943, Neuron patterns controlling transmission of ipsilateral hind limb reflexes in cat, *J. Neurophysiol.* **6**:293.

Loewenstein, W. R., and Skalak, R., 1966, Mechanical transmission in a Pacinian corpuscle: An analysis and a theory, *J. Physiol.* **182**:346.

Maruhashi, J., Mizuguchi, K., and Tasaki, I., 1952, Action currents in single afferent nerve fibres elicited by stimulation of the skin of the toad and the cat, *J. Physiol.* **117**:129.

Merkel, F., 1880, *Über die Endingungen der sensiblen Nerven in der Haut der Wirbeltiere*, H. Schmidt, Rostock.

Miller, M. R., Ralston, H. J., III, and Kasahara, M., 1958, The pattern of cutaneous innervation of the human hand, *Am. J. Anat.* **102**:183.

Mountcastle, V. B., Talbot, W. H., Sakata, H., and Hyvärinen, J., 1969, Cortical neuronal mechanisms in flutter-vibration studied in unanesthetized monkeys: Neuronal periodicity and frequency discrimination, *J. Neurophysiol.* **32**:452.

Munger, B. L., 1965, The intraepidermal innervation of the snout skin of the opossum: A light and electron microscopic study, with observations on the nature of Merkel's Tastzellen, *J. Cell Biol.* **26**:79.

Munger, B. L., 1971, The comparative ultrastructure of slowly and rapidly adapting mechanoreceptors, in: *Oral-Facial Sensory and Motor Mechanisms*, (R. Dubner and Y. Kawamura, eds.), pp. 83–103, Appleton-Century-Crofts, New York.

Nakajima, S., and Onodera, K., 1969, Adaptation of the generator potential in the crayfish stretch receptors under constant length and constant tension, *J. Physiol.* **200**:187.

Nilsson, B. Y., 1969a, Structure and function of the tactile hair receptors on the cat's foreleg, *Acta Physiol. Scand.* **77**:396.

Nilsson, B. Y., 1969b, Hair discs and Pacinian corpuscles functionally associated with the carpal tactile hairs in the cat, *Acta Physiol. Scand.* **77**:417.

Pacini, F., 1840, *Nuovi Organi Scorperti nel Corpo Umano*, Ciro, Pistoia.

Perl, E. R., 1968, Myelinated afferent fibres innervating the primate skin and their response to noxious stimuli, *J. Physiol.* **197**:593.

Pinkus, F., 1904, Über Hautsinnesorgane neben den menshlichen Haar (Haarscheiben) und ihre vergleichenden anatomische Bedeutung, *Arch. Mitroskop. Anat. Entw. Mech.* **65**:121.

Poláček, P., 1966, Receptors of the joints, their structure, variability and classification, *Acta Fac. Med. Univ.-Brum.* **23**:1.

Quilliam, T. A, 1966, Unit design and array patterns in receptor organs, in: *Touch, Heat and Pain*, (A. V. S. de Reuck and J. Knight, eds.), p. 86, Churchill, London.

Ringham, G. L., 1971, Origin of nerve impulse in slowly adapting stretch receptor of crayfish, *J. Neurophysiol.* **34**:773.

Ruffini, A., 1894, Sur un nouvel Organe nerveux terminal et sur la presence des corpuscles, Golgi-Mazzoni, dans le conjonctif sous-cutane de la pulpe des doigts de l'homme, *Arch. Ital. Biol.* **21**:249.

Ruffini, A., 1905, Les expansions nerveuses de la peau chez l'homme et quelques autres mammiferes, *Rev. Gen. Histol.* **1**:420.

Sakada, S., and Aida, H., 1971, Electrophysiological studies of Golgi-Mazzoni corpuscles in the periosteum of the cat facial bones, *Bull. Tokyo Dent. Coll.* **12**:255.

Sherrington, C. S., 1906, The integrative action of the nervous sytem, in: *Silliman Memorial Lectures*, Yale University Press, New Haven; Constable, London.

Straile, W. E., 1960, Sensory hair follicles in mammalian skin: The tylotrich follicle, *Am. J. Anat.* **106**:133.

Straile, W. E., and Mann, S. J., 1972, Discharges in neurons that innervate specific groups of tactile receptors in mice, *Brain Res.* **42**:89.

Talbot, W. H., Darian-Smith, I., Kornhuber, H. H., and Mountcastle, V. B., 1968, The sense of flutter-vibration: Comparison of the human capacity with response patterns of mechanoreceptive afferents from the monkey hand, *J. Neurophysiol.* **31**:301.

Tapper, D. N., 1965, Stimulus–response relationships in the cutaneous slowly-adapting mechanoreceptor in hairy skin of the cat, *Exptl. Neurol.* **13**:364.

Timofeef, D., 1896, Über eine besondere Art von eigenkapselten Nervendigungen in den männlichen Geschlechtsorganen bei Säugetieren, *Anat. Anz.* **11**:44.

Vallbo, A. B., and Hagbarth, K.-E., 1968, Activity from skin mechanoreceptors recorded percutaneously in awake human subjects, *Exptl. Neurol.* **21**:270.

Wagner, R., and Meissner, G., 1852, Ueber das Vorhandensein bisher unbekannter eigenthümlichen Tastkoerperchen (Corpuscula Tactus) in den Gefühlswaerzchen der menschlichen Haut und über die Endausbreitung sensibler Nerven, *Göttingen Nachrichten.*

Werner, G., and Mountcastle, V. B., 1965, Neural activity in mechanoreceptive cutaneous afferents: Stimulus–response relations, Weber functions, and information transmission, *J. Neurophysiol.* **28**:359.

Yamamoto, T., 1966, The fine structure of the palisade-type sensory endings in relation to hair follicles, *J. Electron Microscop.* **15**:158.

Zotterman, Y., 1933, Studies in peripheral nervous mechanism of pain, *Acta Med. Scand.* **80**:9.

Zotterman, Y., 1939, Touch, pain and tickling: An electrophysiological investigation on cutaneous sensory nerves, *J. Physiol.* **95**:1.

Zucker, E., and Welker, W. I., 1969, Coding of somatic sensory input by vibrissae neurons in the rat's trigeminal ganglion, *Brain Res.* **12**:138.

Chapter 13

The Pacinian Corpuscle

Carlton C. Hunt

Department of Physiology and Biophysics
Washington University School of Medicine
St. Louis, Missouri, USA

1. INTRODUCTION

The structure of the Pacinian corpuscle was described by Pacini (1835). It is widely distributed in mammals and is similar to the Herbst corpuscles found in birds. The Pacinian corpuscle is an ovoid structure about 1 mm in length and is easily seen by the naked eye in a number of locations such as the mesentery. On microscopic examination, the lamellar structure of the corpuscle is evident, the lamellae giving an appearance which has been likened to a section through an onion. The corpuscle is innervated by a myelinated sensory axon of medium diameter which terminates within the center of the corpuscle. There it loses its myelin and terminates as an unmyelinated axon. Pacinian corpuscles are highly sensitive mechanoreceptors which respond only to rapid mechanical changes. They are particularly responsive to vibration and appear to subserve the type of sensibility known as vibration sense in man. The corpuscle has been extensively studied as to its morphology, its functional characteristics, and its projection to the central nervous system. The discrete nature and large size of this receptor have made it particularly attractive for the study of receptor mechanisms.

2. MORPHOLOGY

The length of the corpuscle ranges from about 0.5 to 1.5 mm, with an average length of approximately 1 mm; the average width is about 0.7 mm.

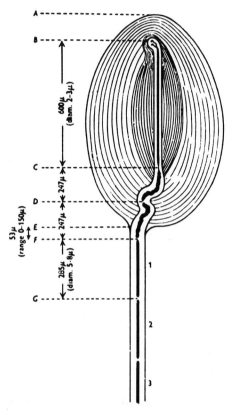

Fig. 1. Diagram of a Pacinian corpuscle. From Quilliam and Sato (1955).

Occasionally, much smaller corpuscles are seen (Quilliam and Sato, 1955.) A single myelinated nerve fiber enters the ellipsoid corpuscle at one end; its course in the corpuscle for the first one-fourth of its length is tortuous and it retains its myelination over this length (Fig. 1). Following this, it enters the central core of the corpuscle and becomes thinner and unmyelinated. It travels along the longitudinal axis of the corpuscle toward the other end of the central core, where it frequently bifurcates. The diameter of the myelinated fiber just outside the corpuscle varies from about 4 to 7 μm. One node of Ranvier lies within the corpuscle; the second node lies between 0 and 150 μm from the central end of the corpuscle. The myelinated fiber in its intracorpuscular course has about the same diameter as immediately outside the corpuscle, although the thickness of the myelin tends to vary more during its course within the corpuscle.

Electron microscopy has provided more detailed information about the structure of the lamellae and of the unmyelinated axon. Pease and Quilliam (1957) found the lamellar structure to differ markedly in the central zone of the corpuscle as compared to the peripheral zone. The peripheral zone is characterized by concentrically arranged sheets of cells separated by fluid spaces. Each lamella on cross-section presents a complete circular profile which is made up of a number of cells whose processes overlap. The spaces between lamellae, which become progressively larger toward the periphery, are filled with fluid. The lamellae in the central region of the corpuscle, called the "central core," show a different arrangement. The spacing between lamellae is smaller, and the lamellar profiles are not full circles but semicircles, with

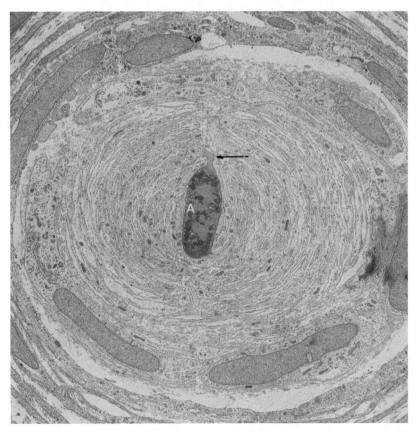

Fig. 2. Electron micrograph of inner core and unmyelinated axon of a Pacinian corpuscle. A, Axon; arrow, footlike protrusion. From Terashima, Lemcoe, and Hunt (unpublished).

gaps between the half circles aligned so as to produce clefts extending from the unmyelinated axon through the central core. At the border between the inner core and outer lamellae, there is thought to be a growth zone where new lamellae are formed. The unmyelinated axon is oval in cross-section, the largest diameter running between the clefts, which are 180° apart. Near the cleft, as Fig. 2 shows, the axon often has footlike extensions which project slightly into the cleft (Nishi *et al.*, 1969). A very prominent feature of the unmyelinated axon is the larger number of mitochondria densely packed beneath its membrane.

Blood vessels supply the Pacinian corpuscle, but capillaries usually do not extend beyond the myelinated region of the axon. The fluid space surrounding the axon and extending through the clefts between the lamellae of the inner core appears to be in contact with the capillary supply to the corpuscle. This must serve as the pathway for the diffusion and exchange of metabolites.

There is some question as to whether or not the corpuscle receives innervation in addition to its principal sensory nerve fiber. Goto *et al.* (1966) described the additional innervation of the Pacinian corpuscle by a small fiber conducting at 0.7 m/s which showed no responses to mechanical stimuli. Santini (1969) has recently described fibers in the region of the inner core which, judged by fluorescence techniques, are adrenergic. These fibers are said not to be related to blood vessels but course in the avascular region of the corpuscle parallel to the principal sensory axon.

3. AFFERENT RESPONSES TO MECHANICAL STIMULI

While some early studies indicated that the Pacinian corpuscle might be a pressure receptor, giving a sustained discharge to maintain pressure, it is now clear that the corpuscle responds only to transient mechanical changes (Gray and Matthews, 1951). Thus if a carefully controlled rectangular pressure pulse is applied to a Pacinian corpuscle, recording from the nerve fiber shows that an impulse is generated at the beginning and at the end of the pressure pulse but not during the plateau of pressure. The corpuscle fires repetitively to the recurrent mechanical changes associated with vibration. Pacinian corpuscles are extremely sensitive to this form of stimulation.

The rate of change of mechanical deformation is a critical factor in determining the response of Pacinian corpuscles. This is evident when movement at a constant velocity is applied. Only when the rate of movement exceeds a critical value does the corpuscle discharge.

Sinusoidal vibration of appropriate frequency is a highly effective stimulus for the Pacinian corpuscle. The most effective frequency is typically between 150 and 200 Hz. At this best frequency, many corpuscles are ex-

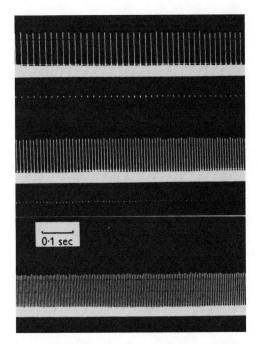

Fig. 3. Response of a Pacinian corpuscle to sinusoidal vibration at varying frequencies. Modified from Hunt and McIntyre (1960).

tremely sensitive, responding to very small amplitudes of vibration (less than 1 μm). The response above threshold to vibration is typically one impulse for every cycle of vibration (Fig. 3). As the frequency is shifted above and below the best frequency, the threshold rises, as may be seen in Fig. 4. The rise in threshold as frequency is raised is at first gradual and then steeper, the maximal effective frequency being approximately 900 Hz. When frequency is lowered below the optimal frequency, the threshold rises somewhat more steeply, reaching a lower effective frequency of about 60 Hz. Temperature change shifts the threshold–frequency relationship. Lowering the temperature from 37 to 24°C shifts the curve toward lower frequencies, as shown in Fig. 4. The difference in the threshold–frequency curves determined from circulated corpuscles at body temperature and from isolated corpuscles at room temperature appears due to the effect of temperature. Pacinian corpuscles from various loci in the cat all appear to have similar behavior to vibratory stimuli. The relationship between vibration frequency and threshold for discharge of Pacinian corpuscles is similar to the relationship between perception of vibration and frequency determined in man (see later).

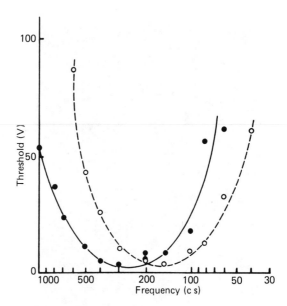

Fig. 4. Relation between threshold and frequency of an isolated corpuscle at two different temperatures: ●, 37°C; ○, 24°C. From Sato (1961).

Near threshold, the corpuscle may discharge less than one impulse per cycle. Strong vibratory stimuli, perhaps by producing harmonics of the fundamental frequency, may evoke more than one impulse per cycle. However, over a large range of amplitudes the response shows a striking one-to-one correspondence between impulse frequency and frequency of sinusoidal vibration. When one records from a nerve containing afferent fibers from many Pacinian corpuscles, as in the interosseous nerve of cat, it is evident that there is a difference both in threshold and in the phase relation between discharge and vibratory cycle among different corpuscles. This may be due in part to the difference in orientation of the corpuscles in relation to the applied mechanical stimulus.

4. MECHANICAL PROPERTIES OF THE CORPUSCLE

The transmission of mechanical stimuli from the exterior of the corpuscle to the region of the unmyelinated terminal is an important determinant of its response. Hubbard (1958) studied this by determining the displacement of lamellae at different distances from the center of the corpuscle when the corpuscle was subjected to the compression of controlled rate and amplitude. Using brief flashes of light, photomicrographs of the corpuscle were taken at varying times during the applied mechanical stimulation (Fig. 5). The displacements of lamellae at three positions within a corpuscle subjected to a compression of 90 μm with a mean velocity of 35 μm/ms are shown in Fig. 6. It may be noted that the lamellae located at a radius of 0.59 relative to the radius of the outer capsule showed a transient dynamic displacement as well as a maintained or static displacement. The lamellae at radius 0.22 relative to the outer capsule showed only a dynamic displacement, whereas the lamellae in position 2 (radius 0.38) showed a large dynamic component and a relatively small static component. The analysis of the displacements into an

100 μ

Fig. 5. Photomicrograph of a Pacinian corpuscle taken with a brief-duration flash. From Hubbard (1958).

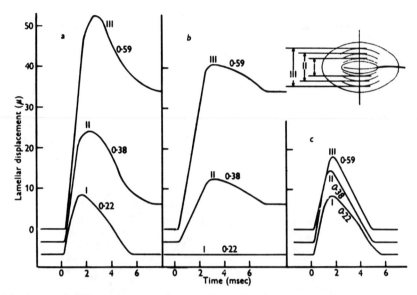

Fig. 6. Lamellar displacements at three positions within a corpuscle. Numbers on curves are ratios of radius of chosen lamellae to radius of outer capsule. Compression of 90 μm at mean velocity of 35 μm/sm began at zero time. From Hubbard (1958).

equivalent static displacement component (b) and a dynamic component (c) is also shown in this figure. The corpuscle acts as a mechanical filter transmitting only transient disturbances occurring at a sufficient rate to the region of the unmyelinated receptor terminal.

5. RECEPTOR POTENTIALS

Alvarez-Buylla and Ramirez de Arellano (1953) found that the nerve impulse at the Pacinian corpuscle was preceded by a local graded potential change in the intracorpuscular portion of the nerve membrane. This receptor or generator potential has been extensively studied by a number of investigators (Gray and Sato, 1953; Loewenstein, 1959; and others). Generally, these potential changes have been detected by recording between the corpuscle and the afferent fiber close to the corpuscle. An air or oil gap surrounding the afferent fiber just central to the corpuscle has been utilized to minimize external shunting. Mechanical stimulation of the corpuscle has usually been achieved by a piezoelectric device transmitting movement to the corpuscle by means of a stylus. A sufficiently rapid movement produces a graded depolarization of the nerve terminal which leads to an all-or-none impulse. Impulse activity may be blocked by procaine or tetrodotoxin, allowing the study in isolation of the receptor potential (see Fig. 7). In the intact Pacinian corpuscle exposed to procaine, Gray and Sato (1953) found that a brief mechanical impulse lasting a fraction of a millisecond evoked a receptor potential which rose rapidly to a peak and then decayed approximately exponentially with a time constant of several milliseconds. In response to a long mechanical stimulus, the rising phase was slower, as was the decay, but the receptor potential declined in spite of the maintenance of the stimulus. They also studied the relationship between stimulus strength and amplitude of the receptor potential. As may be seen in Fig. 8, this relationship is sigmoid, the receptor potential reaching a plateau with large stimulus strengths. The

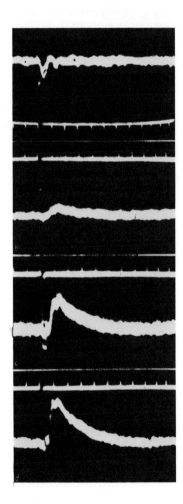

Fig. 7. Receptor potential in response to a brief mechanical pulse of graded strength (b.c.d.). Lower beam shows receptor potential, upper beam 1-ms timing pulses and electrical pulse to piezoelectric crystal. a, Photoelectric recording of crystal movement. From Gray and Sato (1953).

amplitude of the receptor potentials is also related to stimulus velocity. When repetitive pulses of mechanical stimuli are delivered, the receptor potential shows summation at short intervals. At longer intervals, a depression is observed, the second response being depressed for a period up to about 20 ms.

The receptor potential in response to sinusoidal vibration was studied by Sato (1961). The amplitude of the receptor potential was found to vary with frequency of sinusoidal stimulation of constant amplitude. At frequencies of 100–200 Hz, receptor potential amplitude was maximal and diminished as frequency was either increased or decreased.

The responses of Pacinian corpuscles from which the outer lamellae have been removed have been studied extensively by Loewenstein and his collaborators. The removal of the peripheral zone of lamellae and even multiple incisions into the inner core left the receptor potential in response to mechanical stimuli essentially unchanged (Loewenstein and Rathkamp, 1958). Evidence was also presented indicating spatial summation of the receptor potential when different portions of the myelinated terminal were mechanically stimulated.

Hubbard's (1958) study, noted above, suggests that the brief duration and rapid decay of the receptor potential to a long-duration compression of

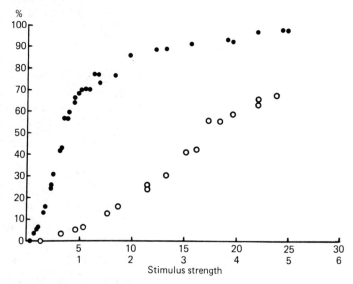

Fig. 8. Relation between amplitude of receptor potential and stimulus strength. Abscissa is the stimulus voltage applied to crystal: ○, 0–30; ●, 0–6. From Gray and Sato (1953).

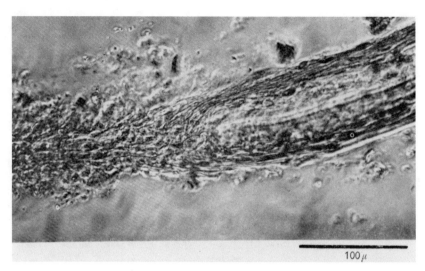

Fig. 9. Photomicrograph of a Pacinian corpuscle from which outer lamellae have been removed. From Ozeki and Sato (1965).

the intact corpuscle might be due to mechanical properties of the Pacinian corpuscle. Only the dynamic component of an applied compression was found in the displacement of lamellae near the inner core. The studies of Ozeki and Sato (1965) and of Mendelson and Loewenstein (1964) confirm this idea. When most of the lamellae are removed (Fig. 9), a prolonged compression results in a sustained receptor potential (Fig. 10). Ozeki and Sato (1965) also noted a hyperpolarization of the terminal on release from long-duration compression. The receptor potential and impulse initiation often seen upon release of compression was attributed to vibration of the stylus.

As noted above, the unmyelinated axon is oval in shape, its longest transverse axis being aligned with the clefts of the inner core. Il'inskii *et al.* (1968) have reported that stimuli applied along the short axis produce depolarization and along the long axis hyperpolarization of the terminal. It is possible that the displacement of the footlike extensions of the unmyelinated terminal into the cleft region produces the membrane changes leading to the receptor potential.

Although the rapid accommodation of the Pacinian corpuscle to mechanical stimuli, i.e., its response only to rapid changes, can be accounted for by its mechanical properties, the axon also seems to accommodate rapidly. Gray and Malcolm (1950) found that long depolarizing current pulses through the corpuscular portion of the nerve axon failed to evoke repetitive firing.

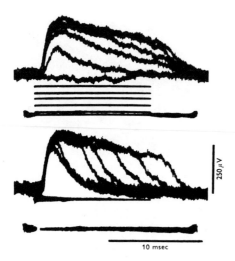

Fig. 10. Responses of a delamellated corpuscle to stimuli of varying strength (upper record) and varying duration (lower record). Upper trace in each record is receptor potential and lower trace voltage applied to piezoelectric crystal. From Ozeki and Sato (1965).

The effect of altering ionic composition on the receptor potential of Pacinian corpuscles has been the subject of several studies. In perfused corpuscles, Diamond *et al.* (1958) found that perfusion with sodium-free solution abolished the nerve impulse and reduced the amplitude of the receptor potential. The receptor potential of Pacinian corpuscles from which most of the lamellae were removed was also studied in sodium-deficient solutions (Sato *et al.*, 1968). Substitution of choline for sodium caused a marked reduction in receptor potential amplitude. Substitution by lithium caused a lesser reduction (*cf.* Nishi, 1968).

Mechanical deformation apparently leads to a conductance change which, in turn, depolarizes the receptor nerve membrane. The nature of the conductance change is not known, i.e., whether it is nonspecific or only to small cations. In any case, a change in conductance to Na appears to be involved.

The application of epinephrine or norepinephrine has been reported to lower the threshold of Pacinian corpuscles to applied mechanical stimuli (Loewenstein and Altamirano-Orrego, 1956). This is of interest in connection with the putative sympathetic innervation of the corpuscle (Santini, 1969).

6. IMPULSE ACTIVITY IN THE NERVE TERMINAL

When recording between the Pacinian corpuscle and its afferent fiber across the gap just central to the corpuscle, both a graded depolarization and an all-or-none response can be seen to occur distal to the gap (Gray and Sato, 1953). Before it was known that nodes of Ranvier occurred within and just adjacent to the corpuscle, this all-or-none response was attributed to the unmyelinated axon. Later, after nodes had been found within the corpuscle, it was generally thought that the unmyelinated axon produced only receptor or generator activity and that impulse initiation occurred at the first node. Two lines of work pointed to this: one was the effect of anodal current passed through the nerve terminal (Diamond *et al.*, 1956) and the other experiments by Loewenstein and Rathkamp (1958), who found that pressure on the first node of corpuscles from which outer lamellae were removed abolished all-or-none activity within the corpuscle.

However, Hunt and Takeuchi (1962) and Ozeki and Sato (1964) recorded potentials from corpuscles which had their outer lamellae removed and found clear evidence for the occurrence of all-or-none impulse activity in the un-myelinated axon in response to mechanical stimuli as well as antidromic stimulation of the axon. Hunt and Takeuchi recorded with wire electrodes external to the inner core, while Sato and Ozeki recorded across an oil–saline interface from a delamellated corpuscle positioned such that the recording was made clearly distal to the first node. Both a graded and an all-or-none negativity in the unmyelinated terminal were demonstrated following mechanical stimulation. Sato and Ozeki found that the amplitude of the receptor poten-

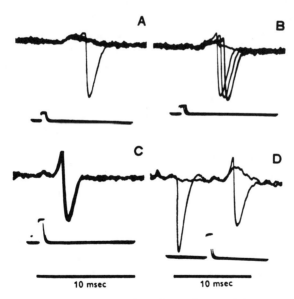

Fig. 11. Response of unmyelinated region of axon in a Pacinian corpuscle. Recording distal to first node in a preparation from which outer lamellae had been removed (termi-nal negativity giving upward deflection). A,B, Responses to near-threshold stimuli; C, supramaximal stimuli. In D, one trace show antidromic impulse, which is followed by receptor potential alone. Modified from Sato and Ozeki (1963).

tial was depressed by a preceding antidromic impulse (Fig. 11). Application to the unmyelinated terminal of procaine blocked its all-or-none response, leaving only the receptor potential.

7. DISTRIBUTION OF PACINIAN CORPUSCLES

In mammals, the Pacinian corpuscle is widely distributed through the body. A number are found in relation to the skin, their axons coursing centrally in cutaneous nerves. In man and in monkeys, large numbers are found in the terminal portions of the digits. In cats, there are large numbers in the vicinity of the footpads. Also, a group is found in relation to vibrissae-like hairs on the cat's foreleg (Nilsson and Skoglund, 1963). Occasional corpuscles occur elsewhere in subcutaneous locations. In some species, such as the cat, a large number of Pacinian corpuscles are found in the mesentery. They are also numerous in certain retroperitoneal structures, particularly around the pancreas.

An important site for Pacinian corpuscles in the deep structures of the limb is in proximity to bone. In the cat, there is a collection of about 50 corpuscles bound to the interosseous membrane between the distal thirds of the tibia and fibula and innervated by the interosseous nerve (Hunt and McIntyre, 1960; Hunt, 1961). Some of these corpuscles are bound by connective tissue to the tibial periosteum. In this locus, the corpuscles are in a particularly effective position to detect bone-transmitted vibration. The interosseous nerve of the cat is a convenient site for recording the activity of a large group of Pacinian corpuscles. This nerve has also been used for stimulation of axons of these receptors for the study of central effects. This nerve does, however, contain afferent fibers from other types of receptors in the interosseous region. A similar collection of corpuscles is found next to the tibia and ulna in birds (Skoglund, 1960). A variant of the Pacinian corpuscles, the so-called paciniform corpuscle, is found in rather small numbers in relation to muscle, and their axons course essentially in muscle nerves.

Certain locations of Pacinian corpuscles are clearly important for the detection of vibration. For example, the corpuscles in the fingertips probably play a significant role in the detection of texture as the fingers are drawn across a surface. The corpuscles which lie in relation to bone must be important for the detection of vibration transmitted from the ground to the body.

What role the corpuscles lying deep in the viscera play is less certain. Such corpuscles may respond to the vibration produced by pulsations of blood pressure, and a number of attempts have been made to determine whether such corpuscles are in some way involved in cardiovascular regulation. This remains an open question.

8. CENTRAL EFFECTS OF IMPULSES FROM PACINIAN CORPUSCLES

The sense of vibration is a well-recognized modality in man. The sensation is specific in the sense of the adequate natural stimulus which provokes it as well as in the quality of the perception. Vibration in the range of about 60–1000 Hz can be sensed, particularly by the fingertips, or when vibration is applied to bone such as the ankle. At lower frequencies, vibration applied to the fingertips evokes a perception somewhat different in quality, which has been termed "flutter." Over the range of frequencies which can evoke a 1:1 discharge in Pacinian corpuscles, a sense of the frequency applied can also be appreciated. It has been claimed that sinusoidal frequencies up to 20,000 Hz can be sensed. Pacinian corpuscles are not capable of responding to pure sinusoidal vibration at frequencies much above 1000 Hz, and it is likely that subharmonics produced by large amplitudes of vibration are responsible for these effects.

A comparison has been made of the threshold–frequency relationship for impulse activity from Pacinian corpuscles of the monkey hand and the threshold–frequency relationship for the perception, in man, of vibration applied to the fingertips (Talbot et al., 1968). The parallelism between these two relationships leaves little doubt that Pacinian corpuscles are the receptors involved in vibration sense and that other receptors are responsible for the sensation of flutter.

9. REFERENCES

Alvarez-Buylla, R., and Ramirez de Arrellano, J., 1953, Local responses in Pacinian corpuscles, Am. J. Physiol. 172:237.

Diamond, J., Gray, J. A. B., and Sato, M., 1956, The site of initiation of impulses in Pacinian corpuscles, J. Physiol. 133:54.

Diamond, J., Gray, J. A. B., and Inman, D. R., 1958, The relation between receptor potentials and the concentration of sodium ions, J. Physiol. 142:382.

Goto, K., Sorimachi, M., Shibazaki, S., and Loewenstein, W., 1966, A dual nerve supply of Pacinian corpuscle, J. Physiol. Soc. Jap. 28:27.

Gray, J. A. B., and Malcolm, J. L., 1950, The initiation of nerve impulses by mesenteric Pacinian corpuscles, Proc. Roy. Soc. Ser. B 137:96.

Gray, J. A. B., and Matthews, P. B. C., 1951, Responses of Pacinian corpuscles in the cat's toe, J. Physiol. 113:475.

Gray, J. A. B., and Sato, M., 1953, Properties of the receptor potential in Pacinian corpuscles, J. Phyisol. 122:610.

Hubbard, S. J., 1958, A study of rapid mechanical events in a mechanoreceptor, J. Physiol. 141:198.

Hunt, C. C., 1961, On the nature of vibration receptors in the hind limbs of cat, J. Physiol. 155:175.

Hunt, C. C., and McIntyre, A. K., 1960, Characteristics of responses from receptors from the flexor digitorum muscle and the adjoining interosseous region of the cat, J. Physiol. 153:74.

Hunt, C. C., and Takeuchi, A., 1962, Response of the nerve terminal of the Pacinian corpuscle, *J. Physiol.* **160**:1.

Il'inskii, O. B., Volkova, N. K., and Cherepnor, V. L., 1968, Structure and function of Pacinis corpuscle (cat), *Fiziol. 2H SSR 1M 1M Sechenova* **54**:285 (English summary).

Leitner, J. M., and Perl, E. R., 1964, Receptors supplied by spinal nerves which respond to cardiovascular changes and adrenaline, *J. Physiol.* **175**:254.

Loewenstein, W. R., 1959, The generation of electrical activity in a nerve ending, *Ann. N.Y. Acad. Sci.* **81**:367.

Loewenstein, W. R., and Altamirano-Orrego, R., 1956, Enhancement of activity in a Pacinian corpuscle by sympathomimetic agents, *Nature* **178**:1292.

Loewenstein, W. R., and Rathkamp, R., 1958, The sites for mechano-electrical conversion in a Pacinian corpuscle, *J. Gen. Physiol.* **41**:1245.

McIntyre, A. K., Holman, M. E., and Veale, J. L., 1967, Cortical responses to impulses from single pacinian corpuscles in the cat's hind limb, *Exper. Brain Res.* **4**:243.

Mendelson, M., and Loewenstein, W. R., 1964, Mechanism of receptor adaptation, *Science* **144**:554.

Nilsson, B. Y., and Skoglund, C. R., 1963, Studies of the tactile hairs and adjacent Pacinian corpuscles on the cat's foreleg, *Acta Physiol. Scand.* **59**:111 (Suppl. 213).

Nishi, K., 1968, Modification of the mechanical threshold of the Pacinian corpuscle after its perfusion with solutions of varying cation content, *Jap. J. Physiol.* **18**:216.

Nishi, K., and Sato, M., 1966, Blocking of the impulse and depression of the receptor potential by tetrodotoxin in non-myelinated nerve terminals in Pacinian corpuscles, *J. Physiol.* **184**:376.

Nishi, K., Oura, C. Y., and Pallie, W., 1969, Fine structure of Pacinian corpuscles in the mesentery of the cat, *J. Cell Biol.* **43**:539.

Ozeki, M., and Sato, M., 1964, Initiation of impulses at the non-myelinated nerve terminal in Pacinian corpuscles, *J. Physiol.* **170**:167.

Ozeki, M., and Sato, M., 1965, Changes in the membrane potential and the membrane conductance associated with a sustained compression of the non-myelinated nerve terminal in Pacinian corpuscles, *J. Physiol.* **180**:186.

Pacini, F., 1835, Sopra un particolor genere di piccoli corpi globulosi scoperti nel corpo umano da Filippo Pacini alumno interno degli Spedali riuniti di Pistoia, Letter to Accademia Medico-fisica di Firenze.

Pease, D. C., and Quilliam, T. A., 1957, Electron microscopy of the Pacinian corpuscle, *J. Biophys. Biochem. Cytol.* **3**:331.

Quilliam, T. A., and Sato, M., 1955, The distribution of myelin on nerve fibres from Pacinian corpuscles, *J. Physiol.* **129**:167.

Santini, M., 1969, New fibres of sympathetic nature in the inner core region of Pacinian corpuscles, *Brain Res.* **16**:535.

Sato, M., 1961, Response of Pacinian corpuscles to sinusoidal vibration, *J. Physiol.* **159**:391.

Sato, M., and Ozeki, M., 1963, Response of the non-myelinated nerve terminal in Pacinian corpuscles to mechanical and antidromic stimulation and the effect of procaine, choline and cooling, *Jap. J. Physiol.* **13**:564.

Sato, M., Ozeki, M., and Nishi, K., 1968, Changes produced by sodium-free condition in the receptor potential of the non-myelinated terminal in Pacinian corpuscles, *Jap. J. Physiol.* **18**:232.

Skoglund, C. R., 1960, Properties of Pacinian corpuscles of ulnar and tibial location in cat and fowl, *Acta Physiol. Scand.* **50**:385.

Talbot, W. H., Darian-Smith, I., Koruhuber, H., and Mountcastle, V. B., 1968, The sense of flutter-vibration: Comparison of the human capacity with response patterns of mechanoreceptive afferents from the monkey hand, *J. Neurophysiol.* **31**:301.

Chapter 14

Receptors in Muscles and Joints

P. B. C. Matthews

University Laboratory of Physiology
Oxford University
Oxford, England

1. INTRODUCTION

Throughout the vertebrata, skeletal muscles are found to be provided with sensory receptors, as also appears to be the case for the joints upon which they act. The function of these receptors is to provide the central nervous system with information about the mechanical state of the body and thus to assist in the central control of muscle action. An engineer faced with the problem of controlling a motor of variable strength working into a variety of loads would undoubtedly incorporate feedback elements to monitor its performance, particularly if the motor were as nonlinear in its input–output relation as is skeletal muscle. Evolution would also appear to have long favored the use of feedback to achieve precision of action and has quite possibly brought about the development of control mechanisms that are more refined than any yet invented by man; at present, physiologists are mostly content with pointing out the analogy between biological control systems and engineered ones, rather than seeking novel principles in the biological ones. It is thus of some interest to describe the various biological transducers which provide the feedback information required for muscle control, even though we cannot yet specify the precise ways this information is used by the CNS.

The increasing complexity of the peripheral organization that has occurred with evolutionary advance may be expected to be matched by an increase in the subtlety with which the information is processed centrally. In part, the information is used to reflexly adjust motoneuronal discharge, as in the well-known stretch reflex by means of which an external stretch of a muscle is reflexly resisted by muscle contraction. In part, proprioceptive information is used by higher levels of the nervous system such as the cerebellum for processes which we cannot yet specify but which can proceed independently of consciousness. In part, some of the information is deployed by the highest levels of the nervous system to influence one's conscious perception of the relative positions of one's limbs and thus assist in the elaboration of a body image. The reflex and other central mechanisms have recently been discussed elsewhere along with a more detailed description of peripheral events (Matthews, 1972). The present account is restricted to the periphery and aims to detail the behavior of each of the main types of receptors. Most of the experimental work performed hitherto has been on the mammal, notably the cat, so the present account is inevitably heavily biased in this direction. The early histological work performed in the second half of the nineteenth century, however, covered a very wide range of species and was particularly well reviewed by Regaud and Favre (1904). The more recent histological work has been dealt with by Barker (1968), and Bone (1964) has discussed fish in detail. At present, we tend to generalize the results obtained on a few selected species to all vertebrates, but in so doing we should recognize the risk of a fall.

2. JOINT RECEPTORS

The capsules which surround joints are supplied by sensory nerve fibers of all sizes. In the knee joint of the cat, which has been the most intensively investigated (Gardner, 1950; Skoglund, 1956; Freeman and Wyke, 1967), the relatively few fibers of over 10 μm are thought to terminate in the joint ligaments in Golgi-type endings which are essentially similar to those in tendons. The more numerous fibers of 5–10 μm diameter terminate largely as Ruffini-type endings in the joint capsule. This type of ending has several separate spray terminals each about 100 μm in diameter arranged in three dimensions in the connective tissue of the capsule. In addition, joint capsules contain a number of lamellated end organs which are smaller and relatively more elongated than the typical Pacinian corpuscle found elsewhere and so are called "paciniform corpuscles." They are normally supplied by medium-sized medullated axons of the same size as those to the Ruffini endings. In addition, there are a number of free nerve endings supplied both by fine medullated and by nonmedullated afferent fibers.

The behavior of these various endings has been intensively studied in the cat by recording the discharge set up in single afferents on moving the joint, using standard electrophysiological methods. The discharge patterns of each particular kind of receptor were established by ablating the very regions of joint capsule or ligament which had just been studied electrophysiologically and then identifying the receptor histologically. The Golgi endings are found to discharge at a rate dependent on the tension in the ligament and to be sensitive almost entirely to the absolute magnitude of the stimulus and hardly at all to its rate of change; in other words, they adapt slowly. The Ruffini endings are moderately rapidly adapting, but they do discharge steadily in response to a steady angular displacement of the knee. However, they fire much more rapidly during phasic movements, showing that they are sensitive to angular velocity as well as to angular position. Their sensitivity can, however, be altered by contraction of the surrounding muscles. The paciniform corpuscles are sensitive to phasic stimuli but not to steady stimuli, and Skoglund (1956) suggested that they primarily serve to signal angular acceleration.

Until recently, it was widely held that individual Ruffini endings each discharged impulses over only a small part of the angular range of a joint and that different endings had different optimum excitatory angles scattered more or less uniformly throughout the whole range of joint movement. Thus the CNS was thought to be able to determine the angle of a joint by detecting which of the various Ruffini endings were firing. Unfortunately, Burgess and Clark (1969), in a more detailed study than any hitherto, were unable to confirm this view for the knee joint of the cat. Virtually no endings were excited with the knee in the mid-position and thus the joint receptors were then failing to provide a signal to enable the CNS to decide on the position of the knee. The presumed Ruffini endings were excited when the limb was moved to one or the other extreme, but many of them were excited equally by flexion and by extension, so that their signals would appear to be irrelevant for helping the CNS to decide between these two contrasting positions. The explanation, if any, of this paradoxical behavior is not yet to hand. But receptors in other joints may well behave more simply; for example, in the costovertebral joint any particular ending is maximally excited at one extreme only, though some are excited by displacement in one direction and some in the other (Godwin-Austen, 1969). Moreover, whichever their preferred direction of displacement for maximal excitation, the majority of costovertebral endings discharge throughout the physiologically normal range of movement of the rib, so that a peripheral signal of joint angle is always available to the CNS.

The reflex effects of joint afferents are comparatively slight; rather, they are normally thought to have as their chief role the providing of sensory signals to allow the highest cortical levels to appreciate limb position and also to detect any passively imposed displacement of the limb. The threshold for detection of dynamic displacement of a joint is often around 1°, but the accuracy with which a given joint position can be recognized is considerably lower. For the last decade, such proprioceptive sensations have been thought to depend entirely on joint afferents, but recent experiments by Goodwin *et al.* (1972) suggest that muscle afferents also contribute.

3. TENDON ORGANS

Tendon organs lie at the musculocutaneous junctions and are often called after Camillo Golgi, who gave them their first full description in 1880. They are found at both the origin and the insertion of a muscle, so that a muscle cannot be deprived of them merely by ablating its tendon. The Golgi tendon organ is derived from a large medullated nerve fiber (10–20 μm in diameter) which breaks up into a series of fine sprays which run between the bundles of collagen fibers. The whole structure may be up to 1 mm long in man. Figure 1 shows an early picture of the tendon organ and emphasizes that an individual tendon organ is directly pulled on only by a relatively small number of muscle fibers; thus it would be expected to respond preferentially to the contraction of only 10–20 fibers out of the many thousands that occur in a muscle of any size.

Electrophysiological recording shows that tendon organs are excited both by muscle stretch and by muscle contraction, as might be expected from their position at the musculocutaneous junction. In this respect, their behavior contrasts with that of the muscle spindle receptors; these are also excited by muscle stretch but fall silent on muscle contraction because they are then relieved of preexisting strain. This difference in behavior is illustrated in Fig. 2. In current jargon, the tendon organs are said to lie "in series" with the muscle fibers, whereas the spindles lie "in parallel"; this arrangement allows nerve

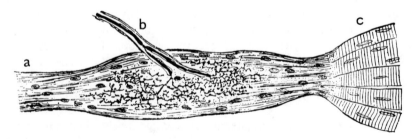

Fig. 1. The Golgi tendon organ as seen by Cajal. a, tendon; b, large afferent fiber breaking up into sensory terminals; c, muscle fibers. From Cajal (1909, Fig. 199).

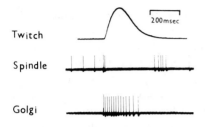

Twitch

Spindle

Golgi

Fig. 2. The contrasting responses of a spindle ending and of a tendon organ during a twitch contraction. From Matthews (1972, Fig. 3.2).

transducers of possibly similar properties to transmit rather different signals to the CNS. Their different behavior also emphasizes the dangers of labeling any receptor that is excited by muscle stretch as a "stretch receptor," without further qualification. At the very beginning of electrophysiological work (Matthews, 1933), the tendon organ was established as adapting rather slowly to a maintained stimulus and as responding to the absolute value of muscle tension, without being greatly influenced by the rate of change of tension *per se*. For many years afterward, there appeared to be little more to say about tendon organs, but there has been a recent revival of interest in the extent to which they are concerned merely with signaling tensions developed by passive stretching of a muscle compared with the extent to which they are concerned with signaling active contractile tension and hence serving as "contraction detectors."

In several muscles of the cat, the threshold of the tendon organs, expressed as a tension, may be sufficiently high for them to be excited only weakly, or not at all, by stretches confined to the physiological range and occurring in the absence of muscle contraction, although they may be excited by very rapid stretches (Stuart *et al.*, 1970; Houk *et al.*, 1971). But individual tendon organs are readily excited by the tension produced by the contraction of a single motor unit, provided that it is appropriately placed to pull directly on the fascicles upon which the particular tendon organ studied lies, as was shown by Houk and Henneman (1967). Moreover, from the appreciable number of different motor units which have been found to influence an individual tendon organ it has been argued that the tetanic contraction of only a single muscle fiber is sufficient to overstep the threshold of an appropriately placed tendon organ. It follows that tendon organs must be excited in the course of even the weakest of muscle contractions. In life, most of the tendon organ discharge would appear to be due to muscle contraction, since comparatively small tensions are normally developed on stretching muscles over their physiological range. But in some muscles, such as the tibialis anterior, a few tendon organs are found to be firing spontaneously in the virtual absence of muscle contraction. Hence there is little point in denying tendon organs a role in signaling passive tensions as well as active tensions, although in practice the latter seem likely to be the most important.

Information on the behavior of tendon organs outside the cat is virtually absent, but their presumed discharges have been recorded in both frog and duck (Ito, 1968; Dorward, 1970). In the frog, they appear to be scanty and to have a relatively high threshold to passive stretches, whereas in the duck they are numerous and have a low threshold. In birds and mammals, at least, they may be looked upon as an essential term of the proprioceptive equipment. In the cat, they are as numerous as the muscle spindles, although occasional small muscles may be without them.

4. MUSCLE SPINDLES

Evolutionary progress has led to the progressive elaboration of a complex end organ out of what was probably originally no more than an afferent nerve fiber terminating on the belly of a muscle fiber, rather than at its junction with the tendon as does the tendon organ. Figure 3 shows a classical drawing of a mammalian spindle and illustrates its complexity. Reptiles, amphibia, birds, and mammals possess muscle spindles in virtually all their skeletal muscles. Remarkably, however, fish, whether body or cartilaginous, appear not to have discovered the muscle spindle, but they may possess other less specialized types of proprioceptive endings, particularly near to or in muscles associated with relatively delicate movements such as those of the fins (Bone, 1964). The swimming muscles of teleosts are currently thought to be completely unprovided with proprioceptors of any kind, but a few have been described for elasmobranchs.

In its essentials, the muscle spindle consists of one or more specialized intrafusal muscle fibers, the central or equatorial regions of which are enclosed in a capsule and have a sensory nerve fiber terminating on them. The capsule contains a certain amount of fluid which presumably has the function of mechanically insulating a highly sensitive sensory terminal from its gross environment and so leaving it free to signal what is happening to the underlying intrafusal fiber. The intrafusal muscle fibers are usually rather thinner

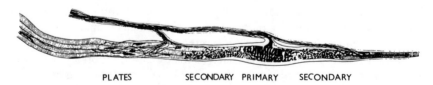

PLATES   SECONDARY PRIMARY   SECONDARY

Fig. 3. The muscle spindle as seen by Ruffini at the turn of the last century. From Ruffini (1898, Fig. 1, retouched).

than the extrafusal muscle fibers of the same muscle, but direct visual observation leaves no doubt that they are contractile and that they are normally triggered into action by impulses descending their motor nerves rather than being spontaneously active like some smooth muscles. The region of intrafusal fiber on which the sensory terminals lie is often poorly striated and contracts less strongly than the rest of the fiber, with the result that the sensory ending is excited when the intrafusal fiber is activated. The intrafusal fibers are attached at their ends to extrafusal fibers or to tendinous filaments; by lying "in parallel" with the ordinary fibers, the length of, and hence the tension in, the intrafusal bundle is constrained to reflect the length of the muscle in which it lies rather than the tension in it. The discharge of the sensory ending thus depends partly on what is happening to the length of the muscle as a whole and partly on whether its own particular intrafusal muscle fibers are contracting.

The increasing evolutionary complexity of the muscle spindle is shown by an increase in the number of intrafusal fibers, by their motor supply being separated from that of the ordinary muscle fibers, and by the appearance of more than one kind of sensory ending within the same spindle. In reptiles, there is normally only a single intrafusal fiber in a spindle, but man, for example, may have up to 14. In reptiles and amphibia, the motor supply to the spindles is exclusively derived from branches of the normal motor fibers to the rest of the muscle, whereas the mammalian spindle normally receives its entire motor supply from specialized fusimotor fibers which are without action on extrafusal muscle fibers. In frogs and reptiles, there is only a single sensory ending within a given muscle spindle, while in mammals there are often two or more differing in their functional properties. However, different spindles in the reptile have sensory endings with different properties, suggesting that a subdivision of function may have been achieved between spindles rather than within a single spindle. In one respect, however, all the types of spindles which have so far been studied have developed the complication of having more than one kind of intrafusal fiber, differing in their speed of contraction. In reptiles with their monofibrillar spindles, this appears to be achieved by having different kinds of muscle fibers in different spindles. These various matters will next be considered in more detail for the few species that have been investigated. It will be appreciated, of course, that the above statements on evolution are based on the study of a few highly developed forms of their kind and so are far from secure.

4.1. Reptiles

It has long been recognized that the muscle spindles of the snake and lizard possess only a single intrafusal muscle fiber (Huber and DeWitt, 1897;

Regaud and Favre, 1904). They thus provide an unusually favorable preparation for experimental analysis, but it is one which has only just begun to be exploited. There are, however, two different kinds of muscle spindles, both of which may occur in the same muscle, although some muscles possess only one of them. One kind has a short, thick capsule, measuring about 40 by 150 μm, and within it the intrafusal fiber broadens out and loses its striations because the myofilaments are replaced by nuclei, mitochondria, lipoid droplets, and various other cytoplasmic constituents. The sensory ending lies on this region, which is nonstriated and thus is very different from the rest of the intrafusal fiber. These spindles are variously called "short-capsule spindles," thick spindles," or "phasic spindles." Other spindles have a thin, elongated capsular region, measuring about 20 by 300 μm, and their intrafusal fiber retains its striations throughout its length so that the sensory ending, which is again disposed equatorially, lies on a striated region of fiber. These are called "long-capsule spindles," or "thin spindles," or "tonic spindles." Outside the capsular region, the intrafusal fibers of the two kinds of spindles appear identical. Electron microscopy shows that the sensory nerve terminals of both kinds of spindles consist simply of crescent shaped nonmedullated terminals some 7 μm broad and 1 μm thick closely applied to the intrafusal membrane and underlying the basement membrane of the muscle (Fukami and Hunt, 1970).

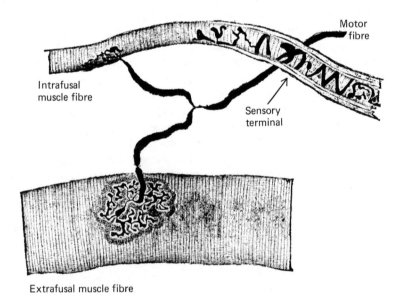

Fig. 4. Classical illustration of the shared motor innervation of an intrafusal and of an extrafusal muscle fiber in the lizard. From Perroncito (1901, Fig. 5).

The intrafusal motor fibers appear invariably to arise as branches from the motor fibers to the extrafusal muscle fibers rather than from separate fusimotor fibers, as illustrated in Fig. 4. Such an occurrence has been recognized from the earliest days. The appearance of the motor terminations may be fairly variable, but two basic types are recognizable, namely, discrete "plate" endings and diffuse "grape" endings, as also found for the extrafusal muscle fibers of the same species. It seems probable that any particular motor axon always has terminations of the same type, whether plate or grape, and irrespective of whether the terminations lie on intrafusal or on extrafusal fibers, and that plates are derived from large fibers and grapes from small ones (Szepsenwol, 1960). The intrafusal distribution of these two kinds of endings, however, has yet to be firmly established. It has been suggested that the long-capsule spindles are innervated solely by plate endings and the short-capsule spindles by grape endings (Szepsenwol, 1960; Barker, 1968); against this, it has been stated that long-capsule spindles sometimes receive grape endings instead of plate endings (Proske, 1969a). The matter merits further study since the morphology of the motor ending may be related to the physiology of the intrafusal fiber that it supplies. Considering a wide range of species, plate endings tend to be found on muscle fibers which contract rapidly and are capable of propagating all-or-none action potentials, whereas

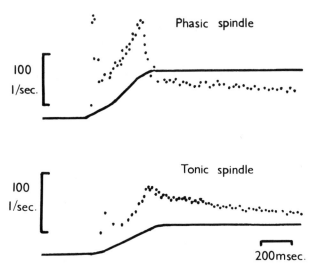

Fig. 5. The contrasting responses of a tonic and of a phasic spindle in the lizard. Responses from spindles in two different muscles to comparable stretches (approximately 5 mm at 10 mm/s). Each dot represents an action potential, and its "instantaneous frequency" is given by the scale on the left. Traced from Proske (1969b, Figs. 5 and 6).

grape endings tend to occur on muscle fibers which contract relatively slowly and which are activated by means of nonpropagated potentials localized to the regions of the motor terminations (Barker, 1968). In the snake spindle, however, limited evidence favors the idea that all intrafusal fibers can give relatively rapid "twitch" contractions and can sustain a propagated action potential (Hunt and Wylie, 1970; Fukami, 1970); any functional differences there may be have yet to be described between intrafusal fibers in thick and thin spindles, and those supplied by plate and by grape endings.

The sensory fibers of thick and thin spindles do, however, differ in their behavior. Those in thick spindles are markedly the more sensitive to dynamic stimuli (Proske, 1969b; Fukami, 1970a). This is illustrated in Fig. 5 and is of particular interest since the same sort of functional difference is found between the two morphologically distinct kinds of sensory endings that occur within a single mammalian spindle, namely, the primary and the secondary endings. In both reptile and mammal, the more dynamically sensitive ending is the one that lies on a poorly striated region of intrafusal fiber. However, not all reptiles have such simple spindles; those of the tortoise are multifibrillar (Huber and DeWitt, 1897; Crowe and Ragab, 1970, but their physiology has yet to be investigated.

4.2. Amphibia

Largely for practical reasons concerned with their maintenance, frogs and toads have established themselves as standard laboratory animals, and so their spindles have been very much more intensively investigated than those of reptiles. The amphibian spindle was described in considerable detail by Cajal (1909), who was among the first to recognize it as a sensory end organ under motor control. As illustrated in Fig. 6, this early work established that the amphibian spindle contains several intrafusal muscle fibers which are well striated except at their equator in the capsule where some or all of the fibers lose their striations. A large nerve fiber, terminating in varicose threads lying along the central regions of the intrafusal fibers, was recognized as a

Fig. 6. Classical illustration of the amphibian muscle spindle. A, Large medullated afferent fiber which branches to give rise to fine nonmedullated terminals arranged linearly along the intrafusal fibers; B, medullated motor fiber. From Cajal (1909, Fig. 198).

sensory terminal, and smaller plate endings, lying more polarly, were recognized as motor terminations. In 1957, Gray made a detailed investigation of the frog spindle as seen under the light microscope and helped establish the view that it contains two separate types of intrafusal muscle fibers which are distinguishable by their size and which are supplied by two separate kinds of motor nerve fibers, both of which are derived from branches of the motor fibers to the extrafusal muscles. By that time, the functional distinctions between the large and small extrafusal muscle fibers had been amply demonstrated by experiment. The large extrafusal fibers are "twitch" fibers which contract rapidly in response to a propagated muscle action potential that is initiated at a typical plate ending by a single impulse in a large motor fiber (diameter above 5 μm). The small extrafusal muscle fibers are "slow" fibers which contract sluggishly even in response to high-frequency activation and which are incapable of generating an action potential across their membrane but instead are activated by localized "small junctional potentials" that are restricted to the region of the motor endings; these latter are grape endings derived from small motor axons (diameter 2–5 μm). Gray's work suggested that the same dichotomy of function should occur within the spindle, though his preparations were actually insufficiently distinct for him to be able to state categorically that the small intrafusal fibers were selectively innervated by grape endings from small nerves and the large intrafusal fibers by plates from large nerves.

Shortly afterward, Katz (1961) made a detailed electron microscopic examination of the frog spindle with particular reference to the arrangement of the afferent terminals, and there have been various subsequent studies (Karlsson *et al.*, 1966; Karlsson and Andersson-Cedergren, 1966; Page, 1966). Among other things, Katz showed that some intrafusal muscle fibers retained their striations and myofilaments throughout the sensory region, though they still apparently received normal afferent terminals, and suggested that these might be "slow" fibers. Page (1966) studied this point in more detail and confirmed the existence of two kinds of intrafusal muscle fibers on the basis of their ultrastructural appearance. One was very similar in its fine structure to twitch extrafusal fibers, and in the two fibers in which the motor ending could be found it was of the plate type. The other kind of intrafusal fibers resembled the extrafusal slow fibers in certain respects (ill-defined H zone, usually no M line) but differed from them in others (the arrangement of the Z line and quantity of sarcoplasmic reticulum), and so Page classified them as an "intermediate" fiber and felt that it would be improper to homologize them with the slow fibers; moreover, not all the intermediate fibers retained their myofilaments throughout the equatorial region. On the three occasions that the motor endings could be found, intermediate intrafusal fibers were supplied by grape endings. Thus a structural dichotomy of amphibian intrafusal fibers seems to be well established, though it is not precisely the same as that for the extrafusal fibers. Nor would this duality of motor function appear to be a universal property of the amphibian spindle, for Page found that some spindles contained only twitch intrafusals and lacked intermediate fibers. Moreover, Brown (1971a) could not produce the expected dynamic sensitizing action on spindles from the sartorius muscle by the injection of suxamethonium (which is thought to produce a prolonged contraction of the slow muscle fibers), even though it did so for the majority of spindles in the iliofibularis muscle. This was taken to suggest that sartorius spindles lack slow intrafusal fibers just as the sartorius muscle itself is almost totally lacking in slow extrafusal muscle fibers.

Katz (1961) found that the fine structure of the amphibian afferent terminals was unlike that of either reptile or mammalian afferent terminals. After subdividing several times and losing its myelin sheath, the nerve fiber terminated as a series of beaded chains, about eight of which lay on any given cross-section of an intrafusal fiber. Each chain was probably over 100 μm long and consisted of bulbous expansions of 2–3 μm diameter connected by 5-μm lengths of thin axis cylinder of only 0.15 μm diameter. The bulbs were commonly situated in cuplike depressions of the intrafusal membrane and sometimes appeared to be anchored to it by fine bridges. Figure 7 illustrates their structure. Katz confirmed that there is only one kind of sensory termination supplied by only a single afferent fiber, but he raised the possibility there might still be a subdivision of afferent function within the spindle, for the beaded chains of microspindles overlay two quite distinct regions of intrafusal fiber, quite apart from the terminations on any small intrafusal fibers. Some terminals lay on a 100-μm-long equatorial "reticular" region of intrafusal fiber which was largely devoid of myofilaments and which contained instead a number of nuclei; furthermore, the fiber was here divided into fins and

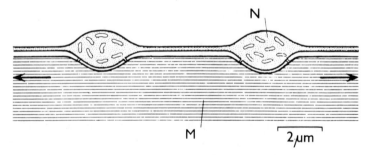

Fig. 7. Drawing of the "beaded-chain" arrangement of the afferent terminals in the frog spindle. M, Muscle fiber; N, nerve terminal with possible attachments to muscle. From Katz (1961, Fig. 38).

branches with the intervening extracellular space filled with a network of fine reticular fibers. Other terminals, and these were in the majority, lay on 300-μm-long "compact" regions of intrafusal fiber which flanked the reticular zone and which have a structure very similar to the polar regions of the fiber with a rich content of myofilaments. In the light of the hypothesis that intrafusal mechanics play an important part in determining the behavior of the ending, Katz suggested that these different sets of afferent terminals might provide different contributions to the overall discharge of the single spindle afferent and more specifically that the terminations over the reticular zone might provide much of the dynamic responsiveness of the whole ending and those over the compact zone much of its static responsiveness. Thus he envisaged a type of afferent specialization rather different from that seen in the reptile and the mammal with their separate types of afferent fibers, but there is as yet no confirmation of this idea.

Experiment has run more or less parallel with the recent histology and has been in very good agreement with it. In 1931, Matthews established electrophysiologically that the amphibian muscle spindle is indeed a stretch receptor, as had long been surmised. In 1949, Katz produced experimental evidence that, in accordance with the histology, the intrafusal muscle fibers were supplied by branches of the ordinary motor fibers rather than by a specialized fusimotor supply of their own. The duality of the motor nerve supply was more firmly established by Eyzaguirre (1957, 1958) by stimulating single motor fibers repetitively. He showed, moreover, that large motor fibers induced a more abrupt change of afferent firing than did small ones which acted on the selfsame spindle. This was in accordance with the view that the fast and slow motor fibers supplied intrafusal muscle fibers with fast and slow contractile properties, respectively.

The first intracellular recordings showed that some at least of the intrafusal fibers were capable of sustaining propagated all-or-none action potentials (Eyzaguirre, 1957; Koketsu and Nishi, 1957), but initially it seemed likely that such behavior was restricted to the large intrafusal fibers and that the small ones would in due course be found to have nonpropagated potentials as do their extrafusal counterparts. However, this idea was soon contradicted by Smith (1964a), who recorded extracellularly from isolated toad spindles and stimulated either large or small motor fibers by means of an anodal blocking technique. As illustrated in Fig. 8, the small motor fibers, like the large ones, were then found to elicit a propagated intrafusal potential as shown by the occurrence of a diphasic action potential. But when the frequency of stimulation of the small fibers was increased above about 5/s the diphasic potential was converted to a monophasic one, showing that the propagation had then failed. In contrast, the large intrafusal fibers were found to be able to continue to propagate potentials at frequencies up to 30/s. Thus

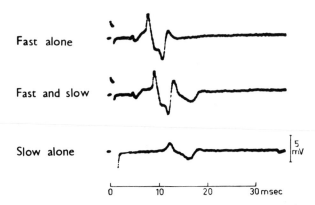

Fast alone

Fast and slow

Slow alone

Fig. 8. Action potentials recorded extracellularly from intrafusal muscle fibers in the toad on stimulating fast and/or slow motor fibers using an anodal blocking technique. Judging by their diphasicity, the potentials elicited by both kinds of nerves were propagated along the intrafusal fibers. From Smith (1964*a*, Fig. 7).

the large intrafusal fibers behaved in much the same way as the large extra-fusal fibers, but the small intrafusal fibers clearly differed from the slow extra-fusal fibers in spite of sharing a common motor innervation with them.

It was particularly fortunate that Smith (1964*b*) proceeded immediately to investigate some of the contractile properties of the two kinds of intrafusal fibers and thereby confirmed the original view that they did differ from each other in spite of both being able to sustain a propagated potential. Smith studied the time course of intrafusal contraction by taking cinephotographs of the contracting intrafusal fibers and subsequently measuring their sarco-mere spacing. One of his graphs is shown in Fig. 9 and demonstrates that the small intrafusal fibers contract more slowly than the large ones, but probably not as slowly as the slow extrafusal fibers, although this could usefully be studied under a wider range of conditions. The significance for sensory action of the speed of intrafusal contraction has recently been emphasized by Brown (1971*b*). Fast-contracting intrafusal fibers can rapidly pull in any slack when the muscle is released, or let it go when the muscle is stretched, thus making the spindle relatively insensitive to length changes. In contrast, during con-traction of slow intrafusal fibers the spindle cannot effectively follow changes in muscle length and would thereby be expected to become sensitized to dynamic stimuli and to small changes in muscle length, in the way familiar for the mammalian spindle during stimulation of the dynamic fusimotor fibers. As illustrated in Fig. 10, the pattern of spindle firing mirrors the pattern of extrafusal tension changes both when large and when small fibers are being activated. Matthews and Westbury (1965) had earlier shown that the large and small motor fibers produce quite different effects on the responsiveness of the frog spindle to ramp changes of length, and ones which are reminiscent, respectively, of those of the static and dynamic fusimotor fibers on the mammalian primary spindle ending.

4.3. Birds

Birds possess a rich supply of muscle spindles which are not unlike their mammalian counterparts (Huber and DeWitt, 1897), but as yet there is practically nothing special to report about them. Individual muscle spindles may contain from one to eight intrafusal muscle fibers, but though these fibers vary considerably in size there is as yet no firm indication as to whether or not they consist of two different kinds as in the mammal and frog. In a recent light microscopic study, all fibers were found to possess "nuclear chains" in their equatorial regions, and there was no bimodality of the distributions of either length or diameter of different intrafusal fibers (Maier and Eldred, 1971). It would, however, be interesting to have the matter investigated with the electron microscope since characteristic differences have thereby been demonstrated between fibers in the mammal. Physiological evidence has demonstrated that avian spindles normally receive a specific

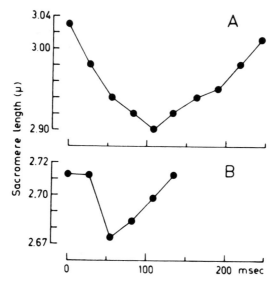

Fig. 9. The differing speed of contraction of different amphibian intrafusal muscle fibers shown by measurement of sarcomere spacing during a twitch observed by microcinephotography on nerve stimulation. (A), Small intrafusal muscle fiber excited by small motor fibers. (B) Large intrafusal muscle fiber excited by large motor fibers. From Smith (1964b, Fig. 4).

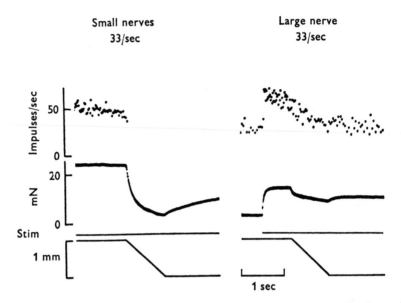

Fig. 10. The comparable behavior of the spindle discharge and the extrafusal muscle tension when an amphibian muscle was allowed to shorten during motor stimulation. Left: Small motor fibers stimulated to give a slow contraction. Right: Large motor fibers stimulated to give a fast contraction. The pattern of afferent firing suggests that the intrafusal muscle fibers behaved similarly to their extrafusal counterparts. From Brown (1971*b*, Fig. 2).

fusimotor supply, but whether or not intrafusal fibers are also supplied by collaterals of normal motor fibers remains an open question (Dorward, 1970).

4.4. Mammals

The fully developed mammalian spindle is a highly elaborate affair with two kinds of sensory terminals, two kinds of intrafusal fibers, and two kinds of specialized fusimotor fibers. In view of this complexity, it is hardly surprising that certain details remain controversial.

4.4.1. Structure

4.4.1a. Intrafusal Fibers. All mammals so far studied have now been found to possess two distinct kinds of intrafusal muscle fibers, which are called the "nuclear bag fibers" and the "nuclear chain fibers" after the arrangement of nuclei found in their equatorial regions. The distinction between them was first made only some 10 years ago by Boyd (1962) and by

Cooper and Daniel (1963) working independently. Figure 11 illustrates the major differences between them as found with the light microscope. At the spindle equator, the bag fibers have a cluster of nuclei lying two or three abreast, while those of the chain fibers lie in single file down the center of the fiber. Outside the central 300 μm of the fibers, they soon come to contain similarly few nuclei, and these are placed at the periphery of the fiber. The bag fibers are commonly longer and thicker than the chain fibers, though this is not invariable.

Features seen with the light microscope, however, appear to some extent to be epiphenomena only distantly related to function, for they may show appreciable variation for spindles from different muscles of the same animal and also between species, without apparently affecting the overall behavior of the spindle. Most notably, the intrafusal fibers of the rabbit all appear to be of the bag type when they are examined with classical histological techniques, and for a time this confused the issue. But electron microscopic and histochemical observations have now confirmed the existence of two kinds of intrafusal fibers in the rabbit as elsewhere (Corvaja and Pompeiano, 1970). Indeed, with the introduction of new techniques of examination yet further subdivisions have been suggested in other species, but these have yet to be shown to be of functional significance (*cf.* Yellin, 1969). Under the electron microscope, the bag fibers are seen to have a regularly arranged array of myofilaments, to contain rather little sarcoplasm with few mitochondria, and to lack the M line which is elsewhere seen in the very middle of the sacromere. The chain fibers have their myofilaments less regularly arrayed,

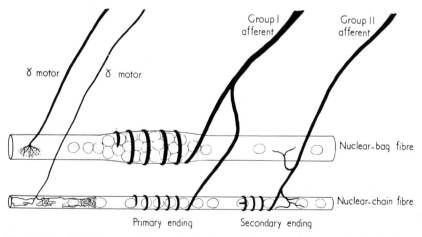

Fig. 11. Simplified diagram of the central region of the mammalian muscle spindle. From Matthews (1964, Fig. 1).

have prominent mitochondria and an appreciable amount of sarcoplasm between the myofilaments, and possess a well-developed M line (Corvaja *et al.*, 1969). The difference in the band structure of the two kinds of intrafusal fibers suggests that the chain fibers contract the more rapidly, for M lines are found in the frog twitch fibers but not in the frog slow fibers.

4.4.1b. Afferent Innervation. There is a general agreement that the arrangement of the afferent innervation on the two kinds of intrafusal fibers is as illustrated in Fig. 11. The primary afferent ending, sometimes called the "annulospiral ending," lies in the central 300 μm of the spindle and is derived from a large medullated fiber (diameter over 12 μm). The afferent fiber branches inside the spindle to send spirals around every individual intrafusal fiber, irrespective of whether it is a bag or a chain fiber. In this central region, the bag fibers contain very few myofilaments, but they do not subdivide and "reticulate" in the way seen in the frog. The chain fibers contain fewer myofilaments at the equator than elsewhere along their length, but some are indeed still present. The regularity of the primary spirals is particularly well developed in the cat, but spraylike and other types of terminations may be found in some other species. The secondary afferent ending lies to one side of the primary ending and is supplied by a medium-sized medullated fiber (4–12 μm in diameter) which terminates partly as spirals and partly as sprays so that the ending was called the "flower-spray" ending by Ruffini (1898). In contrast to those of the primary ending, these secondary terminations always lie predominantly, and sometimes lie entirely, on the nuclear chain fibers.

A spindle invariably contains a single primary ending, but there may be up to four secondary endings, or none at all. It should be emphasized that the crucial difference between the primary and the secondary afferent endings resides in their location within the spindle and relation to the underlying intrafusal fibers, and not in their fine structure. Under the electron microscope, the two kinds of nerve terminals appear just the same except for their size. Both are closely apposed to the surface of the intrafusal muscle fibers, with the muscular and neural membranes separated by only 10–20 μm without any intervening basement membrane. The closeness of contact is often increased by either kind of nerve terminal lying in a groove on the surface of the muscle fiber, sometimes with lips of sarcoplasm partly overlying the sensory terminal. But, except on branching, the terminals themselves are of constant thickness and do not show the beaded chain arrangement that occurs in the frog.

4.4.1c. Motor Innervation. The arrangement of the motor terminals unfortunately still continues to be a matter for controversy. For the last 10 years, it has been agreed that in addition to the plate endings (which have been recognized since the beginning of the century) there is also a more diffuse type of motor ending which somewhat resembles the grape terminations of the slow fibers of the frog. These diffuse mammalian intrafusal endings are now termed the "trail endings" (Barker *et al.*, 1970); an earlier but now discarded name for them was the "γ2 network" (Boyd, 1962). The trail ending differs from the plate ending in having no discrete point of termination as viewed with the light microscope, but instead it wanders some 100 μm along the length of an intrafusal fiber, apparently making repeated synaptic contact with it. Under the electron microscope, there is well-marked postjunctional folding beneath the plate endings but not beneath the trail endings. A given fusimotor fiber is believed to have all its terminations of the same morphological kind, although it should be noted that the distinction between plate and trail endings is not always as clear-cut as that just described. Both types of endings have been seen on both kinds of intrafusal fibers, but, in the main, plate endings occur on bag fibers and trail endings on chain fibers. The chief present uncertainty is as to the extent of the cross-innervation of the two kinds of intrafusal fibers by individual fusimotor fibers. Fortunately the problem is currently being investigated by the elegant combination of electrophysiological and histological techniques, and the matter should soon be resolved (Barker *et al.*, 1973; Brown and Butler, 1973). A degree of cross-innervation undoubtedly exists, but taking the histological findings in conjunction with certain physiological findings it seems likely that the bag intrafusal fibers receive a sufficiently distinct motor innervation for it to be possible for the CNS to control them relatively independently of the chain fibers.

4.4.2. The Functional Distinctiveness of the Primary and Secondary Endings

The responsiveness of primary and secondary endings to a variety of mechanical stimuli has now been amply studied by single fiber recording. Their afferent fibers can be distinguished in the course of an electrophysiological experiment by measuring their conduction velocity. In the cat, with relatively few exceptions, afferents conducting above 72 m/s come from primary endings and those conducting below 72 m/s terminate as secondary endings. For large-amplitude stretches, the difference in behavior of the two may be summarized by saying that the primary ending is very much more sensitive to the dynamic components of any stimulus, but the two kinds of ending are about equally sensitive to changes of muscle length *per se*. In contrast, when very small stretches are used, less than 100 μm in extent, the relative behavior of the two kinds of endings is rather different. The primary ending then shows no particularly greater degree of velocity sensitivity that does the secondary ending, but the primary ending is now the appreciably more sensitive to any absolute change of length, provided that this lasts no longer than a few seconds. The similarities in behavior of the two kinds of endings under various conditions probably reflect similarities in the transducing properties of the two kinds of nerve terminals, whereas the dissimilarities probably depend on intrafusal mechanics and the differential distribution of the endings on the intrafusal fibers. Discussion of such possibilities will be found elsewhere (Matthews, 1972). The present account will merely detail these differences.

Figure 12 shows the contrasting responses of the two kinds of endings to a large, rapidly applied stretch. The primary ending fired the more rapidly during the dynamic phase of stretching, whereas it fired the more slowly at the final length. The velocity sensitivity or degree of "adaptation" of the ending is shown by the amount its frequency of firing fell when the final length was reached and the velocity stimulus removed. Clearly, as is typical, the velocity sensitivity of the primary was much greater than that of the secondary, whereas their static sensitivities were comparable. Figure 13 summarizes in diagrammatic form how the two kinds of afferents respond to various stimuli when the amplitude of stretch is large. In line with the greater concern of the secondary ending with the measurement of muscle length is the finding that when the length of the muscle is held constant the secondary ending discharges appreciably more regularly than does the primary ending (Matthews and Stein, 1969b); this difference probably allows the secondary ending to provide the more accurate signal of length while possibly assisting the primary in signaling phasic events.

The response to stretching of small amplitude is conveniently investigated using sinusoidal stretching, since among other things this readily permits averaging to be used to improve the accuracy of measurement. The sensitivity

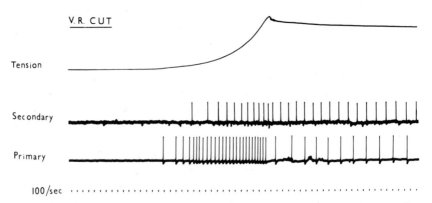

Fig. 12. The contrasting responses of the primary and of the secondary afferent endings of the mammalian spindle on applying a rapid stretch (approximately 14 mm at 70 mm/s) to the soleus of the cat. From Matthews (1972, Fig. 4.2).

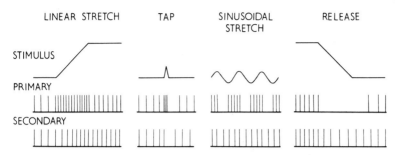

Fig. 13. Diagrammatic comparison of the typical responses of the primary and of the secondary ending of the mammalian spindle to various stretches. From Matthews (1964, Fig. 2).

of an afferent ending to a particular frequency of stretching may be defined as the amplitude of the resultant change in frequency of afferent firing divided by the amplitude of the stretching, to give a value expressed in impulses per second per millimeter. When the amplitude of stretching is sufficiently reduced, the ending fires at all phases of the sinusoidal cycle and the value of the sensitivity becomes independent of the precise size of the stretching. This is the linear range of the ending. Figure 14 shows the response of the two kinds of endings to a range of frequencies when the amplitude was sufficiently reduced for them to be behaving linearly (Matthews and Stein, 1969a; Poppele and Bowman, 1970). For both kinds of endings, the graph of sensitivity against frequency is usually approximately flat from 0.1 to 1 Hz and then begins to increase along the curve which describes the behavior of a system which is sensitive to the sum of the length and velocity components of the stretching. (Poppele and Bowman, 1970, rightly find the relation more complicated.) The "corner frequency" at which the curve begins to rise provides a measure of the relative sensitivities of an ending to length and to velocity; the lower the value the more sensitive is the ending to velocity. Somewhat unexpectedly, the principal corner frequency turns out to be the same for the two kinds of ending, about 1.5 Hz, in spite of the fact that the primary end is much the more sensitive to velocity when the amplitude of stretching is large. The responses of the two kinds of endings to small stretches are, however, far from identical. At all frequencies of stretching, the absolute value of the sensitivity of the primary ending is usually an order of magnitude greater than that of the secondary ending, at any rate in the reasonably physiological preparation of the decerebrate cat with intact motor roots and spontaneous fusimotor activity. At frequencies around 1 Hz, the sensitivity of the primary in decerebrate cats is typically around 100 impulses sec^{-1} mm^{-1}, whereas that of the secondary is below 10. Although the small linear range of the

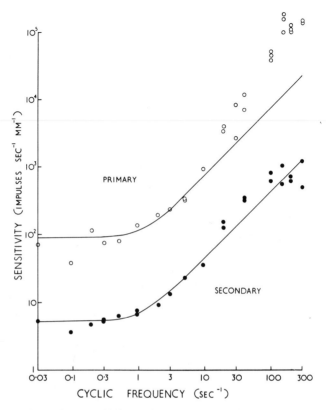

Fig. 14. Comparison of the sensitivity of the mammalian primary and secondary endings to sinusoidal stretching of small amplitude and a wide range of frequency. The sensitivity is defined as the amplitude of the sinusoidal modulation of the afferent firing divided by the amplitude of the sinusoidal stretching; when the stretching is sufficiently small, the value obtained is independent of the precise amplitude of stretching. Results obtained in the decerebrate cat with "spontaneous" fusimotor activity. From Matthews and Stein (1969a, Fig. 5).

primary is only a fraction of the physiological range of movement, the sensitivity of the primary ending within it is sufficiently high for small movements to produce an appreciable modulation of its firing and thus have a physiologically significant action. Moreover, on changing the length of a muscle its spindles can "reset" themselves, probably because of readjustments of the intrafusal muscle fibers, so that the high sensitivity can be transferred to the new length and the endings avoid becoming saturated. On the other hand, the classical response evoked from the endings by large stretches should not now be held to be physiologically unimportant merely because they are "nonlinear." The CNS can be expected to make good use of all the information that it receives and to know the properties of its peripheral receptors well enough to be able to decode their messages, even though at first sight they might appear to be unduly complicated and to be derived from an instrument with a variable calibration.

4.4.3. Fusimotor Control of Mammalian Spindle

In most mammals, it appears that the muscle spindles are no longer supplied by branches of the nerves to the ordinary extrafusal muscle fibers. Instead, they receive a specific fusimotor supply from fibers that are smaller than the ordinary motor fibers (2–8 μm instead of above 12 μm for the hindlimb of the cat) and are therefore called "γ motor fibers." This was first shown by Leksell (1945) by using a pressure block to inactivate the large fibers and then confirmed by Kuffler et al. (1951) by stimulating single motor fibers isolated from ventral root filaments. Fusimotor stimulation produces an intrafusal contraction with marked excitation of the spindle efferents without producing any appreciable tension in the muscle as a whole. However, a shared fusimotor–skeletomotor innervation has been found on occasion to persist in the mammal. Such fibers are currently called "β fibers" to fit in with the preexisting α–γ classification, but there is little logic in this nomenclature since β fibers may fall into either the normal α or γ ranges of velocity, though not usually at the extremes of either. The extent of β innervation in the mammal is still problematical, but it appears to be unlikely to be at all common in large muscles which receive an abundant motor supply. So far, it has only been established in lumbrical muscles, which because of the small numbers of nerve fibers involved have lent themselves to intensive study by both histological and electrophysiological methods (Adal and Barker, 1965; Bessou et al., 1965). The possession of β fibers by such little muscles would appear to allow them to economize in their use of nerve fibers and so might perhaps encourage the persistence of the more primitive arrangement. For the time being, the major emphasis may reasonably be concentrated on the control of the spindles by specific fusimotor fibers of γ diameter, for these appear to be the more usual and the more advanced method of fusimotor control in the mammal.

4.4.4. Static and Dynamic Fusimotor Fibers

Ten years ago, with the histological demonstration of the two kinds of intrafusal fibers, it became natural to seek separate functional roles for each to perform. Following a lead given by experiments (Jansen and Matthews, 1962) on the decerebrate cat, the present author found that fusimotor fibers could be divided into two distinct kinds depending on the effect of their stimulation on the dynamic responsiveness of single primary endings to large-amplitude stretches (Matthews, 1962). The two kinds of fibers were named the "static fusimotor fibers" and the "dynamic fusimotor fibers." Figure 15 illustrates the rationale for this. Stimulation of either kind of fusimotor fiber excites the primary ending when the muscle is at a constant length, and the difference in their action can be seen only at the beginning and end of the dynamic phase of stretching. The dynamic fiber then causes the normal velocity response of the primary ending to be augmented, whereas the static fiber causes the velocity response to be decreased in spite of producing a considerable excitatory action on the ending. An especially important finding supporting the physiological validity of the static–dynamic classification is that when several primary endings can be studied which are all excited by one particular fusimotor fiber they are all found to be influenced in the same way, whether static or dynamic. Since there is only a single primary ending in any particular muscle spindle, this proves that a given fusimotor fiber has a static or dynamic action in its own right, rather than because of some chance relation that it enters into with the intrafusal fibers of one particular spindle. This functional specificity is not, however, matched by any gross anatomical difference between the two kinds of nerve fibers where they run in the main nerve trunk, for in this region the conduction velocities of the two kinds of fibers overlap to a very high degree.

The different actions of the two kinds of fusimotor fibers are also well shown by their action on the response of the primary ending to sinusoidal stretching of medium extent. As illustrated in Fig. 16, the dynamic fiber accentuates the normal dynamic responsiveness to this form of stimulation, whereas the static fiber damps it down. When the amplitude of stretching is

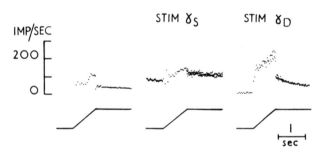

Fig. 15. The contrasting actions of the two kinds of mammalian fusimotor fibers on the responsiveness of the primary afferent ending to ramp stretching. The spindle lay in the soleus muscle, which was stretched (left) in the absence of fusimotor stimulation, (center) during continuous repetitive stimulation of a single static fusimotor fiber, (right) during similar stimulation of a single dynamic fusimotor fiber. From Brown and Matthews (1966, Fig. 1).

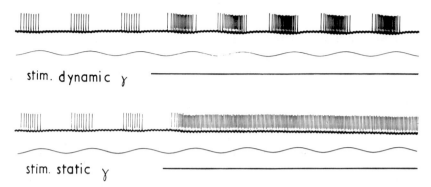

stim. dynamic γ

stim. static γ

Fig. 16. The effect of fusimotor stimulation on the responsiveness of the mammalian primary ending to sinusoidal stretching of medium extent (1 mm peak-to-peak movement at 3 Hz). From Crowe and Matthews (1964, Fig. 6).

further reduced so as to fall within the linear range, characteristic differences are found between the frequency–response curves (Goodwin and Matthews, 1971; Chen and Poppele, 1973). Another important finding is that the secondary ending is influenced exclusively by static fusimotor fibers, which excite it without having an appreciable effect on its dynamic sensitivity. Stimulation of dynamic fibers fails to excite the secondary ending even when the particular dynamic fiber that is being stimulated can be guaranteed to be causing an intrafusal contraction in the very spindle in which the secondary ending studied lies (Appelberg *et al.*, 1966).

The means by which the static and dynamic fibers produce their different effects are still controversial. The original hypothesis was that they do so by each supplying one or other of the two distinct types of intrafusal muscle fibers and that the correspondence is between dynamic fusimotor fibers and bag intrafusals and between static fibers and chain intrafusals (Matthews, 1962). The dynamic fibers, moreover, may be presumed to terminate in plate endings and the static fibers in trail endings. There are still certain difficulties with this hypothesis, and in particular the histological observation of the occurrence of a definite degree of cross-innervation of the two kinds of intrafusal fibers by individual fusimotor fibers. Nonetheless, the hypothesis still appears, in principle, to offer the most profitable approach to the problem. Its essentials remain viable if it be supposed that when a fusimotor fiber supplies both bag and chain intrafusal fibers then the action of the chain fibers predominates and the fusimotor fiber manifests itself as of the static type. Among other things, it fits in with the observation that the dynamic fibers supply intrafusal fibers which contract the more slowly, as judged by their effect on afferent firing (Bessou *et al.*, 1968), and the bag fibers have been observed microscopically to contract the more slowly whether activated by direct stimulation or via their nerves (Smith, 1966; Boyd, 1966). Moreover, it is interesting in this respect that dynamic fibers are found to act by means of nonpropagated local potentials, whereas static fibers may on occasion elicit propagated action potentials (Bessou and Laporte, 1956; Bessou and Pagés, 1969).

5. UNCERTAIN ORIGIN OF ADAPTATION

A perennial problem in considering the internal functioning of the spindle is the origin of its adaptation to a maintained stimulus and why it should be so different for the primary and secondary endings of the mammalian spindle and for the tonic and phasic spindles of the reptile. This is the same as inquiring into the origin of the velocity sensitivity of spindle endings since dynamic sensitivity and rapid adaptation are but two manifestations of the same basic property of the receptor, namely, a sensitivity to the rate of change of the stimulus as well as to its absolute value. *A priori*, the structure of the spindle suggests that it is built to operate on mechanical principles and that the histological differences seen along the length of individual intrafusal fibers are associated with differences in their regional viscoelastic properties. Moreover, it is difficult to see how fusimotor action in the mammal can so drastically change the responsiveness of the primary ending other than by operating mechanically, for the transducing properties of the sensory terminals seem unlikely to be modifiable by intrafusal action. (It is just conceivable, however, that the intrafusal contraction could have its effect by transferring the stretch stimulus from one set of nerve terminals to another with different transducing properties.) The preferred hypothesis for some years has been that during dynamic stretching the viscoelastic properties of the intrafusal fibers act so as to increase the deformation of the central sensorially innervated region of intrafusal fiber above the value it would have for the same extension applied to the spindle under static conditions. This hypothesis, however, has yet to be validated; it is supported by certain observations on isolated cat and rat spindles, but observations on isolated amphibian spindles are against it, although the equator of the amphibian spindle has been shown to be more compliant than its poles (Jahn, 1968). There is no necessity for such different species to behave identically, and for the time being judgment may reasonably be suspended. As argued *in extenso* elsewhere, the present author favors the view that mechanical factors provide an essential though not an exclusive contribution to the adaptive behavior of the mammalian spindle (Matthews, 1972), and the case will not be repeated here, though it should be emphasized that the conclusive experiments have yet to be performed. Certain recent experiments on the amphibian spindle will, however, be briefly described.

The three main sites at which adaptation might arise are as follows: in the transmission of the mechanical stimulus to the receptor nerve terminals, in the mechanoelectric transduction of the deformation of the nerve terminals into a generator potential across the nerve membrane, and in the excitation by the generator potential of all-or-none spikes at some pacemaker region which may or may not be coterminous with the transducer region. In the case of the Pacinian corpuscle, which is discussed in Chapter 13 of this volume, some adaptation would appear to be occurring at all three sites, though with mechanical factors probably predominating in normal function. For the amphibian spindle, it is reasonably certain that the main site of adaptation lies upstream of the pacemaker because the receptor potential shows marked adaptation, as illustrated in Fig. 17. If the pacemaker were to be the major site of adaptation, the receptor potential would be expected to reproduce the wave form of the mechanical stimulus, which it clearly does not do. Likewise, in the snake the receptor potential of a phasic spindle is markedly more phasic than that of a tonic spindle, and, moreover, no particular adaptation is shown by the spike train elicited by direct-current stimulation of the nerve terminals of the phasic spindle (Fukami, 1970b). This leaves intrafusal mechanics and transducer properties as the two likely sites for adaptation. The experiments distinguishing between them are best discussed in relation to Fig. 18, which shows a simple mechanical model of a spindle with inhomogeneous intrafusal fibers, for this illustrates more precisely the way in which regional differences in viscoelasticity can lead to adaptation. Model D, in which the intrafusal pole possesses both elasticity and viscosity, while the equator is elastic, gives a response which is not unlike that of the amphibian spindle and the reptilian phasic spindle; the reptilian tonic spindle could be mimicked by reducing the polar viscosity while retaining its elasticity. The model acquires its velocity sensitivity by virtue of the fact that the polar viscous element resists dynamic stretching but does not resist the final static stretch; as a result, during the dynamic phase of stretching the central elastic region and with it the sensory ending are pulled out beyond their final static equilibrium value.

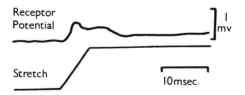

Fig. 17. "Adaptation" shown by the receptor potential recorded from the isolated amphibian muscle spindle. Traced from Katz (1950, Fig. 7a)

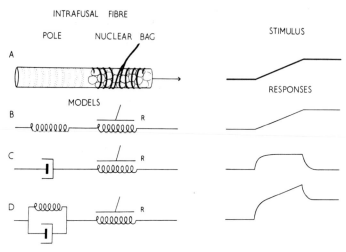

Fig. 18. Simple mechanical models illustrating how adaptation and sensitivity to the velocity of application of a stretch might arise from differences in the regional viscoelastic properties of an intrafusal muscle fiber. (A) An intrafusal fiber which is stretched by the ramp wave form shown on the right. (B,C,D) Left: Models of the fiber composed of springs and of dashpots. Right: their responses to the stretch. The responses may be considered as the receptor potential of the receptor R and are assumed to mirror the extension of the innervated region of intrafusal fiber. From Matthews (1964, Fig. 3).

Two experimental predictions follow if the spindle were to behave like the model. First, if the isolated spindle is observed microscopically during stretching then the central region should be seen to shorten somewhat at the end of the dynamic phase of stretching after being progressively extended during the dynamic phase of stretching. Second, if this shortening of the central innervated region can be prevented then the adaptation of the ending should be annulled. Unfortunately, neither of these predictions was verified when the isolated frog spindle was studied by Ottoson and his colleagues, and so the mechanical hypothesis appears contradicted for this particular preparation (Ottoson and Shepherd, 1970; Husmark and Ottoson, 1971). But it should be emphasized immediately that the isolated spindles which have been studied to date have had virtually the whole of the extracapsular regions of their extrafusal fibers ablated and, as a necessary consequence, have only been studied in the absence of intrafusal contraction. Under these circumstances, the spindle can hardly be expected to display the whole of its normal repertoire of performance. Nonetheless, the very definite adaptation shown by this particular preparation appears incapable of being ascribed to gross mechanical factors, as would also seem to be so for the whole spindle when its intrafusal fibers are not contracting (Kirkwood, 1972). First, Ottoson and

Shepherd (1970) studied the internal deformations of the spindle by using flash photography so that by repeating the same stretch while successively delaying the time of the flash they could chart the internal movements occurring after suddenly stretching or releasing the spindle. The deformation of the central part of the spindle was found to reproduce faithfully the stretch applied to the spindle, whereas receptor potentials recorded under similar conditions showed marked adaptation. There was no sign of the longitudinal creep required to explain adaptation in mechanical terms and as has been seen in the mammalian nuclear bag fibers under broadly similar conditions (Smith, 1966; Boyd and Ward, 1969). Second, in separate experiments, Husmark and Ottoson (1971) stretched the isolated spindle in such a manner that it was maintained at a constant final tension rather than at the more usual constant final length. In a system like that of Fig. 18D, this should abolish adaptation, for it would prevent shortening of the central zone on completion of the dynamic phase of stretching when the tension normally falls. But adaptation of the receptor potential was nearly as marked with a constant-tension stretch as it was with a constant-length stretch, as illustrated in Fig. 19. Related experiments (Husmark and Ottoson, 1970) had shown that although the tension developed in the isolated spindle had superficially the same shape as the receptor potential elicited by the same stretch there was no single relation between tension and potential which was obeyed under both static and dynamic conditions. However, for all this to carry full conviction it needs to be shown that the tension was generated by the intrafusal fibers themselves and not by parallel elastic elements such as the capsule. It would appear from all this that the very considerable adaptation of the isolated frog spindle must be ascribed to the transducer mechanism, or alternatively to mechanical factors acting on an ultrastructural scale and determining the transmission of deformation of the innervated region of intrafusal fiber to its overlying sensory terminals. Investigation could usefully be extended to intact amphibian spindles with contracting intrafusal fibers, for Brown's (1971b) work

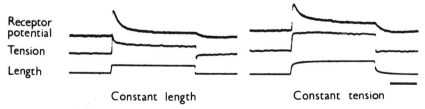

Fig. 19. A comparison of the effects on the isolated amphibian spindle, with ablated poles, of applying a stretch to a constant final length and to a constant final tension. In both cases, the receptor potential shows marked adaptation. Time bar, 100 ms. From Husmark and Ottoson (1971, Fig. 10).

suggests that mechanical factors do indeed then have a part to play, though still not an exclusive one. The progress of this painstaking field of research can be awaited with interest as it seems unlikely that the last word has been said.

6. REFERENCES

Adal, M. N., and Barker, D., 1965, Intramuscular branching of fusimotor fibres, *J. Physiol. Lond.* **177**:288

Appelberg, B., Bessou, P., and Laporte, Y., 1966, Action of static and dynamic fusimotor fibres on secondary endings of cat's spindles, *J. Physiol. Lond.* **185**:160.

Barker, D., 1968, L'innervation motrice du muscle strié des vertébrés, in: *Actualités Neurophysiologiques*, 8th Ser., Vol. 23, Masson & Cie, Paris.

Barker, D., Stacey, M. J., and Adal, M. N., 1970, Fusimotor innervation in the cat, *Phil. Trans. Roy. Soc. B* **258**:315.

Barker, D., Emonet-Dénand, F., Laporte, Y., Proske, U., and Stacey, M., 1973, Morphological identification and intrafusal distribution of the endings of static fusimotor axons in the cat, *J. Physiol. Lond.* **230**:405.

Bessou, P., and Laporte, Y., 1965, Potentials fusoriaux provoqués par la stimulation de fibres fusimotorices chez la chat, *Compt. Rend. Seanc. Acad. Sci. Paris* **260**:4827.

Bessou, P., and Pagés, B., 1969, Intracellular recording from spindle muscle fibres of potentials elicited by static fusimotor axons in the cat, *Life Sci. Oxford* **8**:417.

Bessou, P., Emonet-Dénand, F., and Laporte, Y., 1965, Motor fibres innervating extra fusal and intrafusal muscle fibres in the cat, *J. Physiol. Lond.* **180**:649.

Bessou, P., Laporte, Y., and Pagès, B., 1968, Frequencygrams of spindle primary endings elicited by stimulation of static and dynamic fusimotor fibres, *J. Physiol. Lond.* **196**:47.

Bone, Q., 1964, Patterns of muscular innervation in the lower chordates, *Internat. Rev. Neurobiol.* **6**:99.

Boyd, I. A., 1965, The structure and innervation of the nuclear bag muscle fibre system and the nuclear chain muscle fibre system in mammalian muscle spindles, *Phil. Trans. Roy. Soc. B* **245**:81.

Boyd, I. A., 1966, The behaviour of isolated mammalian muscle spindles with intact innervation, *J. Physiol. Lond.* **186**:109P.

Boyd, I. A., and Ward, J., 1969, The response of isolated cat muscle spindles to passive stretch, *J. Physiol. Lond.* **200**:104P.

Brown, M. C., 1971a, A comparison of the spindles in two different muscles of the frog, *J. Physiol. Lond.* **216**:553.

Brown, M. C., 1971b, The responses of frog muscle spindles and fast and slow muscle fibres to a variety of mechanical inputs, *J. Physiol. Lond.* **218**:1.

Brown, M. C., and Butler, R. G., 1973, Studies on the site of termination of static and dynamic fusimotor fibers within muscle spindles of the tenuissimus muscle of the cat, *J. Physiol. Lond.* **233**:553.

Brown, M. C., and Matthews, P. B. C., 1966, On the subdivision of the efferent fibres to muscle spindles into static and dynamic fusimotor fibres, in: *Control and Innervation of Skeletal Muscle* (B. L. Andrew, ed.), pp. 18–31, Thomson and Co., Dundee.

Burgess, P. R., and Clark, J. F., 1969, Characteristics of knee joint receptors in the cat, *J. Physiol. Lond.* **203**:317.

Cajal, S. R., 1090, *Histologie du Systeme Nerveux de l'Homme et des Vertébrés*, Vol. 1, pp. 485–489, Maloine, Paris.

Chen, W. J., and Poppele, R. E., 1973, Static fusimotor effect on the sensitivity of mammalian muscle spindles, *Brain Res.* **57**:244.

Cooper, S., and Daniel, P. M., 1963, Muscle spindles in man; their morphology in the lumbricals and the deep muscles of the neck, *Brain* **86**:563.

Corvaja, N., and Pompeiano, O., 1970, The differentiation of two types of intrafusal fibres in rabbit muscle spindles, *Pflügers Arch. Ges. Physiol.* **317**:187.

Corvaja, N., Marinozzi, V., and Pompeiano, O., 1969, Muscle spindles in the lumbrical muscle of the adult cat: Electron microscopic observations and functional considerations, *Arch. Ital. Biol.* **107**:365.

Crowe, A., and Matthews, P. B. C., 1964, Further studies of static and dynamic fusimotor fibres, *J. Physiol. Lond.* **174**:132.

Crowe, A., and Ragab, A. H. M. F., 1970, The structure, distribution and innervation of spindles in the extensor digitorum brevis I muscle of the tortoise *Testudo graeca*, *J. Anat.* **106**:521.

Dorward, P. K., 1970, Response characteristics of muscle afferents in the domestic duck, *J. Physiol. Lond.* **211**:1.

Eyzaguirre, C., 1957, Functional organisation of neuromuscular spindle in the toad, *J. Neurophysiol.* **20**:523.

Eyzaguirre, C., 1958, Modulation of sensory discharges by efferent spindle excitation, *J. Neurophysiol.* **21**:465.

Freeman, M. A. R., and Wyke, B., 1967, The innervation of the knee joint: An anatomical and histological study in the cat, *J. Anat*, **101**:505.

Fukami, Y., 1970*a*, Tonic and phasic muscle spindles in snake, *J. Neurophysiol.* **33**:28.

Fukami, Y., 1970*b*, Accommodation in afferent nerve terminals of snake muscle spindle, *J. Neurophysiol.* **33**:475.

Fukami, Y., and Hunt, C. C., 1970, Structure of snake muscle spindles, *J. Neurophysiol.* **33**:9.

Gardner, E., 1950, Physiology of movable joints, *Physiol. Rev.* **30**:127.

Godwin-Austen, R. B., 1969, The mechanoreceptors of the costo-vertebral joints, *J. Physiol. Lond.* **202**:737.

Goodwin, G. M., and Matthews, P. B. C., 1971, Effects of fusimotor stimulation on the sensitivity of muscle spindle endings to small-amplitude sinusoidal stretching, *J. Physiol. Lond.* **218**:56P.

Goodwin, G. M., McCloskey, D. I., and Matthews, P. B. C., 1972, The contribution of muscle afferents to kinesthesia shown by vibration induced illusions of movement and by the effects of paralysing joint afferents, *Brain* **95**:705.

Gray, E. G., 1957, The spindle and extrafusal innervation of a frog muscle, *Proc. Roy. Soc. Lond. B* **146**:416.

Houk, J., and Henneman, E., 1967, Responses of Golgi tendon organs to active contract tions of the soleus muscle of the cat, *J. Neurophysiol.* **30**:466.

Houk, J. C., Singer, J. J., and Henneman, E., 1971, Adequate stimulus for tendon organs with observations on mechanics of ankle joint, *J. Neurophysiol.* **34**:1051.

Huber, G. C., and DeWitt, L. M. A., 1897, A contribution on the motor nerve-ending and on the nerve-endings in the muscle-spindles, *J. Comp. Neurol.* **7**:169.

Hunt, C. C., and Wylie, R. M., 1970, Responses of snake muscle spindles to stretch and intrafusal muscle contraction, *J. Neurophysiol.* **33**:1.

Husmark, I., and Ottoson, D., 1970, Relation between tension and sensory response of the isolated frog muscle spindle during stretch, *Acta Physiol. Scand.* **79**:321.

Husmark, I., and Ottoson, D., 1971, The contribution of mechanical factors to the early adaptation of the spindle response, *J. Physiol. Lond.* **212**:577.

Ito, F., 1968, Functional properties of tendon receptors in the frog, *Jap. J. Physiol.* **18**:576.

Jahn, S. A., 1968, Static elasticity of isolated muscle spindles of the frog and tension development of their intrafusal muscle fibres, *Acta Physiol. Scand.* **74**:384.

Jansen, J. K. S., and Matthews, P. B. C., 1962, The central control of the dynamic response of muscle spindle receptors, *J. Physiol. Lond.* **161**:357.

Karlsson, U., and Andersson-Cedergren, E., 1966, Motor myoneural junctions on frog intrafusal muscle fibres, *J. Ultrastruct. Res.* **14**:191.

Karlsson, U., Andersson-Cedergren, E., and Ottoson, D., 1966, Cellular organization of the frog muscle spindle as revealed by serial sections for electron microscopy, *J. Ultrastruct. Res.* **14**:1

Katz, B., 1949, The efferent regulation of the muscle spindle in the frog, *J. Exptl. Biol.* **26** 201.

Katz, B., 1950, Depolarization of sensory terminals and the initiation of impulses in the muscle spindle, *J. Physiol. Lond.* **111**:261.

Katz, B., 1961, The termination of the afferent nerve fibre in the muscle spindle of the frog, *Phil. Trans. Roy. Soc. B* **243**:221.

Kirkwood, P. A., 1972, The frequency response of frog muscle spindles under various conditions, *J. Physiol. Lond.* **222**:135.

Koketsu, K., and Nishi, S., 1957, Action potentials of single intrafusal muscle fibres of frogs, *J. Physiol. Lond.* **137**:193.

Kuffler, S. W., Hunt, C. C., and Quilliam, J. P., 1951, Function of medullated small-nerve fibres in mammalian ventral roots: Efferent muscle spindle innervation, *J. Neurophysiol.* **14**:29.

Leksell, L., 1945, The action potential and excitatory effects of the small ventral root fibres to skeletal muscle, *Acta Physiol. Scand.* **10**:1 (Suppl. 31).

Maier, A., and Eldred, E., 1971, Comparisons in the structure of avian muscle spindles, *J. Comp. Neurol.* **143**:25.

Matthews, B. H. C., 1931, The response of a single end organ, *J. Physiol. Lond.* **71**:64.

Matthews, B. H. C., 1933, Nerve endings in mammalian muscle, *J. Physiol. Lond.* **78**:1.

Matthews, P. B. C., 1962, The differentiation of two types of fusimotor fibre by their effects on the dynamic response of muscle spindle primary endings, *Quart. J. Exptl. Physiol.* **47**:324.

Matthews, P. B. C., 1964, Muscle spindles and their motor control, *Physiol. Rev.* **44**:219.

Matthews, P. B. C., 1972, *Mammalian Muscle Receptors and Their Central Actions*, Arnold, London.

Matthews, P. B. C., and Stein, R. B., 1969a, The sensitivity of muscle spindle afferents to small sinusoidal changes of length, *J. Physiol. Lond.* **200**:723.

Matthews, P. B. C., and Stein, R. B., 1969b, The regularity of primary and secondary muscle spindle afferent discharges, *J. Physiol. Lond.* **202**:59.

Matthews, P. B. C., and Westbury, D. R., 1965, Some effects of fast and slow motor fibres on muscle spindles of the frog, *J. Physiol. Lond.* **178**:178.

Ottoson, D., and Shepherd, G. M., 1970, Length changes within isolated frog muscle spindle during and after stretching, *J. Physiol. Lond.* **207**:747.

Page, S. G., 1966, Intrafusal muscle fibres in the frog, *J. Microscop.* **5**:101.

Perroncito, A., 1901, Sur la terminaison des nerfs dans les fibres musculaires striées, *Arch. Ital. Biol.* **36**:245.

Poppele, R. E., and Bowman, R. J., 1970, Quantitative description of linear behaviour of mammalian muscle spindles, *J. Neurophysiol.* **33**:59.

Proske, U., 1969*a*, The innervation of muscle spindles in the lizard, *Tiliqua nigrolutea*, *J. Anat.* **105**:217.

Proske, U., 1969*b*, An electrophysiological analysis of responses from lizard muscle spindles, *J. Physiol. Lond.* **205**:289.

Regaud, C., and Favre, M., 1904, Les terminaisons nerveuses et les organes nerveux sensitifs de l'appareil locomoteur, *Rev. Gen. Histol.* **1**:1.

Ruffini, A., 1898, On the minute anatomy of the neuromuscular spindles of the cat, and on their physiological significance, *J. Physiol. Lond.* **23**:190.

Skoglund, S., 1956, Anatomical and physiological studies of knee joint innervation in the cat, *Acta Physiol. Scand.* **36**:1 (Suppl. 124).

Smith, R. S., 1964*a*, Activity of intrafusal muscle fibres in muscle spindles of *Xenopus laevis, Acta Physiol. Scand.* **60**:223.

Smith, R. S., 1964*b*, Contraction in intrafusal muscle fibres of *Xenopus laevis* following stimulation of their motor nerves, *Acta Physiol. Scand.* **62**:195.

Smith, R. S., 1966, Properties of intrafusal muscle fibres, in: *Nobel Symposium I, Muscular Afferents and Motor Control* (R. Granit, ed.), pp. 69–80, Almqvist and Wiksell, Stockholm.

Stuart, D. G., Goslow, G. E., Mosher, C. G., and Reinking, R. M., 1970, Stretch responsiveness of Golgi tendon organs, *Exptl. Brain Res.* **10**:463.

Szepsenwol, J., 1960, The neuromuscular spindle in the lizard, *Anolis cristatellus, Cellule* **61**:21.

Yellin, H., 1969, A histochemical study of muscle spindles and their relationship to extrafusal fibre types in the rat, *Am. J. Anat.* **125**:31.

Chapter 15

Enteroceptors

J. G. Widdicombe

Department of Physiology
St. George's Hospital Medical School
London, England

1. INTRODUCTION

Nervous afferent end organs have been identified in all the viscera, and a complete catalog would be long. They have been studied chiefly by two techniques: histological portrayal, and recording of action potentials from the nerve fibers attached to the endings. For most viscera, there are separate lists of histological appearances and of patterns of fiber activity, without correlation of the two. The reflex actions of different types of receptors have also been extensively studied, but again it is not always possible to collate the reflex with the mediating receptor and its nerve fiber.

This chapter will deal primarily with histology and afferent neurophysiology, and a complete list of receptors, established or claimed, cannot be included. Reflex actions will be mentioned briefly because, although their importance is obvious, they are largely outside the scope of this book. It is worth emphasizing at the beginning what cannot be described. For no enteroceptor, with the exception of the Pacinian corpuscle, do we know the mode of initiation of the receptor and action potentials. For no enteroceptor do we know the intimate physical relationship between the receptor terminals and the surrounding tissue elements, although this information is essential to our understanding of the sensitivity and mode of stimulation of receptors.

There are many thousands of papers dealing with enteroreceptors. Only recent papers and reviews are listed.

2. METHODS

2.1. Histology

The conventional staining methods most applied to enteroceptors utilize methylene blue and various silver stains. Both these techniques can also stain reticulin and elastin fibers, and such artifacts have not always been distinguished from nerve fibers; the literature contains many misinterpretations due to the absence of carefully controlled staining conditions. In addition, when the methods demonstrate nerve fibers, they do not distinguish between afferent and efferent neurons, or between nerve terminals and nerve fibers distant from the terminal. Although in somatic tissues the distinction between motor and sensory endings is usually clear with conventional stains, this often does not apply to visceral innervation.

The problem can be overcome in two ways: (1) The motor innervation of the viscera has preganglionic and postganglionic fibers, the latter being non-myelinated. Selective motor denervation of a tissue by nerve section above the sensory ganglia (e.g., the nodose ganglion of the vagus) will allow the myelinated preganglionic nerve fibers to degenerate, and nerve endings connected to remaining myelinated fibers must be afferent. Selective sensory denervation by nerve section below the sensory ganglion should lead to degenerative changes or disappearance of any afferent end organs, while leaving postganglionic motor fibers intact. (2) Specific histological methods may establish which nerve fibers and terminals are motor, and by elimination the others are afferent. These methods include specific histochemical staining for cholinergic and monoaminergic motor fibers and the electron microscopic identification of motor fibers by the presence of dense-cored vesicles (monoaminergic) or synaptic vesicles (cholinergic). The histochemical methods may be difficult to apply in tissues where there is a rich motor supply, such as visceral smooth muscle, and one has to look for an additional scanty afferent innervation.

Histological methods show enteroceptors of three main structural types:

1. Nerve terminals which break into complex arborizations with terminals that have splayings and knobs (Fig. 1). These are usually assumed to be mechanosensitive, and sometimes have been established as such (e.g., systemic arterial baroreceptors).
2. "Bare" nerve endings, similar to nociceptive terminals in the skin. Histology seldom shows the terminal itself, and sometimes cellular complexes are seen associated with the fiber which could be satellite cells involved in the initiation of the nerve impulse. These receptors are usually assumed to have a visceral nociceptive role.

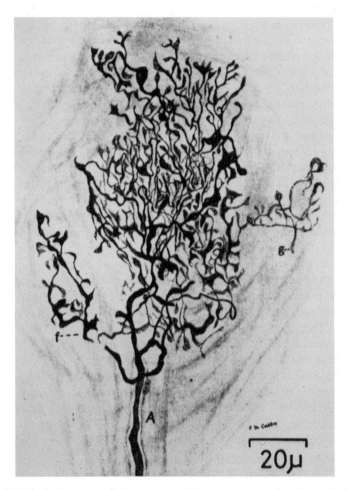

Fig. 1. Histological picture of a human carotid sinus baroreceptor. Tangential section.
A, Large myelinated nerve fiber; g,f, terminal nerve endings. From Heymans and Neil
(1958), after De Castro (1928).

3. More complex corpuscular or encapsulated terminals the function of
which (apart from Pacinian corpuscles—see Chapter 13) is usually
obscure and some of which have been shown to be staining artifacts.

2.2 Physiology

Conventional histology can show in which area or tissue receptors occur
but gives no information about the connections between receptor and tissue

elements. In theory, electron microscopy should contribute this information, but in practice the results have been disappointing. Electron microscopy can show a close proximity between receptor terminal and, for example, smooth muscle cells or collagen fibers but does not show if the receptor is stimulated or sensitized by traction mediated through the collagen or by the smooth muscle contraction. Even for receptors closely studied in this respect, such as arterial baroreceptors, the conclusions from histological evidence alone are tentative and often controversial.

Most of our knowledge of enteroceptor physiology has come from recording action potentials in single afferent fibers from the end organs, a method pioneered by Adrian (1933) and his colleagues. The vagus and glossopharyngeal nerves have been mainly used, partly for ease of experimentation, since it is more difficult to dissect fibers from the sympathetic and other parasympathetic nerves, and partly because the enteroceptive reflexes which have been most studied have their afferent pathways in the vagus and glossopharyngeal nerves. With single fiber recording, it is rarely possible to identify the receptor attached to the fiber being recorded from, but for mechanoreceptors some degree of localization may be determined by probing the appropriate tissue. Therefore, the conclusion that a certain pattern of fiber activity corresponds to an identified type of receptor is nearly always indirect, although in some instances (such as carotid sinus baroreceptors) there can be little doubt about the matter. This may explain why there have been no studies on the precise mode of initiation of an action potential in any of the enteroceptors. Mechanical and chemical stimuli can be applied to the tissue containing the receptor, but what is taking place in the receptor itself is unknown.

For some enteroceptors, the stimulus can be measured precisely, for example, the effect of blood pressure on carotid sinus baroreceptors, but for others the experiments are less quantitative. There have been few quantitative investigations of the relationship between length and tension in smooth muscle and the discharge pattern of receptors there. Similarly, it is not always easy to determine the exact strength of a chemical stimulus acting on a receptor, or to say if the chemical is acting directly or secondarily by changes in the mechanical environment of the ending. Therefore, with some notable exceptions, most of the physiological studies of enteroceptors lack the quantitative precision that has been applied to many somatic end organs.

A further consideration is that receptors with nonmyelinated fibers have been relatively neglected. The reason is obvious, namely, that it is more difficult to record from a single nonmyelinated nerve fiber. However, there is extensive evidence that reflexes conducted by C-fibers from visceral receptors are important and strong, and the problems of their study are not insuperable.

In studying the physiology of enteroceptors by recording afferent impulse traffic, it is usual to cut the nerve trunk before making single fiber preparations.

This breaks the reflex arc and any possible nervous "feedback" to the receptor. A valuable method has recently been introduced by Mei (1970a,b), who has recorded with microelectrodes from sensory ganglion cells of visceral fibers, allowing the study of the afferent pathway and the reflex response at the same time.

When a pattern of impulse traffic in an afferent nervous pathway has been determined, it is still necessary to demonstrate the nature and properties of the reflex conducted by the nerves. Although it is usually possible to establish the main reflex action, by comparing what the tissue stimulus does to effector systems when the afferent nerve is intact with the fiber activity when the nerve is cut, there are dangers in drawing conclusions for the intact animal. Thus most reflex-provoking stimuli in viscera stimulate more than one group of end organ, and the relative contributions and reflex interactions are hard to assess. Again, the reflex responses to a single type of receptor may be manifold, e.g., cardiac, vascular, respiratory, and hormonal, and these responses themselves cause secondary reflex, blood chemical, and hormonal effects. The complexities of studying the primary and secondary reflex interactions of even an isolated afferent system such as the carotid sinus baroreceptors are daunting and explain why so much research on enteroceptors is either qualitative or else restricted to one component of the reflex mechanism.

A particular aspect of the complex mechanism is the possibility of "feedback" to the receptor site itself. This could be either by reflex induction of changes in the intimate vicinity of the receptor (for example, contraction of smooth muscle attached to a mechanoreceptor) or more indirectly by changing the condition of the organ in which the receptors are situated (for example, baroreceptor activation decreases blood pressure which lessens the baroreceptor stimulus). The latter mechanisms have been extensively studied with regard to homeostasis, but the former have only recently been considered and are of greater relevance in this section since they are concerned with enteroceptor properties in relation to their immediate environment.

The sensory action of the enteroceptors is also difficult to study, since it is virtually essential to use unanesthetized man, and this naturally limits the experimental procedure and leads to most conclusions being indirect.

3. CARDIOVASCULAR RECEPTORS*

3.1. Systemic Arterial Baroreceptors

Baroreceptors have been described in the walls of most large blood vessels and of the chambers of the heart, but histologically and functionally they are concentrated at certain points, in particular, the carotid sinus, aortic

* See also Chapter 16 of this volume.

arch, and pulmonary artery. Lesser concentrations are seen at the origin of the subclavian and superior thyroid arteries. Those in the carotid sinus wall have been most extensively studied because of ease of access and ease of isolation and perfusion of the sinus. From the points of view of both histology and reflex action, all baroreceptors present considerable similarities. Carotid sinus receptors will therefore be chiefly discussed.

De Castro (1928) pioneered the histological study of baroreceptors. He described two types, diffuse arborizations and circumscribed glomerular (but not encapsulated) structures (Fig. 1). Most receptors were found in the adventitia of the carotid sinus and appeared to lie parallel to the long axis of the vessel. Other workers have emphasized the diversity of forms of baroreceptors, the terminals showing plates, networks, and coils in various patterns. The media of the carotid sinus is thinner and contains far less smooth muscle and more elastin than other parts of the arterial tree. A comprehensive review of the early literature is given by Heymans and Neil (1958).

These studies with conventional histology give no indication of the relationships between receptor terminals and other tissue elements. Recent electron microscopic studies by Rees (1967, 1968) have suggested that there are three types of carotid sinus baroreceptors. In the deep adventitia, the nerve terminals are closely related to elastin, in the middle layer to collagen, and in the superficial layer to smooth muscle fibers. The possible functional significance of these appearances will be discussed later, but it should be emphasized here that the relationship between nerve fiber and tissue shown by electron microscopy cannot clearly indicate how the receptors would respond, for example, to contraction of the adjacent smooth muscle.

The receptors have myelinated and nonmyelinated afferent nerve fibers. Based on fiber-diameter spectra, the former number about 200–300 for each carotid sinus of the cat (Fidone and Sato, 1969), with fiber diameters greater than 3 μm. The receptors with nonmyelinated fibers are more common, but accurate counts do not seem to have been made; one should not conclude, solely on the basis of receptor counts, that the more numerous are the more powerful reflexly.

Sympathetic nonmyelinated motor fibers run to the carotid sinus wall (Rees, 1967, 1968), and presumably their action is to contract the sparse smooth muscle there. Histological studies, even electron microscopic, have not established the intimate relationship, if any, between efferent nerve, smooth muscle, and baroreceptor.

With normal pulsatile pressures, baroreceptors give a burst of impulses with each systolic increase in pressure, and proportional to it (Fig. 2). Although there is considerable quantitative variation, baroreceptors are slowly adapting and a maintained pressure stimulus can cause discharge for at least an hour (Diamond, 1955). The thresholds for carotid sinus baroreceptors are

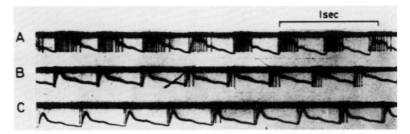

Fig. 2. Activity in an aortic baroreceptor at different levels of blood pressure (A, 125 mm Hg; B, 80 mm Hg; C, 62 mm Hg). Note the relation of the first impulse to the foot of the pressure pulse is fixed. The pressure pulse is delayed as it is recorded in the carotid artery. From Neil (1954).

in the range 80–120 mm Hg in the dog and 60–120 mm Hg in the cat. The thresholds for man are not known, but indirect evidence suggests that if blood pressure is less than about 60–80 mm Hg there is no effective baroreceptor reflex since the stimulus to the receptors is subthreshold. Steady-state pressure–receptor discharge curves are convex upward (Fig. 3), usually approaching a plateau at about 200 mm Hg. Pressures greater than this would therefore not exert a much larger reflex action. Peak frequencies in large-diameter fibers may be as high as 250–350 impulses/s, but frequencies adapted to steady pressure are about 40–70 impulses/s. Receptors with nonmyelinated fibers have been little studied, but they seem to have higher thresholds, lower

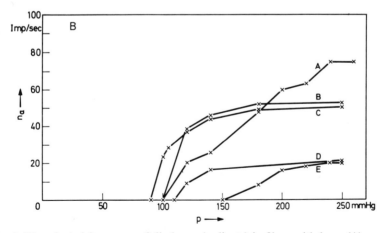

Fig. 3. The adapted frequency of discharge (ordinate) in fibers with large (A), medium (B,C), and small (D,E) spikes (presumably nonmyelinated) at various pressures (abscissa). Note that the frequency of discharge in the nonmyelinated fibers is much less than that in myelinated fibers. From Landgren (1952).

impulse frequencies (50–150 peak, 20–30 impulses/s adapted), and a faster rate of adaptation (Landgren, 1952; Fidone and Sato, 1969).

Baroreceptors also respond to rate of change of pressure; i.e., they have a dynamic component, so that their discharge is greater during increasing pressure than would be anticipated from the instantaneous pressure value. Decreasing pressures have a negative action on the discharge. During pulsatile pressure changes, the instantaneous firing frequency can be approximately expressed as

$$F(t) = A \, dP^+/dt + B \, dP^-/dt + C[P(t) - P_{th}] \tag{1}$$

where $F(t)$ is the firing frequency at time t, $P(t)$ is the pressure, P_{th} is the pressure threshold, dP^+/dt and dP^-/dt are the positive and negative rates of change of pressure, and A, B, and C are coefficients (Christensen et al., 1967).

Physiologically, baroreceptors are subjected to oscillatory pressures, and several studies have shown that pulsatile stimulation of baroreceptors causes greater average discharge than does steady pressure at the geometrical mean of the pressure wave; these studies depend on measurement of either baroreceptor impulse discharge or the reflex response, usually blood pressure change, to the stimulation (Ead et al., 1952; Koushanpour and McGee, 1969). There are several possible explanations. The receptor may have "rectification" properties, so that its positive response to an increasing pressure (A in equation 1) is greater than its negative response to a falling pressure (B). Measurements of receptor rectification suggest that this may be so at low pressures, but possibly not at high ones. Second, if the pressure oscillations overlap with the thresholds of baroreceptors the receptors will be brought into activity by the oscillations but not by the steady mean pressure. Since the threshold range is 60–120 mm Hg for individual endings, it is probable that this latter explanation accounts for nearly all the differences in receptor and reflex response for oscillations compared with steady stimuli. There is disagreement as to whether oscillatory pressures are more effective than steady states at pressures well above threshold for all the baroreceptors, but the measured differences are small and probably not very important (Spickler et al., 1967; Korner, 1971).

Three further comments on oscillatory stimuli may be made. First, baroreceptors with small-diameter myelinated fibers have been little studied, but they probably have a relatively greater dynamic response (Landgren, 1952). The dynamic response and rectification properties of nonmyelinated fiber baroreceptors are not known. With pressure varying over the range of thresholds, these receptors could play an important part in the greater reflex response to oscillatory stimuli compared with steady pressures. Second, it is not clear whether the central reflex mechanism has a different response to phasic afferent input compared with a steady input of the same mean frequency. Third, the fact that the pressure–stimulus receptor discharge curves (Fig. 3) are convex upward means that oscillatory stimuli should have a quantitatively different effect from a steady geometrically-mean pressure stimulus. The fact that, at pressures well above threshold for most baroreceptors, oscillatory and steady stimuli differ little in their action on average baroreceptor discharge or on reflex activity suggests that these last two possible mechanisms are not of great physiological importance.

Considerable interest has been aroused by the possibility that the baroreceptors can have their thresholds and sensitivities affected by changes in the mechanical condition in the vessel wall. There are two possible types of this "peripheral resetting." The first is due to nonphysiological changes in the wall which influence the receptors. McCubbin et al., (1956) and Kezdi (1954) have shown that carotid sinus baroreceptor threshold is considerably increased in chronic renal hypertension. This is presumably a secondary effect; i.e., the baroreceptors accommodate to a maintained change in their hemodynamic environment. Aars (1968) has shown that for aortic baroreceptors in the rabbit this accommodation is rapid, occurring within 2 days, and has suggested that it may be secondary to changes in the interstitial fluid in the arterial wall. Angell James (1971a) has found similar changes for baroreceptors during arteriosclerotic changes in the aortic arch. These results suggest that baroreceptor properties follow hemodynamic changes.

The second way that baroreceptors may have their properties determined at a peripheral level is more physiological. This is by the action of blood-borne catecholamines or of sympathetic nervous activity on the smooth muscle near the receptors. Early experiments showed that catecholamines could change the threshold and response curves of baroreceptors, but the doses needed were so great as to be unphysiological. Stimulation of sympathetic nerves to the carotid sinus can increase the discharge of baroreceptors and set up their reflex responses (Palme, 1943; Kezdi, 1954). This is consistent with Rees' (1967, 1968) observation that some of the receptors seem to be in series with smooth muscle cells. Other studies have been negative (Floyd and Neil, 1952). The most convincing positive evidence comes from experiments on the Virginia opossum (Koizumi and Sato, 1969) which has a prolific sympathetic efferent supply to its carotid sinus, and there may therefore be important species differences.

If there is a sympathetic efferent supply to the region of the baroreceptors which lowers their threshold or sensitizes them, its role in physiology is obscure. If these sympathetic nerves discharge in hypotension, as do many other sympathetic nerves, this would tend to accentuate the baroreceptor activity and thus to increase the hypotension. Both the importance of the sympathetic feedback to baroreceptors and the conditions in which it is activated require further study.

Aortic arch baroreceptors have recently been extensively studied by Angell James (1972b,c,d) and Aars (1968, 1969) by recording single fiber activity in rabbits *in vivo* and *in vitro*. In general, the receptor responses to static and to pulsatile pressures are similar to those of carotid sinus baroreceptors. The newborn rabbit has aortic baroreceptors with activity similar to that in the adult, except that their thresholds are lower (Bloor, 1964). Comparison of the reflexes from the carotid sinus and from the aortic arch could also indicate differences, either peripheral or central, between the two mechanisms. The aortic arch reflex in the dog is less influenced by pressure pulsations superimposed on a steady pressure, but thresholds appear similar (Angell James and Daly, 1970).

The reflex actions of systemic arterial baroreceptors have been extensively investigated (see reviews by Heymans and Neil, 1958; Korner, 1971). The main responses are vasodilation, bradycardia, decreased force of contraction of the heart, depression of breathing, and bronchodilation; other responses have been described, and it is to be expected that baroreceptors exert some reflex effect on all the motor outputs of the autonomic nervous system.

3.2. Pulmonary Arterial Baroreceptors

Pulmonary arterial baroreceptors have been studied chiefly by Coleridge and Kidd (1961, 1963) by single fiber recording from the vagus nerves of dogs with precise localization of the receptors by punctuate stimulation and histological correlation (Fig. 4). The endings lie in both main branches of the pulmonary artery and at its bifurcation, and most receptors have a spontaneous phasic discharge at normal pulmonary arterial pressures. Compared with systemic arterial baroreceptors, those in the pulmonary artery seem to have a more pronounced dynamic response, possibly related to the high distensibility of the pulmonary artery.

The reflex actions of pulmonary artery baroreceptors are similar to those in the systemic arteries, namely, vasodilation, cardioinhibition, and depression of breathing, but the last is especially pronounced. Teleologically, one might expect pulmonary baroreceptors to have a greater action on the right heart, and systemic arterial ones a greater action on the left heart, but this possibility does not seem to have been tested.

3.3. Ventricular Receptors

There have been many histological studies on cardiac receptors (reviewed by Heymans and Neil, 1958), but they have seldom been correlated with

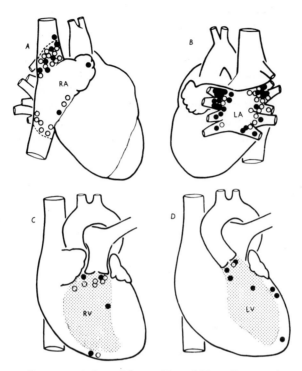

Fig. 4. Diagramatic representation of the position of 92 cardiac receptors each of which had been located by electrophysiological means. Each receptor is indicated by a circle: ○, afferent fiber in the right vagus; ●, afferent fiber in left vagus. A and B show location of atrial receptors and C and D location of ventricular receptors with a cardiac rhythm (i.e., presumably ventricular pressure receptors—see text). In C and D, the stippling represents the cavities of the right and left ventricles, respectively. From Coleridge *et al.* (1964).

physiological investigations, and the diverse histological pictures tell us little about the modes of stimulation.

Two types of ventricular receptors have been identified by single fiber recording, both with afferent nerves in the vagi: baroreceptors with myelinated fibers and epicardial receptors with nonmyelinated fibers. The baroreceptors discharge a high-frequency burst of impulses early in systole, including the isometric phase; thus they respond to intraventricular pressure rather than volume, since the latter is greatest immediately before systole (Paintal, 1963, 1972). This may indicate that they lie in series with cardiac muscle fibers. The extent to which the receptors have a dynamic response, to rate of change of pressure, has not been accurately determined, but simultaneous pressure and discharge records indicate that this may be appreciable. Coleridge *et al.*

(1964) have localized many of the endings in the dog and find them concentrated in both ventricular walls near the semilunar valves. The receptors have conduction velocities in the range 8–19 m/s.

The main reflex from increased pressure in the left ventricle is hypotension and bradycardia, and the ventricular baroreceptors therefore presumably interact with the systemic and pulmonary arterial baroreceptors. Whether there are quantitatively different actions on different systems (e.g., a larger effect on the heart compared with vascular beds for ventricular compared with arterial baroreceptors) is not known, and neither is the relative strength of the reflex.

3.3.1. Epicardial Receptors

Epicardial receptors have recently been investigated by single fiber recordings by Coleridge *et al.* (1964) and by Sleight and Widdicombe (1965). Although called "epicardial," similar endings may also lie in the ventricular myocardium. The left ventricle has a far greater number than the right. Most have nonmyelinated fibers (conduction velocity range 0.4–5.0 m/s). The endings sometimes discharge phasically but more usually have an irregular slow activity at about 1.5 impulses/s. They respond with low-frequency slowly adapting discharges when the ventricle is distended (Fig. 5), but the nature of their response scarcely merits the name "baroreceptor." The physiological event they are most sensitive to is increased force of contraction of the ventricular muscle, induced either by intracoronary arterial injections of epinephrine or by sympathetic motor nerve stimulation (Muers and Sleight, 1972), in which conditions the receptors adopt pronounced cardiac rhythms with peak instantaneous frequencies of 60–70 impulses/s. The endings are strongly stimulated by gentle stroking of the epicardium, and punctate probing indicates that each receptor may have several terminals within an area of about 1 cm².

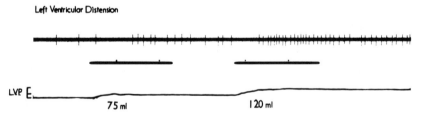

Fig. 5. Action potentials in a fiber from a left ventricular epicardial receptor in the heart of a dog killed by cardiac fibrillation. The upper record shows the response to saline inflation of a balloon in the left ventricle (lowest trace, pressure in balloon; injections of 75 and 125 ml during signals). Time in seconds. From Sleight and Widdicombe (1965).

The reflex actions of epicardial receptors are hypotension, bradycardia, and weak inhibition of breathing, as for arterial baroreceptors. It is not established under what physiological conditions in the intact animal they play a part, nor how important that part is. However, they are probably similar to nociceptive endings in other viscera, and they could be responsible for reflex cardiovascular depression in conditions like cardiac ischemia. It is unknown whether their activity causes pain.

3.4. Atriovenous Receptors

Both the receptors and the reflexes they mediate have been extensively studied, the most definitive work on the vagal afferent pathway being by Paintal (1963, 1972). Since the pressure changes in atria and adjacent veins are virtually identical, the two sites will be considered together; only punctate localization while recording from a receptor nerve fiber can distinguish them. The reflexes from the two areas seem to be identical. On the basis of pattern of single fiber discharge, Paintal has identified two main types, A and B. In the cat these are roughly equal in number, but in the dog those of type B predominate, and the distinction between the two is less clear in this species (Coleridge *et al.*, 1957; Langrehr, 1960). As with ventricular receptors, the atrial ones have not been identified histologically.

Type A atrial endings discharge during atrial systole and give a close correlation between firing frequency and the height of the a-wave of the atrial pressure curve. They sometimes also discharge during diastolic filling of the atria (the v-wave), although Paintal (1972) now calls these "intermediate." With the atrium isolated *in situ*, there is a good correlation between distension pressure and discharge, and the latter is slowly adapting for maintained pressure changes. Measurements of dynamic response have been made by Arndt *et al.* (1971) with isolated atrial muscle, and this component seemed to be so large that they concluded that the receptors were signaling heart rate rather than atrial pressure *per se*.

Type B receptors give a burst of impulses in late ventricular systole, at a time when the atrial volume is greatest (atrial pressure v-wave), and these endings are sometimes called "atrial volume receptors." Maintained distension of the isolated atrium causes a slowly adapting discharge with frequency linearly related to volume; like the A receptors, those of type B have a strong dynamic response. The fact that these receptors are usually silent during atrial systole may indicate that they are not in series with the muscle elements.

There is no difference between the conduction velocities of fibers from A and B receptors, both being in the range 12–27 m/s for the cat (Paintal, 1963). Precise localization is difficult in the cat, because of its small heart, but in the dog punctate stimulation shows that nearly all lie close to the entry of the systemic or pulmonary veins, and virtually none in the auricular appendage (Coleridge *et al.*, 1964). This distribution has some histological support. Several authors have claimed that there is no true difference between atrial A and B receptors, a view consistent with the similarity of localizations and fiber conduction velocities. Thus Arndt *et al.* (1971) could not separate the two groups in their careful study of receptor properties in the isolated atrium. Most workers have found "intermediate" receptors, suggesting that types A and B may be extremes of a range (Langrehr, 1960). The pattern of discharge of an individual receptor may change considerably with varying hemodynamic conditions (Neil and Joels, 1961).

Although several reflexes elicited by increases in volume of the atria have been described, there is no reason to associate any of them with either type A or type B receptors alone. Both groups of receptors could mediate all the reflexes. The main responses to stimulation of the receptors are a regulation of body fluid volume by decreasing the secretion of antidiuretic hormone (Gauer and Henry, 1956; Henry *et al.*, 1956) and a tachycardia mediated by left atrial and pulmonary venous receptors with the motor pathway in the sympathetic nerves to the heart (Furnival *et al.*, 1971).

4. RESPIRATORY SYSTEM RECEPTORS

4.1. Cough and Irritant Receptors

Silver and methylene blue staining and electron microscopy all show afferent end organs under the epithelial layer of cells in the larynx, trachea, and bronchi, with terminals that run between the cells until they nearly reach the cilia (reviewed by Fillenz and Widdicombe, 1972). From their site and appearance, it has been assumed that they are responsible for the cough reflex and the responses to inhalation of irritant gases and aerosols.

Mechanical stimulation of the epithelium of the respiratory tract from the larynx to the bronchi sets up discharges in vagal afferent fibers thought to come from these epithelial receptors. The endings in the lungs have come to be called "irritant receptors" because of their response to inhaled irritant aerosols and gases, and those in the larynx and trachea are sometimes called the "cough receptors" because of the reflex response to their stimulation.

The receptor properties have been studied mainly by recording action potentials from single fiber preparations of the cut vagus nerve. There are properties in common for receptors at each level: larynx, trachea, and intrapulmonary bronchi (Widdicombe, 1964; Fillenz and Widdicombe, 1972). All are stimulated by an intraluminal catheter, and those in the trachea and lungs by distension and collapse of the airway and by intraluminal carbon dust (Fig. 6) (laryngeal endings not tested). The discharges to a maintained mechanical stimulus are irregular and also rapidly adapting, especially for the larynx and trachea. However, the receptors differ in other properties. Those in the trachea, but not the lungs, have an off-response to volume changes (Figs. 7 and 8). The tracheal and especially the pulmonary receptors are stimulated by histamine injections or aerosols because of the contraction of underlying smooth muscle (Mills *et al.*, 1969), but this drug given intravenously does not usually affect the laryngeal endings. The receptors in the lungs are very sensitive to chemical irritants such as ammonia, ether vapor, and cigarette smoke, whereas those in the trachea and larynx are less sensitive.

The lung irritant receptors also have distinctive properties due to their intrapulmonary site. Thus they are stimulated by changes in the mechanical conditions of the lungs that increase the pull of the lung parenchyma on the airway walls: by pulmonary congestion, microembolism, anaphylaxis, atelectasis, and pneumothorax (Ferrer and Koller, 1968; Mills *et al.*, 1970). In general, these receptors seem to be sensitive to any mechanical change in their environment, and their threshold to such changes is low.

The properties of the airway irritant receptors studied by single fiber recording are consistent with the histological appearance of receptors lying between the epithelial cells of the airways. In particular, their sensitivity to inert dust (particle diameter less than 16 μm) and irritant gases and aerosols,

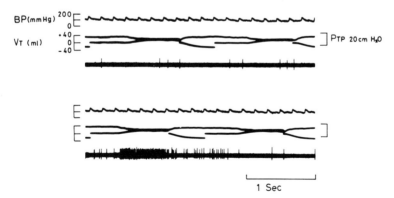

Fig. 6. Response of a lung irritant receptor to inhalation of carbon dust. Traces from above down: Systemic arterial blood pressure (BP), transpulmonary pressure (P_{TP}), tidal volume (V_T) zeroing at points of zero airflow, and action potentials in a single vagal nerve fiber from a lung irritant receptor. Upper record, control showing slow spontaneous discharge; lower record, during inhalation of dust, showing maximum stimulation of the receptor. The rabbit was paralyzed and artificially ventilated and vagotomized. From Fillenz and Widdicombe (1972).

and their stimulation by gentle application of a fine intraluminal catheter, support this site. Furthermore, the recordings are from myelinated fibers, although only the conduction velocities of those from lung irritant receptors have been measured (3.6–25.8 m/s), and the epithelial endings have myelinated connections. Physiological studies have not shown whether irritant receptors occur in airways smaller than the cartilaginous bronchi, although there is histological evidence that they do.

In spite of the similarity of the histological properties of the epithelial receptors at different sites in the airways, and of some of their patterns of response to stimulation, the reflexes that they mediate show clear differences. Mechanical stimulation of the larynx and trachea causes coughing, but in cats laryngeal stimulation produces prominent expiratory efforts and also simultaneous contractions of the inspiratory and expiratory muscles somewhat like retching, while stimulation of trachea and extrapulmonary bronchi causes expiratory efforts alternating with strong inspirations. Stimulation of irritant receptors in the lungs does not usually cause coughing, but instead tachypnea and hyperpnea (Mills *et al.*, 1970; Fillenz and Widdicombe, 1972).

In addition to the reflex action of irritant receptors on breathing, their stimulation causes vascular and bronchomotor changes. Irritation of the larynx and trachea causes hypertension in cats and rabbits, and bronchoconstriction both from these sites and from lung irritant receptors (Tomori and

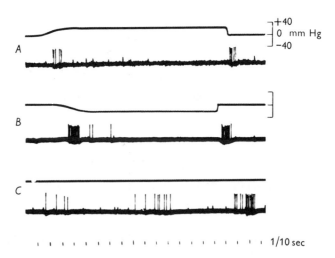

Fig. 7. Action potentials (lower traces) from a rapidly adapting receptor in the trachea of a cat. Upper traces, intratracheal pressure. Inflation (A) and deflation (B) of the trachea cause rapidly adapting discharges from the receptor. In C, the tracheal epithelium was gently touched with a catheter, causing further activity. From Fillenz and Widdicombe (1972).

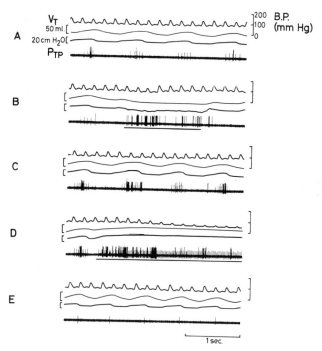

Fig. 8. Responses of a lung irritant receptor (larger action potentials) and a slowly adapting pulmonary stretch receptor (smaller action potentials) to deflation and inflation of the lungs. Traces from above down: Systemic arterial blood pressure (B.P.), tidal volume (V_T), transpulmonary pressure (P_{TP}), and vagal action potentials. A, Control, showing spontaneous discharge from both receptors. B, Deflation of the lungs during horizontal signal mark, showing cessation of discharge of the pulmonary stretch receptor and stimulation of the irritant receptor with an irregular discharge. C, Control after deflation, showing increased firing of the irritant receptor and increased transpulmonary pressure swings. D, Inflation of the lungs during signal, showing slowly adapting discharge of the pulmonary stretch receptor and rapidly adapting irregular discharge of the irritant receptor. E, Control after inflation, showing cessation of discharge of the irritant receptor, inhibition of firing of the pulmonary stretch receptor, and decrease in transpulmonary pressure swings. From Sellick and Widdicombe (1970).

Widdicombe, 1969). There is also considerable evidence that irritant receptors cause or contribute to the unpleasant respiratory sensation of dyspnea in various lung conditions (Fillenz and Widdicombe, 1972).

4.2. Pulmonary Stretch Receptors

Conventional staining methods indicate that airway smooth muscle contains afferent endings, and in some instances the terminal arborizations can be seen to come from myelinated fibers (reviewed by Fillenz and Widdicombe 1972). Although originally called "smooth muscle spindles," they look very similar to the afferent endings found in the carotid sinus, aortic arch, and walls of the heart. Electron microscopy also reveals end organs that look like some of the afferent end organs in the wall of the carotid sinus described by Rees (1967). No connections with the smooth muscle cells have been described. Both conventional and electron microscopy show that these smooth muscle endings are present in the tracheal and bronchial wall down to the small cartilaginous bronchi. Whether they also exist in bronchiolar smooth muscle, and if so how frequently, is less certain.

Adrian (1933) originally recorded action potentials from slowly adapting pulmonary stretch fibers. The evidence that these originate in smooth muscle receptors is indirect. Histologically, the receptors have large-diameter myelinated nerve fibers, and vagal pulmonary stretch fibers have conduction velocities in the range 14–59 m/s (Paintal, 1963). Smooth muscle receptors are present in the tracheal wall, and vagal impulse traffic from slowly adapting tracheal stretch receptors is in general similar to that from pulmonary stretch receptors; the greater simplicity of the trachea compared with the lungs as a site of afferent end organs leaves little doubt that it is smooth muscle receptors being studied (Widdicombe, 1964). Pulmonary stretch fibers are by far the commonest of the myelinated afferent fibers from the lungs, and the most careful histological count of lung receptors in cats and dogs shows that the smooth muscle endings are the most frequent of those with myelinated fibers (Elftman, 1943). The receptors are localized chiefly at the points of bronchial branching where there is most smooth muscle, and where smooth muscle receptors are most frequently seen histologically.

Pulmonary stretch receptors have low volume thresholds, usually within the eupneic tidal volume range or at a volume below functional residual capacity. Thus some receptors discharge continuously during the expiratory pause and are inhibited only by deflation of the lungs. Others are stimulated by deflation as well as by inflation, and this is especially true of endings in the walls of the trachea and extrapulmonary bronchi (Widdicombe, 1964). Impulse frequencies reach maximum values of 100–130 impulses/s in the cat for inflation pressures up to 30 cm H_2O. Although the receptors are "slowly adapting" (Fig. 8), the rate of adaptation to a maintained volume inflation varies greatly between receptors. Part of the adaptation is due to stress relaxation in the lungs during maintained inflation, since the discharge of the receptors correlates better with transpulmonary pressure than with lung volume changes (Davies *et al.*, 1956). The discharge of the receptors varies with the compliance of the lungs. A large lung inflation which increases lung compliance by opening a collapsed lung will increase the volume threshold and decrease the discharge frequency of pulmonary stretch receptors (Knowlton and Larrabee, 1946; Sellick and Widdicombe, 1970; Fig. 8) during subsequent inflations. The receptors are sensitized in pulmonary congestion, edema, and bronchoconstriction, conditions in which there is a greater mechanical pull on the airways due to a decrease in lung compliance. However, except in very severe pathological conditions the degree of change in receptor activity is small. For example, increases in pulmonary venous pressure to 40 cm H_2O increase receptor discharge by only about 20% (Marshall and Widdicombe, 1958).

Whether pulmonary stretch receptor discharge is affected by the tone of surrounding smooth muscle is unclear. Injections of drugs such as histamine that contract smooth muscle usually increase the discharge of the endings, but as indicated above this could be secondary to increased distension of the airways associated with lung collapse. In the absence of this indirect mechanical effect, there is some evidence that smooth muscle contraction induced by drugs inhibits the discharge of adjacent receptors (Widdicombe, 1954, 1964).

The main reflex action of pulmonary stretch receptors is to inhibit inspiratory activity and thus to determine the rate and depth of breathing, the Hering-Breuer inflation reflex (Widdicombe, 1964; Clark and von Euler, 1972). In addition, they cause bronchodilation. Both these actions will influence the discharge of the receptors.

4.3. Type J Receptors

In 1955, Paintal recorded from vagal nonmyelinated fibers from the lungs and studied the physiology of the receptor terminals. Originally called "specific deflation receptors," they are now renamed "J-receptors" (or juxta pulmonary capillary receptors) because of their site. With Richardson's silver method, which stains nonmyelinated axons and their accompanying Schwann cell nuclei, occasional nerve fibers are seen in the lung parenchyma. They are sparse and usually come from the network of nerve fibers surrounding the small arterioles (Fillenz, 1970). Electron microscopy shows axon bundles in intimate relation with endothelial cells of pulmonary capillaries (Fillenz and Widdicombe, 1972), and some of the axons appear to be afferent fibers. Meyrick and Reid (1971) have also observed fibers in the alveolar wall which seem likely to be afferent. One of their pictures shows a cell complex around an afferent nerve fiber in the alveolar wall. These nerves are the only ones so far described in the alveolar wall which could be attached to J-receptors.

The main method of identifying vagal fibers from J-receptors has been by intravascular injections of drugs and by inhalation of halothane. The timing of the responses gives strong evidence that these receptors lie in the lung parenchyma, presumably the alveolar wall. Unlike the other respiratory system receptors described above, J-receptors usually have nonmyelinated afferent fibers, with conduction velocities mainly below 3 m/sec but occasionally as fast as 7 m/s. Impulse frequencies during stimulation reach peak values of 20–50 impulses/s, with average values about 7.5 impulses/s (Paintal, 1970).

The receptors are mechanosensitive, since they can be localized by probing the lungs of open-chest animals. However, their activation on physiological mechanical stimuli (such as large lung deflations or pneumothorax) is weak (Paintal, 1955; Sellick and Widdicombe, 1970). A few are stimulated by large lung inflations, especially in the dog (Coleridge *et al.*, 1965). The pattern and size of their discharges suggest that the receptors play little part in physiological lung volume changes.

The receptors are strongly stimulated in four pathological conditions: (1) pulmonary congestion, caused by occlusion of the aorta, (2) pulmonary edema, caused either by occlusion of the aorta or by injection of edema-producing drugs such as alloxan, (3) pulmonary microembolism, and (4) inhalation of strong irritants such as chlorine gas. The first three conditions, and possibly the last, have in common that they produce an increase in alveolar interstitial fluid, or even overt pulmonary edema. Because of this, Paintal (1970) concludes that the receptors are primarily sensitive to the interstitial fluid content between capillary endothelium and alveolar epithelium (Fig. 9). Whether irritant gases act directly on the endings or by production of interstitial edema is not clear. Guz and Trenchard (1971) have shown that the changes in breathing during experimental pneumonia in rabbits are mediated chiefly by nonmyelinated vagal fibers, and it seems certain that these come from J-receptors. This result extends an earlier observation of Frankstein and Sergeeva (1966) that "pneumonia" produced by inhalation of hot water stimulates lung receptors with vagal nonmyelinated fibers.

The reflex actions of J-receptors include hypotension, bradycardia, and apnea and rapid shallow breathing (Paintal, 1970). They also cause a powerful contraction of the larynx (Stransky, Szereda-Przestaszewska, and Widdicombe, unpublished) and probably bronchoconstriction (Karczewski and

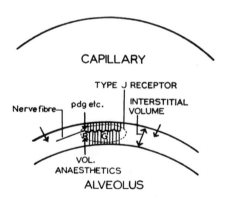

Fig. 9. Diagram of the site and modes of stimulation of a J-receptor. The central structure represents a receptor situated in an alveolar wall. pdg, Phenyl diguanide. From Paintal (1970).

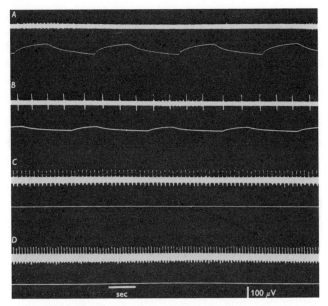

Fig. 10. Nerve impulses recorded from a chicken vagal afferent fiber. Note that the nerve impulse frequency markedly increased as the CO_2 content of the unidirectional ventilatory gas stream was decreased. A, 9% CO_2; B, 6% CO_2; C, 3% CO_2, D, 0% CO_2. In each record, the upper trace represents single unit activity; the lower trace sternal movement, inspiration upward. From Fedde and Peterson (1970).

Widdicombe, 1969). A further action is inhibition of spinal monosynaptic reflexes (Deshpande and Devanandan, 1970). These responses are characteristic of nociceptive reflexes and are consistent with the fact that the receptors are stimulated chiefly by pathological changes in the lungs. Paintal (1970) has suggested that they contribute to the sensation of dyspnea.

4.4. Other Receptors

Of considerable interest is the observation that in the lungs of birds there are receptors which are stimulated by a fall in airway pCO_2 and inhibited by a rise (Fig. 10) (Fedde and Peterson, 1970). Their reflex action is to inhibit inspiratory efforts. No equivalent receptor has been described for mammals, and their histological nature in birds has not been established.

Histological studies of nerve endings in the visceral pleura of mammals have been done (Larsell, 1928; Elftman, 1943). The endings are sparse, seem to have nonmyelinated fibers, and are concentrated at the hila of the lungs. Whether these are afferent, and if so what is their physiological stimulus and reflex action, is unknown.

Vagal single fiber recording can show activity from "mediastinal receptors" (Adrian, 1933; Widdicombe, 1964). These are slowly adapting endings with myelinated fibers, which can be localized to sites in the mediastinum, usually rostral to the heart or near the hila of the lungs. Their reflex function is unknown, and they do not seem to have been studied histologically.

5. ALIMENTARY SYSTEM RECEPTORS

The extensive literature on the sensation and reflexes activated by stimulation of receptors in the alimentary system, in particular the gastrointestinal tract, has been admirably reviewed by Iggo (1966), Sharma (1967), Iggo and Leek (1970), and Leek (1972). The role of the receptors in local reflex control mechanisms has been surveyed by Kottegoda (1970). Here we will consider mainly the types of receptors, based on recording afferent fiber discharge.

5.1. Muscular Receptors

Recording from vagal single fibers has revealed the existence of slowly adapting mechanoreceptors in the walls of the esophagus, stomach, and intestine. These receptors are stimulated by distension of an intraluminal balloon (often used to localize the endings) and by contraction of the smooth muscle, whether spontaneous or drug induced. They are almost certainly in the smooth muscle layers, since their activity is not abolished by removal of the mucosa and the muscularis mucosae, and they are not very sensitive to stroking of the overlying serosa (Paintal, 1954; Iggo, 1957a; Leek, 1969).

In quiet conditions, many of these receptors have a slow continuous discharge, with superimposed rhythmic variations presumably due to local contractions of the smooth muscle too weak to change intraluminal pressure or volume. When stimulated by distension or by isometric smooth muscle contraction, both the spontaneous discharge and the rhythmic variations increase, but isotonic contraction of the muscle has little action on the discharge (Fig. 11). These observations support the view that the receptors are in series with the muscle fibers and that they should be called "tension receptors" rather than "stretch receptors" (Leek, 1972). As with other visceral receptors, thresholds vary considerably. Although slowly adapting to a maintained stretch, the receptors show a clear dynamic component, and also considerable hysteresis. To what extent these are properties of the receptors or of the surrounding tissue is not clear.

The vagal fibers were initially found by Paintal (1954) to have conduction velocities of 6.5–13 m/s, but Iggo (1958), using a different technique, found a range of 0.5–2.5 m/s, both results with cats. The difference is that between myelinated and nonmyelinated fibers, and Iggo has suggested that the fibers

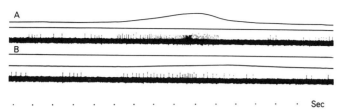

Fig. 11. The responses of an in-series tension receptor in the reticulum during contractions occurring under isometric recording conditions (A) and isotonic recording conditions (B). In A, there is an increase in reticular pressure (top trace in each record) and hence an increase in tension in the reticular wall, no change in reticular volume (middle trace in each record), and a marked increase in the afferent discharge (bottom trace in each record). In B, there is negligible increase in reticular pressure and hence negligible increase in tension in the reticular wall, a reduction in volume (shown as an upward deflection in the middle trace), and only very slight increase in the afferent discharge. From Leek (1969).

may lose their myelin sheaths on passing through the chest to the abdomen. In sheep and goats, the conduction velocities are appropriate for small-diameter myelinated fibers.

Recently, Iggo and Leek (1967) have divided the gastric tension receptors of the sheep into two groups, those with low tension thresholds, which are thought to excite the gastric centers and cause reflex gastric activity, and those with higher thresholds, which have the opposite effect. The equivalent division of types in the cat has not been described.

The actions of the tension receptors are concluded from indirect evidence. Their reflex activity would help to set the level of smooth muscle contraction in the quiescent stomach, and, when the stomach starts to contract, the input from the receptors could control the timing and the force of the contraction. When the contractions become strong, they would be inhibited by the high-threshold endings mentioned above. The sensory response to the receptors is more difficult to study, but it seems reasonable to suppose that they signal the sensation of gastric distension, and this view is consistent with their slow adaptation. However, one would expect the sensation to increase during contractions at constant volume, but not when the contractions were isotonic. It has been suggested that they may mediate "hunger pains" due to strong gastric contractions when the stomach is empty.

5.2. Serosal Receptors

In 1966, Bessou and Perl recorded single fiber activity in the vagus nerves of cats from receptors which responded to light stroking of the intestinal serosa with rapidly adapting discharges at frequencies less than 30 impulses/s.

Being rapidly adapting, they can respond to sinusoidal stimuli, but not faster than 100 Hz. Each unit has several sensitive points in its receptive field, the latter being about 1 cm in diameter. The afferent fibers have conduction velocities of 2–21 m/s, and the endings are clearly distinguished from Pacinian corpuscles which are found in the same region. The receptors discharge when the mesentery is moved, and when the small intestine is distorted by inflation or deflation of a balloon, but they respond only to changes of stimulus and not during a maintained deformation. Physiological movements of the intestinal contents past the receptor site are also a strong stimulus. Neither the receptors nor their reflex actions have been determined.

5.3. Muscularis Mucosae Receptors

In 1957, Paintal recorded single fiber activity in the vagus nerves from intestinal mechanoreceptors which are characterized by spontaneous bursts of activity at 0.03–0.17 Hz, each burst lasting 1–6 s with peak frequencies of 7–26 impulses/s. The receptors can be localized by probing but are not stimulated by intestinal distension. The bursts of activity are present when the intestine is "paralyzed" by atropine and are reinforced by augmented peristaltic movements. However, strong local smooth muscle contractions are frequently without effect on the receptor discharge. Thirty percent NaCl solution stimulates the receptors, but only when it is applied to the mucosal surface and not when applied to the serosa. Several other chemicals did not affect the receptors.

The action of 30% NaCl was Paintal's main evidence that the receptors lie in the muscularis mucosae, since this muscle was contracted by the saline. The role of the endings is uncertain, but Paintal speculates that they are a kind of "flow receptor," since their discharge increases during augmented intestinal propulsion. If this is so, the use to which this afferent information is put has not been established.

5.4. Chemoreceptors

Iggo (1957b) studied gastric receptors in the cat which responded to changes in intraluminal pH. These are of two types, acid sensitive and alkali sensitive. The former have a threshold of pH 3 (Fig. 12) and do not respond to alkali; the latter have thresholds above pH8 and do not respond to acid. Both types of receptors have vagal afferent fibers with conduction velocities in the range 1–5 m/s and are found in all regions of the stomach. They are destroyed by removal of the mucosa. Fairly strong mechanical stimulation excites receptors of both groups, but peristaltic contractions do not. The effective mechanical stimuli are firm stretching of the mucosa, stroking of the

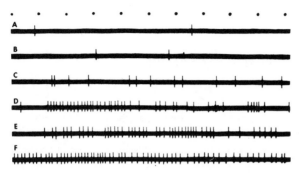

Fig. 12. The response of an acid-sensitive gastric mucosal chemoreceptor to the application of various fluids to the exposed mucosa. A, Distilled water; B, buffer solution at pH 5; C, at pH 3; D, at pH 2; E continued in F, 0.1 N HCl. Time marks 1 s. From Iggo (1957b).

mucosal surface, and overdistension of the stomach. The functions of the receptors are not known, and it is difficult to see under what natural conditions the alkali-sensitive ones would be stimulated.

In the intestine there are also chemoreceptors, and these are stimulated by glucose and certain amino acid solutions (Sharma and Nasset, 1962). Again, the reflex and possible sensory actions are unknown.

5.5. Hepatic Osmoreceptors

The evidence for hepatic osmoreceptors is based chiefly on the work of Haberich et al. (1965, 1969), who showed that when hypotonic solutions are infused into the portal vein of rats a diuresis occurs, but not when the solutions are infused into the inferior vena cava. The response is graded, and glucose and mannitol solutions have the same effect as NaCl. Stretch receptors stimulated by distension of the portal or hepatic vasculature have been eliminated, although the hypotonic solutions could presumably work by osmosis-induced changes in liver cell volume. "Hepatic diuresis" is prevented by cutting the hepatic branches of the vagus nerves, which implicates a nervous afferent pathway rather than a hormone released from the liver (Dennhardt et al., 1971). The afferent nerves control the release of antidiuretic hormone and must interact with atriovenous "volume receptors" and osmoreceptors in the hypothalamus.

Niijima (1969) has recorded from afferent vagal fibers from the liver of the guinea pig and finds that some have their discharge enhanced by increasing the osmolarity of the perfused liver; a change from 315 to 345 mOsm/liter caused a mean increase of 15 impulses/s. Andrews and Stratman (1968) have made similar observations for the perfused rabbit liver. The receptors have not been identified.

6. URINARY TRACT RECEPTORS

6.1. Bladder

Iggo (1955, 1956) has recorded afferent single fiber activity in the pelvic sacral nerves that come from mechanoreceptors in the bladder. These have properties very similar to the gastrointestinal "tension receptors" described above, being stimulated both by passive distension of the bladder and by active isometric smooth muscle contraction. The thresholds and firing frequencies (up to 40 impulses/s) of the receptors show some variation, and the only two receptors localized lay at the neck of the bladder. Simultaneous measurements of afferent fiber discharge and of bladder pressure indicate that the receptors reflexly contract bladder smooth muscle and relax the external sphincter and thus account for the nervously mediated increase in smooth muscle tone as the bladder becomes well distended. At low bladder volumes, there is a reflex relaxation of the bladder and a contraction of the sphincter (Iggo, 1966; Leek, 1972). Whether the same receptors also mediate this reflex is uncertain, as is their role in the sensation of bladder distension.

6.2. Urethra

Iggo (1956) and Todd (1964) have studied urethral "flow receptors," which discharge when liquid flows along the urethra. Maintained urethral distension does not stimulate them. The rate of discharge varies with rate of urine flow, and can be as high as 300 impulses/s; it is irregular, possibly due to turbulence in the flow. These receptors are concentrated near the external urethral sphincter.

There are also rapidly adapting urethral receptors which discharge when urethral caliber is changed but not during maintained distension or during urine flow (Todd, 1964).

Reflexes from the urethra to its sphincters and to the bladder have been studied, and presumably they are mediated by the two types of urethral mechanoreceptors (Leek, 1972).

7. OTHER ENTEROCEPTORS

This survey of enteroceptors has omitted many that have been studied, for example, in the esophagus, upper respiratory tract, kidney, and genital system. There are also probably more yet to be discovered, in particular those with nonmyelinated afferent fibers (from which it is relatively difficult to record nerve impulse traffic). Two types of receptors probably occur in all viscera, mechanoreceptors and nociceptive endings. The particular features of activation of these endings will depend on the nature of the tissue elements surrounding them at each site. Other receptors, such as chemoreceptors and pH receptors, probably occur only in tissues where their specialized properties are appropriate.

In spite of the length of the list of enteroceptors, or possibly because of it, our ignorance of enteroceptor physiology is depressingly profound. In only a minority of cases can we identify the actual receptor responsible for an afferent discharge. In no instance (apart from the Pacinian corpuscle) do we know the biophysical processes that lead to an action potential in the nerve fiber. For mechanoreceptors, we cannot say why some are slowly adapting and others rapidly adapting, why some fire regularly and others irregularly. Often we can only say that we know the receptor is somewhere and that further research is required.

8. REFERENCES

Aars, H., 1968, Aortic baroreceptor activity in normal and hypertensive rabbits, *Acta Physiol. Scand.* **72**:298.

Aars, H., 1969, Relationship between blood pressure and diameter of ascending aorta in normal and hypertensive rabbits, *Acta Physiol. Scand.* **75**:397.

Adrian, E. D., 1933, Afferent impulses in the vagus and their effect on respiration, *J. Physiol.* **79**:332.

Andrews, W. H. H., and Stratman, C. J., 1968, Afferent nerve impulses in the hepatic nerve of perfused rabbit livers, *J. Physiol.* **195**:32P.

Angell James, J. E., 1971*a*, Aortic arch baroreceptor activity in rabbits with calciferol-induced lesions and hypertension, *J. Physiol.* **217**:30P.

Angell James, J. E., 1971*b*, The effects of altering mean pressure pulse pressure and pulse frequency on the impulse activity in baroreceptor fibres from the aortic arch and right subclavian artery in the rabbit. *J. Physiol.* **214**:65.

Angell James, J. E., 1971*c*, The effects of changes of extramural, "intrathoracic," pressure on aortic arch baroreceptors, *J. Physiol.* **214**:89.

Angell James, J. E., 1971*d*, The response of aortic arch and right subclavian baroreceptors to changes of nonpulsatile pressure and their modification by hypothermia, *J. Physiol.* **214**:201.

Angell James, J. E., and Daly, M. de B., 1970, Comparison of reflex vasomotor responses to separate and combined stimulation of carotid sinus and aortic arch baroreceptors by pulsatile and non-pulsatile pressures in the dog, *J. Physiol.* **209**:257.

Arndt, J. O., Brambring, P., Hindorf, K., and Röhnelt, M., 1971, The afferent impulse traffic from atrial A-type receptors in cats, *Pflügers Arch. Ges. Physiol.* **326**:300.

Bessou, P., and Perl, E. R., 1966, A movement receptor of the small intestine, *J. Physiol.* **182**:404.

Bloor, C. M., 1964, Aortic baroreceptor threshold and sensitivity in rabbits at different ages, *J. Physiol.* **174**:136.

Christensen, B. N., Warner, H. R., and Pryor, T. A., 1967, A technique for quantitative study of carotid sinus behavior in: *Baroreceptors and Hypertension* (p. Kezdi, ed.), pp. 41–49, Pergamon, Oxford.

Clark, F. J., and von Euler, C., 1972, On the regulation of depth and rate of breathing, *J. Physiol.* **222**:267.

Coleridge, J. C. G., and Kidd, C., 1961, Relationship between pulmonary arterial pressure and impulse activity in pulmonary arterial baroreceptor fibres, *J. Physiol.* **158**:197.

Coleridge, J. C. G., and Kidd, C., 1963, Reflex effects of stimulating baroreceptors in the pulmonary artery, *J. Physiol.* **166**:197.

Coleridge, J. C. G., Hemingway, A., Holmes, R. L., and Linden, R. J., 1957, The location of atrial receptors in the dog: A physiological and histological study, *J. Physiol.* **136**:174.

Coleridge, H. M., Coleridge, J. C. G., and Kidd, C., 1964, Cardiac receptors in the dog, with particular reference to two types of afferent ending in the ventricular wall, *J. Physiol.* **174**:323.

Coleridge, H. M., Coleridge, J. C. G., and Luck, J. C., 1965, Pulmonary afferent fibres of small diameter stimulated by capsaicin and by hyperinflation of the lungs, *J. Physiol.* **179**:248.

Davis, H. L., Fowler, W. S., and Lambert, E. H., 1956, Effect of volume and rate of inflation and deflation on transpulmonary pressure and response of pulmonary stretch receptors, *Am. J. Physiol.* **187**:558.

De Castro, F., 1928, Sur la structure et l'innervation du sinus carotidien: Nouveaux facts sur l'innervation et la fonction du glomus carotidien, *Trab. Lab. Invest. Biol. Univ. Madrid* **25**:331.

Dennhardt, R., Ohm, W. W., and Haberich, F. J., 1971, Die Ausschaltung der Leberäste des N. vagus an der wachen Ratte und ihr Einfluss auf die hepatogene Diarese—indirecter Beweis für die afferente Leitung der Leber-Osmoreceptoren über den N. vagus, *Pflügers Arch. Ges. Physiol.* **328**:51.

Deshpande, S. S., and Devanandan, M. S., 1970, Reflex inhibition of monosynaptic reflexes by stimulation of type-J pulmonary endings, *J. Physiol.* **206**:345.

Diamond, J., 1955, Observations on the excitation by acetylcholine and by pressure of sensory receptors in the cat's carotid sinus, *J. Physiol.* **130**:513.

Ead, H. W., Green, J. H., and Neil, E., 1952, A comparison of the effects of pulsatile and non-pulsatile blood flow through the carotid sinus on the reflexogenic activity of the sinus baroreceptors in the cat, *J. Physiol.* **118**:509.

Elftman, A. G., 1943, The afferent and parasympathetic innervation of the lungs and trachea of the dog, *Am. J. Anat.* **72**:2.

Fedde, M. R., and Peterson, D. F., 1970, Intrapulmonary receptor response to changes in airway-gas composition in *Gallus domesticus*, *J. Physiol.* **209**:609.

Ferrer, P., and Koller, E. A., 1968, Über die Vagusafferenzen des Meerschwenchens und ihre Bedeutung für die Spontanatmung, *Helv. Physiol. Pharmacol. Acta* **26**:365.

Fidone, S. J., and Sato, A., 1969, A study of chemoreceptor and baroreceptor A and C-fibres in the cat carotid nerve, *J. Physiol.* **205**:527.

Fillenz, M., 1970, Innervation of pulmonary capillaries, *Experientia* **25**:842.

Fillenz, M., and Widdicombe, J. G., 1972, Receptors of the lungs and airways, in: *Handbook of Sensory Physiology*, Vol. 3 (E. Neil, ed.), pp. 81–112, Springer-Verlag, Heidelberg.

Floyd, W. F., and Neil, E., 1952, The influence of the sympathetic innervation of the carotid bifurcation on chemoreceptor and baroreceptor activity in the cat, *Arch. Int. Pharmacodyn.* **91**:230.

Frankstein, S. I., and Sergeeva, Z. N., 1966, Tonic activity of lung receptors in normal and pathological states, *Nature* **210**:1054.

Furnival, C. M., Linden, R. J., and Snow, H. M., 1971, Reflex effects on the heart of stimulating left atrial receptors, *J. Physiol.* **218**:447.

Gauer, O. H., and Henry, J. P., 1956, Beitrag zur Homöostase des extraarteriellen Kreislaufs: Volumen-regulation als unabhängiger physiologischer Parameter, *Klin. Wschr.* **34**:356.

Guz, A., and Trenchard, D. W., 1971, The role of non-myelinated vagal afferent fibres from the lungs in the genesis of tachypnoea in the rabbit, *J. Physiol.* **213**:345.

Haberich, F. J., Aziz, O., and Nowacki, P. E., 1965, Über einen osmoreceptorisch tätigen Mechanismus in der Leber, *Pflügers Arch. Ges. Physiol.* **285**:73.

Haberich, F. J., Aziz, O., Nowacki, P. E., and Ohm, W. W., 1969, Zur Spezifität der Osmoreceptoren in der Leber, *Pflügers Arch. Ges. Physiol.* **313**:289.

Henry, J. P., Gauer, O. H., and Reeves, J. L., 1956, Evidence of the atrial location of receptors influencing urine flow, *Circ. Res.* **4**:85.

Heymans, C., and Neil, E., 1958, *Reflexogenic Areas of the Cardiovascular System*, Churchill, London.

Iggo, A., 1955, Tension receptors in the stomach and urinary bladder, *J. Physiol.* **128**:593.

Iggo, A., 1956, Afferent fibres from the viscera, in: *Twentieth International Physiological Congress*, pp. 458–459.

Iggo, A., 1957a, Gastro-intestinal tension receptors with unmyelinated afferent fibres in the vagus of the cat, *Quart. J. Exptl. Physiol.* **42**:130.

Iggo, A., 1957b, Gastric mucosal chemoreceptors with vagal efferent fibres in the cat, *Quart. J. Exptl. Physiol.* **42**:398.

Iggo, A., 1958, The electrophysiological identification of single nerve fibres with particular reference to the slowest conducting vagal afferent fibres in the cat, *J. Physiol.* **142**:110.

Iggo, A., 1966, Physiology of visceral afferent systems, *Acta Neuroveg.* (Wein) **28**:121.

Iggo, A., and Leek, B. F., 1967, An electrophysiological study of some reticulo-ruminal and abomasal reflexes in sheep, *J. Physiol.* **193**:95.

Iggo, A., and Leek, B. F., 1970, Sensory receptors in the ruminant stomach and their reflex effects, in: *Physiology of Digestion and Metabolism in the Ruminant*, Oriel Press, Newcastle upon Tyne.

Karczewski, W., and Widdicombe, J. G., 1969, The role of the vagus nerves in the respiratory and circulatory responses to intravenous histamine and phenyl diguanide in rabbits, *J. Physiol.* **201**:271.

Kezdi, P., 1954, Control by the superior cervical ganglion of the state of contraction and pulsatile expansion of the carotid sinus arterial wall, *Circ. Res.* **2**:367.

Knowlton, G. C., and Larrabee, M. G., 1946, A unitary analysis of pulmonary volume receptors, *Am. J. Physiol.* **151**:547.

Koizumi, K., and Sato, A., 1969, Influence of sympathetic innervation on carotid sinus baroreceptor activity, *Am. J. Physiol.* **216**:321.

Korner, P. I., 1971, Integrative neural cardiovascular control, *Physiol. Rev.* **51**:312.

Kottegoda, S. R., 1970, Peristalsis of the small intestine, in: *Smooth Muscle*, Edward Arnold, London.

Koushanpour, E., and McGee, J. P., 1969, Effect of mean pressure on carotid sinus baroreceptor response to pulsatile pressure, *Am. J. Physiol.* **216**:599.

Landgren, S., 1952, On the excitation mechanism of the carotid baroreceptors, *Acta Physiol. Scand.* **26**:1.

Langrehr, D., 1960, Entladungsmuster und allgemeine Reizbedingungen von Vorhofs-receptoren bei Hund und Katze, *Pflügers Arch. Ges. Physiol.* **271**:257.

Larsell, O., 1928, The nerves and nerve-endings of the pleura pulmonaris histologically and experimentally, *Phi Beta Pi Quart.*, p. 1.

Leek, B. F., 1969, Reticulo-ruminal mechanoreceptors in sheep, *J. Physiol.* **202**:585.

Leek, B. F., 1972, Abdominal visceral receptors, in: *Handbook of Sensory Physiology*, Vol. 3 (E. Neil, ed.), pp. 113–160, Springer-Verlag, Heidelberg.

Marshall, R., and Widdicombe, J. G., 1958, The activity of pulmonary stretch receptors during congestion of the lungs, *Quart. J. Exptl. Physiol.* **43**:320.

McCubbin, J. W., Green, J. H., and Page, I. H., 1956, Baroreceptor function in chronic renal hypertension, *Circ. Res.* **4**:205.

Mei, N., 1970a, Disposition anatomique et propriétés électrophysiologiques des neurones sensitifs vagaux chez le chat, *Exptl. Brain Res.* **11**:465.

Mei, N., 1970b, Mécanorécepteurs vagaux cardiovasculaires et respiratoires chez le chat, *Exptl. Brain Res.* **11**:480.

Meyrick, B., and Reid, L., 1971, Nerves in rat intra-acinar alveoli: An electron micro-scopic study, *Resp. Physiol.* **11**:367.

Mills, J., Sellick, H., and Widdicombe, J. G., 1969, The role of lung irritant receptors in respiratory responses to multiple pulmonary embolism, anaphylaxis and histamine-induced bronchoconstriction, *J. Physiol.* **203**:337.

Mills, J. E., Sellick, H., and Widdicombe, J. G., 1970, Epithelial irritant receptors in the lungs, in: *Breathing: Hering-Breuer Centenary Symposium* (R. Porter, ed.), pp. 77–92, Churchill, London.

Muers, M. F., and Sleight, P., 1972, Action potentials from ventricular mechanoreceptors stimulated by occlusion of the coronary sinus in the dog, *J. Physiol.* **221**:283.

Neil, E., 1954, The carotid and aortic vasosensory areas, *Arch. Middlesex Hosp.* **4**:16.

Neil, E., and Joels, N., 1961, The impulse activity in cardiac afferent vagal fibres. *Naunyn-Schmiedeberg's Arch. Exptl. Pathol. Pharmakol.* **240**:453.

Niijima, A., 1969, Afferent discharges from osmoreceptors in the liver of the guinea-pig, *Science* **166**:1519.

Paintal, A. S., 1954, A study of gastric stretch receptors: Their role in the peripheral mechanism of satiation, of hunger and thirst, *J. Physiol.* **126**:255.

Paintal, A. S., 1955, Impulses in vagal afferent fibres from specific pulmonary deflation receptors: The response of these receptors to phenyl diguanide, potato starch, 5-hydroxytryptamine and nicotine, and their role in respiratory and cardiovascular reflexes, *Quart. J. Exptl. Physiol.* **40**:89.

Paintal, A. S., 1957, Responses from mucosal mechanoreceptors in the small intestine of the cat, *J. Physiol.* **139**:353.

Paintal, A. S., 1963, Vagal afferent fibres, *Ergebn. Physiol.* **52**:74.

Paintal, A. S., 1970, The mechanism of excitation of type J receptors, and the J reflex, in: *Breathing: Hering-Breuer Centenary Symposium* (R. Porter, ed.), pp. 59–70, Church-ill, London.

Paintal, A. S., 1972, Cardiovascular Receptors, in: *Handbook of Sensory Physiology*, Vol. 3 (E. Neil, ed.), pp. 1–46, Springer-Verlag, Heidelberg.

Palme, F., 1943, Zur Funktion der branchiogenen Reflexzonen für Chemo- und Presso-Reception, *Z. Ges. Exptl. Med.* **113**:415.

Rees, P. M., 1967, Observations on the fine structure and distribution of presumptive baroreceptor nerves at the carotid sinus, *J. Comp. Neurol.* **131**:517.

Rees, P. M., 1968, Electron microscopical observations on the architecture of the carotid arterial walls, with special reference to the sinus portion, *J. Anat.* **103**:35.

Sellick, H., and Widdicombe, J. G., 1970, Vagal deflation and inflation reflexes mediated by lung irritant receptors, *Quart. J. Exptl. Physiol.* **55**:153.

Sharma, K. N., 1967, Receptor mechanisms in the alimentary tract: Their excitation and functions, in: *Handbook of Physiology*, Sect. 6: *Alimentary Canal*, American Physiological Society, Washington, D.C.

Sharma, K. N., and Nasset, E. S., 1962, Electrical activity in mesenteric nerves after perfusion of gut lumen, *Am. J. Physiol.* **202**:725.

Sleight, P., and Widdicombe, J. G., 1965, Action potentials in fibres from receptors in the epicardium and myocardium of the dog's left ventricle, *J. Physiol.* **181**:235.

Spickler, J. W., Kezdi, P., and Geller, E., 1967, Transfer characteristics of the carotid sinus pressure control system, in: *Baroreceptors and Hypertension* (P. Kezdi, ed.), pp. 31–39, Pergamon Press, Oxford.

Todd, J. K., 1964, Afferent impulses in the pudendal nerves of the cat, *Quart. J. Exptl. Physiol.* **49**:258.

Tomori, Z., and Widdicombe, J. G., 1969, Muscular, bronchomotor and cardiovascular reflexes elicited by mechanical stimulation of the respiratory tract, *J. Physiol.* **200**:25.

Widdicombe, J. G., 1954, The site of pulmonary stretch receptors in the cat, *J. Physiol.* **125**:336.

Widdicombe, J. G., 1964, Respiratory reflexes, in: *Handbook of Physiology* Sect. 3: *Respiration*, Vol. 1, pp. 585–630, American Physiological Society, Washington, D.C.

Chapter 16

Arterial Chemoreceptors

T. J. Biscoe

Department of Physiology
University of Bristol
Bristol, England

1. INTRODUCTION

The carotid and aortic chemoreceptors lie within the carotid and aortic bodies. These bodies are of considerable complexity and have been the subject of many studies over the last 50 years. They are concerned with monitoring the gaseous constituents of the arterial blood and have reflex effects, notably on the respiratory and cardiovascular systems. Over the years, there have been a number of reviews concerned with their function and structure, the most recent being those of Biscoe (1971) and Howe and Neil (1971). There are many earlier reviews, and among the most important are the Wates Symposium edited by Torrance (1968) and an article by Comroe (1964). An account of the pioneer work on function by Heymans is given in his reviews with Bouckaert (Heymans *et al.*, 1933; Heymans and Bouckaert, 1939), subsequently expanded in his book with Neil (Heymans and Neil, 1958). Heymans was awarded the Nobel prize in 1938 for his work on these peripheral receptors and their reflex effects. Much of the past research has been about these reflex effects and their elucidation; this discussion is concerned not with that aspect of function but with the problem of the nature of the receptor lying within these carotid and aortic bodies. The carotid bodies have been the subject of most of the research on this problem simply because they are much more readily accessible than their aortic counterparts.

Consideration will first be given to the structure, followed by an account of the relevant functional studies. This leads to an attempt to synthesize the findings to date into a coherent and simple explanation of the nature of the receptor and how it could function.

2. STRUCTURE

2.1. Light Microscopy

It was De Castro (1926, 1928) who first gave evidence that the carotid bodies had a sensory, possibly chemoreceptive, function. He showed the presence of large, rounded cells, glomus or epithelioid cells, lying in groups. The structure was shown to have a very rich blood supply with arteriovenous anastomoses (see also De Castro, 1940, 1951, 1962), and many nerve fibers were present. He concluded on the basis of nerve degeneration experiments that the sinus nerve supply (a subdivision of the IXth cranial nerve) was largely afferent. This description was supported and refined by others, who described, for example, two types of parenchymal cells (Gomez, 1907, 1908; Meijling, 1938; Goormaghtigh and Pannier, 1939; De Kock, 1951, 1954; Pessacq, 1961; Muratori and Battaglia, 1959) and made further studies on the blood supply (Serafini-Fracassini and Volpin, 1966; Goormaghtigh and Pannier, 1939). A similar basic structure was defined for the aortic bodies by Muratori (1933, 1935), the blood supply investigated (Howe, 1956; Coleridge *et al.*, 1967, 1970), and the afferent nerve supply studied (Hollinshead, 1939, 1940).

The view of the nature of the chemoreceptor put forward by De Castro, i.e., that the glomus cell is the detector of changes in blood constituents and that the nerve supply to these cells is afferent, has been universally accepted. It has only been challenged in recent years following the development of the electron microscope for use in biological experiments and hence the advent of detailed studies of the ultrastructure.

2.2. Electron Microscopy

The ultrastructure of arterial chemoreceptors has been well described in recent years and has been reviewed by Biscoe (1971) and Howe and Neil (1971), while Kobayashi (1971*b*) also lists the relevant papers and has made a comparative study. Most of the studies are on the carotid body, but those of Knoche and Schmitt (1963), Knoche *et al.* (1971), Abbott and Howe (1970), and Battaglia and Mariani (1970) show similar structures in the aortic bodies.

A picture has emerged which, in part at least, confirms the findings of the light microscopists.

2.2.1. Blood Vessels

The blood vessels (sometimes improperly called "sinusoids," see Majno, 1965; Farquhar, 1961) are lined by an attenuated, fenestrated endothelium. Around some of the blood vessels, smooth muscle is found (Biscoe, 1971; Biscoe and Stehbens, 1966; Feria-Velasco and Gonzalez-Angulo, 1968; Kobayashi, 1968), and nearby are terminations of sympathetic nerve fibers from the superior cervical ganglia (Biscoe and Stehbens, 1966, 1967; Kobayashi, 1968; Kondo, 1971).

2.2.2. Parenchymal Cells

Ultrastructural studies have confirmed that there are two main cell types and have permitted a more precise definition of their relationships than was possible hitherto. Many names have been given to these two types, and the alternatives have been listed (Biscoe, 1971). Here the two types will be named "I" and "II," a nomenclature which is now being more widely used (Howe and Neil, 1971; Biscoe, 1971; Biscoe and Stehbens, 1966, 1967; Verna, 1971; Bock et al., 1970) and implies nothing about function.

The type I cells have a complex shape and occur in groups of four or five (Biscoe and Pallot, 1972) invested by a type II cell and surrounded by a basement membrane. There are occasional areas of the cytoplasm of the type I cells covered only by basement membrane and not by type II cell. The type I cells may be 10–15 μm in their longest diameter and contain the usual cytoplasmic constituents including a nonmotile cilium. They are the cells widely held to be the receptor cell since De Castro's results published in 1926 and 1928.

The type I cells are recognized by the presence of many electron-dense cored vesicles 100–200 nm in diameter. These vesicles are the site of stores of catechol- and indoleamines, whose presence has been demonstrated by many authors (see Biscoe, 1971, for a summary, and especially Chiocchio et al., 1967, 1971a,b, and Kobayashi, 1971a). There seems little doubt that these amines must play a role in the function of the arterial chemoreceptors.

The type II cells are virtually devoid of electron-dense cored vesicles and surround the type I cells in an attenuated layer. They envelop nerve fibers and nerve endings in a similar way to the Schwann cell.

2.2.3. Nerve Fibers

Myelinated and nonmyelinated nerve fibers are found, and very occasionally a node of Ranvier can be seen or the terminal portion of the myelin sheath giving way to a nonmyelinated fiber. Nonmyelinated fibers are enveloped by Schwann cells or by the type II cell, where they are often very small in diameter, 0.1 μm.

2.2.4. Nerve Endings

The nerve ending associated with the type I cell characteristically contains small synaptic vesicles 50–60 nm in maximum diameter, small mitochondria, glycogen granules sometimes in aggregations, neurofibrils, and an occasional complex vesicle. Such endings have electron-dense junctional regions with the type I cell and are usually separated from the surrounding basement membrane by a layer of type II cell cytoplasm. There have been a number of descriptions which attempt to distinguish different sorts of nerve endings on the type I cell. These distinctions are made on grounds of size and preponderance of a particular set of intracytoplasmic constituents. For example, Al-Lami and Murray (1968) distinguish small "compact and bulbous" from "basket" nerve endings. The latter have a much more extensive contact with the type I cell and may even surround it. Other authors (Bock *et al.*, 1970; Kondo, 1971; Verna, 1971) have described a variety of ending packed with mitochondria which is thought to be the sensory ending. Many of the published pictures show synaptic vesicles in these endings as well as the mitochondria. Other endings without so many mitochondria are also described and supposed to be efferent.

It is quite clear that such distinctions ought not to be made on the basis of single electron micrographs, and serial reconstruction has shown (Biscoe and Pallot, 1972) that the distinctions are invalid. Biscoe and Pallot found that the same nerve ending can have areas of many or few synaptic vesicles, may be applied to the type I cell over a large area in one plane and a small area in another, may have areas of many and areas of few mitochondria, and will always show intermittent electron-dense junctional regions with the type I cells. Thus the appearance in a randomly selected micrograph will depend entirely on the plane of section. In addition, there are usually two or three separate nerve endings on the type I cell, and all of these are supplied by branches of the same axon.

Another group of nerve endings are also found related to the blood vessels and smooth muscle cells (Biscoe and Stehbens, 1966; Kobayashi, 1968). These contain synaptic vesicles, small electron-dense cored vesicles, and small mitochondria and degenerate when the superior cervical ganglion is removed. They are therefore identified as sympathetic nerve endings.

Last, De Kock and Dunn (1966) have claimed to show small nerve fibers terminating in the type II cells, but there is reason to doubt the validity of their findings (Biscoe, 1971).

2.3. Degeneration Studies

Degeneration studies have been concerned with the problem of the nature of the nerve ending on the type I cell. Cutting a nerve is associated among other things with degeneration of the terminals separated from the cell body. This fact was used by De Castro in 1926 to show that nerve fibers in the sinus nerve terminated in the carotid body; he cut the nerve in the position shown as cut 1 in Fig. 1. He used silver impregnation methods and light microscopy, and his findings were confirmed by Biscoe and Stehbens (1967), Hess (1968), and Battaglia (1970) using the electron microscope. It is clear from Fig. 1 that his experiment does not distinguish afferent from efferent fibers, for in either case (pathway A or pathway B in Fig. 1) the ending should degenerate. The experiment did establish the important fact that the structure has a nerve supply.

In 1928, De Castro published the results of the next logical experiment, namely, making an intracranial cut of the nerve supplying the structure, cut 2 in Fig. 1. In this experiment, the fibers following course A (Fig. 1) might be expected not to degenerate whereas those following course B (Fig. 1) would degenerate. De Castro found no evidence for degeneration in the carotid body after 12 days, whereas degeneration had occurred after a similar time when the extracranial operation (cut 1, Fig. 1) was performed. Hence he concluded that the nerve supply was afferent and went on to conclude that the type I cells were receptors.

A similar result was obtained for the aortic bodies by Hollinshead (1939, 1940), who cut the vagus nerve above and below the nodose ganglion, and by Knoche et al. (1971).

With the electron microscope, De Castro and Rubio (1968) confirmed De Castro's 1928 result. There are, however, technical reasons which leave doubts about their findings.

The experiment has also been performed by Biscoe et al. (1970b), who showed there was an absolute, progressive reduction in the number of synaptic vesicle–containing nerve endings in the type I cell as compared with the control nonoperated side. In their series, it was unusual to find normal-looking nerve endings after 2 months. Their counts of numbers of nerve endings were of all structures which could conceivably be recognized as nerve endings and included those which were degenerating. They also showed that chemoreceptor activity could be recorded from the sinus nerve on the operated and nonoperated sides with equal facility at a time when degeneration of the endings on type I cells could be seen. This judgment about facility is of course a subjective one and may be colored by the experience and prejudice of the operator. Nevertheless, recording from the receptor afferents is an important control to eliminate some of the alternative explanations of the results,

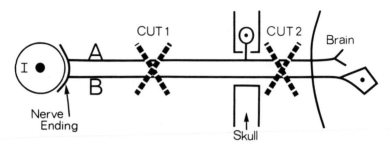

Fig. 1. The two sites at which a nerve supplying an organ may be cut in order to establish the provenance of the nerve ending. In this case, the organ is an arterial chemoreceptor and the nerve ends on a type I cell. A, Course of the nerve fiber and site of the cell body if the nerve ending is afferent. B, Course of the nerve fiber and site of the cell body if the nerve ending is efferent. Cut 1 and cut 2 are the positions at which the nerve has been cut in different experiments. The consequential changes at the nerve ending show whether or not it is to be regarded as efferent or afferent.

namely, that the afferent cell bodies are in the brain stem, that the glossopharyngeal ganglion has been damaged, or that transneuronal degeneration has occurred with cell bodies in the glossopharyngeal ganglion. One is left to conclude that the nerve endings are efferent and that since the serial reconstruction experiments (Biscoe and Pallot, 1972) show that the nerve endings on a type I cell probably all have the same origin they are *all* efferent.

The greatest impediment to the acceptance of this result is the prolonged degeneration time. However, similarly slow rates were described by Biscoe and Stehbens (1967) (and see Battaglia, 1970) though not by Hess (1968) for extracranial (cut 1, Fig. 1) section. Hess (1968), however, did not look at tissue beyond 7 days after cutting the nerve. Such slow rates are not as unusual as may at first appear to be the case, for the literature contains accounts of prolonged time courses (Cheng-Minoda *et al.*, 1968; Lee, 1963; Sherrington and Laslett, 1903; Spoendlin, 1966; Spoendlin and Gacek, 1963; Terayama *et al.*, 1968; Walberg, 1965), especially for nonmyelinated axons. Since the efferent axons probably are nonmyelinated, the result is not too unexpected.

3. FUNCTION

Function is here considered only insofar as it bears on the problem of the receptor and the need to distinguish different types of pathways to or from the receptor complex.

3.1. Types of Activity in the Nerve Supply to the Receptor Complex

The arterial chemoreceptors are known to have two anatomically distinct nerves supplying them. In the case of the carotid body, these are the sinus nerve and a branch or branches from the superior cervical ganglion (Gerard and Billingsley, 1923). The aortic bodies are supplied by the aortic nerve (Hollinshead, 1939) and by sympathetic branches from the stellate ganglion (Mills, 1968).

3.1.1. The Sympathetic Nerves

The predominant spontaneous activity in the sympathetic nerves (Millar and Biscoe, 1966) shows the characteristic respiratory and cardiac rhythms first described in them by Adrian *et al.* (1932). Excitation of the sympathetic supply evokes an increase in chemoreceptor activity from the carotid body (Biscoe and Purves, 1967; Eyzaguirre and Lewin, 1961; Floyd and Neil, 1952) or from the aortic body (Mills, 1968). The other effects of stimulation are described by Purves (1970) and discussed by Howe and Neil (1971).

3.1.2. The Sinus and Aortic Nerves

3.1.2a. Afferent Activity. The statistical properties of the discharge in a single afferent fiber from the carotid body were shown to be those of a Poisson process by Biscoe and Taylor, 1963, so that the probability of occurrence of an afferent impulse is never zero. This finding led to a number of possible conclusions about the mode of impulse generation, which will be considered later (Section 4).

Many of the other studies have been about the effects of changes in blood gases on chemoreceptor activity. The general conclusions from these experiments are that the chemoreceptors respond to independent changes of the steady-state partial pressure of oxygen and carbon dioxide and of pH in the arterial blood. The single afferent fiber results of Biscoe *et al.* (1970a) showed that the chemoreceptor discharge rate increased progressively as the arterial oxygen partial pressure fell below 200 mm Hg.

The other important factor which may affect chemoreceptor afferent activity is the centrifugal path which has been described in the sinus nerve and is discussed below.

3.1.2b. Centrifugal Pathway. The existence of two groups of centrifugally running fibers in the sinus nerve was recognized by Biscoe and Sampson (1967, 1968). One was shown to be of sympathetic origin (see Eyzaguirre and Lewin, 1961); the other most probably arose from fibers with cell bodies in the brain stem. The activity in this latter pathway was nonrhythmic, was markedly increased 10–30 s after the intravenous injection of adrenaline, and was increased when the arterial oxygen partial pressure was lowered or when the carbon dioxide partial pressure was raised. The effects of adrenaline were confirmed and extended to include other catecholamines by Laurent and Jager-Barres (1969). Neil and O'Regan (1969b, 1971b) also described this activity and showed that it was always decreased by cutting the sinus nerve trunk centrally. In addition, they found that an increase in afferent activity could be evoked by chemoreceptor stimulation on the ipsilateral side only when the sinus nerve was left intact. This suggests that there is no central crossing of the pathways, which is surprising.

The depressant effect of this pathway on chemoreceptor discharge was demonstrated first by Neil and O'Regan (1969a, 1971a). Electrical stimulation of the nerve reduced afferent activity, the same result being obtained for the sinus and aortic nerves. Sampson and Biscoe (1970) and Sampson (1971a) confirmed the effect of electrical stimulation and remarked on persistence of the inhibition for 1–2 s after stimulation had ceased, a fact which argues in favor of a chemical transmitter action. They also confirmed that when recordings of chemoreceptor activity were made from a slip dissected off the intact sinus nerve this activity increased if the sinus nerve was cut and further showed that the response curve to change in oxygen tension shifted upward on cutting the sinus nerve. This indicated a tonic inhibitory action and demonstrated that the response curve to steady-state oxygen tension was curvilinear when the nerve was intact. The magnitude of the shift was greatest at low oxygen partial pressures, which finding is commensurate with the increased activity in the centrifugal pathway at low oxygen.

Last, Yates et al. (1970) have shown that stimulation of the sinus nerve is associated with depletion of the electron-dense cored vesicles found in type I cells.

3.2. The Type I Cell

The type I cell is the one proposed by De Castro as the chemoreceptor cell and so described in textbooks. It is the cell which contains many electron-dense cored vesicles.

3.2.1. Structural Considerations

The type I cell has been shown to contain catecholamines and indoleamines by many workers, as noted above. Recently, using electron microscopic methods, Jones and Ballard (1971) and Ballard and Jones (1971) have described the distribution of the cholinesterase enzymes. Butyrylcholinesterase was found around the whole extent of the type II cell membrane, acetylcholinesterase was found in groups of axons surrounded by Schwann cells. The latter site is probably the same as that found predominating by Biscoe and Silver (1966) using the light microscope and nerve degeneration experiments. In these experiments, all of the cholinesterase was depleted by cutting the sympathetic nerve supply, not the sinus nerve. Clearly, Jones and Ballard have much better resolution, but it would be interesting to combine the nerve degeneration experiments with ultrastructural studies. If it is accepted that the presence of cholinesterase is to be equated with cholinergic transmission, then it is to be concluded that the sympathetic pathway is cholinergic and that a cholinergic mechanism is related to type I/II cell function.

3.2.2. The Role of Chemical Transmitters

Apart from the catecholamines and indoleamines in type I cells, acetylcholine has also been found in the carotid body by Eyzaguirre et al. (1965). However, there appears to be an unexplained discrepancy between the amount of acetylcholine and the amount of choline acetyltransferase present in the carotid body (Hebb, 1968), though Hebb did find a relatively high concentration of enzyme in the sinus nerve which led her to suggest that there were cholinergic fibers present and that these could be efferent.

The precise role of acetylcholine in the carotid body has been debated since Schweitzer and Wright (1938) first suggested a transmitter function at the junction between the receptor cell and the afferent nerve ending. In recent years, the most notable proponent of this view has been Eyzaguirre. With his elegant simplifying technique, he has been able to study the performance of the receptor without interference from such extraneous factors as the rate of blood flow, the oxygen content of the blood, and the sympathetic nerve activity. His work (Eyzaguirre and Koyano, 1965a,b; Eyzaguirre et al., 1965; Eyzaguirre and Zapata, 1968a,b,c) has been directed toward showing that the receptor cell hypothesis is valid and that acetylcholine is the transmitter. One of the most important experiments in favor of the hypothesis is one in which Eyzaguirre et al. (1965) were able to show that stimulation of one carotid body caused the release of a substance that excited the downstream carotid body afferents. Later, Eyzaguirre and Zapata (1968b) showed that eserine enhanced the excitation while mecamylamine blocked this eserine effect when the drugs were applied for 1 h and in the case of mecamylamine at a concentration of 10^{-4} g/ml. Eyzaguirre has since carried out further experiments to support this pharmacological evidence (Nishi and Eyzaguirre, 1971). His conclusion remains that the release of acetylcholine presynaptically from the receptor underlies impulse initiation in afferent fibers. However, the earlier and critical findings of Sampson (1970, 1971b) do not seem to be satisfactorily answered insofar as both authors agree that blocking drugs, e.g., mecamylamine, can block the response of the receptor *in vivo* to applied acetylcholine but not to NaCN and natural stimuli, though only Sampson tested the effects of changes in blood gas partial pressures since only he measured them. The failure to record the relevant levels of the appropriate stimulus modalities seems an important omission in the study of a receptor. Because of this finding of differential sensitivity, Nishi and Eyzaguirre (1971) are led to propose that acetylcholine is acting at "relatively exposed 'extra-synaptic' cholinergic sites, probably located in the stem of the nonmyelinated sensory ending." They do not state where this is, and there is no ultrastructural evidence for its existence since the nerve is at all times enclosed either by Schwann cell or by type II cell for the latter cells abut on each other.

One can conclude that acetylcholine and the enzymes responsible for synthesizing and hydrolyzing it are present in the carotid body, possibly in the efferent fibers (Hebb, 1968).

3.2.2a. Chemical Transmitters in Nerve Endings. There is no direct evidence for the location of any transmitter in nerve endings. The indirect evidence referred to above and the presence of synaptic vesicles in the nerve endings on type I cells suggest that acetylcholine may be the transmitter at this site, that is, may be the efferent nerve transmitter whose release leads ultimately to inhibition of chemoreceptor discharge.

3.2.2b. Chemical Transmitters in Type I Cells. Chemical transmitters in type I cells could be released by the action of acetylcholine if this were the transmitter at the efferent synapse and could then cause inhibition of chemoreceptor discharge by hyperpolarizing the receptor. This hypothesis is supported by Sampson (1971a), who has shown depression of chemoreceptor activity from the carotid body by catecholamines, which are known to be present in type I cells. He found that these substances depressed before they excited, the latter response being attributed to their vasoconstrictor action. The catecholamine action was blocked by dibenzyline, which did not affect responses to acetylcholine or NaCN. This depressant action of catecholamines is comparable to the depressant action of catecholamines on the spontaneous activity and the synaptic and chemical excitation of some neurons in unanesthetized cats (Engberg and Ryall, 1965, 1966; Salmoiraghi and Stefanis, 1965; Biscoe and Curtis, 1966; Biscoe *et al.*, 1966). Furthermore, the work of Born and Bulbring (1956) and Burnstock (1958) suggests that adrenaline may increase the membrane potential by stimulating the sodium pump.

4. THE IDENTITY OF THE RECEPTOR

The identity of the receptor is the central problem so far as the chemoreceptor is concerned.

4.1. The Received View

The account to be found in textbooks, originally propounded by De Castro (1926, 1928) and most strongly supported by Eyzaguirre and his associates, is that shown in Fig. 1, pathway A. According to this view, a cell, the type I cell, is the receptor and it initiates nerve impulses in an adjacent nerve ending by the action of a chemical transmitter, probably acetylcholine. From the above account, it should be obvious that it is now possible to doubt this hypothesis on a number of grounds:

1. The structure of the nerve ending adjacent to the type I cell is that of a motor ending not a sensory ending.
2. It can be shown that these endings degenerate when the IXth nerve is cut intracranially (Fig. 1, cut, 2), and therefore they are probably motor not sensory.
3. There is a centrifugal pathway in the sinus nerve whose activity is related to the blood gas tensions.
4. Stimulation of the sinus nerve depresses the chemoreceptor activity.
5. Stimulation of the sinus nerve depletes the type I cells of their electron-dense cored vesicles.
6. Removal of the efferent pathway causes receptor sensitivity to change; it therefore has a tonic action.
7. Acetylcholine has not been shown to be present in type I cells.

The conclusion is that type I cells are part of an efferent system which modulates receptor sensitivity by the action of the transmitters contained within them.

4.2. A New Hypothesis

If the argument of the preceding paragraphs is correct, one must ask what structures could be the receptor. The answer is that the type I cell could be the receptor, though transmitting its response over some distance to nerve terminals enclosed in the type II cell. Alternatively, the type II cell could be a receptor cell transmitting to nerve fibers coursing through it. Both these hypotheses presume the receptor cell and both assume nerve endings in the type II cell. The third possibility to be considered is that there is no receptor cell but that a nerve fiber alone is the receptor. Such nerve fibers could be in Schwann cells or enclosed in the type II cell. Since there no longer are over-riding reasons for accepting the receptor cell hypothesis, this last alternative should be seriously considered, but the role of the type II cell must be borne in mind.

The hypothesis that very small nerve fibers could be the receptor was considered by Biscoe and Taylor (1963) as a possible means for explaining the Poisson distributions of nerve impulses which they had described in single chemoreceptor afferent fibers. At that time, small nerve fibers had not been described in the carotid body. However, more recent studies with the electron microscope have shown them to be present, and so the small nerve ending as chemoreceptor hypothesis should be reconsidered. The case for this hypothesis has been argued by Biscoe (1971). Briefly, the argument can be stated as follows:

The membrane potential of nerve cells is dependent on the ionic gradients across the membrane, and these are controlled by the sodium pump. It is known that this pump is dependent for its activity on metabolic energy, which, in aerobic systems, derives from oxygen. It is clear that under the appropriate circumstances, when all other requirements are in excess, the amount of available oxygen could control the activity of the sodium pump, and so the potassium ion gradient across the membrane and so the membrane potential. It is easy to see how a fall in oxygen tension could, in theory at least, allow the pump to slow down and thus by allowing K ions to diffuse out of the cell lead to depolarization. Such a depolarization would be equivalent to the generator potential of other receptors, which has probably been recently described for chemoreceptors (Eyzaguirre *et al.*, 1970). This generator potential would in turn initiate nerve impulses in the afferent fiber. In the case where there is a large internal volume, or more particularly a low surface area to volume ratio, such changes in the potassium concentration would not be significant. However, where the ratio is high then changes could be very important and the membrane potential could be very responsive to the available oxygen. The possible magnitude and speed of this effect were illustrated with a numerical example by Biscoe (1971) for a nerve fiber of diameter 0.2 μm and making the assumption that the K^+ flux into the nerve and Na^+ flux out were four times greater at 37°C than at 17°C in the squid. The calculation shows that approximately one-fourth of the internal potassium ion could be lost in 1 s, which could cause a change in membrane potential of around 10 mV. If the fiber were smaller, the change would be greater or quicker in onset; e.g., for a diameter of 0.1 μm the change could be 15–20 mV. In addition, if the sodium pump were in part electrogenic then a decrease in pump activity would lead to depolarization by this means. The calculations of Biscoe (1971) show that if one-third of the pump activity is not neutral then this contribution of the membrane potential would be 6 mV, given the assumptions about ion flux.

A further calculation is possible relating to the oxygen consumption of such small nerve fibers (Biscoe, 1971). This again depends on the assumptions about Na^+ flux and shows that the consumption would be about 40 μl O_2/g nerve/s. This is very high and could create steep local gradients in the tissue, and diffusion of oxygen would then become very important. This value may even account for the high oxygen consumption of the carotid body (Daly et al., 1954; Biscoe et al., 1970a; Purves, 1970). The distance of nerve fibers from the source of oxygen would in consequence enter into consideration. If mitochondria were not evenly spaced in small nerve fibers, and they probably are not, then a further factor, the diffusion of ATP down the fiber from the site of production, is relevant.

This account ignores the real biochemical problem posed by the fact that the chemoreceptor responds to such relatively high oxygen tensions. The difficulty is overcome by Mills and Jöbsis (1970, 1972), who have shown that there is a low-affinity cytochrome a_3 present in the carotid body with which reduction goes from minimum to maximum over a pO_2 range of at least 200 torr. The site for this cytochrome is unknown, but Mills and Jöbsis advocate especially the type II cell, and hence a transmitter of some sort. The simplest solution is that the cytochrome could be found in the small nerve endings and hence represents their specialization to perform the chemoreceptor function. One doubt about this idea (Biscoe, 1971) is whether or not the fluorometric method could detect this new cytochrome a_3 if it were restricted to the nerve endings. If the low-affinity a_3 were in type II cells, then presumably its level would affect sodium pump activity and allow release of potassium ions, which would then be the transmitter. The membrane potential of *small* nerve fibers would then be especially subject to this K^+ ion released into their extracellular space. According to such a view, the type I cell inhibitory transmitter could equally effectively act on either type II cell or small nerve fiber and the small fiber would produce a generator potential which would initiate the nerve impulse. As Mills and Jöbsis suggest, the site of impulse initiation would have a normal electron transport chain.

Whether or not the small nerve fiber or the type II cell is the receptor, the small nerve fiber could explain the random discharge of impulses in the receptor afferent fibers, for as pointed out by Biscoe and Taylor (1963) it has been shown by Fatt and Katz (1952) that thermal noise fluctuations in membrane potential would be biologically significant if nerve endings were about 0.1 μm in diameter. It is by no means certain that such variations in a receptor potential would be effective (see Biscoe, 1971; Levitan et al., 1968) in generating a Poisson process, but the possibility remains.

The answer to the question of whether small nerve fibers of the appropriate size terminate in the arterial chemoreceptors will provide the crucial evidence for or against this hypothesis. It is known that in randomly selected micrographs small fibers, 0.1–0.2 μm in diameter, are often seen in type II cells, and some of these become motor endings in type I cells. It is not known whether any of them have terminals enclosed by type II cells, this being the favored position for the action of an inhibitory transmitter released from type I cells, and more so for the action of a chemosensory transmitter from the type II cells. The answer to the question lies with serial reconstructions using an electron microscope.

In conclusion, the presently available evidence suggests that the type I cell is part of an efferent control system whose action on arterial chemoreceptors is inhibitory. This action is mediated by the release of acetylcholine from motor endings which evokes the release of inhibitory catecholamines from these cells. There is an excitatory pathway acting via the sympathetic system probably to alter the pattern of blood flow through the chemoreceptor complex. Last, the arterial chemoreceptor itself may be a small nerve fiber which is specialized insofar as it contains the low-affinity cytochrome a_3 of Mills and Jöbsis (1970, 1972). Alternatively, if this cytochrome should be present in the type II cell, as suggested by Mills and Jöbsis (1972), this cell is the receptor and probably affects the small nerve ending by release of K ion to evoke therein a generator potential.

Note Added in Proof: The reader should refer to Hess and Zaputa (1972) for an alternative interpretation of some of the experiments described here.

5. REFERENCES

Abbott, C. P., and Howe, A., 1970, Ultrastructure of aortic body tissue in the cat, *J. Physiol.* **209**:18P.

Adrian, E. D., Bronk, D. W., and Phillips, G., 1932, Discharges in mammalian sympathetic nerves, *J. Physiol.* **74**:115.

Al-Lami, F., and Murray, R. G., 1968, Fine structure of the carotid body of normal and anoxic cats, *Anat. Rec.* **160**:697.

Ballard, K. J., and Jones, J. V., 1971, The fine structural localization of cholinesterases in the carotid body of the cat, *J. Physiol.* **219**:747.

Battaglia, G., 1970, Ultrastructural observations on the denervated carotid glomus of the rat, *Boll. Soc. Ital. Biol. Sper.* **46**:841.

Battaglia, G., and Mariani, G., 1970, Electron microscopic observations on the aortic–pulmonary body of the rabbit, *Boll. Soc. Ital. Biol. Sper.* **46**:843.

Biscoe, T. J., 1971, Carotid body: Structure and function, *Physiol. Rev.* **51**:437.

Biscoe, T. J., and Curtis, D. R., 1966, Nor-adrenaline and inhibition of Renshaw cell, *Science* **151**:1230.

Biscoe, T. J., and Pallot, D., 1972, Serial reconstruction with the electron microscope of carotid body tissue: The type I cell nerve supply, *Experientia* **28**:33.

Biscoe, T. J., and Purves, M. J., 1967, Factors affecting the cat carotid chemoreceptor and cervical sympathetic activity with special reference to passive hind-limb movements, *J. Physiol.* **190**:425.

Biscoe, T. J., and Sampson, S. R., 1967, Spontaneous activity recorded from the central cut end of the carotid sinus nerve of the cat, *Nature* **216**:294.

Biscoe, T. J., and Sampson, S. R., 1968, Rhythmical and non-rhythmical spontaneous activity recorded from the central cut end of the sinus nerve, *J. Physiol.* **196**:327.

Biscoe, T. J., and Silver, A., 1966, The distribution of cholinesterases in the cat carotid body, *J. Physiol.* **183**:501.

Biscoe, T. J., and Stehbens, W. E., 1966, Ultrastructure of the carotid body, *J. Cell Biol.* **30**:563.

Biscoe, T. J., and Stehbens, W. E., 1967, Ultrastructure of the denervated carotid body, *Quart. J. Exptl. Physiol.* **52**:31.

Biscoe, T. J., and Taylor, A., 1963, The discharge pattern recorded in chemoreceptor afferent fibres from the cat carotid body with normal circulation and during perfusion, *J. Physiol.* **168**:332.

Biscoe, T. J., Curtis, D. R., and Ryall, R. W., 1966, An investigation of catecholamine receptors of spinal interneurones, *Internat. J. Neuropharmacol.* **5**:429.

Biscoe, T. J., Bradley, G. W., and Purves, M. J., 1970a, The relation between carotid body chemoreceptor discharge, carotid sinus pressure and carotid body venous flow, *J. Physiol.* **203**:99.

Biscoe, T. J., Lall, A., and Sampson, S. R., 1970b, Electron microscopic and electrophysiological studies on the carotid body following intra-cranial section of the glossopharyngeal nerve, *J. Physiol.* **208**:133.

Bock, P., Stockinger, L., and Vyslonzil, E., 1970, Die Feinstruktur des Glomus caroticum beim Menschen, *Z. Zellforsch.* **105**:543.

Born, G. V. R., and Bülbring, E., 1956, The movement of potassium between smooth muscle and the surrounding fluid, *J. Physiol.* **131**:690.

Burnstock, G., 1958, The action of adrenaline on excitability and membrane potential in the taenia coli of the guinea pig and the effect of DNP in this action and on the action of acetylcholine, *J. Physiol.* **143**:183.

Cheng-Minoda, K., Ozawa, T., and Breinin, G. M., 1968, Ultrastructural changes in rabbit extraocular muscles after oculomotor nerve section, *Invest. Ophthalmol.* **7**:599.

Chiocchio, S. R., Biscardi, A. M., and Tramezzani, J. H., 1967, 5-Hydroxytryptamine in the carotid body of the cat, *Science* **158**:790.

Chiocchio, S. R., King, M. P., and Angelakos, E. T., 1971a, Carotid body catecholeamines: Histochemical studies on the effects of drug treatments, *Histochemie* **25**:52.

Chiocchio, S. R., King, M. P., Carballo, L., and Angelakos, E. T., 1971b, Monoamines in the carotid body cells of the cat, *J. Histochem. Cytochem.* **19**:621.

Coleridge, H., Coleridge, J. C. G., and Howe, A., 1967, A search for pulmonary arterial chemoreceptors in the cat with a comparison of the blood supply of the aortic bodies in the new-born and adult animal, *J. Physiol.* **191**:353.

Coleridge, H., Coleridge, J. C. G., and Howe, A., 1970, A histological and electrophysiological study of the location, innervation and blood supply of the aortic bodies, *Circ. Res.* **26**:235.

Comroe, J. H., 1964, The peripheral chemoreceptors, in: *Handbook of Physiology* Vol. I: *Respiration* (W. O. Fenn and H. Rahn, ed.), pp. 557–583, American Physiological Society, Washington, D.C.

Daly, M. de B., Lambertsen, C. J., and Schweitzer, A., 1954, Observations on the volume of blood flow and oxygen utilisation of the carotid body in the cat, *J. Physiol.* **125**:67.

De Castro, F., 1926, Sur la structure et l'innervation de la glande intercarotidienne (Glomus caroticuum) de l'homme et des mammifères, et sur un nouveau système d'innervation autonome du nerf glossopharyngien: Études anatomiques et expérimentales, *Trab. Lab. Invest. Biol. Univ. Madrid* **24**:365.

De Castro, F., 1928, Sur la structure et l'innervation du sinus carotidien de l'homme et des mammifères: Nouveaux faits sur l'innervation et la fonction du glomus caroti-cum: Études anatomiques et physiologiques, *Trab. Lab. Invest. Biol. Univ. Madrid* **25**:331.

De Castro, F., 1940, Nuevas observaciones sobre la inervación de la región carotidea: Los quimio-y presso-receptores, *Trab. Inst. Cajal Invest. Biol.* **32**:297.

De Castro, F., 1951, Sur la structure de la synapse dans les chemorecepteurs: Leur mécanisme d'excitation et rôle dans la circulation sanguine locale, *Acta Physiol. Scand.* **22**:14.

De Castro, F., 1962, Sur la vascularisation et l'innervation des corpuscles carotidiens aberrants, *Archs. Int. Pharmacodyn. Thérap.* **139**:212.

De Castro, F., and Rubio, M., 1968, The anatomy and innervation of the blood vessels of the carotid body and the role of chemoreceptive reactions in the autoregulation of the blood flow, in: *Arterial Chemoreceptors* (R. W. Torrance, ed.), pp. 267–270, Blackwell, Oxford.

De Kock, L. L., 1951, Histology of the carotid body, *Nature Lond.* **167**:611.

De Kock, L. L., 1954, Intraglomerular tissues of the carotid body, *Acta Anat.* **21**:101.

De Kock, L. L., and Dunn, A. E. G., 1966, An electron microscope study of the carotid body, *Acta Anat.* **64**:163.

Engberg, I., and Ryall, R. W., 1965, The actions of mono-amines upon spinal neurones, *Life Sci.* **4**:2223.

Engberg, I., and Ryall, R. W., 1966, The inhibitory action of nor-adrenaline and other mono-amines on spinal neurones, *J. Physiol.* **185**:298.

Eyzaguirre, C., and Koyano, H., 1965a, Effects of some pharmacological agents on chemoreceptor discharges, *J. Physiol.* **178**:410.

Eyzaguirre, C., and Koyano, H., 1965b, Effects of electrical stimulation on the frequency of chemoreceptor discharges, *J. Physiol.* **178**:438.

Eyzaguirre, C., and Lewin, J., 1961, The effect of sympathetic stimulation on carotid nerve activity, *J. Physiol.* **159**:251.

Eyzaguirre, C., and Zapata, P., 1968a, Pharmacology of pH effects on carotid body chemo-receptors *in vitro*, *J. Physiol.* **195**:557.

Eyzaguirre, C., and Zapata, P., 1968b, The release of acetylcholine from carotid body tissues: Further study of the effects of acetylcholine and cholinergic blocking agents on the chemosensory discharge, *J. Physiol.* **195**:589.

Eyzaguirre, C., and Zapata, P., 1968c, A discussion of possible transmitter or generator substances in carotid body chemoreceptors, in: *Arterial Chemoreceptors* (R. W. Torrance, ed.), pp. 213–247, Blackwell, Oxford.

Eyzaguirre, C., Koyano, H., and Taylor, J. R., 1965, Presence of acetylcholine and trans-mitter release from carotid body chemoreceptors, *J. Physiol.* **178**:463.

Eyzaguirre, C., Leitner, L. M., Nishi, K., and Fidone, S., 1970, Depolarization of chemo-sensory nerve endings in carotid body of cat, *J. Neurophysiol.* **33**:685.

Farquhar, M. G., 1961, Fine structure and function in capillaries of the anterior pituitary gland, *Angiology* **12**:270.

Fatt, P., and Katz, B., 1952, Spontaneous subthreshold activity at motor nerve endings, *J. Physiol.* **117**:109.

Feria-Velasco, A., and Gonzalez-Angulo, A., 1968, The ultrastructure of the normal human carotid body. II. The tissue elements surrounding the chemoreceptor unit, *Bol. Estud. Med. Biol. Mex.* **25**:291.

Floyd, W. F., and Neil, E., 1952, The influence of the sympathetic innervation of the carotid bifurcation on chemoreceptor and baroreceptor activity in the cat, *Arch. Int. Pharmacodyn. Thérap.* **91**:230.

Gerard, M. W., and Billingsley, P. R., 1923, The innervation of the carotid body, *Anat. Rec.* **25**:391.

Gomez, L., 1907, Studies on the carotid gland, *Trans. Chicago Pathol. Soc.* **7**:104.

Gomez, L. P., 1908, The anatomy and pathology of the carotid gland, *Am. J. Med. Sci.* **136**:98.

Goormaghtigh, N., and Pannier, R., 1939, Les paraganglions du coeur et des zones vasosensibles carotidienne et cardio-aortique chez le chat adulte, *Arch. Biol. Liège* **50**:455.

Hebb, C. O., 1968, in: *Arterial Chemoreceptors* (R. W. Torrance, ed.), pp. 138–139, Blackwell, Oxford.

Hess, A., 1968, Electron microscopic observations of normal and experimental cat carotid bodies, in: *Arterial Chemoreceptors* (R. W. Torrance, ed.), pp. 51–56, Blackwell, Oxford.

Hess and Zapata, 1972, Inervation of the cat carotid body; normal and experimental studies, *Fed. Proc.* **31**:1365.

Heymans, C., and Bouckaert, J. J., 1939, Les chémorécepteurs du sinus carotidien. *Ergebn. Physiol.* **41**:28.

Heymans, C., and Neil, E., 1958, *Reflexogenic Areas of the Cardiovascular System*, J. & A. Churchill, London.

Heymans, C., Bouckaert, J. J., and Regniers, P., 1933, *Le Sinus Carotidien et la Zone Homologue Cardio-aortique*, G. Doin, Paris.

Hollinshead, W. H., 1939, The origin of the nerve fibers to the glomus aorticum of the cat, *J. Comp. Neurol.* **71**:417.

Hollinshead, W. H., 1940, The innervation of the supracardial bodies in the cat, *J. Comp. Neurol.* **73**:37.

Howe, A., 1956, The vasculature of the aortic bodies in the cat, *J. Physiol.* **134**:311.

Howe, A., and Neil, E., 1971, Arterial chemoreceptors, in: *Enteroceptors* (E. Neil, ed.), pp. 47–80, Vol. III/I of *Handbook of Sensory Physiology* (H. Autrum, R. Jung, W. R. Loewenstein, D. M. MacKay and H. L. Teuber, eds.), Springer-Verlag, Berlin.

Jones, J. V., and Ballard, K. J., 1971, Cholinesterases in the carotid body of the cat as seen with the electron microscope, *Nature* **233**:146.

Knoche, H., and Schmitt, T., 1963, Über Chemo- und Pressoreceptorenfelder am Coronark-reislauf, *Z. Zellforsch.* **61**:524.

Knoche, H., Schmitt, G., and Kienecker, E. W., 1971, Beitrag zur Kenntnis der Glomera coronaria der Katze, *Z. Zellforsch.* **118**:532.

Kobayashi, S., 1968, Fine structure of the carotid body of the dog, *Arch. Histol. Okayama* **30**:95.

Kobayashi, S., 1971a, Comparative cytological studies of the carotid body. I. Demonstration of monoamine-storing cells by correlated chromaffin reaction and fluorescence histochemistry, *Arch. Histol. Jap.* **33**:319.

Kobayashi, S., 1971b, Comparative cytological studies of the carotid body. II. Ultrastructure of the synapses on the chief cell, *Arch. Histol. Jap.* **33**:397.

Kondo, H., 1971, An electron microscopic study on innervation of the carotid body of guinea pig, *J. Ultrastruct. Res.* **37**:544.

Laurent, P., and Jager-Barres, M. C., 1969, Activité efferente d'origine centrale dans le nerf sino-carotichen du lapin, *J. Physiol. Paris* **61**:403.

Lee, J. C.-Y., 1963, Electron microscopy of Wallerian degeneration, *J. Comp. Neurol.* **120**:65.

Levitan, H., Segundo, J. P., Moore, G. P., and Perkel, D. H., 1968, Statistical analysis of membrane potential fluctuations: Rotation with presynaptic spike train, *Biophys. J.* **8**:1256.

Majno, G., 1965, Ultrastructure of the vascular membrane, in: *Handbook of Physiology.* Sect. 2: *Circulation,* Vol. III (W. F. Hamilton and P. Dow, eds.), pp. 2293–2376, American Physiological Society, Washington, D.C.

Meijling, H. A., 1938, Bau und Innervation von Glomus caroticum und Sinus caroticus, *Acta Neerland. Morphol.* **1**:193.

Millar, R. A., and Biscoe, T. J., 1966, Postganglionic sympathetic discharge and the effect of inhalation anaesthetics, *Brit. J. Anaesthesiol.* **38**:92.

Mills, E., 1968, Activity of aortic chemoreceptors during electrical stimulation of the stellate ganglion in the cat, *J. Physiol.* **199**:103.

Mills, E., and Jöbsis, F. F., 1970, Simultaneous measurement of cytochrome a_3 reduction and chemoreceptor afferent activity in the carotid body, *Nature Lond.* **225**:1147.

Mills, E., and Jöbsis, F. F., 1972, Mitochondrial respiratory chain of carotid body and chemoreceptor response to changes in oxygen tension, *J. Neurophysiol.* **35**:405.

Muratori, G., 1933, Contributo istologico allo studio dei reflessi aortici della corotide, *Boll. Soc. Ital. Biol. Sper.* **8**:387.

Muratori, G., 1935, Connessioni tra tessuto parangangliare e zone recettrici aortiche in vari mammiferi, *Monit. Zool. Ital.* **45**:300.

Muratori, G., and Battaglia, G., 1959, Caratteristiche citologiche delle cellule paragangliari del glomo carotico, *Boll. Soc. Ital. Biol. Sper.* **35**:1127.

Neil, E., and O'Regan, R. G., 1969a, Effects of sinus and aortic nerve efferents on arterial chemoreceptor function, *J. Physiol.* **200**:69P.

Neil, E., and O'Regan, R. G., 1969b, Efferent and afferent impulse activity in the "intact" sinus nerve, *J. Physiol.* **205**:20P.

Neil, E., and O'Regan, R. G., 1971a, The effects of efferent electrical stimulation of the cut sinus and aortic nerves on peripheral arterial chemoreceptor activity in the cat, *J. Physiol.* **215**:15.

Neil, E., and O'Regan, R. G., 1971b, Efferent and afferent impulse activity recorded from few-fibre preparations of otherwise intact sinus and aortic nerves, *J. Physiol.* **215**:33.

Nishi, K., and Eyzaguirre, C., 1971, The action of some cholinergic blockers on carotid body chemoreceptors *in vivo,* *Brain Res.* **33**:37.

Pessacq, T. P., 1961, Le nevroglie du glomus carotidien, *Archs. Anat. Microscop. Morphol. Exptl.* **50**:289.

Purves, M. J., 1970, The effect of hypoxia, hypercapnia and hypotension upon carotid body blood flow and oxygen consumption in the cat, *J. Physiol.* **209**:395.

Salmoiraghi, G. C., and Stefanis, C. N., 1965, Patterns of central neurons responses to suspected transmitters, *Arch. Ital. Biol.* **103**:705.

Sampson, S. R., 1970, Effects of mecamylamine on responses of carotid body chemoreceptors *in vivo* to physiological and pharmacological stimuli, *Fed. Proc.* **29**:809.

Sampson, S. R., 1971a, Catecholeamines as mediators of efferent inhibition of carotid body chemoreceptors in the cat, *Fed. Proc.* **30**:551.

Sampson, S. R., 1971b, Effects of mecamylamine on responses of carotid body chemoreceptors *in vivo* to physiological and pharmacological stimuli, *J. Physiol.* **212**:655.

Sampson, S. R., and Biscoe, T. J., 1970, Efferent control of the carotid body chemoreceptor, *Experientia* **26**:261.

Schweitzer, A., and Wright, S., 1938, Action of prostigmine and acetylcholine on respiration, *Quart. J. Exptl. Physiol.* **28**:33.

Serafini-Fracassini, A., and Volpin, D., 1966, Some features of the vascularization of the carotid body in the dog, *Acta Anat.* **63**:571.

Sherrington, C. S., and Laslett, E. E., 1903, Observations on some spinal reflexes and the interconnection of spinal segments, *J. Physiol.* **29**:58.

Spoendlin, H., 1966, The organization of the cochlear receptor, in: *Advances in Oto-Rhino-Laryngology*, pp. 28–35, Vol. 13, S. Karger, Basel.

Spoendlin, H. H., and Gacek, R. P., 1963, Electron microscopic study of the efferent and afferent innervation of the organ of Corti in the cat, *Ann. Otol. Rhinol. Laryngol.* **72**:660.

Terayama, Y., Yamamoto, K., and Sakamoto, T., 1968, Electron microscopic observations on the postganglionic sympathetic fibers in the guinea pig cochlea, *Ann. Otol. Rhinol. Laryngol.* **77**:1152.

Torrance, R. W., 1968, Prolegomena to *Arterial Chemoreceptors* (R. W. Torrance, ed.), Blackwell, Oxford.

Verna, A., 1971, Infrastructure des divers types de terminaisons nerveuses dans le glomus carotidien du lapin, *J. Microscop.* **10**:59.

Walberg, F., 1965, An electron microscopic study of terminal degeneration in the inferior olive of the cat, *J. Comp. Neurol.* **125**:205.

Yates, R. D., Chen, I-Li, and Duncan, D., 1970, Effects of sinus nerve stimulation on carotid body glomus cells, *J. Cell Biol.* **46**:544.

Chapter 17

Taste Receptors

Masayasu Sato

Department of Physiology
Kumamoto University Medical School
Kumamoto, Japan

1. INTRODUCTION

Chemical stimuli, applied over the tongue of mammals, elicit impulses in two mixed nerves, the chorda tympani, a branch of the facial nerve, and the glossopharyngeal. The former innervates mostly fungiform papillae in the anterior two-thirds of the tongue, while the latter innervates circumvallate and foliate papillae in the posterior one-third of the tongue. Responses of the glossopharyngeal nerve to gustatory stimuli are different from those of the chorda tympani in that the former is more sensitive to quinine and less sensitive to NaCl (Yamada, 1966, 1967; Pfaffmann *et al.*, 1967). Gustatory nerve responses are also different from one animal species to another (Beidler *et al.*, 1955; Pfaffmann, 1955).

Pfaffmann (1941, 1955) first recorded afferent impulses produced by chemical stimulation of the tongue in single chorda tympani fibers of cats, rabbits, and rats. He demonstrated that the threshold for any one substance is different from one fiber to another, that the frequency of impulse discharge during the first second is approximately a sigmoid function of the logarithm of the stimulus concentration, and that each single fiber preparation is characterized by a different pattern of sensitivity to the taste stimuli representing the four primary tastes. These observations were later confirmed by a number of investigators in a variety of animal species (for references, see Sato, 1971).

2. GUSTATORY NERVE FIBER RESPONSE TO CHEMICAL STIMULI

2.1. Multiple Sensitivity of Single Chorda Tympani Fibers

Relationships between the concentration of NaCl, sucrose, HCl, and quinine and the numbers of impulses discharged during the initial 5 s after stimulation in three chorda tympani fibers of rats are demonstrated in Fig. 1. Each fiber is characterized by a different pattern of sensitivity to the four stimuli. The one at the top is primarily sensitive to NaCl, the middle one is predominantly sensitive to sucrose, and the lowest one is sensitive to NaCl, HCl, and quinine. The threshold and the magnitude of response to any one chemical at a particular concentration differ from one fiber to another, but in all the fibers the number of impulses increases in approximately linear relationship to the logarithm of concentration. However, recent experiments indicate that the relationship between the concentration (C) and the number of impulses (R) can be better fitted by a power function of a form $R = KC^n$, where the number of impulses during the steady discharge phase is taken as the value of R (Sato, 1971). The exponent n for NaCl is about unity (Sato, 1971; Yamashita *et al.*, 1970).

Multiple sensitivity of single gustatory nerve fibers can be seen in Fig. 2, where numbers of impulses discharged during the initial 5 s after stimulation

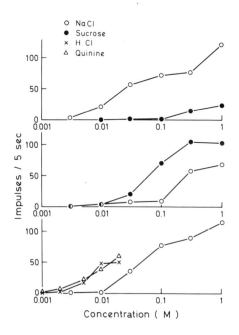

Fig. 1. Concentration–response magnitude relationships for NaCl, sucrose, HCl, and quinine in three chorda tympani fibers of rats. Ordinates indicate numbers of impulses elicited in the first 5 s after stimulation by NaCl, sucrose, HCl, and quinine. Reproduced from Ogawa *et al.* (1968).

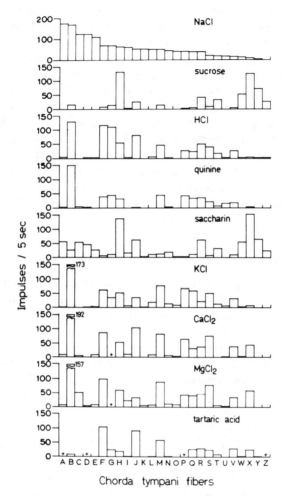

Fig. 2. Response profiles of 26 chorda tympani fibers of rats for various chemical stimuli. Ordinates indicate numbers of impulses elicited in the first 5 s after stimulation, while abscissas represent individual fibers. Stimuli applied are, from the top, 0.1 M NaCl, 0.5 M sucrose, 0.01 N HCl, 0.02 M quinine hydrochloride, 0.02 M saccharin sodium, 0.3 M KCl, 0.3 M CaCl$_2$, 0.3 M MgCl$_2$, and 0.01 N tartaric acid. Crosses indicate the absence of stimulation.

by various chemicals in 26 chorda tympani fibers of rats are presented. A majority of fibers responded to NaCl, but only 50–70% of the fibers yielded responses to sucrose, HCl, or quinine. A statistical analysis of responses of rat chorda tympani fibers indicates that, in general, responsiveness of the fibers to one of the four basic stimuli such as NaCl, sucrose, HCl, and quinine is independent of that to the other three, although responses to HCl are correlated with those to quinine (Ogawa *et al.*, 1968; Sato *et al.*, 1969; Sato, 1971). In the glossopharyngeal nerve fibers of rats, however, responsiveness to any of the four basic stimuli is independent of that to the others, and therefore responsiveness to the four gustatory stimuli is randomly distributed in these fibers (Frank and Pfaffmann, 1969).

It has also been demonstrated by Ogawa *et al.* (1968) that about 50% of rat chorda tympani fibers respond to cooling of the tongue and that responses to cooling are correlated with those to HCl and quinine. Similar findings were demonstrated in hamster chorda tympani fibers. In addition, in hamsters responses to sucrose were negatively correlated with those to NaCl but had a positive correlation with those to warming (Ogawa *et al.*, 1968). Therefore, chemical sensitivity of gustatory nerve fibers is closely associated with their termal sensitivity.

2.2. Neural Code for Quality of Taste and "Across-Fiber Pattern" Theory

Since chemical specificity of gustatory nerve fibers in mammals is not absolute, Pfaffmann (1941) suggested that sensory quality does not depend on the all-or-nothing activation of some particular fiber group alone but on the pattern of other active fibers; i.e., the afferent neural message for quality is probably expressed in terms of the relative amounts of neural activity across many neurons. The across-fiber patterns of responses for a number of taste solutions were first measured quantitatively by Erickson (1963) and Erickson *et al.* (1965), and the significance of these patterns for the interpretation of the qualities of taste stimuli was discussed. Erikson reasoned that stimuli which gave similar patterns should taste somewhat alike while stimuli producing highly dissimilar patterns should have different tastes. A measure of the similarity of these patterns is given by a quantitative correlation between responses produced by pairs of stimuli across many fibers.

As can be seen in Fig. 2, where response profiles of 26 rat chorda tympani fibers for nine kinds of stimuli are presented, the response pattern for saccharin is similar to that for sucrose, and those for quinine, KCl, $CaCl_2$, $MgCl_2$, tartaric acid, and HCl somewhat resemble each other, but the pattern for NaCl is quite different from those for other eight solutions. The above findings are quantitatively demonstrated by the correlation coefficients between the amounts of responses to pairs of stimuli in 26 fibers, shown in Table I. Substances showing similar response patterns have highly significant positive correlations, while substances showing patterns different from one another have small or negative correlation coefficients.

Evidence in favor of the "across-fiber pattern" theory has been obtained in a number of behavioral experiments (Morrison, 1967; Marshall, 1968).

Table I. Correlation Coefficients between Amounts of Responses in Rat Chorda Tympani Fibers to Pairs of Stimuli[a]

	0.02 M quinine HCl	0.01 N HCl	0.5 M sucrose	0.1 M NaCl	0.02 M saccharin Na	0.01 N tartaric acid	0.3 M MgCl$_2$	0.3 M CaCl$_2$
0.3 M KCl	0.94[b] / 0.97[b]	0.76[b] / 0.47[c]	−0.04 / −0.01	0.30 / 0.33	0.14 / −0.06	0.34 / 0.09	0.88[b] / 0.93[b]	0.92[b] / 0.97[b]
0.3 M CaCl$_2$	0.85[b] / 0.97[b]	0.90[b] / 0.57[d]	0.06 / 0.05	0.30 / 0.36	0.03 / 0.01	0.54 / 0.08	0.90[b] / 0.95[b]	
0.3 M MgCl$_2$	0.85[b] / 0.94[b]	0.83[b] / 0.57[d]	0.10 / 0.06	0.32 / 0.36	0.06 / 0.03	0.46[c] / 0.10		
0.01 N tartaric acid	0.17 / 0.07	0.65[d] / 0.58[d]	0.03 / 0.20	−0.02 / −0.26	0.05 / 0.30			
0.02 M saccharin Na	−0.12 / −0.04	−0.05 / 0.10	0.88[b] / 0.94[b]	0.01 / −0.23				
0.1 M NaCl	0.37 / 0.33	0.25 / 0.03	−0.32 / −0.32					
0.5 M sucrose	−0.02 / 0.03	0.03 / −0.01						
0.01 N HCl	0.75[b] / 0.50[c]							

[a] The upper numeral in each cell indicates the correlation coefficient calculated from numbers of impulses discharged during the first 5 s after stimulation in 22–26 fibers, and the lower numeral represents the coefficient based on numbers of impulses discharged during the next 5 s after stimulation.

[b] Correlation is highly significant.

[c] Correlation is probably significant.

[d] Correlation is significant.

For example, Marshall (1968) demonstrated the inverse relationship between similarity of across-fiber patterns, represented by correlation magnitude, and behavioral discrimination. Such behavioral and neural data support a concept that the neural code for gustatory quality is a pattern made up of the amount of neural activity across many neurons.

3. ELECTRICAL RESPONSES OF GUSTATORY CELLS TO CHEMICAL STIMULI

3.1. Innervation and Structure of Taste Bud*

A single chorda tympani fiber innervates a number of fungiform papillae of the rat. This has recently been demonstrated using electrical and chemical stimulation to map the receptor field of individual afferent nerve fibers (Pfaffmann, 1970). There is also evidence for the interaction among fungiform papillae in the rat tongue (Miller, 1971).

Two principal cell types, a supporting cell and a gustatory cell, had been recognized in the taste bud of mammals by the early light microscopists. Recent electron microscopic studies on the taste bud in the fungiform and foliate papillae indicate several types of cells. One of the two principal cell types is dark, while the other is light. However, no conclusive evidence has so far been presented to indicate which one is a gustatory cell (Farbman, 1965; Murray and Murray, 1970). There is, however, good evidence suggesting that these two types of cells merely represent different stages of transition from epithelial cells, since the cells of the rat fungiform taste buds have an average life span of about 250 h (Beidler and Smallman, 1965).

3.2. How Do Gustatory Cells Respond to Chemical Stimuli?

3.2.1. Receptor Potentials of Gustatory Cells

The primary event in the taste receptor mechanism after application of chemical stimuli is assumed to be the formation of a weak complex between the stimulus compound and a receptor molecule located on or near the cell surfaces (Beidler, 1954; Dastoli and Price, 1966). The formation of a complex between the stimulus and receptor molecules is thought to lead to configurational changes in the membrane structure and subsequently to ionic permeability changes in the membrane of the gustatory cell. As a consequence, a receptor potential is generated in the cell. The receptor potential produces a depolarization of the afferent nerve fiber terminal sufficient to generate nerve impulses.

---

* See also Chapter 11 of this volume.

Kimura and Beidler (1961) were the first to impale taste bud cells of the rat and the hamster with microelectrodes and record their electrical response to chemical stimuli. Slow potential changes were recorded from taste bud cells upon application of a variety of chemicals: one cell responded to more than two kinds of stimuli, often as many as four basic substances, although the relative magnitude of response to these substances was different from one cell to another, and the magnitude of response increased with an increase in the stimulus concentration. They assumed from these findings that the slow potentials recorded from the taste bud originated from gustatory cells and might be the potentials that are related to the generation of impulses in the innervating nerve.

More detailed and more quantitative investigations were reported recently by Ozeki (1970, 1971) and Ozeki and Sato (1972) on the electrical properties of gustatory cells of rat fungiform papillae. According to Ozeki (1971) these cells possess a resting potential of about 40 mV and an input resistance of about 80 MΩ, although these properties vary significantly from cell to cell. As shown in Fig. 3, the depolarization or the "receptor potential" in gustatory cells induced by chemical stimulation usually shows a rise time of several seconds, maintains an approximately constant magnitude during

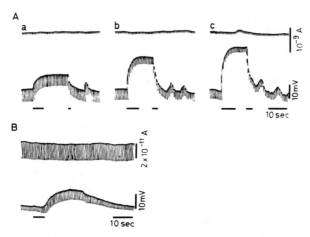

Fig. 3. Receptor potentials recorded intracellularly from rat gustatory cells with superimposed conductance changes. Intensities of applied hyperpolarizing current through the microelectrode are monitored as downward deflections on the upper trace, and the lower trace in each record indicates change of membrane potential. The first signal marker in each record indicates the time of application of a gustatory stimulus, and the second one indicates rinsing of the papilla with 41.4 mM NaCl. A, Receptor potentials of a gustatory cell evoked by 0.3 M (a), 1 M (b), and 2 M (c) NaCl. B, Receptor potential induced by 0.02 M quinine hydrochloride. Reproduced from Ozeki (1970).

the application of stimuli, and decays gradually to the baseline with a fall time of several seconds after rinsing of the papillae with saline solution or water. Both the magnitude and the rate of rise of receptor potentials increase with an increase in stimulus concentration.

A majority of gustatory cells respond to more than two of four stimuli (0.3 M NaCl, 0.5 M sucrose, 0.01 N HCl, and 0.02 M quinine) with maintained depolarizations. The responses vary in magnitude and in time course from one cell to another. Ozeki and Sato (1972) reported that among 109 cells examined 19 cells responded to one kind of stimulus, 28 cells to two kinds, 40 cells to three kinds, and 22 cells to all four. They further examined whether or not the probability of response to each of the four stimuli in gustatory cells is independent of their responses to the other three, and concluded that sensitivities of gustatory cells to these stimuli are randomly distributed throughout the population.

3.2.2. Conductance Changes Associated with Gustatory Cell Response

When electrotonic potentials in response to constant current pulses of 5×10^{-10} A, injected into a cell, were recorded from the cell before and during application of chemical stimuli, a change in magnitude upon application of stimuli was found (Fig. 3). This indicates that gustatory cells undergo changes in membrane resistance or membrane conductance during application of stimuli. On the one hand, conductance increased markedly with an increase in the NaCl concentration, and this was associated with an increase in receptor potential magnitude (Fig. 3A, compare a,b,c). On the other hand, when quinine hydrochloride was applied to the cell, a decrease in membrane conductance associated with the generation of a receptor potential was observed (Fig. 3B, lower trace).

The magnitude of the receptor potential in response to NaCl stimuli of the same concentration varies with changes in the membrane potential level (Ozeki, 1970, 1971). The potential increases in magnitude during hyperpolarization and decreases in magnitude with depolarization. With a strong depolarization, its polarity may be reversed. The receptor potentials produced in gustatory cells by NaCl are therefore analogous to e.p.p.'s (Fatt and Katz, 1951). This similarity between the gustatory cell membrane and the end plate membrane suggests that upon application of NaCl there is an increase in the sodium permeability of the membrane.

Receptor potentials generated in response to quinine behave differently. The magnitude of these potentials decreases upon hyperpolarization of the cell and reverses in polarity upon strong hyperpolarization (Ozeki, 1970, 1971). Taken with the finding that a decrease in membrane conductance occurs on application of quinine to a cell (Fig. 3B), it seems likely that when quinine is applied it brings about a decrease in the membrane permeability to potassium ions.

4. REFERENCES

Beidler, L. M., 1954, A theory of taste stimulation, *J. Gen. Physiol.* **38**:133.

Beidler, L. M., and Smallman, R. L., 1965, Renewal of cells within taste buds, *J. Cell Biol.* **27**:263.

Beidler, L. M., Fishman, I. Y., and Hardiman, C. W., 1955, Species differences in taste responses, *Am. J. Physiol.* **181**:235.

Dastoli, F. R., and Price, S., 1966, Sweet-sensitive protein from bovine taste buds: Isolation and assay, *Science* **154**:905.

Erickson, R. P., 1963, Sensory neural patterns and gustation, in: *Olfaction and Taste*, Vol. I (Y. Zotterman, ed.), pp. 205–213, Pergamon Press, Oxford.

Erickson, R. P., Doetsch, G. S., and Marshall, D. A., 1965, The gustatory neural response function, *J. Gen. Physiol.* **49**:247.

Farbman, 1965, Fine structure of the taste bud, *J. Ultrastruct. Res.* **12**:328.

Fatt, P., and Katz, B., 1951, An analysis of the end-plate potential recorded with an intracellular electrode, *J. Physiol.* **115**:320.

Frank, M., and Pfaffmann, C., 1969, Taste nerve fibers: A random distribution of sensitivities to four tastes, *Science* **164**:1183.

Kimura, K., and Beidler, L. M., 1961, Microelectrode study of taste receptors of rat and hamster, *J. Cell. Comp. Physiol.* **58**:131.

Marshall, D. A., 1968, A comparative study of neural coding in gustation, *Physiol. Behav.* **3**:1.

Miller, I. J., Jr., 1971, Peripheral interactions among single papilla inputs to gustatory nerve fibers, *J. Gen. Physiol.* **57**:1.

Morrison, C. R., 1967, Behavioural response patterns to salt stimuli in the rat, *Can. J. Psychol.* **21**:141.

Murray, R. G., and Murray, A., 1970, The anatomy and ultrastructure of taste endings, in: *Taste and Smell in Vertebrates* (G. E. W. Wolstenholme and J. Knight, eds.), pp. 3–25, J. & A. Churchill, London.

Ogawa, H., Sato, M., and Yamashita, S., 1968, Multiple sensitivity of chorda tympani fibers of the rat and hamster to gustatory and thermal stimuli, *J. Physiol.* **199**:223.

Ozeki, M., 1970, Hetero-electrogenesis of the gustatory cell membrane in rat, *Nature* **228**:868.

Ozeki, M., 1971, Conductance change associated with receptor potentials of gustatory cells in rat, *J. Gen. Physiol.* **58**:688.

Ozeki, M., and Sato, M., 1972, Responses of gustatory cells in the tongue of the rat to stimuli representing four taste qualities, *Comp. Biochem. Physiol.* **41**:391.

Pfaffmann, C., 1941, Gustatory afferent impulses, *J. Cell. Comp. Physiol.* **17**:243.

Pfaffmann, C., 1955, Gustatory nerve impulses in rat, cat and rabbit, *J. Neurophysiol.* **18**:429.

Pfaffmann, C., 1970, Physiological and behavioural processes of the sense of tastes, in: *Taste and Smell in Vertebrates* (G. E. W. Wolstenholme and J. Knight, eds.), pp. 31–45, J. & A. Churchill, London.

Pfaffmann, C., Fisher, G. L., and Frank, M. K., 1967, The sensory and behavioral factors in taste preferences, in: *Olfaction and Taste*, Vol. II (T. Hayashi, ed.), pp. 361–382, Pergamon Press, Oxford.

Sato, M., 1971, Neural coding in taste as seen from recordings from peripheral receptors and nerves, in: *Handbook of Sensory Physiology*, Vol. IV: *Chemical Senses*, Part 2: *Taste* (L. M. Beidler, ed.), pp. 116–147, Springer-Verlag, Berlin, Heidelberg.

Sato, M., Yamashita, S., and Ogawa, H., 1969, Afferent specificity in taste, in: *Olfaction and Taste*, Vol. III (C. Pfaffmann, ed.), pp. 470–487, Rockefeller University Press, New York.

Yamada, K., 1966, Gustatory and thermal responses in the glossopharyngeal nerve of the rat, *Jap. J. Physiol.* **16**:599.

Yamada, K., 1967, Gustatory and thermal responses in the glossopharyngeal nerve of the rabbit and cat, *Jap. J. Physiol.* **17**:94.

Yamashita, S., Ogawa, H., Sato, M., and Kiyohara, T., 1970, Modification by temperature change of gustatory impulse discharges in ch orda tympani fibers of rats, *Jap. J Physiol.* **20**:348.

Index